MW01204739

David L. Craddock

Point of Fate

The Gairden Chronicles

Heritage
Point of Fate
The Twin Crowns (coming fall 2019)

THE GAIRDEN CHRONICLES

Book Two

David L. Craddock

Point of Fate

TYCHE BOOKS LTD.

Point of Fate
Copyright © 2018 David L. Craddock

All rights reserved. No part of this book may be reproduced or transmitted in any form or by any means, electronic or mechanical, including photocopying, recording or by any information storage & retrieval system, without written permission from the copyright holder, except for the inclusion of brief quotations in a review.

The publisher does not have any control over and does not assume any responsibility for author or third-party websites or their content.

This is a work of fiction. All of the characters, organizations and events portrayed in this story are either the product of the author's imagination or are used fictitiously.

Any resemblance to persons living or dead would be really cool, but is purely coincidental.

Published by Tyche Books Ltd.
Calgary, Alberta, Canada
www.TycheBooks.com

Cover Art by Nele Diel
Interior Layout by Ryah Deines
Editorial by M.L.D. Curelas

First Tyche Books Ltd Edition 2018
Print ISBN: 978-1-928025-93-1
Ebook ISBN: 978-1-928025-94-8

Author photograph: Amie C. E. Kline.

This book was funded in part by a grant from the Alberta Media Fund.

Government

To Amie Christine:
My pretty moon, my BFF, my flip.

To Josh Hawkins:
Told you I'd do it.

Author's Note

I'M IN A state of shock right now, so you'll have to bear with me. You see, for a long time, I didn't believe this book would ever be finished. Four years ago *Heritage* landed on store shelves, physical and digital. Now I'm sitting in my home office, indulging in my tradition of writing a note to you, Reader, a tradition in which I partake only when a book is finished or needs only a few more screws tightened.

Point of Fate. Finished. Wow.

Let me explain.

Heritage was my first novel. Not just my first published novel. The first book I wrote, and it was rough. To say that the first draft, brainstormed over 2004 and written in the back half of 2005 was good for nothing more than kindling (get it?) would be an insult to scrap paper. I wrote that first draft for two reasons: Because after years of false starts, I was finally ready to write a complete novel; and because I had short stories due for a creative writing course, and my professor accepted chapters from incipient novels. Two birds, one stone.

I wrote the first draft of *Point of Fate* a few months later, over the spring of 2006. How appropriate: That was a time of new beginnings. I'd written one book, dreaming big dreams of landing a deal on my first pitch and becoming an overnight success. And I was starting not just my second book, but a sequel. I was also falling in love with the woman whose name graces the dedication and acknowledgments sections of this, the finished edition.

i

(Double wow, and double lucky me.)

That draft was worthier of roasting hot dogs and marshmallows, but only just. It was terrible in its own special, mortifying-to-think-about way. But it existed, and that was the key, the lesson I took away from that first draft of my second book. More on that in a minute.

Overnight successes happen, but they're rare, and I don't know that much can be learned from them. At least I wouldn't have learned much. Not nearly enough. I rewrote *Heritage* half a dozen times before it was saleable. I rewrote *Point of Fate*—from scratch, mind—just once. Every time I rewrote *Heritage*, I poured into it all the lessons I'd learned about writing and, equally important, critical and fundamental changes to the world, the characters, systems of magic, cultures—so, so much changed from draft to draft.

In fact, I sold *Heritage* before it landed at Tyche, only for that publisher to go under and send *Heritage* back to me. As disappointed as I was at the time, I would have been even more crushed if that revision of *Heritage* had been the one set in stone. The changes that came after made it exponentially better, but those changes had ripple effects.

I couldn't revise *Point of Fate* until the dust from *Heritage*'s renovations had settled. The sequel sat in the wings, waiting for *Heritage* to finally be finished, and then it waited even longer because after spending so many years with *Heritage* on the brain, I needed a palate cleanser.

I wrote other books: some self-published, some sold through traditional channels. I've done readings, talks, and attended signings at huge conventions like New York Comic-Con. I'm a more confident writer and public speaker than I was in 2014. All of that is surprising, too, because writing really is the only thing on my mind all day, every day. Leaving my Bat-cave to go out into the world and meet people who have actually read my books? That's weird. And scary. And pretty cool.

Now *Point of Fate* is here, which is also weird, and scary, and pretty cool. It's flat-out astounding, if I'm being honest.

I spent so many years thinking about *Heritage*, writing and rewriting it, pouring everything I'd learned as a writer into each new draft, that for a long, long time, I was convinced *Point of Fate* in its complete form would only ever exist in my mind, and as the outline I wrote for my editor, Margaret Curelas, way back in the Long Long Ago of 2015.

That brings me back to how I view first drafts. My foremost goal as a writer is to tell stories that are entertaining, and that make you think a little, too. (Sorry.) My second goal is for each book I write to be better than the last. That just seems natural. If I'm evolving as a writer, each subsequent book should serve as tangible proof of my growth. That's not to say that *Heritage* or *Stay Awhile and Listen: Book I* are unreadable now, only that, in my humble opinion, their successors should be that much improved.

Improved, how? In several ways. Mechanically, to be sure: voice, diction. Creatively, yeah: characterization, pacing. Collectively, what I aim to do with each book is learn from it— one thing or a bunch of things—so that the books that come after can benefit. Lessons such as what to do with first drafts, for instance. First drafts are for getting words down on paper. V. E. Schwab, one of my favorite writers, has a saying that lots of other writers believe, too: Writing is rewriting. It means, roughly, that the real fun occurs as you're reshaping your book, but that's where the real work, the heavy lifting, happens as well.

I like to think of rewriting as sculpting clay, but to sculpt, you need clay. I'm not talking about a jar of Play-Doh. I'm talking corn starch, acetate glue, lemon juice—the works. First drafts are all about making the clay so you can shape it into a porcelain bowl (or a plate, or a bracelet, or a sprawling fantasy epic) later.

Your clay doesn't have to be pretty. It just has to be.

I approach every book with the overarching goal of *This should be better* at the fore of my mind, but I also go in with goals specific to the story at hand. Aside from a page or two worth of text, *Heritage* was centered on Aidan: What he saw, what he thought, where he was, what he was doing. With *Point of Fate*, I wanted to pull the camera back and show a world full of places populated by people with their own motivations, struggles, and objectives—five people in particular.

Five characters. Five points of view. Five stories, many of which ended up being disturbingly prescient, because the world wasn't as upside-down when I wrote or rewrote *Point of Fate* as it is now.

For a book I suspected may never be real, like "One day very soon I'll be able to hold this and turn its pages and inhale the heady scent of paper and words and stories" real, *Point of Fate* turned out really well. At least I think so. I learned a thing or two, and most importantly, I had fun. Hopefully you do, too.

-David L. Craddock
May 31, 2018

Chapter 1:
Doom of the Wild

THE FATHER SOARED through the midnight sky. Curved like the blade of a sickle, he cut his way forward, as bright as polished steel. Silvery flecks winked and swarmed around him. Nichel's mother had called them stars and had likened them to gems woven through ebony fabric, but Cynthia Alston had been Leastonian and the daughter of a wealthy merchant, as enamored with textiles and jewels as Darinians were with stone, iron, and silver. Her mother had found beauty in the night. Her mother had found beauty in all things.

Nichel of the Wolf found beauty in nothing. Her father, Romen of the Wolf, had proclaimed those glittering flecks the Father's Vanguard. Darinians believed that when one died in battle, one's body was interred in Daram Ogahra while one's spirit ascended to the Vanguard. They swarmed across the sky, tens of hundreds of thousands spilling out every which way, riding alongside the Father for eternity and lending their strength to kinfolk in times of strife.

They believed, too, that claps of thunder were rumblings of the Vanguard's endless charge. That flashes of lightning were the sparks of Vanguard steel meeting steel. As a girl, Nichel of the Wolf had closed her eyes and pictured the Father's army, shouting and raising their weapons as they charged across the

1

pantheon time and again.

Now she looked out over the Plains of Dust from where she sat on the top step leading up to Janleah Keep. Her imaginings failed to do the din of this night justice.

Five days ago, the Plains had been empty and quiet, holding nothing but sand and dust and legends and the bones of the clansfolk too weak to survive the Mother's unrelenting glare. Then Nichel had received her silver-wrapped package, and Jonathan Hillstreem had convened with wolf speakers to carry news of its contents. Her clan's speakers had spoken the message to other speakers, and within hours of Nichel losing everything and everyone she had held dear, all the clans had boiled up from the underground and flooded over the Plains of Dust. The land writhed with Darinians for miles around Janleah Keep, the Plains an undulating blanket woven from brown and ebony flesh.

For five days and five nights, they had cavorted as if possessed, singing and baying and drumming their feet against the baked ground of the Plains of Dust. Men, women, and children alike were stripped to the waist, torsos, limbs, and faces painted in tattoos. The older a clansman or clanswoman, the more tattoos covered their flesh, each swirl and glyph one chapter in a lifelong story. Animals drawn with needles and ink dominated chests and backs, shivering and dancing as their hosts' movements breathed life into their still forms. Even infants had at least one emblem, usually the totem that represented their clan: wolf, lion, the poisonous adder, the eight-legged widowmaker, bears, eagles with wings that spanned breasts or broad shoulders.

The clans had gathered on the Plains, but remained separate, each assemblage leaving space between their kind and others. Bonfires as wide as three clan chiefs standing abreast rumbled, tongues of flames licking the cold night air. Heat from the fires coated flesh in a sheen of sweat, bodies sculpted from hard living out on the Plains. Spits turned slowly, and the scent of roasted meshia mingled with the smell of perspiration and body waste. She watched as a pair of Darinians wearing bearskins from the waist down heaved upward on either side of a spit and placed it gently on the ground. Other clansfolk saw it and tensed, but they let their clan chief, a mountain of a man named Guyde of the Bear dressed head to toe in black steel, stride forward and tear a leg free from the carcass. He bit into it, wrenching his head to one side to rip a piece free. Juices dribbled down his chin. Only then did the rest of the bears set upon the carcass, shredding with knives, swords, axes, bare hands, teeth. After they ate their fill, they craned their necks to bellow or shriek at the night sky.

Nichel hunched, fingering the knives at her waist, scanning the Plains. Not all clans ate meshia. Bears, lions, buffalo, exotic birds, and—her fists clenched around her knife hilts—wolves. Fights broke out. Men toppled backward into flames or cried out as steel flashed and flesh became as her mother's pincushions. The peers of those who had proven their strength whooped and bellowed to show their support and approval. The rest rolled around on the ground, punching, stabbing, hacking. Clan chiefs stood apart from the ruckus, coated head to toe in armor, glaring at each other from within ornate helms that resembled the head of their clan's totem.

Nichel of the Wolf turned away. Only two events could result in such a gathering: a call to war, or the death of a war chief. Her people never came together to mourn. They feted the dead through their savage customs before turning to the business of choosing a successor.

Her thumbs played with the hilts of Sand and Silk. Someone nearby was growling. Her hackles rose.

"Would you rather be alone, wolf daughter?"

Nichel looked up and into the face of Jonathan Hillstreem, dressed as always in flowing blue robes. Such attire was practical at night. The Plains of Dust were as cold when the Father took the sky as they were blistering when the Mother's gaze seared the land. Jonathan's face was taut with apprehension. She realized the low growl was emanating from deep in her throat. Her snarling cut off abruptly.

"You shouldn't call me that," she said.

Jonathan winced, noting his slip. He lowered himself beside her to sit cross-legged. She preferred to sit on her haunches. "You're not wearing your dress," he said, speaking loudly to be heard.

"I burned it," she said flatly. Jonathan nodded. He could not have heard her, not over the cacophony. Perhaps he had read her lips. Or perhaps he simply intuited. Her mother had sewn her dozens of dresses, encouraging Nichel to cultivate her Leastonian side as well as her western blood, nurtured by her father who trained her for survival on the Plains. Seeing the dresses in her wardrobe had been painful, so she had flung her wardrobe to the floor and burned it, along with the box that had been sent to her. Not the note that had accompanied it. That she kept.

She dressed more suitably now: trousers and a loose jerkin fashioned from wolf skin—it was acceptable for Darinians of the Wolf to skin pets that died honorably, so that their fur would protect and warm those of the pack who lived—that let her skin breathe during the unrelenting heat of daylight, and boots fashioned from meshia hide.

Nichel kept her hands busy, fighting the urge to growl. Her left hand, her favored hand, tugged Sand from its sheath and slammed it back into place. Again. Again. As if driving it through an enemy's chest. The blade, curved and as thick as two of her fingers side by side, was coarse and rough, like its namesake. It grated against the leather each time she pulled it free and slammed it home. In her right hand, Silk danced and spun across her fingers. It was straight, thin, and easier to maneuver. She barely gave thought to the movements. Her knives were her fangs, as much a part of her body as her hands.

Above them, a sharp crack pierced the din. The sky above the peak of Janleah Keep flared purple, then red, then blue, green to yellow, like a bruise. Color faded, replaced by smoke. Below, the clans' debauchery increased to a fevered pitch. They thrashed and swayed. Lust of all kinds overtook many of them.

Nichel gritted her teeth, resisting the urge to look upward. *I will not acknowledge them. Their decision means nothing to me.* In her mind's eye she saw the silver-wrapped package, saw its contents, saw the blood-splattered interior, saw—

"The ceremony nears its end, I think," Jonathan said, head tilted back to look skyward. Sand rammed home harder. Silk flashed faster.

Jonathan opened his mouth again, then eyed her knives. "I am sure whoever assumes the mantle of war chief will make your father proud," he said in a rush.

Nichel spat. "Superstitious fools and antiquated customs." She turned to glare at him, expecting him to console or placate her. To her astonishment, Jonathan stared out over the Plains, his face twisted in disgust. "They have forgotten him."

4

Sand and Silk fell still. Nichel tried to swallow but her throat had gone dry.

"Romen of the Wolf was an iconoclast," Jonathan continued. "He wanted to take his people away from this sort of savagery." He waved a hand at the naked figures. Noticing her stare, his face blanched. "I'm sorry, wolf daugh—Nichel. I meant no offense."

Nichel did not answer. Jonathan was right. There was a reason foreigners referred to Darinians as wildlanders. Romen of the Wolf had desired to civilize the clans. To take them out of the west and across Torel, Leaston, and perhaps even cultivate the forbidden territory of Sallner. At the very least, he had wished to gentrify the west. To abolish barbaric rituals like the one unfolding before her, and fill the void left by outdated traditions with education and society and prosperity.

Since opening her gift five days ago, she had looked upon her people through new eyes. Their actions—tearing into meat, accosting members of rival clans, men taking women on the ground in acts of passion—became more frantic. Nichel clenched her hands around Sand and Silk so hard her palms ached. None of these people mourned Romen of the Wolf. They were drunken celebrants who had burned his severed head—for there was no body to go along with it—and sent him off to join the Vanguard as quickly and casually as they would have dismissed a foreign messenger. They did not fool her. She had seen their smiles, their furtive glances. They were glad to see one who had dissented from tradition out of the way.

Jonathan was shaking his head. "He did not deserve such an ignoble death."

The memory of her father's glazed and sunken eyes staring up at her from the within the box, of her mother's torn neck and beautiful face ruined by rot and insects, pierced her like a spear to the ribs.

"Will he avenge them?" she asked.

"Who, wolf daughter?"

Nichel ignored the dated honorific. "His successor."

Jonathan hesitated. "I cannot say."

Anger boiled through her like hot water. "The clans are here. All of them. We could march at the Mother's first light."

"We could," he agreed slowly, as if uncertain.

Her head whipped toward him. "Why wouldn't we?"

"There are customs to observe. The war chief makes the decision to go to war, but the speakers must be consulted, the signs observed."

Nichel snarled again. Signs. The speakers clung to their signs like Torelian scholars to their texts. Tears leaked down her cheeks. She made no move to wipe them away. They were not tears of grief. Those had run their course. "It isn't right. It isn't fair."

"It is not," Jonathan agreed. "Romen of the Wolf was a wise chief. He saw the folly in this behavior. When I think of how much he accomplished in such a short time, I never fail to consider what else he might have accomplished had Aidan Gairden not . . ." He swallowed hard.

Her anger lowered to a simmer. "You were his advisor. Did he confide in you? What else did he want to change?"

Jonathan gave her a sad smile. "You."

A muscle in Nichel's cheek twitched. "I do not understand."

"To Romen of the Wolf, you embodied the change he sought. You are the first half-Darinian born in generations, a product of a marriage to a woman outside of Romen of the Wolf's people, let alone his clan. And he rose to clan chief and war chief besides!" His eyes bored through her. "Your father was a progressive man. Why, in time . . ." He came back to himself with a shake. "You should take your place with the other wolves. The time draws near for—"

Her hand snaked out to grip his arm. "In time, what?"

"Well," he said slowly, "your birth was difficult for your mother. Romen of the Wolf knew she would bear him no more children. One has to presume that he hoped for you to follow in his footsteps."

"But I'm a woman, and I am—I was—" *Promised. To him.*

"A woman as hard as any man in the Plains," Jonathan said. "You hunted and killed a meshia when your twelfth name day came, like any Darinian man. You scaled Janleah Keep in nothing but your flesh and paid homage to the Mother during the summer solstice, like any man. You returned as red as the lobsters your mother's father brought in from the Great Sea, so parched you could not speak, your skin blistered and stretched so tight I feared the slightest touch might break it open."

Jonathan appeared to gather his courage. Licking his lips, he cupped her chin in one soft, white hand. "You are a study in contrasts, Nichel of the Wolf. Hard and soft. Beautiful and rough." His nod indicated the knives clenched in her fists. "Sand and Silk. Gifts from your paternal grandparents following the first year of your life. They symbolize your mixed blood. You are Leastonian, but you are Darinian, too, and not only the pride of your father's heart, but of your clan. You would have been a Gairden's queen, but you would have ruled two realms."

"The traditions—"

"Damn the traditions." His fervor made her flinch. "So your father never sired a son," he continued. "So what? Romen of the Wolf stamped out mores not worth keeping. In time, I would venture to guess the speakers would have come to accept a woman as clan chief." His smile widened. "I would venture to guess you would have made them."

He sighed. "To be perfectly honest with you, wolf daugh . . . Nichel, I fear the worst. Your father was a great man, far ahead of his time, but to the speakers and the other chiefs, he was an obstacle. With his death, I fear your people will be all too eager to forget Romen's goals, and Romen himself. A return to the old ways seems likely, even as soon as . . . Nichel? Are you well?"

For a moment, Nichel sat frozen, staring at him without seeing. She sprang to her feet and stepped away from his outstretched hand, her eyes searching his.

"Nichel?" he said, rising. "I'm sorry. I only meant—"

"We will go to war," she said softly. Like silk over sand.

She turned on her heel and charged up the steps, disappearing within Janleah Keep.

JONATHAN WATCHED NICHEL, torn. Part of him wanted to go after her. The other part, the part that won out, decided to leave her be. Nichel was a woman in the eyes of her people, yet fifteen winters—he was Torelian, and would always mark the passage of time as northerners did—was still young. She needed time to think. Time to grieve.

As a woman, she would not be allowed to march with the clans. When they marched. If they marched. Perhaps that was best. Nichel would leave Janleah Keep, giving it over to the war chief and his family, and assimilate back into the wolf pack. She and the other women would travel, and build, and hunt while the men fought. Time and the need to focus all of her considerable wits on survival would heal her wounds.

Turning, Jonathan descended the stairs and threaded his way through Darinians to take his place among the wolves. Eyes followed him as he glided along, like daggers probing and jabbing. Romen of the Wolf had paid Jonathan to advise him. That was one among many new ideas that had earned the war chief enemies among his people. Foreigners were not welcome in the west, at least not for long, and they certainly were not to be given places of honor only a step or two removed from a clan chief.

He did not know how much longer he would be able to stay in Darinia. Romen of the Wolf had been his shield, and Nichel had been displaced. On the morning after she and Jonathan had learned of Romen's death, he had spread the news, as was his duty. Speakers and wolves had materialized at Janleah Keep that very evening as if from thin air. The speakers had read their signs in only a day, and declared that the Mother and Father had called upon Palken of the Wolf, a man two heads shorter than Romen of the Wolf but nearly twice as wide, to lead the clan. Jonathan still called Nichel wolf daughter out of habit, but Palken's girl cub, Kelcyr, had assumed the honorific. Nichel was just a she-wolf, now. Another member of the pack.

A flash of red light drew Jonathan's attention. His eyes trailed up Janleah Keep's pyramidal structure. It had been erected in memory of Janleah of the Wolf, the first war chief, who had fallen in battle eight hundred years ago in the Serpent's War. Now it belonged to the war chief and his clan to use as they saw fit. The Keep stretched for miles across the Plains of Dust and rose in terraced levels. Stone walls separated terraces, and each terrace was slightly less wide than the one below it. The top level was twenty paces wide and long, and it was there that the speakers tended a roaring fire of their own. Sparks fanned out, and colored smoke formed shapes in the sky. The assemblage fell silent as the smoke coalesced into a shape.

A bear, rearing up on its hind legs, maw open in a howl.

Cries rang out, some victorious, others disappointed or despairing. Jonathan's heart sank into his boots. Behind him, the crowd parted, and Guyde of the Bear strode forward, the speakers' vision made flesh. Jonathan eased back. Guyde's helm had been forged in the shape of the animal head that belonged to his clan. The bear's head yawned open in a silent roar. Stony eyes peered out from its recesses. Slowly, Guyde ascended Janleah Keep, armor clanging with each step.

His ascent took time. The clans' ululations heightened. There was no disappointment or anger in those cries. Only acceptance. Jonathan fought to stay calm. There was more than enough firelight for him to shift miles away, even leagues. He knew the desert well enough. He could find his way northeast, back to Torel, or further east to Leaston. A cottage by the sea, a life spent reading and imbibing. He was young, but such an idyllic lifestyle awaited every scholar, though not until they had snow in their beards. Jonathan's cheeks and chin were bare, devoid even of stubble.

Only, there was Nichel to think about. His heart sped up. He could not just leave her. His throat constricted at a sudden thought. What if Guyde encountered her in his ascent to the summit? Nichel was a skilled fighter, but Guyde may as well have been made from steel and metal.

He forced himself to take a deep breath. *All will be well. Wait and see.*

Armored footsteps grew louder, like a soldier coming from far away and drawing nearer. Conversation faded, then dried up like water splashed over the Plains of Dust. Jonathan looked up. The speakers, one for each clan, stood on the summit, each small enough for him to pinch between thumb and forefinger. Guyde of the Bear appeared, and Jonathan understood. The footsteps were the bear's, magically amplified by the speakers, each tread like the far-off rumble of a herd of meshia.

A moment later, the eldest of the aged speakers—a bent-backed woman called Margia of the Falcon, whose braided, coarse, grey hair hung nearly to her feet—stepped forward.

"The Mother and Father have spoken," Margia said in a quavering voice that rang out along the Plains.

"They have spoken," Jonathan and every other voice intoned by rote.

"Guyde of the Bear, the Father bids you come forward," Margia said.

Shrieks and bellows erupted from the clansfolk as the armored bear strode into the center of the circle. Jonathan thinned his lips. The choice made perfect sense. Guyde of the Bear had never crossed the border leading out of the west and into the rest of Crotaria. He was as indigenous to the desert as the mountain from which Janleah's Keep had been cut and shaped. His tongue had never tasted a word of Torelian or Leastonian. His ignorance of any customs besides his own made him the perfect choice for speakers in search of a war chief who would lead the clans according to the old ways.

Margia waved a hand, and the colored fire flared. Smoke fanned out like an expansive storm cloud. A moment later it cleared. Clansfolk gasped and cried out in wonder and fear. Guyde stretched across the sky and towered over them, a giant who stood a head taller than the Keep. It was an illusion, Jonathan knew, but no less awe-inspiring for it. The illusion mimicked Guyde's every movement, though it was transparent. Jonathan could see the Father and his Vanguard faintly through the bear's black armor. His form shimmered as if seen through rain.

"The Mother calls upon you, Guyde of the Bear," Margia said, craning her neck to gaze up at him. "How do you answer?"

"With honor and pride," the big man rumbled. At this, all the bears shrieked and hoisted their weapons. The other clansfolk joined in, though less vigorously. They would follow any war chief the Father chose, but deep down, every clan craved the honor of a war chief being chosen from among their ranks.

Margia inclined her head to Guyde. "Kneel, and I will impart the Father's blessing."

Guyde's armor creaked as he slowly lowered himself to one knee. All the Darinians had gone silent, their faces solemn.

"Guyde of the Bear," Margia began, "as a speaker for our Father, I—"

Murmurs broke out as a growing commotion reached Jonathan's ears. Bare feet slapping on stone. Jonathan frowned, then his gasp joined a chorus of others as a familiar form ascended the summit and shouldered its way up to Guyde of the Bear.

Nichel stood eye level with the speakers' select, but only because he was still on his knees. A great rumbling shook the ground, and Jonathan realized with horror that it was Guyde growling as he unfolded to his full height. The speakers did not grace Nichel with a giant form. The tiny woman, the tiny child, stood her ground, head tilting back to the gaze of the mountainous bear looming over her. Far from angry, the vision of Guyde wore a mystified expression, as if he could not fathom how something so small could stand before him.

"What is the meaning of this, cub?" he asked in his booming voice.

"You forget yourself, Nichel of the Wolf," Margia said, her mouth puckered in a toothless frown. "Return to your clan in shame."

Nichel did not move. When she spoke, her voice was amplified. "Aidan Gairden killed my father. I will avenge him."

At the mention of that name, tens of thousands of lips moved in angry mutters. "*Shorogoyt. Shorogoyt. Shorogoyt. Shorogoyt.*"

Over and over they repeated the insult. Far above, Nichel shuddered. Not in disgust, Jonathan surmised. In ecstasy.

At that, Margia's tone softened. "We all mourn the passing of Romen of the Wolf, but our path is not for you to decide, girl cub. Go. May the Father and his Vanguard light your path."

"I am the wolf daughter. I am worthy of—"

"You were the wolf daughter," the speaker corrected. "Kelcyr of the Wolf is the wolf daughter."

Even from far below, Jonathan saw the blood drain from Nichel's face. She opened her mouth, but Guyde intervened. He rested a boulder-sized hand on Nichel's slim shoulder. His illusion seemed to grip air. "You still grieve, Nichel of the Wolf. I grieve with you, as do we all. But your actions rob you of honor."

Nichel flung his arm away. "I invoke the rite of provenance."

Shocked whispers raced through the throng, most repeating what she had said. Even the speakers appeared shocked. "You are a girl," Margia said, apparently too shocked to do more than state plain truths.

"I am a woman according to our customs, Margia of the Falcon."

"Girl, woman. It all comes to the same. Romen of the Wolf had no son. Your claim is—"

"My claim is valid. An invocation of the rite cannot be denied. You know this. Steel is stronger than flesh, blood stronger than steel. I invoke the rite of provenance," she repeated, and ripped

Silk and Sand free from her belt.

Guyde peered down at Margia. "What is the meaning of this?"

Everyone fell silent, straining forward to hear. Margia of the Falcon was a long time in answering. "An ancient custom. A fallen chief's firstborn may challenge another for the right to lead the clans." She paused. "The challenge is to the death."

Whispers rose in volume. Nichel said nothing, only stared at Guyde unblinkingly, her fists clutching her knives so tightly they shook. Jonathan's fingers bit into his palms just as hard, drawing blood. He barely noticed. Then Guyde spoke, and Jonathan's numbness melted away.

"Challenge Palken of the Wolf to lead your pack, then," he said. "I am the war chief."

"The gods," Nichel said as if the words tasted sour on her tongue, "did not specify which fallen leaders may be challenged. My father was both clan chief and war chief. One and the same."

The bear looked to Margia. The elder's toothless maw opened and closed, as if wanting to say something but thinking better of it.

Guyde slowly turned back to Nichel. "I will not do this," he said quietly. "There is no honor in it."

"You dishonor me by refusing," she said.

Guyde shook his head. "No. I will not fight a woman. It is not right."

All of Darinia held its breath. Bent-backed Margia's mouth worked soundlessly. "You are as impetuous and audacious as your father, Nichel of the Wolf," she said at last.

Nichel did not respond. She held Sand and Silk limply at her sides. Guyde looked at them, then into her eyes. "Your fangs are not sharp enough, cub."

Nichel's upper lip curled. Her posture did not change. Tight-lipped, Jonathan was not fooled. Nichel fought like her father: Coiled, a snake ready to strike. *No*, he corrected himself. *Like a wolf. At ease in front of the hearth like a hound brought to heel, tongue lolling, eyes dancing with laughter, and then on its feet in an instant, teeth bared and snapping around the throat of its prey.*

Margia glanced between them. She slumped as if ready to sag to the ground. "The rite cannot be denied," she said softly.

Guyde's face twisted into a mask of loathing. "This is

outrageous," he said to Nichel. "You should open your veins and let the earth drink of your life water out of shame."

"It is not my blood that will slake the ground's thirst this night," Nichel said calmly.

The bear appraised her while Margia and the other speakers muttered. Abruptly, a gigantic Nichel appeared in the night sky—gigantic, but slight compared to Guyde of the Bear. Talk broke out as clansfolk stared upward at the ethereal warriors.

At last the clan chief raised a hand. At once, a barrel-chested Darinian covered in tattoos hefted a battle-axe as tall as the chief. The bear set off at a staggering run, up the steps into Janleah Keep. Minutes later he appeared, panting and covered in sweat, holding the axe before him. Without turning, Guyde plucked his paw from the man's hands and hefted it over his shoulder.

Jonathan stifled a moan. He'd lifted his axe as easily as a child would lift a pup. Nichel was going to die, and he would follow her to the grave.

THE ROAD TO *the Father's Vanguard is paved with hot coals and sharp stones.*

Romen of the Wolf had spoken those words to Nichel after a hardship. The meshia, the climb, the attempt on her life by an assassin of the Blood. Never before had the words rang truer. Hot coals and sharp stones were as nothing to the man towering over her.

With one hand, Guyde of the Bear removed his helm and tossed it casually over the side of Janleah Keep. It scraped and bounced against stone. The man staring back at her had a hard face carved with scars. His eyes were bright, passionate, pleading.

"Do not do this," he said. "I will avenge your father. Aidan Gairden will pay for—"

At that name, her fear vanished. Nichel darted forward. Silk spun in her right hand as Sand jabbed at Guyde's exposed throat. His eyes went wide, and he backpedaled, giving ground and raising his paw before him—one hand gripping the black shaft near the base, the other choking it beneath its smooth, polished blade—to deflect Nichel's flurry of blows.

Margia scuttled to one side, stumbling and weaving until two other speakers took her by the arms and pulled her to safety down the hatch that led to the summit. Nichel noted this distantly, as vaguely as she registered and dismissed noises from below: howls, shrieks, roars. Firelight glinted off steel as Darinians hoisted weapons high. This, too, she took in, dismissed, snapped her attention back to Guyde. Her body was a blur of motion, booted feet kicking and maneuvering, dancing in and out of his legs. Her knives flashed, Silk probing for openings in his armor as Sand slashed and stabbed.

Guyde's shock lasted as long as rainfall. He planted his feet and swatted at her with the butt of his axe. Nichel raised Sand out of instinct. She may as well have tried to stop a mountain from stampeding over her. The wooden haft, as thick as both her legs, cracked against Sand, sending tremors up her arm. She grunted and stumbled to one side, off balance. Bellowing like his namesake, Guyde threw himself at her, reclaiming ground, cleaving the air with his axe in wide, two-handed strokes. Far below, bears roared. His clansmen were with him. Guyde rode their approval like a wave, roaring in reply. His eyes bulged, bright with the thrill of battle, the anticipation of blood.

Nichel shut him out. She danced back and to the side, circling, appearing to be on the defensive, yet watching. Waiting.

Guyde feinted left, swinging his axe back so far he twisted at the waist. Nichel read his movements. He was preparing to deliver a wide horizontal slice. The maneuver made sense. Given the length of his arms and that of his weapon, such swings covered nearly half the platform. She tensed, appearing indecisive, unsure of which way to go. When he began to swing she would duck under him and—

Without warning Guyde brought his axe up instead of around. He raised it high over his head for a split second and then brought it whistling down. Nichel's grim determination shattered, replaced by fear. The Bear's Paw. It was Guyde's fabled attack, responsible for splitting countless enemies from skull to groin.

Instinctively, she threw herself back. The stone platform shuddered as Guyde's paw crashed down atop it, kicking up sparks. His body shook with the force of the blow. His roar cut off as his teeth clicked together hard enough that Nichel heard it over the tumult of shouts and cheers below. He was slow to lift his axe. The shock of the blow must have been great enough for him to lose all feeling, if only for a moment. A moment was all Nichel needed.

She launched herself forward, not at his throat, but at his legs, where the hinges on his greaves met. Two swipes from Sand, one for each leg, was all it took. The hinges snapped. His greaves fell loosely, exposing dark flesh. In the same breath in which she had swung Sand, Nichel darted in with Silk, stabbing and cutting at hamstrings.

Guyde howled and swung his paw behind him. Nichel rolled and came up hacking and slashing, targeting more weak spots. She was dissecting him, cutting him open and exposing flesh and sinew and bone. Guyde's roars grew more frenzied, anger mingling with pain as blood ran from wounds. He kicked wildly, first with one leg than the other, like a frightened horse.

His right leg gave out first. One moment he was standing upright, and the next he fell to one knee. Fear painted his features. Gripping the handle of his axe, he held the weapon across his chest like an oar, crawling backward.

Nichel did not just see his fear. She could smell it. It filled her nostrils, a mixture of sweat and blood and cold radiating from him in waves. She leaped at him and thrust her knives down.

In an instant, Guyde's expression changed from sheer terror to triumph. He brought his paw up and Sand and Silk bit into wood and held firm. She was wrenching before her feet hit the ground, snarling and trying to rip them free. They were stuck, buried up to their hilts in ebony wood cut from forests in the forbidden realm.

Guyde heaved forward. The shaft smashed into her ribs and sent her flailing. Her feet left the stone and her back crashed against it. Breath left her lungs in a whoosh. Guyde rose, tottering until he achieved balance, snarling as he tried to put weight on his left leg. He ripped Sand and Silk free and hurled them at her feet hard enough that they bounced before skittering out of reach.

She looked up in time to see Guyde pounce. Gritting her teeth, struggling to pull in air, she pushed herself up and threw herself to one side. Too slow. Guyde of the Bear slammed atop her, an avalanche of muscles and steel that stole what little breath she'd managed to regain. She squirmed futilely. His great mass pinned her to the stone. His left knee found her left arm and went still. He shifted his bulk, driving all his weight down on her arm. Something snapped. She screamed, struggled harder, gouging at his eyes with her right hand. Guyde grunted, swatting her hands away, then drove his head against her skull.

Bright colors flashed across Nichel's vision. When they cleared, two Guydes stood over her, blurry as specters through a haze of tears and blood. Blackness threatened to close in. It took all her willpower to cling to consciousness.

Guyde of the Bear stumbled, favoring his right leg. Blood ran down it in a curtain, but Guyde paid it no mind. His mountainous form glared down at the assemblage like some ancient deity descended from the clouds, his expression twisted more by anger than pain. They cried out for him, weapons rattling and fists shaking. They cried out for blood—not just the bears. All of them, demanding sacrifice to the Father.

"This battle is over," he called. "Nichel of the Wolf fought with honor. She . . ."

Guyde's words faded to indistinct mumbling. The world receded. The aches and bruises forming over her body, the fire racing through her broken arm—everything faded. His words were as frilly as the silk of her mother's dresses. For all his talk of honor in combat, there was no way any war chief would let a challenger live. She would be considered a threat to his reign, mercy a sign of weakness. Clansfolk were not known for clemency, nor did they make a habit of forgiving affronts to their honor. A war chief especially could not afford to be seen as soft by clan chiefs who would as soon kill him and take his place than they would follow.

Romen of the Wolf had shown mercy once.

Fresh tears spilled down her cheeks. Her father had done his best to prepare her for this hard life. Now he was gone, and she would follow him to the Father's Vanguard. She stared up at the glowing orb of the Father and at his shining spirits that filled the sky, an army that stretched as far as the eye could see. Would her mother be there? She thought so. The Mother and Father would not separate kindred souls.

Guyde of the Bear's droning reached a crescendo. The roars of his people, of her people, rose to a pitch. They sounded mad, given over to bloodlust. Turning, she saw Guyde's enormous hand reach down and heft his paw, dragging the steel head against the stone. With his other hand he hauled her from her back and turned her over so that she knelt, head lolling, left arm dangling, her neck exposed.

Nichel closed her eyes, but tears still squeezed through her eyelids. "It's not fair," she whispered through bloody lips already beginning to swell. Anger and grief bubbled up.

Guyde must have heard her. His voice grew piteous. "You fought well, Nichel of the Wolf. The Father's Vanguard lit your path and will welcome you home."

His hands choked the haft of his paw. He grunted, whether from distaste at what he knew he must do or from injury. His fists tightened, knuckles whitening. He raised the axe high.

Nichel managed a wet snort. She was not afraid. She was ashamed and heartbroken. Her parents had been slain. It was her duty to avenge them, and she had failed in spectacular fashion. All the while, their killer walked free. Aidan Gairden. The man she had been promised to marry, their union tying unbreakable bonds between Crotaria's northern and western realms. That union would never be. Torel and Darinia would go to war. Hundreds of thousands would die. Aidan would be one of them. She should be the one to spill his blood. To taste it.

Aidan Gairden had betrayed her people. He had betrayed her parents. He had betrayed her. How could he live while she died? It wasn't right. It wasn't fair!

Anger festered, becoming blind fury. Grief rotted into despair. She closed her eyes tighter, bracing for Guyde's axe and hoping the blackness of her eyelids would soon turn to the bright expanse of the Vanguard.

Mother, she thought. *Father. I come to join you.* Peace began to slide over her.

Red eyes opened in her mind. They stared at her, through her, saw inside her. Her thoughts were sluggish, clouded by pain and anguish and wrath so hot her blood boiled.

— *What are you?*

Nichel saw nothing except red pinpricks against darkness. The whispered voice was her own, distant and hazy.

The red eyes intensified, deepening to the shade of molten fire.

Nichel was there, yet not there. Within herself. She gazed into the eyes. They were mirrors, reflecting her pain back at her. Not physical pain. Broken bones and bloodied lips did not exist in this place. Those eyes were mirrors that magnified her wrath and hopelessness tenfold. Those eyes brightened, blinding her, burning her up, filling her, consuming her and the world and everything.

—*Free me.* That voice rumbled, a growl emanating up from the depths of a deep, dark hole.

Nichel opened her eyes.

JONATHAN STOOD ROOTED to the spot, hands wrapped around his stomach. If he moved them, if he so much as loosened his grip, he would be sick.

Spill my dinner, then my blood, he thought vaguely.

A scene of madness played out in the night sky: The giant form of Nichel on her knees while Guyde of the Bear towered over her, towered over all of them. Margia of the Falcon stood with the other speakers further back. Guyde raised his arms over his head. His axe gleamed, reflecting the Father's smile.

Nichel had moments to live. That Jonathan would not outlive her for long crossed his mind only briefly. His thought was of Aidan Gairden and how the wretched prince had broken his love's heart. Out of desperation, he turned to a nearby bonfire. He would leech its light, fill himself with its warmth until he thought flames would burst from his skin. His actions would not save him, but if he could kill enough of the clansfolk, if he could distract Guyde and the speakers, then Nichel might live.

A howl ripped through the sky. Chills ran up his spine. There was a great clatter as weapons slipped from dark hands, like raindrops made from steel and wood. Jonathan's mouth fell open. Above, Nichel pushed herself to her feet. She swayed unsteadily. Her left arm was cradled against her chest, and her eyes . . .

Her eyes were the color of blood and fire.

Guyde let his axe fall and took a step away. Without moving her body, Nichel whipped her head around. Her lips contorted, peeling back into a vulpine smile that bared her teeth.

Does she have fangs? Jonathan thought in dazed wonder.

Nichel flung her head back and howled again. The anguish and rage in that cry broke Jonathan's heart. He fell to the ground, clutching his face in his hands as tears rolled down his cheeks. Looking up, he noticed he was not the only one. All around him, Darinians rocked on their feet or collapsed to their knees, hands clutching heads as if they might split open.

A third howl tore open the night. Jonathan had never heard such loss, or rage. He shivered as if with cold, then realized he was quaking with fright. When he looked up again, Nichel was gone.

In her place stood a wolf unlike any Jonathan had ever seen. It was a wolf, but at least three times as large. Its hair was long and stood on end. Its bared teeth were long and pointed and gleamed in the Father's light. With its head bent, the wolf took an unsteady step forward. Its claws dragged and scraped along the ground. It growled, and the sound rolled and reverberated over the Plains like thunder.

Margia's tan face was bloodless. Her old lips quavered and formed a single, whispered word. "*Nuulass.*"

Darinians took up the chant, first a handful, then a dozen, then hundreds and thousands.

"*Nuulass. Nuulass. Nuulass.*"

Jonathan chanted soundlessly. His throat was dry.

The beast snarled and raised wet, bloodshot eyes to Guyde of the Bear. His visage, carved from stone and scars, wore abject terror. His legs gave way and he crashed to his knees. "Please."

The beast's grin widened, becoming a rictus of pleasure. Its nose twitched, as if it could smell Guyde's fear and was pleased by it. Hungered by it.

It lunged for Guyde's throat.

When it was over, Nichel was a woman once again. She sat on her haunches, naked and covered in blood from head to toe. She stared at her hands, features shifting from confusion to horror to satisfaction, her broken arm seemingly forgotten. When she lowered her hands, she saw what little remained of Guyde of the Bear.

Behind her, Margia's toothless mouth worked. "The Mother and Father have spoken," she said, voice quavering. Her body folded, going prostrate, hands outstretched and lips kissing stone. Far below, the clans mimicked her.

BY THE MOTHER-stained sky the next morning, the speakers entered Janleah Keep and stood before Nichel. They prostrated themselves again. She sat in her father's chair, seat carved from the solid rock of the wall of the great hall where the war chief saw guests, and gazed down at them coldly. Though she had allowed

Jonathan to mend her arm and seal her wounds, she had not bathed. Guyde of the Bear's blood had hardened over her body and flaked off whenever she so much as shifted. Jonathan stood beside her, arms lost in his voluminous blue sleeves.

"What am I?" Nichel repeated, proud of how calm she sounded. Inwardly her temper warred with a fear that threatened to swallow her.

Groveling at the base of her chair, Margia of the Falcon spoke into the stone. Her words came out muffled.

"Raise your eyes to me!" Nichel screamed. Her words rang around the cavern.

Quivering, Margia slowly met her eyes. Her seamed face puckered. Her throat moved. She had to smack her lips together several times before she was able to speak. "The *Nuulass* is the essence of our people."

Nichel pounded a fist on the arm of her chair. "Its name means 'Wild's Doom.' Why?"

Margia shook her head helplessly. "We are ancient. First there was the Mother, then our Father, and then the *Nuulass*, and the clans. That is what the legends say." She looked around at her fellow speakers. They knelt quivering, lips kissing the floor. "Please. I know nothing more."

Nichel's head whipped around to Jonathan. Instantly, she regretted the action. It was too quick, too sudden. Too violent. She was grateful when he only stared at her, unflinching. "You studied the west before coming to my father. What do your books say, scholar?"

He shook his head, appearing sad. "I am sorry, war chief. None of the texts even mentioned a *Nuulass*. What do you remember of your . . . of the change?"

Nichel sat back. "Nothing." That was not entirely true. She remembered blood, first craving it and then tasting it and wanting more. Her temper flared. She could feel it inside of her, feeding on her anger, devouring it.

A hand on hers. Nichel looked at Jonathan. "Whatever this is, you can master it," he said.

"How?" she snapped.

"By mustering all the focus and discipline your father taught you."

My father. Romen's face materialized in her mind, eyes

glazed, mouth ajar, neck torn and bloody where Aidan Gairden had severed it from his body. Her arms shook. This chair was too confining. Her fists tightened around the arms. She could break this chair, bend stone in her hand and snap it like dry grass. All she had to do was continue feeding the thing inside her. Let it out.

— *Free me*, it crooned.

"Breathe," Jonathan said soothingly.

Nichel closed her eyes and breathed. No eyes stared back at her. Silence reigned, and she was grateful.

"What is your command, *Nuulass*?" Margia of the Falcon said.

Nichel's eyes shot open. "Do not call me that. I am the war chief. You will address me as such."

"The *Nuulass* speaks through you," Margia said. "It manifests for the first time in millennia. You must—" She cut off as Nichel went still. The old woman lowered her eyes. "What is your command, war chief?"

"We march on Torel," she answered at once. There had never been any other option.

"When?" Margia asked.

"Immediately."

"What is our destination?"

Nichel glanced at Jonathan, uncertain. He bowed his head, thinking, then leaned in and whispered into her ear behind a cupped hand. He straightened, and Nichel nodded.

"Torelians value commerce from the east," she said. "They eat Leastonian crops and barter for Leastonian goods. We will cut them off. A small force to begin with, to establish an outpost. Gather one thousand clansmen. An equal number from each clan. They will travel by way of the underground and reconnoiter with their folk already in the city."

"The city, war chief?" Margia asked, still speaking to her feet.

Nichel took a deep breath. "They march on Sharem."

Chapter 2:
Stray Thoughts

"CROWN OF THE NORTH!"

"The Guardian!"

"Corpse-slayer!"

"The Guardian!"

Praise chased Aidan Gairden as he rushed across Sunfall's grounds. Just a few weeks ago he would have reveled in them. Folding in ostentatious bows, flaunting his magic, grinning roguishly, soaking up the adulation of Torel's people. His people.

Now their words rolled off his shoulders like snow rolling down the sloped rooftops that capped shops, homes, and temples throughout Crotaria's northern realm. That was the old Aidan. This Aidan was too focused to pay attention to exaltation. Focused and terrified.

The sword at his side rattled in its scabbard. — *For the first time since your Rite of Heritage, your people feel hope*, Grandfather Charles said. *They have embraced you. I thought you would be pleased.*

Unconsciously, Aidan's hand dropped to the sword. His fingertips brushed the egg-shaped ruby, the Eye of Heritage, in the center of the sword's cross-guard, trailed downward to grip the hilt. He grasped it as if it were a branch that kept him from being swept away by a river.

"I'm too frightened to feel pleased, Grandfather," he said.

— *Which is why I am surprised to find you back here, of all places.*

Aidan stopped and peered around as if just realizing where his feet had carried him. Sunfall's eastern courtyard was spacious and tastefully decorated, benches of white marble bordering wide walking paths and lawns damp from melted snow. Spring lasted a short time in Calewind, Torel's capital city nestled at the foot of the Ihlkin Mountains, the season fading as quickly as night gave way to day. Still, the scent of grass calmed him. Just by a hair.

His gaze fell on the stone tower rearing up in front of him, and his ease faded like springtime. He trudged toward it, feet as heavy as stone. A thick wooden door sat at the base. He reached for its brass knob, let his hand fall. He tightened his grip on Heritage.

Habit, he thought. It was meant to be private, a silent admonishment. His grandfather responded anyway.

— *A habit you must break. This place is dangerous.*

"It's where I come when I have nowhere else to go," Aidan said aloud.

The Eye of Heritage flashed. The sword rattled softly.

— *You do have a place to go.*

I can't see Nichel yet. I need to find . . . He let the thought trail off.

— *Just what is it you hope to find here, boy? Besides traps set for anyone foolish enough to intrude.*

Aidan's heart hammered against his ribs. Gathering his courage, he turned the knob and pushed. The door swung inward with a long creak. There were no windows. Bracketed torches cast shadows that danced over stairs that hugged the inner stone wall and curled upward. He stepped in and closed the door behind him. His palms grew damp. Faint as they were, the torches brought a measure of comfort. Darkness made any Touched nervous.

"I don't know what I'm after," he said softly, and snapped his mouth closed. His words echoed. *I thought it would be worth my while to poke around while I wait for Daniel to find the key I need to enter Darinia. I am powerful, even more so with Heritage, but Tyrnen is stronger. He is more experienced, and far more bloodthirsty.*

— And you hope to find some artefact or prayer to gain an advantage, Charles finished.

Something like that.

— Prudent, Charles said, clearly impressed.

Aidan's lips shook as he tried to smile. *You sound surprised I thought of it.*

— I never said that, his grandfather said lightly.

Aidan tried to laugh, but couldn't. He knew why his grandfather was teasing him. Tyrnen's tower had been a place of refuge for Aidan. Now it was ominous. A tomb of memories that were as false as Tyrnen's love for him. Convincing himself he was giving his eyes time to adjust to the gloom, Aidan blinked, then lifted one foot onto the first step. He climbed the next. The next. Around him, shadows twisted and jerked. He thought he heard low laughter and had to stop himself from kindling every torch and releasing a blaze of fire along the path ahead of him.

He hummed a Leastonian ballad, or tried to. His voice rasped and faded. *Christine could sing the tune. She probably knows the lyrics.*

A genuine smile bloomed at the sudden thought. He wished Christine were here. The way she walked, the way she carried herself, her smile that made one side of her mouth curl. Every movement exuded confidence. If she were at his side, he could draw from it like kindling from flame.

He thought of the way her hips moved as she walked, and other pleasant memories arose. Christine wearing a silk nightgown that clung to her pale skin as she had padded toward him. Christine in the low-cut skirt she had worn on the cold, blustery day they had spent in front of the fire at the Fisherman's Pond in Tarion. Christine sitting on his lap, kissing him as he ran his hands through her soft dark hair. Christine, shut away with him in her room in Ralda's Inn, her hair damp and tangled, their bodies pressed together—

A female voice cut into his reverie. *— I don't see how thoughts of your Sallnerian girl are relevant to the task at hand,* Anastasia Gairden said.

Embarrassment led to annoyance. *Can you all hear* every *thought I have?*

— Of course, Anastasia said, as if confused why that could

possibly bother Aidan. *The connection between Gairden sword-bearer and Heritage has always worked thus. Your ancestors are here to help, dear, not to hinder. How can we assist you if we cannot determine what you need?* She paused. *If you insist on thinking of the girl, please imagine her with clothes on. Yes, that's better.*

Aidan reached out to touch the cold stone of the wall. The flush in his body dissipated. At last he halted at the top of the steps. *I could use your help now.*

— *What is it?* Charles said.

He stood before a door identical to the one below, save for a brass knocker in place of a knob. *This only opens from the inside. Every time I visited Tyrnen for lessons, he was already here, waiting to let me in.* Warm memories threatened to rush over him. He shook them away and concentrated, one hand still wrapped around the hilt of Heritage. *I could probably tap into* Ordine'kel *and chop the door to splinters, but I think it wiser to—*

— *test the door first*, his grandfather finished. *Good thinking. Do you know the prayer for espial?*

No. Tyrnen never showed me, nor did . . . He swallowed. *Nor did my mother.*

Charles fell silent. — *Could she be in there?* he asked after a moment.

That's what I aim to find out.

He heard Charles take a steadying breath. — *Very well.* He cleared his throat once, then again.

— *I will guide him, Charles,* Anastasia said gently. *Take a moment to compose yourself. Both of you.*

Aidan scrubbed at his eyes. Guilt and shame fell on him like a sudden snowstorm as he thought back to the last time he had seen his mother, how he had treated her before Tyrnen's imposter had usurped her throne and place in his life.

Grim resolve burned away his grief. Tyrnen had a lot to answer for. *So do I*, he thought.

— *Kindle when you are ready, Aidan,* Anastasia said. *You won't need much.*

Aidan opened his body, a sluice gate that admitted light and warmth instead of water. The torch nearest him, just around the bend in the stairwell leading down, trembled. A trickle of heat crept into him.

— *That will do,* Anastasia said.

He closed himself off and shut his eyes, enjoying the sensation. Like submerging himself in warm bathwater. Gradually, the impression increased, as if the water were being heated. Fire could not be held for long. To a Touched, kindling was like breathing: Inhale to draw in, exhale to expel.

— *Espial is a trifling prayer, really,* Anastasia continued. *Touch the sword.*

His fingers closed around the hilt. The Eye of Heritage flashed, and words in the Language of Light came to him, as if a forgotten memory had suddenly surfaced. Speaking the words, Aidan touched the door and pushed light out through his hand.

Nothing happened.

He frowned. "I don't mean to question your wisdom, Anastasia, but the door still won't open."

— *I can see that,* she said, flustered. *Give me a moment to think.*

— *You studied under Tyrnen,* Charles broke in. *Can you think of what he might have used to seal his quarters?*

The answer came to him immediately. Dark magic. The trouble was, he knew of no way to detect it, much less counteract it.

— *Espial should be enough,* Anastasia said testily. *It's served me well for many years.*

A third voice, smooth and soft, broke in. — *Approximately eight hundred, give or take a decade. Does that sound about right, Mother?*

Anastasia's voice hardened to steel, sharp enough to cut. — *Close enough.*

Aidan's eyes widened. *Mother?* His mind flashed to his family tree, illustrated in vivid detail in a series of stained-glass windows depicting portraits of every member of the Gairden bloodline. They trailed up and around the walls of the sword chamber, beginning with Ambrose and Anastasia and ending with a blank pane where Aidan's likeness would have been engraved immediately following his Rite of Heritage on his sixteenth birthday—had he not failed to accept his duty. Wrinkles creased his forehead as he thought. Beside Ambrose and Anastasia was . . .

"Gabriel Gairden?" he said.

— At your service.

Aidan needed a moment to reconcile the man's voice and speech—slow and smooth, calculated—with the image crafted into his window. Gabriel had been short, bespectacled, and stout.

— Stout, Gabriel purred. *Yes. I like that. Most people described me as "portly" in my day. "Portly" makes me sound like a ship.*

Gabriel's likeness came to him with crystal clarity. Short and stout, with strands of white hair on the fringes of his bald pate and little tufts sprouting from his ears. Like Anastasia, and Aiden's mother, and scores of ancestors he had yet to meet, Gabriel had inherited *Ordine'cin*, the Guardian Light, and had devoted his talent to inventing and scholarly pursuits. His writings were as revered by Torelian scholars as the Lady's teachings were to Disciples of Dawn.

— Was there something you wanted, Gabriel? Anastasia asked. *Aidan is rather busy.*

— Only to help, Mother, he replied. *I believe I know why you failed to open yonder door.*

— Failed? she repeated icily. Aidan shifted his weight, wishing he could escape a conversation doomed to follow him everywhere he went.

— Yes, Gabriel said, not bothered in the slightest. *This door was not sealed by light magic. The boy perceived as much. I am surprised you missed it.*

When Anastasia next spoke, her tone was frosty. *— Very well, Gabriel. I turn the boy over to you. But I will be watching.*

After several long, awkward moments, Aidan spoke up tentatively. *You know about dark magic?*

— A bit, Gabriel said vaguely. *All Gairdens are required to learn a small amount, enough to recognize it so that we can combat it. Your tutelage in that area was cut short. I understand, however, that you are something of a self-learner in the ways of shadecraft.*

Aidan thought about his trip through the tunnels, and his battle against the harbinger who had worn his father's face. *Yes.*

— Very good. Then I can assume that you know how to, what was the term you used, darken?

Aidan's skin prickled with gooseflesh. "Yes."

— Get to it, then.

Aidan turned back to the torch. Its fire was lower than before he had kindled from it, the shadows clustered around it thicker. He opened himself again, but this time he darkened instead of kindled, drinking from the stairway's gloom. The shadows capering along the walls faded slightly. His skin cooled, as if there were a draft.

— *That will do*, Gabriel said. *Now touch the door.*

Aidan complied, placing his palm flat against the polished wood. *I'm ready for the prayer.*

Gabriel's laugh was low and dry. — *Oh, I am not going to cast it. There is more than one way sword-bearers can receive prayers, as you call them, from ancestors. Sending spells, as I call them, through Heritage is convenient, but I view it as cheating. Like plundering a crypt whose doors have already been pried open.*

— *This is unnecessary, Gabriel*, Anastasia said. *Just give the boy what he needs and be done with it.*

— *No.*

Aidan froze.

— *No?* Anastasia repeated, as if sounding out the word for the first time.

— *You taught me that magic is power, Mother. Aidan will never learn to respect this power if it can be handed to him whenever he has need of it. Magic is as much about critical thinking as it is doing. You taught me that, too. Aidan should be learning, not blindly taking whatever we hand him.*

Anastasia was quiet for a moment. — *I still do not think—*

It's all right, Aidan thought, as much to curtail the argument as to dispel the chill creeping through his veins. He brushed at his arm, but the chill intensified. *I would like to learn.*

— *There you have it*, Gabriel said. He sounded neither victorious nor boastful. Merely resolved.

— *Have it your way, then*, Anastasia snapped. Her presence vanished from Aidan's mind. Her abrupt disappearance left a void. His discomfort toward Gabriel increased.

— *Where were we?* Gabriel said, as if blithely unaware of Aidan's feelings, though he could not be. *There is a spell called ensnare that one can use to trap those who attempt to enter an area under its protection. Ensnare can only be executed, perceived, and undone using dark magic. You will attempt to perceive it now. Close your eyes.*

Teeth chattering, Aidan did as he was told. He saw darkness against the backs of his eyelids until, quite suddenly, three words in the Language appeared as if formed from smoke.

— *Touch the door,* Gabriel said.

Aidan's fingertips brushed wood.

— *Open your eyes and speak the words.*

Ice rushed out of Aidan and the relative warmth of the stuffy tower flowed back in. He barely noticed. Crisscrossing black lines rolled down the door like a curtain unfurling. Each line pulsed with a soft, purple glow. They reminded him of the trails that connected the network of tunnels used by the sneaks. Aidan leaned in, chewing his lip. At first glance, the lines had appeared as finely woven as a spider-web. Now he saw that most were knotted and tangled.

What would have happened had I tried to break in? he asked.

— *Nothing pleasant, knowing your old mentor,* Gabriel replied.

That struck Aidan as an odd thing to say. Before he could question the statement, Gabriel continued. — *Now, let me see.* The Eye of Heritage glowed softly. *Yes. You'll need to darken again, Aidan. Not too much. Undoing this spell is more complicated than I had guessed, but not dramatically so.*

The fingers of one hand still splayed on the door, Aidan pulled in more shadows. The darkness around the nearest torch was subsumed by the glow of firelight. Aidan closed his eyes. Six words materialized against his eyelids.

— *Run your fingers over the door as you speak the incantation,* Gabriel said.

His ancestor had placed an emphasis on incantation, as if drawing attention to his purposeful omission of the word *prayer.* Aidan was too cold to pursue the matter. His fingers were numb. Running his hand back and forth over the inky lines, he spoke in the Language. Cold leaked from his fingertips. With each pass, the lines he touched severed and dropped to the floor like remnants of cloth.

Several minutes later, Aidan leaned against the wall and hugged himself. His hands felt clammy, and his airy clothes seemed inappropriate, attire suited for spring instead of winter. *Or for exploring a tomb.*

Gabriel spoke in a detached, scholarly voice. — *The Lord of Midnight and the Lady of Dawn are opposites. Kindling the Lady's light warms your blood. Darkening cools it. Both sap your energy, but darkening is even more dangerous. Draw too much of the Lady's light, and you can burn out your gift. The dark has no mercy. As you tire, your body will break out in gooseflesh. Chills will wrack you. A hacking cough will follow. Push yourself too hard, as you have done quite often as of late, and you will freeze to death.*

Aidan shivered. A lump formed in his throat.

— *Well?* Gabriel said. *Best to get on with it.*

Chapter 3:
Keys

A WAVE OF musty air washed over Aidan as he stepped inside Tyrnen's tower. The structure's one and only room was redolent of tattered scrolls, oiled leather, and brittle, yellowed pages. Aidan had not always enjoyed reading or listening to lectures, but the scent of old parchment had been both soothing and stimulating. There was magic in this room, knowledge that was his for the taking. All he had had to do was ask.

Lessons were given by day. Nights in the tower had been some of the best of Aidan's sixteen winters. When Kahltan took the sky, Tyrnen would light a fire and they would sink into spongy armchairs. Aidan would nurse a cup of hot cocoa and listen as Tyrnen told stories of heroes and villains, and of fantastical creatures that had walked Crotaria long ago. Outside, winds howled and Tyrnen's single window frosted over as snow fell. But inside, the fire crackled and suffused Aidan in warmth and safety.

The old man had been a master storyteller. He would kindle to alter his voice for each character, knowing precisely when to speak a thundering intonation or drop to a clandestine or tremulous whisper. Tyrnen would slowly lean forward, building tension that boiled over when he leapt out of his seat and gestured wildly at exciting parts.

Closing his eyes, Aidan breathed deeply, permitting himself a moment of reverie. The first thing he saw when he opened his eyes was the hearth. It sat cold and full of ashes.

Gripping Heritage, he moved from bookcase to bookcase, scanning them and running his fingers over cracked spines. Trunks painted in wild colors sat wedged between them. Glass display cases coated in dust contained trinkets.

Gabriel?

— *Yes?* His ancestor's reply was low and sibilant.

You know why I'm here?

— *You hope to ransack your old mentor's home and purloin objects to give you an edge when the two of you meet to decide the fate of the world.*

More or less. You said you have experience with dark magic.

— *I said all Gairdens receive some training,* Gabriel corrected swiftly. After a moment, he continued more evenly. *I collected artefacts diplomatically referred to as "tainted" in order to better understand how they functioned. I was notorious for allowing my curiosity to get the better of me. Why do you ask?*

Because I don't know what I'm looking for, exactly.

— *There are sensations one trained in either magical discipline can learn to feel when one draws close to a magical artefact. I have perceived no such sensations in this place. Quite surprising, given the old man's reputation.*

Aidan wandered over to the hearth. A half-empty mug of tea sat on the small table between armchairs, and an open book rested facedown on an armrest. Aidan picked it up and thumbed through it. Boisterous calls drifted up from below, muffled by the stone and the closed window behind Tyrnen's desk.

The Guardian! Crown of the North! Corpse-slayer! The Guardian!

He went to the desk. On one side, books rose in lopsided steeples. Some were open, their pages yellowed and creased. Trinkets and scrolls, some held open by inkpots, were scattered over the other side. The center of the desk was bare. Aidan dragged a finger over the surface and raised it. His fingertip came up clean.

"You've lapsed in your reading," he said quietly, and smiled.

— *Fond memories?* Gabriel said.

Just remembering words Tyrnen said to me. Very often.

His memories were fond, but spoiled, like meat with spots of mold. He had loved Tyrnen like a grandfather, but had Tyrnen loved him? Or had he been acting under the influence of Luria Thalamahn, only pretending to care for Aidan while grooming him, waiting for him to take up Heritage so he and his mistress would have control of a sword-bearer?

Anastasia's presence reappeared as abruptly as it had departed. — *Does it matter?*

"I don't know," Aidan snapped. Being the sword-bearer was beginning to feel like living with every member of your family in a one-room house with no windows.

— *Before you knew of his duplicity, your memories of him were some of the happiest of your life,* Anastasia said. *It is understandable for you to mourn a time that has passed. But do not ever forget that he is your enemy, and the most dangerous threat Crotaria has ever faced.*

Aidan offered no reply. He knew Tyrnen was his enemy. That did not make the thought of killing him any less complicated. He would do it, because Tyrnen deserved death.

— *Worse than death,* Charles said softly.

Unbidden, Aidan recalled again the last time he had seen his mother. He had not seen her in the flesh. Annalyn Gairden's form had appeared through the misty haze roiling in Tyrnen's spirit stone, a glass orb no larger than Aidan's fist. She had pressed her palms against the glass and opened her mouth in a silent scream. Then the mists had swallowed her, like storm clouds consuming everything in their path.

Frustrated, he pounded the clear portion of the desk. Vaguely, he was aware of the voices from below, still shouting. He drummed his fingers absently over the surface as he ran his eyes over Tyrnen's bookcases yet again. *There must be something here I can use.*

— *Daniel should be along soon,* Grandfather Charles said. *Time grows short, Aidan. Your command over the Lady's light has kept you alive so far. Trust in Her. Leave this place, find Daniel, and get the key you need to travel the tunnels.*

He nodded and started toward the door when his arm caught on something. Turning, he saw that his arm had plunged through the desk. Its bare surface remained visible, but his arm was half submerged, as if he had plunged it into a murky pond without breaking the surface. His hand thumped against the desk's solid front as he tried to walk away, hooking him back around.

Are you seeing this? he asked no one in particular.

— *Not only can we see it,* Gabriel said, *but I now detect something inside the desk.*

Aidan yanked his arm out and clutched it to his chest. Visions of whispers, shadowy creatures whose laugh sounded like dry leaves skittering across stone, swam through his mind.

— *Wait,* Gabriel said, confused. *It . . . it is gone. Its presence vanished the moment you withdrew your arm.* He sounded cross, even offended. As if Aidan choosing to protect his limbs had been an act of selfishness.

— *Whatever it was, it was powerful,* Gabriel said. *And familiar.*

Aidan's curiosity was piqued. *Familiar?*

— *I cannot be sure unless I see it.*

Aidan picked up on Gabriel's unspoken command. He ran his hands through his hair, then froze. The tumult from below had grown louder, but he ignored it. He pulled Heritage free of its scabbard and held it before him, both hands wrapped around the hilt. The blade, as white and pure as freshly fallen snow, sparkled in the Lady's light shining in through the window.

He blinked. When he opened his eyes, every object—books, papers, shelves, furniture, cracks along the walls, the walls themselves—appeared as black outlines set against a white canvas. Aidan looked down at the desk. The books and papers pushed off to either side stood out like charcoal sketches. In the center of the desk, as exposed as a trunk with the lid thrown open, he saw the outlines of a cavity. A lone book sat at the bottom. Shifting Heritage to his right hand, Aidan reached for the book, then grunted in surprise. His brushed the surface, hard and unyielding as any block of wood.

He frowned. The desk had been solid when he first touched it, then had opened while still appearing whole.

— *You were tapping on it,* Charles reminded him.

Aidan rapped his knuckles along the desk. Nothing happened. He knocked again. A third time. His fist sunk through. He smiled and wiggled his fingers, which looked like wriggling black snakes through the screen of Sight.

— *It is back,* Gabriel said tensely. *Whatever treasure lies within Tyrnen's hiding place, I can detect it again.*

Aidan's smile melted. *All right. I'm going to try to remove it.* Eight hundred years' worth of Gairdens drew a collective breath. He paused, considering. He could chop the desk to splinters—he wouldn't even need *Ordine'kel* to manage that—but the idea struck him as prosaic, and obvious. Tyrnen would have planned for just such a solution.

— *You know his mind well,* Anastasia said.

I do.

— *Then what should you* . . . She trailed off, and Aidan realized she had picked up on his next idea. *I think you have dabbled quite enough in the forbidden arts for one week.*

Aidan understood her reticence toward darkening, though he did not agree with it. He had seen acts committed with light magic that the Lady of Dawn should never have permitted, yet dark magic had been perceived as somehow different from—

— *It is not for you to agree or disagree, Aidan,* Anastasia went on. *You are a Gairden, and the Guardian. You are sworn to uphold the Lady's laws. Just because you are the first of our line blessed with both halves of* Ordine *does not give you leave to rewrite scripture.*

"We don't have time for anything else." His eyes fell on a shadowy corner of the room, untouched by the light filtering through the window. He darkened and spoke in the Language, invoking ensnare. No lines crawled over the book or the desk's hidden cavity. Giving himself no time to think, he reached in and pulled the book free and dropped it quickly. It landed on the surface of the desk with a heavy thump. Aidan scrubbed his hand against his shirt as if he'd plunged it into a bedpan.

Another blink and Sight fell away. Sheathing Heritage, he held the book in both hands. It was twice as large as any of Tyrnen's other tomes, and stuffed with crinkly pages that looked swollen, as if dipped in water and left out to dry. The cover was wooden, painted black with a lacquered finish. Ornate scrollwork spelled out *Approbation for the Moon.* Below it was a large silvery orb.

"Moon," Aidan whispered, drawing out the unfamiliar word. A chill came over him as he looked from the title to the silvery orb. Kahltan? It had to be. He opened the cover to reveal the first of hundreds of pages, tattered and yellowed with age.

A folded parchment fluttered to the floor. Distracted, Aidan picked it up, opened it, and read. In the center were two letter Vs, each turned on its side so their openings faced one another. *A key.* He clutched the paper. *This is obviously important if Tyrnen went to the trouble of hiding it.* He refolded the paper, stuffed it into a pocket, and turned his attention back to the book.

The title was repeated in the center of the first page. Beneath it, written in a flowing hand, were the words *Aaren Bridgegil.*

An author attribution, Aidan pondered, already turning pages.

— *Yes,* Gabriel said absently. *He gave it to me.*

Aidan's hand froze. Gabriel's explanation was so matter-of-fact that he needed a moment to process it.

Anastasia got there first. — *Explain. Now.*

Gabriel took his time in answering. — *I acquired that book from a scholar.*

— *Why didn't you mention this before?* Anastasia demanded.

— *Because of how you are behaving at this very moment, Mother. This occurred after the Serpent's War. I was fifteen winters old. Sallner was nearly twenty winters in its grave, but the wounds from the war were still fresh. For a Sallnerian to be found in possession of such a book—*

— *Your scholar friend was Sallnerian?*

— *He or she would have been burned on the spot,* Gabriel concluded.

— *Indeed.* The Gairden matriarch's voice shook with anger. Her next words went unspoken: *And so would you.*

A heavy silence draped Aidan's connection with the sword. Below, the shouting from the courtyard had grown wild.

— *As I was saying,* Gabriel resumed in a lazy drawl, *I met this young scholar in Sharem one spring day. He was a refugee from the Territory Bridge—*

Anastasia hissed in a breath.

— *who had paid his debt and earned his freedom,* Gabriel continued, speaking over her. *He had come into possession of the book from his elderly father, who had died from . . . Well, we've all been to the Territory Bridge. Young Bridgegil knew that he could not risk carrying the book into the realms, so he gave it to me.*

Aidan reeled with questions. So did Anastasia.

— *How did the young man know where to find you? How did you hear of him? What—*

— The details of our meeting are not important, Gabriel said. *Suffice it to say, I was interested in the book purely from a scholarly point of view. It pays to know our enemy, does it not? Knowing your and Father's views on the south, I chose to keep it to myself.*

Why did you want it? Aidan said.

— Knowledge is power.

It's odd, though, Aidan thought, *that he gave you the book in secret, yet wrote his name in it.*

The silence that descended was heavy. *— That is curious,* Charles said.

— I didn't think to question him, nor did I think much of the attribution until later, Gabriel replied. *Shades are a vainglorious sort, Charles. We all know the type.*

— Some more than others, Anastasia said darkly. Gabriel hesitated, as if he wanted to say more, but fell silent.

Aidan leafed through pages. They were crowded with words written in the Language. Annotations clogged the margins. Some listed measurements and calculations. As he read, a hollowness opened in his stomach. The author wrote in elegant, flowing script. Despite that, there was a guttural quality to the Language. He recognized it. When a Touched kindled the Lady's light, the prayer he spoke was lyrical, like a hymn. Darkening was far from mellifluous, words in the Language turning low and gravelly.

He closed the book and studied the cover. *Approbation of the Moon.* His fingers touched the orb. It looked like it had been drawn with chalk, but his fingers bore no residue. There was something recognizable about it, too, more than its resemblance to Kahltan. He squinted at it.

— It's vile, Charles said. *Burn it, Aidan. Erase this filth from existence.*

Aidan hesitated. *Gabriel.*

— At your service, the man purred.

This . . . He opened the book to its first page. *This Aaren Bridgegil. He was a practitioner of dark magic?*

— They're known as shades. And, yes, he was. Quite experienced, given the book's contents. That's remarkable considering how tirelessly our dear friends in the Temple of Dawn work to purge all traces of Touched blood on the Bridge.

And you're certain he wrote it?

— I know what you are thinking, Aidan, and you are wrong. Neither Dimitri nor Luria Thalamahn could have written this book.

Why?

— Because they knew not a fraction of the potency of shadecraft, much less the spells documented in that book, Gabriel answered heatedly. His tone softened. *Read the book, Aidan. Cover to cover. Not a single spell documented within it was used in Sallner eight centuries ago.*

His next words were spoken through a sneer. *— You associate dark magic with death. That is one of its functions, I admit. Dark is light's opposite. If light gives life, darkness brings death. That does not make dark magic inherently evil.*

"How do you know so much?" Aidan asked. "From reading this?"

— From studying it firsthand. Aaren Bridgegil was one of the most powerful Touched in the history of Crotaria. I should know. I studied under him.

A shriek from outside shattered their conversation. Aidan raced around the desk and peered through the window. Below, the eastern courtyard had filled nearly to capacity. Cobblers, bakers, and other common folk in plain garb mingled with scholars and nobles draped in snowy robes. Wardsmen wearing steel and snow—polished boots, gleaming white mail, conical helmet—pushed and shoved their way through them. The crowd broke, people running this way and that.

Aidan pressed his hands against the glass and discerned the source of the shouting. The Wardsmen wore flat expressions. Their eyes were glazed. The face of one hung askew, exposing a skull mottled with rot and moss.

Vagrants.

Just ahead of them, two other Wardsmen sprinted away from the undead and toward the tower. One of those wore a helm lopsided, red hair spilling out like sloppily bundled straw. The fiery-haired man reached the tower door first. He threw himself against it and staggered back, as if he'd struck a stone wall. His helm flew from his head and skittered across the paving stones. Then, as if he felt eyes on him, the man peered up and he locked gazes with Aidan. He glanced over his shoulders at his pursuers, then back at Aidan, and shrugged, lips stretched in a tight smile.

"Daniel's in trouble," Aidan said, reaching for his sword.

— *Wonder of wonders*, Grandfather Charles muttered.

Chapter 4:
Chain of Command

AIDAN KINDLED THE Lady's light streaming in through the window, closed his eyes, and shifted. A gust of wind scattered papers and toppled the stacked books on Tyrnen's desk. Air rushed over him. The scent of musty parchment was gone, replaced by crisp spring air. The shouts, no longer far below and heard through stone and glass, exploded in volume. He opened his eyes and stood at the base of the tower beside Daniel and the second Wardsman, a man his age whom Aidan recognized but whose name he could not place.

Daniel jumped as if Aidan had leaped out from behind the tower. "My hero," he said. He raised his *Sard'tara*, a smooth black pole with curved blades at either end.

Aidan gave no reply. He tightened his grip on Heritage and blinked. Sight draped over his vision, washing the world in charcoal-on-canvas shading. A wave of men, women, and children ran pell-mell over the courtyard, pushing and prodding and trampling in their desperation to get clear of the man whose face dangled behind his head like a lowered hood. Aidan saw the rest of his skull clearly through Sight, as well as the skulls of the vagrants charging up to stand on either side of the exposed undead. The three drew steel and waded in.

Aidan's feet carried him forward. He was dimly aware of

Daniel and the other Wardsman shouting at him, but he could not have stopped even if he'd wanted to. With Sight came *Ordine'kel*, the second half of the *Ordine* gift, and with it, the presence of Ambrose Gairden. Aidan was like a marionette under the control of the world's greatest puppeteer. His grip on Heritage, clumsy and ineffectual without *'kel*, became strong and sure. As if he had been holding a sword since before he could walk.

The first vagrant, fleshy mask askew, tried to veer past him. Heritage flashed in Aidan's hands, slicing through its decayed neck. It met no resistance, cutting as cleanly as a ray of the Lady's light through fog. The body slumped to the ground. Its head dropped a moment later, rolling to a stop against a bench leg. Aidan was not precisely sure how he had swung, how he had cut with such speed, precision, and strength. That was because he hadn't, in a way. His body was like a suit of armor that the Gairden patriarch had stepped across centuries to wear, the sword an extension of his arm.

— *One down, two to go*, Ambrose shouted.

Exhilaration heated Aidan's blood. He was enjoying this because his ancestor was enjoying it. He planted his feet and held Heritage before him, hands wrapped around the hilt, waiting to see which of the two vagrants would come for him first. Which would die first. His prey not slow, tearing toward him. And then, as if they were a wave and he a great rock, they split around him and raced at Tyrnen's tower.

— *What under the shade?*

Ambrose's confusion was an echo of Aidan's. He—they—turned in time to see the vagrants bear down on Daniel. The other Wardsman leaped in from the side and plunged his short sword into a vagrant's chest. The creature staggered to a halt, then cocked its skull, as if this new arrival had done something curious instead of lethal.

"The head!" Daniel shouted. Not in time. The other man raised his sword to deflect a blow that would have taken him in the right shoulder. Sparks flew as blades met. Caught off balance, the Wardsman stumbled and lost his footing. He raised his sword again, face pale with terror.

The vagrant spun and advanced on Daniel. Aidan's heart jumped into his throat, but Daniel appeared unruffled. The

Sard'tara in his hands became a blur. Two sharp cracks rang out as each end of the weapon knocked away the sword of one vagrant and then the other. The blades spun over the pathways to land in the grass with soft thuds. The other Wardsman recovered, hauling himself to his feet and, face pinched in concentration, stabbed one vagrant cleanly through its skull. Bone cracked and fragments scattered along the stone path, skittering like stones. The body gave a jerk and folded. In the same instant, Daniel swung his *Sard'tara* up in an arc. One curved blade gleamed as it severed the remaining vagrant's head from its shoulders.

— *A good fight*, Ambrose said approvingly.

Aidan blinked. The patriarch's presence drained out of him, leaving him disoriented. When he opened his eyes, color had returned to the courtyard. His heart still pounded with the thrill of battle. A feeling of disappointment lingered. He breathed hard although he was not winded. With the patriarch in charge, he had wanted to cut down a vagrant. Both vagrants. All vagrants.

Daniel held his *Sard'tara* parallel to his body, face shiny with sweat. "We really must stop meeting like this," he said.

Aidan took one last deep breath. "I was waiting for you. Did you get the . . .?" His words died away as his gaze fell on a sword sheathed at Daniel's waist. Ordinarily his friend never carried a sword—he was about as proficient with a blade as Aidan was without Ambrose's hand to guide him—but the sword Daniel carried bore an eerie resemblance to Heritage. It was identical in form, but ebony instead of snowy. A sapphire was embedded in its curved guard. Its jewel-encrusted hilt stuck up from a scabbard as black as Kahltan's heart and was painted in bile-colored swirls. The Serpent's Fang.

Someone in his mind—he thought it was Ambrose—hissed a breath.

Daniel cleared his throat loudly as the other Wardsman, short with black hair that ended in a tail at the nape of his neck, hurried over to join them and gave an unsteady bow.

"Apologies, Crown," he stammered. "Aidan, I mean. I had never seen . . . those creatures, they . . ." He gulped air, his complexion still pale.

"They are what we're up against," Aidan finished. "Torel, and all the realms."

"Undead," Daniel said. "They're called vagrants. Aidan and I have fought them before, and there are more—"

"Under Tyrnen's command," Aidan finished. Daniel shot him a sharp look but said nothing.

The Wardsman glanced at them, back at the bodies along the ground. Dark, viscous blood oozed from their necks. He flashed a shaky grin. "Now that it's over and the Lady still warms my bones, it was kind of exciting, wasn't it? Fighting creatures out of stories." Toeing a corpse, he said, "What makes them move? How do they—" He cut off after noticing their grim expressions.

"Dark magic," Daniel said.

Aidan stayed quiet. He had placed the Wardsman: Jak Merrifalls. Sixteen winters, same as Aidan. Also like Aidan, he enjoyed a good story and pulling pranks. Now, however, Aidan felt removed from him. Distant. The events of the past few weeks had forced him to shed his childhood and childish distractions like clothes that no longer fit. *Mere weeks*, he thought, head swimming. He looked away.

"These creatures killed our friends, Jak," Daniel said quietly, "and they would have killed us if it wasn't for our Crown, here." He nodded at Aidan.

Jak's grin faded. "You're right, Daniel. I didn't . . ." One look at Aidan and he lowered his gaze to the stone path. "Sorry, Crown."

Aidan patted his shoulder. "It's all right. Go back to your post. West gate, isn't it?"

"Yes, Crown." Jak snapped off the Ward's salute, making a fist before raising his forefinger and small finger and placing his hand to his heart, then set off at a run.

"Wait," Daniel called.

Jak skidded to a halt and looked over his shoulder.

"Go to the south gate instead of the west," Daniel said. "They're shorthanded there."

Jak frowned at him, his eyes wandering to Aidan. Daniel jerked as if pinched. "Oh. If that's all right, Aidan. Crown."

"Of course," Aidan said. "South gate, Wardsman. May the Lady keep you warm."

Jak saluted again and took off at a run. They watched him go. After he vanished, Daniel removed one of his gauntlets, fished inside it, and removed a crumpled and sweaty piece of parchment. "This key will put you about ten miles south of Janleah Keep."

Aidan said nothing. Daniel followed his eyes to the Serpent's Fang at his waist. "Don't be mad," Daniel began. "I'm only carrying it because, well, it doesn't seem the sort of thing to leave lying around even if it is a fake." He swallowed. "It is a fake, right?"

Aidan nodded tightly. "You should have it destroyed anyway."

Daniel shrugged. "I kind of like carrying it. It makes me look, I don't know, more regal. Decorated."

Aidan choked back a laugh. Daniel had a gift for dispelling worry. "Ten miles?" he said, gesturing for the key. "That far?"

Daniel handed over the parchment. "If there are tunnels that lead directly into the Keep, no sneaks know about them."

Aidan unfolded it. In the center was a crude drawing: an "I" with tiny black dots on either side. He stuffed it in his pocket. "Thank you, Daniel."

His friend shrugged. "Anything for you, Prince of Passion." He paused. "I keep forgetting that you're a king, now. They'll let anyone sit on the throne these days."

"Watch your tone, or I'll have you exiled."

Daniel's face grew sober. "Are you leaving immediately?"

"Yes." Aidan waved at the vagrants. "Where did these come from?"

"The south gate," Daniel said quietly. "That one was Stanwick Yarah." He nodded at the body nearest Aidan's feet. "I was on my way there. Soon as I arrived, a pack of vagrants charged. There were about five, but Stanwick and the others lost their wits at the sight of them." Daniel shuddered. "Can't blame them for that, I suppose, though it's the smell that bothers me most. Worse than a Wardsman who hasn't bathed in a month."

Aidan stared at the body. He knew Stan, or knew of him. He had made it a point to learn the names of as many of his mother's—now his—Wardsmen as possible, for a smoother transition when he, Aidan, took the crown. Stan Yarah. Forty winters, a wife and two daughters. "His family should know."

"I've already sent pigeons." Daniel hesitated. "One of those creatures was with them, Aidan. The ones with the empty eye sockets and strings of flesh over their mouths."

"Harbingers," Aidan said. The word conjured up memories of

the blank, eyeless faces that had haunted his dreams, the creatures that had worn his parents' faces and his mother's soul.

"There was just the one, but one was enough," Daniel said. "I saw Stan die. And the harbinger, it just looked at him and crooked a finger, and Stanwick was back on his feet, only he wasn't Stan anymore."

"How many of ours fell?" Aidan asked.

"All three Wardsmen. Stan, and old Barty Klenger, and little Jaret Belgin." He barked a harsh laugh. "Little, I say. He was around our age."

"There were only three guards at the gate?"

"With the rest of the army marching to Darinia, we've got fifteen hundred soldiers to spread around all of Calewind," Daniel said. "Three men to a gate is all we can spare. We're reinforcing them as quickly as we can. Anders Magath assigned me to the south gate to relieve Stan. He'd been on duty for nearly a day and a half. Anders can't keep up with everything. He's pulling out the last few tufts of hair he's got, and I don't blame him. He's the highest-ranking officer left, with Brendon Greagor leading the march. I told Anders I'd spread the word at the gate but then I had to get back to you. That calmed him down a little."

Daniel shook his head. "Better him in charge than me. I can't wait until you kill Tyrnen so I can go back to guarding doors. It's nice and quiet in the throne room." He scratched behind an ear. "Well, not lately, I guess."

"What about the harbinger? Did it get inside Calewind?"

Daniel shook his head. "After it, cast, uh . . ."—he waved a hand to indicate magic—"on Stan, it did the same to the other two, and then it . . . it eyed me, and just disappeared. Shifting, I think you call it. Anyway, the square was crowded, people were panicking, so I tried to get the vagrants to give chase. It worked." He knuckled his back. "I'd better go. Anders is probably bald by now." He eyed the vagrants. "Three down, and only, what, another ten thousand to go?"

"If we're lucky." Aidan closed his eyes and pinched the bridge of his nose. Exhaustion was creeping over him. Aidan had no control over his movements under the sway of *Ordine'kel*, but his body still suffered wounds and fatigue.

Suddenly, Daniel pounded a gauntleted fist against the tower. "The shade take Tyrnen and his undead."

Aidan looked up. "You just gave me an idea."

He ducked into the tower and bounded up the stairs, Daniel following on his heels. At the top, Aidan found *Approbation of the Moon* where he had left it in his haste to help his friend. He hefted the book in both hands and held it out.

Daniel's eyebrows rose. "I'm afraid I don't have much time to read. I'm also afraid it would take me two lifetimes to get through a book that size."

Tucking the book under one arm, Aidan said, "Watch this." He knocked on the desk three times and lowered the book into the hollow cavity.

Daniel whistled. "We could have used that back when we were swiping your grandfather's ale."

"Which we only did the one time," Aidan said quickly, shooting him a meaningful look.

Daniel looked from Aidan to Heritage. "Right! Of course."

The Eye of Heritage flashed red.

Aidan opened the compartment again, removed the book, and stuffed it behind a bookcase. "I don't want Tyrnen coming back and getting his hands on that book. Find the most powerful Touched in Calewind and give it to him." He thought of Christine. "Or her." He stepped closer and spoke in a whisper. "It's full of dark magic. If word got out, it might start a panic. But the fact is, we need every advantage we can get."

Daniel nodded, though he appeared reluctant. "What is it?"

"There aren't many Touched left in Calewind. Tyrnen—"

"Ordered them to march with the Ward," Aidan finished. He brought a hand down hard against a bookshelf. As the Eternal Flame of Crotaria, Tyrnen was the Lady of Dawn's will personified, and spoke with her voice. *Christine, I hope you're well on your way.*

"You know," Daniel said slowly, "you could probably use the prayers in that book. Tyrnen and your mother always said you were the most powerful Touched in . . . well, ever."

Aidan shook his head. "I can't. I need to speak with Nichel."

"The Ward is on the march. What makes you think the clans aren't as well? They're probably halfway here by now."

"I've got to start somewhere."

"Start here, then." Daniel's tone was strained. "You've sent

Christine and your father on errands. Anders can't do everything himself. Are you sure you can't—"

Aidan held up a hand and fought to keep his tone even. "If I stay here and Nichel is on the move, I won't be enough to stop the clans from burning and pillaging every town and city they cross on their way to Sunfall's gates. If she's not there, then I'll look elsewhere. I don't want to go, Daniel. I have to. I have to try."

Daniel's lips thinned. "As you command, Crown."

"That's not fair. I'm doing the best I know how."

Daniel stared out the window. "I know," he said. "I'm just frightened." He gave a small smile. "I think I was less frightened when it was just the two of us out on the open road, hunted by dead bodies and a grumpy old man."

Aidan broke into a grin. "That makes two of us."

Outside, Daniel and Aidan crossed to a stone bench near the center of the courtyard. It had been pushed aside, revealing a hole that sloped downward. Daniel frowned at the bench. "Must have gotten jostled during the fight," he began, sounding doubtful.

Aidan's jaw tightened. "If we know about the tunnels—"

"Then Tyrnen probably does, too," Daniel said, scrubbing a hand over his face.

"You think someone came through," Aidan said. It was not a question.

Daniel let his hand drop. His eyes were wide and frightened. He shook himself as if throwing off his fear. "Maybe, maybe not. Nothing can be done about it now. What I can do is seal this one behind you."

"How will I get back?"

"You know." Daniel waved his hands in a flourish.

"Of course. What was I thinking?"

"You weren't. Lucky you've got me to do that for you."

Shouts caught their attention. Aidan, crouching to slip into the hole, began to straighten.

"Don't," Daniel said. "The sooner you leave, the sooner you get back."

Aidan tried to respond but could not. Tension wrapped iron bands around his chest. Leaving felt wrong.

"Go!" Daniel shouted, pushing him.

Aidan scrambled into the tunnel, Daniel close behind him.

Chapter 5:
Circle

A SMILE LIT Christine's faced as she threaded her way through Sunfall's southern courtyard. Aidan's last kiss lingered on her lips. One cheek was still warm from where it had rested against his chest. *When this is over.* His last words to her before he had left, not looking back. She was glad for that. If he had, she might not have let him go again.

She lengthened her stride. The sooner Tyrnen's head adorned the tip of Heritage, the sooner she could begin the next chapter of her life. *Christine Lorden Gairden.* Her smile grew so wide her cheeks hurt. Her right hand moved to rest on her belly.

Out of habit, Christine sidestepped and wove around Torelians too preoccupied to look where they were going. Too preoccupied to acknowledge her existence. She supposed they had an excuse this time. Minutes earlier, Aidan had ascended to Crown of the North, and had revealed that the war between Torel and Darinia was a lie perpetrated by Tyrnen. Aidan had vowed to reunite Darinia and Torel against Tyrnen's forces. Calewind was abuzz with excitement, and terror.

She grazed the shoulder of a man in a snowy robe. "Pardon," she murmured. He glanced at her, gave a quick nod, looked away, and then looked back. His expression hardened as he took in the shape of her eyes, the silky texture of her raven-colored hair. He strode away. Christine's back stiffened, though she forced her stride to remain casual, graceful. Her father was Torelian, her mother Sallnerian, and she had inherited her mother's features. As if her thought had impelled them, a few more Torelians hurrying along noticed her. Their gazes burned with suspicion and hostility.

Christine put a spring into her step. Her appearance had been met with prejudice since long before she was capable of understanding why everyone on Crotaria seemed to hate Sallnerians—and especially hybrids—on sight. She took after her mother, true, but she had her father's Touched blood. Christine and her brother Garrett had created a lucrative business that earned more than enough coin in all denominations to afford the best of everything: food, clothing, the finest rooms in the grandest cities of any of Crotaria's four realms.

But did that matter to Torelians? No. So, why should it matter to her?

Her back straightened. She held her head high. She was not perfect. She had made mistakes, but Aidan had forgiven her. He loved her, and she loved him, and none of these petty northerners could change that.

Slowing, Christine looked west, her gaze piercing the obstacles that separated her from Aidan—Sunfall's gates and ornate statues, Calewind's buildings and high walls, the rolling hills and thick woods of the northern realm, and the endless, golden expanse of the Plains of Dust— to stare at the exact spot where he stood. Though she could not see him, she could sense him across the distance that separated them. Her chest ached. He had been close minutes ago, only to abruptly jump thousands of leagues west. *How can I miss him so much already?*

Christine wondered if he missed her, too. She twisted the gold ring on her right forefinger, brushing the pad of a finger against the amethyst set in its center. She was linked to Aidan, a bond forged by Tyrnen—the thought sent a shudder through her—but it had limitations. She knew only that he was far to the west. As long as he wore his Band, she could point right to him even if the Lady and Kahltan and every star in the sky vanished and left Crotaria in darkness.

Nearing the gate which led down the mountain pass that opened into Calewind, Christine spotted her party. Four men and women wearing green robes stood in a circle. She made a conscious effort not to rush over to them. If her good fortune held out a little longer, she would soon be Christine Gairden, Queen of Torel, and one of those eight figures: A member of Torel's Dawn, the most elite group of Cinders in the four realms.

I might have to speak out against the robes, though. Abhorrent fashion.

An older woman with shoulder-length red hair stepped out of the cluster as Christine approached. "Are you ready to depart?" Keelian Faltan asked.

Christine did not answer. To Keelian's left stood General Edmund Calderon, resplendent in snowy-white mail and tabard. Steel and snow, Wardsmen called their armor. Edmund stood apart from Torel's Dawn, left hand resting on the hilt of Valor. He smiled when he saw Christine, but the smile did not touch his eyes, which were bloodshot and haunted.

Keelian arched an eyebrow. "Sorry," Christine said, gathering her wits. "I'll be ready in just a moment. I would have a word with General Calderon."

"He will be accompanying us to Sharem," Keelian said. "Surely your conversation can wait a few more minutes."

Another apology perched on the tip of Christine's tongue. She swallowed it. She was done deferring to Torelians. "This will not take long."

Keelian eyed her, noting her attire and the skin it left exposed, and rejoined the group. Christine realized her shoulders were hunched, like a scolded child. With just a few words, Keelian had punctured her good spirits. *She was so friendly a few minutes ago, before . . .*

Before she and Aidan had shared a passionate and public goodbye. Had Keelian witnessed their display? It was possible. Aidan and Christine had not wandered far from Torel's Dawn before sharing affections. Keelian was Torelian, they all were, though no Touched swore allegiance to any crown. Not before they graduated to the rank of Cinder and received their Band, and certainly not after. Though they had to follow the law of any land where they dwelled, the magically gifted followed the Eternal Flame. No longer. Tyrnen Symorne was a traitor to the realms, and Torel's Dawn had sworn support to the Crown of the North.

Still. For all their renown, even those eight Cinders were only human. Allegiances could be sworn, but prejudices were harder to set aside. Those eight had been born and raised in the north, taught Torelian mores, and had seen the northern king openly display affection for a Sallnerian.

For a snake.

Christine felt eyes on her. Edmund's face was a smooth mask, but his hand lingered on Valor's hilt. Christine's cheeks burned. *Does he hate me, too? Do they all hate me?* Suddenly she hated them right back. Not for their inborn scorn and bigotry, but for letting her hope they might one day accept her as one of them.

So what if his father hates me? So what if they all do? Aidan doesn't. Nothing else matters.

Edmund moved toward her, walking with a slight limp. Before he could reach her, Christine spun away and strode over to Keelian Faltan. "I am ready."

"Are you sure?" the Cinder asked.

"Yes."

Keelian gestured. "Join the circle."

Christine did as commanded. Around her, the eight members of the Dawn clasped hands. Christine took Keelian's offered left hand and reached for the Touched to her right. When he did not take it, she turned to him, a question on her lips. He had moved, leaving a gap in the circle. Edmund stepped into it. Wordlessly, his attention directed straight ahead, he took Christine's hand, still held outward. His palm and fingers were rough and calloused, the hand of a man more accustomed to holding steel than flesh.

She looked away quickly. She knew this was how a circle worked. Edmund was Untouched and had to stand between two who had been blessed by the Lady of Dawn in order for the circle's magic to flow through him, connecting him to them like a link in a chain.

Christine fidgeted. *Why did he stand next to me?*

"Embrace the light," said Coren Landswill, a stern-looking man with groomed auburn hair and a goatee, standing across Christine. She kindled, opening her body to receiving the Lady's light. A sliver of warmth flowed into her veins. She had never needed much light, even for difficult spells. That restored her confidence. In all likelihood, she was more powerful than any two members of the Dawn together. Torelians could look down their noses at her all they liked. She had earned the right to stand beside them.

And above them.

Guilt flooded her. *Is that how you think of them? The same way they think of you?*

Edmund's hand tightened around hers. Not enough to hurt, but enough for her to look up. His face remained smooth, but his eyes were wide with wonder. Christine understood. Magic now raced through him like a stream that had broken through a dam. No matter how many times she experienced it, there was nothing quite like the heady sensation of magic lacing one's veins.

She bit her lip. *Almost nothing like it*, she amended, thinking back to the night she had shared with Aidan.

"To Sharem," Coren said, drawing her attention. "The hill outside the north-facing wall."

Christine knew the location. In unison, all save Edmund spoke in the Language of Light. Gusts of wind kicked up and buffeted passersby, who gave them a wider berth. Robes cracked like whips. Their surroundings—the golden spires and arched bridges of Sunfall that gleamed under the Lady's bright gaze, the cobblestoned courtyard and its high, smooth walls, where Christine had sat hoping to catch a glimpse of Aidan Gairden as he passed through on his sixteenth birthday—smeared.

All around her, the Dawn closed their eyes. Christine lived with her eyes open. She laughed as wind rushed over her, through her, tugging at clothes and hair. A roar filled her ears. The sensation, like racing on horseback at impossible speeds, and the sight of nature and manmade creations streaking like paint on canvas, made even some of the most famous Touched retch. Christine loved it. Magic was a gift, even if it came from a goddess who had doomed her and her people to a lifetime of hate.

As suddenly as the shifting began, it was over. Streaks of color snapped into place, becoming rolling fields and leafy trees. Another gust of wind erupted from the circle. Christine stood frozen with shock. Beside her, Edmund gasped, and his hand went limp and slipped free. Hills rolled, verdant and picturesque. A few trees on the outskirts of the forest that bordered the eastern side of Sharem swayed in a gentle breeze.

The rest of the forest, and the earth immediately in front of and around Sharem's northern gate, was a ruin. Firs that had grown three hundred feet tall had been burned to piles of ash. The ground was charred and gouged. Weapons sat in piles of steel-colored slag amid the remains of armor and helms fashioned in the shapes of animal heads. Grisly remains rotted under the Lady's hot gaze.

Christine pressed the back of her hand to her mouth. She closed her eyes, tried to breathe in, nearly retched. *Aidan did this.* He had told her about the battle outside Sharem, about what he had done. What he'd had to do. Her lips pressed into a line. *Tyrnen did this.*

She straightened and glanced at Edmund. He stood motionless, face ashen. "We will stop him," she said quietly.

After a moment, he spoke. "Tyrnen did not do this."

Guilt twisted her stomach into a knot. Christine wanted to correct him. To explain that Tyrnen had manipulated Aidan, just as he had manipulated her. *I helped. I was Tyrnen's dog. Dawn and Dusk.* Instead, she said nothing. *I did not need much convincing. I wanted Tyrnen's approval. I wanted to be part of Torel's Dawn. I still do.* Her resolved hardened. *I will earn it.*

The group stood silently for several minutes. Finally, Coren Landswill studied them each in turn. He appeared unruffled by the sight of the massacre. *Or the smell.*

"Come," Coren said, and led the procession toward Sharem. They picked their way down the hillside carefully. Christine tried to imagine what Aidan had felt, what he had thought, as the battle unfolded.

"My Wardsmen should have removed these bodies," Edmund said. His voice was strained, as if he were trying not to breathe too deeply.

"I imagine they will soon enough," Coren said, looking back over his shoulder. "The snows only melted recently. And remember, General, that the Darinians were considered enemies of Torel when your son . . . Well. I suspect it was more important to the Wardsmen stationed here to fortify the Torelian district in the event of another attack by the Darinians than it was to organize clean-up duty."

No one spoke again until they reached the northern wall. Keelian turned to Edmund. "General," she said, gesturing toward a horizontal slot in the guard tower that stood beside the gate. Edmund rapped a gauntleted fist against it. The slot slid to one side, and a pair of eyes peered out. Christine was close enough to see them widen at the sight of Edmund.

"We will pass," Edmund said.

The eyes flinched. "Sorry, General. We, ah, we haven't been letting traffic in or out since the attack. I'm afraid . . . Ah. I'm afraid I'll need you to confirm your identity, for you and your, ah, party to enter. It's protocol, sir," he finished quickly.

Edmund's face had grown stonier by the word. His left hand choked Valor's hilt and then ripped the blade from its scabbard. Steel sang in the fetid air. "Is this not enough?" Edmund said, speaking softly so that Christine and Torel's Dawn had to lean in to hear. "I gave you three demerits two winters past for brawling in the Crown's Promise after hours while wearing steel and snow, Leif Moggery. If I do not hear the creak of that gate within a heartbeat, I will paddle you with the flat of my blade in the Crossings for all to see and assign you to janitorial duty for so long that your grandchildren's grandchildren will have to carry out the remaining decades of your sentence and—"

The slot snapped shut, muffled orders were barked, and the gate swung open. Edmund jammed Valor back into its sheath and marched ahead. Christine and the others followed in his wake. Leif Moggery danced alongside Edmund as the general strode past, babbling apologies and explanations. "Back to your post," Edmund barked, and Leif hurried off.

They stood in Sharem's Torel District, its architecture and layout modelled after the features of its realm. Roads were wide and orthogonal, lined with stalls and buildings cut from marble or white stone bearing sloped roofs designed to let rain and snow slough off. The clamor of city life filled the air: Torelian citizens in white clothing hurrying along, ignoring the shouts of merchants from their stalls and doorways; scholars in flowing white robes walked side by side with their heads bent together; Wardsmen marched in groups of three or four, expressionless as they patrolled. Horses clopped along pulling wagons or gilded carriages, the latter displaying red orbs painted on either door. The riders within those carriages were clad in crimson robes and stared ahead. A few whisked curtains closed, as if the roads and their contents offended them. *Bloodrobes see dirt everywhere* was a popular saying where Christine had grown up. It was seldom repeated in the north, where the Disciples of Dawn were greater in number, not unless you wanted to be dragged into the Temple of Dawn for a lecture or worse, depending on the shape of your eyes.

Frowning, one hand splayed on her belly, Christine studied the scene. All the shouting, the hustle and bustle of daily life—it was a veneer, she realized. Faces were pale and drawn. Guarded. Pedestrians hurried rather than strolled. Even the merchants, Leastonians dressed in bright trousers, boots, and shirts, seemed nervous, only the promise of coin keeping them from packing up their wagons and racing deeper into the east.

Christine heard mention of her name and turned to Coren. "Pardon, Cinder. I'm quite tired. You were saying?"

Cinder Coren smiled. "Of course. It occurred to me that the Second would be at the Temple of Dawn this time of year, ahead of assessing prospective graduates from the Lion's Den. We will find him there, I think, rather than at the university. Will you accompany us?"

Christine's heart took off at a gallop. Everything was happening so fast. Before she could invent some excuse—too tired, too busy, too afraid—Edmund intervened.

"I wish to speak with you," he said to her, smiling wanly. "And, I must admit, I need to keep my feet on solid ground for a short time. Shifting is . . . I never will get used to it. My wife loves it."

Christine was not the only one who caught Edmund's use of present tense. She looked at the ground. A lump formed in Edmund's throat. His eyes, bright and interested a moment ago, turned to stone.

"Very well," Coren said. "We will continue on to the temple to inform your father of all that has transpired. He should know of the Eternal Flame's betrayal so he can begin the formalities involved in aligning the Touched with the Crown of the North. Temporarily," he added, a reminder that the Touched would once again swear fealty to the Eternal Flame once the war had ended and a new leader of Crotaria's magically gifted could be chosen.

The group moved away, following the wide, straight lines northward. Two members hung back. Christine recognized them: Kerevin Hoven and Deletar Jan, two of the Dawn's most senior members. Both had fair skin, but Kerevin had a bare face and bald head while Deletar, at least ten winters younger, kept his moustache and pointed goatee neatly groomed.

"We will meet you at the harbor in one hour," Kerevin said to Edmund.

"Don't you need to rest first?" Edmund asked.

"No," Kerevin said. "Forming a circle enabled each of us to share the burden of kindling. Deletar and I have more than enough strength between us to carry the three of us to Ironsail."

Edmund inclined his head. "One hour, then." The other men returned the gesture and set off after their compatriots, seeming to glide up the road. To Christine's surprise, a cloud seemed to lift from Edmund's eyes. Before she could react, he pulled her into a hug. She stood rigidly, arms at her sides, absolutely stunned. Several passersby stared before hurrying on their way. Her shock must have shown on her face when Edmund pulled away. His face was the color of a Disciple of Dawn's robes.

"I apologize for being so forward." He took a breath, seeming to search for words. "You helped my son. For that, he owes you his life. He is my life. He is all I have left, Christine. I owe you my life as well."

She murmured that it was nothing, nothing at all. Shielding his eyes, he squinted up at the Lady. "Would you share a drink before I depart?"

Now more curious than tense, Christine nodded. Edmund gestured for her to walk beside him. They set off, strolling along the latticework of uniform streets. Unconsciously, her right hand rested on her abdomen. She noticed Edmund's left hand holding Valor's hilt and wondered if he was using it as a form of support. His limp was becoming more pronounced.

Wardsmen banged their fists against their chests when they spotted the general. Scholars and civilians murmured and bowed to Edmund. At the sight of Christine, they gaped, no doubt wondering why the general of Torel's Ward would be seen with a Sallnerian woman. *Just the general of Torel's army out walking a mutt*, Christine thought. Shame warmed her cheeks. Edmund had been nothing but kind to her. *So far*, a voice in the back of her mind whispered.

They turned down a side street and stopped at a broad stone building. A lacquered wooden banner depicting a Wardsman's shield resting against a lantern exuding a warm glow hung above the entrance. *Ward's Haven* was written on the sign in flowing strokes.

"All the men on day shifts come here after Dawnfall to relax, so it should be quiet for a little while longer." Edmund grimaced. "I need to rest my feet."

"It's fine," she said, and followed him inside.

The Haven's common room was spacious and softly lit, reminding her of the Fisherman's Pond and Martha Elenstrobe, its innkeeper and a second mother to her and Garrett. Round tables and stools were scattered across the polished floor. Edmund saluted to the innkeeper—"Retired Wardsman," he told her by way of explanation—and crossed to a table in the center of the room. Christine understood perfectly. Men in taverns exchanged gossip the way Leastonian merchants traded wares and favors. It wouldn't do for the general to be seen tucked away in a dark corner with another woman so soon after his wife's death, especially Aidan Gairden's lover.

No one knows you're his lover, she realized. Word of Tyrnen's deceit, and the death of Annalyn Gairden, had likely not reached Sharem yet. As far as these people knew, Edmund Calderon was still king of Torel, husband to the Crown of the North and father to the prince.

"Two swamp waters," Edmund said to the Torelian serving woman who bustled up.

"Just water for me," Christine said. The server returned seconds later carrying two tall tankards. She bowed deeply to Edmund, shot Christine a curious look that was probably supposed to be discreet, and hurried off.

"I apologize for being presumptuous," he said, nodding to her glass. "I just assumed . . ."

"It's all right. Normally I'd take you up on the offer, but I want to have a clear head when I talk with my father. He can be . . ."

"Intense?" Edmund offered. She smiled. He took a draft from his tankard and pushed it aside. "I'll follow your lead. Swamp water numbs the body and the mind." He folded his hands on the tabletop. "I understand congratulations are in order."

Christine felt a flash of panic. When she offered no reply, Edmund continued. "My son loves you, Christine."

Her anxiety dissipated, replaced by giddy flutters in her belly. "He said that?"

"He did. I gather you care for him."

"I love him," she said simply. Her heart soared. It felt so good to say that to someone other than Aidan. It made their love feel more real somehow.

Edmund's smile failed to touch his eyes. "Any woman patient enough to put up with my son must be quite special. Annalyn did her best, but . . ." His face clouded over.

"She did wonderfully," Christine found herself saying. She noticed that the tension had drained out of her back and shoulders. She felt at ease with this man and found herself grateful for his company. "As wonderfully as any mother could have done with that one."

He chuckled. "Indeed."

She hesitated, not wanting to ruin the mood. "General—"

"Edmund. Please."

"Edmund, then." She crossed her legs under the table and adjusted her skirt. "Are you well? I noticed your . . . that is, your leg . . ."

He shifted in his seat. "I'll be fine. Shifting is unsettling, but less painful that supporting my own weight, much as it pains me to admit it. Sitting for a time helps. Besides, I have business to attend here before I continue on."

Christine ventured a guess. "Torel's Ward."

He nodded. "When I returned to Calewind, I made reconnaissance my primary focus. I needed something to hold on to." His voice became flat. "Tyrnen had already taken Anna from me. Aidan was missing, and for all I knew, he was dead, too. I convinced myself not to act rashly. I skulked, and I listened. Tyrnen and his pets were to march toward Sharem. Ripe for the picking—that's how the old man described the city. Thanks to Aidan's . . ." He shuddered, and chills swept up Christine's spine. "Tyrnen wanted to raze Sharem to the ground. Probably still does. A city known across Crotaria for its trade, positioned at the heart of the realms? It's a prime target. My guess is he's pulled strings to direct the clans here, too. The Ward and the clans will meet, Sharem will fall, and the armies will be decimated—truly easy pickings for Tyrnen's creatures."

Christine's throat went dry. She sipped her water. "What will you do?"

"Speak with the Ward when they arrive. It shouldn't be long now. Touched travel with them—more of Tyrnen's pets among them, I wager—but even so, an army that size cannot move from

Calewind to Sharem in a few blinks. I expect them soon, however. My lieutenant colonel must be told of recent events. The Ward and the clans must not fight."

"Aidan needs you in Ironsail," she pointed out.

"He does." Edmund held her gaze. "Which is why I hoped you could help me."

"Anything," Christine said at once, and was surprised. She trusted this man, and trust had never come quickly to her.

"I will prepare a document that conveys my orders. Would you be willing to deliver it?"

She swallowed. "Can I do that?"

"I am general of Torel's Ward, and I say you can. Will you?"

"Yes. But, if I may ask, why not ask Torel's Dawn to carry the missive? They have aligned themselves with Aidan." She paused, reading his expression. "You don't trust them."

Edmund leaned back, chewing his lip. "I don't know them. My wife would tell you that the Touched unsettle all those not gifted with the Lady's light, and I suppose that is true in my case. I'm a fighting man, and some habits are hard to break. I've spent my life studying ways to combat the Touched—to combat opponents of all sorts, even my own people if it comes to that—and I sometimes find myself surveying everyone I meet, friend or foe or family, for weaknesses even as I shake their hands and pass rolls at dinner."

"Did you do that with me?" she asked, hoping she did not sound as uncertain as she felt.

Edmund shook his head. "Aidan trusts you, so I trust you."

Christine took a long drink to hide her flushed cheeks. "And Torel's Dawn? Annalyn must have trusted them, too."

"Not exactly. My wife did not mistrust them, you understand, but . . ."

"But they belonged to Tyrnen," she finished. He nodded. "You have nothing to worry about, Edmund. Torel's Dawn are Touched first and foremost. Tyrnen formed the group as the north's most elite Cinders, but they served him because he was the Eternal Flame. They are loyal to that title, and Tyrnen no longer holds it." Her stomach lurched. "According to the hierarchy of the Touched, my father will ascend."

Edmund turned over her words. "Aidan would be wise to seek your counsel whenever possible."

"You tell him that. He can be stubborn."

"Now that you mention it," he said, and they shared a laugh. To Christine's ears, only hers sounded genuine.

Edmund took another pull from his tankard. He set it down empty. When they stepped outside, the streets were nearly deserted. Young students in white robes went from lamp to lamp, flicking a hand ostentatiously and wearing a smug expression when the empty glass globe burst into luminescence. Christine suppressed a fit of giggles. She had been a student once, too, and beyond impressed with her ability to light lamps.

Edmund stood admiring the horizon, and Christine stood with him. The sky glowed molten orange, and the Lady hovered over the mountains far in the west.

"Aidan should be there by now," he said. "I hope he can talk sense into that poor girl."

Her good mood drained away. Nichel. The wolf daughter. On the day of Aidan's birthday, he and Nichel would have married, further solidifying the alliance between Torel and Darinia. Christine and Garrett had been in the southern courtyard outside Sunfall, packed tightly together with a mob of tens of thousands of Crotarians that spilled down through the snowy streets of Calewind, though she was fairly certain she was the only Sallnerian within miles of the Torelian capital. No one wanted to be the first to leave. Voices—Edmund's, Annalyn's, Aidan's, Tyrnen's, and those of visiting dignitaries who lavished the crown prince with gifts—had reached from the throne room where Aidan's Rite of Heritage took place out into the courtyard thanks to magical amplification. Every moment of the ceremony, every action, passed through the courtyard and down into the city, eliciting a ceaseless babble of excited whispers.

When Christine had heard Romen of the Wolf and his wife admit that the wedding between Aidan and Nichel would have to be postponed due to the cub's illness, sighs and moans had swept through the crowd. Christine had not joined them. She had hoped the girl would make a swift recovery, though not too swift. She had been enamored with Aidan even then, and had anticipated his sixteenth birthday with a mixture of eagerness at seeing him up close—she and Garrett had paid an exorbitant amount of Torelian marks for their prime spot in the courtyard—and trepidation at his impending vows. *There's still a chance*, she remembered thinking after news of the postponement lifted her heart into the clouds. *He could still notice me, and I could get away from my sycophant brother and start a new life as—*

And then he had seen her. Had looked right at her. The doors into Sunfall had opened, and Tyrnen was gesturing, trying to get Aidan's attention so they could conclude their march into the palace. But Aidan had had eyes for her. He had stared as if transfixed. Christine remembered how blood had thundered in her ears, drowning out cheers and screams. She had wrapped Garrett and herself in a heat bubble that melted the snow before it could touch them, but right then and there, she and Aidan had been in their own bubble. She had grinned like a fool, and had kept on grinning until Tyrnen had steered the prince into Sunfall and the doors had closed behind them.

Now her stomach clenched. Would it take a wedding to build a bridge over the river of blood that lay between Torel and Darinia? Jealousy made her hot and dizzy. She wanted to be beside Aidan, needed more than anything to feel his arms around her, to hear his promise of the future that awaited them after all this ugliness was settled. The fingernails of her right hand dug into her abdomen, and she relaxed her grip.

"He is promised to her," she said softly.

"Was," Edmund corrected. "Aidan and I discussed this very subject . . . why, it was earlier this afternoon."

She wiped at her eyes, careful not to look at him. "What did he say?"

"That he cares deeply for you. I reminded him that, in all likelihood, his betrothal to Nichel no longer stands, given all that has happened. I also told him that his love life will still be waiting for him after more important matters have been settled."

Christine took a deep breath. Edmund was right, but his words sparked a new fear. Aidan was thousands of leagues away, walking alone into the jaws of a vengeful pack of wolves and bears and Dawn knew what else. "I should be there with him," she said. "I should be helping him."

"You can," he said. "By talking to your father, and by helping me."

She turned to him, determined. "Tell me what to do."

CHRISTINE WAITED ACROSS the street from the northern guard

tower, adjacent to where they had entered the city. Edmund had invited her inside, but she did not want to ruin a pleasant day by inviting stares and whispers. The tower door opened, and Edmund stepped out holding an envelope sealed with the Gairden crest.

"Here you are," he said, handing her the missive.

She examined it. There were two seals. The second depicted the letter "V" with a sword—Valor, she presumed—stuck through it diagonally. The wax was still hot.

"I must continue on to Ironsail," Edmund said. "When the Ward arrives, demand to speak to Brendon Greagor. He's my second in command. If anyone gives you trouble, just show them that."

Christine pocketed it. "What does it say?"

Edmund smiled. "Orders for how to handle the clans, should they arrive before Aidan."

"You can count on me, General," Christine said, then caught her mistake. "Edmund!"

He gave her another small smile. It was a flame without warmth. "Will you be all right?" she blurted out.

Edmund's smile broadened, though it still did not reach his eyes. "As well as I'll ever be."

Chapter 6:
Homecoming

CHRISTINE WATCHED EDMUND'S retreating back and did her best to ignore the flock of butterflies in her belly. Torel's Dawn waited for her in the heart of the city. So did her father. It was said the Eternal Flame waited on no man, not even kings, and that his Second was only slightly less impatient.

Her lip curled into a smirk. *Well, I am no man.*

Besides, the afternoon light waned. Surely the rest of her father's day would be filled with bureaucracy and Dawnfall canticles. Better to wait to see him until morning.

Coward, she thought.

Oh, hush, she chided herself.

Her ears attuned to voices and music. Christine turned east, brightening. *Early spring,* she thought. *It's Festival!* She headed toward the Leastonian district. Wide, orthogonal roads and men and women clad in robes of varying shades of white and grey gave way to narrow, winding streets that curved like Kahltan's narrowed eye as she walked to the east side of the city. The ground became coarse with sand tracked in by merchants and captains and galerunners who had journeyed to Sharem by barge or ship. She passed through an archway painted in the colors of the rainbow, leaving behind Torel's snow-white buildings and sloped rooftops for structures of myriad shapes and sizes and colors.

As if the archway were a portal to a magical realm, Christine's good cheer swelled the moment she crossed it. One day she would live in Sunfall, as far north as one could go, and she would weather the ice snug and safe with her husband inside the palace's golden walls. But every year, she would emerge from hibernation to visit the east and celebrate the Festival of Blossoms. As a girl she'd spent months beforehand each spring hand-making her costume: a radian flower one year, an eagle another, a fantastical beast—a horse with an ivory horn jutting from its forehead—still another. She and Garrett had performed in Leastonian cities every night during the three-day celebration, when coin and wine flowed freely. Next year would be different. Next year she would be married, and she and Aidan would attend the Festival of Blossoms and celebrate the rebirth of spring together.

The Leastonian quarter was more subdued than usual, but for easterners, subdued meant lowering their shouts to yells. Christine lost herself in the press of bodies bedecked in masks and face paint. Meats sizzled on skillets set atop glowing coals. Her stomach growled. Keeping one hand on her middle, she fished through her purse and paid a single Torelian coin for two skewers of grilled meat seasoned with spices. Her mouth watered as her teeth sank into the sizzling flesh. It was tender and pink in the middle, just the way she liked it. She devoured her meal in seconds and licked juices off her fingers as she walked. She would need to eat again soon. She would find an inn, eat a bowl of stew— a large bowl, the largest on offer—and wash it down with . . . Not with a glass of Leastonian slush, a dish made of ice cream flavored with grape wine pressed from vineyards further east. She wanted slush, craved it, but would refrain.

Water again, she thought sourly. *Damn you, Aidan Gairden.*

Christine followed the curvature of the east district northward. Reaching the heart of Sharem, she gave the Temple of Dawn a wide berth. Sharem sat in the heart of Crotaria and was divided four ways, like a pie cut into four perfect slices. Each district fell within the boundaries of its realm and was governed accordingly. The Temple of Dawn sat at the center of Sharem and, thus, the center of the realms. Although the Disciples of Dawn were powerful and respected throughout Crotaria, they were not the authority in Leaston, nor the Leastonian district of Sharem. Instead of Wardsmen, Christine passed groups of Azure Blades, men and women in sea-green leather Armor and carrying *Sard'tara* instead of axes and polearms and swords, their eyes as alight with merriment as the civilians and captains and merchants they were paid to protect. In the western district, a rotation of clansfolk held sway, mostly silversmiths and other craftsmen looking to trade their wares for exotic foodstuffs before heading back out onto the Plains.

A block of ice formed in Christine's stomach. *They can't still be here,* she thought. *No after what happened.* If clansmen still inhabited the western district, no one would be celebrating anything. There would be fighting, and blood flowing instead of slush. Still steering far clear of the temple, she fell into a brisk walk, then a jog. Uneasiness set in, building until her throat felt parched.

The road leading into the Darinian quadrant ended at a long, tall, wrought-iron gate that stretched for miles to either side, blocking entry into the district. Gripping two of the bars, she peered through it. Darinians did not build according to Torel's neat, orderly roads, nor did they mimic the winding avenues of Leaston. If a plot of land was deemed suitable, they built there. Far from appearing arbitrary or cluttered, Darinian cities evoked an earthy, natural quality. Most structures were squat and unadorned, slabs of stone welded together—lodgings, the clansfolk called them. Darinian cities consisted primarily of lodgings. The clansfolk were itinerant. Cities dotted the Plains of Dust, usually next to oases, but no clan settled for long. Lodgings were simple so that they could be abandoned on a whim and claimed by the next clan that wandered by. The west's portion of Sharem was no different.

Low on the horizon, the Lady winked from between dark, empty lodgings. Just ahead, an elaborate fountain with a wide, broad lip sat dry and empty. Six stone animals reared up in its center: bear, wolf, falcon, lion, elk, snake. They stood back to back instead of fighting and clawing and snapping at one another. Unified.

Nichel. The wolf daughter's name rose in her mind, and Christine's mouth twisted. Nichel was Aidan's childhood friend, and his betrothed. Not after all that had happened. Surely not. A rash of jealousy flushed her cheeks. Guilt followed, and her face burned hotter. Christine banished Nichel from her mind. Dwelling on her was futile. She recalled Edmund's assurances, and told herself she had no reason to worry. *Aidan is there as the Crown of the North. He seeks to reestablish their alliance. That is all.* She thought back to the first evening they had spent together, wrapped in each other's arms in front of a fire while a storm shook walls and rattled windows. A storm battered at them now, threatening to sweep them away.

One hand strayed to her middle. So long as they held on to each other, they would be safe.

"Fool," she muttered. As Edmund had said, Aidan had put the good of the realms ahead of personal matters. She would do the same. She was not some doe-eyed girl. She was Christine Lorden, Cinder, daughter of the Second, and independently wealthy. Being a queen would not define her. Being the wife of a Gairden would not define her. But Sharem's abandoned western district might. The block of ice in her stomach hardened. She had been Tyrnen's source inside Sharem—part of her requirements for eligibility into the Dawn, he had hinted—but from Aidan's account of the battle, Tyrnen had twisted the intelligence Christine had fed him, luring Aidan into a false sense of security and, with the collusion of the harbingers posing as Annalyn and Edmund, pushed him to slaughter the clansmen who had taken the city.

Aidan had been manipulated. So had Christine. The difference was that Aidan had accepted responsibility for his part in the conflict between Torel and Darinia. Tyrnen had been behind it, but if Aidan could own his mistakes, so could she.

Christine rested her head against the cool bars. *I did this. This was my fault.* Straightening, she considered her Cinder Band. It seemed uglier to her. Wrong. Her mouth tightened. Without the Band, Ernest Lorden would see only his daughter, purveyor of cheap parlor tricks. The ring spoke to strength and experience. *And I did earn this.* She breathed slowly and steadily. The Lady was a molten ball set against an orange sky. Her feet ached. She wanted to find a bed and sleep until Dawnrise—maybe later—but she had one more stop to make.

She retraced her steps to the heart of Sharem, slipping through the courtyards and gardens surrounding the Temple of

Dawn. Instead of mounting the steps leading up to broad, ornate doorways, her feet carried her along the South Road. Crotaria's North, East, South, and West roads began in Sharem, from each respective entrance of the temple, and extended into each realm. Christine followed the South Road until she came to a stone edifice taller and wider than the gate barring admittance into Sharem's Darinian district. In the center was a portcullis. It was down. It was always down. A door sat on one side. Christine marched up to it and rapped her fist against it twice. A slot near the top snapped open and a Wardsman glared out.

"No entry or exit after—" he began. Christine flashed her Cinder Band. His mouth snapped shut, and a moment later, so did the slot. Inside, a crank began to turn, and the portcullis slowly rose. Christine swept through with her head held high and entered a dark tunnel. Heat climbed her neck. *He never would have treated a Torelian Cinder with such disrespect.* She had half a mind to march back to that guardhouse and . . .

No. She reminded herself she was a grown woman with important work to do. And that work would be done . . . tomorrow. For tonight, she wanted to pay her respects. Her footsteps echoed in the tunnel. There were no torches, but she knew the way. All Sallnerians did. The passage tapered, constricting so that travelers had to walk single file. She emerged in the Sallnerian district. Her heart sank. It was in an even poorer state than when she had left eight winters ago. Paving stones buckled, giving weed-choked roads the appearance of mild waves frozen in mid-swell. Paint peeled from buildings cobbled together from boards foraged from carpenters' scrap piles. Shanties, taverns, and shops were crammed shoulder to shoulder. Many structures leaned as if weary. Not for the first time, Christine thought an errant breeze would knock one into its neighbor and set off a cascade effect.

Sallnerians in grey robes shuffled up and down the streets. They looked up, noticing her. Christine immediately felt self-conscious. Her brocaded skirt and blouse had been tailored by a renowned seamstress in the eastern city of Temperdine. She had purchased her elk-leather boots from the most expensive cordwain in the Pincer's Heart market of Ironsail. Here, the Sallnerians' robes were threadbare. Some wore shoes; most did not. Her mind went back to the interior of the Ward's Haven:

clean, polished, orderly. There was only one tavern in Sharem's southern district: The Bog, its owner had proclaimed it centuries ago, embracing the ruin of his people rather than allowing their eternally soiled reputation to be used against him as a weapon. The Bog had no floor. It was four shabby walls and a leaky ceiling suspended over dirt.

Christine moved briskly down the main street, hurrying toward the entrance to the Territory Bridge. Like the tunnel leading into it, the Sallnerian district narrowed. Dilapidated buildings thinned out as a screen of leaves and boughs rose up, choking the path and weaving a canopy that thinned the Lady's dying light to wispy tendrils. Pockmarked stone trailed off into dirt and grit.

She paused. Fifty paces ahead stood another checkpoint guarded by Wardsmen. *I'm not ready for this.* She turned to leave.

Her skin cooled.

Christine whipped toward the trees to her left. "Who's there?" A breeze sighed through branches, stirring leaves. She froze. The wind was still. There had been no breeze.

A rustling in the undergrowth behind her. "I am a Cinder," she said. "Come out now, or I will have to report you to—"

Suddenly, a humanoid shape exploded out of the undergrowth and charged down the road, away from her and toward the Territory Bridge checkpoint. Scared and angry at feeling scared, she took off after the retreating shape. Their heavy breathing mingled with the susurrations of wind stirring leaves.

A Wardsman stepped into the road and threw up a hand. "Halt!"

The figure Christine pursued stumbled and crashed face first to the dirt road. A groan filled the air. Armor clattered as another Wardsman rushed up to the first. Christine reached the fallen form—a man, by his build—an instant before the guards and cursed under her breath when she recognized him. Lam was gangly, had been since they were children, though he was a head shorter than Aidan. A mop of dark hair crowned his head. His face was distinguished by sharp, angular features, tightened further by anger.

Steel hissed as the Wardsmen yanked swords from scabbards. The second one, an older man with grey hair and creases in his face, noticed Christine's Cinder Band.

"Stand back, if you please, Cinder. This is Ward business. We'll handle it."

The first Wardsman hauled the Sallnerian man up from the ground by the collar of his shirt. The man tried to shake him free. "Stop struggling," said the Wardsman, raising his sword to the man's throat. "It will go easier if you hold still."

The Sallnerian obeyed.

"Do you have a pass?" the older one asked.

The Sallnerian muttered unintelligibly.

"Speak up," said the older Wardsman, his voice neutral.

The other Wardsman, shorter and no more than twenty winters, swatted the man's head. "You were given an order by a sergeant in the Ward."

"You have no right to treat him that way," Christine said.

"He's off the Bridge after curfew without a pass," said the younger Wardsman in a pompous tone. Christine gave him a withering stare. He swallowed and glanced at his partner.

"You haven't asked me for my pass," Lam said. Christine shot him a warning look, but the Sallnerian's expression was defiant.

"Do you have one?" the younger Wardsman said.

"There. Now you've asked," Lam said. The younger guard's face turned purple.

Dawn and Dusk, Lam, please shut up.

"You have no authority here, Cinder," said the older Wardsman, his tone respectful but firm. "We answer to the Crown of the North, not to your Eternal Flame. Move along."

"My friend is with me," Christine went on, gesturing to the Sallnerian. "He has no pass because he is out on my authority."

"And who are you?" the younger Wardsman said. "A Sallnerian wearing a Band?" He sneered. "Now I've seen everything."

"You couldn't possibly have," Christine said, "since you are barely old enough to have removed your lips from your mother's—"

"Please answer his question, Cinder," the older Wardsman said.

"I am Christine Lorden, Cinder and daughter of the Second."

The younger Wardsman opened his mouth then closed it. "What business do you have on the Bridge?"

"My business is my own. Lam of Domicile Four is with me," she repeated.

"And his business?" the younger Wardsman snapped.

"Same as mine," she said.

"Which is?"

"Not yours." The young man's mouth opened and closed again. "You really ought to keep your mouth open or closed," Christine added. "You look like a fish." She fought back a smile when his eyes bulged.

The older man turned to Lam. "Do not leave the Bridge without a pass again, Sallnerian. Not even in the company of a Cinder. Since Christine Lorden is a Cinder, she knows the laws." He held Christine's gaze for a long moment, then released Lam.

Lam made a show of smoothing his rumpled grey robe and brushing dust from his shoulders. "I'll keep that in mind."

"I'll be watching you," the younger Wardsman said, drawing himself up to his full and inconsiderable height.

Lam wiggled his eyebrows. "Lucky you," he purred.

The Wardsman went for his sword, but the older man put a hand on his arm. "Calm yourself, Dirik. Remember your station."

"Our business is concluded for this evening, Lam," Christine said loudly. "Come. I will escort you home." Christine strode past the Wardsman, sweeping through the checkpoint and toward the Territory Bridge. He hurried behind her as the road grew rougher, and fronds the color of burnished emeralds closed in. Two pairs of eyes boring into her back.

Lam fell into step beside her. "I was just thinking about you."

"I'll bet you were. That was stupid, Lam."

"Thinking about you? Never. You've grown quite fetching."

"Do you want to tell me why you were out without a pass?"

"Do you want to tell me why you decided to come back?" he replied. "And don't tell me it's because you missed the food. No one who leaves misses the food."

Christine bit her lip to stifle a laugh. Lam noticed and nudged her with an elbow. Their boots crunched over loose stones and dirt. Her stomach churned. She was here, on the Territory Bridge. *Home*, she thought. Her feet dragged. Firelight twinkled up ahead. Vague forms draped in white tabards milled about squat wooden huts.

"Who'd you lift the Band from?" Lam asked, touching her ring.

"You know very well I didn't have to lift it."

"But you could have. It's the principle of the matter, Chris."

"Nobody calls me that anymore. Besides, it's a boy's name."

"Oh, would that you were a boy. It would have made things so much simpler." He leaned his head on her shoulder. Christine made a sound of annoyance and shrugged him off.

"There's grilled meat over on the east side," she said. "Are you hungry?"

"I should stay on the Bridge. I really don't have a pass. Come on. Myrthel still makes stew after Dawnfall."

Christine wrinkled her nose. "Is her stew still stringy?"

"Stringier. You know Myrthel. She lives to defy expectations."

"I think I'll pass. I'm not feeling well today."

Lam's grin slipped. "Don't tell me you haven't spent long nights yearning for the taste of home."

"A friend once told me no one who leaves misses the food."

"Your friend sounds wise. And handsome." Lam tried his best to look casual. "Here to see your father?"

"Yes."

"And after that?"

Christine gave no answer. Lam's features tightened. "Well, you'd best be off. I'd hate to deprive you of a warm meal and a warmer bed."

"Please don't start this up again, Lammy."

"We began this conversation years ago, *Chris*."

"And we're certainly not going to finish it now." Christine glanced over her shoulder. The Wardsmen still watched them.

"Fine," Lam said. "Be seeing you." He picked up his pace to cut in front of her.

She reached out to take his arm. "You need to explain what happened back there."

"Is that an order, Cinder?" he asked.

"You know it isn't."

Lam did not meet her eyes. "You were there. A couple of snowmen dirtied their hands touching a snake. Same story, different day."

"I sensed you," she said quietly.

Lam jerked, caught her eye, looked down at the ground. "I'm not sure what you mean."

"Touched can sense kindling. The skin grows warm. I'm sure

you've felt that." Hurt bubbled up inside her. "Why didn't you ever tell me?"

"You weren't here to tell."

"I mean before. Why didn't you tell me before I left?"

"I didn't know."

Tears stung her eyes. She scrubbed at them.

Now Lam did look at her. "What's wrong with you?" He sounded surprised and confused. "This is the first time I've seen you act like such a . . . a girl."

"Nothing," she snapped, and felt a helpless fury when tears spilled down her cheeks. *Damn you, Aidan Gairden.* "Who else knows?" she asked, swiping them away.

He hesitated. "No one."

"You're lying."

"I am not!"

"You never could lie to me, Lammy."

"If you call me that again, I'll make it my life's work to see that everyone calls you Chris for the rest of your days."

"Who else knows?"

He bit his lip. "Feter."

"Can he Touch?"

Lam nodded once.

"He'll stay quiet then," she said.

"Yes. Besides, we've got other secrets to keep."

Christine gave him a level stare. "I can talk to my father."

"About Feter?" Lam looked horrified.

"No, you shade-stricken idiot. About kindling. He'll be discreet. He can get you the training you need—"

Lam took a step back. "Don't you dare tell him. The Second knowing I can Touch is the last thing I need."

"You need someone to guide you. If any of the snowmen find out . . ."

"I'm careful," he said, sounding petulant.

She narrowed her eyes. "There's something you're not telling me."

"You're suspicious, as usual."

"And you're not suspicious enough, as usual."

Lam threw back his head and laughed. "You haven't changed."

To her surprise, Christine smiled. Fresh tears welled up, these of joy. "Oh, Dawn and Dusk," she muttered.

Lam was staring at her as if she were some new species of swamp frog. "What is wrong with you?"

Giddiness swept over her. She was dying to tell someone. Why not her oldest friend? "I've got news. Big news."

Lam took her hands. "Tell me."

"Not here. Too many ears."

His bushy black eyebrows climbed his forehead. "That big?"

"Bigger."

"Come on. Domicile one thirty-seven is still waiting for you. We'll get a bowl of Myrthel's stew—probably two apiece, if she can spare them; it really is thinner than ever—and you can see the others. Feter will be over the . . ." He paused. "Over Kahltan to see that you're back."

Christine bit her lip. "I have to see my father first thing in the morning."

His expression grew tense. "Don't tell him. Please."

"I won't. It's about an unrelated matter."

Lam relaxed. "So, stay in one thirty-seven tonight."

"I really should stay close, Lam. I need to see him at Dawnrise. Much has happened."

He dropped her hands. "You're too ashamed to stay in your old place."

"No! It's not that."

"It was good seeing you, Christine," Lam said. He spun on his heel and strode off in the direction of the domiciles.

Christine raised a hand and tried to call for him. The words dried up in her throat, and her hand fell limply to her side. The urge to cry returned. She whirled and march off toward the eastern district.

"Damn you, Aidan Gairden."

Chapter 7:
Traveling Companions

SHAREM WAS BATHED in the hazy gold of Dawnfall by the time Edmund reached the Leaston district's port. Men wearing brightly colored shirts and pants tied or untied ropes from moorings and formed lines to pass crates and bags to and from ships and down to solid ground. Their tan arms glowed with sweat. Sandals and bare feet pounded up and down the docks, which were slick with water splashed up from the Avivian River.

The Avivian unspooled through Torel and Leaston like blue ribbon. It was not the only water route that connected the realms, but it was by far the busiest and most profitable due to its smoothness and width. Peddlers travelled land routes in coaches or wagons, but affluent merchants relied on sails and galerunners.

Edmund choked Valor's hilt. Cinders Kerevin Hoven and Deletar Jan were late. To a man who had spent every morning of his adult life running and giving drills long before the first glimmer of Dawnrise in the east, tardiness was as grievous a sin to Edmund Calderon as blaspheming the Lady's name was to her disciples.

That's not the only reason you're upset, Anna whispered.

He closed his eyes. As always, his conscience assumed his wife's voice. She was right. He had passed off military work to Christine. To someone outside his brothers in the Ward. When had he ever done something so irresponsible? Since Tyrnen had killed his Anna and set out to manipulate their son. That was when.

It occurred to him that he did not feel the pang of guilt that usually ate away at him before, during, and after perpetuating some wrongdoing, no matter how small. That did not bother him, and that would have been even more worrisome had he the capacity to worry about anything. He had not always been so conscientious. Then he had met Anna. She had changed his life for the better. She had saved him.

Still, her voice materialized in his mind at the most inopportune times, such as when he eyed confectionaries at dinner, or when he discreetly encouraged some of Aidan's more endearing bad habits, even ones that amounted to—

"Just a bit of harmless fun, Anna. All boys duel with sticks."

His wife's thin eyebrows soared. "Do all boys poke their queen's head cook in her hindquarters with their sticks?"

Edmund's mouth quirked. "I will admit that it was a dishonorable blow. Helda's backside was unarmed."

One of Anna's feet began to tap. Edmund allowed a grin to break through. He could read her body language as easily as she read her prayer books. She was annoyed, but amused, too. On some occasions he could tip the scales in his preferred direction. She seemed open to that today, but . . . "I'll talk to the boy."

"Oh no you won't," she said in a single breath. "That did no good last time. If Aidan had been anyone else, Helda would have flattened him like dough."

Edmund propped himself on an elbow. He was reclining in their marriage bed after a long day in the barracks, watching Anna undress after her long day at court. "That would make him easier to handle."

Anna unfastened her favorite pair of sapphire earrings—a gift from Aidan and Edmund for her last birthday—and placed them in her jewelry box. "He was born with Ordine'cin, Ed. He'll never be able to wield a blade like you, but that does not mean—"

"That he should disregard lessons in handling one safely. I agree. I will talk with him."

She gave him a level stare. Edmund crossed their bedchamber to her. Their tall window was dark and coated with frost. Candles suffused the white stone walls in warmth. He ran his hands over Anna's bare shoulders, lifted her Dawn-kissed hair to caress the nape of her neck.

"*A serious discussion,*" *he said.*

"*Do you promise?*" *she murmured. Her chest rose and fell faster.*

"*On our peach pit.*"

Anna bit her lip. "*Aren't you sweet.*" *Her eyes danced with light. She let him lead her to their bed, and then they—*

"—Calderon? General?"

Confusion broke his reverie. Edmund's gaze flitted this way and that, landing on but not connecting with the barges, the quays, the burly crew members hustling and bustling around him. *Sharem. I'm in the eastern district of Sharem.*

His heart sank. His memory of that night with Anna had felt as real as it had been six winters prior. He would have given anything to trade this world for memory.

"General Calderon? Are you well?"

Edmund focused on a stout man wearing a wide-brimmed blue hat and oiled brown beard sprinkled with grey hairs. He leaned on the rail of the harbor's largest river boat, his stubby fingers bedizened with rings. It took Edmund a moment to place him. When he did, excitement coursed through him. "Jamian Rolf," he said, lifting a hand.

Jamian waved back and descended a ramp down to the dock. Trailing behind him was a woman whose colored vest fit as loosely as any of the clothing worn by the men working the ships. Flaming curls spilled over her shoulders. At least a dozen bangles clacked and jingled over her arms as she walked. Edmund caught one look at her chest and directed his attention elsewhere. Her vest was open in a wide V, exposing smooth, tan skin and the swells of her breasts. He was not embarrassed. He had visited Leaston far too often to allow their nonchalant attitude toward nudity to set his cheeks aflame, yet he would observe the north's proprieties.

Jamian was breathing hard by the time he reached Edmund. He bowed elegantly, a gesture of respect and equality. Leastonians paid allegiance to their wallets first and the merchant's guild second. A guild on which Jamian sat. Perhaps Edmund would not need to travel all the way to Ironsail after all. *The sooner I gain the guild's support for Aidan, the sooner he'll be taken care of.*

Edmund inclined his head. "Good tidings, Captain. I'm amazed to see you so far from your seat in the Prefecture."

Jamian beamed at him. "Did you know, General, that I am one of the youngest members of the merchant's guild? I'm fifty-two. Fifty-two!" He snorted. "Those old codgers call for an interlude during lunch because eating a whole drayfish saps what little vitality remains in them."

"You must grow bored."

"Aye," Jamian said, and looped an arm around the waist of the woman at his side. She watched Edmund curiously, as if trying to work out how any person could breathe under so much steel. "I almost had Cyrolin take us further north. Sharem isn't the friendliest place these days." He tried to look casual, but his eyes shone with curiosity.

The woman, Cyrolin, said nothing. Now that she stood so close, Edmund noticed the tattoo near her left collarbone. A cloud with a human face, mouth open and lips extended in an "O" as if exhaling. Three wavy lines extended outward, ending in another cloud-like puff.

"How do the winds treat you, galerunner?" Edmund asked formally.

Cyrolin glanced at Jamian. "You may answer," he said.

Her lips tightened, but she replied. "The Lady's breath grows warmer to the east, but still chills my bones even so far from the north."

Jamian swatted her backside. "Show respect."

"General," Cyrolin added.

"What brings you to Sharem?" Jamian asked, scratching at his facial hair.

"I'm on my way to Ironsail."

"Ironsail! You've got a walk ahead of you. Once you get there, you could always sail back on the *Crown Prince*."

"One of yours?"

"No, Edmund. Yours. Or should I say, your boy's, when he comes to claim it."

Edmund frowned until he remembered what Jamian was talking about. Several members of the merchant's guild had travelled north for Aidan's sixteenth birthday some weeks past and had gifted him a deed to a ship of his very own. *The Crown Prince*. A name all too fitting. "Aidan won't be along to collect his gift anytime soon, I'm afraid. I assume your fellow guildmasters reported what happened on his birthday."

Jamian nodded, his face sober. "Terribly embarrassing. No matter. He'll get past it. He's a Gairden, and a Calderon besides." The captain ran his tongue over his lips. "Is it true what people are saying about the attack here? Aidan did this? The north and the west are at war, then?"

For the first time, Edmund picked up on the differences on the docks. Men moved faster, out of fear rather than alacrity. The sooner they could bed down—probably in the east district—or set out on the Avivian, the better. There was less shouting and cursing. Jamian appeared to be the only captain in attendance. The others were probably sequestered in their cabins.

"How did you hear?" Edmund asked, fighting to keep his tone even. He knew the answer before the question hopped off his tongue.

"You know how word travels to the east," Jamian said with a sly expression. "I'll admit it surprised me, though. The viciousness of it. I thought it might be exaggerated. Not that I've seen the site of the battle yet. Still, I wouldn't put it past a Leastonian merchant to tell a tall tale, even one of the guildmasters."

"It's true," Edmund said. His lips felt numb. "There's more to it, though. Aidan was . . . influenced."

The captain doffed his hat and ran a hand through his hair. "Stars and spray, Edmund. You must have a story to tell."

Edmund did. He opened his mouth to give his friend the abridged version. Before he could get a word in, Jamian raised a hand. "Tell it, but later. Just tell me what you need."

Edmund could have sagged with gratitude. With Jamian's voice added to his, the guild would be that much more likely to consent to Aidan's needs. "The Azure Blades."

Jamian fingered his hat. "The guild doesn't often let the Blades get involved in foreign affairs, as you well know."

"We're not fighting Darinia, or we're not meant to be. Tyrnen Symorne has . . ." Rage and grief choked off his words.

"Say no more," Jamian said. "You've got my cell, but the others, well, I don't speak for them. You'll need an audience with the guild. Can't be helped, but some things can be sped along, and I can put in a good word." He patted the woman's backside again.

"Cyrolin here is one of our best galerunners. She can get us to Ironsail in five days. Maybe four. In fact . . ." Jamian planted his hat back on his head. "Nothing stopping us from leaving now, I guess. It was a short journey—always is, thanks to Cyr—and we're stocked on provisions. I'd hoped to make a few trades before returning east, however." He raised his eyebrows at Edmund.

"The Crown is generous to allies," Edmund said.

Jamian's eyes grew brighter. "What do you think, Cyr? Do we need to wait until Dawnrise?"

Cyrolin scoffed. "Lanterns will do fine. Two, I think, to last me through the night. Sailing the winds is not so difficult, if one knows how to weave the Lady's light properly. Many galerunners kindle too much at once, and become fatigued by midday, when Her light is brightest. I prefer to weave light the way a seamstress threads a needle: a constant stream, slight, yet pliable, and not too taxing." Cyrolin studied the evening sky. A breeze picked up, and her mouth curled into a lopsided smile as it played with her curls and vest. She seemed to relish the wind's caress the way Annalyn had enjoyed the Lady's warmth.

"The wind favors you, General," she said. "You will stand before the guild before week's end."

"Thank you," Edmund told her. "But I had a faster method of travel in mind."

She frowned. "Shifting."

Nodding, Edmund's mouth went dry. He pushed his discomfort with shifting away. *My boy needs me.*

"Galerunners are not proficient in that prayer," she began.

"The galerunner will not be necessary."

Edmund spun, hand on his sword. Cinders Kerevin Hoven and Deletar Jan glided toward them, hands hidden in their sleeves and crossed at their waists. Jamian glowered at the two Touched. "Who are your companions, Edmund?" the captain asked, his tone cheerful.

Before Edmund could speak, Kerevin filled the gap. "We are of Torel's Dawn. We have been asked to escort the general to an audience with your guild."

"And I was just asking Jamian and the lady if they would join us," Edmund said.

The Cinders' eyes narrowed in unison, darting from Edmund to Jamian and Cyrolin. Edmund's hand rested on Valor's hilt. His chest felt tight. In the back of his mind, he analyzed his distrust of the two men. Annalyn had been Crown of the North and a Gairden born with *Ordine'cin*, yet she had been of the people, like her father Charles before her, and Charles' mother before him, and so on down the Gairden bloodline. Tyrnen's assemblage of Touched radiated superiority. Even now, they stared at Jamian—a decorated captain and a member of the ruling body of Leaston—and his galerunner as if they were Sallnerians fresh off the Territory Bridge.

Jamian looped his thumbs behind his belt. "Rather late for a jump, even with my Cyr to lend her power to yours."

Kerevin directed his gaze at Cyrolin. His smile widened, as if amused at the idea of the woman's power amounting to more than a trickle of water. He raised his left hand. A gold band hugged his forefinger. It glowed brighter like a candle's flame. Edmund had seen that particular luminosity once before.

"A lamp," he said.

Kerevin nodded. "Of the sort Aidan Gairden received from Torel's inventors on his birthday. Very good, General."

Edmund bristled. Kerevin sounded as if he were praising a dog clever enough to fetch a twig and return it to its master.

Deletar exposed his hands to show off a ring of his own. "Cinder Kerevin and I will need to stand before the guild as well, Edmund, to assure them of the Touched's cooperation in the conflict. Perhaps the captain and his galerunner should join us. It will make the journey to Ironsail that much smoother, and leave neither Cinder Kerevin nor myself fatigued."

Edmund said nothing. A voice in the recesses his mind, one that only materialized when matters of life or death arose, spoke up. *Do not trust them.* It was a young voice, boyish. It was not his conscience; it was his survival instinct, and he trusted it implicitly. Christine's words from earlier joined it like a chorus: *Tyrnen may have formed the group, but they served him because he was the Eternal Flame.* He trusted her, but for reasons he could not put his finger on he could not bring himself to trust Torel's Dawn.

Jamian stole a glance at Edmund. "It would take us several days to return to Ironsail by the river, and I will need to be present when Edmund addresses the guild."

"The four of us can depart immediately," Kerevin said. "We

need only form a circle, a process with which General Calderon is familiar. I am afraid we cannot accommodate any of your crew, however. They will have to make their way back east on their own."

"My galerunner comes with me," Jamian said.

Deletar smiled, amused. He pointed up to the sky. "Kahltan reigns, my lady, and you lack our advantages." He waggled his fingers, showing his lamp.

"Galerunners are proficient in protracting light over several hours, and I am the best of my kind," Cyrolin responded. Her voice held not so much as a whit of arrogance. She was stating fact. "In my hands, a wink from the Lady's last rays carries a ship as far as her midday luminescence in the hands of any other."

Deletar and Kerevin shared a look.

"The five of us, then," Edmund said. He did not want to give them time to suggest an alternative.

Kerevin and Deletar looked at him, to Cyrolin, back to Edmund. "Very well. Form the circle," Kerevin said. He gestured imperiously at the galerunner. "Place yourself between the two Untouched."

Cyrolin shot him a cool look, then glanced at Jamian. "Go on," he said.

She did as commanded. Edmund stepped up to her left. Jamian took his place on her right. Deletar stood beside him, and Kerevin flanked Edmund on the left. They joined hands. Edmund, heart hammering harder than ever, was dimly aware that Cyrolin's palm was soft and clammy. She was nervous. That was good. Nervous people were on their guard, and he needed a Touched on his side. Just in case.

He let his left arm hang loosely, so that wrist brushed Valor. He could rip it free and sheathe in the throat of either member of the Dawn before they could blink.

The Touched kindled. Heat rushed through him, a sudden fever. The world tossed and turned. Edmund closed his eyes and thought of Anna.

Chapter 8:
Our Place

THE WIND STOPPED, there and then gone as suddenly as it had started. The invisible hands tugging at Edmund's steel and snow dropped away. A salty tang tickled his nostrils. *We have arrived.*

He kept his eyes closed. He and Annalyn had something of a tradition when they visited Ironsail. They would stand together, facing one another, hands clasped, eyes closed. and just listen. To the cry of the gulls, the rumble of waves rolling in from the Great Sea, the slow *hiss* as surf drained away.

Edmund repeated the tradition, letting the sounds and smells of Ironsail wash over him. When he opened his eyes, he was confused. Anna did not stand before him, smiling patiently, eyes full of love and—

"—*patience,*" *he muttered, staring at the ground.*

A slim finger touched his chin and pushed up gently until he met her eyes. "There is no need to thank me. The Lady knows you exhibit more than your fair share of patience when I need it."

"You are my wife."

"And you are my husband." Anna spoke so matter-of-factly, as if there was nothing abnormal about the Crown of the North having to soothe her general after every shift in their long journey east.

87

A breeze teased her hair. Anna looked radiant, framed by the pink of Dawnfall that stained the western horizon behind her. She squeezed his hands. "The sooner we enter the city, the sooner we can hide away in our place."

"You've convinced—"

"—me? General? Can you hear me?"

Edmund opened his eyes. The woman frowning at him, watching him as if he might dissolve at any moment like a snowman on the first day of spring, was not his wife. *Cyrolin. The galerunner.* Hot tears stung his eyes. Anna was gone. His serenity and elation receded, swallowed up by the void in the pit of his stomach. Its blackness had consumed everything. There was nothing left. Since infiltrating Calewind in search of Aidan days ago, he had stood on a narrow perch at the center of that nothingness. One step in any direction, one breath, and he would lose his balance and fall. Falling would be so easy, and would bring such relief. Such peace.

Aidan. His son's name was like a single star in a sky as black as Kahltan's heart. He forced himself to remain upright. To balance for just a little while longer. Annalyn's soul belonged to Tyrnen. The thought of the traitorous Eternal Flame set his blood to boiling. That was good. Anger and hate pushed away the nothingness, filled him with purpose.

Skin slid away from his left hand, leaving his palm cool. "General Calderon?"

Cinder Kerevin's smooth, unctuous voice stoked Edmund's temper. He took in his surroundings. They stood to one side of the East Road. The broad route, paved in sandstone, began just outside Sharem's eastern district, extended fifty leagues to the east, was swallowed up by jungle, reappeared and unrolled another seventy leagues, unspooling near cities and plantations, and ended at Ironsail's front gate. They stood just outside the large, sand-colored walls of Leaston's capital. A fresh breeze carried more sea air, and a tumult rose over the city walls.

The Lady had abandoned the sky this far east, turning it over to Kahltan and his stars. Jamian and Cyrolin stood in between the two Dawn members. Appearing anxious, Jamian kept glancing over his shoulder to the west, back the way they had come. Cyrolin gazed around coolly. Kerevin and Deletar remained impassive.

"Are you well?" Kerevin asked.

It took Edmund a moment to realize the Cinder spoke to him. Before he could answer, Jamian spoke up. "You look like a man who needs to heave over the rail of his ship," the captain said, squinting at him.

"Your compassion is noted, Jamian," Edmund said. "Let's enter the city without further delay. The sooner I speak with the guild, the sooner I can return to my son."

"They'll already have disbanded for the night," Jamian put in, "and you're unlikely to find room and board this time of year. You can bed down at my estate, and I'll call an emergency gathering at first light."

Edmund gave him a puzzled look. *This time of year?* Before he could inquire, a panel of the stone wall slid aside and a brown-skinned man in sea-green armor stepped through, *Sard'tara* held loosely in his left hand. "Admission?" the Azure Blade asked, eyeing each of them in turn. Recognition flickered when his gaze landed on Jamian. "Guildmaster. We didn't expect you back on foot."

"I seem to have misplaced the *Cutter*, Blade Kilam," Jamian said.

"I see," Kilam said, though he plainly did not. He was studying Edmund's steel and snow, the sword at his waist. His stance was casual, but his grip on his *Sard'tara* tightened.

"General Calderon," Jamian said by way of introduction. Kilam saluted in an easygoing way, placing his gloved right hand against a silver pin depicting a fist closed around a double-bladed spear like the one he held. "Let us through, Kilam," Jamian said. "Guild business."

The Blade shrugged and stepped aside. Jamian led them through the portal, Cyrolin following, her gaze on her feet. Kerevin and Deletar glided behind her, and Edmund took up the rear. His boots passed over grass, then stone, then crunched atop fine grains of sand that coated the streets.

"Welcome back to Ironsail, General," Jamian said, waving his hand across the eastern capital like a man unveiling a feast. Ironsail emblemized the stark contrast between the eastern and northern realms. Where Torelian cities were plotted along neat grids, Ironsail's roads curved in gentle arcs. Homes, shops, stalls, and palm trees bordered every sinuous path. The night air was balmy instead of freezing, and carried the scent of the Great Sea. Cyrolin, wearing a short skirt and an open vest that exposed the swells of her breasts, was overdressed. Men and women walked shirtless through the streets, talking and laughing. Those who were clothed wore brightly colored garments like Cyrolin's, vests open halfway or all the way so as to feel the Lady's heat and warm breath on their tanned chests. Gold loops adorned ears, silver studs sparkled in one nostril or another, bracelets clicked and clacked.

From up ahead came the dull roar of waves rushing in and out. *The Great Sea speaks, and Ironsail listens*, went one saying. Those who listened profited. Commerce was the beating heart of Ironsail. Farmers, peddlers, merchants, and fishermen and women did so much business that the capital needed two harbors, North Haven and South Haven, located at either end of the city. In some ways, the havens were mirror opposites. South Haven was dirtier, hosting more taverns and dens of iniquity where one could gamble away fortunes and fingers. Rumor said the sneaks held their base of operations there. Edmund knew that was true, but could not have pinpointed that base if his life depended on it. North Haven was colorful to the point of garishness, its streets lined with theatres, art galleries, bookstores, clothing shops, and banks. The realm's most prosperous traders made a point of depositing a fraction of their wealth in banks throughout the east. *A coin in the bank is better than ten at hand,* merchants said.

Both havens maintained harbors. Ships came and went at all hours, setting sail for the Great Sea or lumbering down the Avivian or one of many other rivers that connected Crotaria's realms. *The Havens never sleep* was another eastern saying.

"It feels odd to enter from the road," Cyrolin said from Jamian's other side.

"Aye," the captain said.

"Is there any chance you could convene the guild tonight?" Edmund asked the captain.

"We have business with the guild as well," Kerevin said.

"We wish to speak with your colleagues about enlisting the galerunners to Aidan Gairden's cause," Deletar added. "Provided the Second gives his consent for the Crown of the North and the War Chief to add the Touched to their ranks."

"Your fellows indicated that wouldn't be a problem," Edmund said.

"It shouldn't," Deletar replied. "We're doing our due diligence, same as you, General."

"We are all fatigued from travel," Kerevin interjected smoothly. "I know I could do with some refreshment."

Jamian's eyes lit up. "We might as well wet our tongues."

"The guild—" Edmund began.

"Has adjourned for the day," Jamian said.

Edmund ran a hand over his face. "Very well. I could use a drink. Just one." His heart gave a sharp pang. "The Frosted Cup?" he asked, hoping he sounded nonchalant.

Jamian clapped him on the shoulder. "No finer establishment in the city. Come."

A swell of foot traffic flowed around them as they walked. Most Leastonians were tall and fit. Men shaved their heads bald to discourage bugs and to stay cool; women wore their hair long, done up in plaits and bedecked with gems. They wore sandals, and most of the women painted the nails of their feet and hands.

Edmund did not disapprove. Quite the opposite. Growing up in a village that straddled Crotaria's northern and eastern realms fostered within him a greater tolerance for different skin tones and cultures. Leastonians were relaxed, not indolent as many believed. Their easy smiles and flowing body language were infectious and calming. Jamian weaved around a pile of animal droppings without looking and sauntered through an open doorway. A sign out front depicted a chilly mug drawn in chalk, waves of frothy blue-and-green water spilling over its edges. *The Frosted Cup*, read crude, childish script. Another sharp tug nearly wrenched Edmund's heart from his chest. *Our place.* He looked away and crossed the threshold.

One step inside and he froze. Every surface, from the floors and benches to chairs, stools, even the walls, teemed with vagrants. They made no effort to disguise their rotting forms. Green and pink gore covered chests and limbs. Their faces were misshapen and inhuman, sporting leathery skin in a mix of colors. Tusks sprouted from mouths. Horns, some long and curved, others small and stubby, grew from heads and ligaments.

The vagrants were acting strangely. They appeared to be laughing. And carousing. And drinking, and paying for their drinks with coins that glinted in the light of candles swaying from chandeliers. Lanterns shivered and shimmied as celebrants jostled one another and pounded their fists along tabletops and the counter that wrapped around an island of drinks and glasses in the center of the common room. From the corner of his eye, he watched a vagrant holding a tall glass in one hand peel away his face—pink and hairy and dirty, like that of a pig—to reveal a human countenance. His hair was dump and plastered to his tan skin. He wore stubble at least three days old, and his eyes were filmy, though from drink instead of death.

All at once, Jamian's comments about the guild disbanding early for the day and scarce room and board in Ironsail clicked together. "The Festival of Blossoms," he said, words swallowed in the cacophony. Someone tugged at his elbow. He focused on Jamian, who waved for Edmund to follow him as he pressed through the crowd. They stopped near a table in the rear. Jamian flashed his merchant's guild pin, a multi-colored disc. Grumbling, a group of rough-looking men and women covered in tattoos and piercings gathered up their drinks and squeezed out. Edmund and his party slid into their seats.

Edmund was last in. Jamian sat nearest the wall, leaving Cyrolin wedged between them. The galerunner folded her hands in her lap and pinched her shoulder blades to make herself as tiny as possible. Cinders Kerevin and Deletar sat comfortably opposite them. Jamian raised his guild pin and a serving girl appeared as if from thin air, elbowing her way through the crowd. Jamian said something incomprehensible and held up five fingers. The girl nodded and shoved her way to the bar. Kerevin pressed a finger to his lamp-ring while his lips moved. Silence blanketed the table. Edmund watched the crowd. Bodies bumped and squirmed, mouths moved, but no sound permeated the bubble surrounding their party.

"Much better," Jamian said.

"Is every establishment in the city so overcrowded?" Deletar asked.

"As sure as the sea is salty," Jamian replied. "The festival lasts for the next few days. Surely you've attended before?"

"The Eternal Flame keeps us quite busy," Kerevin said.

"Kept," Deletar said.

"Indeed," Kerevin said, shaking his head. "To think Tyrnen

Symorne could betray the realms and our Lady."

Edmund said nothing. The mention of Tyrnen's name brought back flashes of his desperate fight against the old man's undead at Lake Carrean. Under the table, his left hand groped for Valor's hilt. His fingers touched warm skin. Beside him, Cyrolin started and yanked her hand away. Edmund mumbled an apology.

"What will the Touched do?" Jamian asked.

"Appoint Ernest Lorden as Eternal Flame and align our people with the Crown of the North and the War Chief," Kerevin said.

"We presume your guild will vote similarly," Deletar said.

Before Jamian could answer, the serving girl sidled and squeezed her way to their table, a tray of frosty mugs held high over her head. Tendrils of steam wafted from the heads of each glass as she clapped them down on the table. Pausing after handing out the second glass, she blinked, registering the void of noise in which they took shelter.

"Don't suppose you've got room for one more," she said.

Jamian appraised her, his gaze lecherous. "Only one spot left, I'm afraid." He glanced down at his lap. The girl tucked her tray under an arm, looking thoughtful. Cyrolin studied the tabletop.

Edmund said, "Not now, Jamian." Cyrolin glanced at him and then away just as quickly, her expression unreadable.

Jamian's lips dipped into a moue. "Work, work, work." He winked at Edmund, then turned back to the girl. "Stop by later. And keep the slush coming. Grape, if you please." He dug into a vest pocket and held out his closed fist. The girl's face lit up and she held out her tray. Leastonian marks clinked and rattled atop it. "Shoo, shoo," Jamian said, and she scurried away.

"She can't be a day older than Aidan," Edmund said.

"Which means she's old enough," the captain said, raising his glass. Wisps of steam curled around his beard as he drained the slush in a single pull. A shiver ran through him. He brought the cup down with a hard thump and dragged his sleeve across his mouth. "Colder than Kahltan's shade, but fruitier, if I had to guess." He grinned. The captain's lips and teeth were stained a purplish-blue.

When the server returned, Kerevin placed a hand on her arm. "Perhaps we should keep our wits about us, Captain." For once Edmund agreed with the man.

"I suppose one will be enough," Jamian grumbled. The woman plunged back into the press of bodies. Jamian nursed his glass as if it were a babe.

"We were discussing the possible course of action the guild might take," Deletar said.

"No, we weren't," Jamian said, sitting back. "Because there's nothing to discuss. There's only one possible course of action, and that's to align ourselves with the Crown of the North."

Relief flooded through Edmund. The guild's alliance was as good as done. A political victory hundreds of leagues from Torel's throne, probably the easiest victory he would ever earn, and he was one step closer to Annalyn.

Jamian chuckled and waggled a finger at Edmund, clearly misreading his relief as surprise. "I know what you're thinking. Easterners are nothing but a bunch of sandworms, more likely to bury our heads in the sand than lift the sharper end of a *Sard'tara* to throw in with our allies in the north. Well, you're mistaken, General. Leastonians love a good war . . . as long as the price is right."

"And you feel certain the other guild members will agree," Kerevin said, studying Jamian intently.

"Like I said: if the price is right. And it has been for decades. Trade with Torel is where most merchants get their income. I feel certain any man or woman on the guild would march to war for Annalyn Gairden or her boy. Torel was good to us under her reign. Once the others learn what your old Eternal Flame did to her, they'll order the Azure Blades to march."

"And the galerunners?" Deletar asked. Cyrolin raised her eyes.

"That'd be your new Eternal Flame's decision, I'd wager."

"More or less," Kerevin replied, giving a hint of a smile. "All Touched on Crotarian soil are expected to heed the Eternal Flame's command. That allegiance supersedes even your bond."

"It sounds like your Eternal Flame and the guild would see eye to eye," Jamian said, and took another drink.

Kerevin sat back, looking satisfied. "I see. Very good."

Jamian either did not hear or ignored the Touched. He picked up Cyrolin's cup. "Drink it," he told her. "Good spirits shouldn't go to waste."

Obediently, Cyrolin raised the glass to her lips. Edmund watched her throat shimmy up and down once, twice, three times. She lowered the cup with a gasp, drew a deep breath, and ran her tongue over the purple liquid staining her lips, savoring every drop.

"There," Jamian said. He turned to the two Touched. "They say a galerunner moves the winds, the winds do not move her. Her captain, though. That's another story."

Cyrolin glared at him, chest still heaving. Kerevin and Deletar looked puzzled. Edmund was curious, too, albeit in a vague sort of way. He knew little of the bond between captains and galerunners and might have inquired in different circumstances. Today, he cared not one whit. "Let's get going," he said. "I'd like to get a good night's rest so I can be up before—"

Kerevin held up a hand. "A moment, General." He leaned closer still, and even though there was no need, he spoke in a whisper. "Tyrnen infiltrated the north. For weeks, an abomination ruled Torel in Annalyn's name. It seems possible, even likely, that Leaston could be under his sway as well."

Jamian frowned. "I don't think so. The Azure Blades and galerunners stationed in the Prefecture would have detected anything amiss."

"From what I have observed, galerunners detect only what their captains ask them to detect," Kerevin said.

"Tell them," Jamian said. Cyrolin sat very still, her folded hands away from her empty cup.

"A fact that makes it even more likely Tyrnen could have intruded on your realm unnoticed," Kerevin said. "And Azure Blades? They are Untouched men and women."

"It took Aidan's magic to expose the creatures in Sunfall," Deletar pointed out. "And that was after they had manipulated and plotted their way into a war against the clans."

Jamian fell silent, troubled. Fear and impatience heated Edmund's blood. "We cannot just sit in a watering hole and drink."

"Agreed, General," Deletar said. "But caution is paramount."

"What do you have in mind?"

Kerevin and Deletar shared a look. "One of the reasons Tyrnen was able to displace you and the Crown of the North was due to Torel's power being so centralized," Kerevin said.

"Remove the Crown of the North, and you've won the north," Deletar said.

Edmund only nodded. His throat was too constricted to speak.

"Leaston is very different," Deletar went on. "Its power is spread between eight guildmasters. Therefore, it stands to reason that word of any plot or strangeness, no matter how seemingly inconsequential, would reach at least one guildmaster."

"Unless some have been compromised," Edmund put in.

The group went quiet for a moment. "Unlikely," Jamian said at last. "Each of us has a cell of Azure Blades assigned to us. They cost a small fortune, but we all have big fortunes to protect."

"Where is your cell, Captain?" Kerevin asked.

Jamian swatted at the air. "Left half back in Sharem."

"You were correct nonetheless," Kerevin said. "And the remaining half?"

"At my estate."

"You should gather them around you right away," Deletar said. Jamian fidgeted as if eager to be off. Edmund mulled over their words. The pair of Touched were right. He felt exposed, naked. He had grown accustomed to having Anna, or Aidan, or Tyrnen—the Lady take him into Her embrace and sear the flesh from his bones—by his side to help him think through entanglements that involved the arcane.

His chest tightened. He squeezed Valor until his palm ached. "What do you have in mind?"

Deletar pursed his lips. "Just because the merchant's guild does not convene until Dawnrise does not mean we can do nothing tonight. Kerevin and I can speak to the galerunners, and—"

"Actually, Deletar, we cannot," Kerevin said. "Not without permission."

Deletar looked confused for a moment. "Ah. Yes. The captains prefer not to allow their galerunners to associate with . . . what is it you call our lot, Captain?"

"Lightwalkers," Jamian said, a grin spreading across his face. "It's nothing personal, our separating your lot from the galerunners. We just wouldn't want them getting ideas."

Cyrolin made a rude noise.

"Shut your clam, Cyr," Jamian said. The words passed his lips without a trace of anger or command, but Cyrolin went silent immediately.

"Most intriguing," Deletar murmured, watching Cyrolin.

"How does the contract work, exactly?"

"Trade secret," Jamian said, looping an arm around Cyrolin's shoulders. The galerunner's face was stony. "This one could help, but she gets fidgety without me around to mind her manners for her." Cyrolin's face hardened further. "I'll go with you to speak to the galerunners," he went on. "Word of a captain is second only to that of a guildmaster in the east, and I happen to be both. Besides, you wouldn't know where to find our galerunners. That's a trade secret, too."

"What can I do?" Edmund asked.

Kerevin tapped his fingertips together. "Get some sleep."

"I am not a child to be—"

"I meant no disrespect, General," Kerevin said lightly. "My words were meant in friendship. You heart has suffered a terrible loss, and your body has suffered grievous wounds. My fellow Cinder and I have seen the way you move. Were we more adept at healing, either of us would be glad to—"

"That won't be necessary," Edmund said stiffly.

"They're right, Edmund," Jamian said. "Use my manor house. Cyr will accompany you."

"She does not need to do that," Edmund said. "She could go with you to help—"

"I am sitting right here," Cyrolin snapped.

Heat crept up Edmund's neck. "My apology, Galerunner."

"I have a name."

Warmth spread from his neck into his cheeks. "Most people address me by title, so I . . . just out of habit . . . I meant no offense."

Cyrolin started to reply, her face twisted in anger. She jumped and gave a yelp, looking down at the bench. "I hate when you pinch me."

"And I hate when you disrespect my friends," Jamian said, unperturbed.

Cyrolin's eyes were as sharp as *Sard'tara* heads. "Apology accepted," she said stiffly to Edmund.

Jamian burst out laughing. "I never thought I'd live to see the day anyone could knock General Edmund Calderon back on his heels." He slapped the table. "No time to waste, then."

"Agreed," Deletar said, still watching Cyrolin with a curious expression.

Jamian unclasped his guildmaster pin, held it aloft, and shouted to the room at large, "Move your asses, you bunch of asses!"

"The asses can't hear you," Cyrolin muttered.

They did not need to. One look at the lamplight glinting off Jamian's pin and the sea of revelers parted, squishing and bunching up to either side and opening a vein through the center of the room. The five of them scooted off their benches and stepped out of the bubble. Noise rushed in like water bursting through a dam. They hurried down the narrow track.

"I'll be home in two hours," Jamian said to Cyrolin.

"Two hours," she responded. Jamian nodded, and he turned on his heel and marched off, Kerevin and Deletar flanking him.

"You will follow," Cyrolin said brusquely, and took off down the street in the opposite direction.

Chapter 9:
Enclaves

EDMUND WAS TALLER than Cyrolin, had longer legs, and was accustomed to marching for days with only brief periods of rest. Yet the galerunner, shorter by a head and at least ten years his junior, managed to stay a good four strides ahead of him.

Shade take this damn limb, he thought as he limped in her wake. Pain stabbed through him with every step. He pounded at his left leg with a fist. It was his fault, that was the worst part. He had not given the wound proper time to heal. Had not and could not, not with Anna gone and Aidan alone.

Aidan has never been defenseless, he told himself. *Childish and petulant at times, but never defenseless. Especially not since Tyrnen had taken his mother from him.* A strained smile appeared on his face. Anna's death, Tyrnen's betrayal, the situation with Nichel of the Wolf. Each was a blow to Aidan, as if he were metal to be forged by a Darinian smith's hammer. But his son did not break or bend. Life's hammer forged him anew. His boy had become a man.

At that, the lightning bolts coursing up his leg faded. *He'll be fine, Anna. He has Daniel, and Christine.* Rather than assuage his worries, the thought brought new ones. Aidan's relationship with a Sallnerian would cause friction between Sunfall and the Temple of Dawn. Certainly, he would face overwhelming opposition if he went so far as to wed Christine. And there was Nichel of the Wolf to think about. Anna and Romen of the Wolf had promised their children to one another shortly after Aidan was born and shortly after Romen had even impregnated his Leastonian wife. Annalyn had met with the war chief and his wife, and had asked to touch Cynthia Alston's belly. Most women did not show the signs of pregnancy for months, but a Touched could detect a budding life almost instantly, Edmund knew. Anna had known about Aidan almost immediately.

"A daughter," his queen had whispered. The Alston woman had glowed like the Lady at noon and had wrapped her arms around her stomach. Edmund had stood by in silent opposition. Not because of any ill will toward the clans. He'd always felt people should have some say in who they married. Anna had called him—

"—a hopeless romantic," she said, smiling fondly.

They were at Lake Carrean, outside the cabin, picnicking on one of Torel's few glorious spring days. Aidan, swaddled in a blanket beside them, slept soundly. Helda, the head cook who came on as Aidan's nursemaid at Anna's exhortations, had prepared bread, meat, cheese, and fruit before disappearing with her husband, Old Beld, for a hike in the woods. Edmund relished private time with his family even as anxiety simmered on a low flame in the back of his mind. Defending them was his job. Although the lake was peaceful, Edmund, a soldier since boyhood, since the day Anna had saved what remained of his life, was never truly at ease.

Anna reached over to stroke his cheek. "I know how you feel. But there are considerations to anticipate, my love. Alliances to strengthen."

"Torel and Darinia have remained allies for over eight hundred years," he pointed out.

"Due to diligence and nurturing from both our realms."

"Even the strongest steel can bend if held in the flames for too long."

"I see you've been spending time with Romen again," she said.

"Do you disagree with the expression?"

"Not in the slightest. But Romen of the Wolf agrees with me. He possesses a keen mind and incredible foresight, a gift few

chiefs have demonstrated. He wants to gentrify his people. He knows they cannot survive on the Plains forever."

"I understand his reasoning, Anna." Her face lit up, as it always did when he used the sobriquet. It was so informal, so taboo from any lips except his. "I only speak for our boy because he cannot," he continued, rocking Aidan's bassinet gently, "not out of disagreement with your political motivations."

She stiffened, and her hand froze over the fresh rolls Helda had baked. "I'm looking out for our son, too."

"I know. But we've taken away his choice. Imagine if we hadn't been given a say in our futures."

"My father would not have refused to wed his daughter and only heir to the general of his army."

"I was not always general of the Ward."

"No, but you were always destined for great things. I knew it the moment I set eyes on you."

His face became incredulous. "Really? Catching me stealing food in the west district market seemed to you a strong indication of a bright future?"

"You were desperate."

"I was still a thief." Sitting up, he took her hands in his. "The point I'm trying to make is that we fell in love many, many years before I was worthy to kneel before your father. Or you. If I had taken a different path—still a good one, a just one, but one that had ended in a commoner's job instead of a place of the highest prestige and duty one can attain in the north without carrying that sword," he nodded toward Heritage, lying within Anna's reach, "or if I had remained what I was when we met, would we have been able to pursue our feelings?"

"Pursue? Yes, I think so."

He looked doubtful.

"I do think so. I did not turn you in, did I?"

"No. You bought me dinner."

"That was my first time in a tavern," she said, smiling a little.

He smiled, too, then grew serious again. "But," he prodded.

Her face fell slowly, like storm clouds rolling in to blot the Lady. "But you're right," she finished. "More than likely we would not have been able to be together." She bit her lip again. Despite the tone of their discussion a wave of heat swept through him. Dawn and Dusk, she was beautiful.

"I made this decision for Aidan for the good of the realm, and for Crotaria. You know that, don't you?" Anna asked, a pleading note lifting her voice.

"Of course, I do."

Her chest rose as she took a deep breath, held it, and let it out in a whoosh. "I'm still having a difficult time finding a balance between wife, mother, and queen."

"I suspect you always will. You've got three difficult jobs. I don't envy you."

"Thank you, dear. You do know how to lift a lady's spirits."

Edmund laughed, and she smiled, and her smile was—

". . . rest all night," someone was saying to him.

Edmund blinked. The lovely vision of Lake Carrean, and his boy, and his Anna, popped like a soap bubble. Without the reverie to distract him, pain came rushing back. "I only need a moment longer," he said, leaning against a waist-high wall. His face shone with sweat.

"Over here," Cyrolin said. She crossed the street to an ornate bench. Edmund collapsed with a grateful sigh. Sitting beside him, Cyrolin crossed one leg over the other and folded her arms across her chest to stare straight ahead. Happy to ignore anyone who wanted to ignore him—a luxury he could not often indulge in his position—Edmund removed his gauntlets and bent to massage his leg. He kneaded flesh like Helda kneaded dough. His agony lessened, from white-hot fire to a low pulsing.

Around him, Leastonians in masks depicting feral beasts and body paint that glowed in the night flowed past. Clusters stopped at stalls to pick up mugs of drink or baskets of food. On the other side of the street, directly across from them, sat a nondescript building that no one seemed to notice. "What is that?" Edmund asked, pointing.

Cyrolin looked. She licked her lips.

"It's an enclave, isn't it?" he asked. Without waiting for answer, Edmund pushed himself to his feet. Cyrolin rose beside him.

"We're supposed to go to my master's estate."

"I'm sure he wouldn't mind a slight detour." Edmund waited for a break in the tide of celebrants then limped across the street and rapped on the plain wooden door.

Cyrolin spoke up from beside him. "One cannot enter an

enclave without permission," she hissed. "That's why my master had to accompany the Cinders."

"I'm General of Torel's Ward," he said by way of explanation. She gave him a doubtful look.

The door opened and Edmund found himself staring at the top of a head of wild hair. "General Calderon," an Azure Blade in sea-green leather armor said. Edmund looked down. The Azure Blade who had greeted him was a reaver, diminutive folk from somewhere across the Great Sea whom Leastonian pirates liberated and hired on in their militia when they returned to Crotaria. Though half the height of most Leastonians, what reavers lacked in stature they made up for in ferocity. Like all of his race, the reaver's skin was brown and craggy. A thick red beard covered the bottom half of his face and trailed to his belly. "Welcome to the east." The reaver laughed and gestured for him to enter. Cyrolin followed, looking dumbfounded.

They stepped into a cool, dimly lit room, as round as Ironsail's streets were wide. A few tables and sets of wooden chairs carved from ebonywood sat in the center. Cots were arranged neatly along the back wall. Other Azure Blades stood or sat: Leastonian and reaver, men and women, talking or reading or sharpening *Sard'tara*. One bed was occupied, and its inhabitant, a bare-chested, ebony-skinned man, sat up sharply. Pairs of eyes flashed between Edmund and Cyrolin.

"Hahrzen," the reaver said, and extended a stubby hand.

Edmund shook it. "I don't recall having met you, Hahrzen. How did you recognize me?"

"Your face is famous in the east," the reaver said.

Edmund gave a small smile. Unless he missed his guess, one of the many sneaks that scurried through the underground network of the tunnels like rats in a pantry had recognized him. If Azure Blades at one enclave recognized him, all the others surely would.

"What brings you here?" Hahrzen continued. "Does the Crown travel with you?"

"No, but I am here on Crown business. Tell me, Hahrzen. Whom do you serve?"

"Guildmaster Filtek, so long as his coins flow like water from the hot springs in the west."

"The Plains of Dust are dry, Hahrzen," one of the men said

from a nearby table. Kiwi juice dripped down his chin.

"The hot springs are real," Hahrzen said. "I have heard rumors."

"Have you heard of any sort of mischief or malfeasance as of late?" Edmund said.

"Such as?"

"Disturbances, your guildmaster acting strangely. That sort of thing."

Hahrzen shrugged. "No, nothing. Well, no more than usual this time of year. The festival makes extra work for us all, but the pay is good. Guildmasters require double security when they venture into the city."

"Where is Guildmaster Filtek now?" Edmund asked.

"Out frolicking, under the protection of his second cell."

Edmund nodded. He knew each guildmaster travelled under escort of a personal guard of Azure Blades at all times. The rest of that cell reclined at their enclave until needed. Azure Blades who kept families saw them only occasionally.

Hahrzen's features grew hard. "What sort of mischief do you mean, General?"

Edmund took a moment to think. He wondered briefly if he should explain to the Blades about vagrants and harbingers, but dismissed the idea. The occurrence of the Festival of Blossoms complicated matters. All manner of oddities would walk Ironsail's streets for days. Besides, the more he discussed Tyrnen, the greater the chance word of Edmund's presence would reach the old man.

"Has the Eternal Flame met with Guildmaster Filtek recently?" Edmund asked.

"Not to my knowledge, and I'd know."

Edmund nodded. "Good."

"What's this about?" Hahrzen asked. The other Blades were listening openly.

"I have a report to deliver before the guild," Edmund said. "It would be better to wait to share details until then."

"That serious?"

"Yes."

Hahrzen glanced at Cyrolin. The galerunner remained expressionless. "Where is Guildmaster Jamian? No Blade has ever seen him apart from his galerunner for more than a night."

Hahrzen grinned again. "Not even a night, at that."

Cyrolin glared but said nothing.

Edmund clapped Hahrzen on the shoulder. "Thank you for your time. We'll see each other soon, I think."

"Of course," Hahrzen said, and showed them out.

As soon as the door closed, Cyrolin set off without a backward glance, her strides carrying her far ahead once again. After a time, she slowed. "There is another bench ahead. We can stop to—"

"I don't need to stop," Edmund snapped. The lie took less energy to explain than yet another recitation of Tyrnen's ambush. It was no less embarrassing, however. He had taken pride in becoming the Ward's most accomplished swordsman. Many claimed he was more proficient than Ambrose Gairden had been in his prime. Such boasts did not stoke Edmund's pride. He did not fight for glory. He fought to defend his realm, and to defend his family above all.

He had failed.

Cyrolin's scowl cracked. "Have you seen a healer? One of the disciples?"

"This injury is recent. There was no time to seek healing."

"I don't know much about the healing arts," she said quickly.

"I didn't ask." He stamped his left foot against the sandy street. "Let's keep going."

Cyrolin resumed walking. Even with Cyrolin's leisurely pace, his leg began to throb within minutes of starting out. Stopping would only invite pain all over again. He let his mind wander, reviewing his conversation with Hahrzen and what he already knew of Leaston's militia. There were eight guildmasters and twice as many enclaves. A cell of Azure Blades remained by their guildmaster's side at all times. Other cells patrolled the streets or stood guard at the Prefecture and guildmaster estates. They were everywhere, and like all Leastonians of a certain class, were tied to the sneaks' underground network. If Tyrnen or his servants were in Ironsail, chances were the Blades already knew. That made him feel better. Likely he would walk into his audience tomorrow morning to find a merchant's guild ready and willing to take action.

Around them, Ironsail's crowds grew more boisterous. Costumed revelers carried translucent green wine bottles laced with vines that glowed myriad colors. "We're almost there,"

Cyrolin said over her shoulder. Edmund, in too much pain to speak, nodded. Looking undecided for a moment, Cyrolin veered toward the wall of a stall and leaned against it. Edmund staggered over and slumped, leaning on one shoulder.

"I just need a moment," he said between breaths. Sweat ran down the bridge of his nose and dripped off the point.

Cyrolin watched him. "I could try to heal you," she said at last.

"No."

"You don't want my help?" she asked, voice testy.

I don't deserve it, he thought.

Cyrolin made a noise of disgust. "Captains, generals, merchants, kings . . . Men are all the same. Why won't you ask for help?"

"It's not in my nature." Edmund straightened. "I can walk, now."

She mulled that over. "Stand behind me."

"Why?"

"You are slowing us down. I can assist." She resumed walking without waiting for a reply. Edmund followed, and a gentle breeze tugged at him, then pulled. He felt like a hook on a fishing line. He walked at his normal, limping gait, but buildings blurred by. He looked down. Every stride devoured ground, and moreover, he felt only slight discomfort, a light pinch compared to razor-like teeth that gnawed at his leg. All around him, something unseen pressed in—firm, yet comfortable. A strong wind pulled at him from the front, tugged on his steel and snow, his hair, his cheeks. Wind screamed in his ears. The droning hum of conversation and laughter rose to a pitch as they grew close and then dropped away just as quickly, their painted faces and wild costumes there and gone. He breathed in and out. Whatever the magical force at Cyrolin's beck and call, it was powerful but gentle. If a cloud were able to be at once fluffy and as hard as steel, then a cloud was what buoyed him now.

Keeping his legs moving, Edmund looked ahead. Cyrolin walked in front of him in long, languid strides. She cut a path through the crowded streets like a gopher chewing through earth to dig a tunnel, never colliding with anyone nor seeming in danger of doing so. The strong currents that hauled Edmund gently yet implacably along did not bowl them over. They were lightly pushed, as if jostled. He turned and caught a few glances over their shoulders before they rescinded, lost in the crowd.

Cyrolin began to angle herself, turning slowly like a ship coming into port. They stepped onto a side road that was narrow and short, a tie between the longer curved roads.

"Right," she said.

He turned and, in a single step, swung far and wide, wide, gliding into the side street. "How are you able to do this?" he called over the rush of air.

"I am a galerunner," she shouted back. "I herd the winds like a shepherd herds sheep."

Edmund looked down at his left leg. It still hurt, but not so badly. Because, he reasoned, he was taking fewer steps, making each one count. Cyrolin was doing the hard work. Sconces flickered wildly as they passed, shuddering in fear of her power. He realized she was kindling from them, skimming from source to source like a stone over water.

They slowed. The cloud propelling him disappeared. He continued walking, resuming his normal pace, only now normal seemed sluggish, as if he waded through a swamp.

Cyrolin turned and grinned. Her cheeks were flushed and her hair was tangled and windblown. Her chest heaved, but her eyes shone with pleasure. "I thought you might need to rest," she said.

"I feel fine, actually," he said, surprised to find he was breathing hard.

"You never get used to it."

"To what?" he asked.

"The feeling of having the gales at your back. Without it, movement, breathing, life—it's . . ." she shook her head, gasping, and not from exertion. She was excited. She was alive.

"Disappointing," he finished.

Her grin widened. "Yes."

Two figures in light-gold robes glided up to them. Kerevin and Deletar. "Cinders," Cyrolin said, surprised.

They ignored her. "General," Kerevin said. "How fortunate to meet you here."

The weight of his mission, of his life, rained down on him like an avalanche. "Yes. Did you have any luck?"

Deletar chewed on his lip for a moment.

"You found something amiss?" Edmund said.

"No, and that's the problem," Deletar said. "We found nothing amiss at all. No sightings, no mention of any meetings with Tyrnen since late last spring."

"Which only makes sense," Kerevin added. "Tyrnen stayed quite busy in the north last spring."

"Helping with preparations for Aidan's sixteenth birthday," Edmund said, remembering. The old man had been a constant presence at Sunfall, never far from Anna or Aidan.

Kerevin steepled his hands and tapped his fingertips. "The Azure Blades and galerunners present a force almost as great as the Ward and the clans. We cannot assume Tyrnen has not made a move to manipulate them."

"So, we stick to the original plan," Edmund said, feeling the usual rush of anticipation that preceded a battle. Of being active. "We go before the guild tomorrow." His left hand strayed absently to Valor's hilt.

Cyrolin looked around. "Where is Jamian?"

For the first time, Edmund noted the captain's absence. Kerevin and Deletar shared another exasperated look. "Captain Jamian imbibed on more slush during our, ah, expedition," Kerevin said.

"The merrymaking was too powerful for him to ignore, it seems," Deletar added. Edmund detected a faint trace of raspberries and grapes on his breath. Noticing, the Cinder explained. "We joined in, but he got to be . . ." The Cinder stole a glance at his companion.

"Unruly," Kerevin finished. "We thought it best to leave him to his fun." He eyed Cyrolin. "How does the captain feel now?"

"I have no idea," she replied.

"Your bond does not make you privy to his state of mind?" Deletar asked.

"No. If it did, I would be consumed by lechery."

"Interesting," Kerevin murmured.

Edmund ground his teeth. This was just like Jamian. It occurred to him that while he liked the man well enough, all their interactions before today had taken place in short bursts.

"Do you know where he is?" Deletar asked Cyrolin.

"The bond does not work that way. If I had to guess, back at his estate. It is not so far. The gales can carry us there in half the time it would take to walk unaided."

Deletar licked his lips. "I don't suppose you'd be willing to teach us how you manipulate—"

"I cannot."

"Cannot, or will not?" Kerevin asked. He sounded curious rather than hostile.

"Cannot. Galerunners are sworn to secrecy by their masters."

"Pity," Deletar said. He yawned. "It is late, and we have travelled much today. Until Dawnrise?"

Cyrolin nodded. After the Cinders had vanished around a corner, she asked, "Are you ready to continue?"

Edmund took a step toward her in answer, and the familiar and comforting sensation of a cloud at his back returned. Cyrolin walked far ahead. They did not speak, only walked. Torches, warm glows spilling out of windows and doorways, and colorful tendrils curled around wind bottles melded and rushed by in a dizzying haze. Minutes later they arrived at Jamian's estate, a rambling edifice of marble. Sweeping courtyards dotted with palm trees and fountains hugged the mansion. Jamian's front door, tall and wide and painted red, stood slightly ajar. No light bled from the doorway. It was dark. So were the apertures where glass should go. Leastonians forewent glass panes so the sea breeze could flow through structures.

"Does Jamian normally leave his door open?" Edmund asked.

Frowning, Cyrolin started forward. Before he could stop to think, Edmund stepped in front of her. Years of shielding Anna compelled him to act. She glared at him. He ignored her, drawing Valor and easing through the entryway.

"Jamian?" he called softly.

No answer.

Edmund tightened his grip. "Wait here." He moved, footsteps scratching against paved stone speckled with sand. The entrance hall branched off to the left and right, and extended straight ahead. Edmund sidled to the right. He found himself in a guest room, spacious and lined with exotic furniture, rugs, and pillows piled on top of a bed. Gauzy drapes puffed out from glassless windows on the far wall. Edmund got a fantastic view of the Great Sea, cerulean waves sparkling under Kahltan's silvery glow. The low crash of waves and rush of the tide sighed through the room.

"Jamian?"

Nothing. To the left was a dining area. Countertops held spices, bowls, utensils. Back in the hall, he squinted straight ahead. "Jamian?"

The sound of retching answered him. Glancing back at Cyrolin, he followed the sound into a room dominated by a bed carved from cherry oak. Jamian sat bent over a pail. He was naked, his clothes discarded along the floor. He looked up. His face shone with sweat. He was as pale as his sheets.

"Must've drank too much," the captain grunted. His eyes widened and he lunged face-first into the bucket. Gagging followed by wet splatters against the wood. He reeled, wiping an arm across his mouth. "Take care of me, Cyr."

Edmund looked over his shoulder to see the galerunner. Wordlessly, she brushed past him. "Careless," she said, standing over Jamian.

"And be nice," he grumbled.

Cyrolin made soothing sounds under her breath. Edmund, gaining some insight into how their bond must work, was under no such compunction. "What were you thinking, Jamian?"

"Sorry," Jamian muttered. "I don't remember drinking more than a few."

"At each stop?" Edmund said sarcastically.

Cyrolin glared at him. "You speak to a guildmaster on the merchant's guild of Leaston."

"He is that," Edmund said. "He is also a fool."

Before Cyrolin could retort, Jamian spoke up. "He's right, Cyr." He took a deep breath and met Edmund's eyes. "I am sorry. Truly. I don't remember drinking so much. Our friends matched me cup for cup."

The hairs on Edmund's arms stood at attention. "Go on."

"We had four, maybe five at the most, and nothing too strong. No swamp waters. I lost my stomach for the stuff years ago, I'm ashamed to say." Jamian grinned shakily. "Maybe they've got stronger stomachs for spirits."

Edmund doubted that. He had met captains who could drink the burliest Darinians under a table, and Jamian was one of those. Jamian's eyes widened and he lunged into the bucket again. When he came up he handed it to Cyr, arms trembling. "I need to sleep. And don't you worry, Edmund. First light. You can count on it."

"If you're well enough," Cyrolin said, shooting Edmund a warning look.

"I'll be well enough," Jamian said, lying back. "Cyr, show Edmund to his quarters."

She left his side and crossed to the doorway. "Follow me," she said, and disappeared. Edmund watched Jamian. The captain's eyes were closed, and he was breathing evenly. He caught up with Cyrolin in the entry hall, followed her into the airy guest room with the open windows.

"There are refreshments on hand," she said, gesturing to a side bar stocked with cups made from crystal and a decanter filled with water.

"Thank you," he said. She did not acknowledge him, only turned to go. "Cyrolin?"

She turned in the doorway. "What is it?"

"The Touched advised Jamian against drinking earlier. Why would they drink with him?"

Cyrolin frowned. "Yes. That was odd." Lithe and tall, she drummed her painted fingernails on the lintel. "We're all tired from the day's events. Shifting consumes a great deal of energy, even in a circle. Perhaps . . ." She shrugged.

Edmund felt his eyelids growing heavy. All he wanted was to sleep. Both of his legs had turned into stone lumps.

"If there's nothing else . . ." Cyrolin said. Edmund shook his head. She left, and he fell into the feather mattress's embrace without bothering to shed his steel and snow. *Anna hates when I do that.* He drifted off smiling.

Chapter 10:
Butcher

AIDAN'S BREATH PUFFED out in little clouds as he hurried through the tunnels. The trail was cramped and wending. He held Heritage like a torch, the Eye's stormy glow pushing back the blue-black light that pulsed from the inky veins running along either wall. Susurrations rose and fell, rose and fell, forming words. He shut them out.

He emerged in a waypoint, a cavernous chamber honeycombed with arched entryways identical to the one from which he had followed. Veins snaked up and down along the walls, vanishing into archways and flickering like lightning behind clouds. Rope latticework covered stone between points of egress like webbing. The murmurs swelled and faded, swelled and faded, echoing around the chamber.

Aidan strode to a table at the center of the waypoint. Its plain surface was cluttered with supplies: maps, quills and inkpots, parchment, water skins, tinderboxes, two lanterns, and a stack of rectangular bars wrapped in shiny paper. His stomach gave an angry growl. Unable to resist, he scooped up one of the bars, unpeeled the wrapper, and bit into it. Smooth, milky chocolate dissolved on his tongue. He popped the second half in his mouth, wiped gooey fingers on his pants, and pocketed two more bars. He took up a lantern and tinderbox, and hooked a water skin through his belt. *They call it the Plains of Dust for a reason.*

Looping the lantern to his belt, he fished Daniel's key out of his pocket and gazed around the waypoint. The "I" flanked by two dots waited by a tunnel halfway up the far wall. Aidan crossed the cavern and placed one foot in a loop at the bottom of the netting.

— *There is an easier way.*

Aidan paused. Gabriel's voice melded with the chatters swimming through the waypoint. His ancestor had been quiet since Aidan had turned *Approbation of the Moon* over to Daniel.

What do you mean?

— *Think back to your fight against the harbinger.*

Aidan immediately understood. He had travelled through shadows, seamlessly melding with one and stepping through others. It had been similar to shifting, only stepping into and out of patches of darkness had been like submerging himself in cool water instead of warm Dawn. And more exhilarating.

— *Infinitely more so,* Gabriel purred. *And faster. And less taxing. Even a Gairden with your prodigious talents must favor efficiency.*

Riding the shadows, Aidan thought.

— *A clever but flamboyant term,* Gabriel sent back. *Some call it shadewalking.*

And could I . . . shadewalk all the way to Darinia from here?

— *That is how one is meant to travel the tunnels. If you are asking if you could shadewalk from here into the west under your own power, I would not attempt it. That would be too much even for you.*

Aidan's head tilted back. The aperture he sought waited above five others. He was not averse to climbing. Aching fingers and sweaty clothes would be minor aggravations compared to the trials he had suffered over the past weeks. Still . . .

He opened his ears and mind to the murmurs. Words crystalized, and he recognized them for what they were: prayers formed in the Language, but not in supplication to the Lady of Dawn. *Touch and spirit me away, Lord of Midnight.*

Aidan's brow furrowed. *When I travelled the tunnels before, I darkened from the veins along the walls.*

— *Naturally.*

What's the difference between darkening from the veins and darkening from shadows?

Gabriel's laughter was soft and raspy, parchment sliding over dry skin. — *Shadows are puddles compared to the oceans of darkness these conduits carry. Theirs is the oldest source of energy on Crotaria, perhaps even the world. Darken from these veins, and you draw from their innate energy, not your own.*

Aidan shivered as if he could feel Kahltan's frigid gaze through layers of dirt and stone. *They are sources of dark magic.*

— *The purest.*

How were the sneaks able to tap into them? Were they shades?

— *Hardly. The sneaks discovered the tunnels and appropriated them as their own.*

Then whoever did build them, Aidan thought, *would be the oldest source of life on Crotaria?*

— *Correct,* Gabriel said.

But who— Aidan began.

— *The tunnels have always been here, so far as any scholars are willing to say.*

— *Nonsense,* Anastasia interjected. *The histories say—*

— *Who wrote the histories, Mother?* Gabriel asked.

— *The Disciples of Dawn,* she replied after a moment's hesitation.

— *Ah,* her son replied.

Aidan tried to shut them out. He placed two fingers in the vein and winced. The viscous substance felt like mud flecked with ice. Looking up at the entryway, he darkened. Ice flowed into him, coursing through his bloodstream—and then he was standing inside the tunnel entrance, the ground far below.

— *I find the sensation of shade in my veins soothing,* Gabriel said. *Refreshing. Like a drink of ice water after days walking the Plains. Don't you?*

Aidan did. Deep down, he did. He spotted the key and let his fingers rest in the vein that ran just beneath it. Concentrating on the key, he darkened again. Then he stood at the mouth of a tunnel, looking down at another waypoint. It was identical to every other—rocky floor, table loaded with supplies—except the tunnel where he now stood was set lower along a side wall.

I'm in Darinia. I'm thousands of leagues from home. The rapidity of shadewalking would never cease to amaze him.

— *It is rather incredible,* Anastasia admitted.

— *How big of you to say, Mother,* Gabriel said, satisfaction radiating from his words.

Aidan ignored them, turning away from the view of the waypoint to stare down the dim, serpentine tunnel. The path would take him approximately ten miles outside Janleah Keep. His heart raced. Now that he was in Darinia, the prospect of confronting Nichel loomed large.

I wish Christine were with me. She's fearless. Her face swirled into focus. The way her eyes lit up when she looked at him; the curve of her lips when she smiled, indicating that she was entertaining a particularly mischievous notion; and the curvature of her . . . His blood heated.

— *Young people,* Anastasia lamented.

Embarrassed and highly annoyed by his lack of privacy, Aidan shoved the thoughts away. That only made him angrier. They were his thoughts. He should not have to curtail them just because his mind had become a palace made of glass instead of stone and marble. He wished, and not for the first time, that he had a way to—

— *There is a way,* Gabriel cut in.

Excitement tingled in Aidan's belly. *Tell me.*

— *This goes against tradition,* Anastasia said sharply. *The sword-bearer and his or her ancestors must remain in contact at all times for the good and safety of the sword-bearer.*

— *Not at all times, Mother. You would not understand because you and Father were the first to hold Heritage. As such, you have never lived in a glass palace, as Aidan so eloquently put it.*

— *Even so, Gabriel,* Charles interjected. *I think Aidan would be better served by—*

Aidan had had quite enough of his family deciding what would serve him best. *Tell me,* he thought again.

— *As my sword-bearer commands,* Gabriel said. *Now, I will send you the spell through Heritage, as is our tradition.* He drew the last word out, biting off every syllable. Gabriel's raspy laugh wormed through Aidan's mind, and he could not suppress a shiver. *It is known as scrim, and it was created by Aaren Bridgegil.*

The author's name sent another wave of gooseflesh up and down Aidan's arms.

— Before I send it, however, you should know how to reverse it, because I will not be able to explain it to you, Gabriel said.

Aidan suddenly had a new focus for his anxiety. *What do you mean?*

— Walls of stone and marble, remember? Now pay attention.

Aidan listened. Heritage thrummed in his hand. A prayer to Kahltan formed. Absently, he stuck his fingers into a conduit and darkened. A breeze caressed his mind. No, not a breeze, exactly. A sheet as light as a feather fluttering over his thoughts. A whisper made silk. Abruptly he realized he was alone in a way he had not been since the morning of his sixteenth birthday.

"Gabriel?" he said aloud. Nothing. Then, tentatively: *Grandfather?*

Only the low chatters of the magic coursing through the tunnels answered.

He let out a long, deep sigh, and walked along the winding path. He thought of Christine, of home, of Christine, of his mother and father, of Daniel, and of Christine. No disembodied voices broke in, telling him what to do or reminding him of this or that.

Bliss.

The path sloped upward. Aidan hunched as the ceiling lowered. The conduits ended abruptly. Aidan groped in the darkness until his fingers brushed solid stone, then coiled rope. He raised Heritage. The Eye reddened, revealing a rope ladder dangling from above. Sheathing Heritage, he mounted the ladder and climbed. Faint light shone through cracks above. At the top he probed at the darkness around the edges of light. It was a boulder set over a hole in the ground. Holding the topmost rung with one hand, Aidan heaved against the rock. It rolled to one side. Rust-colored sky greeted him. There was no wind. Heat settled over him, thick and heavy. Panting, he clambered onto the surface and got his bearings.

The Plains of Dust extended in all directions, dry earth baked reddish-brown. Tall pillars bearing carved faces dotted the landscape. The Lady of Dawn held a different vantage here than she did in the other realms. By now, Kahltan ruled the sky in Calewind, but here She was halfway submerged in the western horizon. Blues and purples leaked into rusty Dawnfall, but the Lady's warmth was slow to dissipate.

He squinted. Off in the distance, shimmering behind a curtain of heat, he saw a pyramid with serrated edges. Janleah Keep. Aidan took a draft from his water skin. Just a short one. Oases and their wells were prized territory in the west due to paucity of water. He bent down and rolled the boulder back into place. Taking a deep breath, he started the long walk toward the Keep.

Aidan's mind wandered. Not all of the Plains were bare. Darinians were renowned for smithing and building. Fabulous cities hewn from stone had sprang up around oases, land worth more than gold and silver to the clans. According to the histories, the Darinians roamed the west and settled cities long enough to build a well, refill water skins, hunt game, or fight rival clans over territory. Then they moved on, the city left behind like a picked-over carcass, waiting for another clan to come along and breathe life into its shops, domed halls, and roadways.

A breeze caressed his skin. He closed his eyes, basking in it.

Not all clans moved from outpost to outpost. Some made permanent homes in mountains or sand dunes. Outsiders could walk atop a dune and never realize that they passed directly over a sprawling Darinian city. They—

Aidan jerked to a halt. *A breeze? From where?* He looked around nervously and caught a flash of movement to his right. Pillars of stone stretched up to the stars like fingers. Something had moved behind them. He blinked. *Ordine'kel* fused with *Ordine'cin* draped his vision in black and white. His eyes saw through a pillar far ahead and to his right to perceive a crouched form holding two hatchets. The form barely moved, hardly breathed. It was coiled, ready to strike.

Aidan released Sight and resumed walking, maintaining his unhurried gait. Janleah Keep grew larger. Overhead, blue light faded to a plum-colored purple. He wrinkled his nose. The air carried a sickly-sweet smell, and something fouler, like excrement sitting in chamber pots for days. Swallowing, he blinked, sheathed Heritage, and walked on. More pillars dotted the landscape. Carvings decorated them, but the Lady's light had grown too faint for him to make out words or symbols. His ears picked up soft rustlings of cloth. He let one hand drop to his sword hilt and summoned Sight. More black-on-white forms crept along before him, flowing from pillar to pillar like shadows. Some were tall, some short, all lithe. Women.

I thought clanswomen did not fight alongside their men? Aidan thought.

No response. The scrim was still in place. Aidan heard low keening. The breeze from earlier. His throat went dry. No air ruffled his shirtsleeves. His ears pricked. It was not wind he heard, because there was no breeze. Low voices, repeating the same words. Chanting.

Trying to appear casual, he kindled a thread of the Lady's dying light and murmured a prayer in the Language of Light, repeating Gabriel's incantation backwards, per his instructions. The feather-light cloth over his mind lifted and voices crashed into him, scattering thoughts like startled birds.

— no longer feel his presence, Charles was saying frantically.

*— the meaning of this! You will explain—*Anastasia.

— could feel 'kel earlier, but I could not speak with him, Ambrose said.

— If you would all quiet down for just a moment, Gabriel said, *you will notice that the Crown of the North has returned.*

The shade's cool tone cut through their shouts and protestations like a knife. Aidan felt a pang of guilt. Cold fear emanated from his grandfather in waves that threatened to suffocate him.

I'm here. I've been here.

They pounced on him, talking over one another and demanding that he never cut himself off from them again. That made him angry, but another flash of movement off to one side ripped his attention away from his mind and back to the Plains.

We will discuss this later. There are—

— We know, Charles said sharply. *We saw through the Eye. What should I do?*

— What can you do? Ambrose said. *You can't fight them. You're here to discuss peace, not . . .*

Aidan could not read the patriarch's thoughts the same way Ambrose could read his, but he got a sense of what the other man had been about to say. *Not spill more blood.*

He walked on, aware of darting movements and soft, padding footsteps. The last rays of light vanished as the horizon swallowed the Lady of Dawn. Kahltan's milky white light lit his path. Within three miles of Janleah Keep, the columns ended abruptly. Eight clanswomen spilled out from behind them, flanking him four to a side, lines of hard flesh and harder faces replacing stonework. Some were nude, some half-clothed in animal skins. Glittering eyes peered out from helms molded into eight different heads: wolf, snake, lion, bear, falcon, elk, stallion, tiger. Chanting made guttural by steel slipped out through their helms. The words were still indecipherable, but the sharpness of their delivery conveyed meaning well enough.

Aidan paused. Sweat ran down the back of his neck. His right hand twitched, wanting to grab Heritage. He balled it into a fist and held it stiffly at his side, walked onward. They matched his pace, chanting and watching as they moved in two straight lines.

— *You could shadewalk*, Gabriel purred.

No.

— *The alternative is offering yourself up for slaughter. That is the only way this ends.*

Vanishing now and reappearing inside the Keep would be perceived as hostile, and seal my fate just as surely.

Heritage rattled in irritation.

Aidan got to within twenty paces of the broad steps that unfurled from the entrance to Janleah Keep when the chanting stopped. Wolf and elk stepped from the head of each line to bar his path.

"Shorogoyt," they said in unison. "Shorogoyt. Shorogoyt." The other six picked up the chant.

What does that mean? he asked.

— *Butcher*, Anastasia replied softly.

Chapter 11:
She Who Reigns Within Herself

"BREATHE IN. OUT. Breathe in. Out. Slowly, wolf daughter."

Niche's lips peeled back in a snarl. "Do not call me that."

"Apologies, war chief. In, and out. In. Out. That's it. Concentrate on my voice. Hone your thoughts as we discussed."

Nichel stared at the backs of her eyelids. She took slow, relaxed breaths. It was forced relaxation. Jonathan had no right to keep her here. She was the war chief. She should be marching at the head of the clans, a wolf's head on the shoulders of a body made up of one hundred thousand clansfolk ready to pillage and maim and kill and—

She stood at the center of a cave. Green light illuminated wet stone walls that extended up into darkness. The light wavered, as if reflected from water. Ahead, the light faded, giving way to darkness. Darkness above, darkness in front, darkness behind. Two shining red orbs appeared in the center of blackness far ahead.

Nichel's eyes flew open. Jonathan sat cross-legged on her bed across from her, palms on his knees, watching her. His expression was serene. Nichel sat on her haunches. She wanted to claw his eyes out.

"It cannot harm you if you suppress it," he said.

"I can't suppress it," she hissed between clenched teeth. "You don't understand what it's like. It's always there."

"Remember what your father said."

Nichel became aware of biting pain in her knees. She looked down. Her nails dug into her flesh, just short of drawing blood. She relaxed her hands. "Only he who reigns within himself is king," she muttered.

"Indeed." His smile became sympathetic. "Might I suggest a slight alteration? Only she who reigns within herself is queen."

Queen. She would have been Aidan's queen, if he had not—

"I can't do this," she said.

"Nor can you run from it. You must face the *Nuulass*, and you must suppress it."

Nichel's glare became as sharp as Sand and Silk. He stared back calmly, and it was she who looked away. "Let's try again," she said, lowering herself to sit cross-legged.

"Very good."

It took all of Nichel's control to clamp her eyes shut.

"In, and out. Deep breath. Exhale. See the lake. Be the lake."

Her chest rose and fell, rose and fell. She imagined her lake as she had described it to Jonathan days ago: A glassy body of water bordered by grass and flowers of every conceivable color. Forming the image was difficult. She had seen water only once, staring out at the Great Sea during her single trip into Leaston. It had been vast and never-ending. Like the Plains of Dust, only liquid and rippling and blue. Her favorite color from a past life.

Nichel breathed. Her lake's surface was crystalline, reflecting a cloudless sky. Jonathan's voice faded to a murmur, and she was glad. His scent wafted in. He smelled of spring water and soap. Fresh and clean, the way her mother had smelled. Although an honorary member of the wolves and a Torelian, Jonathan harbored a passion for beauty. Leastonian merchants ventured along prescribed paths through the Plains, and he always traded for soaps and spices and fabrics and books.

Most Darinians believed Jonathan's predilections made him weak. Nichel disagreed. Her father had taught her to embrace other cultures. She had been born half Leastonian and half Darinian, and had she wedded Aidan, would have become queen of the north.

The water rippled.

Nichel's lips twitched, exposing a flash of bared teeth. Aidan again. She thought of how he would look as Sand sawed through his throat, blood spurting from his neck and running down his chest, wide eyes going glassy as he sank into death's embrace.

That called to mind the heads of her mother and father. Faces sunken, eyes glazed, blood caked on the torn edges of their throats.

Grief punctuated anger, mingled with it. Nichel's eyes stung. Wetness seeped down her cheeks.

A soft hand took hers and squeezed. She squeezed it back.

"Slow your breathing, Nichel. Easy. Easy. I am here. You are safe."

The cave existed deep inside her. It lived in the cave, and it lived inside her. She was there, too, as immobile as if steel spikes had been driven through her feet. Darkness before her, darkness behind her. Red orbs, so bright and hot, floating toward her. No, not floating. Growing. Swelling. Filling the blackness, emitting heat that threatened to sear flesh and burn bone to ash—

The lake! Her mind sought it, scrambled for it, clung to it. It appeared, but changed. Brown, dead grass. Wilted flowers. Steam rising from a surface that had begun to boil.

Her clans. Her people. They travelled belowground, utilizing passageways whose function had been understood long ago but had since been lost, devoured by time. So, they marched on foot, hidden from the Mother's gaze and from the Father's Vanguard, and they did so without her. Jonathan was her advisor, and he had advised that she stay behind until she could bring it under control. A trifling detail. The clans would emerge soon, boiling out of holes in the ground and washing over Torelian man, woman, and child, and she would join them as soon as—

Not red orbs. Eyes. Pupils that burned like liquid gold ringed by fire. They bulged, wide and bright and burning. Heat washed over her, scalding, unending, but she did not melt or burn away. There was nowhere to go. Nowhere but forward.

Light wavered, bouncing off wet stone walls. Ahead, the red eyes waited. A deep growl shook the earth beneath her feet. One step. That was all it would take. One step into the center of the Nuulass and she would join with it, and there would be no more loss. No more pain. Only rage, an ancient and eternal fury strong enough to level mountains and raze cities.

Spring water and soap. Jonathan was there. She could smell

him. Jonathan was—

Dead. All dead. Romen of the Wolf. The pale queen who had birthed the wolf daughter—dead. Her people—dead. All at the hands of the man she loved. The man she had thought she'd loved.

Grief threatened to swallow her. Nichel's feet itched to step forward, to leap into those blazing eyes. Were they closer? They were. Tongues of flame ringed those eyes like lashes.

Her courage had been burnt to cinders. Nichel swept it up and clung to it as she turned her back on the Nuulass. *Its howl reverberated through her mind. Its scream was shrill and feminine. She spun back and the eyes had receded.*

GO!

Her command overwhelmed the Nuulass. *It shrieked and fell back.*

The blackness of the cave was not without end. She had built this place, had willed it into being. She flexed her will like a muscle and pushed. The Nuulass *flew back and away and down, the cave floor curving downward into a pit. A vault deep within the recesses of her soul. The* Nuulass *existed within her, but it could be contained. It roared in frustration, but that roar receded and Nichel slammed a seal over it. The seal trembled with the force of its blows, to no avail. It had been forged by Darinian hands, her hands, wrought from steel and marble and diamond.*

Still, it trembled. The Nuulass *craved freedom. It craved control. It craved. Blood. Aidan's blood. It battered at the seal until the walls trembled and dust curtained down and—*

Only she who reigns within herself is war chief.

YOU WILL BE STILL.

Her willpower crashed against the seal, fusing with steel and marble and diamond. They did not reinforce her will. Her will reinforced them. The seal did not move again. She jumped from the cave to her lake, to green grass and bright flowers and a surface as still as a mirror.

Nichel's eyes fluttered open. She became aware of her ragged breathing, of sweat that plastered clothing to her body. Jonathan stood over her, his face drained of color. "Are you all right? I thought you were . . . I thought it had . . ."

"I triumphed. Are you surprised?"

His body sagged. "No, not surprised. Relieved."

"I've conquered it."

"No, Nichel. I told you it cannot be conquered. Only suppressed."

Tears welled up again, not from grief. "I cannot fight this battle forever."

"You can, and you will, because you must. You are the war chief. The mightiest of your people. They know it. So do I, and so must you."

Tension leaked out of her. Jonathan took her hand again and kissed her knuckles. "You do not fight alone, Nichel. You will never be alone." His other hand stroked her curly hair. His scent altered. Lust, musky and sharp, hung over soap and spring water like humidity. She went rigid.

"Do you want me to stop?" he said softly.

Nichel could not answer. She did not know what she wanted. Jonathan took her silence for permission and leaned in. His breath warmed her lips.

A coppery scent teased her nostrils. Blood. Another scent: wolf hair.

Emotions followed: anxiousness, like a strand that quivered.

Nichel gently pushed him away. "Ulestren and Ipadia approach," she said, rising smoothly, at once proud and astonished at how even her words sounded.

"How do you know? The scents," he answered himself.

Her bedroom door flew open, admitting a tall woman with long legs and short-cropped silvery hair. Anyone but Ulestren of the Wolf would not have dared enter without permission. Ipadia of the Adder, fair skinned and coppery haired, shuffled in behind her. Her eyes held Nichel's, but they appeared strained, as if desperate to fly away. Nichel felt a low growl rise in her throat. Had Ipadia opened her door without knocking, she would have gutted her where she—

The seal trembled.

Nichel took a moment to gather herself. "What sets your nerves on edge, wolf sister?" she said, pointedly directing her attention at Ulestren. Ipadia bristled at not being included in the war chief's address, but wisely kept her mouth shut.

"We came ahead to deliver the news, war chief. The pack has him."

Thought and reason fled. "Has who?" As if she needed to ask.

Ulestren stole a glance at Ipadia before answering. "Aidan Gairden."

The seal trembled.

Chapter 12:
Keeper of Doors

DANIEL PAUSED OUTSIDE the entrance to the Crown's Promise, removed his helm, patted his hair, smoothed his steel and snow. Taking a deep breath, he flung open the door and strode in.

The Crown's Promise was the largest and busiest tavern in Calewind's southern borough. On a normal night, a tidal wave of sights and sounds and smells would have ushered him into the common room. Patrons shouting and singing, clay mugs pounding against tables, calloused hands clapping backs draped in leather jerkins, serving girls in white blouses and skirts setting down drinks and scooping up Torelian or Leastonian marks—Leastonian coin bought more and better spirits—fluted bottles and crystal glasses cluttering the long, rectangular tables in the inn's private dining room. Horace Winlow, the mustachioed barkeep, would be dancing between four barrels as wide as his chest, turning spigots and filling icy glasses with foamy drink, his face red and shiny with sweat.

Tonight, the common room was full but subdued. Fire blazed in the hearth that spanned half the length of the back wall, but people packed in around tables as if for warmth. Conversation was low, like wind sighing through trees. Laborers in white shirts and breeches nursed drinks or stared at tabletops or stared straight ahead, eyes haunted. Serving girls meandered, wiping tables and listlessly gathering empty glasses. The private dining room to one side typically hosted Calewind's more affluent citizens, who drank Horace's finest vintages from crystal goblets. Tonight, the dining room sat empty.

A purple haze hung over the common room. Daniel wrinkled his nose. He would recognize the sweet scent of windrose tobacco smoke anywhere. Of course, he would. He had harvested enough crops in his lifetime. *Enough to last me two lifetimes,* he thought. Everywhere he looked, patrons stamped wads of it into pipes or took long drags from rollups.

Daniel went toward a small table at the back and dropped into a bench. He propped his *Sard'tara* against the wall, mindful to angle the curved blades at either end away from him. He let his hand linger on the weapon's smooth shaft. It was a gift from his father. A symbol, Rakian had said, that Daniel had come of age. To Daniel's way of thinking, he had not come of age so much as he had been forced to join Torel's Ward. Rakian had taught him how to handle the weapon, but Daniel had stashed it away after noticing the odd looks some of the Wardsmen were giving it, and him. *Sard'tara* were an eastern weapon. Northerners fought with swords, axes, polearms, spears. He hadn't thought to retrieve it before fleeing Sunfall with Aidan in the dead of night. Secretly, Daniel had been almost grateful to leave it behind.

Absently he wondered why he had decided to retrieve it earlier that morning. A pang of homesickness ran through him. He turned away from the *Sard'tara*. It was ridiculous that he would miss Rakian Shirey, of all people. As he adjusted his weight, the black sword at his waist scraped against the bench. Daniel rolled his eyes. *Should have let Aidan take the Dawnburned thing with him.*

A raucous gale of laughter came from a group of round tables across the room. Daniel stole a glance. A tall Wardsman whose face he could not make out held court, leaning in to talk in a low voice and then slapping the tabletop when his joke reached a crescendo. The other Wardsmen, helms at their feet or beneath the tables, threw back their heads and laughed. Several dipped their heads to pull from mugs, revealing the taller man's handsome face and coifed blonde hair.

Daniel hunkered lower in his seat. He did not feel up to a confrontation with Karter Rosen. Folding his hands on the tabletop, he took one last look at the group, and paused. One Wardsman sat apart, helm on, nursing a drink. He was staring right at Daniel.

Daniel looked over his shoulder, wondering if the Wardsman was trying to catch the attention of someone sitting behind him, when he remembered his back was against a wall. He turned back slowly. The other man continued to stare. Daniel stared at the tabletop, looked up, back down again. He knew all of his brothers by name—the ones stationed in Calewind, anyway—but he couldn't place this one.

A serving woman wandered into his line of vision. Daniel patted his hair again before she wandered over. She was young, her face curtained by auburn hair. "What'll you . . ." She trailed off, recognized him, and beamed.

"Why, Master Shirey. I thought you'd forgotten all about me."

"That's Lieutenant Shirey now, Mara," he said, trying not to look too impressed with himself.

Her face brightened. "You got the promotion?" she said, setting down a clay mug from her tray.

His smile faltered, so he stretched it. "Just before I stepped inside."

Mara looked him up and down. "I thought lieutenants would be . . . cleaner."

Daniel grimaced, looking down at his dirty hands and shirt sleeves. "Aidan wanted me to—"

"The Crown of the North?" she interjected, wide-eyed.

"One and the same. The Lady save us all. Anyway, he—Crown of the North—asked me to do a little job for him."

"Really? You, personally?" She stepped closer. He drew in her scent: flowery perfume masking a faint brew of sweat, roasted meat, and spirits. "I knew you and Aidan were friends, but I didn't realize . . ."

Doing his best to appear nonchalant, he took a swig of ale. "There's work to do, and some of it's bound to get dirt under a man's nails. You heard the Crown's announcement earlier."

"No, I was working. I've heard talk, though."

"What kind of talk?"

Mara dropped onto the bench across from him. "My feet could use a rest. They're saying . . ." She blinked. "What is that?" she asked, pointing.

Daniel followed her finger. "A *Sard'tara*. It's one of those—"

"Oh," she breathed. "Like the Azure Blades use? I've never seen any Wardsmen use those," she rushed on without waiting for an answer. "Are you any good?"

"Yes," he said. It was not a boast. During his boyhood, any time not spent tending crops or doing chores had been consumed by Rakian's training. Daniel had not had much opportunity to demonstrate his aptitude with the weapon. Throne room doors did not often stage uprisings in need of quelling. "You were saying, about talk around the city," he prompted.

Mara leaned in. "They're saying that the Crown talked about dead bodies rising from the grave to attack us. And something about the Eternal Flame turning traitor."

"You don't sound surprised."

"It's not hard to believe. The part about the Eternal Flame, I mean. You know what Calewind was like while Aidan—the Crown—was on the run."

"Actually, I don't. I was with him."

Mara's mouth fell open. "Really?" She got up and sidled onto the bench next to him. Daniel scooted over to give her space. She scooted closer until he was crammed between her and the wall. "What was it like? Where did he go? You were helping him?" She shook her head. "From standing around guarding the throne room doors to helping the Crown flee Calewind."

Daniel smiled tightly. "Exhausting. What was the city like while we were away?"

Mara bit her lip. "Cold. It was a cold place, and I don't just mean the snow. The Wardsmen harassed people. There was a strict curfew, and executions almost daily against anyone who spoke out against Queen Annalyn."

Her face had gone pale, so Daniel covered her hands with one of her own. Mara gave him a grateful smile. "Listen to me prattling on. I don't mind admitting that I'm scared. Queen Annalyn and General Calderon didn't lift a finger to rein in the Ward. Turns out they weren't themselves after all, I guess. People who attended Aidan's trial say he exposed them as . . . as walking corpses. Horrible creatures with tight skin and no eyes."

Mara scooted closer until she was halfway on his lap. "Aidan killed them, though." She shook her head. "Magic. To some people it's a gift. I think it's a curse. Just look what it's capable of.

To think the Eternal Flame can call upon the power of Kahltan, too. People are scared. Have you ever seen it so dead in here?" She swallowed. "Not the best choice of words, I suppose."

"It will be all right," he said lamely.

She smiled at him. "Of course. The Eternal Flame stands no chance against a Gairden. Especially not one with friends like you. Calewind will be safe again, and Torel, and all of Crotaria besides."

Her hand settled on his leg, drifted up to his thigh. "Perhaps you'd be willing to escort me home."

Daniel's thoughts scattered. "What?"

Her eyes smoldered. "I have a few more drinks to serve, a floor to clean, and then I'm done."

His face burned, and his cheeks hurt. He became aware he was grinning in what he felt certain was a foolish way. "Sure. I mean, yes. I'll need to be up early, though."

"Important work planned for tomorrow?"

"Have to be at my post before Dawnrise." The words were habit, routine. Daniel could not have stopped them from spilling out had he tried, but he regretted them as soon as they left his tongue.

Her hand froze. "Your post?"

"Yes," he said more evenly. "The throne room."

"I . . . I thought you would be helping the Crown of the North with . . . something."

Daniel's good mood evaporated. "I am helping him. Those doors aren't going to guard themselves."

Mara stood up and ran her hands down the front of her dress. "More ale?"

"No," he said quietly. "Something warm. Tea, I guess."

"Fine." She started to leave, then looked back. "You shouldn't have led me on."

"How did I lead you on?"

"You're not a Wardsman. You're a doorkeeper." She stormed off.

Daniel pushed his empty cup away and studied his hands. Mara returned a few minutes later and slammed his mug of tea down so hard that it sloshed over the sides and burned his wrists. He hissed in a breath, but she didn't notice, or at least pretended not to. Muttering, Daniel sipped. Warmth spread through him.

He felt better. A little better. He closed his eyes and pictured his mother's kitchen. She had fixed him a mug of tea every Dawnrise. Sometimes they had talked. Other times they sipped and watched the Lady light the east.

His mind's eye fixed on a new scene: Snow-covered hills dotted with skeletal trees. He ran, heart thundering in his ears, breath ghosting out in front of him. Aidan ran just ahead, throwing terrified glances over his shoulder. They were being pursued by creatures that had been men yesterday, or the day before, or hundreds of years earlier, before Tyrnen had dug them up and ordered them to pursue Aidan to the ends of Crotaria and back.

Remembering their adventure, the sickening fear that had left their stomachs as blocks of ice, was strangely calming. Daniel smiled. He and Aidan had run for their lives from decaying corpses, but when had he ever felt as alive as he had those cold and harrowing days and nights? Never. Their pursuers had caught up to them more than once, but Aidan had survived because Daniel had been by his side. He had watched over Aidan as they trudged through snowstorms, outwitted thieves in seedy taverns, and fled vagrants and whispers and harbingers and Kahltan only knew what else.

You're a doorkeeper. That's all.

Affecting a cough, he scrubbed palms over eyes that suddenly stung.

When he looked up, the Wardsman from across the room was standing over him.

Chapter 13:
Twins

"Is this seat taken?" the Wardsman said gruffly.

Daniel was momentarily at a loss. "Uh . . . Not anymore."

The Wardsman slid onto the bench opposite, smoothing his steel and snow. Daniel studied the newcomer. His face was plain and partially concealed by his helm, which was pulled down low. "Are you new?" he asked, rotating his head as if to work out a knot in his neck. He was trying to peer underneath the helm to get a look at his guest's eyes, but it was no good. His face was cloaked in steel and shadows, and he seemed to be staring down at the table intentionally, a sharp contrast from his bold looks across the tavern just a few minutes before.

"Yes," the Wardsman said.

"That explains it, then."

"Explains what?" the Wardsman said, looking alarmed.

"I noticed you staring at me earlier," Daniel said. "I couldn't place you."

"You know every Wardsman in the Ward?"

"All the ones in Calewind."

"I'm a transfer," the Wardsman blurted.

"Where'd you come in from?"

"Ah. Um. Gotik."

"You don't sound certain."

"It's been a long day," the Wardsman said.

"Oh," Daniel said softly. "I'm sorry. I should have . . . How bad is it? I issued orders to evacuate that village first."

The Wardsman looked impressed. "You did?"

Daniel hesitated. What he had said was not precisely true. Earlier that morning, Aidan had ordered Daniel to organize the evacuation of villages, towns, and cities around Calewind, and escort their citizens to the capital. Vagrants were camped four leagues outside Calewind's walls, but those walls—carved by Darinian smiths—were taller and sturdier than the wood that enclosed villages. Daniel had passed the instructions to Lieutenant Anders Magath, who had promptly pulled out the first of his last tufts of hair.

Daniel had not stuck around to confirm that the order to evacuate had been followed. Aidan had needed him. So, in a roundabout way . . .

"Yes," he said at last. "I did."

"That's why I wanted to talk to you," the Wardsman said. "You were sitting alone, so I thought perhaps . . ."

"Perhaps I was an officer?"

The Wardsman nodded.

Daniel smiled. "You're in luck."

Mara reappeared. Pointedly ignoring Daniel, she flicked a strand of hair out of her eyes. "What'll you have?" she asked, then stared at the Wardsman before whipping her head toward Daniel. "Is this your way of showing me up?"

Nonplussed, Daniel looked between the barmaid and the Wardsman. "I have no idea what—"

Mara sniffed and looked back to the Wardsman. "And what do you think you're doing dressed like that? They'll jail you if you're caught trying to—"

"Swamp water," the Wardsman said quickly, in a voice so deep it sounded as if it had floated up from the bottom of a well.

Mara narrowed her eyes and stomped off.

"Do you know her?" Daniel asked.

"I only know one person in Calewind. My brother."

"Who's your brother?"

Just then Mara returned and set down a clay mug filled to the brim with a thick, brownish-green liquid. "Nasty stuff," she said primly. "We should ban it, just like we should everything else that slithers up from the south."

"Get lost," the Wardsman snapped. Mara stiffened and stormed off a third time.

"I realize we just met," Daniel said, "but I like you." He raised his tea mug.

To his surprise, the Wardsman blushed and clicked his mug against Daniel's. "She struck me as an unpleasant person," the Wardsman said. He pulled from the swamp water, and his complexion turned a deeper shade of red. Throwing an arm across his face, he coughed and sputtered. Brown and green flecks spattered over his white sleeve and onto the table.

"First time?" Daniel asked.

The Wardsman took a moment to catch his breath. "Yes."

Daniel blinked. The voice that had answered him was lilting and pleasant. "What's your name?"

The Wardsman went still. After another cough, he dragged his sleeve across his mouth. "Rufus Merrifalls." His voice was deep again. Almost too deep.

"Merrifalls," Daniel repeated. He snapped his fingers. "You must know Jak."

Rufus brightened. "Jakob's my younger brother. He enlisted—"

"Shy of a year ago," Daniel interjected. "He's showing an enormous amount of promise."

Rufus straightened, looking proud. "I'm relieved to hear that. He was something of a louse back at home. My mother and father thought joining the Ward would be good for him. Discipline, structure, and all that." Rufus waved a small hand as if brushing away a fly. "So, Jakob enlisted. He's a good man, but he's lazy. Too lazy to run a farm. Father told him to choose: The farm, or the Ward."

Daniel sipped his tea, then took a larger swig. It had grown tepid. "I'm familiar with just that circumstance."

"Really?"

"Mm-hm."

"I guess you decided to enlist."

"Not exactly. My father . . ." Daniel pushed his tea away. "It's a long story."

Rufus only nodded, and Daniel felt a swell of gratitude. Rufus Merrifalls would learn his history and reputation soon enough.

Saves me the trouble of having to sick it all up again.

A thought occurred to him. "You said Jak is your younger brother?"

"That's right." Tentatively, Rufus lifted the swamp water back to his lips and took a sip. This time the drink went down smoothly. "Why?"

Daniel shrugged. "In Leaston, the firstborn son takes over the plantation."

Rufus froze in the act of raising the glass again. "Torel's customs sometimes differ in that regard."

"Not in my experience," Daniel said lightly. He gestured around the room. "Torelians can't farm year-round like us Leastonians—the weather in the north being what it is—but many of the brothers who live here chose to enlist rather than work their family's land or study at a university. I don't mean to pry," he added. "I didn't care much for milking cows, either."

Rufus swallowed, licked his lips. "You're from Leaston?"

Daniel took another swallow of tea. He'd said too much. "We were talking about your brother."

"Yes," Rufus said. "You know where to find him?"

"I sent him to help fortify the southern district."

Rufus's complexion turned pasty. "That's where those . . ." He shuddered.

Daniel leaned forward. "You've seen them?"

"Just one," Rufus said quietly. "I saw it down in . . ." His mouth snapped shut.

Daniel frowned. "Down where?"

The swell of laughter and voices grew louder. Daniel looked up and saw the tall Wardsman standing over him, surrounded by a contingent of friends. *Friends,* Daniel thought, scoffing. Like runts in a litter of pigs, the Wardsmen trailing after Karter Rosen stuck close. He chased skirts and drank from Dusk until Dawn when left to his own compunctions, and was generous enough to toss table scraps to the hangers-on. Karter stood at least a head taller than Daniel, with broad shoulders. Though they had removed their polished white helms, Karter and the others still wore their steel and snow. The Gairden crest—an *H* with a sword sheathed through the connecting bar—on their left breasts gleamed under the lantern light. Each carried a tall mug, and each face was flushed.

"Evening, doorkeeper," Karter said, smirking. His followers chortled.

Daniel gave Karter a cool look. Rufus Merrifalls scooted over to the wall and pressed himself against it, as far from the others as possible, and made a careful study of the lacquered tabletop.

"Did you hear me?" Karter said.

Under the table, Daniel's left hand clenched the hilt of the false Serpent's Fang he had carried from Sallner. *For Aidan. Because he asked me to.* "I appreciate you coming over to check on my hearing," he said. "Very kind of you. Now leave."

Karter's smile dropped away. The other Wardsmen were watching him carefully. He was twenty-eight, twelve winters older than Daniel and at least forty pounds heavier, all of it muscle. Karter leaned in close, breathing loudly through his nose. "Mighty confident, aren't you? Must be nice, being friends with a Gairden."

Blood pounded in Daniel's ears like drumbeats. He took another swig of tea even though his cup was empty. The bigger Wardsman's lip curled. "Cushiest job in the Ward, that's what you got. All thanks to your prince friend."

"Crown of the North," Daniel corrected without thinking.

Karter straightened, smirking. "Crown of the North. My mistake. Better get it right, else you'll snitch on me, eh?" His chest shook with laughter. "You'd do that, wouldn't you? Daniel the Sneak. Daniel the Doorkeeper. Although now that Aidan's on the throne, you're due for advancement, I guess. Suppose you'll be helping him bathe and dress next."

Karter's bootlickers chuckled as if on command. For some reason, their low chuckles bothered him more than foolish insults. Karter leaned in close again. "You look upset, Daniel the Doorkeeper. What's wrong? Did I hurt your feelings?"

"No," Daniel said. "Your breath is horrid."

Rufus snorted.

The color drained from Karter's face. His arms snaked forward and grabbed Daniel by the collar of his mail and yanked him off the bench. The table scraped loudly against the wooden floor. The Wardsmen around Karter fanned out. All around the Crown's Promise, muted conversation died out. Daniel saw other Wardsmen—the ones who liked him, or at least tolerated him— stand up from their tables, drinks still in hand.

"You look frightened, Shirey," Karter whispered. "Gonna turn that steel and snow yellow?"

Daniel said nothing. Blood rushed through his body. His muscles were tense, but not from fear. He felt alive in a way he had not since returning to Calewind to find that Aidan and General Calderon had chased Tyrnen and the harbingers off. His mind flashed back to a night from weeks earlier, when he and Aidan had taken shelter at a disreputable-looking tavern called the Hornet's Nest. There had been thugs, just like Karter, except not wearing Torelian colors. Daniel had given them a tongue lashing, and then Aidan had done that new trick where he touched Heritage and his eyes turned white. Heritage had come to life in Aidan's hands in a way it should not have. Aidan had been born with *Ordine'cin*, rendering conventional weapons useless to him. Unfortunately for the street toughs in the Nest, Aidan had been revealed as an exception to the Gairden rule.

Aidan had saved Daniel, or so the Crown had thought. One of the toughs had yanked Daniel out of his seat, just like Karter had done. But Daniel had not needed help then, and he did not need help now.

"You should let me go." As he spoke, his right hand eased toward his *Sard'tara*.

Karter snarled. "Begging already?"

"Do I sound like I'm begging?" Every pair of eyes in the tavern were on them. *Good,* Daniel thought. *A few more seconds, one quick cut in the side, and—*

Karter jerked. A grunt of surprise and pain passed through his lips. A knife was poised against the stubble covering his throat. Rufus Merrifalls held it easily, sliding off his bench and pressing up against Karter's back. Sweat broke out on Karter's face. "Who in Dawn's name?" he began.

"Drop him," Rufus said. Once again Daniel noticed that the voice was light, almost musical.

Karter dropped him. Daniel had not realized his feet had been hovering just over the floor. He landed hard and caught his balance before he could stumble and fall. All the while his eyes remained fastened on Karter's. A bulge in the man's throat bobbed just above Rufus's blade. Steadily, Rufus lifted the knife from Karter's throat. When it was clear, Karter spun and lunged, grabbing Rufus by the shoulders and slamming him against the wall so hard it shook. One big hand wrapped around Rufus's throat. The Wardsman dangled, heels drumming against the wall, fingers clawing at Karter's grip. Raspy pleas escaped his throat. No one stepped forward to help. Karter's other hand balled into a fist and cocked back.

Without thinking, Daniel plucked up his *Sard'tara* and pressed one blade against Karter's throat. "Drop him."

Karter growled, tightening his hold. Rufus yelped. Daniel pressed the blade against Karter's throat until a dark drop of blood welled up. "They're small words, Karter, so I know you understand them."

Karter let go. Rufus fell, crumpled to the floor in a heap, coughing and rubbing at his throat. Roaring, Karter swung one arm out in a backhand. In one smooth motion, Daniel rapped Karter's kneecaps with the *Sard'tara*'s twin heads—first one, then the other. Karter squealed and fell as if his legs had been cut out from under him. He tried to rise but Daniel gripped his *Sard'tara* just below either head and shoved him, pressing the weapon's shaft against his chest.

Karter's eyes flitted around the room like a bird freed from its cage. "You got lucky," he said. "But you're not your father. In your hands, that fancy stick is just a—"

Stepping back, Daniel adjusted his grip so that he choked the *Sard'tara* beneath one of its blades and swung it at Karter's face. The second blade whistled as it cleaved the air. Karter screeched. Daniel stopped it a hair's width from a stubbled cheek. The Wardsman gaped at it, made another strangled noise, and his eyes rolled back in his head.

A cheer rose up from across the Crown's Promise. One of the Wardsmen—Tomas Sinderwell; Daniel recognized his short-cut black hair and brown face—raised his cup. More cheers followed as Karter's bootlickers dispersed, slowly at first, then making a break for the door. Daniel let the cheers wash over him. For a moment, he was back by Aidan's side, in the thick of the action, fighting and fleeing from vagrants and harbingers and the old man who had ruined his friend's life.

Then he remembered Rufus. "Are you all right?" he asked, extending a hand to the Wardsman, who still sat on the floor.

Nodding, Rufus took his hand and let Daniel pull him up. The man was surprisingly light. His helm was crooked. Rufus pawed at it, pulling it down low again. "Thank you," he said. The words came out raspy, and mellifluous.

That was when Daniel knew. "Jak Merrifalls doesn't have a—"

The door flew open and crashed against the wall. Every head turned to take in the Wardsman framed in the doorway. His face was a bloody mask. Green splatters covered his steel and snow like badges. Daniel placed him as Nathaniel Bree.

"We need help," Nathaniel managed, eyes bulging and rolling. "The south gate is being overrun by . . . by . . ." He shook his head, unable to finish.

Tomas Sinderwell leaped to his feet. Around him, others took up helms and weapons. "How many of you are there?" Tomas asked.

"Just three," said Nathaniel. "Two now. They sent me to get help. It's Terrence Cline and Jak Merrifalls. There were four of us. Bradley Jarom was there, too, but he died, and then they— and then they . . . they . . ." His eyes grew haunted.

Daniel knew. *They brought him back.*

Rufus Merrifalls bolted to the door, shoving past Nathaniel and racing out into the night. Cursing, Daniel grabbed his helm and gave chase.

Jak Merrifalls doesn't have a brother, he had been trying to say. *He has a twin sister.*

Chapter 14:
Charge

RUFUS MERRIFALLS WAS a her instead of a him. That made her a liar, in Daniel's view. For her next trick, she became a thief.

Daniel grabbed his *Sard'tara* from the bench and charged out of the Crown's Promise. Out on the road, the backs of his brothers greeted him. Wardsmen dashed and bustled at the front of the inn, untying bridles from wooden posts and leaping into saddles and tearing off in a storm of hooves and shouts.

"He stole my horse," one of the Wardsmen shouted.

Daniel squinted. Far ahead, a horse carried Rufus—if that was her name, and he seriously doubted it—down the long, straight road that unwound all the way to the southern gate. Another of his brothers, Graham Ritterhad, flung himself into his saddle and buried the heels of his boots into his horse's flanks. The mount whinnied and took off at a gallop. Tomas Sinderwell shouted an order as he too thundered away.

"Wait!" Daniel called, waving his arms as Tomas disappeared in the distance. He let his arms fall. Wardsmen who patrolled Calewind's market districts, residential areas, university campuses, and cathedral grounds were assigned horses. Doorkeepers guarded their post on their own two legs.

The street was dark and quiet again. Grumbling, Daniel set off at a jog. Sprinting would do no good. The weight of his steel and snow would tire him too quickly. Already his breath puffed out in front of him. *Spring indeed,* he thought. Kahltan shone like a burnished coin from high in the night sky, bathing roads and buildings in milky light. The clink and rattle of Daniel's armor echoed throughout the vacant district. Lanterns and candles shone from a few open windows. Most had been shuttered to keep out the night. He had never seen Calewind so empty. He thought back to what Mara had said. *People are scared.*

They had reason to fear. By sending the bulk of the army off to fight a false war, Tyrnen had cut the head off the Ward, leaving an emaciated body of leaders consisting of Lieutenant Magath and a handful of sergeants to command the fifteen hundred Wardsmen who remained.

Footsteps up above made Daniel look up. Lieutenant Magath had been busy. Bulky shapes cloaked in shadows crowned every other building along the road. They were siege weapons to be manned in the event Tyrnen's undead breached Calewind's gates. Most of the fortifications were in various states of production. Wardsmen, two to a building, crawled around rooftops, building and securing their charges. *We're not ready. Dawn and Dusk! I shouldn't have let Aidan leave.*

"What's going on?" one called down.

Daniel slowed, doubled over with hands on knees. "There's been . . . an attack," he shouted back, winded. "Southern gate." Wardsmen scrambled down ladders hidden in the blackness of narrow alleyways. From those narrow streets, he heard horses whinny and set off at gallops.

"Wait! Wait, you Dawnburned sons of—Wait!"

The pounding of hooves faded, swallowed up by the night. Still cursing, Daniel picked up his pace. His breathing grew labored. Reaching the next block of buildings—tall and peaked with spires—he noticed something that froze his belly. The lanterns lining the street were unlit. Normally, children of twelve winters or older walked the streets near Dusk, lighting lanterns with metal poles tipped with fire. A few stalls were still piled high with produce, jewelry, rugs, furnishings, weapons. Daniel's worry sharpened. Most stall vendors were Leastonians who would take their eyes off their own children before they would leave their wares. Theft was low in Calewind—few cutpurses were brave or foolish enough to operate so near Sunfall—but with the Ward depleted and fear over the coming attack worsening, all it would take was one spark of panic to set the whole citizenry, which vastly outnumbered the Wardsmen who had been left behind, aflame.

The pungent aroma of smoke burned his nostrils. Up ahead, steel clashed against steel, and men screamed in pain and fright. A flickering white glow licked at the night sky. Daniel poured on speed and half ran, half stumbled into the southern square. There were four entrances into the capital. The north entrance led from the city and up a shallow mountain pass to where Sunfall sat amid the lower peaks of the Ihlkin Mountains. Entering Calewind from the north was impossible unless one came from Sunfall, which could not be breached due to the precipitous cliffs and peaks that bordered it. The east, south, and west gates were located in broad courtyards. There, those preparing to depart could prepare wagons, carts, and caravans before setting out, or stretch their legs after arriving in Calewind.

Pandemonium reigned in the southern courtyard. The gate was dented and singed. White fire raced up the guard tower. Wardsmen battled vagrants clad in moldy clothes. Some of his brothers, faces as pale as their tabards, ran pell-mell around the square. Suddenly, one Wardsman turned on his brother and thrust his sword into the other's belly. Daniel jerked to a halt. The man, slumping to his knees and clutching at his torn belly, was Jak Merrifalls. The vagrant—*It must be a vagrant, its eyes are lifeless*, Daniel thought half in a daze—whipped its head up and fixed him in its blank stare.

Movement from above caught his eye. More vagrants scrambled to the top of the gate from outside. The gate, and the wall bordering it, stood four times the height of a man, but the vagrants threw themselves over, spilling to the ground and rushing into the fray, dragging broken legs and torn arms behind them. A few charged pockets of Wardsmen barely holding a single undead at bay. Others spotted Daniel and charged for him.

All at once, calm fell over him like a blanket. Daniel took a deep breath. As he inhaled, he imagined he was drawing in all his emotions, thoughts, and worries, as his father had taught him. He saw the courtyard, saw vagrants and Wardsmen fighting, shrieking, dying. He exhaled, and on his breath were all those concerns. Without them weighing him down, his body was light.

Nimble. His mind went blank. His eyes swept the courtyard again, and now he saw neither humans nor walking corpses. He perceived tactical advantages and opportunities.

The vagrant that had stabbed Jak opened its jaw in a shriek and advanced on Tomas Sinderwell. Daniel tightened his grip on his *Sard'tara* and closed the distance between himself and the vagrant in three long strides. He swung. There was a sharp crack, like old pottery shattering on stone. His curved blade erupted through the front of the vagrant's skull. Bone fragments sprayed outward. Daniel jerked his weapon free and was moving before the body hit the ground. Tomas gaped up at him like a fish, amazement painted on his face.

Daniel did not notice. Four vagrants stampeded toward him, axes and swords raised high. He sprinted forward to meet them, *Sard'tara* a whistling blur. The weapon's bladed heads flashed in the light of the fire. Tremors ran up the shaft as he batted away thrusts, cuts, lunges. With a flick of his wrist he went from the defensive to the offensive, neatly severing two hands clutching axes and swords. The two vagrants stumbled back, weaponless, just before their skulls burst into pieces and their bodies dropped. The remaining two waded in, chopping and swinging. Daniel danced, evading and lunging and slicing. One swing severed a skull from its neck. Daniel let his momentum carry him forward, twirling the *Sard'tara* up and around to cleave up through the fourth vagrant from jaw to temple. The skull split, and the body pitched over on its side.

Daniel planted his legs, his breathing deep but even, assessing the battlefield. Three more vagrants were coming for him. *Why me?* A question to be answered later. He was dimly aware of a Wardsman beside him. The man had fallen to his knees and was cradling Jak's head in his lap. Telling his brothers to mourn their dead later would do no good. For most, this was their first encounter with the dead. His lips quirked in a half smile. *Theirs, but not mine.* More vagrants clambered over the gate. Blood thundered in his ears. His heart beat so hard and fast his body seemed to quiver. Daniel charged forward.

An explosion rocked the gate. Dust and stone flew every which way. Daniel threw one arm over his nose and mouth, squinting to maintain vision. Something unseen had rent a hole through the middle of the gate. It was just wide enough for a large man to squeeze through. His body tingled with anticipation. No matter the threat that stepped through, he would meet it.

Wet gurgling from behind him. Tomas Sinderwell staggered through the cloud of debris. His hands clutched his throat. Blood spurted through Tomas's fingers and ran down his hands, arms, and steel and snow like water. His eyes were bright and terrified. His lips moved soundlessly. Then the light in his eyes winked out, and Tomas pitched forward to the ground.

"Steel and snow!" Daniel shouted, raising his *Sard'tara*. "To me!"

His brothers—he counted three who still lived, including the one holding Jak—did not hear him. Did not hear, or ignored. Half a dozen vagrants had cornered the two on their feet. At that moment a red-robed figure stepped through the hole in the gate. The wasted skin of its face was stretched taut over its skull. Its mouth was open as if in surprise. Fleshy bars stretched from lip to lip, like cell bars. A harbinger. Its empty sockets fixed on Daniel.

Daniel stood his ground. Harbingers possessed the souls of slain Touched. It would do him no good to rush it. Yet he could not wait for long. Beside him, his brothers were dying. He took a step toward them, and that was when the harbinger raised a hand holding an ornate lantern. A small flame danced within its glass walls. Abruptly the flame grew, warped, into the contours of a familiar face.

Garrett Lorden's visage shimmered like a reflection on the surface of a pond disturbed by a breeze. It looked around, smiling pleasantly, and found Daniel.

"Ah," Garrett said, voice low and predatory. "There you are."

Daniel's mouth went dry. Memories broke through the dam of his concentration. A small, plain cabin somewhere deep in Sallner. Walls splashed with blood. His grunts and screams. Heavy blows rained down on him over and over. And those eyes: wild and icy blue, set below blonde hair pulled back in a ponytail.

Daniel's legs shook. His mind willed them to spring into action, to carry him far away from Garrett Lorden, apparition or flesh. Instead, he stood frozen to the spot.

Garrett laughed. "We have unfinished business, you and I," he said. His lips twisted into a moue of childish disappointment. "But not yet. My master says I must wait. He says Calewind is mine to sack. And I will, Daniel. I will sack it from within. Show him."

The harbinger raised its free hand and swept it outward, like a man showing off his land. All around the square, the bodies of Wardsmen stirred, pulled themselves to their feet, chins tucked against their chests and weapons held in limp fingers. Suddenly their heads snapped up as if at a command. Flesh and hair sloughed away like loose masks and dropped to the ground, revealing bloody skulls. Every head swiveled, every pair of empty sockets settled on Daniel.

His blood ran cold.

"You see?" Garrett said. "It's so simple to turn them. My army—his army—grew tonight. I'll fatten our ranks on the rest of your brothers." His voice dropped. "I can find you, you know. I have its scent. No matter how far you run or where you hide, I can walk right up to you and I will pick up where we left off and I will flay you, and break your spine, and—"

The tip of a blade burst through the harbinger's neck. It jerked, loosening its hold on the lantern. Garrett Lorden's eyes bugged in shock that became outrage. He opened his mouth. Before he could speak, the harbinger's fingers went limp and the lantern hit the road in an explosion of glass and flame. Garrett's apparition sputtered out on the stone.

Daniel blinked, let out a long, shuddery breath. It was as if Garrett Lorden's sudden absence had freed him from a trance. He turned, wetting his throat to thank the Wardsman who had saved him. Rufus Merrifalls stared back at him, Jak's sword trembling in her hands. She was panting. Her green eyes were wide and glazed with shock. She blinked and seemed to notice her sword for the first time. The blade was covered in green, gummy blood. Her mouth snapped shut. Swallowing hard, she knelt to wipe the blade clean on the vagrant's robes. Tears streamed down her cheeks.

A chorus of sibilant hissing brought Daniel back to himself. Vagrants surrounded them, but they were retreating, backing toward the ruined gate. More departed than had entered. Daniel counted nine. Nine of the twelve who had run from the inn to the aid of Jak Merrifalls and the other sentries at the southern gate. Nine skulls where flesh and stubble and life had been. Nine brothers of the Ward conscripted into Tyrnen's horde.

Two of his brothers had survived. Red and green gore painted their bodies and faces, but they limped toward Daniel.

He concentrated on Rufus. "Are you all right?"

She did not answer right away. She stared down at the body of the harbinger with a mixed expression of horror and revulsion. Its mouth was still open. The fleshy strips between its lips sagged inward.

"That was my first," she said softly.

"First time what?"

"Killing someone."

Daniel's anger at being duped lessened. "That's not a someone," he said gently. "That's a something."

Her head shot up, and she glared at him. "Someone. Something. What does it matter? I killed it." Her eyes were wet. She blinked hard and looked away.

Daniel was at a loss. Wardsmen were not supposed to cry, but then, she was not a Wardsman. Or a man. "I'm sorry. I only meant that you didn't kill it. It was already dead."

She turned back. "What was that thing?"

Before he could answer, the pounding of hooves announced reinforcements. From their saddles, Wardsmen shouted and raised swords, axes, and spears. Anders Magath, his wild white hair framing a leathery face distinguishable by the deep scar that ran along his cheek, rode at their head.

"Are you going to let our gate burn, doorkeeper?" he barked as he yanked on his reins, bringing his mount to a halt. "Or do I have to save you from burning where you stand, too?"

Daniel's cheeks burned. The dull roar of fire eating away at the guard tower adjacent to the gate had been mere noise during the battle. Now Daniel realized he was baking in its heat. "I . . . need water."

Anders' scowl deepened. "Damn right you do. I wouldn't expect a fire to snuff itself." He thrust a finger at the smoke. "There's a throng of gawkers standing around watching you stand around. If I were a gambling man, I'd bet a hundred Torelian marks and Heritage itself that most of them live around here and would be happy to get you some water. Now move!"

Daniel dashed into the crowd. Within minutes, he had a line of merchants, innkeepers, laborers, and Wardsmen passing buckets of water down a line to him. He tossed each bucketful at the flames and then passed empty pails back down the line for replenishment. Daniel's arms grew heavy. Sweat poured down his face. Their efforts amounted to droplets of rain. It was no good. The flames glowed white, and water seemed not to affect them.

As efficient as harvesting crops with your toenail instead of a scythe, his father would have said. Daniel's face tightened. Rakian Shirey never missed an opportunity to criticize his son's efforts.

The sound of heavy panting caught his attention. A large man in white robes draped with a yellow sash that ran from his right shoulder down to his golden belt caromed down the street, red-faced and perspiring. *A Hand of the Crown,* Daniel thought, and sagged with relief. The fat man took one look at the fire, raised a hand, spoke a few words in what Aidan called the Language of Light, and the snowy flames winked out. Daniel let the empty bucket in his hands drop to the street as he inspected the guard tower. It was charred, inhospitable. Tendrils of smoke curled up into the night sky.

The Hand of the Crown dropped his hand and nodded in satisfaction, as if he had won some contest between himself and the fire. Anders Magath strode up to him with hands planted on hips, talking in a low voice.

"You don't look good," a woman said.

Daniel glanced at Rufus Merrifalls. Her steel and snow were singed, and her hair reeked of smoke. "Neither do you." He planted his fists against his spine and leaned back, wincing in pain and pleasure as bones popped. "You helped with the buckets?"

"I stood right beside you!" she said, indignant.

"Oh." He shrugged, winced as pain flared in his shoulder.

"Want me to rub them? I do it for Jak all the time," she added quickly when Daniel gave her a strange look. As if just realizing what she had said, her face went slack. Fresh tears cut tracks across her soot-stained cheeks.

"I'm sorry about your brother," Daniel said quietly. "I couldn't reach him. I tried," he finished lamely.

Rufus scrubbed an arm across her eyes. "I know. I saw." She straightened, and Daniel saw she was crying harder than ever. Her lips trembled, and her face was wet. "I tried too. He taught me how to use a sword. My little brother! Taught me!" She laughed.

Some of the tension and fatigue drained out of him. Her laughter sounded strained, yet melodious. Like bells that jingled merrily even as storm winds threatened to rip them away. Abruptly, her laughter turned to tears. Daniel stood awkwardly, watching her shoulders bob as she cried, unsure what to do. He cleared his throat. "So, uh, even though you're not a Wardsman, you handled yourself well."

She looked up, eyes wet and red. "I'm not?"

"Well . . . no."

"I fought alongside you, didn't I?"

"That doesn't make you a Wardsman."

"Where can I enlist?"

"You can't."

"Why not?"

"Man. Wardsman. Last I checked, you weren't—"

"You haven't checked, and you certainly never—"

"Will you two shut up?" a voice roared from beside them. Daniel and Rufus jumped. Anders Magath stood before them, eyes as bright as bolts of lightning.

"Sorry, sir," Daniel said.

"Oh, it's fine," Anders snapped. "You were only loud enough to call down the rest of the shade-spawn camped outside our gates."

Daniel swallowed past the lump in his throat. "Apologies, sir. I saw a lot of my brothers die tonight. I'm feeling . . ." He shook his head. "Out of sorts."

Color returned to Anders' face. "I suppose you're entitled. Take a moment to compose yourself, then help your brothers clean up this mess." He turned and waved at the scene behind him. The vagrants were splayed out on the ground, skulls and splinters of bone scattered around them. Daniel's brothers stood in a line, directing the crowd back to their homes and inns. Every now and then, a Wardsman would throw a glance over his shoulder at one of the corpses that wore steel and snow.

Daniel stood straighter. "Yes, sir." He moved toward the line of Wardsmen, and Rufus fell into step beside him.

Anders grabbed her by the shoulder. "You! Who are you? I haven't seen you before, and I know every man in the Ward." His gaze turned stony. "Are you one of those spies General Calderon warned me about? An emissary of the Eternal Flame's come to infiltrate our ranks? Answer me true, and if I think you're lying I'll open your wrists and let the color of your blood speak for you."

Rufus's mouth worked. Anders was glaring at her, his face turning scarlet. With a glance at Daniel, she removed her helm. Auburn hair, freed from its confines, collapsed over her shoulders.

"Alix Merrifalls, sir. My friends call me Alix. Alix with an 'i.'"

Lieutenant Magath gaped. "You're a woman."

Alix went red. "Thank you for noticing. Sir."

"Where'd you get the steel and snow?" Before she could answer, Anders shooed the question away. "Never mind that now. Merrifalls . . . Merrifalls . . ." He blinked as the answer slid into place. "You're Jakob's sister."

"Yes, sir," she said. Her eyes were wet again.

Anders' face softened. "I'm sorry for your loss. Jak was a good lad and an even better Wardsman. He gave his life defending the north. That might not mean much to you now, but it means a great deal to me and to our Crown."

Alix's lips trembled. "Thank you, sir."

"But I'm afraid I cannot allow you to wear the steel and snow," Anders continued.

"Why not?"

"Because you're a woman," Anders said.

"So what?"

"Women can't fight in the Ward," the lieutenant said in a tone of barely restrained impatience. *Better to ask why the Lady rises in the east instead of the west,* Daniel thought. *She just does, that's all.*

"This one can," Alix countered. She thrust her finger in the direction of the harbinger sprawled in front of the charred gate. "Do you know what that is?"

Anders followed her finger. His frowned deepened as he took in the billowy robes, the ruined head, the too-tight skin. He made a sound of disgust. "A vagrant, and a particularly loathsome one by the looks of it."

"In a way, sir," Alix said, speaking quickly, sensing opportunity. "It's a . . . He called it a . . ."

"He?" Anders interrupted. "He, who?"

Alix pointed at Daniel. She looked sheepish. "I'm sorry, I don't recall your name."

"You never bothered to ask for it," Daniel replied. She flushed. Turning to Anders, he said, "It's called a harbinger, sir. A dead body possessed by the soul of a Touched and controlled by the Eternal Flame. It can raise the dead, sir, and turn them into . . . into vagrants. We saw it happen right in front of us."

Anders' complexion had gone ashen yet again. "The Lady save us all."

"I killed it, sir," Alix said loudly. "Snuck up behind it and buried my brother's sword in its head. They're strong, but they die the same as any man. I saw it raise the dead, sir, and . . ." Alix stole a glance at Daniel. He could tell she was about to tell Anders what else she had seen: A man's face in the flames of the harbinger's lantern, taunting Daniel.

Anders looked askance at the Hand of the Crown. Daniel watched the rotund man standing near the hole in Calewind's south gate. A few Wardsmen clustered around him, holding torches. Two others shuffled into view, each gripping one side of a slab of icestone as thick as a door and as tall. The Hand pointed at the gap. Grunting and sweating, the Wardsmen toddled over to the hole and held the icestone against it. As Daniel watched, the Touched raised one hand toward the flame of a nearby torch, placed the other against the block of icestone. The flames shrank, like water seeping through cracks in a foundation. The Touched lowered his hand and, appearing winded, said something to the Wardsmen still holding the slab in place. Exchanging uncertain glances, they removed their hands. The icestone held, congealed against the gate as if it had been a part of the structure for years.

Tapping a finger against his hairy chin, Anders stared at the Hand until the round man came slowly up to their little group. "The icestone will hold," the Hand said, raising one sleeve to wipe a line of sweat from his brow. His face gave off a soft red glow, as if he were afflicted with fever. Without waiting for Anders to give him leave, the Hand nodded and began shuffling away down the street, shoulders drooping.

Still quiet, Anders watched him go, finger tapping his chin.

"Sir?" Daniel asked quietly.

Anders' finger stopped, lowered. "Can we trust them?" he muttered to no one in particular. Alix shot a confused look at

Daniel. He gave a slight shake of his head. Now was not the time to explain that he knew exactly who the lieutenant meant. The Touched. Those able to kindle the Lady's light and shape it into magic. They hailed from all four realms of Crotaria and were expected to live according to the laws of those realms. However, they answered only to the Eternal Flame. A chill swept through Daniel at the thought of Tyrnen at the head of an army of undead and Touched.

Anders shook himself and seemed to remember they were there. Alix stared at him expectantly. "The answer is still no," he said.

Her fists clenched. "But, sir—"

"I'm sorry, young lady," he said, and he sounded sincere. "I don't make the laws. I only uphold them."

Alix's mouth tightened. "And does the Crown forbid women who are not part of the Ward from fighting?"

Anders' mouth worked.

"Let her fight!" cried a female voice from the crowd. Anders whipped around, glaring daggers. The assemblage had grown rather than thinned. A line of Wardsmen held their arms out to either side to hold them back. Onlookers wore expressions that ran from curiosity to horror as they looked from the Wardsmen to the blood streaking the square. A few women sobbed openly. He hardened his heart against their grief.

"I thought I told you to help your brothers remove the bodies," Anders growled. Snapping to attention, Daniel formed the Wardsmen's salute and touched his fist to the Gairden emblem at his breast. Before he could turn away, Alix spoke again.

"I saved him, sir!"

Daniel froze. She and Anders both stared at him. "Saved who?" the lieutenant asked.

Alix ran her tongue over her lips. "Him," she said, nodding at Daniel. "He froze like a rabbit cornered by a bear when the . . . the harbinger appeared, and I killed it. Even though I'd just lost my brother, I killed it."

Every head in the swiveled to where the harbinger lay dead, back to Anders, Daniel, and Alix. Their mutters rose in volume. The Wardsmen restraining them shifted, looking uneasy. Fresh tears rolled down Alix's cheeks. "I deserve the chance to avenge my brother. I refuse to cower like a maiden from the stories. I can fight, and I will fight. In your steel and snow, or in my plainclothes. With a sword or spear, or with a shovel or pitchfork. It's my right. Torel is my realm, too."

Anders gnawed at his lower lip, studying Alix with eyes that burned like coals. Around them, the crowd seemed to be holding its breath. Some of the Wardsmen threw glances over their shoulders at the lieutenant, arms still spread. Daniel tensed. His brothers were shaken by what they had seen, and by their losses. For all their training and discipline, Wardsmen were still flesh and blood. They were scared, tired, confused.

He stepped forward. "Sir. We need all the help we can get. And she . . . she's capable. She did save me, like she said."

Anders narrowed his eyes. "You're vouching for her, doorkeeper?"

The title jabbed like a knife point. "Yes, sir."

"Fine. Then she's your responsibility."

Daniel's mouth fell open. "Sir, I didn't mean for—"

"No arguing, or you can keep each other company in the depths."

"Thank you, sir," Alix began, "I won't let you—"

"And you, girl." His raspy growl stopped Alix cold. "I don't know where you found that armor, and I don't want to. I only know that I want it returned immediately, and if I see you wearing it again, I'll throw you in the depths. Disperse. Now. I'll see you both at Dawnrise."

Whirling on the crowd, he shouted, "Get back to your homes, all of you! You're in violation of curfew!"

"What curfew?" a man threw back in a surly tone.

"Safe in your beds by Dusk or a night in the depths," he roared.

At that, the assemblage scattered. Anders stormed off without a backward glance. Daniel's brothers watched the onlookers go and then broke ranks, breaking into groups to move bodies and clean up debris. Daniel moved to join them. Alix caught his wrist.

"Thank you," she said.

"I didn't do it for you. I did it for Jak. Now, come on. We've got a long night ahead."

She followed without protest. They went to Jak's body, Daniel at his feet and Alix at his head. Averting his eyes so that he would not have to watch Alix cry—

Wardsmen don't cry, but she's not a Wardsmen, so I guess

that's all right—

Daniel bent at the waist and grabbed Jak's booted feet. Alix took hold of him under his arms. They carried his body and laid it by the smoking remains of the guard tower. Straightening, Daniel removed his helm and raked a hand through his hair.

"There's no need for you to—" he began.

Alix scrubbed the back of her hand across her eyes. "Come on. There's work to be done."

Chapter 15:
Old Friends

NICHEL STALKED ACROSS the council room. When she reached the far end, she spun on her heel and strode back toward Jonathan, who stood with arms folded near her father's stone chair. Emotions roiled, changing as fast as she could cross the room.

Aidan was here. Aidan, the man she loved. Aidan, the man she wanted to kill. Love or hate. Create or destroy. Life or death. She could not have it both ways, yet it was, and the dichotomy threatened to tear her apart.

Memories flashed through her mind. Aidan as a boy cub, laughing and running as she chased him through Janleah Keep's tunnels and Sunfall's galleries. She had tried to catch him and kiss him. Another image: Aidan, grown, and she chased him, and she caught him and sank her teeth into his throat. Like Guyde. She had torn Guyde's throat with her fangs. His flesh had ripped so easily, like wet parchment. Coppery blood had gushed down her throat and into her belly.

She hadn't known whether to vomit or drink more. She still didn't.

Nichel closed her eyes, not needing to see to navigate the wide stone hall ringed with towering effigies of war chiefs long buried. In her mind she saw the lake with its grass and its flowers swaying in the breeze and—

The cave. Cold and coarse, its tremulous green light turning her stomach. The seal trembled.

The lake. The cave.

She heard a low moan and did not realize it had come from her throat until a sharp pain in her head made her open her eyes. She was gripping two fistfuls of hair. She let her hair fall and the pain lessened.

"In and out, Nichel," Jonathan murmured. "Remember your father's words."

Nichel slowed. *Only he who rules within himself is king.* Wise words from a wise man. Shame filled her. Romen of the Wolf would be mortified by the animal savagery deep within her. Romen had wanted to build, to expand, to gentrify. The *Nuulass* wanted to raze, to diminish, to regress. *Nuulass.* At the very thought of its name, of what it meant, gooseflesh broke out over her body.

Rubbing one prickled arm, she pictured the cave in her mind and forced the entity deeper into its pit. Strengthened the seal that contained it. Her will was tougher than steel, stronger than diamond.

Nichel smelled him before she heard his footsteps. He was still two hundred paces off, and her pack escorted him. Nichel disregarded the other scents and fixed her heightened sense of smell on the one: cold and crisp, with a tinge of firewood. Like winter morning. She did not let herself dwell on how her senses had increased. The seal held. It must hold. Her hands hooked into claws. Unless she decided Aidan deserved to—

No. The lake. Think of the lake.

Ulestren of the Wolf and Ipadia of the Adder entered, flanking one of the openings that ringed the council room.

"They're coming, sister," Ulestren said. Her eyes scanned the room, her body tense. Nichel moved to the center of the center of the council chamber, facing the entryway where his scent grew stronger. The other three exchanged uncertain looks, then moved in behind her.

"We are with you," Jonathan said softly.

Nichel did not trust herself to speak. Jonathan's scent changed, spring water and soap mixing with heat. Not lust this time. Anger. Raw hatred toward the man who had slain his war chief.

Aidan materialized, arms tied behind his back and flanked by dark-skinned women covered in tattoos. Nichel watched Aidan. He was taller than when she had last seen him. His legs were long. No longer a cub. A man. Except . . . except his face was still boyish, but lined with worry. He was right to be worried. His eyes were bright and focused on her. Nichel's Darinian side dismissed the notion of love at first sight as foolishness. Her Leastonian side embraced it as her reality. Her legs had chased him through the Keep and Sunfall. Her heart had been running after him ever since.

Love, her mother had sighed once. *A magic hotter than the Lady's summer light.* Cynthia had laughed as she stroked Romen's arm and watched him squirm in his chair, his stony face turning red until a grin broke through.

Aidan had ruined Romen's grin. Aidan had silenced her mother's laughter. Aidan had stolen them from her. Aidan had stolen himself from her. Aidan had stolen her life.

Hatred flowed into love, turning it rancid. Love and hate. She could not hold both. The hackles on her neck rose even as her heart raced like a wolf pursuing meshia.

Aidan's scent changed. A heady blend of fear and confusion permeated cold northern morning. She searched his eyes. They were wide and directed at her. He looked as if he had never seen her. It took a moment to become aware of herself. She stood hunched, teeth bared and hands hooked. She straightened, took three breaths, and reassessed the situation.

Seven of her pack surrounded Aidan. Each woman's visage was blank, and none had drawn her weapon. Their eyes blazed with the desire to kill. To quench their war chief's thirst for vengeance. "*Shorogoyt,*" one said in a calm voice. Aidan flinched as if struck.

"*Shorogoyt,*" Nichel agreed. "Bring him to me."

Two of the pack marched Aidan across the intervening space. They were firm, not rough. She became aware of their scent: rage barely held at bay, like hounds on a leash. That scent turned her stomach. *Is that how I would smell to them if they were animals, like me?*

They stopped five paces away, gazes fixed on hers. Their reticence to look away even for a moment spoke to loyalty and to fear. They knew what prowled inside of her, waiting for an opening so it could bite and claw its way out.

"War chief," said Lensit of the Stallion. Like her clan's namesake, she was tall with long legs and brown hair that flowed down to the small of her back. "We found this one approaching from the east. He . . ." The scent of shame, like human waste, burned Nichel's nostrils. "He appeared suddenly, and nearly caught us from behind." Her jaw tightened.

"Be at ease," Nichel said. "Aidan Gairden has become known for ambushes."

Aidan looked pained. "I can explain, Nichel. I—"

Ulestren crossed the distance in three long strides and slapped him. "You will address her as war chief, and you will not speak unless spoken to, *shorogoyt*."

"*Shorogoyt*," said Grivah of the Eagle from behind Aidan. Nichel studied Aidan. He had closed his eyes just before Ulestren's blow. *He sensed it coming yet made no attempt to turn away.*

Ulestren's hand left a bright pink mark on Aidan's cheek. He spared her a glance, then faced Nichel, standing straighter. "I did not come here to ambush you, war chief. I came to turn myself over to your judgment."

Nichel opened her mouth to speak, then abruptly closed it. She realized she had no idea what words might spill out. Every beat of her heart brought forth a conflicting suggestion. Condemn Aidan to death by the Mother's Kiss, as was custom for criminals in Darinia. Grant him leave to speak. Cut his throat where he stood. Throw her arms around the boy she had loved since girlhood.

Turning to Jonathan, she nodded slightly. Jonathan stepped forward. "Aidan Gairden, you come to us armed," he said, inclining his head to the sword at the prisoner's waist. Jonathan frowned as he addressed the pack. "You allowed this man, who murdered so many of your kin, to carry steel in the war chief's presence?"

Grivah's nose, hooked not unlike a beak, twitched as if she smelled something unpleasant. "We tried to remove the sword, war chief, but could not."

"Could not?" Nichel repeated.

"No, war chief." Grivah's brow wrinkled. "It is the Gairden totem, wrought from magic."

Nichel looked closer at the sword. Heritage. Of course. Aidan was sword-bearer and Crown of the North.

"What is this trickery, Aidan Gairden? What are you plotting?" Jonathan asked.

"I plot nothing."

Ulestren sniffed lightly.

Jonathan's sleeves fell back as he raised his arms, revealing a gold ring set with a purple amethyst on his right hand. Nichel observed that Aidan wore an identical ring on the same finger. "I am a Cinder, boy," Jonathan said. "If you think I will stand by when you could harm the—"

"He may keep the weapon," Nichel said.

Every head in the room turned to her. "War chief?" Jonathan said.

Nichel did not respond right away. She had expected Aidan to reek of deception and murder but, strangely, perceived nothing of the sort. Nothing at all. It was as if his emotions were walled off. "My pack surrounds Aidan, and I am far from helpless." She thumbed the hilts of Sand and Silk. "Besides, Aidan is *Ordine'cin.* He cannot draw from the Mother's light because our Father rules the sky, and his gift precludes him from swordplay."

Aidan opened his mouth to say something, then glanced at Heritage, as if listening.

Jonathan looked doubtful, but nodded. "Aidan Gairden, the Darinian clans hold you responsible for the slaughter of over one thousand clansmen outside of Sharem. Do not attempt to deny this accusation. Word of their deaths was carried to us by our speakers when they communed with the creatures of the Shared Wood, of which many perished when you razed the trees and our people to the ground. The punishment meted out in the west for such transgressions is death by our Mother's Kiss. You will be . . ."

Jonathan's words faded to a buzz. Nichel's heightened senses were attuned to Aidan. Every word Jonathan spoke leeched the light from Aidan's eyes. He looked repentant and reeked of guilt. A man could shape his face the way a builder shaped clay, but he had no control over his scent.

She froze. More than guilt emanated from him, and his face reflected it. Regret, and sadness. Like rain carried on the wind. That confused her. The speakers had reported the fate of the contingent of Darinians she had sent to Sharem. She had mourned them, but they had been warriors slain in battle. In a war.

"Tell him of the other crime," she said.

At her voice, Aidan blinked. Jonathan paused in mid-sentence. "Are you certain, war chief?"

"Tell him," she repeated, staring at Aidan.

Jonathan's face grew as hard as his tone. "Aidan Gairden, Nichel of the Wolf, war chief of the clans, finds you guilty of the deaths of Romen of the Wolf and Cynthia Alston."

The force of Aidan's reaction nearly lifted her from her feet. His mouth dropped open. Scents careened into her: shock, followed swiftly by confusion, then sudden realization devoured by white-hot rage.

Deep within her, the *Nuulass* stirred. Like a predator out on the Plains, it stalked anger, feeding on it for sustenance.

The seal trembled.

And then, as suddenly as it had surfaced, Aidan's anger lessened. It became an undercurrent buried beneath layers of anguish so heavy it might as well have been her own. A stinging sensation pricked her eyes.

Aidan's body sagged. "Nichel, I did not do this." His voice was barely a whisper.

"You claim innocence?" Jonathan asked.

"Of the deaths of Romen and Cynthia, yes. Of the others, no."

Karta of the Spirits grabbed a fistful of his hair and yanked back, exposing his throat. She placed a hand on it, her long nails caressing his flesh. "You have more blood on your hands, *shorogoyt*. My husband has not returned from your realm. Where is he?"

Aidan tried to swallow. "Your husband?"

"Cotak of the Spirits, and our clan chief."

Aidan closed his eyes. "Dead, but not by my hands."

Nichel saw Karta's fingers tense. Faint lines of blood ran down Aidan's throat. "Enough," Nichel snapped.

Karta whipped around. "He lies, war chief. He—"

"He will be judged."

Karta's face tightened, but she released Aidan and stepped back. Jonathan shook his head in disgust. "Whether Cotak of the Spirits' blood stains his hands or not, he has confessed to the massacre of your people at Sharem, war chief. All that is left is to pass sentence."

Nichel's emotions went to war again. Aidan faced her. He was not . . . calm, not exactly. Resigned, and sad. "May I speak, war chief?" Aidan said.

"You wish to confess," Jonathan said.

Aidan hesitated. He glanced down at his sword, and his brow furrowed. Jonathan's voice cracked like a whip. "Perhaps you would be willing to share your conspiratorial whisperings to which the rest of us are not privy."

At that, Aidan went still. He raised his head to face his accusers. "I wish to speak with Nichel alone."

"Denied."

Aidan ignored the advisor. "Your father was a good and just man," he said to Nichel. "He would give an enemy the opportunity the chance to speak or fight."

"And you offered Romen of the Wolf neither," Jonathan said, his words ringing through the chamber. Behind Aidan, the pack stirred and muttered.

"*Shorogoyt. Shorogoyt.*"

"Aidan Gairden, by the authority of the war chief of the clans, I—" Jonathan began.

"Leave us."

Jonathan spun. "Nichel. War chief. I must advise against this. The Gairdens are as sly as foxes and as cunning as wolves, and—"

"And I am a wolf, advisor."

"I only meant . . ." He raised his hands and took a moment to choose his words. "I only meant that his guilt is known. The atrocities he committed against your people are testament to his guilt. Allowing him to speak will only open old wounds." His voice softened. "I would not see you suffer again."

Fondness for the man swelled within Nichel. Part of her wanted to agree with him. All she had done, all the plans set into motion—the coup in Sharem, the march of her people into Torel, who should be storming into the north even now—it had all been for this moment. Yet not even the faintest trace of deceit wafted from Aidan. Only grief and contrition. The part of her that clung desperately to reason and humanity cooled her anger slightly, a handful of water flung onto burning coals.

"Leave me with him."

Jonathan stood firm. "He is a Gairden. A sword-bearer. He is dangerous."

His counsel rang true. So, too, did Aidan's words. Romen of the Wolf had heard out his enemy when she and her mother had almost . . . Without thinking, she shot a sidelong glance at Ipadia of the Adder. The other woman looked away.

Nichel's words were colder than Aidan's natural scent. "He may hold his sword. If he attacks me, at least I will see it coming."

Relief rose from him, the first cool breeze of fall after a long summer. No victory. Only relief, and not strong enough to dampen his sadness. *Anger, too. Held at bay.* She knew something about anger that potent.

At last, Jonathan nodded. "He is Touched, war chief. I insist that you let me Tie him."

Before Nichel could lash into him, Aidan surprised her by stepping forward, extending his bound wrists. "I submit to Cinder Hillstreem's request."

"It was a demand, boy," Jonathan snapped. Nichel and Aidan ignored him. He simply stood waiting, watching Nichel with his arms extended. Doubt wormed its way into her thoughts. Why was he so compliant? Aidan had to know that he would not leave Janleah Keep with his life. She nodded at Jonathan. The Cinder stepped forward and cupped Aidan's head in his hands. Aidan stiffened, and then relaxed.

"It is done," Jonathan said, stepping back. At the same instant Ulestren strode forward. Steel flashed in her hand, and the rope around Aidan's wrists fell to the floor in coarse strands. Lips forming a line, he massaged his hands.

"You have my leave," Nichel said.

To his credit, Jonathan did not argue. He bowed and swept from the room. Nichel's pack fanned out, each exiting through a separate doorway. A moment later, doors boomed closed, and Nichel was alone with the man she loved. With the man who had ruined her life.

Chapter 16:
Division

—*SOMETHING IS NOT right with that girl,* Anastasia whispered.

She's grieving, Aidan returned. *I can sympathize.*

Yet that was not it. Not all of it. Aidan watched Nichel steadily. She no longer hunched. Her fingers, no longer bent into claws, rested at her sides. They brushed the cold steel of the knives he had seen her carry since her girlhood. He could not remember their names. Her stance was rigid, as if she might spring forward at any moment.

Nichel's eyes testified to Anastasia's judgment. They were red, as if she had been crying, but the redness went deeper. Darker. Fire behind a veil of smoke, as if her soul burned. The rest of her was still as stone, but those eyes trembled as if attempting to break free of her skull.

Something lurked behind them, in the fire. *Anger? No. Hatred.* Aidan's stomach twisted. He had never thought anyone could hate him so much.

— *Feral.*

Gabriel had only whispered, yet Aidan stiffened as if he had shouted. — *Feral,* his ancestor purred again. *There is darkness within her, more than within most wildlanders. Hers is a darkness so ancient and total it makes the brightest noontime as midnight. Tread lightly.*

163

Gabriel's casual usage of vulgarity made Aidan's skin crawl. Before he could comment, Nichel spoke in the biting language of Darinians. "Are you prepared to use that? You will not find me so easy to kill."

Aidan followed her gaze to where his left hand gripped the hilt of Heritage in a stranglehold. He let his fist relax. — *We can unTie you,* Grandfather Charles said. *You need only give the word.*

No.

Slowly, he pulled his sword free, watching Nichel as steel hissed against scabbard. Her eyes glittered, but she remained still. Poised. Heritage sang as Aidan pulled it free. He knelt, placing it at his feet, and kicked it toward her. It scraped and spun across the stone floor.

— *This is unwise,* Ambrose said. Ordine'kel *is your only means of protection.*

I know what I'm doing.

Without looking, Nichel stopped Heritage with one foot. "I said you could keep it."

"I wanted you to know that I mean you no harm."

Her face contorted in a vulpine grin, and Aidan's skin crawled again. "I do not fear you."

"I came to talk, Nichel."

"It is too late for talk."

"You don't believe that. If you did, I'd be dead."

She only watched him. — *Like a wolf studying its prey,* Charles murmured.

"Nichel, I am so sorry for your loss. I swear to you that I had nothing to do with what happened to them."

"Lies," she snapped. "Our realms enjoyed eight hundred years of friendship. If you wanted to go to war, my father would have observed formalities. He would not have done what you did."

"Our families were friends. You can't believe I would have—"

In her fury, Nichel reverted to the Darinian tongue. "He would not have murdered your mother and sent you her head in a gift-wrapped box!"

Her words echoed around the room. Nichel's eyes shone brighter. Her hands had fastened around her knives. Aidan rocked back on his heels. "I . . . I had no idea. Nichel, I am so sorry. I knew he had killed them, but I didn't know the lengths to which . . . They were good people. I'm sorry. I don't know what else to say."

"There is nothing you could say. You have severed the alliance between our realms, and between us. You were my friend. More than that. We were to marry. Our families were to become one!"

She shook her head roughly. "I feel nothing for you, now. Nothing but pity." She paused. "You are the monster."

Her final words sounded forced, as if trying to convince herself as much as condemn him. "I am a monster," he agreed quietly.

Her expression shifted from anger to wariness. "You do not deny it?"

"I deny that I played any part in what happened to your parents. But I do not deny that I have done things since their deaths that I regret. I was manipulated, but I will not make excuses. Outside Sharem, Nichel, I—"

"I know what you did. My speakers communed with the woodland creatures. Those that survived. They spoke of the agony my people suffered at your hands. Blood stains those hands. It will never wash off."

"I know."

"So, you admit it. You confess."

"To Sharem. To killing men in an act of war." His throat went dry. "Not that that makes it any better. I didn't believe in the war between our people. Not then, and not now. As for your parents, Nichel—"

She ripped her knives free. "I told you—"

"It was Tyrnen Symorne."

Her eyes narrowed. "The Eternal Flame?"

"Yes. My mentor. And my friend, or so I thought."

"I told you I would not listen to lies."

"And you told me that you would let me speak," he countered.

Nichel looked astonished that he had rejoined her. War chiefs, he suspected, were not used to arguing.

— *Neither are Crowns,* Charles murmured.

— *Watch your tongue with this one, Aidan,* Anastasia said.

"Speak," Nichel said at last.

He did, starting with what had happened on his birthday and relaying all that had happened since. She did not interrupt again. Occasionally her nose gave a little twitch that Aidan thought he was not supposed to notice. His voice cracked when he told of his mother's fate, and he thought he saw sympathy flicker across Nichel's features.

"I left to see you immediately following my coronation," he said several minutes later. "I would have come sooner, but my people deserved to know what Tyrnen had done, and that a Gairden sat on the Crown of the North again, and that Darinia is not our enemy, and never was."

For a moment, he thought she might not have heard. She stood rooted, staring. Her nose gave a final twitch, and she lowered her knives. "You did not kill my parents."

It was not a question, but he answered it as one. "No."

"And you claim Torel is not my enemy."

He shook his head.

"My people took Sharem peacefully. Did you know that? No one was allowed to enter or leave through its gates, but no harm came to them. Not even your Wardsmen. It was not the inhabitants of trading outposts I wanted. It was you."

"You were there?" he asked.

"No." Her tone was testy. Aidan decided not to pursue his inquiry. "You made no attempt to convene with my clansmen," she said. "Doing so might have prevented deaths for both of our realms."

"I wanted to," he said quietly. "But I was afraid."

"Of what?"

"Of defying my parents. The creatures I thought were my parents."

"You attempt to hide behind your action by justifying it as an act of war. You could have defied those imposters, even if you had known what they were. Instead, because of your cowardice, over one thousand clansmen lost their lives."

Aidan dropped his gaze, but could feel hers still on him, weighing him.

— *She is doing it again,* Gabriel said.

Aidan glanced up. Nichel's eyes were closed. She sniffed at him, and her expression indicated she did not care for what she smelled.

NICHEL FOCUSED ON her breathing, and on the shadows flickering over her eyelids.

Men carve lies from words as easily as our builders carve

spires from stone, her father had said. A man could not disguise his scent, however. Aidan was not lying. He smelled dirty and malodourous, but from guilt, and only when talk turned to Sharem. Even then, guilt mingled with sincerity, pain, and loss.

All at once her emotions calmed. Nichel revelled in the stillness. It was the first equanimity she had enjoyed in months. Silence so loud it was deafening. *And Aidan is responsible for it.*

Nichel opened her eyes and saw the man she loved. He watched her uncertainly. She resisted the urge to go to him. She was a woman, but the woman's needs would have to wait.

"Where is Torel's Ward now?" Nichel asked.

"Marching toward Sharem. They will use the city as a staging ground for their invasion of the west."

She tensed. "On your orders?"

"No. On orders given by the harbingers who usurped my mother's throne."

She nodded slowly. "The clans converge on Sharem as well. I should have marched with them. I wanted to. I just . . ." She glanced at Aidan. He waited patiently. *Tell him. Tell him what you are.* No. She was not ready. The *Nuulass* was quiet. She wanted it to stay that way.

"We could go to them together," Aidan said. "My father is on his way to Ironsail to warn the merchant's guild of Tyrnen, but I ordered him to stop in Sharem first so that he could pass on my commands to the Ward. They will not attack your clans. You have my word. Still, given all that has happened, I think it would be best to announce our new alliance together." He paused. "If that's what you want."

Nichel was impressed. "You gave your father orders?"

Aidan immediately reeked of discomfort. "Yes. It was . . . strange. I am the Crown of the North, and the sword-bearer, but this is all still so new to me. Those titles are just words."

Nichel nodded eagerly. "It is the same for me. When Margia of the Falcon—she is the first of the speakers—when she calls me war chief, I feel . . ." She frowned, searching for the right words in Torelian. "Wormy."

Aidan smiled. "You mean squirmy. Like worms in your belly."

"Yes." Squirmy was the perfect way to describe how she had felt when she had stood before the speakers on the night the *Nuulass* had emerged, and the perfect way to describe how she felt now. Her heart beat wildly. *The way it used to,* she realized. Before her life had been torn to shreds.

"Ruling is difficult," Aidan said.

Her grin faded. "It is."

"Do you want to know something funny?" She nodded, and he continued. "Growing up, I was so afraid of becoming Crown of the North. I thought I was doomed—doomed!—to a life spent listening to nobles bicker over land and trade routes. Now, that doesn't sound so bad. At least I'd be alive to let merchants and nobles bore me to sleep." He barked a humorless laugh. "I haven't even sat on the Crown of the North yet. Not once. Sometimes I wonder if I ever will." Aidan frowned at his sword.

Nichel sniffed. *He is sad again. And afraid.*

"I believe you." The words spilled out of her in a rush, but she did not want to take them back. Aidan looked up at her, but he was not smiling, like she expected. He looked frightened.

Everything happened at once. Aidan shouted, but she could not make out his words and did not need to. His fear stabbed her nose like a spike. His eyes bored into her. No, into something behind her. She did not stop to think. Still gripping Sand and Silk, she spun. As she turned, she got one look at her attacker: A man, tall, wearing snow-white armor and a helm, rushing at her from behind an effigy and raising a sword above his head. His faceplate was open, and his eyes were flat, and her nose perceived something rank for the briefest of moments before another thought came screaming into her mind.

A Wardsman.

The seal trembled.

She plunged Sand and Silk into his gut. Steel pierced mail and tasted flesh. The Wardsman grunted, clutched his belly, and fell face down.

For a few moments, the council room was silent save for the pops of the torches. From behind her came the sound of boots scuffing against stone. She spun and saw Aidan, crouched and in the act of rising. He gripped Heritage, raised as if to strike. His eyes glowed white. He blinked. His gaze returned to normal.

"Nichel," he began, lowering Heritage.

She could not hear him. The *Nuulass* battered at his prison, roaring. Fury over his betrayal filled her, consumed her. She smelled fear. Aidan's terror. Fear for her? No, fear of her. Of what she would do to him because he had betrayed her. He had lied to her.

Spring water and soap tickled her nostrils. She looked up. Jonathan and the pack stormed in. They surrounded Aidan, the women holding their weapons and Jonathan's sleeves thrown back to reveal outstretched hands. Aidan dropped the sword and called for her.

He is afraid, I can smell his fear, I can taste it and it's so good—

The council room swayed, a blur of stone and fire and painted bodies. When it stopped, she stared up at the darkness cloaking the ceiling. Footsteps around her. Aidan called her name again, a pleading note in his voice. She could not decide if she wanted him dead or alive.

Jonathan decided for her.

Chapter 17:
Into the Temple

DAWN TWINKLED THROUGH the brocaded curtains of the broad window of the finest room on the highest floor of the Eastern Pearl. Christine mumbled and turned away. Bells clanged. She buried her head in her pillow and squeezed her eyes shut. The bells thundered. In one motion she kicked the covers away and swung her legs over the side of the bed. She stood slowly, stretching, and padded across the polished wood floor to a gilded bureau. She liked large spaces. They gave her room to breathe.

Pulling towels from drawers, Christine entered the adjoining room and found a cast-iron tub filled three-quarters full of water. Over the tub was a small, circular window. She kindled a sliver of Dawnrise. Steam rose from the water. She stripped off her nightgown and took her time slipping into her bath one leg at a time, sighing as warmth enveloped her.

Christine picked up a cake of soap from a ledge over the tub and dropped it into the water with a *ker-plunk*. She kindled again. Suds bubbled over the surface. She sank up to her nose. Hot water worked kinks out of her neck. Tension melted away. The backs of her eyelids called again, and she answered. Aidan appeared there. A smile tugged at her lips, then faltered. He was still so far away. Stuck in that wasteland until the she-pup could be made to see sense.

Unbidden, Christine thought of Lam. Her eyes fluttered open. The bathroom was dimmer than when she'd fallen into reverie. She glanced up. Grey clouds smothered the Dawn, and her spirits. She washed, dried, and reentered her bedroom. The outfit she had chosen the night before, a blue blouse and riding skirt with knee-high boots, was laid out by her bed. She toweled her body, but not her hair. It gave a silky sheen when wet, and would dry as she walked.

She checked her reflection in the mirror, nodded, and strode out of her suite and down the winding staircase. The common room of the Eastern Pearl was vast. Tables round and rectangular filled the space. A marble hearth took up one wall. The spring morning was cool, and a low fire murmured, making the cavernous room cozier. Patrons rubbed sleep from their eyes while serving girls in colorful clothing bustled around carrying trays of eggs and bacon with tall pitchers of freshly squeezed orange juice.

Christine approached the bar and ordered a glass of juice. The innkeeper, a portly, bronze-skinned man with wisps of grey hair, glared. She fought down her temper. Even easterners looked at Sallnerians askance. Fortunately, Christine knew the Leastonian language. She dug through her purse and tossed four Sallnerian marks on the bar.

The man made no move to take them. "Leastonian or Torelian coin only."

Tight-lipped, Christine slapped down two Leastonian coppers. He scooped them up and called her order through a door leading into the kitchen. A moment later, he placed a glass in front of Christine. She took it and turned to go to a corner table where she could be alone and unseen.

"I'm sorry."

Christine turned back to the innkeeper. His shoulders were hunched. "I've got nothing against southerners." His lips twitched in a tight smile. "I don't exactly blend in with the snow myself. But Sallnerian marks don't circulate well in Sharem. They're no better than stones."

"I understand," Christine said.

He squinted at her, and his face shone with recognition. "Say, you're Christine Lorden. How long's it been?"

"A long time."

"Here to see your father?"

Christine's heart thudded. "I am."

The innkeeper set his towel aside and spread his hands on the counter. "We've been wondering when the Second or the Flame would intervene. Sharem's seen more than her fair share of unpleasantness lately, though I don't suppose you know much about that."

Christine rested a hand on her belly. "No. What happened?"

"Darinians took the city. All four districts"—he snapped his fingers—"just like that. No violence from what I heard, though more than a few of the clansfolk were unhappy."

"How so?"

"Like they were impatient to start skinning hides and wearing them as coats." He leaned closer. "Sneaks brought back word," he whispered. "As they tell it, Wardsmen were taken hostage. Then the Crown sent Wardsmen from up north, led by the prince himself."

"I saw the field." Christine's voice sounded distant.

The man nodded. "Lightning and fire rained down from the sky. Hundreds of wildlanders . . . I shouldn't talk like that. Hundreds of Darinians died. Not a single Wardsmen, not from the prince's regiment. And then the rest of the Darinians just vanished. There one day, gone the next."

Christine forgot all about her juice clutched in one trembling hand. "What more do our friends have to say?"

"More Wardsmen, lots of them, coming from the north, and fast."

"And the west?" she asked. At that, the innkeeper looked uncomfortable. Almost embarrassed. Her eyes widened as realization sank in. "Nothing?" she asked.

Before he could answer, the front door opened. Four men, two northerners in white shirts and trousers and two Leastonians in billowy shirts dyed multiple colors—blues, purples, pinks, oranges, yellows—walked in and headed for the bar. They noticed Christine and stopped, staring, then pivoted and went to a table along the far wall. The northerners sat with their backs to her. Their eastern companions faced her. One man's eyes lingered on the creamy skin exposed between her skirt and boots. Christine ignored them. *Northerners. If they're not looking at me like I slithered out of a swamp, they're undressing me in their mind.*

"How could the sneaks know nothing?" she asked, more to herself.

The innkeeper rubbed thumb and forefinger together. Christine dipped her hand into her purse and placed two more Leastonian marks on the countertop. They were gone in a flash. "They have a theory," the man said.

"And that is?"

"The Darinians had Sharem. The Torelians took her from them. She belongs to all four realms, not to one."

"You think the Darinians will try to take the city back?"

He nodded. "Only thing that makes sense, and probably not without bloodshed this time. Calewind's got to be heavily fortified, right? Crown of the North sits above it like a . . . well, like a crown. Take Sharem first, make her a staging ground. That's their best move." He rubbed his chin. "It'd be the best move for Torel, too."

Christine rose. "Thank you."

The innkeeper eyed her untouched glass. "You paid for the juice."

But you didn't think I would, she thought, and left.

Christine hurried through the eastern district, cutting across wending roads to the Temple of Dawn. Her heart raced. One hand cradled her belly. Things were moving fast, faster than Aidan had predicted. *Maybe we're not too late. Maybe there's no sign of clan movement because Aidan talked to Nichel.* Christine looked westward. He was still there. *What could be taking so long?* Jealousy pulled her lips back from her teeth. She focused on her objective.

There were four main entrances to the Temple of Dawn. Four Wardsmen guarded the north, south, and west gates. A handful of Azure Blades were posted by the eastern entrance. One disciple stood with each group, swathed in a blood-red robe. She approached the eastern gate, not bothering to show her Cinder Band. The disciple caught sight of her. His face turned stern, then recognition smoothed his features. He waved a hand and the high, ivory-colored gate rose smoothly upward. She followed a marble path through a well-manicured courtyard.

The Temple of Dawn was a towering edifice of white and red stone. Had the sky been clear and bright, it would have sparkled. Spires soared, tapering to points. Flowers in shades of red and gold bordered colonnades where men in robes walked, some reading from books, others with heads bent in conversation. Christine shivered. Approaching a set of wide steps, she scaled them two at a time. There were fifty in total. She dragged herself up the final four, panting and muttering curses. The steps had never tuckered her out before. She doubled over, hands on her knees, catching her breath.

Damn you, Aidan Gairden.

Resting a hand on a column, Christine straightened. She caught the sharp, metallic scent of a brewing storm and rolled her eyes. *Aidan would appreciate this heightened drama.* She beamed at the thought of him, then grimaced. *Cursing him in one breath, missing him with the next.* Her emotions were harder to hold on to than a sneak.

The vestibule was as posh and elegant as any gallery in Sunfall, judging by what little she had seen of the northern palace. Grand staircases swept upward to the temple's eastern and western wings: classrooms and worship halls on the east, offices and libraries to the west. Rugs of red and gold fabric were spaced evenly across polished floor. Near the peak of the vaulted ceiling was an enormous, circular window composed of a single golden pane. Normally, golden light bled through the bottom of the glass. As the Lady climbed higher, the foyer would be suffused in Her radiance. Today, the stormy weather draped the temple in a haze. Lanterns were affixed to columns and walls.

Torelians meandered around the hall. White-robed scholars pored over books and whispered together. Pontiffs in golden robes listened to red-robed priests as they walked along, lecturing and pointing. Pontiffs and priests were both disciples, but pontiffs ranked below priests, who were considered just below the Second, who ranked below the Eternal Flame. Christine threaded her way through robes of all colors, heading toward the eastern staircase. She climbed it slowly, feet growing heavier with each step. On the second floor, tables and chairs carved from imported woods sat scattered. Both staircases continued up. Her father's office was on the fourth floor. She climbed steadily. The butterflies in her stomach became an avalanche of boulders.

On the third floor, three men and three women dressed in robes the color of thunderclouds dusted a line of tables and chairs encircling bookcases. Their hair was dark and silky, just like hers. Their eyes were slanted, just like hers. Their skin was creamy. Just like hers. The oldest was maybe a few years younger. One of the women looked up and locked eyes. Christine gave her a disarming smile and raised her right hand in greeting. The woman's eyes fell on her Cinder Band. Her face colored and she hastily turned back to her dusting.

Christine thought of Lam and his threadbare clothes, of the rundown buildings in the southern district, of the stormrobes before her, cleaning up after disciples and scholars. *The tables and chairs on each floor cost more than every domicile on the Bridge,* she thought. *Dusk, their robes cost more than the domicile where I grew up.* Annoyance heated to ire. She took the next set of steps two at a time.

The fourth floor was mostly empty. Her father's door was at the end of a long corridor. Another group of stormrobes scurried about, rolling up sheaves of parchment and replacing books on shelves. Christine's feet dragged.

Her father's door was closed. Christine raised her hand to knock, let it drop. There was a chair against the wall to one side of his door. She sat, crossed her legs, and jiggled one foot twice. She stood up, paced, forced herself to stand still. She leaned against the wall beside his door, arms folded beneath her breasts. Slowly, ever so carefully, her head drifted to the door until her left ear pressed against the cool wooden surface. Nothing. Not even a muffled whisper. Disciples had a way of wrapping their offices in screens that dampened sound.

Christine paced. Patience is a virtue, her father liked to say. *Well, some of us are less virtuous than others.* None less so than Sallnerians. Her lips rose in a sneer. Had she been any other man's daughter, she too would likely be wearing a stormrobe instead of dressing as she pleased and flaunting a Band.

She placed a hand on her belly. That settled her nerves a little. *Who could he be talking to?*

Then she knew. Torel's Dawn. Why else would her father cast a screen to block conversation?

The door opened, and Christine jumped. Cinder Terrence Saowin, dressed in a crimson robe and hands clasped at his waist so that the pads of his thumbs touched, stepped out and closed the door softly behind him. He was a head taller than Christine, almost Aidan's height, with broad shoulders and smooth cheeks and cold eyes.

Terrence noticed her and blinked. "Well. If it isn't our little runaway."

"Hello, Cinder Terrence." Her right hand found her midriff.

Terrence followed the movement. "A Cinder Band? Who gave you that?"

"No one gave it to me," she said. "It was earned."

"I did not see you at winter commencement." It was not a question, yet he awaited a reply. Christine opened her mouth to give one. Fighting years of conditioning, she closed it. Bells clanged again, louder here, so close to the temple's bell tower. Terrence immediately bowed his head and began to mutter. Low murmurs rose up from the lower floors. Christine let her chin touch her chest, but she did not close her eyes, nor did she recite the benediction.

Oh, Lady of Dawn,
Let me live this day by answering the great end for which
You made me:
To glorify You who gives us life,
To praise You who gives us warmth,
To walk in Your light and abstain from shade and shadow,
To do good in Your name.
Truly, our lives are meaningless without this noble purpose.

Terrence and the others ran through morning canticles until the bells stopped ringing. Their clangorous echoes took several moments to fade. Christine lifted her head as Terrence raised his.

"You were telling me when you received your Band," he said.

"I wasn't, actually."

He flashed a winning smile. "No matter. The Second is responsible for overseeing the valediction of all students to Cinder rank. Such an advancement would not have escaped his notice."

Christine's irritation and urge to rebel grew. Terrence had a habit of stirring up those sorts of feelings. "My father is inside, then?"

"He is. But I'm afraid this is not a good time to speak with him. He has a full agenda. I was just informing him that—"

Christine gave Terrence a curt nod, turned the handle, stepped through, and closed the door not-so-softly behind her.

The Second's offices contrasted starkly with the rest of the Temple of Dawn. Cold, stone floor unadorned by rugs. A block of wood for a desk covered in books and documents. Four chairs, three on one side. Plain walls covered in charts and maps and proverbs. A large window over the Second's desk let in grey light.

Ernest Lorden looked up, and Christine's chest hitched. His hair and beard exhibited more grey than the last time she had seen him, just one winter ago. His eyes were a piercing blue dulled somewhat by pouches sagging beneath them. He sat back, folding his hands and frowning. Christine felt a flutter of rebelliousness. He knew why she had slammed his door. She decided to preempt a lecture.

"Why is he so insufferable?" she asked.

"So that I do not have to be." Rising, Ernest skirted his desk and came to stand before her. His hands fidgeted at his sides, as if he were trying to decide between raising them for a hug or waggling an admonishing finger. Christine, too, was torn by indecision. Part of her wanted to throw herself into his arms. Another part, the part that won out, kept her feet fast to the floor.

"Surprised to see me?" she asked.

"No. I received word that you were in the city."

Torel's Dawn. Relief that she would not have to be the first to bring news of Tyrnen's deception to her father and the temple ran through her.

"You look well," he said.

"Thank you. So do you."

He scratched at his beard. "Your father's got ash in his beard."

"Not because of me. Not anymore."

His lips quirked. "Always. You'll have children one day. Then you'll understand."

Christine's lips compressed. "For someone so concerned about his daughter, you seem to have forgotten how to write."

"I never know where to find you. You could be anywhere."

"Please don't start."

"I'm only trying to explain."

"Tell you what. Before I leave, I'll write down my schedule. Every minute of every day."

"Christine."

"That way you know where to find me: when I plan to eat, to sleep, to bathe, to dress, to work, to breathe—"

"Quills and parchment work two ways, you know," he snapped. "You needn't wait to hear from me to get in touch. You are an adult."

She opened her mouth to lob a volley of retorts: that he had been hovering her entire life, that she and Garrett had been forced to grow up almost immediately after learning how to walk because Ernest Lorden, the man who had sired them, had all but vanished after . . .

After.

"I don't want to fight," she said at the same moment he said, "We shouldn't do this."

An awkward silence descended. She tucked a lock of hair behind her ear. Ernest's gaze dropped to her Cinder Band. "Who gave you that?"

"It's legitimate."

"I never said it wasn't."

"You were thinking it."

Ernest's shoulders descended. "Christine, please. I was only asking a question anyone would ask. Many of the most gifted Touched don't graduate and receive a Band until their twentieth winter. Most quite a bit older. To receive a Cinder Band at the age of sixteen—"

"Seventeen."

"—is a grand accomplishment. I worried I had missed a private ceremony."

You did. "It's new," she said. "A month old."

Ernest opened his mouth to say something, then shook his head. "Never mind. We don't have to talk about it if you don't want to." He exhaled slowly. Christine wrinkled her nose. His breath smelled of sour berries. "You've been busy, then?" he asked.

Her stomach gave a nasty lurch. "Yes. Working. Mostly."

He nodded. "Your . . . show. With your brother."

"Yes."

"Do you need money?"

"I make money, Father."

"I know, I know." He took in her clothes. "Fine garments."

That brought back the memory of the haggard Sallnerians

drifting through the southern district, and of Lam, and of the Sallnerians tidying up in the temple. "Any cloth is finer than a stormrobe."

His expression became pained. "I hope you don't use that word where any of the disciples can hear you. Terrence has been ranting and raving about the thralls all morning."

"About the Sallnerians?" She dragged out all three syllables, letting them roll on her tongue.

Ernest gave her a level look. "I apologize. Thrall entered my lexicon against my own volition, believe me."

"Would that I could."

Ernest gave her a pained look. Shame heated her cheeks. Her father's attempts to converse with her were painful, but they were genuine. Maybe, she considered, her attitude was anticipatory. Ernest always managed to lecture her on something or other, or make her feel responsible for something entirely out of her—

"There was an incident on the Bridge last night," Ernest said. "You were there, or so reports indicate."

There it is. "Oh, it was nothing," she said lightly. "Lam and I were just out walking."

"He was out past curfew."

"He was out with me."

"I don't make the rules, Christine. I only enforce them."

"You could make the rules, and you know there isn't one against a Sallnerian being accompanied by a Cinder after curfew."

Ernest eyed the ring again. "It's not the first time Lam and a few others have left their domiciles, and the Bridge. I'm as lenient as I can be, given my position, but Terrence is pushing for tighter security. Earlier curfews, a larger Wardsmen presence on the Bridge—"

"It's a good thing he's only a disciple, then."

"—even a reduction in the Sallnerians' wages."

"He can't do that!"

"No, he can't. But I'm under terrible pressure, Christine. Many of the disciples agree with Terrence." Unconsciously, Ernest rubbed his forehead and closed his eyes. "I know he's asking around, recruiting supporters."

Christine suddenly felt a wave of sympathy for him. "It doesn't matter whether he has two supporters or two hundred. You are the Second. You have authority."

"Not absolute, and only in lieu of the Eternal Flame."

"Still, you could—"

His voice lost all intonation as he recited: "The Eternal Flame is a manifestation of Dawn's light and burns not half as bright. The Second holds the Flame in place, a lamp to steady Dawn's grace. Together, the Flame and the Second—"

Her sympathy popped like a bubble, pierced by years of neglect and hurt simmering over a low fire. "You always do this. You fall back on Temple precepts and verses and precedent instead of acting."

"There is nothing to act on, Christine. Terrence knows I am carrying out the Eternal Flame's orders and would not dare countermand them."

Christine smoothed her shirt at her belly. He was right, and that annoyed her.

"Although the Flame has been away a great deal as of late," Ernest went on. "I imagine it has to do with that business in Torel. You haven't been in the north, have you?"

She opened her mouth to answer.

"Well, stay out," he continued. "It's not safe. Not even Sharem is safe."

Christine disregarded his command. "Have you heard from Tyrnen?" A deep frown wrinkled his face. She made a sound of impatience. "The Eternal Flame. Has he contacted you?"

"No," he said, going behind his desk. "Not in weeks. I considered traveling to Sunfall to speak with him. I understand why he maintains a home at Sunfall, though last I heard the boy had earned his Cinder Band."

Troubled, Christine said nothing as she lowered herself into a chair opposite her father.

"He led the attack, you know," Ernest continued in a quieter tone. "Prince Aidan." He shook his head. "A nasty business, Christine. The north and the west are at war, and the Eternal Flame has gone silent." He scrubbed a hand over his face. "I don't know where the Touched stand, or if we're standing at all."

"Father," she said slowly, "You said Tyrnen—oh for Dawn's sake! The Eternal Flame has not contacted you at all? Not even through a liaison?"

His eyes widened. "Is that why you're here? He gave you your

Band? He must have."

Christine crossed her legs and played with her skirt. "He did."

A grin split Ernest's face. "Christine, this is cause for celebration! I admit, I had my doubts your ascension would ever happen."

"What's that supposed to mean?"

He waved away her indignation. "I meant only that you were never committed to your education. Your attendance at the Lion's Den was spotty at best, especially after you left the Bridge. I'd have thought your upbringing would have encouraged you to take your schooling more seriously, especially at the most prestigious school in the four realms. Don't look at me like that. You were always quick-tempered, Chris. Just like . . ." His throat moved.

A tingly sensation spread through her chest. Her father rarely spoke of Monumei Lorden, formerly Monumei of Domicile 137. Ernest cleared his throat and blinked hard several times. "Where is your brother?"

"I have no idea," she said coldly.

"In the city? He must be. Will you two be performing tonight? I'll attend. Terrence, too. He's had fun before. He must have. At least once." He laughed.

Christine wanted to shrink into her chair and keep shrinking until she disappeared. Her father looked so proud. It was the first expression of joy she had seen on his face in . . . *Ever. I've never seen him look happy until this moment. And now I have to shatter the illusion.*

"Father, have any members of Torel's Dawn paid you a visit?"

Ernest did not answer right away. Color drained from his face.

Christine tried to swallow, but her throat had gone dry. "I'll take that as an answer in the affirmative. You must have many questions. I will attempt to answer them, but Aidan will probably do a better job of . . . Father?"

Color rushed back into his face until his cheeks were redder than ripe tomatoes. "I always knew you were talented," Ernest said slowly. "But I never imagined you would be invited into Torel's Dawn. Christine, this is wonderful!"

"Father, you don't understand. I'm not—"

"My daughter, a member of Torel's Dawn!" He brought his hands together in a clap that made her jump. "Your talent would take you great places. I've always known it."

"Father."

Ernest swept around his desk. "Where are you staying? Somewhere in the northern or eastern districts, I hope."

"Father, there's something—"

"You're moving to the temple. I'll send for your things. Where are you staying? Oh, I know you don't care for Terrence, but he wouldn't—"

Christine shot out of her chair. "Father, please!"

He froze, one hand on the doorknob. "What is it?"

"Please sit down."

He lowered himself into the chair beside her, concerned. Christine took a breath. "I have a lot to tell you. I thought they would have found you first—they were supposed to, Dawn blind them—"

"Christine!"

"So, I will have to be the one to do it."

"You should not take the Lady's name in vain, especially not in this office, and in front of me. You're a grown woman, and a Cinder, and—"

Christine brought her palms crashing down on the arms of her chair. "Will you please let me get through this without interrupting?"

Tight-faced, he stared at her.

"Thank you," Christine said. Her tongue darted out to wet her lips. It felt like a dry paintbrush. She swallowed once more and began to speak.

Chapter 18:
Old Friends and New Secrets

DISCIPLES MURMURED GREETINGS at Christine. She swept past them without a word, ignoring sounds of disapproval that hit her back like stones. She was a Sallnerian. Her skin was too hard to be pierced by stones. Up ahead, wide doors leading out into the courtyard stood open. She stormed through them and paused, pulling in a breath. Fresh air tasted sweet and settled her stomach. Not enough.

Wrapping a hand around her middle, Christine descended the stairs as quickly as she dared. Her cheeks puffed out. She gulped in air and fastened her mouth closed again. Upon setting foot on the path cutting through a courtyard bordered by flowers crawling up lattice walls, she hurried down it. Fifty paces away, she glanced around to make sure she was alone. Then she doubled over behind a topiary pruned in the shape of a horse and retched. She braced one trembling hand against a knee. The other deftly gathered her silky black hair into a tail behind her. She vomited again.

A tendril of bile drooped from her lip. She spit. Her stomach gave one last violent heave. Nothing came up. She wiped her mouth, straightened, and sank onto a bench. Her hands shook. A breezed caressed her, cooling checks damp with sweat and carrying the scent of rain. She wanted to curse, needed to, but lacked the strength. Secretly, she feared opening her mouth only for more bile to come rushing up her throat.

Thunder rumbled. The light in the garden faded. Christine thought of what today still held in store. Her stomach lurched. She closed her eyes. *Best not to think about it until I have to.*

She rose slowly and began walking. She did not know where she was going until she reached the checkpoint on the Territory Bridge and flashed her Cinder Band. Two Wardsmen, different from the night before, opened the portcullis without a word and stared at her as she passed through. Christine wanted to lash out at them, but did not. Still, it was not fair. Her Sallnerian blood and features were no more her fault than was the weather. *This is the life we've been given,* Garrett had said once, when Christine's eyes had got them turned away from a northern inn. They had been thirteen, and it was the first time Christine had been keenly aware of how different she and her brother looked. *We can embrace it, or run from it.*

That had been easy for Garrett to say. He favored their father: tall, with blonde hair and blue eyes, and skin that browned instead of reddened. Sallnerian disgrace, men called it. Why else would their skin burn and peel like a molting snake beneath the Lady's gaze? Still, Christine had taken Garrett's words to heart. From the way she dressed to the way she walked to the words she chose, she exuded confidence in who and what she was.

The memory brought her comfort. Small, but it was enough. *For all my brother has become, he taught me that much.*

Trees sporting leafy fronds thickened around her, weaving a canopy and walls of thorny branches on either side. Scalethorn, the brambles were called, because snakes who tried to escape the Bridge by fleeing into the woods would get caught up in them, leaving behind skin. Her stomach clenched at the thought of Lam crawling through the undergrowth. *He could have gotten cut, or an infection, or . . . or worse. Fool.*

As she walked, the sounds of waves crashing, the hiss of tide flowing in and out, grew stronger. The Territory Bridge was three miles long and just as wide, a sinuous strip of land that connected the main body of Crotaria to Sallner. Leafy fronds, scalethorn, and rough trunks ended abruptly, replaced by walls of jagged rocks. Torelian historians said the Ihlkin Mountains had once hugged Crotaria from the north where they began, all the way around down to what was now the Territory Bridge, the path leading into Sallner. The southern portion of the mountain chain had been obliterated by Touched following the Serpent's War. The walls of tall, sharp remnants stood in their place, locking together without so much as a fingernail-sized gap and extending out into the Great Sea for half a mile. Too far for any ship to sail close, or for Sallnerian thralls to swim to freedom.

Her stomach roiled again. *It's not a bridge. It's a cage,* she thought, not for the first time. *A cage wrought from brambles, rocks, water, and those Dawn-damned checkpoints.*

As she walked, uniform rows of squat, shabby domiciles up ahead grew larger. Sallnerians in grey robes drifted down narrow dirt roads separating each row, steering clear of the pair of Wardsmen standing guard at the end of each lane.

One last step and she emerged from beneath the canopy. A light mist tickled her skin. She felt a familiar twinge of irritation: Rain would churn dirt to mud, and bare and sandaled feel would get dirty, cold, possibly infected. As if in a trance, she angled left and headed down a row of domiciles close to the western edge of the Bridge. Halfway down, she stopped before a hovel that looked the same as any other but for the splintered, wooden plaque nailed to its door: *Domicile 137.*

She reached for the rusty door handle when a reedy voice cracked like a whip. "Hey! What are you doing?"

Habit took over: Christine spun toward the voice, let her hands dangle so that the Wardsmen speaking to her could see that she held no weapon—no steel, no sticks or stones, not even a fork—and fastened her eyes to the ground.

"Chris? Is that you?"

She lifted her gaze and stared at the grinning visage of Feter of Domicile 20. Christine gave a shaky smile back. Feter was tall with a mop of brown hair and a smooth, almost girlish face. As a boy, he had been lanky and scrawny. As a man, his face was gaunt and his grey robe hung loosely. Before she could speak, Feter enveloped her in a hug. Christine embraced him in kind, careful not to squeeze too hard.

"Let's have a look at you," he said, eyes shining. "My goodness. You did fill out nicely."

She giggled. "All grown up, Fet. Like you."

He tsked and planted his hands on his hips. "Grown up, yes. Not out, though. Not like you. I'm so glad you've come to visit.

Does Lam know? He could use cheering up."

"He's not in trouble, is he?"

"Trouble? Lam? From the moment he wakes up until he goes to sleep." Feter nodded at Domicile 137 and wiped a sheen of rainwater from his face. "Are you on your way in? It's still unoccupied. Let's get out of this miserable dampness."

"No," Christine said quickly. She took his arm. "Let's go to your place."

He looked confused for a moment, then his expression became sympathetic. "Of course."

Of course? she thought, confused. Then: *Because I don't want to enter my old home.* Fet was thoughtful that way, always considering the feelings of others.

They hurried down a lane and turned right, passing half a dozen rows of domiciles before turning right again and hustling up to Domicile 20. Feter clasped the handle and pulled it open, gesturing for Christine to enter. She shook her head. "You first. Just stand in the doorway."

He obeyed without question, another habit of being a stormrobe. She kindled and spoke two words in the Language of Light. The Lady's light crawled rather than flowed into her, as if slow to awaken. His eyes widened for an instant, then his face relaxed as his robes and skin dried.

"Magic must be so handy," he said as she dried her own body and followed him inside. "And you make it look so easy, too. Always have."

She made a noncommittal sound. A prayer that normally called for a single word—a monosyllabic grunt, really—had taken two thanks to the grey clouds smothering the Lady's light.

Feter's domicile looked like any other: one door, one window, one room five strides long and five wide. It was a mess, which struck her as odd. A pile of empty containers sat in a corner. The square window on the back wall was filmy with dust. In the center of the floor lay two pillows and two blankets, each thin as parchment. The boy she had grown up with had insisted on neatness. But then, he never had spent much time in his domicile. No Sallnerian did.

"You're lucky no Wardsmen have come by for inspection," she said. Noticing that his bedding took up most of the floor, she squatted to roll it up and set it aside.

"Don't," Feter said sharply.

She straightened. "All right. Sorry."

He laughed and ran a hand through his hair. "The floor's filthy."

"So are my boots." She smiled.

"Just leave them by the door, and we'll sit on the sheets."

Christine braced herself against a wall with one hand as she used the other to pull off her boots. Feter whistled. "Those are beautiful. I love the leather. Where'd you get them?" he asked, removing his sandals.

"Oh, these?" she replied, hoping she sounded nonchalant. "Somewhere back east. I don't remember. How have things been?"

He lowered himself to sit cross-legged. "Oh, you know. We eat like Gairdens and gather around the fire pits to tell stories and drink ourselves silly."

She raised an eyebrow. Feter shrugged. "Well, Gairdens deposed from their throne and made beggars, and fire pits with flames kept low according to the rules, and drink consisting of muddy water. No complaints about the stories, though."

She laughed. "Stories are a good way to pass the time."

"Stories are a good way to forget," he said quietly. "Stormrobes, indeed. An ironic name, but milquetoast robes doesn't have quite the same ring to it." Feter shook himself and forced a smile. "You must have many stories, Chris. I never thought I'd see you again after you ran away."

"You didn't get in trouble, did you?" she asked quickly.

Feter shook his head. "No one even suspected us of helping you. Turns out it was unnecessary. They passed that edict around the same time: Thou shalt be permitted to flee the Territory Bridge if thy blood is only somewhat muddied by snake's venom. I think that's how it goes. Anyway. We've kept up with your exploits as best we can. How is Spectacle doing? Where have you travelled? Performed for any Gairdens lately?" He leaned forwardly, face eager.

Christine bit her lip. She could not tell her father about Aidan, not until Tyrnen had been dealt with, but she wanted to tell someone. *Why not your oldest friends?*

Feter took her silence for answer. "I thought not. But don't be disheartened. You and Garrett are gaining a reputation. Word trickles into Sharem. It's all the little ones on the Bridge talk about. Not that there's much else to discuss aside from work hours and wages and cursing disciples and snowmen, which we always do under our breath because, well, swords are sharp and fire has a nasty habit of burning, and—"

"The prince," she said softly.

"What?"

"I performed for the prince."

"The prin . . . ? Oh!" Feter's eyes grew wide. "Aidan Gairden? Really? When? Are you lying? May your skin molt right here and now if you are."

Christine met his stare. His eyes nearly popped out of his skull. "Shade cool my bones," he breathed. "You're not joking. How could . . . ? Ah! His birthday was just a short time ago, wasn't it? Imagine, performing for a Gairden on his birthday! And I've heard Aidan Gairden is quite handsome. Oh, and he turned sixteen! You must have seen Heritage. What does it look like? And the food. What did you eat? Were there—"

"It wasn't on his birthday." She kept her face smooth, but could not help the heat rising in her cheeks.

Feter stared at her. "You and the prince of Torel?"

She nodded.

He clapped and let out a crow. Christine made a shushing motion. "You can't tell anyone, Feter. Promise me."

"Why not? If I'd bedded a prince, I'd climb to the highest tower of Sunfall and shout it down to Calewind. You did bed him, I assume?"

"Feter!"

"What? It's what people who fancy one another do, Chris." He shook his head.

She shifted, self-conscious. "What?"

"Nothing, it's just . . ." His throat moved. "Assuming you're not lying"—he glared at her until she let out an exasperated sound—"assuming you're not, you've come so far, Christine."

"Because I've seen a prince naked?"

He gave her a playful swat. "Because of all you've done and seen. I'm proud of you." Tears glistened in his eyes.

Her own eyes began to burn. She sniffled and wiped at them before tears could spill. *Damn you, Aidan Gairden.* "You don't think I abandoned you? Abandoned our people?"

"Abandoned? Christine, everyone on the Bridge dreams of getting away. You and Garrett got out from under the temple's thumb and felt sunlight on your faces as free Sallnerians. Be proud of that. I would."

She frowned. "Sunlight?"

Feter laughed. "Listen to me prattling on. Tell me more about your prince. You love him, and he loves you, and you're going to make lots of Gairden babies. Or just one, in this case."

Christine went rigid, panic coursing through her like icy water. Then she forced herself to breathe. He was referring, of course, to the precedent of the Gairden's gift: A Gairden heir could be born with *Ordine'kel* or *Ordine'cin*, one or the other, and each Gairden would only ever produce one heir.

"It's complicated," she said in what she hoped was a neutral tone.

"Complicated?" His eyes grew flinty. "Let me guess. He doesn't want anyone knowing he's been slithering around in the dirt with a snake?"

"Aidan's not like that."

"Ah. The trouble between Torel and Darinia. Is that it?"

"Yes," she said simply, grateful he had saved her another recitation of all that had transpired. Then, curious, she asked, "What was the Bridge like with all of that going on?"

"All the stormrobes working in the city when the Darinians took Sharem were sent back to the Bridge and put under guard. The Lady be praised," he added after a pause. It sounded perfunctory, but Sallnerians held little regard for the Lady because she seemed to hold little regard for them.

"We heard the battle well enough, though," Feter continued. "When the first boulder hit, we thought it was a storm. When we realized it was one of the walls coming down . . ." He shivered. "The screams were worse. They say your prince burned men alive. With those white flames you Touched make." Abruptly, he sat forward. "Shade! That's why you're here, isn't it? To talk to your father about allying the Touched with your prince."

"I already did," she said, stretching out her legs. "I spoke to him this morning."

"And?"

She rolled her eyes. "My word alone isn't good enough. He's calling a full conclave around noon."

"Will your prince be by your side?"

Christine thought of Nichel and her hands balled into fists. "As I said, it's complicated."

"I'm sure you'll be fine."

A flutter of panic sent tingles through her chest. "I wish I could be as calm as you."

Feter waved a hand as if swatting a fly. "Let someone else incur the Gairdens' wrath for once. Better the snowmen and Darinians kill each other." He blushed. "I'm sorry. I'm talking about your love. I'm sure Aidan is a wonderful man. Just don't give him reason to hurl white fire in my direction."

"I'll see to it," she said.

Feter shook his head. "A Sallnerian *seeing to* a Gairden. Wait until Lam hears this."

As if on cue, the door flew open. Habit drove Feter to his feet in a flash, and Christine was only a breath slower. They each pressed against a wall and dropped their hands to their sides palms out. But the man silhouetted in the doorway against grey clouds and a haze of mist was not a Wardsman. Lam's grey robe was the color of charcoal, soaked with rain. His hair was plastered to his head, but his eyes shone like cinders.

His face twisted when he saw Christine. "Are you lost? The east quarter, where the streets are paved and the beds are soft, is that way." He jabbed a thumb behind him.

Feter tsked and reached out to take Lam's hand. "You're letting out all the heat. It's not much, but it's mine."

Lam yanked his hand away and heeled the door closed. "I wasn't aware you had company."

"I stopped by to say hello to you and Feter," Christine said lightly.

"Christine's in Sharem on business," Feter said. He reached for Lam, and Lam stepped back. Feter looked hurt and confused.

"She's a Cinder," Lam muttered.

"I wouldn't tell!" Christine said, stung.

Lam shrugged, but he averted his gaze to the floor.

Feter clasped his hands in front of him. "You don't seem surprised to see Chris."

"We crossed paths last night."

Feter's eyebrows knitted. "When last night?"

Christine looked between them. "You didn't tell him?" she

asked Lam.

"You said not to tell anyone."

"Feter is not anyone."

"You snuck out after curfew again, didn't you?" Feter asked.

"You were hungry," Lam said.

"I can go hungry for a night," Feter snapped. "Better that than seeing you given to the Lady's embrace." Scorn dripped from the goddess's name like water droplets from Lam's robe.

Christine gasped. "They still do that? I thought my father—"

"Your father's a Torelian," Lam said, "and the Second. He cares about snakes as much as any other Touched." His gaze flicked to her ring, then he sneered. "Like father, like daughter, I guess."

Feter gasped. Outside, thunder rumbled, and the rain picked up. She and Lam glared at one another. He looked away first, but Christine took no satisfaction from it. Choking back tears, she took a step toward her boots. Her bare foot caught on something and she staggered forward. Lam steadied her with a hand.

"Got you," he mumbled.

Christine shook free of him and crouched, rubbing her big toe and glaring at the floor. There was a small protrusion beneath the blankets.

"Probably a rations container," Feter said. He went to stand over it.

Lam touched her shoulder. "I'm sorry," he said softly. "Are you all right?"

Christine stepped into her boots. "I'm fine," she said, voice tight with pain both emotional and physical. Her toe throbbed in time with her heart.

"You don't have to go," Feter said. "Please, Chris. We have so much catching up to do."

"I have to see my father."

Before Lam could interrogate her, Feter stepped in. "Come back afterwards. I insist. Please."

Her eyes moved to Lam. Not looking at her, he raised one shoulder, let it fall. Thin-lipped, Christine opened the door and stepped out into the rain, trying her best not to limp until she was out of view.

Chapter 19:
The Second and the Flame

THUNDER RUMBLED OUTSIDE the Temple of Dawn. Christine shivered. The sound, muffled by the temple's thick walls, sounded like the far-off charge of Darinian clansmen stampeding toward Sharem to raze it to the ground.

Christine banished the image from her mind. *Aidan is safe. He'll reason with Nichel, and then he'll come back.* She focused on her surroundings. She sat on a gilded bench in a vestibule lit by dozens of standing lamps, hanging lanterns, and candelabras. Across the broad corridor stood two stone doors. Detailed engravings depicted bearded men in robes lifting their arms in supplication to a ball of radiance high overhead. In the corridor, disciples in red or gold robes hurried along, glancing at her and frowning. Christine stared straight ahead.

If memory served, the domiciles lining the Territory Bridge were as leaky as they were rickety. Christine tried to remember Wardsmen or disciples seeing to repairs during her brief time in Domicile 137, but could not.

Another peal of thunder. Light rain pattered the window above her. She balled a fist. *I'll speak to Aidan about conditions on the Bridge as soon as he returns. He'll make things right.* The thought brightened her. Focusing on what they would do during their life together made the uncertainty and fear of the present less important somehow. Something to be disposed of quickly so she and Aidan could move on to bigger and better goals.

Christine fingered her Cinder's Band. She grabbed a fistful of her shirt and polished the gold ring and purple amethyst until they gleamed in the firelight. She turned her hand this way and that, admiring the ring.

A disciple in a red robe slowed, watching her with narrowed eyes. She looked up, and the suspicion on his face turned to recognition. He murmured a "The Lady shine on you, Christine Lorden" and hurried on. Her mood darkened. *Christine. No "Cinder," I notice.* She stared at the Band. She had studied. Not as long as many, but only because Touching had come easily to her. Prayers that required most men to speak incantations of a dozen words in the Language of Light took her three or four at the most.

Not that it mattered. The disciple who had demurred to her had not seen her band. He had seen the shape of her eyes, the fairness of her skin, the color and texture of her hair. People saw her and drew conclusions based on deception committed by her people eight hundred years ago, not all she had made of herself in the present.

Christine leaned her head back against the wall and closed her eyes. *It isn't fair.* One hand went to her belly. Calmness rolled over her like a cool, silk sheet. Just as she began to feel better, the stone doors across the corridor swung open. Terrence stepped out, hands tucked into his sleeves and arms folded across his chest. He was wearing a golden robe. The Disciple of Dawn looked her up and down, lingering on her legs and chest. Rising, Christine made a point of fidgeting with her Cinder Band.

Terrence's mouth twisted. "We are ready, Christine Lorden," he said.

She continued fidgeting, turning the Band so it flashed. Terrence said nothing. Her mouth tightened. "Very well, Terrence."

His face turned crimson. Christine glided by him, eyes set straight ahead. She took two steps into the audience chamber and froze.

The Hall of Morning was a cavernous chamber with smooth, marble walls that rose in a dome. A band of glass wrapped up and around the curved walls, unravelling to a skylight at the pinnacle of the dome that filtered in grey light. The glass seemed to bubble as raindrops struck it and slid down. Standing lamps ringed the expanse. The floor was composed of white tiles, and a floor mural of a golden circle with bright blue eyes and a luminous smile dominated the center of the room. Eight painted rows extended outward from the circle, each tapering to a point.

Christine expected to see eight disciples in crimson robes seated at a long table in the center of the mural. She would stand before them, present her case, and leave. Instead, she saw eight high-backed chairs situated at the tip of each row, and a disciple in each one. The Hall of Morning's arrangement for a trial.

Chairs creaked as the disciples shifted to stare at her. Seven wore shimmering gold robes. Only one man, seated directly in front of her with his back to the door through which she entered, did not turn. Unlike his companions, he wore a voluminous blue robe. Unless Christine missed her guess, he had a long, thick beard as white as snow.

Her heart pounded.

"Take your place."

Terrence's voice came from over her shoulder. Christine walked forward on wooden legs, refusing to look at the man in blue. Christine stopped in the center of the mural, facing the Second, who sat across from her. Ernest Lorden's face was pale and drawn. His gaze was fixed on a sheaf of papers held in trembling hands.

Booted footsteps thudded over the tiles behind her. Terrence swept past. Christine followed him with her eyes and noticed the empty chair to her father's right. She watched in a daze as Terrence crossed the span of the mural and took his seat.

At last, Ernest Lorden looked up. "Good afternoon to you, child." His voice was weak and shaky, but the acoustics of the room made it seem like he stood right in front of her.

"Good afternoon, Second." Christine was pleased at how even she sounded.

Ernest cleared his throat, a sound like thunder directly overhead. "You requested an audience before the Lady's servants, and we have gathered."

This is happening. It's really happening.

"Given the severity of the matter, one among us saw fit to call for a trial to judge your claims," Ernest continued.

Terrence spoke next. "The Lady's light surrounds us. It comes from everywhere—"

"—and so shall the Lady's judgment," said a brown-bearded man to Ernest's left.

"For there is nowhere Her light does not touch," said another man, this one to Terrence's right.

"No shade in which Her children may seek shelter from justice." A fourth.

The other three spoke, but Christine did not hear them. She turned in time with their voices, facing each to acknowledge that the Lady's judgment did in fact surround her, and that she stood in light so as to not hide in the shade. Finally, she faced the man in blue.

Tyrnen Symorne, once the Eternal Flame of Crotaria, sat with one leg crossed over the other, wizened hands steepled under his chin. His Cinder Band and Eternal Band—a golden loop fitted with a sapphire—glinted in the firelight. His gnarled hands held the head of a cane.

"Do you agree to be judged?" Tyrnen said, finishing the opening procedure.

Christine stood as still as stone. There was only one answer to give. Any other was tantamount to guilt. "I agree."

Tyrnen sat back. "Second," he said, voice strong and clear, "you may begin."

Christine turned away a little too quickly: The room spun. She extended her arms at her waist, as if dipping to curtsy, to steady herself.

"Are you well, Christine?" Ernest asked. His frown was one of concern.

"I am," she answered.

Disappointment flashed across his face. That confused Christine. *Because I didn't use his formal title?* That was probably it. Ernest Lorden clung to formality as tightly as Kahltan to midnight.

"You are here," Ernest continued, voice shaking, "because you have accused Cinder Tyrnen Symorne, Eternal Flame of Crotaria, Beacon of Dawn, Hand of the Touched, of treason against his kind and the Lady of Dawn Herself."

Now Christine shook, but not with trepidation. "I made the accusation in private."

"Such a claim cannot stay behind closed doors," Terrence interrupted.

Ernest raised a hand and the disciple fell quiet. Terrence's face reddened, and his lips pursed in a pouty moue. "Our disciple is correct," Ernest said, sounding a trifle begrudging. "Any accusation levelled at the Second or the Eternal Flame, even in private, must be brought before the Hall of Morning."

"Had you studied harder," Tyrnen said from behind her, "you would have known that, Christine Lorden."

Christine's hands clenched at her sides. "You gave me my Cinder Band. Perhaps you should hold yourself responsible for this oversight."

Tyrnen chuckled, but said nothing.

"Please," Ernest said, spreading his hands. "We will adhere to protocol. Will the accuser state her name." It was not a question.

"Cinder Christine Lorden."

"State the crime and the accused."

"Father, you know who—"

"I am not your father here."

She bit back a retort. "The accused is Tyrnen Symorne. The crime is grand treason toward the Lady's servants on Crotaria, and all served by them."

Gasps rang out. Christine stiffened. It was one thing to confide the truth to her father in private. Speaking in front of the Hall was another.

Ernest sat forward. "Christine, you—"

"*Cinder* Christine Lorden, Second."

Ernest closed his eyes for a moment. "Cinder Christine Lorden, you have levelled a serious charge at the most honored of our kind. The time has come for you to make your case. If you are found to have given false testimony, you will stand guilty in the eyes of the Lady of Dawn." His tongue wet his lips. "The punishment for such a crime is death. Do you understand and accept?"

Christine mustered every ounce of willpower she possessed to keep her hands from straying to her belly. "I do."

Ernest took a deep breath. "I advise you to hold nothing back."

"This is highly irregular, Second," Terrence said loudly. Mutters broke out around the room.

Ernest gestured for silence. "She is newly ascended and may

not be familiar with trial custom."

"She should be," Terrence said. "She wears the Band, does she not?" The unspoken accusation, that she had stolen rather than earned her ring—just like a snake—revealed itself in his smirk.

Christine chewed her bottom lip. The Second counselling an accuser was indeed unorthodox, and her father knew very well that she understood the customs of the Hall. She had grown up in Sharem.

"Speak," Ernest Lorden commanded.

Christine hesitated. Where to begin? She opened her mouth and it all came tumbling out: The attack on Sharem and Aidan's part in it; how her proficiency as a Touched had caught Tyrnen's eye and spurred him to enlist Christine and Garrett to find and recover Torel's prince; her betrayal of Aidan and helping his friend, Daniel Shirey, escape, though she left out where Tyrnen had taken them; and Aidan's explanation concerning how Tyrnen had manipulated Darinia and Torel against one another.

Rain fell harder, but Christine's words, delivered steadily, drowned it out. Her father interrupted her only once: "He is the Eternal Flame, child; show proper respect." The other disciples wore expressions of shock, disbelief, and horror. Tyrnen did not so much as flinch.

When she finished, Terrence struggled to speak for several moments. "How dare you?" he said in a choked voice. "This is blasphemy! The dead rising from their graves! Utter absurdity. And to accuse our Eternal Flame, the Lady's earthly emissary of . . ." He drew a deep, shuddering breath.

Ernest, whose face had remained stoic throughout Christine's account, rubbed his eyes. "Is your testimony complete?" he asked quietly.

Terrence whipped his head around. "You cannot be considering anything this child says."

"I assume you can offer some sort of proof," Ernest said to Christine.

"Torel's Dawn," she began, but Terrence interrupted her.

"Outrageous! That you would think to bring forward those who escorted you here to blaspheme—"

"Be silent, Terrence," Ernest said.

"What manner of proof could the girl bring forth?" the disciple continued. "A corpse able to move of its own volition? And why does she come before us alone? Convenient, don't you think, that Aidan Gairden—newly anointed Crown of the North, if this girl is to be believed—has gone to the west? Why would a Gairden not bring such dire news himself?"

Ernest slowly raised his head to fix Terrence in his gaze. Christine's breath caught. She knew that look. "Terrence, your behavior is appalling. A supplicant called an audience and we are obligated to hear her case."

"And so we have," Terrence shot back, "one rotten with sacrilege and predicated on lies. The Eternal Flame could not wield the Lady's light against any of Her servants, much less a Gairden. He sits among us! We could ask him! Not that I would debase myself or dishonor him in that way. And if the Flame had attempted such wickedness, the Lady would have rejected him. I firmly believe that."

"Then you are a fool," Ernest said.

Christine gasped. Hers was not the only one.

"Ernest Lorden," Terrence said shakily, "the edicts—"

"I am aware of the edicts better than you, Terrence Saowin. The Lady gave us free will. She is not a shepherd who tirelessly safeguards Her flock from harm. She lets them roam where and when they will. There have been crimes committed with Her light, and you know that as well as I. You have passed sentences on them is this very room, though one would never suspect it for all the ignorance you display. Oh, close your mouth, Terrence. You look like a simpleton. I have half a mind to assign you to the grey robes and keep you scrubbing floors until next spring. You serve the Lady of Dawn. Comport yourself accordingly. As for the Eternal Flame, he will be given his opportunity to speak, as process dictates. In the meantime, you have squandered yours. I do not want to hear your voice again until we call for judgment."

Terrence's mouth worked. The Second massaged his temple between thumb and forefinger. "You must admit," Ernest said, "that it is both odd and troubling for the Crown of the North, whoever that may be, to fail to come to the Temple of Dawn and deliver this news. Doing so would lend greater weight to your accusation."

Christine saw Aidan in her mind's eye. He smiled at her, and the warmth of that smile melted away trepidation. "I am the Crown's . . . friend. He sent me here."

"Do you normally take orders from any crown?" one of the other disciples asked.

"I obey the laws of the realms, as Touched are commanded to do except when those orders contradict edicts from our Eternal Flame or his Second," she answered. The disciple nodded, satisfied. "And I did not come alone," Christine finished.

"Yet no one stands with you," Ernest said.

"I was elaborating on the subject of proof before I was interrupted."

"This—" Terrence began.

"*Be silent.*" The Second's voice cracked like a whip. Terrence went white as a sheet. "Speak," Ernest said.

Profound gratitude welled up within her. *It's the closest he's come to defending me all my life. Dawn, I shouldn't need his support. I don't. But I want it.* She blinked hard to squash the tears threatening to spill out. *Damn you, Aidan Gairden.*

"Thank you, Second. Torel's Dawn knows the truth as well. They were at Sunfall when the Eternal Flame attacked Aidan and his father, Edmund Calderon. They accompanied me to Sharem and told me they would speak with you shortly after we arrived. That was yesterday."

"They have not," Ernest said.

A block of ice formed in her stomach. Her confidence wavered. "I . . . we arrived last night. I went to find a room in the eastern quarter, and they . . . Cinder Coren Landswill and Cinder Keelian Faltan. You know them?" She colored. *Of course, he knows them. Dawn!*

"I do," Ernest said, not unkindly.

"They said they would seek you out immediately."

"This was last night?"

She nodded.

Ernest peered around the Hall of Morning. Five of the disciples shook their heads slowly Terrence shook his so hard Christine expected it to spin to the floor. Tyrnen sat motionless.

Ernest straightened. "No one has seen Cinder Coren Landswill, or Cinder Keelian Faltan, or any member of Torel's Dawn for many months. Do you have another way to validate your accusations?"

Christine shifted her weight, thinking. Aidan was in the west, Daniel was back in Calewind, and Edmund was probably on a ship to Ironsail by now, a galerunner speeding him to the merchant's guild. Her eyes widened. *Edmund!*

"I do," she said breathlessly. "A document. Signed and sealed by General Edmund Calderon."

The disciples watched with obvious interest. "What are its contents?" Ernest asked.

Christine hesitated. Truthfully, she did not know what words Edmund had written explicitly. But why would he have given it to her, with orders to turn it over to his chief lieutenant in the Ward, if it was not damning to Tyrnen?

"It was not my place to read it," she answered.

Ernest exchanged looks with the disciples. "We could read it," he said slowly. "It is an urgent matter. Breaking the seal may ruffle some feathers up north, but given that Torel seeks the Touched's aid . . ." He nodded as if to himself. "Do you carry the missive?"

Christine fumbled at her skirt. Her pockets were empty. "I left it at the inn."

Ernest's expression changed, from tolerant and open-minded to afraid. "I see. So, you could retrieve it?"

"Yes."

"Very well. I call for a brief recess. This audience will convene no later than one hour from now, in this room. At that time, Cinder Lorden, I expect you to have—"

Terrence shot out of his chair. "To have what? To have forged a document bearing Torel's general's signature?"

"How could I forge his seal?" Christine shouted.

Ernest stood. "Quiet, both of you. You go too far, Terrence. Yet again."

All the air had been sucked out of the Hall. Terrence did not shy away from the Second. "This child is clearly receiving special treatment. Who else could come before our conclave and accuse the Eternal Flame of a crime, only to be granted time to retrieve proof they should have had at the ready for the trial they requested? It is outrageous!"

Christine spoke up. "I requested an audience, not a trial. Had I known I was walking into an ambush"—she resisted the compulsion to shoot her father a withering glare—"I would have come prepared."

Terrence's face turned bright red. "You lying sn—"

Several things happened at once. Ernest Lorden barked a short prayer in the Language of Light. Candles dimmed. Disciples gasped as Terrence spun to face the Second, fear painted on his face, replaced swiftly by defiance. The light grew dimmer. Christine stepped in front of her father and kindled. Several other candles winked out.

Across the room, the stone doors crashed against the walls. Everyone jumped, startled, and released the light they held. The room brightened as candle flames blossomed and resumed their shivering. Coren Landswill and Keelian Faltan swept into the room, their crimson robes fanning out behind them. They took their place to either side of Tyrnen, who rose slowly from his seat, putting his weight on his cane.

"Such disorderly conduct," the old man said as he straightened.

Rain hit the domed roof like a waterfall, a steady droning like thousands of beating wings. Christine barely heard it. Her mouth went dry as she stared at Coren and Keelian.

"I believe," Tyrnen said, "that this is the point in a trial's proceedings when the accused is granted permission to speak. May I, Second?"

"We haven't resolved the matter of General Calderon's document," Christine said, shooting her father a pleading look.

"I think you'll find the document unnecessary, Second," Tyrnen said. "May I?"

Ernest's attention swung between his daughter and his superior. He dipped his head. "Please, Eternal Flame." He took his seat, eyes fixed on his clasped hands.

Christine trembled with anger. How many times? How many times had her father turned away from her, from Garrett, from their mother, and toward his duties as Second? *Daily,* whispered a nasty voice in a dark corner of her mind. The same corner where memories of long, cold nights and days spent shivering beneath thin blankets while rain leaked through the roof of Domicile 137 resided.

Tyrnen shuffled to the center of the mural to stand beside Christine. She took a step away. Tyrnen said nothing, though his eyes glittered. *With amusement,* she realized. Her clenched fists shook as Tyrnen began to speak. With every word, her fury threatened to boil over. In his version of events, Aidan had been rejected by Heritage on his sixteenth birthday, and he had fled Torel rather than participate in the war, only to return and, with his father's aid, usurp the Crown of the North from Annalyn Gairden. Tyrnen, appalled and caught off-guard by Aidan's true nature, tried to reason with the prince, failed and, under mortal threat, fled to his private home in Sharem's northern district. He did not emerge, and spoke to no one, until Torel's Dawn had come to him with further news of events transpiring in Torel.

As much as she hated to admit it, Tyrnen's manipulations impressed her. He refuted each and every one of her points, not by dismissing it with conjecture, but with the truths and half-truths he had used to turn Torel and Darinia against one another.

Tyrnen fell silent. Rain drummed against the windows, the roof, rain down the walls. "And Christine?" Ernest said at last. "Where does my . . . where does Cinder Lorden fit into your account?"

Tyrnen managed to look dismayed. Christine, he explained, was Aidan's lover. A bright and ambitious half-Sallnerian looking to raise her station by marrying into Torel's ruling family. Keelian and Coren had accompanied her, as Christine had testified, but under a false pretense. They believed her mad and accepted her request—her demand—to shift to Sharem with them and speak with the Second so that they could deliver her to her father, who knew best how to handle her "rapidly deteriorating mind," as Tyrnen put it.

When Tyrnen finished, the conclave sat stunned. All except Terrence, who only shook his head and wore a sad but resigned expression. Ernest opened his mouth to speak. No words came out. He cleared his throat and tried again. "Your account contradicts Cinder Lorden's at every turn, Eternal Flame."

Tyrnen's expression was grave. "On the subject of her title, Second, it saddens me to say that I played no part in presenting your daughter with her Cinder Band."

"Liar!" Christine said.

"It is authentic," Tyrnen continued as if she had not spoken, "but given to her, I suspect, by Aidan Gairden in an attempt to reach out to Touched who may look to the Second's offspring as a symbol of the Touched's unity with Torel. A unity I advise strongly against. Torel and Darinia are at war, but the Touched have aligned with the north on my authority. I will order all Touched from both realms to return to the Temple of Dawn and—"

Ernest raised a hand. Had raised it before Tyrnen had invoked his authority, but the old man had only just now noticed. He blinked, adopting a confused expression. "Eternal Flame," the Second said slowly, "you are involved in a trial. According to custom and edict, you set your authority aside until the matter is resolved."

Tyrnen's lips rose in a placating smile. "The realms are at war, Second. Surely, in such a circumstance . . ." His smile faltered as Ernest Lorden shook his head.

"Those are our laws. You know them as well as I. No circumstance, not even war, may erode them." He sounded deeply apologetic, even abashed. Ernest began to quote from the law. "For Her light fades only temporarily, when the Lord rules the sky, but always returns at Dawnrise to—"

"I know the laws," Tyrnen snapped. Every head swiveled toward him. Christine fought to keep from grinning. The old man gathered himself. "What is it you suggest, Second?" he said in a more respectful tone.

Ernest stared at his lap for a long while. "Christine claims that she arrived last night with Cinders Keelian Faltan and Coren Landswill," he said, looking up. "You made the same statement, Eternal Flame, though you claim it was for different reasons." He turned to the two members of the Dawn. "I would hear from you. Did this occur?"

"Yes," Coren said.

"You should have come to me directly," Ernest said. "Why didn't you?"

Keelian stepped forward. "We swore allegiance to Aidan Gairden publicly for fear of what he might do if we refused. He is stronger than the two of us combined, Second."

"Surely Aidan could not have stood against the united force of all eight members of Torel's Dawn."

"No, but an act of violence against the Crown would have put all Touched at risk," Keelian said. "Privately, our unit feared for the realms. Coren and I sought the Eternal Flame's counsel."

Christine's throat moved. *And the others? Dawn and Dusk. Edmund!*

"And you knew you would find him here?" Ernest sat back.

"We knew of the Second's private residence," Coren answered.

Tyrnen interjected. "Surely the fact that I came to you earlier this morning, Second, carries weight."

Christine narrowed her eyes. Ernest had said he had not heard from Tyrnen in months. Had the old man been watching her, waiting for her to leave her father's office so that he could continue weaving his web?

Ernest studied the floor at his feet. Terrence straightened. "The word of the Eternal Flame carries all the weight in all the realms. The testimony of two of his most trusted advisors adds that much more. I think we have heard enough to reach a verdict." His lidded eyes fastened onto Christine's. She stared coldly back at him.

Ernest looked up. "There will be no verdict given here today." Terrence looked shocked, but the other disciples nodded. "This conclave must adjourn to sort through all we have heard," the Second continued. "Until we reconvene and the accuser and accused are summoned to the Hall of Morning, I ask that none of you"—his gaze took in Christine, Tyrnen, and Coren and Keelian—"leave Sharem. To do so will serve as a tacit admission of guilt."

Tyrnen waited until the last echoes of Ernest's words had died away. "A wise decision," he said, folding his wrinkled hands at his waist. "I will take up my quarters in the temple."

Ernest nodded, then shifted his attention to his daughter. "Christine Lorden? Where—"

"The Eastern Pearl," she responded stiffly. Without another word, she turned on her heel and stormed to the door.

"Christine," her father called.

She slowed, looked back to him. Ernest was standing with one hand extended toward her. Hope swelled in her chest. She crossed to him and reached for his hand.

Ernest withdrew it slightly, looking pained. "Your Cinder Band."

Christine let her hand fall. "Why?"

"Until proof of your ascension can be obtained . . ." He trailed off.

Fighting back tears, she slid the ring from her hand and dropped it into her father's palm. The Second tried to close his fingers around hers along with the ring. Christine jerked her hand away as if burned. Ernest's face creased. When he spoke, his voice was steady.

"Summons will be sent to—" he began.

The Hall doors swung open. A tall disciple with a close-shaved brown beard stood framed in candlelight. Ernest's face turned as crimson as the man's robe. "We are in council, disciple."

"Apologies, Second," the man said, dipping his head. "You wanted to be notified if . . ." Noticing Tyrnen, he trailed off. His head bobbed deeper. "I am sorry, Eternal Flame. I did not see you. I—"

"Let the Lady guide your tongue, man!" Ernest said.

The disciple gathered himself. "Of course. Second. Eternal Flame. I thought you should know: Torel's Ward is two leagues outside the northern gate."

Christine left the room at a run. Behind her, Tyrnen turned to Keelian Faltan, and the red-haired woman followed on her heels.

Chapter 20:
The Steward

FROM THE HILLTOP, the Ward's encampment looked like a field of snow. Below, rows of white tents stretched northward. Straight lines of brown and green ran between them, like seams in a blanket. Fifty thousand men clad in steel and snow jingled and clanged as they hurried up and down those lines, rainfall plastering hair and clothes to their bodies, or sitting beneath awnings eating from platters of meat and roasted vegetables, or sharpening swords or axe heads or spear points, or leading horses by bridles to where the animals were penned in neat lines of rippling brown and black flesh, tails swishing irritably.

The flies had found their way over from the latrines. The latrines had appeared within seconds. The one hundred Touched who had marched from Calewind alongside the Ward kindled from the Lady's light—threadbare as it was—to cut through the earth like hot steel through cloth. They milled about, red-robed forms ducking in and out of tents or stopping by fires and holding out their hands. For warmth? Possibly.

Lieutenant Moser spoke up. "Satisfied, sir?" he shouted over rain that poured down in sheets.

Colonel Brendon Greagor offered no reply. Fat, cold raindrops pressed his dark hair to his head. Beneath him, his horse waited patiently. One of his ears twitched. Otherwise Acker remained statuesque. The sky might as well have been blue and bright with the Lady's warmth instead of grey and pouring down rain. Acker was more disciplined than many of the sergeants they had left in Calewind. Brendon's hands tightened on the reins. Had General Calderon been present, he would have been the one inspecting the encampment from afar. *At the Lady's shoulder*, Edmund liked to say. Had liked to say. The general had not been himself of late.

He should be here. I should be by his side.

His left hand shook. Without looking around, Brendon gripped his left wrist until the shaking subsided.

Lieutenant Moser raised a spyglass and stood in his stirrups to look west. "No sign of any wildlanders," he said, squinting through the brass tube.

"Clansfolk," Brendon corrected automatically, still staring ahead.

Moser lowered the tube. "Right, sir. Sorry, sir. I'm just a little on edge."

Brendon pressed his lips into a line. His sword, not yet named, hung at his left hip. He resisted the urge to throttle its hilt. Another habit of the general's, one Brendon had picked up by spending so much time with the man. His left hand resumed trembling. Once again, he squeezed it until it fell still. "Should we return?" Brendon asked. Too late he realized the mistake.

Moser eyed him. "That's up to you, sir."

Without another word, Brendon flicked Acker's reins. The horse ambled forward. Moser fell in beside him. They rode wordlessly down the hillside toward palisades leading into rows between tents. Three Wardsmen stood abreast before each palisade. Most had their heads together. They saw the colonel approaching and straightened. Brendon resisted the urge to send Acker into a gallop. Such a spectacle would communicate imminent danger to the Ward. He had to move at a stately pace. The Wardsmen snapped crisp salutes as he passed through, hands bunched into fists, thumbs across fingers to form an "H."

The sounds and smells of an encampment washed over him. Booted footsteps sloshed through earth churned to mud. The scent of meat wafted out from tent flaps. Conversations flowed together into a buzz. Blades rasped on whetstones. Every so often they came to crossroads, and the goings-on were the same at each: Men stripped to the waist cracking wooden practice swords together, weapon racks standing full nearby. Mud stained their pants, but no one lost his footing. The clansfolk were unlikely to call off the war due to poor weather.

"With your leave, sir," Moser said. Brendon looked around. They were halfway through the encampment. He nodded, and the lieutenant turned his horse down a side lane and headed toward a tent at the far end. A hollowness opened in Brendon's stomach. He continued on, snapping off salutes, giving orders in a firm tone just shy of a bark, dressing down men whose steel and snow did not appear freshly pressed and polished.

Two Wardsmen and a Disciple of Dawn stood just inside his tent, framed in the doorway so that they could see anyone who approached. Brendon swung one leg over Acker and stepped down to the ground. Before his second foot followed the first, two other Wardsmen had appeared to lead the animal away. "See that he's fed," Brendon called.

"Aye, sir," they called, and hurried off.

Brendon stepped into his tent. Rain drummed against the canvas, which did not sag. Northern tents sloped like northern buildings so that snow and water ran off. The Wardsmen stepped forward, saluted, and launched into reports. Brendon listened as he stripped out of wet clothes and changed into fresh steel and snow.

"Would you care for a fire, Colonel?" Cinder Ellis asked.

"Please," Brendon said. He watched the Touched from the corner of one eye as the man stepped over to a pit surrounded by lone stone walls. The man kindled from a nearby lamp. There was a *whoosh* and flames licked out from over the top of the stones. Slowly, heat suffused the cavernous tent. It was far from luxurious. The space was filled with tables covered in maps and diagrams, weapons, clothes, untouched meals, chairs scattered here and there. Torel's Ward had stopped only an hour ago. They had marched long and hard between four jumps—shifts, the Touched call them—carried out by the four dozen disciples who had travelled with them. Scouts had brought no reports of Darinians anywhere nearby: Not approaching Sharem, nor within it. The western district sat abandoned, they said.

The disciples confirmed those reports based on intelligence from their own sources within Sharem. They cooperated with the

Ward not out of any loyalty to Torel or the Crown, but on the Eternal Flame's command. Still. Brendon watched the Touched who had started the fire as he returned to his post in the entrance. Beside him, the Wardsmen droned on and on: food stocks were high, disciples had boiled water for safe drinking, shelters had been built for the horses, weapons were counted, all present, and being sharpened.

Brendon held up a hand and the reports stopped. He started to phrase his command as a question, then caught himself. "I need a moment."

The Wardsmen clapped fists to chests in the Gairden salute and marched to the entrance. Brendon went to his cot and forced himself to sit down slowly. He wanted to drop. He wanted to sleep for a day, if not a week. He wanted—

"Sir."

Brendon's feet cried out for rest, but he hauled himself upright. "Yes?"

The Wardsmen by the entrance stepped aside, revealing Cinder Keelian Faltan of Torel's Dawn. Her emerald robe and red hair appeared untouched by the rain. The sight of her set his heart racing, but not with desire.

"Cinder Faltan," he said. "Why aren't you in Calewind?"

"I was only yesterday, Colonel. I stand before you now at the behest of the Eternal Flame."

Despite the warmth of the tent, Brendon suppressed a chill. "Tyrnen Symorne is here?"

"The Eternal Flame"—he did not miss her emphasis—"is in Sharem, with orders for me to pass on to you. You are steward in the absence of your crown and general, are you not?" Without waiting for him to answer, she continued. "The Eternal Flame's intelligence informs him that the clans draw near. Prepare for battle at Dawnrise, if not sooner." She turned to go.

Brendon's eyes did a quick sweep of the tent, landed on his sword. It stood propped in a chair, too far away from him to retrieve nonchalantly. "The Ward does not march on your Eternal Flame's command," he said. Then the oddity of her words struck him. "Why did he seek me out? Shouldn't you be speaking with General Calderon?"

"General Calderon is not here, as the Eternal Flame well knows," Keelian said patiently.

Brendon's lips formed a thin line. Of course, Tyrnen would know that. The Flame had been present when General Calderon had ordered Brendon to lead the Ward south to Sharem. That order had been given minutes after Prince Aidan had returned to Calewind and the general had arrested him and had him dragged off to the depths. The severity of Edmund's reaction had surprised Brendon almost as much as the fact that he had given the order at Tyrnen's bidding.

Brendon realized Keelian was studying him, waiting for him to speak. "I will take the Flame's orders under advisement, but will wait for further news from General Calderon."

Keelian's expression became amused. "Have you forgotten that your general and crown gave the Eternal Flame consent for him to speak on their behalf?"

Brendon's throat moved. He had not forgotten, particularly because he had not been by Edmund's side when consent had been given. He had found out about it later, from Tyrnen himself, with Edmund standing silently by his side the way Lieutenant Moser had stood by Brendon on the hilltop.

Relief, faint but growing stronger, eased the lump in his throat. Tyrnen did speak for the Crown and general. That bothered Brendon and was further testament to the odd behavior of both Annalyn and Edmund since Aidan's . . . incident on his birthday. Perhaps odd behavior was to be expected. There was no precedent for Heritage rejecting Gairden blood.

Still. Tyrnen commanded the Touched, and Disciples of Dawn marched alongside Torel's Ward. Perhaps Edmund saw an opportunity to consolidate command.

Perhaps.

Across the tent, Keelian nodded as if the matter had been decided. "I will tell the Eternal Flame you complied. He will be pleased." She said this as if Brendon should be pleased that Tyrnen would be pleased. "This evening, he will explain further what—"

There was a loud thud from the doorway. The flaps at the entryway billowed as if caught in a sudden storm. The Wardsmen at the entrance ripped swords from scabbards and brought them together over the entryway. Brendon's attention fell on a Sallnerian woman, young and beautiful with long, silky black hair untouched by the weather. Her eyes were fierce. One hand gripped a parchment so tightly her knuckles were white.

"I need to see Colonel Brendon Greagor," the woman said loudly.

"Did you make an appointment?" one Wardsman asked.

"I have orders from—"

Cinder Ellis came forward. "You attempted to shift into this tent," he said coldly.

The woman scowled. "I was told I could find the colonel here."

"Do you have a day pass?" Ellis asked.

Her scowl twisted into rage. She raised her right hand. "I am no stormrobe. I am Christine Lorden, and I am a Cinder. You will not speak to me like—" She cut off, noticing her finger was bare. Brendon could just make out a pale line of flesh, like where a ring would have rested.

"Young lady," Cinder Ellis said. "You will address disciples and members of Torel's Dawn with respect, or we will have no choice but to Tie you and confine you to your domicile."

The woman raised her right palm. Lamps in the tent flickered. Shouts broke out as Wardsmen raised swords and Cinders Keelian and Ellis raised hands. Brendon went to his blade. Touching its hilt infused him with confidence. He stepped in front of Keelian, holding the sword. He did not raise it. It hung limply at his side, but did not go unnoticed.

"Colonel?" Keelian said.

"I will grant this woman an audience."

"Sir," one of the Wardsmen said, "she materialized out of thin air and—"

"She carries orders from your general," Brendon said. All eyes fell on the woman. She held the envelope aloft like a shield. Edmund's crest, a "C" that cradled the Gairden "H" with Heritage sheathed through the middle bar, sealed the flap.

Keelian spoke first. "This Sallnerian stands in judgment before the Hall of Morning," she said. As if Brendon should know what that was supposed to mean.

"Tyrnen is on trial," Christine fired back.

"You would show disrespect toward—"

"Silence!" Brendon roared. Everyone stared at him in surprise. "This is my tent. We will comport ourselves according to our stations." Swords and hands lowered, all save Christine's. Brendon glared at her.

She sneered. "I'm just a snake. If I agree I'll only deceive you later. Isn't that right?"

Keelian laughed darkly. The woman's eyes flashed, but Brendon spoke first. "I see you, Christine. Now lower your palm."

Christine's mouth fell open. Her hand dropped.

"Colonel," Ellis said, "I must advise strongly against—"

"I know what you must advise strongly against, but I have made my decision. She carries a missive from General Calderon."

"A forgery," Keelian declared. "Nothing but a fraud."

"Like your Eternal Flame," Christine said.

Keelian's hands twitched as if she intended to raise them. She balled them into fists. Her lip curled. "Read the damn missive. Let us be done with this farce."

Brendon eyed her. He waited several moments, then extended his hand. Christine handed it to him. He took it to his desk. The others followed in a tight cluster, save for Christine, who hung back, arms folded beneath her breasts. He sat, broke the seal with a knife, set it aside, and read.

Bren,

Do not engage with Darinia. Negotiate peace when they arrive. Aidan holds the sword. I will explain more when I join you. I will be coming from the east.

Given my absence, I appoint you general of Torel's Ward until such time as you see fit to appoint a successor. I will continue to serve Torel as counsellor to the crown.

You march with Disciples of Dawn at your side. Always remember that the disciples and Wardsmen serve the Lady together, but in their own way.

I have every faith you will serve in the post of general with honor.

Edmund
Counsellor to the Crown of the North
"Valorous"

Brendon's left hand trembled.

Keelian thrust out a hand. "I have the right to read it and report to—"

Brendon handed it to her. Keelian's eyes scanned it. "It is from

General Calderon," she said, sounding surprised. Her visage darkened as her eyes moved down the missive.

"There," Christine called from where the Wardsmen watched her by the entrance. "A northerner said it, so you can be sure it's true."

Stunned silence. Keelian folded the letter and held it. For a moment, Brendon thought she intended to set it aflame. Then she handed it back to him. "Those are not the orders the Eternal Flame sent," Keelian said finally.

"They were never my orders, Cinder." His voice came out clearly and evenly. Right then he felt emboldened. "You can tell the Eternal Flame I said so, or send him to me, and I will tell him the same."

"Send him?" Keelian repeated, as if the words were in a foreign tongue. "Without your compliance, Colonel, we may be forced to withdraw our support from the Ward." She gave Brendon a moment to digest the weight of his words. Brendon did not need that long.

"You will address me as general, Cinder. And you may withdraw if that is what the Eternal Flame decides is best." *Always remember that the disciples and Wardsmen serve the Lady together, but in their own way.*

Keelian did not respond at first. Her eyes grew faraway. She gave a slight shake of her head. Her eyes were clear. "I will remain in the encampment as the Eternal Flame's steward, to see that his wishes are carried out."

"You mean the Lady's wishes," Brendon said.

"They are one and the same," Keelian replied. She turned to the disciple. "If you have no other duties here"—Ellis colored at the word duties—"I would ask you for a tour."

Ellis started to turn toward Brendon, then thought better of it. "Of course, Cinder," he said. They withdrew without asking permission.

Christine turned to go.

"Wait," Brendon called.

The swords barred her way again. Her back stiffened. "I am not a bird to be trapped in a cage, General," she said over her shoulder. "I have delivered Edmund's orders. I am free. To go," she added.

"Where did you see him? The general?"

216

"He was in Sharem just yesterday."

I will be coming from the east. "Where did he go?" Brendon asked.

Christine gave no answer. "Speak up," one of the Wardsmen said gruffly. She glowered and remained silent.

"You don't have to answer," Brendon said.

"I know."

He raised his eyebrows. "Why are you so hostile?"

"Because . . ."

"Because I'm Torelian." He gave her a half smile. "You must see the irony."

Christine's lips became a thin line. "Why did you say that before?"

"Say what?"

"That you see me."

Brendon raised and lowered a shoulder. "To calm the situation. You seemed angry."

"I wasn't," she said. "Not until I set foot in your camp and was treated like a thief from the moment I—"

"You did shift," he pointed out.

"So? The disciples do it all the time, I'll bet. But of course, they're Torelian, so it is allowed."

"No. Because we're aware of them. You arrived unannounced."

"So did Keelian."

"Fair enough. My point is, I have not treated you unfairly."

"We've only just met. Give it time."

Brendon smiled. "How do you know the general?"

Christine wet her lips. "I am Aidan's . . . friend."

"The prince is well?" He thought over what he had just said. "He holds Heritage?"

Christine seemed to swell with pride. "He does." All the pride rushed out of her. Her pretty features twisted. "He is in the west. With Nichel."

The wolf daughter? A thousand questions assailed Brendon. He chose one from the maelstrom. "And his mother?"

Christine's tone softened. "You should wait for Edmund."

Anxiety crept back in. "I will." He waved at the Wardsmen. "Let her pass. And apologize for how you treated her."

The men looked poleaxed, but mumbled apologies. Christine

appraised them coolly and swept toward the exit. Before she could step outside, she paused. "Thank you."

Brendon knew for what. "You're welcome."

"Why aren't you like the others?"

Brendon knew what that meant, too. "Edmund—General Calderon—and I grew up together in the lower north. We did not come from wealth. Far from it. We had a hard life. Not as hard, I'm sure, as your friends on the Bridge," he appended when her eyes flashed, "but hard. Life is different closer to Calewind."

Christine nodded slowly. "Thank you," she said again. Then she stepped out into the rain and promptly vanished. Raindrops splattered against the air above her, as if striking a glass ceiling.

Brendon stared after her. Overhead, the sky darkened. Absently, he gripped his left hand.

Chapter 21:
Visitor

CHRISTINE WALKED SHAREM'S eastern district in a daze, ignoring the inns and taverns and shops with painted rooftops, men and women and children in costumes and face paint, arms thrown over heads in a futile attempt to shield themselves from rain that fell in cold sheets. For a moment she considered going back to Domicile 137. Back home. Back to her old blanket, to memories of early childhood, of Garrett and her mother. The thought of facing Lam turned her feet into blocks of stone.

No matter how high she rose, no matter who she loved, people would only ever see her as a snake. Terrence was one of them. So was Lam. The unfairness of it gnawed at her. In recent memory, only two people had treated her as a person. Aidan, and Brendon Greagor.

I see you, Christine.

What did that mean? Never mind. *He can't be trusted. If I hadn't been carrying a missive from his general he'd have let the disciples throw me back onto the Bridge.*

A fist closed around her heart. Aidan. She needed him. Christine looked west. *I can't go to him, and he can't come to me. He's out there. Safe, for the moment.*

She huffed out a breath. Aidan had been in Darinia too long. Then again, convincing Nichel of his innocence would not be an easy matter. Christine had seen evidence of the bloodshed first hand, just outside Sharem's walls.

I swear to the Lady, if that wolf-girl harms one hair on his head I'll rip her fangs out with my bare hands and gut her with them.

Christine stepped under a portico and watched rain fall in a curtain. Thunder cracked and lightning flashed. She had delivered Edmund's message, leaving her with nothing to do than wait to see how the Ward and clans would get along, and for her father to decide her fate. Waiting. So much Dawn-damned waiting. For the first time since she and Garrett had left Sharem with nothing but the clothes on their backs, she felt lost. Displaced.

Do you know what you need? It was the pampered voice, as she called it. The voice that had begun speaking up after she amassed a tidy sum and could afford the finer things in Crotaria. Nice rooms, large beds, edible delicacies. *You need a bath.*

But I've already taken a bath today, Christine replied. A grin teased the corners of her mouth.

So what? You deserve another. And a drink of slush to go with it.

Drinking in the tub? How decadent.

How perfect, you mean.

Christine stepped back out into the storm and released her prayer for a heat bubble. Rain drenched her, soaking her clothes and plastered her hair to her face, her shoulders, her arms, her back. She lifted her face and laughed. The drops were fat and soft, not small and hard like stones. The Lady's irritable mood could dampen her skin, but never her spirit.

Christine followed curving streets back to the Eastern Pearl. The inn was lit up like a torch when she rounded a corner and saw it, the glow of firelight spilling out of every window. She picked up her pace, hurried through the front door, and ran shivering to where a fire roared in the mantel that stretched the length of the common room. The flames ebbed ever so slightly. A long moment later and her clothes were dry. She could feel eyes on her as she strode back across the common room. Some bored between her shoulder blades like knife points. Others were admiring and stoked her confidence.

At the top of the ornate staircase, Christine stopped, one hand lingering on the polished banister. The topmost floor of the Pearl was quiet and dimly lit. There might have been murmuring from behind closed doors lining the hall, but the rain pelting the roof smothered them. *So why is my heart beating so fast?*

Slowly, she moved down the length of the hall to her room. The door was ajar. She pushed it open. A fire murmured in the hearth across from her bed. Tyrnen sat in the padded chair where she had laid out her clothes for the day, holding his cane on his lap.

Christine did not stop to think or ask questions. She raised a hand to the fire and felt heat suffuse her, coursing through her bloodstream as the fire cowed. She pointed at Tyrnen.

"That won't be necessary."

For reasons she could not explain, Christine did not lash out. She could have. She perceived no cramping in the stomach, the painful sensation that signaled to a Touched that he or she had been Tied. Her finger remained levelled at the Eternal Flame's chest.

"What do you want?"

"In the short-term, I would like for you to return the heat you stole. I am an old man, Christine. My skin is as thin as parchment."

Christine narrowed her eyes. He was lying. They both knew the real reason she dared not strike out against him. The trial. She waved a hand at the hearth. Heat rushed out of her. In the same instant the fire leaped up, twice as high as it had been, then settled.

"We have nothing more to say," she said.

Tyrnen crossed his legs. "I was surprised to find you here."

Christine bristled. "I can afford this room. You know I can."

"Of course. I paid you handsomely."

"I was wealthy before I met you. And I don't want to talk about that. That part of my life is finished."

"I was not referring to the room, Christine. I spoke more broadly. Here, as in Sharem. Then it struck me. It is obvious, now that I think about it. You are here because Aidan thought you would be the best choice to speak with the Second." Tyrnen nodded. "Very wise. He's grown into a discerning young man." He looked almost wistful.

"No thanks to you."

His features hardened. "Don't be foolish. He owes much to me. Whatever my intentions, I raised Aidan as surely as his mother and father."

"Then why did you betray him?"

"Even the Eternal Flame answers to higher powers."

"You don't mean the Lady. You mean Luria Thalamahn." Christine took another step into the room. "What would my father say if he knew who really stood to gain from the conclave's verdict? That body may be yours, but you forfeited your mind and soul centuries ago. Aidan told me. You're nothing but a hound. A lapdog."

The shadows in the room deepened. The flames in the hearth shrank as if touched by a breeze. Christine opened herself to light, ready to kindle. Tyrnen laughed.

"What's so funny?" she snapped.

"Did you know, Christine, that some say Luria Thalamahn did not go along willingly with her husband's experiments? Some say she was one of his experiments. His first, in fact."

"I thought you were Luria," she said, the room's deepening shadows forgotten.

"No. Nearly, I will admit. I keep her close." His left hand jerked toward his side, as if intent on seeking something there.

"Or she keeps you close," Christine said.

He shrugged. "I meant what I said before. You could join Torel's Dawn. You are more than capable enough."

Her mouth twisted in distaste. "I'll have nothing to do with—"

"Whatever you think of me, my dear, know this: I am as powerful as you think I am. More so. And I do not recruit lightly. Those Cinders were the brightest minds of their time. Even receiving a hint of an invitation to join is an honor for any Cinder."

"Except according to you, my Cinder Band was a lie."

"It was not." Tyrnen uncrossed his leg and crossed the other. "Which is precisely why I am surprised to see you here. You so callously dismiss me as a lapdog, yet it appears we are both doing the bidding of our masters."

Christine felt her nails dig into her palms. "I volunteered for this. I wanted to . . ." She swallowed. *I'm letting him bait me.*

"A bold decision," he said, rolling the cane in his palms. "Foolish, though. You do know about Aidan and Nichel, I presume. They are betrothed. Unless I miss my guess, that upsets your plans for the future considerably."

Christine's voice shook with anger. "Their parents made that promise before Aidan could even form words."

Tyrnen's bushy brow lifted. "I always took you for such a confident woman. Beauty, intelligence, poise . . . It has only been a few short weeks since we last spoke, and on friendlier terms. Did Aidan manage to wrap you around his finger so quickly? Then again, I am not surprised. The boy has a way about him."

His voice dropped to nearly a whisper, as though he were talking to himself, and his gaze went through her. "I loved him like a grandson. That's true, whatever you think. The boy saw more of me than he did his parents. Mother running a kingdom, father leading an army that had nothing better to do than put down barbarian invasions along the coastlines. Aidan and I took to each other right away. I was hard on him, but I am hard on all my students. Him less than others, I admit. He charmed his way out of countless lessons, not that he needed many of them. He's the fastest learner to study under my tutelage, a breath quicker even than you."

Tyrnen smiled faintly. "I don't need to tell you about Aidan's charm. You know all about it. So does she, you know. When her father would pay the north a visit, Nichel trailed Aidan like a shadow. Laughed at every word he said. Fawned over him. He loved every moment. Even the most humble of men have egos that swell when fed, and Aidan is far from humble. He is susceptible to beauty, and Nichel has grown into a woman as beautiful as her father was ruthless—"

Christine's left hand clasped around her midriff. "Get out." Her right hung limply, or so she hoped the old man believed. Her body was weightless, an empty vessel waiting to be filled with light and ready to hurl fire.

To her surprise, Tyrnen braced himself on his cane and stood. He ambled across the room to the door, leaving his back exposed. Christine would never have another opportunity. It would not take much, no more than a sliver of firelight. The Eternal Flame was flesh and blood. Flames crackled in the hearth. Rain beat down on shingles and ran down the walls of the inn like tears.

"You won't kill me, Christine."

She jumped. His words were soft, barely audible over the rain.

"You need me alive," he finished.

Her throat moved. "Why?"

"You stand in the heart of Crotaria. Kill me, and every Touched on this continent will chase you from one end to the other. Aidan would be obligated to join in the hunt, with his wolf by his side. It's almost poetic: Torel and Darinia unified against Sallner. Again."

"Go."

Tyrnen went. Christine stared at the spot where he had stood, listening to the tap-tap-tap of his cane down the corridor. A moment later, her skin warmed. She poked her head out into the corridor. Tyrnen was gone. Shifted. *To where?* Probably the Temple of Dawn. He was safe there, nestled to the Lady's bosom while her father and his shade-cursed conclave deliberated testimonies.

Christine hugged herself. The fire still burned, but she no longer felt warm. Tyrnen was gone, but his words lingered like frost over spring grass. She dropped onto her bed. Heedless of her boots, dry but caked with dirt, she hugged her legs to her chest. She tucked her chin on her knees and stared. She did not see the door, the polished wooden paneling, the luxurious carpets and bedspread. She saw Aidan and his wolf. His betrothed. Smiling at one another. Laughing the way they had as children, if Tyrnen could be believed.

Since when do you trust Tyrnen Symorne, you Dawn-blinded idiot?

That made her feel better, and so did the Lady's grand reappearance. Blinking, she looked up. The room brightened as storm clouds parted and glorious, mood-buoying light bled through the patina of water on her window. Christine crawled over on her knees and looked out, smiling. Within minutes, Sharem's east quarter was so busy she never would have guessed a storm had driven everyone inside.

Her smile faded as red-robed disciples emerged, coming from the temple, from side streets, from every which way, mingling with Leastonians in their bright clothing. Her hands tightened on the window sill when she saw disciples clad in green robes. Torel's Dawn. *Why had they lied?*

Christine knew why. They were allied with Tyrnen. *Willingly? Or because he holds their souls in his pocket?* She leaned forward, letting her forehead touch cool glass. Getting involved in a trial only stalled what Tyrnen could have accomplished with a simple command. He was the Eternal Flame. The Touched were his.

A malaise settled over her. She felt as if she had descended into the deepest, darkest cave, with no hope of escape. Christine took slow, even breaths. Each inhalation drew hope back into her body, each exhale a rejection of Tyrnen's darkness. She tapped her fingers against the glass. Tyrnen's intentions were obvious, now that she had the clarity to see them. He was here to stall. Aidan needed the Touched's support to stand a chance against the undead.

Her eyes narrowed. *Aidan and the Darinian she-dog.*

Growling, she turned from the window. She loved Aidan, and he loved her. He had said so.

No, he hadn't. Not explicitly.

Christine closed her eyes and recalled their last conversation, less than a day gone. *"When this is over."* Those were his exact *words. What could he mean?* That they would be together. Obviously.

Besides, Christine had shared an experience with Aidan that the wolf cub would never be able to take away from her. *I'll tear her throat out first.*

She forced herself to laugh. *Tear her throat out? Dawn! Who's the wolf now?*

Christine took a few more moments to chide herself. Jealousy over a man? She was above such behavior. *And there is no reason to worry.*

"I need to get out of this room," she said aloud. Throwing a green cloak around her shoulders, she swept out the door and down the stairs.

Chapter 22:
Apologies

DANIEL'S EYES SHOT open. For a moment he thought he was back in the cabin, and that the hammering sound was the harbinger pounding on the closed door, demanding to be let in. Its arrival was a mercy. Garrett Lorden would have to stop hitting him, kicking him, scratching and clawing him, to confer with Tyrnen's servant.

The hammering came again, louder and more insistent. Daniel blinked and focused on his surroundings. A large chamber, ornately furnished. Bedsheets woven from silk, and a thick duvet stuffed with down feathers, all white as snow. *Aidan's bedchambers.*

Aidan's door shuddered in its frame. "Who in Dawn's name is it?" he yelled.

"Alix Merrifalls."

Daniel glanced at the window. The panes were dark and coated in a thin glaze of frost. *Spring, indeed.* "It's not even Dawnrise. Go away."

The doorknob rattled, and the hammering continued.

"All right, all right!" he roared, throwing away the covers and wincing as his bare feet made contact with the stone floor. Pushing himself off the bed, he hopped across the expansive room and threw open the door. Alix held a torch in one hand. She wore sturdy leather boots, breeches, shirt, and gloves. Her chopped, auburn hair framed her face unevenly, the right side hanging longer than the left. Her eyes were bright, like emeralds set against snow.

If his open-mouthed stare bothered her, Alix gave no sign. She glanced down, coughed, and looked away. Daniel followed her gaze and realized he was bare from the waist up. His trousers were wrinkled from sleep. Freckles dappled his chest and forearms. His biceps were well-formed from years of working fields and running drills.

His cheeks bloomed scarlet. He wasn't sure whether to slam the door in her face—or just stand there. He just stood there, trying and failing to look unflustered.

Alix met his gaze. "Good morning."

"What are you doing here?" he blurted.

"I came to apologize."

"For what?"

"For lying to you."

Regaining his composure, he gave her a shocked look. "You mean your name isn't Rufus? I'm astounded. Simply astounded."

Alix brushed away a strand of hair. "Rufus is my father's name. I wasn't sure if I should use it. Someone might have recognized it and connected it to Jak. But I couldn't think of anything else."

"You should have thought harder. A false name makes a better disguise than a mask," he quipped by rote.

She arched an eyebrow. "You sound as if you speak from experience."

Daniel mentally cursed himself. *Loose tongues topple realms.* Another favorite saying of his old guildmaster. "Just common sense."

"It fooled you. You say Jak was your friend, yet you knew nothing about a sibling."

"Jak didn't talk much of home." He regretted the words as soon as they leaped from his tongue.

"He never mentioned me?" Alix asked, forehead crinkling.

"Not that I recall," Daniel admitted.

Swallowing hard, she looked away. "He couldn't wait to leave."

"Look," Daniel said, softening his tone, "I know the old walrus assigned you to—"

"Old walrus?"

"The lieutenant," he said in a near whisper, looking up and down the corridor as if Anders might have folded his barrel-sized frame and hid behind a sconce.

"Oh." She giggled.

"I appreciate your diligence, but we don't need to be at our post until Dawnrise."

"That's not so far off. I want to be there before the morning canticle. I hate morning canticle." Alix slipped past him and into Aidan's bedroom. He gritted his teeth and closed the door.

"This is the Crown's room?" she asked, gazing around.

"It is. Who told you I was here?"

"I asked around. Why are you using it? Are you and he . . . you know . . ."

"I'm afraid I don't."

Alix glanced at the bed, then back at him. Her meaning sank in like a needle. "What! No! Nothing like that."

"There's nothing wrong with it," she said, spinning to face him with her arms crossed.

"I didn't say there was. I'm just not that way."

"Jak was that way. There was nothing wrong with him. He just had different tastes."

"It makes no difference to me. He was my friend."

"Thank you." She uncrossed her arms. "How do you know the Crown?"

"Aidan and I are friends. Have been since boyhood."

"Really?" She gave him a weighing look, as if reevaluating an opinion.

Daniel puffed out his chest. "Well, if you must know, he thinks of me as an older brother. I'm sort of his keeper."

"Then why aren't you keeping him now?"

"Would you mind waiting outside?" he snapped.

Alix swallowed again and sat on the edge of Aidan's bed. "To tell you the truth, I don't want to be alone." Her eyes were wet.

Daniel cleared his throat. "Fine. That's fine. I'll be ready shortly." He busied himself gathering his steel and snow, then stepped behind Aidan's wardrobe screen to dress.

"I came here to bring Jak home," Alix said loudly. "Even though he would have resisted."

Daniel said nothing. He remembered what Alix had said about

Jak not talking about home, and thought he understood why.

"I'm doing this to feel close to him," Alix continued. "Thank you for helping me."

"I didn't," he said, stepping out from behind the screen, armor jangling as he moved. "You grafted yourself onto my hip."

Her green eyes were cool, her tears shimmering like ice. "It's the least you could do."

"For what?"

"I owed you an apology. You owed me your life. I killed that . . . that harbinger."

"I had the situation in hand," he snapped.

She rolled her eyes. "And Kahltan is warmer than the Lady of Dawn. I can handle myself in a fight, and now the lieutenant knows that."

"Wardsmen train for years. Just because you banged sticks together on a farm with your brother doesn't mean—"

Alix stiffened. Daniel raised his hands. "I'm sorry. I shouldn't have said that."

Taking a deep breath, she stood. "It's all right. You really did look like you were in trouble. That face in the lantern . . . you looked like you'd seen . . ." She laughed humorlessly. "Like you'd seen a ghost."

"Garrett Lorden is very much alive," he said tightly.

"Who is he?"

"He serves the Eternal Flame and sits at the head of the army outside Calewind's walls."

Her features sharpened. "He killed my brother." It was not a question.

"In a way," Daniel said slowly.

"Then he's the one I'm fighting."

"Yes, but not as a member of the Ward."

She raised her chin. "I don't want to wear the steel and snow." She hesitated. When she continued, her voice had hardened. "No, that's not true. I do."

"You know the law."

"The law says all sorts of things. Mostly things pertaining to women and men like my brother. It isn't fair."

"No, it's not. But I'm not in a position to change it."

"You're friends with the Crown. He could—"

"And maybe he will, but he's got other problems to deal with at the moment, and I'm trying to help him."

Alix shifted from foot to foot. "Jakob and I grew up working. Up at Dawnrise, mucking out stables, feeding chickens, milking cows, harvesting crops. It was a hard life, but a peaceful one."

Daniel waited silently.

"Jakob and I didn't want it, though. We talked of leaving home all the time. Of going out into the world and having adventures. But working the farm was . . ." She lifted her arms, flexing her fingers as if trying to grasp at an elusive concept.

"Constant," he finished quietly. "Steady. There."

Alix's face lit up. "Right! I didn't care for it at first, but I got used to it. I had to. Cows and chickens and pigs don't care if you're happy, or sad, or sick, or tired." Alix tucked a frayed lock of hair behind one ear. It slipped free, too short to find a hold. "Does that make sense?"

Daniel nodded. "It was the same for me. For a while, anyway."

"What changed?"

He opened his mouth to answer, closed it. "Long story."

She nodded, accepting. "I thought if Jak came home, he could help us. I was too late to save him, and I can't do anything to help my folks back in Gotik. Do you think they'll evacuate the village soon?"

For a moment, Daniel stared blankly. Then he remembered his conversation with *Rufus* in the Crown's Promise, and his proclamation that he had given the order to evacuate. "I'm sure," he said quickly.

"I hope so. Calewind's gates are closed. Do they only open when evacuees arrive?" She nodded before he could answer. "That makes sense." Her chest hitched. "I need to help. I need to do something. I can't just sit in a tavern, waiting and wondering."

"There are ways to help besides fighting on the front lines."

"I told you, I—"

"The Wardsmen are trying to protect people from the monsters outside our gates, and you want to step right into their open jaws. You don't even have a—" He cut off, noticing for the first time the sword at her waist. She thumbed the hilt. Daniel recognized it. "Jakob's," he said.

"I took it last night. It's all I have left of him."

He sighed. "You can come with me."

Her lips tugged upward in a trembling smile. "Really?" Daniel gestured at the door for her to step out. She paused. "I really am sorry for deceiving you."

He plucked his *Sard'tara* from where it lay propped against the wall beside Aidan's bed. "No, I'm sorry for what you're about to do."

Alix gave him a curious look as he pulled Aidan's door closed.

Chapter 23:
Brilliant Ideas

DANIEL PASSED THROUGH Sunfall's corridors and galleries in long strides, holding his *Sard'tara* so it was parallel to him. Grey light filtered through arched windows. Servants in snowy livery dusted portraits and furnishings, carried linens and trays of food.

He glanced over his shoulder. "Keep up," he said—and realized Alix Merrifalls walked beside him, matching his pace step for step. Her stride spoke to a childhood spent racing across fields for fun. The duty they approached was not fun, and she was none the wiser.

Overhead, bells broke out in clangorous song. Daniel could hear bells ringing throughout Calewind, as they would be throughout every city in the north all the way down to Sharem. Servants froze, knelt gracefully, set aside baskets and trays and rags and soaps, and pressed their foreheads to the gleaming floor. Within the palace and without, every voice chanted in near-perfect concert.

Voices tapered off after three verses, those that had fallen out of harmony trailing like echoes in a cave. Daniel had not paused—Wardsmen were on duty, and thus exempt from canticles—but noticed his were the only footsteps he heard. Slowing, he saw Alix a few paces back, halfway between standing upright and kneeling. Daniel gestured for her to follow. She did, looking grateful. After several moments, dozens of voices repeated the prayer. From the corner of his eye, Daniel watched Alix's face turn a deeper shade of red with every word.

By the time they reached the great doors of the throne room, the bells had stopped and palace activity had returned to normal. Daniel frowned. No Wardsmen stood guard outside the entrance, nor in the spacious vestibule that led in from the southern courtyard. *Dawn, we're shorthanded.*

He threw open the doors and was greeted by familiar sights. Galleries ringed the room. A row of torches hung in brackets between each gallery, unlit during daylight hours. Four great stained-glass windows, one in the middle of each wall, admitted pre-Dawn light. A red carpet split the floor, unrolling from the doors and up a handful of stairs to the foot of two thrones, one larger than the other and bearing the same name as the monarch who should have been seated there.

Daniel closed the doors and faced the thrones. A pang of loss tightened his chest. He was used to seeing Annalyn and Edmund far across the way, beaming at him in greeting over the heads of Hands of the Crown and supplicants crowding the thrones. Most of all, he missed his friend. He had a sudden vision of Aidan sitting the Crown of the North, looking troubled. Frightened, even. Then he glanced up, noticed Daniel, and a grateful expression smoothed his features. *"Thank the Lady you're here,"* Aidan would say. And they would depart Sunfall again, off on another adventure where he was useful and respected.

"What in Dawn's name are you grinning about?"

The gruff voice scattered Daniel's reverie. At the foot of the stairs, a long table sat parallel to the red carpet. Eight sergeants sat four to a side. They were staring at him. Karter Rosen scowled at him from his seat at Lieutenant Anders Magath's right hand. The lieutenant loomed from where he stood at the head of the table, big hands splayed on its surface. "You're late."

"Sorry, sir. I got . . . Sorry."

Anders shook his head, then noticed Alix. "What are you doing here, Merrifalls?"

Facing the lieutenant, she cleared her throat. "Doing what you told me to, sir. Torel is my kingdom. I want to help. Sir."

Anders straightened, weighing her. Weighing them both. Someone at the table coughed. Karter leaned in to whisper something to one of his brothers. The sound of Anders' bare hand slapping the smooth surface was like a crack of thunder. Everyone jumped.

"Did I give you leave to speak, Sergeant Karter?" Anders boomed.

When the last echoes of Anders' question faded, Karter mumbled, "No, sir."

"Repeat?"

"No, sir," Karter said, clearer and louder.

"I will not tolerate men under my command speaking out of turn, and I have even less tolerance for men who would use such language to refer to a lady. Merrifalls is as brave as the Lady is bright, which is to say far braver than you ever have been and ever will be. Where were you at the attack at the gate last night, Sergeant Karter? Probably drunk in a gutter or hiding. Or both. That's my wager. If I had the authority, I would strip that crest off your steel and snow, and hand it to Merrifalls. She may have breasts, but I look around this room and I see two women, may the Lady burn my bones to ash if I'm lying."

Karter stared at his lap. His face was the color of Dawnfall.

Anders looked up. "You are not a member of the Ward, young lady. However, I applaud your courage." His gaze flicked to Daniel. "I remind you that Mistress Merrifalls is under your auspices. She is to obey your orders the moment you give them and not an instant later."

Alix could not possibly have stood any straighter. "Sir! Yes, sir!"

"Good. Now, Wardsman Shirey, brief her on the job at hand so that we can continue with our work."

Alix turned to him, her expression eager. "What do I do?" she whispered.

"Be quiet and stand by the door."

She nodded, looking expectant. "And?"

"That's it."

"That's it?"

He shrugged.

Her words grew heated. "You never told me—"

"Do you find your duties confusing, Merrifalls?" Anders roared.

Alix jumped. "No, sir!"

"Good. Now be quiet and stand by the door."

Daniel choked down a grin. "Told you," he mouthed.

Alix glowered. Ignoring her, Daniel faced forward, *Sard'tara* by his side, the butt against the floor. He heard Alix fidget, then imitate his stance. Glancing over, he saw her fist wrapped around the hilt of Jak's sword. Anders returned his attention to his sergeants. "Where were we?" Even his normal speaking voice sounded like the promise of a storm.

Sergeant Edward Bailey consulted leaves of parchment. "Food and water are plentiful, sir. We can hold out through late spring, maybe even summer."

"Fine. Sergeant Karter. Report."

Karter coughed, shuffled through parchment. "Enlistments are up, sir."

"Up? Every able-bodied man in Calewind has been ordered to report to Sunfall's southern courtyard to receive orders. There are fortifications that needed finishing. Dawn and Dusk, there are fortifications that need starting. The gates are undermanned. The streets are undermanned."

"I know, sir. I'll spread the word: Enlistments are mandatory."

"That they are, Sergeant. So, what's the problem?"

"Word of last night's attack is spreading, sir. People are afraid."

"Afraid of what?" Anders snapped.

"Of . . . of the dead, sir. Of fighting the dead."

Anders pounded a fist on the table. "Where are the bodies of the vagrants that were killed last night?" His eyes flashed around the table until another Wardsman spoke up.

"The graveyard, sir." The man—Sergeant John Steele, middle-aged, his face creased with wrinkles—hesitated, added, "Where you ordered them taken, sir."

Anders pinched the bridge of his nose. "Yes. I forgot."

Daniel stared at Anders. It was the first time he had heard the lieutenant speak at a volume lower than a bark. He sounded tired. Human.

"Spread the word, Sergeant Karter," Anders said. "Able-bodied men will either hold a spear or the bars of a cell down in the depths if they haven't enlisted by noon today."

"Yes, sir."

Anders squared his shoulders, studied the faces of the men

gathered at the table. "How go our defenses?"

Papers fluttered in reply. "Slowly, sir," said Sergeant Gavin Kaurr, whose thick moustache stood out against his pasty face like an ink blot. "We're shorthanded there as well. Palisades have been erected in front of the east and west gates. Construction on a palisade for the south gate began last night immediately after the bodies were cleared away."

"What of the pitch? The trebuchets? The ballistae?" The lieutenant brought a fist crashing onto the tabletop, making every sergeant jump. "Shade and shadow! We'd better be making progress somewhere."

Uncomfortable silence.

"Still under construction, sir," Gavin went on, speaking quickly. "The men are working as fast as they can. We need more help," he finished lamely.

Anders deflated, appearing even more worn than before. "A slight change in plans," he announced. "Inform able-bodied men that they may hold spear, cell bars, or a hammer and nails."

Talk turned to other matters: Plans for defenses in progress and others yet to be built. What to do about the populace in the event the enemy breached Calewind's walls, as they had last night. On fortifications in the city's north district, should they penetrate that deeply into the capital.

Daniel's attention wandered. He opened the hand around his *Sard'tara*, letting the weapon list to one side, then caught it with his other hand. Back and forth he passed it. Overhead, the Lady's light grew brighter, filling the stained-glass windows with color. *I wonder how Aidan is faring with Nichel. They've probably caught up on old times. Now they're assembling the army. Aidan will be riding at its front, Nichel by his side. I should be there with him.*

Leaning back, he pressed an ear to the door. Silence. No surprise there. The doors to the throne room were oak, and triply as thick as other doors in Sunfall, able to withstand a siege should enemies infiltrate the palace. Still, the total absence of sound worried him. He could usually hear something: the low murmur of the voices of his brothers standing guard on the other side, the footsteps of servants, the impatient and imperious voices of nobles.

Alix stirred beside him. He blinked, coming back to himself, to the room, to her. She stood stiffly, fist clenching and unclenching around the hilt of Jak's sword. *She's taking this seriously. More seriously than I am.*

She stared intently across the room. Daniel followed her gaze and let Anders' words sink in. "... the surrounding outposts," the lieutenant was saying. "There's no way to warn them, much less reach them in time. General Calderon gave me orders: Evacuate northern villages and cities, and defend Calewind, but I do not have the manpower to do both." He hesitated. "We can do more here, men."

Silence swallowed his unspoken decision. The other Wardsmen exchanged glances, a different emotion on every visage: anxiety, resignation, disgust. Not at the lieutenant, Daniel realized. At the truth of his words. A spike of fear drove through his chest.

"But, sir," spoke up Sergeant Kieran Wood, Daniel's elder by only two winters. "What about the rest of the Ward?"

"What about them?" Anders snapped.

"So many abominations walk under the Lady's light," Wood said. "Surely the Ward would have encountered them on their march toward Darinia."

"They would have sent word," said Sergeant Raymond Porter, his deep voice uncertain.

"Unless the vagrants killed them to a man," Anders said. "How many Touched remain in Calewind?"

"Most of the city's disciples marched with the Ward, at the Eternal Flame's command," Sergeant Markus Hallwell answered.

Daniel frowned. Much as he loathed to admit it, Tyrnen's plan was quite clever. Emptying Calewind of disciples and soldiers, Touched who specialized in battle, ensured that any Touched left in the capital were unsuited for the coming conflict. That left Calewind at an even greater disadvantage.

"Torel's Dawn travelled with General Calderon to Sharem," Hallwell went on. He hesitated. "Sir, a force the size of the Ward could not move without attracting attention. There must be a safe route down south to reach villages and cities safely."

Anders did not respond. Karter shot to his feet, chair clattering to the floor. "We can't just abandon our people!"

For the first time since the gathering had begun, Anders dropped into his seat. "I know, lad."

Karter remained standing, fists quivering. "We could go. I could go. Two Wardsmen to each village, town, and city in the north. We could bring their people back here."

"You'd never make it back," Anders replied.

"How can you know that? There are horses in our stables faster than Darinian stallions."

"Speed isn't the problem," Anders said. "The enemies outside Calewind's walls—that's the problem."

"They're leagues away!"

"Doesn't matter." Anders scrubbed his hands over his face. "They likely gathered after the Ward marched, or we would have engaged them already. Maybe we have. Dawn and Dusk, I don't know. What I do know is last night they hit us from the south, and we have to assume they've got us surrounded and protect Calewind accordingly."

Karter licked his lips. "We wait until Dawnfall, then slip out. We follow the north road to every northern outpost. Warn them, and then move on." Anders squinted, considering. Sensing that he was getting through to the lieutenant, Karter plunged ahead. "Just a small contingent, sir. Nothing that would hurt our numbers here. Three of us. There are Wardsmen stationed in every northern town and city. When we arrive safely at our destination, we send one or more of them out to pass the message on. Cover more ground."

Anders drummed his fingers on the table, studying them. "I can't allow it."

"Why not?" Karter's voice was high and shrill.

"Because there are few of us as it is. The Crown of the North—"

"To shade and shadow with the Crown!" Karter fired back. Anders' face turned scarlet. Karter paled, but pressed on. "Where is Aidan now? He left us! He left us here to die!"

Rising, Anders placed a hand on his shoulder. "You're not the only one with family outside these gates, lad." Although he whispered, his words carried around the room. Karter collapsed into his chair.

Sympathy cut through Daniel like a knife. That annoyed him greatly. *First time I've felt sorry for you, Karter. First and last.* The vow made him feel better. A little. His chest was still tight, as if he had cinched a belt of steel around his chest while dressing that morning. He leaned back against the wall and closed his eyes. There was no point worrying about his father and mother. Their farm was far to the south, a long way from the threat facing Calewind.

". . . all we can do for now," Anders was saying. Daniel opened his eyes and saw the lieutenant standing beside Karter, one hand on his shoulder. He turned to each sergeant at the table, fixing them with a hard gaze. "The Crown of the North will mend our alliance with Darinia and turn the Ward around. Never doubt the Gairdens. In the interim, we must do our best to protect Calewind and her people." He let his hand fall from Karter's shoulder. It curled into a fist. "As much as it burns me up inside, as much as it makes me feel a coward, the truth is we simply cannot spare our brothers as couriers to villages and cities that may already be . . ."

The lieutenant trailed off and loosed a long, heavy sigh. Many of the sergeants regarded him with wide, haunted eyes. Others stared at their hands.

Alix stirred. "I thought you said the villages were being evacuated," she whispered.

He swallowed. "I . . . That is, I thought . . ."

Lips trembling, Alix turned away and stared blankly across the room. Daniel's heart pulsed in his throat and ears. *What can I do?* On the run with Aidan, he had known precisely how to act— except for when he had fallen ill and become a burden.

Daniel wilted against the wall. He was fooling himself. Aidan had been the hero, not him. Aidan could shift between Gotik, and Sordia, and Tarion, round up their people and bring them back here to safety.

The solution slammed into him with enough force to propel him forward from the wall. "The Hands of the Crown," he blurted.

Every pair of eyes landed on him. Alix's gaze settled heaviest of all. "What do you mean, Shirey?" Anders barked.

Daniel flinched. His confidence cowered under all those stares. "Well . . . that is . . . just an idea . . ."

His mumbled words faded into silence. Shaking his head, he took one shuffling step back to his position by the door. Then he saw Karter's face. No sneer curled the big man's lips. His expression was desperate, and familiar. Karter was looking at him the way Aidan had looked at him their first night on the road, in the cave, when Daniel had been trying to start a fire to keep them from freezing to death. He had failed. Aidan had saved them.

Aidan wasn't here, but in a way, wasn't he still relying on Daniel to save him? Wasn't everybody?

"Well?" Anders said.

"The Hands of the Crown, sir."

"You said that before. What of them?"

Each stare was like a weight on his chest. Daniel raised his vision to a spot on Anders' red forehead. "How many Hands of the Crown are in Calewind?" He forgot to append *sir*. Before he could rectify the mistake, Anders spoke.

"Eight. Two in each district. What of it?"

"All Hands are Touched. They can shift. We send them out, one or two to each outpost. The closest ones first, so they don't have to shift far—that tires them out—and once there, they can—"

"Pass the message on to the Hands stationed in each town and village to facilitate evacuation," Anders breathed. He slapped a meaty hand to his forehead. "Dawn and Dusk, why didn't I think of that?" Then he frowned. "It's still too dangerous. Some of the villages are leagues away, and as I understand it not even two Touched linked could make that . . . that what-do-you-call-it, that shift."

Daniel had considered that and had an alternative at the ready. Before he could voice it, Alix spoke up. "There's an underground tunnel in Sunfall's eastern courtyard, sir."

Daniel gaped. "How do you know about that?"

"I used it to get from Gotik to here. If there are others, we could send people through them."

"The one you speak of is sealed," Daniel said.

Once again, every pair of eyes pinned him to the wall.

"You knew about this, doorkeeper?" Anders said.

Daniel flinched. "Yes, sir. Aidan departed through it yesterday. He ordered me to seal it behind him, and I did."

Alix's face fell. Daniel licked his lips. "But there's another."

"Is it sealed?" asked Anders.

"Not yet."

"Why not?"

Daniel's face warmed. Truth be told, he had forgotten about the second tunnel. Perhaps that had been a blessing. "I thought it best one be left open, sir, in case of, uh, just such an occasion."

Anders studied him with narrowed eyes. "Your knowledge of

these tunnels. Do they have anything to do with your past?"

"Yes, sir," he said stiffly.

"They're Touched, Shirey," Anders said. "They may not honor their duty to the north. Tyrnen may have them."

"All we can do is ask, sir," Daniel said.

Anders was silent. At last he nodded. "It's worth a try. Good thinking, Wardsman Shirey."

Pride spread through Daniel like hot cider on winter's coldest night. A toe nudged his boot. "Alix Merrifalls helped come up with it, sir."

"That she did," Anders said. He nodded at her. "Good thinking, young lady."

"You can't think of everything, sir. You're exhausted," Alix said, voice high and excited.

"I am at that," Anders admitted. "The Lady could descend from her throne and dance naked in front of me, and I'm liable not to notice." Laughter rang around the table. Every sergeant wore grins of relief and hope. Unless Daniel was mistaken, Karter's was widest of all.

A hand took his and squeezed. Alix Merrifalls beamed at him. Her eyes shone like polished pearls. "Thank you," she mouthed. Daniel thought his face might burn to ashes. He shrugged, and she dropped his hand, still grinning.

Another crack of thunder as Anders' hand met tabletop. "It's settled, then," he boomed, sounding alert and almost jovial. "Sergeants, I want the Hands of the Crown rounded up and brought to me in the palace's southern courtyard. Spread out: two of you to the south district, two to the west, and two of you to the east. Rosen, Steele, you're on recruitment duty." Anders jabbed a thick finger at Daniel. "Wardsman Shirey and his, uh, charge will summon the two Hands who reside in the Spire."

More dazed than ever, Daniel only nodded.

"Good," Anders said. "This meeting is adjourned. We will reconvene at noon." Once again, he pointed at Daniel. "Be here. You as well, Merrifalls."

With that, he strode away from the table and toward the doors. Daniel hastened to swing open the closest, gesturing for Alix to do the same on her side. They threw open the doors just as Anders marched through. When he reached Daniel, he slowed.

"Good on you for speaking up," he said quietly. Then he was

gone, striding out of sight. Alix smiled at Daniel, expression aglow with approval. Seeing her look at him that way made him lightheaded.

Near the thrones, chairs scraped back, and armor jangled as five sergeants exited. On his way past, Karter paused, seemed about to say something, then gave a curt nod and hurried out.

Chapter 24:
Cinder Toban Kirkus, Hand of the Crown

"WHERE IS THE Spire?" Alix asked as she and Daniel crossed the southern courtyard.

"North district. We're not far. Once we're there, just follow my . . . Alix?"

She had stopped short at the gate that opened onto the mountain trail down to Calewind, slack-jawed. Daniel followed her line of sight and gave a small smile. He had lived in the capital so long that he sometimes forgot how splendid the city looked just after Dawnrise.

Calewind lay spread out before them, a monument to the precision and order that ran through Torel like lifeblood. Roads were broad and orthogonal, each as straight and finely measured as lines on a grid. Buildings flowed proportionally. One-story residences filled the southern district. Shops and homes rose two stories across the lower half of the eastern and western districts, giving way to three- and four-story mansions in the upper halves. In the north, universities and cathedrals stood tallest, capped with turrets and gleaming domes. The gradual ascent of buildings—each as white as snow—starting in the south and flowing north was like a staircase paved from rooftops. Sunfall soared above them all, perched in the Ihlkin Mountains like a crown, its fluted towers like fingers reaching for the heavens.

In the east, the Lady rose from the horizon and climbed to her perch. Pink light stained the morning sky. Calewind's rooftops sparkled like frost. Daniel's smile melted away. Every building in the capital, every marble fountain and statue, every colonnaded plaza and extravagant manse, every block of stone and wedge of gold and slab of marble had been cut, shaped, and placed by Darinian builders centuries ago. Unless Aidan repaired that alliance, unless the north and west could defeat Tyrnen, blood would run through those streets. Manmade works of splendor would be reduced to dust and ash.

"Let's go," Daniel said quietly. He opened the gate himself. There was no Wardsman posted to it.

The path down was narrow and sinuous. Ice coated it during the winter, but never for long. Touched students patrolled every street and path in Calewind, practicing their kindling by keeping trails safe for passage. They entered through another gate that opened onto the northern road, Calewind's primary artery. The city was pristine, and less crowded than usual. Only a few carts and carriages trundled along the streets. Merchants, most Leastonians festooned in brightly colored clothing and jewelry, shouted and leaped behind stalls piled high with fruits, vegetables, chocolates, clothing, rugs, lumber, tools, and weapons, their cries piercing the morning's calm.

"It's so . . ." Alix said softly then shook her head. "So big. So . . . majestic."

Daniel said nothing. He was observing. From the rooftops came the clatter of preparation: footsteps, hammers pounding nails, saws chewing wood, men shouting orders and cursing. Wardsmen and laborers clambered, installing drums and casks and cookpots that would be filled with boiling pitch. Lieutenant Magath doubted that the vagrants would penetrate so deeply into the city. Nevertheless, he said, it paid to be prepared.

Most passersby wore leathers to ward off winter's last breaths. Some wore robes of white, gold, or red. Boots were polished, clothes freshly pressed, collars straight, hair slick and shiny with oils. Women wore lace gloves. Affluent men wore no gloves, revealing soft hands more accustomed to holding wine glasses or quills than chisels or swords. Laborer or fop, their faces were pale and tight.

"Why do the buildings sparkle like that?" Alix asked.

"Icestone."

"Like . . . stone made from ice?"

"It's like marble, but stronger. Enhanced by kindling."

"How?"

"You'd have to ask a Touched."

Alix soaked up more sights as they walked. "Jak loved the city. He wrote letters to me describing the places he saw, the things he did. I thought I had a picture in my mind of Calewind. But this? It's more wonderful than I imagined."

"You didn't notice it yesterday?"

"I arrived in the dark and found my way to the Crown's Promise only because Jak said he spent time there." Alix laughed under her breath. "There are houses in the western district bigger than our barn." She regarded him thoughtfully. "Did you feel like that when you arrived here? Overwhelmed and awed?"

"Can't say as I did."

"Nothing impresses Daniel Shirey, farm boy and Wardsman?"

"I lived in a city before I worked a farm."

"As big as this?"

"Big enough."

"Which one?"

"Ironsail," he said gruffly.

Alix either didn't notice his terseness or ignored it. She blew uneven locks of hair out of her face. "White sands and ocean spray. I'd love to see it one day."

"Maybe you will. Come on."

They headed deeper into the northern district's wing of universities. The Spire was its largest, an icestone cylinder that stretched up to the clouds. Wide steps led to its entrance, which stood open. *The doors of learning are always open,* its scholars liked to say. Daniel guessed it probably got cold during the winter.

They entered a foyer, round and cavernous. Bands of glass wrapped around the room, and sconces hung below. The Lady's light streamed through the windows. Dust motes fell like snowflakes. Men and women spoke in low tones, their white snowy whispering as they walked. Others reclined in chairs with their noses buried in a text, or perused bookcases and pulled out dusty scrolls and manuscripts.

Above them, a mezzanine jutted out like a crescent. Above and to one side of it, another crescent platform could be seen. A third hung over and beside the second, and a fourth stretched high above their heads. Together, they formed a broken spiral staircase.

"Dawn and Dusk," Alix murmured, eyes as wide as tea saucers. Daniel was speechless. He had never set foot inside the Spire. He was a thief, a farmer, and a doorkeeper. The streets of Ironsail had been the classroom where he learned his first trade. His father had taught him the second.

He started forward, and Alix caught his arm. "Remember what Anders said."

"About finding the Hands of the Crown and sending them off to deliver our message?"

"No. The other thing." She glanced around and stepped closer. "We don't know whose side they're on."

Daniel licked his lips, suddenly more attuned to the atmosphere of the Spire. It was hot, hotter than sconces could have made the air. There was magic everywhere in this place: in the air, the parchment stuffed in bookcases, coursing through the veins of the men and women who appeared at ease in their chairs and absorbed in their texts, but who could immolate either of them with a quick prayer and a flick of a wrist.

His fingers trailed down to the scabbard at his waist, came away empty. The imitation Serpent's Fang! He'd forgotten it back in his—in Aidan's—bedroom when he'd dressed that morning. His *Sard'tara* was strapped to his back, one bladed head inches from the floor.

Daniel glanced over at Alix, saw her hand clutching the hilt of Jak's sword. Anxiety hit him like a sudden blizzard, leaving him cold. *Why did I have to speak up? Anders would have thought of sending the Hands out to warn Torelian outposts eventually. I should have just kept quiet.*

Before he realized what was happening, Alix marched up to two women and a man wearing a bushy beard and singed white robe. They sat in a cluster of squashy chairs. The man was absorbed in conversation with one of the women, his hands gesticulating. Their companion wore thick spectacles and frowned over a scroll. All three wore a gold ring topped with an amethyst on their right forefingers.

"Pardon me," Alix said. The man and woman broke off and

looked up, blinking in confusion. The second woman remained bent over her scrolls. "We're looking for a Cinder."

Their expressions turned to mild amusement. "I'm afraid you'll have to do better than that," the man said. His female companion chuckled.

Alix blushed. Daniel stepped forward. The Cinders took in his steel and snow, the Gairden crest on his breast. Bushy eyebrows rose. "We're looking for the Hands of the Crown who reside in this district. Where can we find them?"

"Only Cinder Toban Kirkus remains," the man replied. His elbows were perched on armrests, hands folded beneath his chin.

"Remains?" Daniel said. Then a chill swept through him, and he knew.

The woman nodded, shifting in her seat. "All the others marched with the Ward." A deep frown creased her features.

"Cinder Kirkus spends most of his time in the main library," the man said. He pointed. "Step onto a lift and ask it to take you to level four."

"Thank you," Daniel said, and spun to cross to the hearth. Two pairs of eyes settled on his back.

"Where are these lifts?" Alix said, craning her neck to stare upwards.

"Here, I think," Daniel said. They stepped onto a wide stone plate beside an unlit hearth. The plate's surface was embossed with a flame. "Level four," Daniel said.

Nothing happened. "Could you take us to level four, please?" Alix said.

A low whirring filled Daniel's ears. At the bottom of his periphery he noticed a soft blue light. The bottom of the platform glowed cerulean. Then it shot upwards. Daniel and Alix both fell into a crouch, throwing their arms wide for balance. Their fingertips touched. Alix looked over at him and laughed. "The Cinder did say to ask," she said.

The first mezzanine rose and then fell below them as their lift climbed. It was wide, and covered in chairs, bookcases, lecterns, and tables holding clay pitchers and goblets. The third held much the same. Several scholars in white robes wearing Cinder Bands broke their conversation to watch them pass. At their feet, the platform hummed and glowed.

"Are you all right?" Alix said, straightening carefully, arms still extended to either side.

Daniel followed her to his feet. "Just feel out of place, I guess."

"Me, too. My mother and father only have two books: The Book of Dawn, and a cookbook passed down by my mother's side for generations. This place would leave them speechless." She looked away. "Jak would have loved to have seen Mother speechless."

"She'll be here before the day is out," Daniel said.

"You don't know that."

"I don't know it, but—"

"What if this Kirkus person doesn't agree to carry our warning?"

"We have to try," he responded, hoping he didn't sound desperate.

Alix flashed him a smile. "You're right, farm boy."

His breath caught in his throat, and it had nothing to do with the air rushing past him. He was struck by her beauty, more stunning than the Lady hanging in the sky on a cloudless summer day.

"What is it? You look sick," she said.

Daniel cleared his throat and put on his best Wardsman-doorkeeper face. "I haven't eaten breakfast yet. Someone made me late for work."

The lift's glow faded, its upward momentum slowed. It stopped smoothly in front of the fourth mezzanine. An ornate rail ran along its edge. There was a rattling sound, and a partition slid away into the wall. Daniel and Alix stepped onto the mezzanine. The rail clattered back into place and the lift shot back down to the ground floor.

"A beautiful woman greets you at your door first thing in the morning, and you complain," she said.

"A beautiful woman in desperate need of Leaston's best hair stylist," he quipped. She pushed him playfully.

"This is neither the time nor the place for roughhousing," barked a deep voice.

Daniel placed him immediately. Across the fourth level, the rotund man who had repaired the southern gate after the attack stood before a gilded bookcase, a large blue tome open in hands the size of bear paws. His eyes squinted from beneath pouches of fat. Pinned to the collar of his blood-red robe was a gold brooch fashioned in the shape of an open hand reaching up through a crown.

Daniel cleared his throat and straightened. "You're a Hand of the Crown."

"Cinder Toban Kirkus, Hand of the Crown, Disciple of Dawn, to be precise." He snapped the book closed. "You're a Wardsman."

"I am, and I'm here with a request from the Crown."

"If it isn't of the utmost importance, I haven't the time for it." Toban dropped into the nearest cushy chair. The cushion wheezed under his weight. "It's that gate, you see. One block of icestone won't do it. I need to reinforce all of it. Better yet, you could be guarding it. There are too few snowmen—"

Daniel stiffened, but the Cinder took no notice.

"—to guard the gates, and I'm alone, or as good as."

"What about the scholars and inventors?" Daniel said. "We ran into some below."

Toban's laugh made his body jiggle. "Fools. Useless. Too absorbed in their studies to pay attention to what's happening around them. Busy inventing baubles that won't do a damn bit of good. Not all Touched are soldiers, boy. One must train in the art of magical combat. I have that training. So did the other Hands, but they left. They followed . . ." His expression darkened. "They followed *him*." He wiped a hand over his face, closed his eyes, fell silent. His chest rose and fell in the rhythm of sleep.

Daniel glanced at Alix. She shrugged. "Um, Hand Tob—" he said.

"It's Cinder!" he snapped, slapping his hands on the armrests. "Cinder Toban Kirkus, Hand of the Crown!" Cinder Toban Kirkus, Hand of the Crown, sat up straighter. "A message," he blurted, gaze fixed on Daniel. "You said you bring a message from the Crown. Is he back?"

"No," Alix said. "Lieutenant Anders sent us to deliver our—"

"Anders? He said the message came from the Crown," Toban said, jabbing a finger at Daniel. "If Aidan isn't back—"

"Please," Alix said, wringing her hands. "It's urgent, and it comes from the lieutenant. He's the highest-ranking officer in the city. You must know that."

Cinder Toban Kirkus, Hand of the Crown, stared at Daniel. "You look familiar. Red hair . . . Red hair . . . Ah. Shirey. That's right. You're the Crown's friend. The doorkeeper. Is that how little Lieutenant Anders thinks of a Hand of the Crown? He sends a doorkeeper to deliver an urgent message? I've never been so insulted!"

Daniel chewed his lip.

"Well?" Cinder Toban Kirkus, Hand of the Crown, sputtered. "I am one man, and I am busy. Busy and exhausted. Out with your message, doorkeeper. Out with it, and then get out."

Daniel's mouth went dry. The Spire suddenly felt too big. What was he doing here?

"Well?" the Cinder boomed. Daniel closed his eyes, wishing he could disappear into his boots.

"You need to show more respect."

Daniel's eyes shot open. Alix stood in front of him, glaring at the Cinder, who gawked at her in amazement. "I need do no such thing, young lady. How dare you—"

"Daniel Shirey is a servant to the Crown of the North, same as you."

"Ha! We are hardly equals. I—"

"According to the oath you swore, the Crown comes before all other powers, second only to the Eternal Flame, who speaks for the Lady of Dawn." Alix shielded her eyes and gazed around. "I don't see the Lady of Dawn here. That means the Crown is your first priority. Not the Touched. Aidan Gairden and his orders."

Cinder Toban Kirkus, Hand of the Crown, quivered like a mound of red pudding. "I will not be insulted this way." He pinched the collar of his robe between thumb and forefinger and held it out so the light streaming in from the skylight glinted off the pin at his collar. "All who wear this crest are afforded a due amount of respect."

"I know," Alix said crisply. "My father wears the same badge."

"Your fa . . . ? Who is your father?"

"Rufus Merrifalls, Hand of the Crown at Gotik."

Daniel started. Alix ignored him.

A smile crept over Cinder Toban Kirkus's face. "Gotik? The tiny village to the south?"

"Unless you know of another Gotik," she said crisply.

Toban's smile melted. "Has he been Touched by the Lady's light?"

"He's . . . yes, but not . . . that is, he's not that powerful. He—"

"Ha!" Toban shouted, as if he had just won an argument decisively.

"That doesn't matter," Alix said, practically shouting to be heard. "You know the oath. 'Whether right or left, all Hands serve the Crown of the North in equal measure.'"

Cinder Toban Kirkus did not appear to take kindly to his oath being flung at him. "I will not be lectured by the likes of some . . . some farm girl."

"I am a farm girl, and the Hands of the Crown are supposed to serve the peop—"

"You've offended me," Toban said with an imperious gesture. "Leave. Or I shall have no choice but to remove you against your will."

"But our message!"

Cinder Toban Kirkus gave a great harrumph that rippled over his body like a wave. "You should have served your message before you served your insults. Be gone. Now."

Alix's mouth froze, words dying mid-breath. Daniel had looked up from where he had been making a thorough examination of the plush blue carpeting. At the insult to Alix, a sliver of heat lanced through him. Two long strides closed the distance to Toban.

"Apologize," he growled, his knees pressed against Toban's.

The Hand blinked. "What?"

"Apologize to my friend. She is an honorary Wardsman, never mind her gender. You have insulted her. I could have you imprisoned."

"You wouldn't dare."

"I have the authority. I may be a doorkeeper, but I am a servant of the Crown, just like you."

"I am a Touched, and am—"

"Above such petty rudeness, or should be."

Toban colored. "Sorry." He shot them a venomous look. "Deliver your message and be gone."

"The surrounding villages and cities are in danger," Daniel said. "You are to shift to them, warn them of the threat, and evacuate them to Calewind."

"As I told you, I am alone—"

"That is your order."

Toban ground his teeth. "Fine. But even a village as scrawny as Gotik has too many for a Touched to evacuate by shifting."

Without taking his eyes from the Cinder, Daniel reached into a pocket and offered him a folded sheet of parchment. "Which is why you're going to use this."

Toban took the paper, unfolded it, stared blankly. "I don't understand." He held the paper out to Daniel and Alix. She leaned in, frowning. Near the top was a square with a circle drawn in each corner. At the bottom were two horizontal bars, parallel, with a vertical bar between them, like an "H" on its side.

"It's a key to the tunnels used by the sneaks of Leaston," Daniel said.

"The sneaks are real?" Toban asked.

"You're talking to one."

Toban's gaze changed from surly to interested. "How will I—?"

"There's at least one tunnel that leads in and out of every village and city in the realms. First thing you'll do is shift to Gotik. Look for the key near a lone shack or pile of rocks on the outskirts of the village."

"Behind the Hand's garden," Alix put in.

"Enter the tunnels and follow the path until you come to a waypoint," Daniel continued. "It's a large room with dozens of other tunnels. Find this one"—he tapped the key—"and press your hand against it, then gather the group around you and invoke the magic you need to run the tunnels."

Toban blinked. "Run the tunnels? I'm afraid I don't understand."

"Use the words written at the bottom. Any Touched can do it. Even Aidan figured it out, so it can't be that hard."

"Via the Lady's light?" Toban asked, eyes scanning the text written at the bottom of the parchment.

"Not exactly."

Toban's brow climbed his forehead. "Touch the key . . . pray to Her inverse . . . Inverse . . ." His head whipped up. "Shadecraft?" he said in a strangled whisper.

Daniel nodded. "Did I fail to mention that? Oh, wipe that look off your face. Aidan has run the tunnels on more than one occasion. You're not going to be thrown in the depths for following the Crown's lead." He smiled grimly. "Of course, you don't have to—what is it you Cinders like to say?—walk in the shade to use the tunnels. You could always just walk. Find the key, walk from tunnel to tunnel. But something tells me you'd prefer dark magic to using your legs."

"Dark magic," Cinder Toban Kirkus murmured.

Daniel straightened. "You're to depart immediately." When Toban did not respond, Daniel gestured to Alix and returned to the railing. From below, a platform rose. Daniel hardly saw it. Blood pounded in his ears.

"Dawn," Alix mumbled, standing close to him.

"Wait."

Daniel turned. "What is it?"

Cinder Toban Kirkus heaved himself up from his chair and waddled toward them. Glancing around, he composed his features. "Suppose I refuse," he said quietly.

Daniel fought to keep his mouth from dropping open. "You can't."

"Of course, I can. You're asking me, on behalf of the Crown of the North—the Lady of Dawn's most trusted, revered servant—to violate one of Her commandments. If word of that were to get around . . ."

"And who would you tell?"

"I'm sure the Disciples of Dawn would relish an opportunity to install one of their own in Sunfall."

"Aidan wouldn't—"

"Aidan isn't here."

Daniel gritted his teeth. "What do you want?"

"What can you offer?"

Daniel considered. His gaze fell on the book sitting in Toban's abandoned chair. "Magic," he said.

Toban's eyes lit up. "I'm listening."

ANDERS MAGATH WATCHED his sergeants squirm. Throats cleared.

"You delivered your messages as Wardsman Shirey instructed?" he boomed.

The sergeants snapped to attention: sitting up straighter, their expressions rapt. "No, sir," said Jareth Byrn, a middle-aged man with specks of salt mixed in with his brown goatee.

"Why not?"

Karter, looking sour as always, spoke up. "The Hands are gone, sir. All but one somewhere in the northern district. They followed the Eternal Flame to war."

"What alternative action did you take?"

"We found scholars, sir," Karter said. "Two per district. They can carry missives as well as Hands, I guess. I didn't think we should come back empty-handed, sir."

Anders pursed his lips. "You all did this?" Nods around the table. "And Wardsman Shirey?"

"We didn't convene with him, sir," Karter said.

"You don't care for him, do you, Sergeant Karter?"

Karter's face turned stony. "No, sir."

"This is not the time for petty feuds, Sergeant."

"No, sir." Karter hesitated again.

"What is it?" Anders said.

"Cinder Jacelyn, one of the scholars I spoke with, confessed some concern over one of the instructions that . . . that Wardsman Shirey had us deliver, sir."

"Which one?"

"She showed me. The line read . . . something about praying to Her inverse."

Anders tapped the back of his chair, pondering. "Means nothing to me."

"Me neither, sir."

The sergeants glanced toward the closed doors of the throne room. Daniel was conspicuously absent from his post. There was no humming, no clatter of *Sard'tara* on the floor indicating that the boy had dozed off or missed grabbing the weapon while tossing it from hand to hand. "He must still be in the north district, sir," Byrn said. "Shall I fetch him?"

"No, no. I'll go. I could use fresh air. You men talk amongst yourselves. I'll expect four suggestions from each of you concerning ways to bolster our defenses when I get back."

They clapped a fist to their chests in the Gairden salute. He mirrored them, turned on his heel, strode to the doors, threw them open. All at once a frisson of unease wormed its way into his belly. The vestibule was empty and silent. There was usually some scullery maid moving about, or Hands or common folk waiting for an audience. No Wardsmen were stationed outside the doors today. There was no point. He was shorthanded and needed men out in the streets more than he needed them standing around in Sunfall.

Behind him, the doors clicked closed. The sound echoed in the empty hall. Light streamed through stained-glass windows, painting squares over the gleaming floor. Shirey had been told to fetch Hands in the northern district. Cinder Toban Kirkus, Anders knew, purportedly the only one still in—

Movement to his left. He whirled and saw a dead man. Jak Merrifalls stood framed in the mouth of a corridor. His skin gave off a healthy, lambent glow, standing as he was in the colored light pouring in through the window above him. Except he had died in the attack the night before. Anders had seen his body, met the man's grieving and infuriatingly brash sister. Except . . .

The eyes. Jak's eyes were dull and flat.

Jak looked up and saw Anders. He smiled and retreated down the corridor.

For a moment, Anders considered storming back into the throne room and calling his sergeants to arms. His heart drummed against his ribs. That decided him. Tightening his grip on his blade, he plunged after Merrifalls.

"WELL?" DANIEL ASKED.

Toban looked up from the book. His ruddy face had gone ashen. The book shook in unsteady hands. "You say this belonged to the Eternal Flame?"

"Kind of," Daniel said. He had neither the time nor the patience to explain that Tyrnen was, in fact, a possessed Touched who had lived on hatred and dark magic and a lust for power for over eight hundred years, and that the trove of magical books and scrolls and trinkets he had accumulated had more than likely belonged to the Touched he had killed to harvest souls for his harbingers.

Toban placed the book on Tyrnen's cluttered desk. His breathing was loud and shallow. "It's forbidden. All of it."

Daniel held his exasperation in check. "But powerful."

"Very," Toban admitted.

"You wanted magic. I've given you powerful magic, with Aidan's blessing to use it."

Toban pursed his lips, staring at the book. "*Approbation for the Moon*. What is this moon the title speaks of?"

"No idea."

Toban sat heavily in Tyrnen's chair, which creaked under his

257

weight. "Tell me again what the Crown said. Every word."

Daniel searched the ceiling. "The book is full of dark magic, and that I should give it to the most powerful Touched in Calewind." *Which might not be you,* he added to himself. *But you're susceptible to bribery, and you're the best I've got at the moment.*

Toban had straightened at the last words. "And it's mine?"

"On loan," Daniel said. "To protect Calewind."

Toban opened the book, leafed through pages. "I'll get started immediately."

Daniel crossed the room toward the desk. Toban glanced up, saw him coming, tried to hug the book to his chest. Daniel plucked it deftly from his grip.

Toban started. "How did you—?"

"I'm a sneak, remember?" He caught himself. *Was. I was a sneak.*

Toban shot to his feet. "Return that book this instant."

"Or what?"

"Or I'll turn you into a human torch," the Cinder said. Behind him, Daniel heard Alix pull her sword free. He raised a hand without turning. Daniel held the book aloft, waving it in front of the Cinder's face. Toban reached for it. While he was distracted, Daniel drummed on the desk three times with his free hand. Its surface turned from wood to air, and Daniel dumped the book inside. Toban watched the book's descent the way Leastonian fishermen watched a bobbing line. He stared from the desk and back up to the Wardsman. He dipped his hand toward the desk and cried out when his knuckles rapped solid wood.

"Shade and shadow, boy!" he said, cradling his fingers. "What did you do?"

"Protected my investment. Now you can't set me on fire."

"Give it back!" Toban demanded in a petulant tone.

"No."

"You said the Crown asked me to—"

"You'll get the book when you deliver the message. Make the rounds, return to Calewind, and you can get started tonight."

Toban glared at him. "Fine. Where to first?"

"Gotik," Alix said from beside Daniel. He nodded.

"Fine," the Cinder said again.

"One more thing," Daniel said.

"What is it now?"

"You're to share the magic you learn in that moon book"—his mouth twisted around the arcane word—"with other Touched when you return. Crown's orders."

Toban spoke in a clipped tone. "There are few Touched still in the city. My colleagues in the Spire are scholars. They deal with inventions. Practical applications. I was a soldier before I became a Hand. Combat is my specialty. I will defend this city single-handedly, if I must."

Daniel frowned. He sensed no arrogance in the big man's words. If anything, he thought he'd detected shame. "You know what happened last night isn't your fault."

Toban stiffened. "What?"

Alix drew a breath. Conscious of their eyes boring into him, Daniel took a moment to gather his thoughts.

"We're up against the Eternal Flame. His forces outnumber ours five to one. Maybe more, maybe less. Numbers aren't exactly my strong suit. His army consists of dozens, probably hundreds of souls of men and women widely considered the most powerful Touched of their time. He uses people. He sucks them dry, and then, when they're nothing but husks, he holds on to what he needs and discards their flesh like old rags."

His thoughts turned to Garrett Lorden, and a mixture of fear, anger, and pity washed over him. "Tyrnen has forgotten more about dark magic over the years than one person will ever know. All we can do is our best. That means working together. The scholars may not be as powerful as you, but they are Touched, and they're all we have. There must be something they can do. Delegate. Give them simple tasks that will ease your burden. And you will be carrying a heavy burden, Cinder Toban. Relaying messages will be easy." *Provided the villages due to receive them are still standing, and you don't find a pack of undead villagers waiting for you.* "What comes next, when you return? That's the hard part."

Daniel crossed his arms and shrugged, staring down at the floor. There was nothing else to say. Alix's hand alighted on his shoulder. Her touch was gentle and soothing. He looked up and caught Toban's eye. The Cinder was staring at him in wonder.

"Dawn burn me to ashes if you're wrong," Toban said softly. "I'll return before Dawnfall. See that you're here to greet me." He muttered a word and vanished. A gust of wind kicked up loose papers.

"Dawn," Alix said again.

"What?" Daniel asked, feeling defensive.

"You have a way with words. I'm impressed, farm boy."

"Yes. Well. I had plenty of time to talk growing up. Cows make for attentive audiences. Come on. We need to get back. Anders'll be pulling out what little hair he still has, and when we get back, he'll start pulling mine, and—"

Alix placed a hand over top his. "Thanks," she said.

His heart skipped a beat. "For what?"

"You're helping to save my parents. They're all I have left."

Daniel looked at her hand. "We should get back."

Neither moved. Alix was staring at him intently, eyes coruscating like the sapphires embedded in the hilt of Aidan's sword.

There was a sharp knock at the door. Daniel leaped back and adjusted his helm. Alix straightened more slowly, smoothing her shirt and looking highly annoyed. The door creaked open, and a bearded scholar wearing a singed white robe poked his head in.

"Forgive the interruption, Wardsman Shirey."

It took Daniel a moment to place him: The inventor who had pointed them in Toban's direction. "How did you find us?"

"I followed you." The man entered, hands clasped at his waist and looking around. His eyes grew wider and wider. "The Eternal Flame's sanctuary," he breathed.

"What did you need, Cinder . . . ?"

"Emerus," the man said. "Emerus Saul. I meant to speak with you earlier, only I couldn't place you right away. You are Aidan Gairden's friend."

"Yes."

Emerus inclined his head. "Calewind has been in turmoil since the Crown's birthday, and I have much to share with him, now that he has been installed to the throne."

Daniel shifted. "Between you and me, Cinder Emerus—"

"Just Emerus will be fine."

"—I don't know when Aidan will return. I expect it will be soon, perhaps even this evening," he went on in a rush at the look of alarm dawning on Emerus's face. "In the meantime, I could take you to speak with Lieutenant Magath. He's the senior officer in charge until Aidan, or Edmund, or Brendon—"

The Cinder swallowed. "I really need to speak with the Crown, or another of our kind who would understand the news I have to share. It's in regard to the lamp." He stared meaningfully.

Daniel gaped. "I'm afraid I don't . . ." Emerus's appearance clicked. "You gave Aidan the lamp on his birthday."

Emerus beamed. "That I did. I helped create it, though I can't take all the credit. I worked with colleagues in the Lion's Den, and—" He drew in a breath, and his voice quivered with excitement. "I do prattle on, but the lamp is why I wanted to see the Crown. Using what I learned in assisting with the production of the first artefact, I—that is, my associates at the Spire and I— we made more."

"How many more?"

"Lots more."

Daniel straightened. "Show me."

They followed Emerus through Calewind and back into the Spire, where a lift carried them up to the third level. Alix gasped. A table had been shoved against the railing. A handful of inventors milled around it, bending down to inspect the objects lying upon it. There were six: a bracelet, a necklace, three rods each as long as Daniel's arm, and a small knife curved like a beckoning finger. Each was gold and glittered in rays of the Lady's light.

"I don't know what they are," Alix murmured, "but they're beautiful."

Emerus crossed to the table. Daniel and Alix trailed behind him. The necklace consisted of a gold strand as fine and delicate as hair. A glass-like cylinder as long as his forefinger hung from it. It pulsed with strong, golden light. Alix reached for it tentatively, but a stern look from one of the other inventors—a woman as tall and severe looking as Helda, mistress of Sunfall's kitchens—made her jerk it away.

"Lamps," Emerus said proudly. He indicated the necklace. "Go on, dear lady, go on."

Alix shot the woman a triumphant look and lifted her hair. "Help me with it?" she asked Daniel.

Bumbling a little, Daniel fastened it around her neck.

"An exact replica of the one I gifted the Crown on his birthday," Emerus said, tapping his fingertips together. "I trust he put it to good use."

"Very," Daniel replied.

The inventor beamed in delight.

"How do they work?" Alix asked, the necklace's cylinder hanging settling between her breasts.

"Ah," Emerus said, face lighting up. "When near a source of light, the lamp fills, and a Touched may kindle from it even at Kahltan's darkest hour. The Crown's is the twin to the necklace you wear."

"It saved our lives," Daniel said.

The inventor's brow soared. "Really? Splendid! These are our newest prototypes." His lips puckered as if he tasted something sour. "Two members of Torel's Dawn marched in yesterday before departing, demanding we turn over what we had. I gave them two necklaces. Those were all I could spare. Our first three prototypes, made based on the one gifted to the Crown, went to some of the disciples marching with the Ward. I expect they'll find use for them."

Daniel nodded absently. He was watching Alix, who stared at the necklace. "It's so beautiful," she murmured.

The female inventor scowled. "Are you a Touched?"

"No," Alix said. "My father is, but . . . " She shrugged.

"Then you won't be able to use it."

"It's still pretty."

Emerus smiled. "Indeed. We strived to combine form and function, but even the form has a purpose beyond storing light. To the uninitiated, it is merely jewelry."

"Do all the other lamps work like the necklace?" Daniel asked, waving a hand to take in the table.

"Fundamentally, yes. All lamps conserve Her light. But these other lamps also combine form and function in unique ways." He hefted one of the three rods, holding an end in either hand. "This rodule can be used as a cane. As a Touched walks, he or she can kindle light from the rodule, soothing aches and pains as they move about."

"Maybe it's just the Wardsman in me talking," Daniel said, "but I see another use."

Emerus nodded, looking grave. "To bludgeon. Indeed." He sighed, replaced the rodule on the table. "That's why I came looking for you. All of us here in the Spire know of the threat against Calewind, and who is behind it." His voice grew quiet. "I was in the assemblage three days ago. I stood there, watching, as the Eternal Flame prepared to order Aidan executed. And the general just watched. He just stood there and watched."

"That wasn't—" Daniel started.

"I know," Emerus said. "That's what made me realize that something was wrong. Treason or not, Edmund Calderon wouldn't have been so quick to sentence his only child. And Annalyn? I know her." His face tightened. "That is, I knew her. She loved Aidan more than she loved her own life. She wouldn't have . . ." He shook his head. "I saw what Aidan did when he held Heritage. Touching the sword pulled back the veil over the faces of those imposters. And Tyrnen didn't deny it. How could he? Instead, he attacked, and I knew at once that he was our enemy. That's what I wanted to talk to the Crown about, you see."

Silence fell. Alix's hand drifted to her throat, fingered the necklace absently.

"When I think of our Eternal Flame dipping into the Well of Night, it makes me feel dirty," Emerus continued. "I oppose Kahltan and his shades. I would confront Tyrnen myself, if I thought I stood a chance of walking away."

Daniel held his tongue. He wondered what Emerus would think of Aidan if he had overheard the Crown's orders to share the moon book with able Touched in the service of protecting Calewind. As an Untouched, Daniel viewed magic as a tool. A hammer could be used to drive nails into wood, or to shatter a man's skull. It was not inherently good, nor inherently bad. It was an instrument at the disposal of the man who wielded it.

Emerus gestured at the table. "We'd been working on the lamps for some time. But ever since that day at Sunfall, I redoubled my efforts and came up with these." He hesitated, viewing them askance. "I admit to feeling shame at what I have made here. I do not believe the Lady intended for us to harness her light as a weapon. I respect what soldiers do—my brother, also a Touched, followed that path—but I preferred to channel my talents toward productivity."

Emerus squared his shoulders and picked up the knife, fingered the point of the blade. "Consider these lamps, and our service, a gift. We'll have more ready by Dawnrise tomorrow. And we will fight alongside the Ward, if you'll have us."

"We will," Daniel said. "More Touched are coming."

"Oh?"

"Cinder Toban," Daniel said. "That's why I was looking for him. He has been sent to northern villages and cities with word of the impending attack. Their Touched will bolster your numbers."

Nodding, Emerus returned his attention to the lamp-knife. "This is my greatest creation," he said quietly. "And my worst. I call it the Nail of Dawn. The blade stores light, of course, and can be kindled from, like any of the others. But it has another purpose." He thrust the Nail toward the wall. As he did, his sleeve ruffled and fell back, exposing pale flesh. "Stab this into a man's belly, and the light within—"

Bells clattered from the Ihlkin Mountains.

"Afternoon worship?" Alix asked uncertainly.

"An alarm," Daniel said tightly. "Sunfall is under attack."

Chapter 25:
Promotion

DANIEL AND ALIX burst into the vestibule outside the throne room. Their gasps for breath were deafening in the deserted space. The throne room doors were closed.

"I don't understand," Alix said. Her face was shiny, and her hair hung in damp, crooked strands. "Where's the attack?"

Daniel sucked in two breaths, straightened, and hurried to the throne room doors, one hand extended to wrench them open. Far down the corridor to his right came the sounds of struggle: shouts, steel against steel, snarls, a scream of pain. They took off down the corridor, racing past galleries and portraits and framed documents. Not a single servant, disciple, scholar, or Wardsman appeared.

"Do you see them?" Alix shouted.

"What?"

"Footprints."

His gaze flicked to the floor. A trail of muddy tracks weaved a drunken path up the hallway and around the bend that led to the sword chamber and Aidan's quarters. Up ahead, the Lady's light filtered through a window, framing a muddy footprint. *No,* he corrected, slowing to study it. Not mud. *Vagrant blood.*

"How'd they get in? The gates?" Alix said.

Daniel said nothing. Most people knew nothing of the tunnels that snaked beneath Crotaria. Daniel did, and was quite certain that if he were to visit the only unsealed access point in the city—below a stall in the western district that had been mysteriously vacant for years—he would find it split open like a scabbed wound and bleeding undead into Calewind.

He skidded around a bend. Up ahead, Aidan's door was closed. Daniel braced his shoulder and threw himself at the door. The wood yielded to his steel and snow. The first thing he saw was the ruined body of Anders. The lieutenant had been cut open from stem to stern—one of Rakian Shirey's favorite sayings—and lay discarded in a corner. His eyes had been cut free like pearls from oysters, and his innards lay draped over him like gaudy Yule decorations. Blood dark as wine painted the walls, floor, and bedding.

Bile climbed up Daniel's throat. *We're alone. Anders left us alone.*

"Gimme a hand, farm boy," Alix said, grunting.

Her voice brought him back to himself. His eyes swept the room, taking everything in. Two other Wardsmen—Markus Hallwell and Dylan Gaines, who had only taken the steel and snow two winters past—lay on the floor, eyes blank, blood pooled beneath them. Red and green flowed together, creating murky puddles. A vagrant lay nearby, its skull smashed to pieces. The bed was undisturbed by bodies or gore. A black sword lay atop the sheets. *The false Fang.*

At the far end of the room, three vagrants had Karter Rosen backed against the wall. He held his spear horizontally, shoving at vagrants as they darted in. Two broke from the pack and separated, moving to flank him. The third wore a human face that hung limply, like a loose mask. Daniel thought it looked vaguely familiar.

Alix screamed and ran forward. Daniel sprinted after her without thinking. The sight of her charging headlong into danger, into certain death, left him cold with fear. She reached the vagrants first. Raising Jak's blade in both hands she cleaved through the shoulder of the vagrant on Karter's right. It stumbled back, more surprised than hurt, and spun to face her. She gasped. Its mask still hung askew, but Daniel finally recognized that face. Jak Merrifalls' eyes were flat and dead, his visage twisted in a mixture of hatred and contempt.

Alix spread her feet and raised her sword. Tears stained her cheeks. "Get the others." Then she launched herself at her brother.

Daniel's gaze flashed to Karter. He had managed to break away from the vagrant coming in on his left, swinging and thrusting to hold its axe at bay. Daniel leaped forward, looping his arms underneath the vagrant's and lacing his hands across the back of its neck so it could not lower its hands. "Now!" he shouted, lowering his head and tucking it beneath one rotten shoulder.

There was a sickening crack as Karter's spear exploded out the back of the vagrant's skull. Its body went limp in Daniel's grip. He let it fall. Karter staggered forward, gasping and clutching his side. Blood seeped through his fingers. His face was ashen. "Get back," Daniel snapped.

"Don't order me, doorkeeper," Karter said through clenched teeth. He raised his spear, took a wobbly step forward, and promptly sank to his knees.

Daniel wrested Karter's spear from his grip and spun to face not-Jak. Alix hammered at him with her sword. He deflected her blows easily, twisting his axe to turn them aside, but could find no opening to retaliate. Without warning, Alix flipped her sword, seizing it like a dagger and driving it at not-Jak's head. Daniel yelled. Her momentum was too weak, the thrust too ineffectual. Her blade glanced off his axe, leaving her exposed. Daniel ran for her. His movements were sluggish. He felt like a deer bounding through snow.

Suddenly, Alix crouched and sprang at her brother. At the same time, she flipped her sword in her hands, gripping it properly, and drove it toward not-Jak's chin. The undead stepped back, and Alix's blade sank into his throat. She fell against him, recoiled at the bib of green blood that ran from its throat to soak its chest. She wrenched her blade. It held fast. Her eyes widened in fear. Not-Jak's face twisted in a rictus. He brought his axe up.

Daniel held his spear at the base and batted away the axe. Not-Jak staggered to one side, off balance. Alix ripped her sword free with a squelch. Roaring, the vagrant came at Daniel, swinging its axe wildly. He raised his spear, turning aside the first swing, the second. The third bit through the spear shaft and sent tremors up Daniel's arms. Fragments sprayed to the floor. Daniel threw the bottom half away and adjusted the top half, holding it like a sword. Not slowing, he crashed headlong into not-Jak, throwing an arm across its chest like a bar and driving his shattered haft at the vagrant's left eye socket.

Alix's brother seemed to have retained his foxlike reflexes in un-death. He jerked his head to one side, sending Daniel stumbling forward. Behind him he heard not-Jak's axe whistle as it cut the air. The hairs on the back of his neck stood up. He closed his eyes. *Lady of Dawn welcome me into your warm embrace.*

"Jak!"

Daniel spun at Alix's shriek. So did her brother. Before it could attack, Daniel recovered and drove the point of his spear through the back of not-Jak's skull. The vagrant jerked, went limp. Its axe clattered to the floor. The body followed, and Alix slumped down beside it.

Daniel threw his shattered weapon aside and reached for her. She flinched, made a mewling sound. "It's just me," he said. "You're all right."

Her eyes cleared, fastened onto him. Her hands—clammy and shaky—found his and brought them up to cup her face. Her cheeks were wet with tears. "I killed him," she whispered.

"No. You freed him." Even as he said the words, Daniel knew they probably were not true. Aidan had told him about Tyrnen's spirit stone, and how the souls trapped within it could be used over and over until it was destroyed. *She doesn't need to hear that. Not now.*

Hope lit Alix's face. "I can stand." He helped her to her feet.

Something moved behind them. Daniel whirled, raising his fists. Karter, paler than ever, flinched, but did not move away. "You all right?" the sergeant asked.

Daniel nodded, looking his rival up and down. "Better than you."

"I'm alive," Karter said simply. "Thanks to you."

Feeling uncomfortable, Daniel shrugged. "You wear the steel and snow. We're brothers. You would have done the same for me."

"Dawn," Alix muttered from behind him.

Karter ran a hand through his hair, smearing a red-green paste through it. "I don't know that I would've. Not because I dislike you. And I do dislike you." He managed a weak smile, and

Daniel found himself returning it. "I was so afraid. I just stood there and watched as . . ." His eyes flicked to the bodies of the two Wardsmen, then to Anders. "I froze. I could have saved them." His fists clenched. He seemed to be gathering himself to say something unpleasant.

"Thank you."

Daniel was not sure how much more of Karter Rosen treating him like a human being he could take. "I need to get you to the infirmary."

"No, I can walk on my own." Karter lifted his hand from his side, stared at his blood. "One of them grazed me, is all. It looks worse than it is."

Daniel realized Sunfall's bells had stopped ringing. "Where are the others? The sergeants?"

"There were more of them," Karter said from the door. "The undead. Ran out of the southern entrance when the bells started. The others followed them. I started after, but Dylan and Markus and I saw the footprints leading here, and we . . ." He shook his head. "I froze."

"Don't focus on that," Daniel said. "We need to determine where the vagrants came from and stem the flow."

"I wouldn't know where to start."

"I would," Daniel said.

Karter regarded him. "These tunnels you spoke of?"

"I think so. When the others get back"—*if they're still alive*—"I can draw a map. They're easy to find, once you know what to look for."

"You're going to do better than that, Sergeant. You're going to take us to them."

Daniel scratched his head. "That would be easier." His hand froze. "Wait. What?"

"Sergeant," Karter repeated. "We need men able to take charge, and that's what you did here." He barked a humorless laugh. "Handled yourself better than I did, that's for sure."

"I only . . . you can't just promote me like—"

"It's what he would have done," Karter said, gesturing at Anders' body. "Now that Lieutenant Magath is . . . gone, we're the highest-ranking officers in the capital. That means I, and any of the other sergeants, can promote you. Which I just did."

Daniel's stomach fluttered. Alix squeezed his arm.

"I'm headed to the infirmary," Karter said. "If there's even anyone there. Dawn and Dusk, there'd better be someone there. Clean this place up and meet me and the others in the barracks in two hours. The throne room is too isolated. We didn't hear Anders until it was already too late."

With that, he stepped gingerly over the shattered remains of the door and disappeared. Daniel and Alix listened to him shuffling down the hall.

"Dawn," Alix said yet again.

Three servants arrived with two carts and cleaning supplies. Daniel helped them load headless vagrants onto one cart while Alix set to work scrubbing blood from the walls and floor. When they finished, the servants stripped Aidan's bed and threw the sheets over the undead. Jak's body went onto the second cart with Anders' remains and the bodies of Dylan Gaines and Markus Hallwell.

"Those were Wardsmen," Daniel said. "They're to be given proper burials."

The servants exchanged looks. "I'm sorry, Wardsman," one said, "but they will all be burned."

Alix looked up in alarm.

"Burn the vagrants if you want," Daniel said quietly. "The others deserve proper burials."

"I truly am sorry, Wardsman," the servant repeated, "but Lieutenant Magath issued strict orders that—"

"Lieutenant Magath is dead," Daniel said. "Pieces of him are on this cart. I'm a sergeant now, and you will do as I say." He softened his voice. "Your families would want the same for you. Only . . . " He glanced at Alix. "Remove and burn their heads. If you don't, they could rise again."

She paled, but nodded once. The servants bobbed their heads and wheeled the carts away down the corridor. "Thank you," Alix said.

"Of course," he said, voice unsteady. Without another word, he went to the bucket, took up a sponge, and knelt to help her finish cleaning. They worked in silence. The blood was still wet and wiped away easily. A short time later, Daniel stood and knuckled his back, sighed as it popped. Glancing at the splintered remains of the door, he grinned.

"What's funny?" Alix asked, standing and wiping frayed

strands of hair out of her face.

"Aidan needs a new door."

"And you find that amusing because . . . ?"

"This is the second time vagrants have smashed their way into his bedroom."

She raised an eyebrow. "That was you, farm boy."

"Yes, but vagrants were involved."

"Your secret is safe with me." She tossed her sponge into the bucket. It landed with a *plop*. Water sloshed over the sides. "Maybe it's a good thing, you getting promoted."

"Why's that?" he asked, trying to sound casual.

She waved at the pieces of wood. "The Crown of the North's door met its fate at your hand. Or rather, at your shoulder. As I understand the position, a good doorkeeper keeps doors. He does not destroy them."

For a moment, he gaped at her. A burst of laughter exploded out of him, and his tension vanished. Alix's grin split her face. "We've had quite a day, haven't we?"

Daniel dropped onto Aidan's bed. "Is it still the same day? It can't be."

Alix stood. "The excitement never ends when you're with me."

Her clothes were damp with sweat and blood. "You're a mess," he said.

"Thank you," she said again. Her cheeks colored. "Not for telling me I'm a mess. I'm well aware of that. For before, I mean."

He raised his hands. "Karter Rosen showed me gratitude today. Willingly! I'm afraid I've reached my quota. Besides," he went on quietly, "you shouldn't have had to be the one to . . . you know."

"I don't think I could have," she admitted. "If you hadn't been there, he would have killed me. My own brother." She stared at her boots.

"No," he said, standing and taking her by the arms. "That thing looked like Jak, but it wasn't him."

Her eyes found his. "I hesitated. He—it—could have killed you."

"But it didn't, and I don't think you would have let it. You're strong, Alix Merrifalls. Look at all you did to get into Calewind. You're a member of the Ward, now, or as good as. Jak, the real Jak, would be proud of you."

"You, too," she said softly. "Strong, I mean."

"I hesitated, too. I took one look at this room and wanted to run."

"But you didn't, and thank the Lady for that. You saved lives today, and not just mine."

"Alix—"

"And if you contradict me," she said, putting a finger over his lips, "I'll get Karter to come back in here and compliment you again."

"There's no need to be cruel."

She laughed and shoved him with her raised finger. Daniel stumbled, caught his foot on the frame of Aidan's bed, and tumbled onto his back. Alix stood over him. Her eyes shone. He could feel himself slipping away in them, like a ship caught in a vortex, swirling down, down . . .

He wasn't sure whether he pulled her on top of him or she tackled him. One moment they were separate, and the next their lips were locked and their hands were groping at clothes. Alix worked deftly, feeling her way to the clasps of his armor and undoing them faster than a sneak picking a lock. He sat up, spread his arms, still kissing her, and felt his chest piece drop to the floor with a clang. Climbing on top, she straddled him, raised her hands. He tugged her leather vest over her head. Her hair rose with her shirt, tumbled back into place over her bare shoulders. She bent toward him, but he held her in place, drinking in the sight of her, running his hands over her curves, feeling the smoothness of her skin.

Daniel stood hastily, breathing hard. "Alix, wait."

"I don't think I can." She reached for him, and he stepped back.

Daniel ran his hands through his hair. "Today has been . . . We've been through so much in such a short time. We just met, but it feels like . . ."

"Like we've known each other for years?"

He nodded.

"We haven't," she said. "But, so what? I know enough, and I feel the rest."

He took a deep breath. "We don't have to do this."

Hurt twisted her features. Anger followed on its heels. "Are you implying that I'd give my body to you out of gratitude?"

His mouth worked. She took silence as his answer. Alix made a sound of disbelief, crossed rigidly to where he had discarded her shirt on the floor.

"Alix, please. I—"

"Just stay away from me." She shrugged into her shirt and hurried from the room. Daniel sank onto the bed, wanting to call her back but unable to find the words. He laced his hands behind his head and stared at the ceiling. Footsteps reached his ears. He sat up and turned to the doorway, hoping she would materialize out of the darkness. Karter Rosen appeared instead. He still limped, though his gait appeared steadier. He came to the splinters that clung to the bottom of the doorway like broken teeth.

"Did you forget?" Karter asked. Daniel blinked at him. Karter rolled his eyes. "Garrison. Two hours. You. There."

"Right," Daniel said, scrambling to his feet and throwing on his shirt.

"What about that?" Karter pointed at the bed as Daniel eased back into his chainmail. Daniel followed his finger and jerked in surprise when he saw it: The false Serpent's Fang, still sheathed, the tip of the scabbard poking out from underneath the bed. He bent over and grabbed it. "Where'd you get such a strange blade, anyway?" Karter said, coming over to look at it.

Daniel didn't respond. His lips had become a thin line. His palms were slick with sweat.

Karter frowned. "All black. It looks almost like . . ."

"I think this might be what drew them here," Daniel said.

"Who?"

"The vagrants." Daniel explained how he had come to possess the sword. Karter's frown deepened as he listened to the tale. "Why would the Crown leave such a blade with you?" he said when Daniel finished.

"He didn't want it to fall into Tyrnen's hands." Daniel's eyes were fixed to the ebony blade. "He told me not to touch it, but that was when we thought it was the real Serpent's Fang."

"The one that belonged to . . . to . . ."

"Dimitri Thalamahn, Serpent King of Sallner." Daniel's voice sounded hollow.

Karter turned pale. "We were drinking in the southern district last night."

Daniel nodded slowly, remembering Garrett Lorden's face in the lantern. The madman had not appeared surprised to see Daniel. "I think they can track the sword. Magic, probably." Guilt cut him like a knife. "It's my fault. All of it."

Silence hung between them. His stomach clenched. The urge to bolt, to tear across the leagues separating Sunfall from his parents' farm deep in the southeast, grew overwhelming.

Karter scoffed. "You may be a sergeant, now, but you're not that important."

"No, I'm not. But this sword. I should have known."

"You couldn't have. Even the Crown thought it was harmless. Either way, we'll take care of it right now. Old Harold Beld in the east district refuses to leave his forge. I say that's fine. We'll give him a project."

"What project?"

"I'll explain on the way." Karter looked around as if realizing something was out of place. "Where's your woman?"

"She's not my woman," Daniel said hastily.

Karter scrutinized him, flicked his gaze to Daniel's bare chest. "All right."

"She's not," Daniel said, sounding glum.

Karter shook his head and stepped over the fragments of Aidan's door. "You picked a shade-cursed time to fall in love, Shirey."

Daniel dressed and walked beside Karter Rosen. Their footsteps echoed through Sunfall's empty halls. Out in the southern courtyard, a single Wardsman—at least a winter younger than Daniel, which explained why he didn't recognize him—stood staring down the sinuous path that led down the mountainside and into the city. His shoulders were hunched, his spear held in loose fingertips. Three men in plain clothes—white breeches, white shirts, and lightweight white coats—exchanged uncertain glances at the sight of Daniel and Karter emerging from Sunfall. The men held short swords at their sides, as if the blades were too heavy to lift.

Daniel and Karter shared a look, then saluted the Wardsman. Their gauntleted fists clapped against their chainmail, and the man jumped in surprise. He took them in, straightened, snapped a salute. The civilians studied him and imitated his pose.

"Attack could come from anywhere, Wardsman Holtik,"

Karter said.

"I know, sir. I'm sorry, sir."

Karter looked as if he wanted to berate the man further. He gave a small shake of his head. "As you were."

"Yes, Sergeant."

Karter harrumphed as he and Daniel started down the path. "I usually take a bit more pleasure tormenting the snowflakes."

"Don't I know it," Daniel grumbled.

"But it's different, now," Karter continued. "Maybe it's everything going on. I've . . . never been this afraid before." Karter flicked a glance at Daniel, his face stony, daring him to laugh.

"We're brothers," Daniel said simply.

Karter's face cleared. "I suppose we are."

They passed through the gate into Calewind. The Lady arced toward the western horizon. Shadows were beginning to lengthen, and the streets were nearly empty. Shops stood closed, stalls abandoned but packed away properly. Song spilled out of taverns, but the harps and voices and clinking glasses sounded quieter than usual. Subdued.

They followed the perfectly measured streets to the east, passing between shops and estates and seminaries where Torelian children learned how to read, write, calculate numbers, and received testing from Disciples of Dawn to determine if they were Touched by the Lady's light. As they neared the east district, Daniel heard the steady ring of hammer on anvil. Old Beld was old indeed, but still as big and brawny as an ox. His beard was the color of dirty snow, but his face and arms were leathery and taut with muscles. As one of the only smiths in Torel whose work was considered on par with Darinia's best, Beld stood little chance of retiring until he found an apprentice he deemed worthy of taking over the business.

Daniel and Karter handed Old Beld the blade and explained what they wanted done to it. At first, Old Beld eyed it with undisguised interest. Daniel watched him nervously. *Blacksmiths lust after steel the way Leastonians lust after gold*, his father liked to say.

"It's tainted," Karter said softly. Beld lifted an eyebrow.

"Dark magic," Daniel said.

That did it. Old Beld's face twisted in disgust. "Fat lot of good it'd do me, then."

"That hammer's gone and damaged his hearing," Karter muttered to Daniel.

Old Beld snorted and went to work. He stoked the bellows, filled his vat with liquid fire, and lowered the false Fang into it. When the blade was half submerged, he began a long count, his lips moving beneath thick layers of moustache. Daniel watched, counting along in his head. At one hundred, Old Beld lifted it out and inspected it. The upper half of the blade was gone. Liquid fire oozed from the midpoint of the shaft.

"Good 'nuff?" Beld asked. His eyes shone.

"All of it," Daniel said.

"Gem, too?" Beld said, nodding to the sapphire embedded into the hilt.

"All of it."

Old Beld snorted again. Transferring the remainder of the false Fang to a pair of tongs, he submerged the remainder and held it.

"Just let it go, Master Beld," Karter said softly.

Old Beld shrugged, lifted the tongs from the pool of fire. They held nothing.

"I advise letting the fire cool and then disposing of it," Karter said.

Beld peeled off his gloves and wiped them on his sooty apron. "Lady bless me," he said. He turned his attention to Daniel and Karter. "That all? I got a wife to get home to."

"You're married, Master Beld?" Daniel said, hoping he didn't sound too incredulous.

"'Course. Old Helda."

Daniel thought his eyes might pop out of his head. Karter wore an identical expression.

"Good woman," Old Beld said, beaming. Many of his teeth were dark with soot, like black squares on a tiles board.

"Better cook," Daniel said.

Old Beld threw his head back and roared laughter. "Ain't no bigger truth!" He was still roaring when Karter pulled on Daniel's arm and steered him away.

Once they were out of earshot, Daniel turned and said, "We ought to put them on the front lines" at the same instant Karter said, "They could hold the city alone."

They stopped and grinned. "Come on," Karter said. "The day

is still young, and there's work to be done."

"I'm not sure I like this sergeant business," Daniel muttered.

"You're in good company, then. Now, on the matter of building a bulwark in the east, I'm thinking that's not the best place to utilize your talents."

"My talents?"

"I want you greeting refugees when they start to arrive—which could be any moment—and directing them to outposts. I'll give you a list so you know where we're shorthanded. When you're not assigning refugees, I want you training new recruits in using staffs and spears. All these farmers are more apt to plough crops with these weapons than stick vagrants with them. Show them what you did to me."

"To you?" Daniel asked. Then he remembered their confrontation from the night before. "Oh. That."

"Yes, that," Karter said, and gave him a wry smile. "It hurt, and I never saw it coming. After that, go ahead and . . ."

Karter's words faded to a buzz as Daniel's thoughts turned to Alix. *What a difference a day can make*, he thought, thinking of how her sudden appearance that morning had irritated him to no end. He wondered where she was, and who she was with, and was thoroughly annoyed to realize he missed her.

Chapter 26:
Noncompliance

EDMUND WAS AWAKENED by the sound of padded feet dashing into his room. "Have you seen him?"

He opened his eyes. It took him a moment to remember where he was, and to place the woman's voice. *Cyrolin. I'm at Jamian's estate.* Edmund lay on his belly staring at a sand-colored wall pointy with stucco. Seagulls called off in the distance. The scent of saltwater touched his nose.

Groaning, Edmund pushed himself upright, his body cracking and popping. His left leg was the worst. It was numb, as if asleep. He turned to face Cyrolin. Her hair was in disarray. Her face was tight with worry. Her robe, made of a diaphanous material, hung open down the middle. He palmed his eyes, as much to rub away sleepiness as to avert his gaze, until stars filled his vision.

"Jamian's gone," Cyrolin said. She rushed from the room.

He removed his palms. When the stars faded, he saw bright, blue morning sky. "Damn it. We're late."

Edmund stood. *Slept in my armor.* Anna had once told Aidan that—

"—your father sleeps in his steel and snow."

The family sat out on one of the south patios, dining on breakfast and looking out over Calewind as the Lady ascended her throne in the east. Far below, down the mountain path, people the size of ants trickled out of their homes and into the streets.

Aidan, eight winters old, did not observe any of this. He was staring open-mouthed at Edmund, who sat across from the boy and his mother. "You do not!" *he said.*

Edmund, dressed in his armor, took another bite of eggs and raised his eyebrows.

"Haven't you noticed what your father wore to breakfast this morning?" *Anna asked.*

"You wake up very early," *Aidan pointed out to his father.* "Right when the Lady begins to rise. You could dress before breakfast."

"I rise before the Lady," *Edmund said.*

Aidan's eyes widened. "Before her? People do that?"

Anna caught Edmund's eye. Her lips quivered. He directed his attention to his plate, concentrating on military drills, inventory, tours of the barracks. Anything to keep from bursting out laughing.

Then Aidan spoke up. "Is that why your steel and snow smells so bad?"

Edmund's discipline failed him.

The sound of furniture scraping across tiled floor broke his reverie. Grimacing at the stiffness in his bad leg, he set off down the hall toward the source of the commotion. He found Cyrolin in Jamian's bedchambers, rushing from the bed to the bureau and back, overturning pillows and blankets and folded clothes.

Spotting him, she froze. "Jamian's gone," she said again.

Edmund removed his gauntlets, tossed them on the bed and ran his hands through his hair. "Slow down. Does he usually step out first thing in the morning? For a walk, or . . . ?"

"No. I have no idea where he could be." She sank onto Jamian's bed. "I expected him to bring home pretties. That's what he calls other women. But he did not come in. I would have awakened."

"You sleep in his bed?"

"Why is that important?"

"Ordinarily, it wouldn't be. But if you share his bed, it would be difficult for him to slip out unnoticed."

Looking guilty, she averted her gaze.

"What is it?" he asked.

Cyrolin fussed at the bedding. "I do sleep in his bed most nights. He enjoys my company. Sometimes he even asks me."

Heat crept up Edmund's neck. "Asks you?"

Cyrolin did not reply right away. "Although he is a guildmaster, sometimes his tongue runs away with his mind. The city is crowded with strangers come for the festival. What if he said the wrong thing to the wrong person? What if he's passed out somewhere? What if he . . . ?" She bent, head in her hands.

Edmund's anxiety over missing their morning audience dissipated. Just slightly. The more he learned of a galerunner's contract with her captain, the more he viewed it as slavery. Still, she obviously worried over Jamian. He began a slow circuit of the room, looking but not touching the captain's furniture or belongings.

"What are you doing?" Cyrolin asked, standing.

"Anna does this sometimes," he said. "She has an appointment or some other obligation, but since she's the Crown of the North, she usually leaves me some indicator of where she's going if I cannot attend. That way her guards and I know where to look in case she's absent for too long."

"Anna. Your wife. I thought she . . ."

Edmund jerked to a halt a few steps from a lacquered wardrobe. "She is. I forget sometimes." His eyes burned.

"I'm sorry," she said, and sounded as if she meant it.

Edmund did not look at her. He focused on the steady murmur and sigh of the Great Sea and resumed searching. He pulled the wardrobe doors open, gave the inside a cursory glance—several pairs of boots, colored shirts with ruffled sleeves, variegated pants, gold cuff links—and closed the doors. Then he patted around on top. His fingertips came away dusty. He moved to the bed, inspecting the ruffled sheets, and . . .

There, by the floor. He bent down and picked up a sheet of parchment.

"What does it say?" the galerunner asked.

Edmund did not answer, his eyes scanning line to line.

Cyrolin,

I'm feeling better this morning, so I've gone ahead to assemble the guildmasters. Evening is the earliest we'll be able to convene. Our agenda is full today. The late start works to our advantage. Make sure the general does not come to the Prefecture empty-handed. Traditions must be observed.

I will meet you here beforehand. Bring the general's offering for my approval.

Jamian

Edmund handed the note to Cyrolin. She read quickly, then lowered it with a frown. "I knew of no morning meetings on his agenda."

"Perhaps he forgot to mention them."

"Unlikely. He uses me to spirit him to and from the Prefecture. Jamian does not care much for walking."

I'd never have guessed, Edmund thought distractedly. His mind had turned to more pressing matters. "What does he mean about observing traditions?"

"Your trade offering."

Edmund let out his breath in a hiss. The trade offering. Or, as the Darinians called it, *Infarct bry cest dasm.* In the common tongue shared between north and east, it translated to *Scratching a friend's back.* Guildmasters expected dignitaries from other realms to buy favors with favors. Merchants loved cutting deals on imported materials, paying lower tarries on roads, cozying up to a ruler in order to scoop a trade agreement out from under a rival. The greater the favor a supplicant performed, the more apt the guild was to reciprocate in turn.

He shoved his anger away. He needed to focus. Jamian had shown no indication of expecting a favor in exchange for helping Edmund convince the other guildmasters to ally with Aidan and Nichel. *The agenda,* he remembered. Of course. Jamian had obviously met with the others earlier this morning. The other guildmasters probably had reminded Jamian that even General Edmund Calderon of Torel's Ward would be expected to bring something of value before them. *Sentimentality is worth less than nothing,* Leastonians liked to say. Everything had a price.

As general, Edmund wielded the authority to grant favors in Torel's name. He had been king under Anna's rule, and his son held Heritage now. *Something material. But what could I purchase in Ironsail that the guildmasters do not already own?* There was also the matter of coin. His purse contained emergency funds only, not nearly enough to convince the guild to help fund a war.

He frowned. Would Cinders Kerevin and Deletar be expected to offer a favor in the name of the Touched? *They mentioned nothing of any such dealings when we saw them last night.* He opened his mouth to ask Cyrolin if she could recommend a gift, but the words dried on his tongue. She was perspiring, and her visage was contorted in anxiety. "What's wrong?" he asked.

"Let's go," she said, lifting her hands to her shoulders.

"Go where?"

"The Pincer's Heart."

Edmund recognized the name. It was the busiest shopping district in Ironsail, and the most expensive. Before he could respond, Cyrolin pulled her nightgown over her shoulders, exposing smooth, pale skin, and a rash that spread from her belly up to her breasts. From there it fanned out across her arms.

He turned away. "I'm sorry. I did not mean to look. But I noticed . . ."

"The verrucae," she said. Fabric rustled against skin.

"Is that the redness?"

"Yes. It is my punishment."

"For what?" he asked, bewildered.

She came around in front of him, wearing a skirt and vest streaked in pinks and purples. "For noncompliance."

THEY WALKED SIDE by side, following the lazy loop of Ironsail's roads. The city was quiet and still. Most of the merrymakers were sleeping off the first night of festival. The sandy streets were littered with empty bottles, their colored vines dark or flickering. To the west, the Great Sea susurrated, sharing secrets few were awake to hear. No wind sped them forward. Edmund had not suggested that Cyrolin use her talent. There was no need to hurry if the guild could not receive them until later, much as that grated on his nerves.

Cyrolin had been quiet since their departure. Her sandals scratched over the sandy roads. Edmund cleared his throat. "You did nothing wrong that I can see."

"Of course, I did," she said without looking.

"What could you possibly have done?" He thought he knew, but wanted confirmation.

"Jamian gave me an order, and I dawdled."

"Jamian was not present to give you an order."

"He did not have to be."

Edmund fell silent. Her reply confirmed his suspicions on two counts: That galerunners were compelled to obey orders given verbally or in writing, and that Jamian had written the letter. If it had not been written in his hand, he doubted Cyrolin would have been forced to obey. His features hardened. *To comply.*

"He abuses you through the bond you share."

Cyrolin slowed and turned to him. "No, he doesn't. I do."

"How? By hesitating even an instant after being given an order?"

"Yes." She rubbed at her right arm.

"That's inhuman."

"It is how things work."

"I don't understand—" he started.

Her scratching intensified. "Could we please walk as we talk?" she said in a small voice.

"Of course. I'm sorry."

They set off again. Cyrolin grew more relaxed. Her scratching ceased, her face smoothed out. "Please explain it to me," Edmund said.

"Why should I?" She seemed suddenly defensive. "What concern is it of yours?"

"I just want to understand."

She stared straight ahead. Around them, Ironsail began to stir. Leastonians in colorful garments strolled up this road or that one. Revelers wearing costumes or smeared face paint shuffled in groups of two or three, bleary-eyed and talking in low tones.

"A galerunner is bonded to her captain in exchange for his payment."

"Jamian pays you?"

"No. He bought me from another captain who took me from a faraway realm when I was a child. I don't remember its name, or where it's located, or anything about it, other than it was rainy. I also remember being hungry. I remember the voyage across the Great Sea to Leaston. To this city. I remember seeing your Lady on these shores for the first time. We had a different name for her where I came from. I remember that, too. Sol."

"Sol," Edmund repeated, feeling it on his tongue. "A pretty

name. Lyrical."

Cyrolin's lips quirked. "Yes."

"How old were you?"

"A child. Perhaps four or five summers."

"You've been with Jamian since childhood?"

"No. I was trained by other galerunners to ride the Lady's breath. To manipulate it. Without that skill, I had no value. Jamian came along when I was sixteen summers. He bonded me then. It's a curious thing, the bonding. Almost like your Torelian marriages. We join hands, like so"—she reached and took his hands, cupping them as if to drink water, resting her palms against his—"and another galerunner folds his or her hands overtop ours, and says an incantation. There's a warm feeling, and then . . ." She shrugged.

"And then you must comply with him forever," he said, unable to keep the bite out of his voice.

"As long as he is my captain."

"And you must do as he says, when he says it, or else—"

"Or else the verrucae," she said, absently running her nails up and down her exposed midriff. Her rash had faded from an angry red to a light pink.

"What does he make you do?"

She held his gaze as they walked along. "Whatever he wants me to do."

Cyrolin guided him down a side street. They emerged in a wide square lined with shops and stalls painted in varying shades of red. Any surface not painted was draped in rosy banners. The Pincer's Heart was congested even at so early an hour. Merchants positively sparkled, their nose, ears, fingers, and clothes festooned in gems and loops of gold and silver. They paced in front of their stalls, displaying ornaments, weapons, fruit, exotic animals, carpets, tools, books, puzzles, clothing, cheeses, spiced meats, toys made from wood or metal. One merchant let her breasts spill out to attract eyes to her supply of iridescent figurines carved from glass.

Across the square, two young men walked hand in hand. Not far from them, an ebony-skinned man shouted and waved, gesturing at a small group of children who sat huddled in a pen looking frightened and confused. The boys were not human children, but reavers. The girls looked like Cyrolin: red hair, dark green eyes, creamy skin. At the sight of them, Cyrolin went rigid and looked away. Galerunners in training, Edmund guessed, as a few men and women wearing captain's garb stopped to examine them.

Edmund's heart sank. The sight of the two young men made him glad. Such public displays would not go unpunished in Torel, yet in the same breath he had seen two people free to express their love, he had witnessed children being sold to the highest bidder. It was a grim reminder that Leaston, for all its open-mindedness in some ways, was ultimately a realm made up of people, and people tended to work against their fellow man if it would earn them so much as a single coin.

"What will you buy?" Cyrolin asked.

"I don't know. I didn't come to Leaston for a shopping excursion."

"Let me point you in the right direction," she said, gesturing for him to follow.

They meandered, inspecting "the ripest fruit this side of Sharem," and jewels "cut by hands more deft than a wildlander smith's," and "silver so fine you'll swear a Darinian fashioned it, but"—the merchant spoke in a conspiratorial whisper—"no Darinian silver could be bought for prices as low as those I offer."

The Lady's light grew hotter with each passing minute. So did Edmund's temper. They were wasting time. "I don't care. That one," he said, waving a hand at a medium-sized trunk.

The merchant, a man fatter than Jamian, rushed over. "Ah, yes. A fine choice, fine choice. Handmade, carved from ebonywood." He took in Edmund's steel and snow. "Ah, a Wardsman! A discount in exchange for your bravery."

"How large of a discount?" Edmund said.

The merchant ran his tongue over his lips. "Let us say . . . fifteen Leastonian marks. Or eleven Torelian, if that's all you carry." His tone suggested he would be much more satisfied with the former. Not that it mattered. Edmund had only eight Torelian marks to work with. He opened his mouth to tell Cyrolin they should look elsewhere.

To his amazement, the galerunner snorted. "An insulting offer. Come, General. There are other merchants in the Heart who would be more than happy to—"

The merchant sputtered. "General? Of the Ward?" He glanced

at Edmund's waist, saw Valor. "Forgive me, sir—General Calderon the Valorous. I did not recognize you."

"That you would ask more than three Leastonian marks for such a box is insulting enough," Cyrolin snapped. Edmund watched her carefully. Her slouched posture indicated boredom, but her eyes radiated excitement.

"My dear, I . . ." The merchant got a better look at Cyrolin. "Captain Jamian's galerunner," he said under his breath. A plaintive note had entered his tone.

"The very one," Cyrolin said loudly. "We should look elsewhere, General. Jamian has told me of much better deals to be found closer to North Haven."

"Ah! Forgive me, galerunner, but I beg to differ. You won't find better trunks in all of—"

"A trunk is a trunk," Cyrolin said.

"But only this trunk is suited for . . . for . . ." He looked at Edmund. "Who are you buying for?"

"His sister," Cyrolin cut in. "A young noble in the north."

The merchant frowned. "A sister? I had not heard that the general—"

Cyrolin began to turn away. "I saw other gilded furniture across the market."

"Ah! Her first trunk, then!" the merchant shouted jubilantly. "I can take . . . ten Leastonian marks."

Cyrolin's eyes brightened. Edmund, catching on to what was happening and wanting to be done with the charade, broke in. "I can offer you eight."

"Eight snowflakes?" The merchant cleared his throat. "Forgive me, General, but that's a pittance in light of—"

"Eight," Edmund cut in.

"Fourteen!"

"Eight."

"General, be reasonable. How about ten?"

Edmund narrowed his eyes. "Five."

Now the man's eyes were as bright as Cyrolin's. "All right, all right. Six snowflakes, and a stall in Calewind the next time I visit."

Edmund pretended to turn that over. "When will that be?"

"Within the month."

Edmund stuck out his hand. "Done."

The merchant nearly wrenched his arm out of joint. "Excellent, General. You'll be most pleased with it, General. Your sister, too."

Edmund kept a firm hold on his patience as he dug six Torelian marks out of his purse and handed them over. The other man snatched them away as if worried Edmund might change his mind. "If you'd like, I can have one of my apprentices—"

Before he could finish, Edmund bent at the knees and grabbed the chest at either side. As he straightened, a bolt of pain shot up his left leg. He bared his teeth to stifle a grunt. "Thank you, I'll be fine," Edmund said.

The merchant smiled. "And I'll send word ahead of my visit, General? In, say, three weeks' time?"

"Very good," Edmund said over his shoulder as he and Cyrolin strode off. *If either of us is still alive by then.* He was in a black mood. He had never owned a box worth more than a single *snowflake*, and he was less than thrilled about owning one worth six times as much. It was wide enough to store linens and clothing, making it awkward to carry, and he banged his knees against it with every step. By the time they exited the plaza his face was covered in sweat.

"It's a chest. A work of art," Cyrolin said. She had seemed to read his mind.

"There are eight guildmasters. I'm bringing a single box—"

"A chest," she corrected.

"—a single chest for eight people. What will they give me in return? A single Azure Blade?"

"The trade is just a formality. An observance of tradition, as Jamian said."

Hearing the captain's name brought Edmund's temper up another notch. "He had better be ready."

"Admit it," Cyrolin said. "You enjoyed yourself."

"The barter?" Edmund shrugged. "Not as much as you."

"I am a Leastonian," she replied simply. "More or less a Leastonian, after so many years. Do you intend to keep your word?"

Edmund remembered his promise to the merchant. "If Calewind is still standing, he can sell his *chests*."

Grinning, Cyrolin shook her head. "Once a Leastonian trader gets his foot in the door, he'll chop it off rather than allow it to close."

"Meaning?"

"Meaning, your new friend will reap a profit, and then petition you for better locations, offers of trade. If that does not work—or even if it does—I would not be surprised if your son caught word that a generous merchant cut his father a deal. What Crown of the North would refuse a request made from the man who helped his father in his time of need?"

Edmund did not challenge her prediction. He hated commerce and politics. Those had been Anna's territory. She was intelligent, quick, and cunning. He could wield a sword and protect his family.

No, he thought. *You can only do one of those things.*

Cyrolin read his face. "We're almost back to Jamian's estate," she said.

Edmund only nodded. He was so tired. So numb. So ready to be finished.

"Stop here," Cyrolin said. Edmund did. His arms were on fire. "Step away," the galerunner said. Edmund did. Her lips moved. With a wave of Cyrolin's hand the box lifted into the air. "Come. It will follow." She resumed walking, and the box bobbed along behind her.

"Thanks," he grumbled. *I could have used that ten minutes ago.*

"I was not sure I could perform the spell," she said. That time, he guessed, she had read his tone rather than his mind. "Galerunners learn how to manipulate the winds, and not much else."

They continued on. More revelers in wild costumes and paint flooded the streets: a man in midnight-black attire and a fox mask, his eyes a burnished gold; a woman with snakes coiled along her arms and body, maybe real, maybe not; a handful of men wearing caps, white face paint, a mouthful of fangs; two larger men ensconced in old leather, curved horns atop their heads and legs ending in cloven boots.

Uneasiness pierced his apathy like a sword point. Some of the costumes were too real after the things he had seen. "Thank you for getting involved," he said, in need of a distraction.

Cyrolin glanced at him. "Involved?"

"With the merchant. My head is . . . in a different place. I was as likely to stab him and take the chest than muster the wits needed to barter with a Leastonian."

"I didn't do it for you," she said simply.

"Jamian?"

"In part." She scratched idly at one arm. Edmund noticed the rash there had nearly faded. Cyrolin gestured at the chest, which gave a little leap, like a tiny dog happy to see its master. "I think they'll like it. They appreciate craftsmanship, and this is beautiful work."

"You obviously enjoy bartering," he said. "At the very least, you're good at it."

"I do, and I am," she said after a moment's thought. "I watch Jamian. I listen. But back there, I . . . wanted to barter. I did that for myself." Her expression grew tense.

"You should tell Jamian to let you do the talking more often. You could save him a great deal of money."

Cyrolin made a noncommittal sound. They rounded a bend and the high walls and tall palm trees ringing Jamian's estate came into view. Cyrolin touched the ornate iron gate, and Edmund heard a faint click as it swung open to admit them. He crossed the courtyard behind Cyrolin, who strode through the manor's front door.

"Jamian?" Cyrolin called, stepping into the foyer. Edmund stepped in behind her, then stopped. His nostrils flared, and he perceived a faint, sickly-sweet scent.

A loud crash behind him made him jump. The chest had clattered into the doorframe, too wide to fit. The furniture paused, as if considering, and then bumped into the doorframe again. Again. An instant later it thudded to the ground just outside the door.

"He's still not here," Cyrolin said.

Edmund's fists clenched. "We should go now."

"No," she said. "He will not be ready. He said so. Besides," she added, "you look unwell."

"I'm fine," he snapped. She disappeared back toward Jamian's bedroom. Edmund sank onto the bed, trying and failing to ignore the throbbing in his bad leg. He lay on his back, staring at the ceiling, trying not to think.

Voices woke him.

Edmund sat up, breathing hard, once again forgetting where

he was. He remembered faster this time, but the Lady was much lower in the sky. His aches had faded to dull rumbles. Then he remembered the cry.

He found Cyrolin standing over Jamian, who was sitting up in his bed. The captain was dressed and appeared in much better health. His complexion was ruddy, and his characteristic smirk was in place. Only dark circles under his eyes betrayed exhaustion and tension from the previous night.

"You're all right," Edmund said.

"Of course," Jamian said. "My fever broke before Dawn, so I got an early start. I look forward to seeking my bed earlier than usual tonight. But first," he continued, rising to face Edmund, "there are pressing matters to attend to. I offer my apologies for the delay, General."

Edmund inclined his head. He was in no mood to accept apologies. He would have forgiven a legitimate illness, but Jamian's irresponsible behavior the night before threatened the fate of Crotaria. More importantly, it threatened Edmund's only reason for living.

Suddenly, Jamian turned and coughed into the crook of an elbow. "I believe I'm coming down with something," he said.

Perhaps you'll find a cure at the bottom of a bottle, Edmund thought.

Cyrolin frowned at the captain. "You need to rest. You—"

Jamian's voice was low. "Cyrolin. Do not argue with me. You will accompany me now."

The galerunner's mouth snapped shut. She immediately fell into step behind him as he swept from the room. *He looks ill, but not does move like it*, Edmund thought absently. His thoughts had turned to the impending audience.

Out in the foyer, Edmund caught the too-sweet scent again. "Does anyone else smell that?"

Jamian paused in the front doorway. "Ah. I bought a side of pork from a street vendor this morning. I brought it out to the patio to serve, thinking you would both be home when I returned. I must have forgot about it." He gave a smile that did not touch his eyes. "I confess, I still feel ill. Come. The sooner we call on my associates, the sooner I can . . . and what is this?" He toed the chest, which lay on its side near the doorway.

"The general's trade offer," Cyrolin said. She waited outside with her shoulders hunched and her arms at her sides.

"Of course. You got my note." Jamian appraised the box and nodded, lips quirking in a small smile. "It's perfect." Cyrolin held one hand over the box. It stirred like a leaf caught in an eddy of wind. "No," he snapped. "Leave it."

Cyrolin let her hand drop. The box clattered to the ground. Jamian rubbed his hands together. "Thank you, Edmund. If my compatriots ask, I'll tell them you followed our custom to the letter, and that we settled the matter privately." He winked. "Should they ask. I'd prefer they didn't, truth be told. It's a fine chest and will look splendid in my master bedroom. Don't you agree, Cyrolin?"

"Yes," she answered, eyes downcast.

"Come," Jamian said, and started toward South Haven. Cyrolin spun on her heel and walked in his shadow.

Edmund hesitated. Something didn't feel right. Then his thoughts were filled with visions of Aidan taking the battlefield, watching Wardsmen and clansfolk torn to shreds by undead, his eyes wide and frightened, wondering where his father was, why Edmund had failed him.

Had Anna wondered? Had she felt alone and betrayed in the end? No. His wife was too strong for such frailties. Aidan, too. Edmund was the weak one.

The fist around his heart tightened. Edmund put one foot in front of the other.

Chapter 27:
Before the Guild

IRONSAIL'S STREETS LOOPED into South Haven, where they tapered and straightened into a neat grid marred by squalor. That squalor, Edmund had come to find, was intentional.

Beyond rows of taverns, brothels, tenements, and unmarked shops where one could peruse and purchase illicit goods, South Haven served as Ironsail's warehouse quarter. Less scrupulous businesses were a screen for narrow lanes lined with granaries, silos, and storehouses. Merchants, captains, and peddlers came to South Haven to unload stock from their buildings and sell it. Some materials were loaded onto barges and shipped up and down the rivers that unspooled across the realms—excepting Sallner—like blue lace. Others were transported by seafaring vessels that left for the Great Sea, waters charted only by Leastonian captains or pirates. Peddlers carried goods along the West Road, passing through cities and villages and continuing on into Sharem or further north toward Calewind.

The Prefecture sat in the center of South Haven. Wide stone blocks made up a forecourt where patrons could mingle on carved benches or on the rim of fountains molded from bronze. Broad steps lined by gilded columns ascended to a wide stone edifice crowned by a golden globe twice as wide as the Prefecture itself. On the western horizon, the golden globe of the Lady of

Dawn receded, staining the sky in deep shades of orange and red and setting the Prefecture's ornament to sparkling. The globe's resemblance to the Lady was no mistake. To Leastonians, trade was the center of the world, and they viewed Ironsail, not Sharem, as the true center of Crotaria's four realms.

Every piece of the Prefecture, from the blocks of the forecourt to the globe itself, was shabby, as if the building had been raised and then left to rot. That, too, was by design. The wealthiest men and women in all of Leaston sat on the guild. They assembled to hold council in the Prefecture, but their vast sums of coins and material goods were stored elsewhere, in their manor houses and in banks across the eastern realm. Thieves hoping to loot the Prefecture and make off with prized jewels would come away empty-handed, if the guildmasters left their hands intact.

Edmund counted ten Azure Blades milling around the forecourt as he approached with Jamian and Cyrolin, *Sard'tara* at their sides. None were men, women, or reavers he recognized. That was fine. No one looked surprised to see him. That meant he was expected.

One of the Blades, a woman with short, chestnut-colored hair and flinty eyes, came forward to meet them. "Guildmaster," she said, nodding at Jamian.

"A fine evening to you, Blade Nita," the captain returned. "I am here to meet with my fellows. They are inside." It was not a question.

Nita hesitated. "They are, Guildmaster."

Edmund caught her pause. All at once his senses sharpened, as if a peaceful camp had been disturbed an arrow out of the dark. He scanned the broad courtyard extending out from the Prefecture and studied the Blades more carefully. What he had taken for milling was actually patrolling. The Blades moved in set patterns, back and forth. Their eyes were alert. Around them, warehouses sat quiet and dark. Edmund was reminded of sepulchers. Outside South Haven, laughter and shouts rang out. *Festival*, he remembered.

"Was there something else?" Jamian asked Nita.

"I only just arrived," she said. "Things have been rather chaotic."

"How so?"

"I'll let someone with more knowledge of the situation

explain."

Nita strode toward the Prefecture. A section of the rectangular building slid down to provide ingress. She stepped through and the panel slid up, like a jaw snapping shut.

"We were not asked to wait inside," Edmund said quietly.

Jamian was frowning. A minute later, the panel opened again, and Hahrzen the reaver came stomping up to them. "Sorry to make you wait," he said gruffly.

"What's the problem, Blade?" Jamian said. "I waited only out of courtesy. I am a guildmaster, and can come and go as I damn well—"

Hahrzen raised his hands. "Peace, Guildmaster. I'm only following orders from your peers. A situation has come up. Forgive me for saying so, but you look a bit worn."

"I imbibed last night," Jamian said.

"How much? If you don't mind me asking."

"Half a bottle of slush at most, and I believe I do mind. Explain yourself."

Hahrzen scratched at the back of his neck. "There's a bug going around. Several other guildmasters sent missives explaining that they were bedridden. It was only your request for an audience that dragged them here."

"Will the guild still be able to meet?" Edmund asked sharply.

Jamian glanced at him. "What symptoms?" he asked.

Edmund felt a barely perceptible pang of guilt. He and Anna knew the guildmasters and liked most of them. But he could not afford more delays.

"Aches, chills, fever, retching," Hahrzen said. He lowered his voice. "Some of their galerunners and members of their cells have been taken with it."

"Have you heard rumors of any disease, Hahrzen?" Edmund asked. "A plague, perhaps, carried from overseas?"

"From the visitors come for festival, more like," the Azure Blade replied. "We're taking steps to contain an outbreak."

"What steps?" Jamian asked.

"Guildmaster Gewnan ordered all gates closed an hour ago. Maybe too late, but it's something."

Jamian frowned. "Some of the others did seem more tired than usual."

Edmund quelled a spasm of anxiety. A plague in the east did

not make his own assignment any less urgent. "I need to meet with the guild, Hahrzen," he said. "That situation I spoke of yesterday . . ."

The reaver lifted an eyebrow. "The situation you danced around and refused to make clear?"

"That's the one. It's urgent, even more dire than what might be happening here. Jamian can attest to that, and has."

Hahrzen took a deep breath. "Guildmaster Osphera looks barely able to sit up under her own power, and the rest are as worse for wear." He frowned. "She came in good health, but by the time you left, Guildmaster Jamian, she was complaining of chills and had come down with a case of the shakes."

"She did look unsteady," Jamian said.

"I hate to say it, but you might have been one of the first infected," Hahrzen said. His gaze flitted to Edmund. "Unless you brought an illness with you, General."

"I am hale and hearty," Edmund replied. No offense was intended. Hahrzen was a soldier doing his duty.

"The audience is of great import," Jamian replied. "This must be done. Then we will adjourn."

The reaver's brow furrowed. He knew he could not argue with a guildmaster. Stepping aside, he waved them through. Jamian took the lead. Edmund let Cyrolin fall in behind him. They approached the nondescript wall from which the reaver had emerged. Jamian brushed a hand against it, and a panel slid upward. Before entering, he looked up at the sky.

"There will be fireworks," Jamian said softly.

For a moment, Edmund forgot the urgency of his mission. When his father was out of earshot, Edmund's mother had told him of blasts of color that bloomed in the sky like glittering flowers and boomed like the most fearsome storms. Fireworks were outlawed in the north, but Leaston had no such compunctions.

Jamian smiled, as if to himself. "Oh, yes. The festival will reach its apex tonight, General."

They stepped inside. Like its exterior, the Prefecture's interior was a study in humility. Simple rugs and portraits decorated otherwise plain walls and flooring. Cabinets and tables sat against the walls, but they too were artless, utilitarian. In the center of the building, Edmund knew, stretched a theatre with a wide stage and sweeping rows of seats from which—

Run.

Edmund froze. It was his inner voice, honed over a boyhood spent monitoring every drink of spirits his father took. Three bottles were safe. Halfway through a fourth, James Calderon's eyes turned bleary and bloodshot, signaling that the time had come for Edmund to go to his safe place to wait out the coming storm. His inner voice had been honed to a razor's edge over thirty winters serving his realm and the Crown of the North in Torel's Ward. It was less a voice and more an awareness able to consider his surroundings and shape calculations and instincts into words.

For the first time since watching Anna bleed out over the snow at Lake Carrean, Edmund felt afraid. Unconsciously, his left hand strayed to Valor and throttled its hilt.

Behind him, the panel slid closed. Jamian and Cyrolin were far ahead. He followed. Three pairs of boots rose and fell almost in unison. Standing lamps flickered and murmured. Closed doors stood between cabinets and portraits. Jamian led them up this hall and down that corridor until they arrived at a narrow staircase leading up into the golden orb of the Prefecture.

Another narrow passageway. Through a door at the far end. They emerged in a round room. A single bench made of dark, polished wood ran along the far wall. Eight doors stood behind the bench. Between the doors and bench were eight chairs. Far above in the center of the vaulted ceiling, a skylight admitted the Lady's fading light.

Edmund's eyes took in more than the audience hall revealed. Eight doorways, one skylight. Nine points of egress, including the one through which they had entered *No. Ten.* In between the eight doors behind the guildmasters' bench was a span of wall slightly wider than a door. It led to the tunnels, or so he speculated.

"Here you are, General," Jamian said.

"You won't stand alongside me?"

"I'll be taking my customary place at the bench," he said. "We'll join you shortly."

Edmund did not move. His stomach churned with the nerves he often felt just before a battle broke out. He opened his mouth, wanting to point out that the guildmasters might be more receptive if they saw Jamian by his side. Then the captain surprised him.

"Stay with him, Cyrolin," Jamian said. The galerunner fixed him with a confused expression. "Edmund is our ally, and deserves a show of our support. I would provide it, but, alas, am compelled to sit with my associates."

Blinking once, Cyrolin said, "You do not wish me to stay by your side?"

"What I want is for you to refrain from questioning me."

She dropped her gaze and clasped her hands at her waist. Jamian faced Edmund and, grinning, snapped the Ward's salute. His expression gave the gesture a mocking air. Edmund returned it stiffly. The door leading into the chamber closed behind Jamian.

Cyrolin stood in the center of the room, unable or unwilling to look at Edmund. "Jamian does not seem himself," he said quietly.

A muscle in her jaw twitched. "I find him the same as ever."

Edmund gazed around, trying to distract himself when a sharp crack sounded from outside. "What was that?" he asked sharply.

"Fireworks," Cyrolin said, studying him with one eyebrow raised. "You've never heard them."

"Or seen them," he muttered. The prospect no longer excited him. Another crack followed the first, and Edmund was reminded distinctly of the sound of a lightning bolt stabbing the earth.

"They're beautiful," Cyrolin said, "and not so different from thunder in a storm. I am used to thunder. We see lightning sometimes, Jamian and I, out at sea. If he permits it. I typically steer us clear of inclement weather. Edmund? Are you all right?"

Her voice faded. The room faded. Reality faded, giving way to—

—*snowy earth stained red. Anna screamed as her legs exploded. Blood and flesh and bits of bone sprayed everywhere, painting ground and trees and ice. The flash of the lightning bolt had been bright, but Edmund did not close his eyes. He could not.*

Anna's legs were gone. Her eyes rolled. Edmund thought dimly that she was lying where they had picnicked with Aidan a lifetime ago. Tyrnen stalked toward her, reaching into his robes, and then Anna said something that made the old man rush forward. Edmund became aware of himself, muscles straining to break the grip of the hands that held him. And then Edmund stepped in front of Edmund, some doppelganger, and—

"—want me to get Jamian?"

The voice cut through his trance like a knife ripping silk. Edmund focused on it, pulled on it as if it were a rope and he were suspended over a crevasse. Cyrolin was there, face framed by auburn hair. "I'm sorry," he said. The words came out hoarse and shaky.

"Do the fireworks bother you?"

"They bring back painful memories."

Before Cyrolin could respond, the eight doors opened. Edmund adopted his customary military bearing: stiff-backed, stoic, left hand on his sword hilt, right hand clapped to his side.

Five men and two women filed in, the fabric of their shawls and skirts and trousers whispering as they moved. Jamian, clothed in a yellow shirt open at the collar and a pair of baggy trousers, wore the most sensible attire of the bunch. Four of the men were ensconced in rainbows of velvets: silver shirts, red pants, green sleeves, blue sandals, purple turbans embedded with gaudy yellow stones. Osphera, a woman at least ten winters Anna's senior, wore a flowing black dress and a hat capped with a feather nearly half her height. The feather caught in the doorway and then flicked upright as she passed through. The billowy sleeves of another guildmaster, a lady Edmund did not know, sagged nearly to the floor.

Azure Blades trailed behind them, dressed in their sea-colored leather vests and leggings. Each gripped a *Sard'tara*, Darinian for Star Splinters. Dakran of the Anvil, the Darinian smith whose soul had long since taken its place in their Father's Vanguard, had forged the first *Sard'tara*, and had named it by spreading the legend that he had fused it from a sliver of midnight sky topped with the soul of a brave warrior. The name and legend stuck, and the Darinians had carved one thousand *Sard'tara*. The merchant's guild of that era snapped them up, then begged and exhorted for more. The war chief had refused. It was not a question of money. Their Father could spare no other souls from his Vanguard.

The *Sard'tara* had taken on mythical status among the Azure

Blades. Not a single Splinter had been lost. Commanders were known to reorient battle plans, shifting Blades from primary objectives to recovering *Sard'tara* dropped by fallen brethren. According to rumor, no weapon had even been broken, cracked, so much as scuffed. Another rumor intimated that a Splinter could cross with Heritage, and the Gairden's blade would break first.

Hahrzen and Nita entered, and Edmund recognized a handful of other Blades who entered with them. The Blades took their customary places to either side of their respective guildmasters and faced forward. Edmund experienced a flash of professional respect. Man, woman, or reaver, all Azure Blades were trained well, and would serve his son ably against Tyrnen's horrors.

Whispering fabrics and creaking chairs subsided into silence. Edmund narrowed his eyes. Seven guildmasters, seven seats filled. There was a click as a door on the far right opened. Gewnan Ferinold, the eldest guildmaster, tottered out. His back was hunched, his lips puckered in a moue. He was dressed plainly, having little time or patience for ornamentation: brown trousers and shirt, long sleeves, no hat to cover his soft head of wispy curls, and spectacles with lenses as thick as the decorative panes in Sunfall.

Gewnan lowered himself into his chair with a sigh. Two Azure Blades flanked him, the heads of their *Sard'tara* scraping softly against the floor. Jamian leaned forward in his chair. "Are you sure you're well enough to attend, Gewnan?"

The old man waved a spotted hand. "Only tired from all the commotion. I didn't catch this bug you and the others came down with."

"How fortunate," Jamian said.

"Now, then," Gewnan said, squinting. "Are we all here? Excellent." He adjusted his spectacles and cleared his throat. "General Edmund Calderon." He peered down his nose at Edmund, who inclined his head. "We are always happy to receive you, General, though I understand these are grave circumstances."

"Thank you," Edmund replied. The hand around his heart squeezed for all it was worth. From far away, a trio of explosions went off. *Boom, crack, boom.* Colored light flashed through the skylight, bathing the room in shades of green, blue, red.

"Normally, a meeting during our festival would be a most inopportune time," Gewnan went on. "But we would never refuse an audience with our allies in the north. Please, speak."

"Thank you, Guildmasters," Edmund said. They stared at him with hands steepled and elbows resting on the bench. Most wore cool, distant expressions. "I believe Guildmaster Jamian has already shared with you the purpose of this council, so I will get to the heart of the matter."

"Jamian has told us nothing," Osphera said in her stern voice.

Edmund glanced at Jamian. The captain sat back in his chair, rocking slightly, hands folded around his belly, face expressionless. At a loss, Edmund looked at Cyrolin. The galerunner was frowning.

Crack. Boom. Voices far across the city rose in awe and merriment.

"My apologies," Edmund said. "I was under the impression—"

"We are under impressions of our own," Gewnan said sternly. "Please share yours so that we can reach a consensus."

Consensus? A sudden chill raced up Edmund's spine. Could Tyrnen have reached the guild ahead of him? His left hand itched, a desperate longing that could only be scratched by clasping Valor's hilt. Edmund ignored it. Reaching for a weapon would not be received well in present company. He took a breath. "Approximately one month ago," he began, "the Crown of the North and I were ambushed by Tyrnen Symorne, Eternal Flame of Crotaria. He spirited us away to Lake Carrean, a site to the southeast of . . ."

He told them everything, speaking in a monotone voice and trying not to linger on the visions that accompanied the scenes he painted in words. As he spoke, the fireworks continued. Vibrant flashes of light brightened and dimmed just as quickly, like Dawn fading to Dawnfall then to Midnight in seconds. Every explosion hit Edmund like a wild heartbeat, the kind felt when one wakes sweating and gasping from a nightmare.

". . . why we need your aid," he continued. "The Ward and the clans stand divided and confused. With the support of the Azure Blades, for which Torel will pay a handsome commission, the realms can unite and send Tyrnen and his vagrants back to their graves."

He swallowed. His throat was parched. He could have done

with a drink, but no one moved to serve him. The guildmasters stared. Only Cyrolin seemed affected by his words. She no longer studied the floor. Her eyes had settled on him. Her visage was pale, her body rigid.

The lanterns flickered and murmured, and the shadows of their flames danced over the walls. Silence lay heavily over the room, and Edmund realized the fireworks had finally, mercifully ended.

Gewnan stirred, the folds of his robes susurrating. "Quite a tale," was all he said. Some of the guildmasters nodded. The Azure Blades remained perfectly still, their gazes trained ahead.

"It is the truth, Guildmaster," Edmund replied.

Osphera and the younger woman exchanged neutral looks that Edmund interpreted as doubt. "Have you any proof?" Jamian asked.

Edmund gaped. *Proof?* Then he understood. The other guildmasters now knew as much as Jamian had known since yesterday, yet Edmund had yet to verify any of his claims. Jamian was not trying to intimidate or dispute him. He was trying to help him build his case. These were not men and women accustomed to contracting the Azure Blades on a whim. They were the ruling body of the east, as powerful and revered as Anna in the north, or the war chief in the west, and would require solid evidence to act. Moreover, it was only natural that they question his account. If anyone had tried to tell him five or six weeks ago that corpses could be reanimated, he would have laughed.

Unfortunately, he had left so hastily that he had no such evidence at hand. Suddenly, he realized that he did . . . after a fashion. "Torel's Dawn," he said. "Two of their rank accompanied Jamian and me to Ironsail."

"The Eternal Flame's cabal?" Gewnan said, eyebrows raising.

"Summon them and I assure you they will corroborate every word I've told you."

Gewnan tapped his chin. "That won't be necessary. Your traveling companions are already here. Before you arrived, they gave us quite a different account of events that transpired in the north last winter."

Edmund's blood ran cold. *What's going on?* Before he could put the question to them, Gewnan continued.

"What's more, the Cinders have brought a witness of their

own. Her account corresponds to theirs, General Calderon. Not yours."

The door behind Gewnan opened, and Cinders Kerevin Hoven and Deletar Jan stepped out. Their stony expressions deepened the chill hanging in the air. They flanked the doorway and waited. Faint footsteps grew louder, and their witness entered the chamber.

Edmund supposed he had known that Tyrnen would never be content to let her soul rest. Not so long as he had it to bend to his will. His wife looked as he remembered her: short, with curly brown hair streaked with the Lady's light. Regal. Composed. Annalyn Gairden, or the thing that passed for her, swept dead eyes over the council.

Her attention landed on Edmund. No emotion registered.

"Greetings, men and women of the guild," the harbinger said in his wife's dulcet voice. "I understand there is some confusion around Torel's succession. Allow me to enlighten you."

Outside, a deafening series of explosions announced the renewal of the fireworks.

Chapter 28:
Her Account of Events

BEYOND THE PREFECTURE, Ironsail exploded in a fit of colors. Edmund ignored the display. It was her, yet not her. Anna's soft, snowy skin. Her fortitude and unblinking stare that added a foot and a half to her diminutive height. Her very soul. The vagrant wore these features like props in a theatre costume. A perfect disguise.

Edmund did not realize he was strangling Valor's hilt until the echoes of the final explosion subsided and he became aware of a faint rattling coming from below him. The hand gripping his sword hilt quivered, rattling the steel in its scabbard. He loosened his grip.

Annalyn took a breath. "Peace and quiet. At last."

"We appreciate that the north does not condone the usage of fireworks, Crown. We hope you can respect our customs in turn."

"Naturally," Annalyn said. "Though you are aware of the origin of fireworks, are you not, Guildmaster Gewnan? A Sallnerian invention, born of forbidden experiments and—"

"Enough pleasantries." Edmund's voice sheared like a serrated blade. He thrust a quivering finger at her. "That is not my wife."

Every head in the council chamber turned to consider Annalyn. "It certainly appears to be," Jamian said.

"I told you how harbingers work," Edmund said. "Tyrnen harvests souls and implants them in bodies."

Annalyn's face grew sad. "It is as I told you before, guildmasters. My husband is delusional. His condition has worsened since Aidan failed his Rite of Heritage. I had hoped to resolve this misunderstanding quietly, but"—she fixed Jamian with a penetrating look—"it seemed a meeting of the council was in order."

Jamian squirmed. "Guildmaster Gewnan thought this way best," he said slowly, as if choosing his words. "He is hale and hearty, you see, and felt such a dispute should be settled according to guild protocol."

"I do see," Anna said. "I cannot hold you responsible for this inconvenience."

Jamian visibly relaxed.

Edmund shoved his emotions down deep and concentrated. There had been no dispute until Tyrnen's harbinger had emerged to challenge his story. He looked at Jamian, who avoided making eye contact, and then at Kerevin and Deletar, who likewise ignored him.

Annalyn squared her shoulders. "What can I do to assuage your fears and doubts?"

"We have neither, Crown," Osphera began.

"On the contrary," Gewnan said, frowning at his fellow guildmaster, "I feel as if my head is spinning. Crown, your husband provided a summation of events that contradicted yours at every turn."

"Yes," Annalyn said, her bearing considerably frostier. "And since when does the word of a general—a former general at that—hold more weight than the word of a Gairden?"

Gewnan did not flinch. "You are not being accused. Yet there is a fair amount of confusion hanging over our council like a fog at sea. A good captain makes sure of his path."

A chuckle, as light and musical as chimes caressed by a breeze, rippled through Annalyn. "Your maritime metaphors are as apt and convincing as ever. Very well."

She stared at Edmund, as if daring him to challenge her. He did not. He could not. It took all of his willpower to stop himself from leaping at her and sawing her head from her shoulders. The thought pleased and sickened him. She was not Anna, yet she was

Anna.

"Aidan failed his Rite of Heritage," the harbinger began. "I do not know why, nor do my ancestors. Edmund and I left with Tyrnen to receive his counsel in private. While we were away, we were attacked by Romen of the Wolf and some of his wildlanders. Upon returning to Calewind, it came to Tyrnen's attention that the clans had taken Sharem. Aidan reclaimed the city as instructed, but refused to cooperate further and fled Sunfall. While he was . . . away, Edmund's mind began to slip. Perhaps it was his son's betrayal, or the war. Edmund and Romen of the Wolf were close. I am certain Romen's betrayal cut Edmund as deeply as any blade could have done. Or . . ."

She looked Edmund dead in the eye. "Or perhaps it was a lifetime of personal struggles that my husband had fought so hard to suppress, only for him to see them manifest in his son."

"I'm not sure I understand," Gewnan said.

"Cowardice, guildmasters. When Edmund was young, he—"

"No!"

Edmund's stricken tone drew all eyes to him. Cyrolin gaped, and he knew his face must have mirrored hers. The harbinger's words had struck him like an open-palmed slap. Every muscle in his body had gone as rigid as steel. "Lies," he whispered, though he did not mean to whisper. His throat was raw.

"It's all right, dear," the harbinger purred. "We are among friends."

His heart thudded. She—it—imitated Anna's soothing tone flawlessly, the one she reserved for when old terrors found him in his sleep and he woke up shivering like a boy of five winters. He was forcibly reminded that the harbinger resembled Anna in more ways than physical. It possessed her memories, her soul. They had been in love, were still in love if Anna's soul had not been tortured past remembering, and with that love came a level of intimate knowledge shared only by spouses. That knowledge served as a key. With it, all the hopes, dreams, secrets, and fears of the heart could be unlocked.

"He tried to kill me, guildmasters," it continued. "My own husband. He cornered me in my throne room, held my family's blade to my throat. People saw. Wardsmen, my subjects . . ."

"That was not Anna," Edmund shouted. "It was a harbinger."

"Edmund," Anna replied patiently. "We have discussed this. If a harbinger needs one's soul to appear as that person, how could a harbinger adopt your appearance, as you have claimed, let alone mine?"

"That was a vagrant," Edmund said, though he faltered even as he said it. Did Tyrnen need one's soul to mold a body into one's image? He did not know. Aidan would. Anna would. But could he trust her?

"You do not deny threatening the life of the Crown of the North?" the younger of the two women on the merchant's guild asked him.

"I deny threatening my wife. I threatened the creature wearing her face."

"Ah, yes," Jamian said with amusement. "These vagrants you spoke of."

"Harbingers," Edmund snapped. "A harbinger is a body able to—"

Jamian waved a hand. "Come, Edmund. You must realize how this sounds. How can you prove the veracity of such an allegation?"

By painting the walls green. His left hand strayed toward Valor. Anna saw it and played her part. Gasping, she took a step back, one hand to her chest. Like statues come to life, the Azure Blades leaped into action. Most formed tight clusters around their guildmasters. Hahrzen jumped over the bench as fluidly as water.

"Stop him, Cyrolin," Jamian snapped. "Let no harm come to the Crown of the North."

"Please," Anna said. "Do not hurt him. My husband is confused and frightened."

"He has acted this way before, Crown?" Gewnan asked.

Edmund ground his teeth. They were talking about him as if he were a simpleton. Cyrolin had not moved. She wore an expression Edmund could not quite place. Puzzlement?

Annalyn nodded. "He has, yes. Back at Sunfall. I ordered him arrested. I had no choice. He fled, of course. Torelians like to say my husband is a swordsman on a level with my family's patriarch. They are wrong. My husband is Ambrose Gairden's better. He slaughtered the Wardsmen who tried to apprehend him. Now I find him here, sowing his madness."

"Or trying to," Jamian said. "That we've allowed this council to go on this long is a travesty. Edmund Calderon's deception—"

"No," Annalyn interrupted. Her voice was thick, as if fighting back tears. "I described his actions as madness, and I believe that to be true. My husband does not need to see the inside of your prison, Jamian. He needs help. Help I can give him."

Grim nods around the bench. All except Gewnan, whose eyes flickered between Edmund and Annalyn. The old guildmaster leaned back in his chair, considering. "Where is the Ward now, Crown?"

"Marching southwest, I expect," the harbinger answered. "My husband's loose grasp on his mental faculties do not change the fact that the clans are a threat to my realm, and yours."

"Those marching orders correlate with what you told us, General," Gewnan said.

Edmund had the wherewithal to shake his head. "Not quite. The Ward does march to the southwest to meet Darinia in battle, unless Aidan can stop them."

"Aidan?" Anna echoed, feigning astonishment. "You have been in contact with our son?"

"The general claims Aidan Gairden travels west on his own, to confer with Nichel of the Wolf," Jamian said.

"Yes," Annalyn said softly. Her brow crinkled, and a fresh wave of grief nearly knocked Edmund to the floor. He knew the expression well. Annalyn had been caught off guard and was thinking fast on her feet. Had she been anyone else, he would have pounced, poking holes in her story. *Better to poke holes in the putrid vessel holding her soul.* Edmund did neither. He felt dazed, as if a breeze might carry him away. As if he might let it.

"You seem unsurprised by your son's course of action, Crown," Gewnan observed.

"Aidan protested the war," Annalyn said. "He asked for time to question the clans. But we were past talk. Blood had been spilled. No amount of parlay could erase Romen of the Wolf and his wildlanders making an attempt on our lives. I am the Crown of the North. I have a responsibility to my people, the same you have to yours."

"Your sword," Edmund blurted. Everyone looked at him. He pointed at Annalyn's waist. "If you are the Crown of the North, then where is . . . ?"

Edmund trailed off as Anna drew Heritage. Slowly, like the

Lady rising at Dawn. At last it emerged, and Edmund's stomach sank. Firelight flashed against the long white blade, the crescent guard, the egg-shaped ruby embedded in the hilt studded with sapphires.

An imitation. It must be. Tyrnen had orchestrated the same trickery during Aidan's trial. Only this time, Aidan was not here to counteract him.

Jamian leaned over the bench. Anna held the sword out for him to inspect. "It appears genuine," the captain said, sitting back and casting a doubtful glance at his associates, who peered closely at it.

"I must concur," Gewnan said slowly.

Edmund ignored him. "Hahrzen. You can corroborate what I have said." He swept his gaze around the room to take in the other Azure Blades. "As can many of you."

"What's this?" Annalyn asked.

"Yesterday, Cyrolin and I"—Edmund gestured at the galerunner, who was still watching Jamian—"we visited the headquarters of Hahrzen's cell. I asked them . . . I asked . . ."

Hahrzen cocked his head. "You spoke in the most ambiguous of terms, General," the reaver said. "You asked if we had seen or witnessed any suspicious activity. We had not, at least nothing abnormal for the Festival of Blossoms. When I pressed for more details, you would not confide in me. You were guarded and vague, perhaps intentionally so."

Gewnan pulled off his spectacles and rubbed his hands over his eyes. "Crown, I hope you understand that Leaston cannot take action one way or the other until we learn more."

"Of course, Guildmaster. I will be happy to stay a little longer if that is what it takes to convince you."

Gewnan nodded. "As for you, General Calderon, I'm afraid your actions could be construed as inciting discontent. Back north, I suspect your Crown would label them treason."

"I can help him," Anna interjected, voice ringing with emotion. "We need to talk, he and I. My training in the healing arts will soothe him."

Gewnan stood. "Do what you need to do, Crown."

Edmund had no response. What was the point? Anna and Aidan had been his first line of defense against magic, as he had been theirs against steel. He was isolated, with no way to expose the ruse.

The room and its occupants faded away, and Palit materialized around him. The village was dark. His father was drunk, and Edmund had . . . done what needed to be done. He was only twelve winters old. He fled Palit with nothing but the shirt on his back and trousers caked with dirt and soot and blood. He hadn't owned shoes or sandals, but that was fine. Twelve winters of walking barefoot across hard, rocky ground had hardened the soles of his feet until they were as tough as boots. He smiled faintly. Anna had once said—

"You could kick down the door to my kingdom using nothing but your bare feet."

They were in bed, holding one another, basking in the afterglow. She was not Annalyn, Crown of the North. She was Annalyn, wife, nestled in the crook of her husband's arm, dozing while he stroked her Dawn-kissed hair.

Edmund said nothing. Anna liked to tease him about his feet, only because she knew he did not mind. They had softened over the years, a sharp juxtaposition to the rest of his body, forged under the hammer of Torel's Ward: drills, exercise, combat training, a diet optimized for nutrition instead of taste, cold nights and colder days out in the mountains battling barbarian invaders and holding vigil over friends as they breathed their last breath.

He was there, in the present, with her. Not always, though. At times he was transported back to his boyhood, back to Palit, and he was alone. Trapped in his family's hut, his father drunk and screaming and hitting his mother. She tried to fight back. She stopped struggling. Stopped screaming. Stopped doing anything. Then James Calderon had gone looking for his son, and Edmund had grabbed a broken bottle and—

Survived. He had survived.

The Prefecture snapped back into focus. His senses attuned to the scene. Shouts and cries and thunderous explosions from outside. Anna, the thing that dared to wear Anna's face, was talking.

". . . lapsed into one of his trances. I fear his condition is worsening."

Edmund scanned the room. All eyes were on him. Gewnan's held pity. The rest held nothing. No emotion. No thought. Blank.

Dead.

Edmund let his hands drop to his sides. His fingers brushed Valor's hilt. Only Cyrolin noticed. She was standing beside him.

"What do you feel should be done, Crown?" Jamian asked.

The harbinger adopted an imperious pose. "Azure Blades. Take my husband into custody. But be gentle. I will talk with him privately."

As one, the Blades raised partitions in the bench that flipped open like lids and poured onto the floor. Edmund was surrounded. He did not move. "Tell your allies to come no closer, Hahrzen. I do not want to fight you."

Hahrzen, at the front of the pack, stopped and threw out one arm, stubby but corded with muscle, holding the rest back. For the first time, his eyes showed wariness. Edmund experienced a moment of doubt. Could Hahrzen still be alive?

Behind them, every member of the merchant's guild except for Gewnan had risen to their feet. Kerevin and Deletar flanked Annalyn, rolling back the sleeves of their robes.

"What are you waiting for?" the Anna-thing said. "Torel's general has no authority here."

"Neither do you," Edmund said. He turned to Gewnan. "Since when does the Crown of the North give orders to Leaston's guild or their militia?"

Kerevin and Deletar slowly raised their hands. Edmund noticed and pointed to them. "And isn't it odd that members of Torel's Dawn follow her lead? The Touched swear allegiance only to the Eternal Flame."

"We act in accordance with Tyrnen Symorne's commands," Kerevin began.

"Whom you said you have not seen in weeks," Edmund interrupted.

Jamian slapped a hand on the bench. "Cyrolin. Arrest the general."

The galerunner reached for him at once.

"You don't have to do this," Edmund said quietly. Outside, the explosions grew louder.

Suddenly, Cyrolin jerked her hand away. Comprehension dawned on her face.

"Arrest them both!" Jamian screamed.

Hahrzen hesitated. The rest of the Azure Blades shouldered

him aside and charged. Valor sang as Edmund ripped it free. He thrust and slashed, aiming for exposed skin. All he needed to do was draw blood, and his claim would be proven. But the Azure Blades were good. Their *Sard'tara* flashed and spun, deflecting every blow. Unlike his Wardsmen, who flanked their enemies, the Blades closed ranks and thrust with their *Sard'tara*. Fighting them was like fighting a giant pin cushion.

Cyrolin stood frozen. A *Sard'tara* stabbed at her. She opened her mouth to scream. Without thinking, Edmund lunged with Valor. Something stung his hand an instant before his sword encountered resistance. Steel clattered as one of the *Sard'tara*'s heads fell to the floor.

Whirling around to face his oppressors, Edmund caught a glimpse of Gewnan's dark-green robes disappearing through the door he had entered. Four Azure Blades hurried after him.

The Annalyn-harbinger shouted incoherently and pointed at Edmund. Kerevin and Deletar raised glowing palms.

Edmund backed toward the door. "Go!" he shouted, grabbing Cyrolin's sleeve and shoving her toward the door. "Run!"

Chapter 29:
Honor and Dignity

EDMUND SHOT OUT of the Prefecture. South Haven appeared deserted. The night air was cool on his face. Wind carried shouts and cries from several streets away. He allowed himself an instant to take in his surroundings and then sprinted for the nearest building, a three-story warehouse cloaked in darkness. None of the standing lamps bordering the street had been lit. The only light came from fireworks blooming overhead, bathing the streets in shades of color.

Weeks of pushing himself without seeking healing for his injuries had caught up with him. Rounding a corner, he made the mistake of bringing all his weight down on his left leg. It gave out like a dry twig expected to support Sunfall. Edmund collapsed in a heap, his steel and snow banging and scraping against the pavement. Sucking in breaths, he grabbed hold of the undercarriage of a nearby wagon and pulled himself to his knees, looking back the way he had come.

Azure Blades boiled out of the Prefecture and fanned across the street. Annalyn, Kerevin, and Deletar strode out behind them. The Anna-thing spoke and gestured, pointing at alleyways. Around her, streets and buildings flashed red and gold and blue and green. Fireworks boomed and crackled. The Blades broke rank and set off, disappearing down streets. Three raced abreast in his direction. Edmund hauled himself to his feet and toppled backward into a shadowy doorframe. Pressing himself against the door, Edmund held his breath. The three Blades sprinted by without looking at him. He closed his eyes. He was exhausted, dirty, and afraid. Most of all, he was angry.

All at once the excitement pumping through his veins leaked out of him. His leg throbbed and shrieked. He scratched idly at the back of his right hand. His fingers came away wet. He raised his hand to his face and stared at it as if he had never seen its like. *Blood?* Then he remembered the *Sard'tara* that had almost cut Cyrolin's throat. It was a minor wound in and of itself, but one wound too many. His nagging leg, another harbinger usurping Anna's face and body and memories and soul, the thought of Aidan somewhere in the west, depending on him. Too much. All too much. He could have dropped right here. He was tempted. All he had to do was step out of the doorway. The vagrants would find him, and—

Instinct and training took over. Edmund pictured himself bundling his emotions, thoughts, and bodily pains into a ball, wrapping that ball in a knapsack, and dropping that knapsack down a well. He had a problem and needed a solution.

Silence. Opening his eyes, Edmund leaned forward and peered up and down the road. No sign of Azure Blades or his dead wife. Despair flooded through him again. It took every last scrap of discipline to keep from sitting down and waiting to be found. Edmund stepped out. He took another step. A third. One foot in front of the other. A cacophony from overhead made him look up. Spheres of bright red lines bloomed in the sky like flower petals in springtime. He felt the explosion deep in his chest. Then the lines of color faded, and all was quiet. Almost quiet. The Great Sea whispered and chattered.

A gust of wind buffeted him from behind. Edmund whirled and there she was. His Anna. She raised a hand, extended as if in offer. "I know where to find—" she began.

Edmund closed the distance in two steps and drove Valor through her face. Green gore gushed out, spraying the walls and street and his steel and snow. The harbinger choked and went limp. Its dead weight pulled at Valor. Before it even hit the ground, Edmund kicked the corpse off. It pulled free with a squelching noise and sagged to the street. He stared down at it.

Its face was ruined, but Anna's eyes stared up at him. Through him.

Edmund turned and retched. A screen of tears clouded his vision. *It's not her. Not her. Not her. Not her.*

The words rang false. Sometime later—time no longer had meaning—he stood upright and dragged his sleeve against his mouth, turning so he did not have to face the body. No one, no thing, had come running. Shade hung beneath awnings and in alleyways. With the absence of fireworks, only Kahltan's silvery light revealed cobblestones and faint features of buildings. He breathed in the salty tang of the Great Sea.

Edmund pushed himself off the wall and fell into a slow, even trot. His leg complained. He ignored it. His choices were either move and deal with the pain, or stand still and die. Pain it was. For now.

He glided from doorway to doorway, holding his breath and scanning the street. His steel and snow made only the faintest rattle. He thought of Anna, and the torment her soul must be suffering at Tyrnen's hands. His chest tightened as his stomach roiled. A grim resolve grew in him, festered, black and poisonous. He lived for Aidan's life and Tyrnen's death.

He kept moving, doorway to alleyway to doorway. Breathing slowly, evenly. It was a trick Wardsmen learned to stay calm and aware on the battlefield. As he moved north, sounds of merriment—laughter, catcalls, glass bottles shattering on pavement—grew louder. Edmund slowed, thinking. His steel and snow was conspicuous. An Azure Blade would recognize it, and him, instantly. He shed his white tabard. A good start, but not enough. Jamian's estate floated into his mind's eye again. He could go there to rustle up some clothes. *And then what?*

That was a question for later.

Edmund set off again. The warehouse district ended abruptly, narrow streets giving way to wide, curving lanes bordered by standing lamps and braziers. Foot traffic went from nonexistent to suffocating. That worked in Edmund's favor. He fell into a casual stroll and walked among celebrants wearing paint and costumes. No one gave him a second glance. Why should they? Everyone was drunk or happy or both. He tensed at the realization that some of those glowing skeletons, field beasts, and other aberrations might be composed of dead flesh instead of paint and fabric. Vagrants could be anyone. Oh, well. He had no control over that.

The crowd flowed along. Edmund let them carry him, keeping his eyes open for side streets and sidling toward them. A few turns later he caught sight of Jamian's high walls. His gate stood open. Edmund frowned. There were no Azure Blades stationed outside the property, along the walls. He would have planted men there had he been the one planning an ambush. *Unless he wants to take me quietly.*

Edmund strolled along the wall. His eyes darted this way and that, searching for . . . *There!* A palm tree just inside one wall hooked above and over it, so that its head hung over the street. Without slowing, Edmund stepped onto the wall with his right foot and boosted up, scrabbling at the top of the wall and shimmying up the palm tree, hugging it with his legs and thighs. As a boy, he had taken pride in his ability to climb any surface no matter how slick or sheer. Hungry children had to know how to climb, and swiftly, if they wanted to steal food and evade vendors and Wardsmen.

He pulled himself up and sat atop it as if it were a horse and he its rider. Catching his breath, he watched the street below. No one so much as glanced up. Only his bad leg paid him any attention. He balled a fist and beat it into submission, or at least numbness. Then he shimmied down the slippery trunk and onto Jamian's grounds. Edmund crouched behind the trunk, draped in darkness, and studied the expanse.

Azure Blades swarmed the courtyard. They fanned out between the columns of the portico and into the grass or mingled by the gate. Jamian's front door opened. Two Blades lumbered out, each lugging one end of something big and heavy. Edmund swallowed a curse. It was the chest. Bending at the waist, they set it down and waved in the direction of a gate. Hahrzen came forward, hand gripping the wrist of a man in richly colored robes. Edmund took a moment to place him. The merchant from the bazaar, who had sold him his chest. His face was pale and confused. At the sight of the trunk, his eyes widened.

Hahrzen's lips moved. The merchant nodded, mouth moving. Edmund was too far to make out what they were saying, but their body language conveyed meaning well enough. Hahrzen gestured at the chest. The merchant nodded and puffed out his chest, a vendor proud of his wares. Yes, it was his making. Hahrzen asked him a question. The merchant's lips formed the words *steel and snow*, and then *General Edmund Calderon.*

Edmund cursed under his breath.

Hahrzen gestured to one of the other Blades. The man stooped forward and threw back the lid. The merchant recoiled, one soft, beringed hand covering his nose and mouth. The Blade with Hahrzen reached in and lifted something out. Edmund caught a glimpse of shredded, brown flesh and colorful clothing, and a whiff of the sickly-sweet smell he remembered from earlier that day. He had a good idea what the box held. Jamian's corpse. The man who had walked and talked like Jamian, who had betrayed him in front of the guild minutes ago, was not Jamian, but it very likely possessed his soul.

The merchant straightened, scrubbing an arm across his mouth. Hahrzen waited for him to get himself under control then jabbed a finger at the chest. The merchant looked horrified and took a step away. He pointed at the chest and said the words *Edmund Calderon* again. Edmund's head swam. He was watching himself be implicated in a murder he had never committed. With that, he had seen enough. Turning, he settled his right foot on the palm's trunk. He vaulted upward at the same instant a hand clapped around his right wrist.

Edmund's boot scraped loudly as he dropped to the ground. Stumbling, he let instinct take over, riding momentum into a crouch and tugging Valor free with his left hand. The sight of Cyrolin stopped him cold. She raised a finger to her lips and pointed. Two Azure Blades stood talking nearby.

Cyrolin tugged at Edmund's wrist. He followed in a crouch. They settled into the ferns hugging Jamian's walls. "I'm sorry to surprise you," the galerunner whispered. "When I saw it was you, I thought . . . I didn't know if you were . . ."

"Still alive?"

She nodded.

"Jamian isn't," Edmund said.

Her expression did not change. "I know."

"How?"

Cyrolin lifted up her shirt, exposing her stomach. Edmund stared at her in amazement. "The verrucae. It's gone. How?"

She let her shirt fall. "Back at the Prefecture, when he ordered me to detain you, I felt no compulsion to obey. Usually, the need feels different at that early stage. Like a fly settling on bare skin. A tickle that grows to an itch, and then begins to burn. I felt no tickle, no itch, no burning. I felt nothing. Jamian spoke, but it was . . . not him."

Edmund's mind raced, flitting back to earlier that evening when Jamian had resurfaced at his manor. "He gave you commands before we left for the audience. What did you feel then?"

Cyrolin's brow knitted. "Nothing. I must have obeyed out of habit."

"Congratulations, Cyrolin," he said quietly.

"For what?"

"You are free."

"Free," she mouthed, a new word that did not quite fit. Her features were tight, more frightened than overjoyed. "Free." She sighed the word, a long, pleasurable exhale.

Edmund found himself smiling. "It must feel strange."

"It is . . . like being in a new city. Not knowing where to go. Except"—her voice grew more excited—"except I can go anywhere I want." Her body began to shake, as if freedom pulled at her from all directions. She began to rise.

Edmund caught her wrist. "Wait. Where are you going?"

"Wherever I please. Isn't that what freedom is?"

"I hoped you might help me."

Cyrolin yanked her hand away. "Help you what? Escape?"

"Not right away, but, yes, eventually. That man who looked like Jamian isn't him, Cyrolin. My wife is . . ." He cleared his throat. "The creature wearing her skin has compelled the guildmasters, who are probably dead, too, to close Ironsail's gates. No one in or out. This plague they mentioned isn't a sickness. It's death, and Tyrnen or his creatures inflicted it."

"How would we escape?"

"I was thinking of the tunnels."

"I do not know where to find them," she said quickly.

"Nor do I. That leaves shifting, then."

"I cannot do that."

A muscle in his jaw twitched. "Can't, or won't?"

"Can't. The captains do not allow us to learn."

"You helped shift us here."

"No," she corrected, "I gave my power to a circle. They performed the shifting. Galerunners are not taught the art."

Edmund chewed his lip. "Your captains don't want you trying to escape," he said.

Cyrolin nodded.

He ran a hand through his hair. Teaching galerunners to shift would offer innumerable benefits out at sea. In the event of a storm, a galerunner could shift her captain and treasures to safety. "You must have seen what Torel's Dawn did when we were in the circle. You could try. This is important, Cyrolin. My son is depending on me to return with the Azure Blades at my back. If I do not—"

"That is not my concern."

"Actually, it is. You saw what happened at the Prefecture. You know what's become of Jamian. The merchant's guild has fallen. Tyrnen has gained a foothold in the east. If his power grows, he will kill you and everybody else. You're a Touched. He'll probably turn you into one of those . . . those . . ." His thoughts drifted to Anna, and his heart gave a nasty lurch.

"Then I will leave the east," Cyrolin said. "I will find a ship and return to my people."

"The Azure Blades will be looking for you, too."

"Why would they?"

"I ran, and so did you. The creature wearing your old master's face knows what you are: Human, and in control of your destiny. They intend to frame me for Jamian's murder, and unless I miss my guess, they will name you my co-conspirator."

She brushed his words aside. "I can move unseen. I will steal a ship to my liking, and I will leave."

"You don't even know where your island is located."

"I will find it. I have time."

"You'll sail the Great Sea looking for a single isle? You're talking madness."

"To be free is not madness. To be free is . . ." She took a deep breath. "It's everything."

"Freedom does not mean turning your back on people who need you," he said.

Her face turned crimson. "That is exactly what it means. People have seen how Jamian treated me. He was kinder than some captains, but worse than many. Did anybody help? Did they say something? No. They had their freedom. They were free to count their coins and drape themselves in fancy clothes and look the other way."

Edmund's anger faded, replaced by pity. "You did not deserve that."

"And yet you argue with my logic. I sympathize with your plight, General, but your problems are your own. My concern is restoring my pride and my dignity. I will do that by choosing my own path."

She turned away.

"I saved your life," he hissed.

Cyrolin froze in the mouth of the alley. "What?"

Edmund breathed through his nose, his fists clenched so tightly his nails dug into his palms. "At the Prefecture. The *Sard'tara* that almost took your damn head off. You'd be dead or worse right now if it wasn't for me."

Cyrolin had gone pale. "I was never in any danger. I would have—"

"You would have been killed." He held up his right arm, exposing the back of his hand. Blood oozed from a scratch. "I paid for your life with blood."

"Why? We have known each other for two days. Less than that. Why would you risk yourself to save me?"

"Because it was the right thing to do. Because doing what is right is how I keep my honor intact. And because . . ." He hesitated.

Cyrolin stood frozen, her gaze intense. "Because?"

"Because you're my friend. What different does it make how long we've known one another? You said it yourself. Actions and choices matter. Just as important is the wisdom to make the right choice and take the right action."

All the color drained from her face. "I am choosing prudently. I am choosing for me."

"You are making the wrong choice."

"That is not for you to decide."

With that, Cyrolin vanished. Wind buffeted Edmund. Voices carried across the yard. Edmund glanced over his shoulder and saw an Azure Blade looking in his direction. He held perfectly still, waiting for the man to convince himself he was jumping at shadows. A few moments later, another Azure Blade called for him, and the man ran off.

Edmund wasted no more time. He scrambled up the palm tree and crouched on the wall. Looking down, the pavement and crush of bodies seemed far away, making him lightheaded. He would have jumped without thinking, preferably without looking, but he doubted his bad leg could take much of a shock. Turning, he eased his legs down first, then lowered himself until he hung by his fingertips. He braced his feet against the wall, then let go, dropping back first to the ground.

Instead of hitting the ground, he fell into a cluster of Leastonians. Grunts and cries of surprise rang out. Edmund bounded to his feet and reached down to help them up. He gave them a dazed, glassy-eyed smile. They returned his expression and raised half-empty bottles wrapped in glowing lights as if in a toast. He let them take the lead and fell in behind them. He trailed to the next turn, took it, flowed along the turn next to that, and ended up near the open gate leading into Jamian's manor. Two Azure Blades stood in the portal, backs to the street. Edmund got in close. Had one of them turned or so much as glanced to one side, he would have been spotted. The risk did not bother him as it might once have. His leg was not the only part of his body that felt numb. Slumping against the wall as if drunk, he listened.

". . . first guildmaster murdered in my lifetime," one, a younger man, said.

"Just you wait," said a gruffer, older voice. A reaver similar in stature to Hahrzen, but with blue hair and bells woven through his braids.

"How are we supposed to find this Edmund Calderon?"

The reaver shrugged. "He's got nowhere to go. Every way in and out of Ironsail has been sealed. He'll turn up. The guildmasters have questions for him, and for the woman."

Edmund let the crowd push him along past the gate. At the next side street, he broke from the pack and hurried to a doorway. The Azure Blades confirmed his suspicions, but he had no time to chase after Cyrolin. Nor did he know where to start. *She's gone, then. Fine. I have my own problems.*

Ironsail had been sealed. Only the surface? There were dozens of tunnel nodes in the east's capital. Not that that mattered. He knew of them, but did not know where to find them. The guild preferred that foreigners refrain from using the tunnels so as to avoid accidentally exposing them to realms outside their own. Cyrolin was his only chance to find them.

He sagged against the door. *Annalyn*. He needed to be near her, but he couldn't. He could go somewhere where he felt near her. Not dressed as he was. He needed a disguise. A normal pair of clothes, or what passed for normal in the east.

The door behind him flew open. Edmund toppled forward. When the world stopped spinning, he was staring up at what appeared to be a boar, its tusks dull and dirty. It reached up and removed its head, revealing a tangled mass of damp hair and an ebony face shiny with perspiration. "Are you all right?" the man said. Edmund grunted and stood. The man's eyes narrowed. "Good. Perhaps you can tell me what you were doing outside my—"

Edmund ripped Valor from its scabbard and clipped the man's head with his hilt. The man had no time to think, let alone shout. His eyes rolled and he began to drop. Quick as a blink, Edmund sheathed Valor and got his hands under the man's armpits before he could fall. "Sorry," he muttered, and dragged the man inside.

He changed quickly, leaving the costume's owner naked on his floor. *A not uncommon sight during Festival, I imagine.* He slipped the mask over his head. Immediately his breathing became loud and raspy. The mask itself was heavy. Still, it would be impossible to recognize him. *It might be impossible to see at all.* Edmund strained to see through the mask's eyeholes, each narrow slit the size of a keyhole. Fumbling at the door, he stepped outside and picked his way into the flow of foot traffic.

The din was incredible. No one talked. They shouted. No one laughed. They guffawed and roared. Smells assaulted him. Fresh fish, cooked meat, stale sweat, sugars and salts and spices, cheese, slush. Edmund's breathing picked up, growing hoarser. He scratched at the wound on his right hand, digging in to get through the fabric of his ridiculous costume. It itched and was beginning to burn. He went along until he spotted the Frosted Cup just up ahead. Once again, he prodded and elbowed his way out of the throng. He opened the door and squeezed in. The common room was less packed than it had been the previous night, perhaps because so many people were enjoying fresh air and fireworks.

Edmund approached the counter and waved over a harried man wearing a stained apron. "How much for a room?"

"What?" the man yelled back.

Gritting his teeth, Edmund pulled off the boar's head. He held his breath, expecting the man to raise an alarm. The innkeeper's expression changed. "General!" he bellowed. "Sea and shores, it's good to see you!"

"And you, Garol," Edmund said, forcing himself to smile. "Do you have any vacancies?"

"No," the innkeeper said. "But . . ." He glanced around as if to make sure no one was listening in. "There's a basket of peaches waiting for you upstairs, General."

The room spun. Blood pounded through his ears like a Darinian war drum.

Garol jerked a thumb toward the stairwell. "The usual room." He leaned in close. "I'll make sure no one knows you're here."

Edmund did not hear him. He drifted toward the stairwell as if in a trance, leaving his boar mask on the countertop. The stairwell was narrow, dimly lit, and stuffy. He followed it up to the fourth floor. The corridor here was long, with only two doors, one on either side. Luxury suites. The best rooms in Ironsail outside of a guildmaster's manor house.

He crossed to the door on the left. Wistfulness settled over him like a filmy curtain. This was where they had stayed. Edmund opened the door, and she was lying on the bed as she had been that night, only this time she was fully clothed.

Anna grinned a vulpine smile. She rolled a peach between her palms, back and forth, back and forth. "As I was saying: I know where to find you, Ed. You cannot hide from your wife."

Chapter 30:
A Basket of Peaches

"CLOSE THE DOOR," Anna said.

Edmund's legs wanted to move. He stood his ground. "You're not her."

"I am."

"Just because you wear her face and speak in her voice—"

Anna leaned back on her palms. "Do you remember what we did here?" She ran her tongue over her lips. Her eyes glittered with lust. "We made love in this bed countless times, but one stands out. You know the one. What was it I said? It was so long ago, but I remember. What would they—"

"... *think if they learned a Gairden heir was conceived in another realm?*" Anna murmured, hands on her belly. She stroked it fondly, smiling.

Edmund stood over her, the goblets of wine in his hands forgotten. "You're sure?"

Anna nodded. "I would not turn down a glass of slush otherwise."

"How can you be sure?"

"A Touched can learn of her pregnancy moments after conception."

"And you're certain? Really certain?"

She laughed and ran a hand through his hair. "I'm certain."

"Well," he said, and licked parched lips with his dry tongue. "Well."

Anna studied his wide eyes and pale countenance. "Why so surprised, General? We weren't taking steps to avoid this."

Carefully, Edmund set the goblets on a side table and sat beside her. "I'm not surprised. Not in the way you mean. I suppose it's just . . . I'm going to be a father. I'm going to be a father," he repeated. It was unreal. Like one of his Wardsman had shared the happy news with him: he was happy for the other man, but it was not happening to him.

"Are you excited?" she asked softly.

"Yes," he said, glad she could not see him. Anna would have seen the truth in his eyes. Edmund was not excited. He was—

". . . terrified," Anna finished. "I could feel terror radiating from you, but I did not speak of it. You preferred to leave your father back in Palit, where you—"

"Stop."

Anna pursed her lips. "This was our room. Our place when we came here. Looking at it now . . ." She gazed around, brow raised. There was a bed, a wardrobe against the adjacent wall, and a small table that held a lantern and a basket of half a dozen Leastonian peaches. His favorite. "Well," the harbinger said, features pinched in disgust. "We were young, and I needed a change of pace. Growing up in a palace was all well and good . . ." She trailed off again, watching him. Waiting for him to finish the words she had uttered so often.

But even luxury grows dull. I crave change. Difference. I want to see the world.

Anna had said the words to him the first time they met, and every time they travelled thereafter. That was why they bedded down at inns instead of in palaces or mansions. On a guildmaster's estate, they would be pestered by servants or traders or guildmasters or Hands of the Crown. Proprietors like Garol gave them a hiding place. *"A place where we can both pretend to be anyone we want to be,"* she was fond of saying.

"Those are my memories," Anna said, one finger tapping against her chin. "I am her, whether you acknowledge it or not."

"You have her memories. That is not the same as—"

"It was a summer night," she continued, still tapping her chin. "We decided on Aidan. But why that name?" It smiled, a cold expression that did not touch her eyes. "Ah, yes. After your brother. The one who—"

"That's enough. You will not manipulate me."

The harbinger's finger slowed, stopped. Rising, it chuckled throatily. "I am not manipulating you, Edmund. If I wanted to manipulate you, I would do this." Anna cupped his left cheek in her right palm. Her skin was soft and smooth. Hers.

Edmund recoiled and slapped her. The crack of open palm on face was like a whip. Anna left her feet and slammed against the far wall, sliding to her hands and knees. Her expression changed, from shocked to delighted.

"I will remember that." The harbinger giggled as it pushed itself to its feet. "You still don't understand. You are a fool. Even so, I think Tyrnen is going about this the wrong way."

Edmund's fist went to Valor. "Where is he? Is he here?"

"Of course not. He's far too busy dealing with . . . other matters."

Edmund jerked Valor free. "If he's harmed my son, I swear on the Lady I will—"

"You don't want to do that," it said lightly.

"I've killed you twice already. That's less than you deserve for perverting her memory."

Anna plucked a peach from the basket and bounced it from palm to palm. She managed to keep it in the air for ten bounces before it dropped and rolled across the floor. "You taught me that," she said. "I remember. I remember everything. I have died three times. Once at Tyrnen's hands, on the shores of Lake Carrean. In almost the same spot where we picnicked. You remember." The harbinger shivered. "Excruciating, blinding pain. My mother and Helda told me childbirth was the most pain a person could suffer. With all due respect, they never had their legs sheared off by lightning."

Realization set in. A hollow pit opened in Edmund's stomach, swallowing everything.

"The second time," Anna continued, "was at your hands. In the lake. I remember that death vividly. It was not as painful as the first, and yet, in a way, it hurt more. I grabbed you. The harbinger wanted to kill you. That was Tyrnen's order. But I only wanted to hold you. To embrace until you stopped breathing. We would have been together, afterwards. I thought you'd have wanted that."

Anna resumed her seat on the edge of the bed. "The third death, I should have seen that coming. I underestimated you. I've always underestimated you. Did you know that? As much as I respected your bravery and strength, I never quite believed you were worthy of me up here." She tapped her forehead. "Poor Edmund. Do not misunderstand. I loved you. Truly, I did. What I loved more was the fantasy you represented. Nights in seedy inns, drinking in taverns, making love in some . . ." Her nose wrinkled. "Some hole in the wall. That is what your princess, your queen, needed. Most women would be content growing up in a palace with wardrobes larger than the shanties on the Territory Bridge. Not me. I needed an escape. You were that. And to think I owe my escapism to your affinity for Leastonian fruit."

Reaching over, she took another peach from the basket. "So, I thank you. I don't believe I ever said that. It's never too late for a Gairden to put things right."

The room tilted, wavered through a blur of hot tears. Valor slipped from his fingers and clattered to the floor.

Annalyn fussed with her skirts. "And how do you repay me? By killing me. Not once, but twice. The bodies are expendable. Corpses can be found anywhere, especially in the backstreets of Ironsail, and are as pliable as clay. But the memories, Edmund. Those will live on in me forever, right next to the sweeter ones we made here, and back in our home. Edmund the Valorous. General. Husband. Father. Killer."

His mouth worked. Finally, the words spilled out. "I didn't know."

"I know, dear," she said, her voice as musical as chimes in a breeze. "But you do now, and you can make it up to me." Anna rose and sauntered over to him. She cupped his cheek in a palm. "It will not hurt, Ed. Not for long. That's what you want. Escape. An end. My eyes are lifeless, but so are yours. You will fall asleep, and then we will be together again. An endless fantasy."

Her breath, the harbinger's breath, was fetid. Like stale air from a grave. Edmund could not look away. She crooked a finger and her second peach floated up into her grip. She raised it to his lips. "Take a bite."

Forever, she had said. *One endless fantasy.*

Edmund closed his eyes and opened his mouth. The fuzz of

peach skin brushed against his lips, nearly as soft as his Anna. *Fitting that it should end this way*. Teeth broke skin.

Behind Edmund the door flew open and crashed against the wall. There was a loud thud followed by a bestial scream. Edmund opened his eyes in time to see Annalyn crumple to the floor. The peach hung suspended in the air a moment longer, then dropped. Annalyn was back on her feet before it hit the floor. Her back was bent and her hands were hooked like claws. She stared daggers at him, past him.

Cyrolin stood in the doorway.

Chapter 31:
Equals

ANNA HISSED LIKE a cornered animal. A chill ran through Edmund. All at once the harbinger's hold on him shattered into a million pieces. It possessed Anna's soul. It looked like her, moved the way she did, spoke with her voice, and could call up any memory the way the librarians at the Spire could take a disciple right to the book or scroll of his choice. Despite all of that, the harbinger was not her.

Annalyn Gairden, his Anna, was not an animal.

Grief and anger flooded Edmund, raw and fresh, as if he had lost her all over again. He raised Valor high and lunged. Or, rather, he tried to. His feet would not obey. They dragged instead of lifted, heavy as Darinian anvils. He collapsed to the floor. Valor clattered beside him. Abruptly he became aware of heat flushing his face. His body felt ponderous and unwieldly.

The harbinger struck quick as an adder, snatching Valor from the floor. Adjusting its grip to clutch the sword by its blade, the creature murmured words. Its palms glowed white hot. There was a snap like ice cracking underfoot, and Valor fell back to the floor in two jagged pieces.

Edmund stared at it, then looked up. The harbinger stood over him, grinning Anna's grin, only the expression was too wide, inhuman. There was a scraping noise and the harbinger grunted.

Its smile faded into an expression of almost comical confusion. Hands went to the broken blade of Valor protruding from its belly. Its expression cleared, twisting into a snarl.

"The head," he said weakly.

Valor's lower half pierced the harbinger's skull. Anna's face went blank. The body crumpled to the floor. Bony fragments fell like hail, skittering on the wood. Green blood spurted and dribbled, staining Anna's dress and the polished floor. Edmund did not remember crawling over to the body. He found himself staring down at it, pulling his broken sword from her skull and shoving it into his scabbard. *Instinct. All instinct.*

The next minute hands grabbed him beneath his arms and pulled him upright. Edmund was powerless to resist. Thick creepers crawled over his mind, blotting out thought and emotion. "Can you stand?" he heard Cyrolin ask as she hauled him upright.

Edmund tried. His legs betrayed him again. He pitched forward into the galerunner's arms. She drew a deep breath and spoke two words. Something at her feet flickered. A lantern, Edmund observed. Cyrolin pushed him to a standing position again and let go. He slumped, and something caught him. Something invisible and soft. *Cloud*, he thought. He stopped trying to help and let his body sink into it. His arms hung loosely.

He faced Cyrolin, whose attention flitted around the room. It landed on the basket of peaches, followed it to the lone piece of fruit lying discarded near Anna's bloody corpse. Picking one up, she sniffed it. "Did you eat any?" she asked. Then she noticed the puckered wound on his hand. She took it and brought it close, turning it this way and that. "The *Sard'tara* cut. You were poisoned. Almost doubly," she amended, tossing the peach onto the bedcovers.

Her news elicited no reaction from Edmund. Gently, Cyrolin touched his wound with one fingertip. Edmund tried to cry out but could not. Her touch was feather light, but felt like a nail being driven into his flesh.

Voices called from below as footsteps pounded up the stairs. Cyrolin hurried to the window at the far end of the room and threw it open. She climbed through and spoke a word as she beckoned to Edmund, who floated forward obligingly, his body angling so he hovered parallel to the ground. His head poked through the opening. He stared down at rooftops that crowned buildings of myriad shapes and colors. People flowed along the streets like debris in a stream.

Cyrolin crouched on the inn's rooftop. Her features tightened when boots thundered outside their room. Fists hammered at the door. Edmund registered all this absently. He felt small and tightly packed away somewhere deep in his mind. From his vantage, he could watch events unfold, but was not an active participant.

Cyrolin straightened and jumped off the rooftop. The cloud cocoon that embraced him drifted to the edge after her. Then he plunged. Wind played with his hair as pavement rushed to meet him. *I'm going to die*, he thought. The realization brought neither joy nor sorrow. He floated in emptiness.

The wind dropped from a roar to a low whistle, to nothing. The world held still. Edmund could not move his head, so he rolled his eyes. He was in a narrow side street. Somewhere in the distance, a horn sounded. Cyrolin's head whipped in its direction. She held up a hand as if to silence him.

Another horn. Groggy, Edmund tried to focus. The second blast had come from the opposite direction, somewhere deep within Calewind.

"Can you stand?" Cyrolin asked.

Edmund opened his mouth to explain that his legs refused to obey him, then tentatively took a step forward. Another. "I guess so," he said. The cloud at his back vanished.

Cyrolin took his right hand, careful to avoid pressing on his wound. "I need to draw the poison out." Edmund nodded and turned away. He did not trust himself to speak. Cyrolin turned her attention to his hand. Edmund was not afraid. He felt like a fool. *I knew* Sard'tara *were poisoned. How could I have gone so long without thinking to leech it out myself?*

Because you're not focused, he answered.

A cool sensation like flecks of ice flowed into his angry red wound. That coolness filled him, moving from his hand to his arm and through his body to wash away feverish heat. Cyrolin released his hand. Edmund flexed it. It was stiff, but the soreness was gone.

"Thank you," he said. "I thought *Sard'tara* poison killed instantly."

"Some do. Azure Blades use many types of poison. Some corrode the bloodstream and stop the heart within seconds. Others creep through the body more slowly, numbing limbs or causing sickness. Your enemies do not wish you dead, I think. Not yet."

Shouts from above. "We should go," Cyrolin said.

"Where?" he asked, displaced. Jamian was dead. Tyrnen's vagrants had gained a foothold in Ironsail. Aidan was all the way across Crotaria. Anna was dead, yet aware of everything that was happening around her, and to her. His throat constricted. His left hand strayed to Valor and found the hilt and jagged tooth of a blade. His courage had been broken and lay in pieces in his and Anna's place.

Edmund let his hand fall away. Valor was just a sword. It could be replaced. "Lead the way," he said.

"Stay close," she said, then stepped into the flow of foot traffic. Edmund followed on her heel. Every now and then a horn sounded. Some were high and sharp, others sonorous. Cyrolin followed, or tried to. He quickly lost track of how many times she backtracked, went forward, and turned again, going left where she had turned right minutes before. At last she made a sound of disgust and abruptly turned left when she had been poised to head right.

Buildings and wide lanes gave way to North Haven's harbor, a grid of wide docks with ships and barges anchored or setting off into the night. The reflection of Kahltan's silvery eye gleamed on wet, wooden docks over rippling water. Bare-chested workers— men and women—hauled cargo, secured lines, readied horses for merchants preparing to enter Ironsail. The air sang with curses and shouts and laughter, perfumed by the Great Sea's salty tang.

Cyrolin followed the docks to a ship that towered over the others. A man with dusky skin and a bald head was bending to pick up a box. Looking up, he smiled at Cyrolin. "Good evening, galerunner. We're preparing for Captain Jamian's voyage in the morning."

"You are ahead of schedule, I trust," she said.

"Of course!" he said, affecting mild outrage.

She laughed. "Very good." Gesturing at Edmund, she continued, "The captain has instructed that I show one of his guests, a dignitary who will be joining us on our voyage, to a cabin for the night."

The man nodded. "Probably few vacancies left in the city."

"None that we could find."

Cyrolin began a steep climb up a gangway. Edmund followed, aware of the man's eyes on his back. She led him onto the deck and proceeded into a cabin. Closing the door behind him, Cyrolin fumbled in the dark before Edmund heard the scratch of a match. A lantern flared, painting the walls shades of orange. Edmund glanced around. *This must be Jamian's quarters.*

A large desk dominated the center of the cavernous space. Maps and logbooks and charts cluttered its surface. A high-backed chair sat behind it, two smaller chairs in front. Edmund was drawn to a strange instrument in one corner. It was a ball, large and painted blue, with masses of green and brown over its surface. *A map,* he decided, *but why round?* The ball sat perched in a metal stand. Curious and in need of a distraction, he touched it. Areas painted green and brown protruded and felt bumpy.

"Be careful with his globe," Cyrolin said.

"Globe," Edmund repeated. Touching a single finger against it, he pushed to one side. Hinges squeaked as the globe turned, revealing a larger splotch of green and brown. Elegant script proclaimed *CROTARIA* in its center. He recognized the continent from his own charts and maps. Small green bumps were speckled in the sea of blue around it. Those must be islands. He knew barbarian invaders came from distant lands, but had never thought of them as a man's home. *Could one of them be Cyrolin's homeland?*

Edmund turned to find her rummaging through an armoire. "Here," she said, withdrawing an armful of clothes. "You need to change."

He waited until the door closed behind Cyrolin, then stripped out of his boar costume. He moved slowly, like a man of eighty winters instead of forty. Cyrolin knocked a few minutes later, and Edmund gave consent for her to enter. "I expected you to be halfway across the Great Sea by now," he said as she sat in one of the smaller chairs. "What changed?"

"You were right. There is no way out of Ironsail."

"I'm glad you stayed."

Cyrolin tensed. "Why?"

"I'm happy to have company." Edmund blinked. He had

meant to say *help*. He walked stiffly to the chair beside her and lowered himself into it, wincing.

"Your leg?" Cyrolin asked softly.

"Interminably," he answered.

She slipped out of her chair and crouched beside him. "May I?"

Edmund took a deep breath, then nodded. Cyrolin placed one hand on his calf and the other on his thigh. Color rose in her cheeks. "I can provide only temporarily relief."

"I'll take what I can get."

The lantern on Jamian's desk flickered. Edmund relaxed as warmth seeped into his skin, his blood, his muscles. His leg loosened, leaving him limber and relaxed. The gradual sensation reminded him of slipping into the baths after a long day running drills for his Wardsmen, steam and hot water kneading his muscles like sure hands.

"What were those horn blasts?"

"Cells of Azure Blades. It's how they communicate to one another, like their own language." Her lips pressed together. "Each cell has a different style of horn so their calls are unique. I don't know how to decipher them." She huffed a breath. "Would you like to tell me about the fruit?"

Edmund shifted, remembering the soft peach fuzz on his lips, and the way the harbinger had tried to feed it to him. The same way Anna had always done. His shoulders slumped.

"I'm sorry," Cyrolin said. "I do not mean to pry."

"It's all right. Maybe I need to talk about it." He began a study of the ceiling. "I met Anna when I was twelve winters old. I'd been in Calewind for three days, and I was hungry. Starving, actually."

"What were you doing when you met your wife?" she inquired. Heat flowed through him.

"Stealing peaches."

Cyrolin tensed. Edmund followed her line of sight to his left hand. It gripped Valor's hilt. He forced his fist to unclench and folded his hands in his lap. "I'm not going to attack you. It's a nervous habit."

Cyrolin relaxed. "Because you are a general? A habit from fighting wars?"

"Torel has fought fewer battles than you might think." He licked his lips and, as if coaxed, the story he had told only one other person spilled out of him. Not fast and wildly, like water from a falls. Gradually, like pus from an infected wound.

"I grew up in Palit, a small village in the southeast of Torel. Maybe the smallest. A few huts, some fields, dirt roads that turned to mud in the rain and snow, and it rains often along the southeastern border. I had few friends. One was a boy two winters younger than I, named Brendon. He and I ran with a couple of older boys who kept us around because they found us amusing. There was little to do in our village but chores or get into trouble. We chose the latter. Once, when a Leastonian peddler came to call, one of the older boys—I don't even remember his name—dared me to steal a dagger set on a pair of hooks just inside his wagon. I waited until the peddler was busy with some of the adults, then I snuck in and lifted it. I might have made a good sneak.

"The older children urged me to sell it. I refused. When they tried to take it, I turned it on them. They threatened to go to my father. I told them that if they did, I would cut their throats in the night. I meant it, every word. I kept it with me at all times. Right here." Edmund patted Valor at his waist. "I knew I would need it one day, but I was afraid."

Edmund's throat moved. "My father was a farmer, and not a very good one. Maybe that wasn't his fault. Our village wasn't suited for farming, but we had no money to go anywhere else, and he knew no other forms of labor. My mother had no occupation, as many women in the north do not. She was a drunk, and a very good one. Drink was all they had in common. He was a large man, my father, and when he failed to exert authority over his wife through wealth and accomplishment, he resorted to hitting her. And me. He was good at that.

"One night, he hit my mother. Nothing unusual. I heard her hit him back. Just once. He struck her again, and again, and again. I remember she screamed once, then went quiet. I remember lying in the back of the hut, huddled beneath my blankets, eyes squeezed shut, pretending to be asleep. All the while he kept hitting her. If you've ever heard a butcher slap raw meat onto a block, that's what I heard that night."

Cyrolin's warmth faded, but her hands lingered. Edmund said nothing. His head was tipped back. His eyes were open, but he did not see Jamian's cabin.

"He said her name. Then he screamed it. He sounded afraid and confused, like a man who has awakened from a nightmare only to realize he was not dreaming. Then he called for me. He sounded angry. I don't know if I made a sound or if he saw my blankets shivering, or if his booze-addled brain still functioned enough to deduce that there were only so many places I could hide. I heard him making his way to me, stumbling and dragging his boots, tripping over chairs and empty bottles. I knew he would kill me, too. Kill me and leave our bodies and then leave our village to make a fresh start somewhere else. Somewhere far away where the Ward could not find him.

"And then I clutched the dagger's hilt, just like this, and this calmness fell over me. I waited. I squeezed the hilt so hard it left an imprint on my hand, but I didn't notice that until later. His footsteps grew closer, stopped. He kicked me in the side. I bit my lip hard enough to draw blood, but I didn't cry out. I didn't say anything. I just waited. He bent over. I could smell his breath through the blanket. It was very thin. My eyes were open. I could see him through the cloth. I saw his big hand reaching. He tore the blanket away, and I sprang up, and he was leaning right over me, and I slashed with my knife."

Edmund suddenly found it difficult to breathe. "I'd never seen so much blood. I still haven't. It got all over me. I couldn't change my clothes because I didn't have any other clothes. I ran outside and out of my village until I found the North Road and then I just kept running. I stopped here and there to sleep and steal food. I didn't want to steal. I had to. By the time I reached the capital, I had a plan. I'd seen Wardsmen once. A couple of them passed through Palit a handful of times every spring through the autumn, before the roads got bad. I couldn't help staring at their swords and spears, and the way they carried themselves, and their armor. The steel and snow. They seemed so confident. As if nothing and no one could frighten them or harm them. I know better now, but as a boy . . ."

"I understand."

Edmund glanced at her. He had been lost in reverie and was ashamed to admit he had forgotten Cyrolin was there. A slight pressure on his leg made him look down. She pulled her hands away. Edmund sat up and stretched his leg.

"You joined them," she said. "The Wardsmen. When you got

to the capital."

It took him a moment to answer. "That was the plan."

Cyrolin gave him a wry smile. "Plans do not always go according to plan."

"They do not," he agreed. "I was starving. My shirt was still bloody, even though it had dried. I mixed in some mud to hide it. I could have washed it in a lake or a puddle, but I wasn't thinking. I just ran. It sounds funny now, but I expected to look over my shoulder and see my father chasing after me, shambling along the North Road, his throat torn and his chest and legs and arms bloody."

Edmund cleared his throat. "I entered the city, telling the Wardsmen at the southern gate some lie about my father being here on trade. They hadn't heard of him—not surprising, he had no reputation to speak of—but they let me in anyway. The people of Calewind are . . . different. More lax."

"Because they live in the capital?" Cyrolin asked.

He nodded. "They can look up and see Sunfall perched above them like a golden crown. The Gairdens will protect them. Why should they be afraid? I wandered the streets, and my head was not in a good place. I was exhausted and afraid. I grew rash. I finally entered the east, where Leastonian peddlers sell harvests. And I saw this peach." His mouth began to water. "I swear it was as big around as the Lady at noon, and as orange as Dawnfall. I could have sold the knife. I still had it, but for some reason I couldn't bring myself to part with it. So, I waited until the vendor turned his back, and I gripped the knife's hilt, and I was calm again. Brave. And then I swiped the peach and took off running.

"There were shouts, and I could hear footsteps, but I was used to running. I turned this way and that, and I had no idea where I was going but neither did they. I stopped in some alleyway, and do you know what amazed me? There was no trash anywhere. Like I said, Calewind is different. I sat down, giving no thought to who could see me, and I started to take a bite, and the peach was ripped from my hands. I remember the sound of my teeth snapping together. A click. I looked up and saw the most beautiful woman in the world standing over me. She was a girl. Fourteen winters. She was wearing a grey cloak and hood. And she said, 'I saw you.'

"I didn't know what to say. I couldn't say anything. I could barely think or feel, I was so tired and hungry and frightened. So, I"— his cheeks grew warm—"just started crying. I didn't blubber. I had some dignity. She told me later I just sat, with tears cutting tracts down the dirt on my cheeks. She took pity on me. We were near a tavern, and we went inside and got a table at the back, and she gave me my peach. No one bothered us. No one recognized her."

Edmund laughed, and it was real. "She'd slipped out of the palace, away from her nursemaid, Helda, who's her cook now if you can believe it. She told me all about running away and not wanting to be the Crown. How she wanted to see the world. I told her about Palit. Not about my father, though. That came later. Besides, I wasn't thinking about my father. For the first time in weeks, he was the last thing on my mind."

"What were you thinking about?"

"Her. Anna. I couldn't see past her, and I didn't want to. We stayed there until the proprietor shooed us out, thinking we were a couple of street rats. He was half right. After that, we walked and walked, oblivious to Kahltan's circuit through the sky and barely aware that Dawn had come again. I was two winters younger than she, but I was taller, and things I had seen and done gave me a maturity and experience she felt drawn to. That's how she put it. Then she said she had to go home. I pleaded with her to stay. She didn't want to go, she said, but she told me she could help me. I believed her. Less than an hour later a Wardsman came looking for me."

Cyrolin gasped. "She turned you in?"

Edmund smiled. "I was taken to Sunfall, given a fresh change of clothes, and led to the throne room for an audience with Charles Gairden, Crown of the North and Anna's father. Anna was there, resplendent in white and with jewels in her hair that glittered like dewdrops under the Lady's light. She smiled at me, and my heart filled, and I don't know how I got through the rest of the audience. When I left, I was given a room in the barracks and began my training. I was—

"—a Wardsman, now," Charles said, looming from his throne.

Edmund rose from bended knee, fighting to keep from gaping at Annalyn. Her smile fell on him. The pride in her eyes could have lit a clear path on a starless night. "Thank you, ah,

Your Majesty. I will make you proud."

"See that you do," Charles Gairden said gruffly. He was taller than he was burly, but he was the Crown, and he cut an impressive figure as he unfolded himself from his throne. "Your training begins immediately. Well? Go on, then."

Turning away from her was physically painful. A Wardsman guided him through Sunfall and to the western courtyard. It was a large stone expanse. All around him, men brought swords to bear against straw dummies, groomed animals, polished armor, sharpened steel, ran drills. Across the way sat a wide edifice bare of ornamentation. "Go straight to the barracks and report to Sergeant Rakian Shirey," the Wardsman said. His mouth twisted as if he had tasted something sour. "He's briefing another new recruit. Once you've met with him, you—"

"You are relieved, Wardsman."

Her voice set Edmund's cheeks afire. He turned and saw Annalyn, back straight and chin jutted out, looking every bit the daughter heir.

"Your pardon, Princess," the Wardsman said, bowing. "Your father asked me to show my new brother to the courtyard."

"And so you have, and now I would speak with him. Return to your station."

"Yes, Princess," the Wardsman said, bowing again and hurrying off. Annalyn watched over her shoulder. When the sounds of his steel and snow faded, she whirled to face Edmund. Her face lit up with pride and joy.

A hand touched his arm. Edmund started in his chair. Then he remembered. Cyrolin. Jamian's ship. *Anna. Dead.* His heart ached. He cleared his throat and looked away. "Sorry. I don't know what came over me."

"Exhaustion," Cyrolin said, "and perhaps lingering effects from the *Sard'tara*. You need rest."

He scrubbed a hand over his face. "There are many things I need and slim chance of getting them."

"We should stay here for tonight. Festival ends tomorrow. The crowds will thin."

"And go where?" Edmund said. "Ironsail is closed." He tried to stand, needing to pace, but he was not used to putting his weight on a leg able to support it and overbalanced.

Cyrolin was by his side in an instant. "You need to rest," she said again.

"There's no time."

"We can talk through ideas just as easily from these chairs as we can on our feet. Besides, there is no safer place for us at the moment."

"At the moment?"

Cyrolin resumed her seat. "Did you hear the horns earlier? Before we left the inn?"

"I vaguely recall hearing something," he said slowly.

"I have only heard that call twice in my life. Once when pirates attempted to raid North Haven—"

"I thought Leastonians were pirates."

"From other lands," she said patiently. "And again tonight."

"What does it mean?"

"It is a call to arms issued from a cell of Azure Blades that finds itself against overwhelming odds. Any Blades able to hear the call are expected to rush to their compatriots' aid, sounding their own horns to signal their imminent arrival."

Edmund processed her words. "So that means that other cells are still alive."

"At least some," she said. "The only cells exempt from answering are those protecting a guildmaster at the time of the call. In the event of a widespread attack, they abandon their bunkers and meet at a secret location."

"Do you know how to find them?"

Cyrolin scowled. "No. Only Azure Blades know where to gather. Horn blows coordinate those locations as well. It's a language, of sorts. I do not know it, so I brought us here." She uncrossed her legs and stood, beginning to pace. "I do not know if any of Jamian's cell are still alive. Our best chance lies in their bunker."

"The one they've probably abandoned?"

Cyrolin nodded. "Cell members rotate shifts. Those who make the decision to abandon a bunker would need some way of informing other members of where to relocate. If we go to the bunker, we might be able to find a clue indicating where they have gone, for those who would come after." She hesitated, looking as if she wanted to say more.

"If they're alive," Edmund said. Cyrolin nodded. Edmund

massaged his leg and mulled over her words. "It's as good a plan as any. We stay here tonight and set out at Dawn. No, before. The less populated the streets, the better." He braced himself against Jamian's desk and pushed himself to his feet. "You sleep here. Before you settle in, show me to another cabin where I can . . . Cyrolin?"

She had frozen in mid-stride, her expression white as snow. "Do not give me orders, Edmund."

He thought back on what he had said. "I'm sorry. I was only agreeing with you."

"We are equals now," she said slowly, as if working out her words as she went along. "I am a free woman. I am not beholden to Jamian, or to you, or anyone else."

"Of course," he said softly.

Cyrolin swallowed. "I . . . like you, Edmund. You are a friend," she went on quickly, "and you saved my life."

"And I saved yours."

"Yes, exactly. We are equals. We must work together. Do you agree?"

"I do."

"Then, when the time comes for us to make a decision, we should make it together."

"Agreed," he said.

At that, her face took on its normal ruddy complexion, and her shoulders loosened. "Good. I am glad." She took a deep breath. "I think you should sleep here. I am not used to such large quarters. I will take a smaller cabin. And I would like to keep the lantern with me, if that is all right."

"Of course."

"Good." She smiled. Despite the turmoil of his life, Edmund could not help smiling back. He was happy for her.

Shadows wavered and danced over the walls as Cyrolin picked up the lantern. "Until Dawn, then."

"Before. If that suits you," he added.

"It does. Good night." She moved to the door.

"Cyrolin."

She turned, one hand on the latch.

"Thank you for saving my life," he said.

Cyrolin seemed to breathe in his words. "Thank you for saving mine."

Chapter 32:
Honor or Survival

VISUALIZING THE LAKE and holding that image, clutching it, squeezing it, was like sculpting from water instead of stone. One instant Nichel pictured it, serene and verdant, a breeze sending ripples over the surface and teasing her skin. In the next instant it was gone, swallowed by darkness. She was in the cave again. A set of crimson eyes seared a hole into her mind and spirit.

The lake. Aidan sat on the shore, legs stretched out, skimming stones across the water. He turned to her and laughed, eyes sparkling with mischief and humor. That was the Aidan she had known. He was still handsome and carefree now, but more so. Fully grown, fully developed, yet as ebullient as a cub chasing its tail. Her heart filled with love.

Then he was gone, consumed by darkness. The eyes of the *Nuulass* radiated fire hotter than a smith's forge, hot enough to reduce love to ashes and stoke hate deep in the furnaces of her belly. Words thundered, echoing throughout the cave and rattling her teeth, her bones, her soul.

— *The boy-cub lies.*

Aidan and the lake. The *Nuulass* and the cave. Love and hate. Back and forth, over and over.

Nichel tore her gaze away from the demon's and stared up at a silver square high above, embedded in darkness. It was the seal. She was on the wrong side. The cave was supposed to represent a prison within the deepest recesses of her mind, one where dark thoughts and darker urges lay sealed away from the light. She sped toward that seal, appeared on the lakeshore, found Aidan. He opened his arms and she took a step toward him.

The cave again. Not for the first time, Nichel thought that the blackness was thicker and larger, seeping from her prison to spread through her like a blight.

She felt hands on hers, gently pulling her fingers away from her head. Nichel opened her eyes and saw Jonathan easing her hands from her hair and into her lap. "Breathe," he said softly.

She inhaled and let out air slowly. As she did, her bedchambers came into focus. All eight members of her pack formed a ring around her bed. They stood with their backs to her, postures stiff. Color rose in her cheeks. Were they rigid out of vigilance for their war chief, or out of embarrassment because of their war chief?

Only one clanswoman had the courage to look her in the eye. Ulestren's head of cropped silvery hair turned so she viewed Nichel over her shoulder. Her face was carved from stone, but concern shone in her gaze.

Sitting up, Nichel ignored her. "How did I come to be here?" Right on its heels she asked: "Does he live?"

Jonathan blinked, unsure which inquiry to answer first. "He does. We brought you here, Nichel. You . . ." He hesitated, then lowered his voice. "You were overcome. It's understandable, given the circumstances."

Nichel closed her eyes. Fainted. The war chief, leader of all the clans, had fainted. Her attention swiveled to Ulestren. Her friend's expression had not changed. Nichel swung her feet over one side of her bed and rose. Only Ulestren and Jonathan watched her bare feet touch the stone floor. Only they saw her sway, one hand lashing out to grip a bedpost and then return to her side, quick as an adder uncoiling to strike.

Her pack parted as she rose from the bed and crossed to her door. The knob would not turn. She clenched her fists. "Why am I locked in?"

Jonathan hurried over, fussing with a set of keys. "Not locked in. We locked Aidan out. For your protection. After the assassin . . . I saw no reason to assume that Aidan was alone, so I—"

Aidan. Love and hate. Her hands went to her head. She could

feel it again. The *Nuulass*, a presence in her mind and soul attempting to claw its way out. She took a long breath and pictured the seal. It trembled but held.

"Where is he?"

"The Crevasse," Jonathan said after a moment of hesitation.

Nichel took another soothing breath and broke into a fit of coughing. The scent of perfume—lilies and marigolds, roses and orchids, mixed with peaches and berries and cream—abraded her nose like a sandstorm abraded the flesh, cloying to the point of nausea. Tears welled and seeped down her cheeks. Nichel scrubbed her palms over her eyes and turned to face her pack. Since when had any of them taken to wearing Leastonian scents? Her vision cleared, and their visages froze her next breath, taken through her mouth, in her throat.

Four of her pack, including Ulestren, wrinkled their nose but otherwise remained still. Grivah of the Eagle, Lensit of the Stallion, Drisa of the Leopard, and Shonliuhl of the Bear stared at her with expressionless faces. Their skin was pale and glistened with a coat of perspiration. Their stances not just stiff but utterly still, as if shaped from wax. They did not so much as blink. The other four were more animated, now shifting from foot to foot.

Nichel sniffed the air, testing. Fragrances assaulted her. She sneezed and scrubbed at her nose with the back of an arm.

"Are you well, Nichel?" Jonathan asked.

Nichel scrubbed until her nose felt raw. "Perfume," she said thickly.

Jonathan nodded. "Yes," he said under his breath. "I didn't want to say anything, but one or more of your pack appears to have taken a liking. It's a bit . . . overwhelming, to say the least."

It? Her heightened sense of smell picked out no fewer than half a dozen aromas. Who wore them? She couldn't tell. "No more," she said in a steady voice that still sounded thick, as if with illness. Grivah, Lensit, Drisa, and Shonliuhl gave no indication that they had heard.

Jonathan returned to unlocking her door. The jangle of keys brought her to her senses.

"I will see him."

He paused. "Nichel, that is not a good idea."

She ignored him. "Who will accompany their war chief?" Her

voice was steady, though she hoped Ulestren would be the first to volunteer. If Grivah, Lensit, Drisa, or Shonliuhl were ill, she needed to avoid them.

Ulestren was the second. Ipadia of the Krait stepped forward. "I will attend, war chief."

"No."

Ipadia flinched as if struck a blow by the heat in Nichel's tone. Her olive skin darkened. She dropped her eyes to the floor.

"I will attend you, war chief," Ulestren said.

"Good. Jonathan, how long does it take to unlock a door?"

As if her words served as a key, Jonathan swung the door opened and stepped into the corridor. "At least let me—"

"No. Stay with the others." She shuddered as another wave of odor assailed her. "Tell them to bathe. Ulestren and I go alone."

Her friend fell into step behind her as they rounded the first corner leading down into the Crevasse. Brightly colored shapes and figures decorated the walls. Some drawings were elaborate. Others were simple, figures drawn from circles and jagged lines. Each stone panel told part of the story of her people, but Nichel ignored them. She set her attention ahead, letting her feet carry her while her mind delved deep below the ground.

Aidan. Her palms grew clammy. Nichel had no idea what words would spill from her lips when she saw him. It was possible she would forego words entirely, opting to drag Sand across his throat while Silk poked holes in his belly. Stabbing and carving, blood cascading down his chest and legs.

Heat flushed her skin. She ran her tongue over dry lips. Absently, her hands strayed to her belt. Her left fist tightened over Sand's wider, coarser hilt. Her right fist closed on air.

She stopped. "Where is Silk?"

"The council room, perhaps."

"Perhaps?" Nichel growled the word.

Ulestren shrugged. "Our concern was for you, and for apprehending the *shorogoyt*. Not for your fangs."

Nichel ground her teeth, staring up through stone. The council room was two layers above her. She could send Ulestren to retrieve Silk and go on ahead to speak with Aidan.

"You fight a losing battle."

Her attention snapped to Ulestren. "What do you mean?"

Ulestren's features had softened. She took Nichel's hands,

forcing her to stop walking. Loosening her hold on Sand caused near physical pain. "I know you, Clan Sister," Ulestren said. "The war you fight in your heart shines through your eyes. Your grief and rage threaten to consume you. You must not let it. Your father—"

Nichel braced. If Ulestren dared echo the negative sentiment that the other clans had shown toward Romen of the Wolf in life and in death, not even her status as Nichel's clan sister would save her from the *Nuulass* tearing her limb from limb.

"—was a rational and courageous man. I mourn him, too. On the night I learned of his entry into the Father's Vanguard, the Plains of Dust drank my tears as greedily as we thirst for the Mother's Milk. Romen of the Wolf was our clan leader, but he was like blood to me."

Tears stung Nichel's eyes. "I miss him, Clan Sister. Both of them."

"As do I, Clan Sister." Ulestren's tone hardened. "But Romen of the Wolf would scoff at your lack of control. You dishonor him. He looks down upon you from his place of honor in the Father's Vanguard, and what he sees shames him."

Nichel's throat went dry. Not even Margia of the Falcon would dare speak to her this way. Ulestren must know she walked dangerous ground, but showed no sign of fear or contrition. "You must be as rational and courageous as your father, if not more so. You are no longer a cub. More than that, you are a woman, Clan Sister. You walk a path only clansmen have trod. Think with your mind and not your heart. You can do this. You are wise. You would have been a great speaker for our clan one day." Ulestren appeared to steel herself. "What is done, is done. I did not come forward to fight by your side out of respect or awe at the creature that sleeps within you. I fear it, but I do not fear you. It is inside you, not you inside it. Do not sleep at its feet. Bend it so that it sleeps at yours. Focus. You can, and you must."

Nichel said nothing. It took all her willpower not to turn away.

"I am here," Ulestren said. She gave Nichel's hands a squeeze. "We will discover the truth together." Her face split in a wolfish grin. "I will be the Sand to your Silk."

As her friend continued to speak, Nichel felt her lips curl into a smile.

AIDAN OPENED HIS eyes and saw darkness. He inhaled, then gagged and breathed through his mouth. Stables that had not been mucked out in a week smelled like Leastonian perfumes compared to the Crevasse.

Stirring, he winced as pain stabbed his head. Someone had hit him there, but why? He closed his eyes—there was no difference in the darkness that surrounded him—and thought. *Nichel. The council room.* His eyes popped open. *The Wardsman!* And then Jonathan and Nichel's guards—her pack—had raced in, and . . . And now he was here, in the Crevasse, the second lowest point in Janleah Keep.

Aidan stretched his hands in front of him. They were his eyes, and his eyes perceived rough, damp stone, straw, and rusty bars. Gingerly, he pulled himself to his feet, one hand on a bar that extended up past his height. He groped. His fingers left one bar and brushed another, and another. At eight paces, his booted toe rattled against another bar. He turned right, followed another eight paces, turn right again. A third time.

A cage, he thought at the exact moment Grandfather Charles sent the same thought.

Where are you? Aidan asked.

— *A small room adjoining the council chamber,* his grandfather said. *That young man, Jonathan Hillstreem, is here, as are half a dozen of Nichel's pack.* His voice grew troubled. *Strange that they're not with her.*

— *Why are you still here?* Gabriel asked.

It took Aidan a moment to realize the scholar had addressed him. *What do you mean?*

— *I mean, we un-Tied you before you allowed Nichel's pack to truss you like a chicken to market, and that handsome lout of Nichel's failed to detect it. You can leave any time.*

There's no light down here.

— *You're a shade. You don't need light.*

Aidan offered no reply.

— *Loathe though I am to admit it, Gabriel raises a valid point,* Anastasia said.

— *For once we agree, Mother,* Gabriel said.

Aidan's headed pounded. He sank to the ground, laced his hands behind his head, and leaned back against the wall. The throbbing subsided. Not much, but even a little brought blessed relief.

I can't.

— *You can.*

I won't, then.

— *We will act in your stead,* Gabriel said.

No. Aidan was well aware that the Gairdens had some agency through Heritage. They had demonstrated it to help him expose the Annalyn-harbinger during his trial. But there was a catch.

— *How did you work it out?* Anastasia asked quietly.

Aidan gave a small smile, for once not minding that they were sifting through his thoughts like a thief pillaging a man's home. He had not been certain, not entirely, that a sword-bearer had to issue a request for aid or open himself or herself so that an ancestor could touch the world through Heritage. Not until his desperate flight from the Hornet's Nest with Daniel, Christine, and her brother, when Anastasia had healed Daniel through him.

— *You cannot just sit here,* Anastasia said.

Aidan barely heard her. His chest rose and fell rapidly. Darkness might as well have been walls to a box that pressed in against him. A tightness welled up in his chest. Cold sweat broke out. His clothes grew damp and heavy.

Christine. He thought of her smile, the way her eyes lit up with happiness and mischief when she looked at him. Memories of the brief but sweet touches they had shared became a candle in the interminable darkness of the Crevasse. *At least she's safe with her father.*

— *Breathe,* Grandfather Charles said gently.

Aidan forced himself to take slow, deep breaths. A few minutes. He just needed a few minutes to gather his wits and calm his mind. Then he would plan, and act. In his mind he sat in the chair in front of the hearth at the Fisherman's Pond inn, Christine's weight pleasant in his lap, her hair soft and smelling of—

— *As much as I enjoy the sight of the Sallnerian girl prancing through our young heir's mind wearing nothing but a smile— ah, there she goes now—he needs to concentrate,* Gabriel said.

Aidan's mouth tightened. It occurred to him that he did not care for the man.

— *Your feelings are of no matter to me,* came Gabriel's purred reply. *It is not my job to be adored. It is my job to keep sword-*

bearers alive, and you are making my job difficult. You will explain why you refuse to act.

Why don't you steal it from my thoughts?

— *Because the last time I tried, you shut me out.*

Aidan rubbed his eyes with his palms. *I had Nichel convinced. The assassin cast doubt in her mind. It was a vagrant. The Sight showed me that, but I never got a chance to show her.*

— *She might not have listened,* Ambrose said. *Turning around and seeing you holding Heritage, ready to strike . . .*

I was trying to save her!

— *We know that,* Anastasia said. *But, well, think of how you must have looked.*

Aidan sighed. *I know. The Wardsman's appearance was convenient.*

— *You think Tyrnen sent it,* she said.

Who else?

— *You will not find the truth sitting down here,* Gabriel said.

No, but any action I take other than waiting will be construed as hostile. Shadewalking to freedom will make me look guiltier than I already do. He shot a leg forward, kicking loose stones. *She believed me. That has to count for something. If I break her trust now, I'll never win it back.*

The silence drew out, long and endless. He wondered why they did not press him to reconsider, and realized he desperately wanted them to. The darkness was closing in, suffocating him.

— *You are the sword-bearer,* Ambrose said. *We respect your decision. But, Aidan, can you risk leaving this matter in Nichel's hands? The girl is . . . unstable. She could decide to execute you.*

Aidan ran his hands through his hair. How he wished he could hold Heritage just long enough for Anastasia to soothe his aching head. *She hasn't yet.*

— *It is not a question of if, but when,* Gabriel said. *She is disturbed. Utterly mad.*

She's not mad, Aidan thought, leaping to Nichel's defense. *Grandfather, you knew Nichel. Tell them she isn't mad.*

Charles was a long time in replying. *She did behave irrationally, Aidan. She seemed barely in control. You must have noticed.*

She lost her parents in a horrible way, Grandfather. She may be a woman according to the customs of her people, but she's still young. "We both are," he muttered.

A thought occurred. *Gabriel, you said you detected a darkness within her.*

— *Not a darkness,* he said. *I detected* the *darkness, as pure as that which flows through the tunnels. Not that that comes as a surprise. After all, the wildlanders—*

They are our allies, and Nichel is my friend. You will afford them respect.

— *Apologies,* Gabriel purred.

Aidan doubted he meant it, but moved on. *You said no one knew who built the tunnels.*

— *I said no one knew because no scholar had written down the answer. You did not ask if I knew the answer, and I do. The Darinians constructed the tunnels and infused them with dark magic.*

Gasps resounded through Aidan's mind. Aidan did not add his to them. He was thinking.

— *Darinians are men and women, flesh and blood,* Anastasia protested shakily.

— *After a fashion,* Gabriel said.

Meaning? his mother asked.

— *The Darinians were some of the earliest practitioners of dark magic.*

Did they create it?

— *Don't be a fool, boy. I said the . . . the westerners practiced it. No man created Nocturne, the wellspring of darkness from which shades draw, and none knew more of the Nocturne than did the clans. It flows through their blood, and through the blood of all Touched. They were simply among the first in recorded history to harness it effectively.*

And in unrecorded history? Aidan asked.

Gabriel's laugh was soft, dry. — *You are learning.*

Answer the question.

— *Is that a command from my Crown?*

It is.

When Gabriel spoke again, his words sounded different, as if spoken through a grin that Aidan imagined as vulpine. — *As far as I know, they are the first. That is the truth.*

Aidan frowned in the dark. *What did you mean when you said they were men of flesh and blood after a fashion?*

— *There are rumors, legends that grew from myths. That the totems of Darinian clans are more than symbols. They are gods that assumed the forms of animals and other, non-corporeal forms, according to their speakers' interpretations.*

I thought Darinians worshipped the Mother and Father.

— *Their speakers know the truth. I cannot say for certain. Other myths purport that certain Darinians were able to assume the forms of those totems.*

How? Through dark magic?

— *Again, I cannot say for certain.* Gabriel sounded hesitant.

Because you don't know.

— *I do not.* Now Gabriel sounded annoyed.

A thousand and one questions flooded Aidan's mind. He sifted through them and grasped the most important. *What you detect in Nichel, is it one of those totems? Those gods?*

— *I believe so.*

How would you know?

— *Light magic burns all it touches. It is instantaneous, bright and hot and final. Dark magic is tenebrous, and cold, and long-lasting. It carries . . . weight, for lack of a better term. The weight of the magic I sense in Nichel is heavy. Ancient.*

— *Did you sense it from other Darinians during your time?*

— *No.*

A fresh outbreak of sweat dampened Aidan's skin. *Do you know of a way to manipulate it? A curse, or . . . or something?*

Gabriel was silent for several moments. — *Curse is such an ugly word,* he said finally.

Aidan leaned forward, peering intently into infinite darkness. *Such a spell exists?*

— *A spell exists for nearly everything, Aidan. You will not find this particular spell in any book of light magic, however. The Lady frowns on influencing the minds and emotions of others. The Lord of Midnight has no such qualms.*

Aidan mulled over his ancestor's words. *Tell me more.*

— *The spell is called coercion. With it, a shade can . . . let us say encourage certain behaviors by strengthening certain emotions.*

— *You're talking about forcing someone to act against their will,* Charles said sharply.

— *I am not,* Gabriel replied. *Coercion intensifies. It cannot* create emotion where none exists. *Coercion is not a mallet. It is a chisel, an instrument of precision. The stronger the emotion, the less coercion one needs to bring about a desired result.*

Aidan frowned. *I'm afraid I don't understand.*

— *Quite all right. It is a complicated subject. Human beings rarely feel only one way about any matter. Imagine a woman whose husband abuses her, yet at one point, their love was strong. He dies, leaving her a widow. She mourns him, or perhaps she mourns for the love that was lost more than the man himself. Yet, she is also glad to be free of him. The two feelings are not mutually exclusive. It is natural, even common, for humans to feel two conflicting emotions. Emotions are as stones on a scale, and a Touched may use coercion to add stones to either side. If the desired emotion is stronger, coercion will act faster. If the opposite emotion is dominant, the Touched will need to add several stones. Not all at once, or the spell may backfire.*

Aidan worked through Gabriel's explanation. *So, working from your example, a Touched could have coerced the woman into killing her husband.*

— *Indeed. She loved him, and yet she hated him. The strength of that hate in relationship to its converse emotion would dictate how much coercion was needed to tip the scales. If she were desperate, angry, fearful for the wellbeing of her children, I venture she would not have needed much convincing.*

Aidan stared into nothingness, his mind working.

— *What is your point, Gabriel?* Anastasia asked. She sounded cautiously intrigued, and more than a little horrified.

— *I could explain it to you,* he replied, *but Aidan knows. Don't you, Aidan?*

Aidan did. One by one, his ancestors caught on.

— *This is not right,* Anastasia said.

— *Nichel believes him,* Gabriel said. *Not past tense. Such an emotion cannot be wiped away.* His tone grew thoughtful. *Not many stones would be needed, I think.*

— *Charles, surely you do not condone this,* Anastasia said.

Aidan's grandfather did not answer right away. — *Escape, or coercion. Those are Aidan's choices, and as he pointed out, any attempt to escape would likely end in disaster.*

The part of Aidan's mind occupied by Gabriel swelled in

triumph.

Meanwhile, Anastasia diminished, as if giving ground. —*Ambrose?*

The Gairden patriarch took his time in answering. — *When I served Torel's Ward, before I became general, the men had a saying: In life, fight with honor. In war, fight to survive.*

— *Which means?* Gabriel asked. Aidan detected no trace of the sarcasm Gabriel used to goad his mother into arguments.

— *It means that veteran warriors who want to survive learn to exploit any advantage they can. Nichel is not our enemy. Nevertheless, she and Aidan are engaged in a battle of sorts. If Aidan loses, Crotaria loses.*

— *Wise words,* Charles said, though he sounded troubled.

— *I can't believe I'm hearing this,* Anastasia said. *Gabriel, as you explained it, part of Nichel still believes Aidan. I also believe a part of her wants him dead. She may want one outcome more than the other, but she still wants both. Using coercion would force her to choose the result we want. It is manipulation, however you choose to present it.*

— *Would you rather she mounted your grandson's head on a spike?* Gabriel asked.

— *No. I'm only saying—*

— *The choice is for Aidan to make,* Charles interjected.

— *So it is,* Gabriel said. *What is your choice, Aidan?*

Aidan's fists trembled. His family's legacy had led him here, to this place, this moment, this choice. — *It is never easy,* Anastasia said, *to wear a crown. Nor should it be*

There was a loud, rusty squeal. Soft voices followed by a candlelight that grew brighter as two pairs of footsteps drew nearer. Nichel emerged from the darkness like an apparition. One of the pack, Ulestren of the Wolf, followed on her heels. They stopped well short of the bars of his cage, their eyes hot enough to sear flesh from his bones.

"It is time," Nichel said. The words were a harsh staccato.

Feral, Gabriel had called her. Aidan found he had to swallow. "Time for what?"

"To die," Ulestren cut in.

ULESTREN'S DECREE OF death hung in the air. As they agreed, Nichel showed no reaction. She just watched. Aidan squinted into the candlelight, trying to make her out. Her eyes were sharper than his. Had she a desire, she could have counted each scuff on his boots and the individual stones in the wall he sat against. However, her nose saw what not even her eyes could make out.

Aidan emitted no fear or guilt. Only . . . Her nose twitched, and she stifled the urge to flee. Compassion, as warm and pacifying as a blanket on a cold night out under the Father's Vanguard. Hesitating only a moment, she allowed his compassion to fill her heart.

The seal trembled.

A moment's hesitation was all the *Nuulass* needed. Aidan's empathy soured. Warmth heightened until her blood boiled. She closed her eyes and pictured the lake, breathed in and out, in and out. Blackness crept in around the edges of her haven. All it would take was one more moment of weakness and it would wash over everything like tar.

— *Let me in,* the voice purred. *Let me drown thought and reason.*

"No!"

Ulestren spun, frowning. Her hands went to Talon, her own fang. Nichel made a gesture, and Ulestren relaxed. Aidan spoke into the silence.

"Nichel, please," he said, climbing to his feet. Nichel could not help noticing that he came no closer to the rusty cell bars. With an effort she pushed the *Nuulass* away, locked it below her seal.

"Silence," Ulestren said. "You killed Romen of the Wolf and his mate, and then you travelled all the way here to return his young to the ground. But not by your own hand. You are too cowardly for that." She spat at him. Aidan flinched as it spattered his cheek.

For a moment, Nichel forgot all about the *Nuulass* and her pain. Spitting was considered the ultimate insult among Darinians. Such a flagrant waste of moisture was reserved only for the most extreme insults. The only response was combat to the death.

Aidan raised a hand and wiped away Ulestren's spit. He did not step back as she approached the bars of his cage. "The war chief killed your assassin. Be grateful. Had he lived, your man would have suffered to his last breath. I would have seen to him personally."

"I did not send him, and that man is no man at all."

Ulestren narrowed her eyes. Before she could insult or taunt him again, Nichel cut in. "Explain."

"He is a vagrant, one of the creatures I told you about. I believe he—it—was sent by Tyrnen to incriminate me. And perhaps to kill you, if you appeared to believe me."

Ulestren snorted. "The war chief is too intelligent to be taken in by the likes of—"

"Leave us," Nichel said.

"You cannot be serious," Ulestren said, eyes wide.

"Do you disobey your war chief?"

"Jonathan Hillstreem said I was not to leave you alone with him."

Anger bubbled up, and for once it was not directed at Aidan. "I am confused, Ulestren of the Wolf. Do you swear allegiance to Cinder Hillstreem, or to me?"

Ulestren stiffen. "To you, of course." Her voice did not quaver, but Nichel smelled her shame.

"Jonathan bound his magic," Nichel went on evenly, "and the *Ordine* blade is . . ." Her gaze flickered to Aidan. "Safe. Somewhere he cannot reach it. You reminded me of who and what I am. I am not afraid of this man." *Stay calm. Focus.* "Wait for me just outside. I will not be long."

Ulestren hesitated, then whirled on Aidan. "If I do not see her standing before me by the time our Mother perches over the mountains, they will call me *shorogoyt* by the time the night is through."

She began to leave, then paused at the edge of the light cast from Nichel's candle. Nichel handed it to her. "Take it."

"Thank you, war chief."

There came the sound of stone grating on stone as Ulestren departed. Gathering herself, Nichel faced Aidan. He shifted from foot to foot, eyes darting around. Her nose caught the scent of anxiety: Faint, like a tendril of smoke curling up from a fire.

"Nichel?" he said, his voice doubtful as he cast his gaze around. "Have you stayed to execute me?"

The seal trembled.

— *You smell his fear,* the *Nuulass* whispered. *He is prey. We can hunt him.*

With an effort, Nichel shoved the voice down deep. "No," she said, surprised at the tremor in her voice. Her heart was in her throat. She swallowed, waited until it faded from a drumbeat to a muffled thumping. "Not yet."

Relief tinged with caution wafted from him. He stepped forward, his hands groping until they curled around the cell bars. "It was a vagrant. I did not lie."

"Its appearance was convenient."

"I could have proven it to you." He smiled a little. "You killed it too quickly."

She straightened, then caught herself. *Taking pride in your enemy's words? Fool!*

"Yes," she said, "which is why I am surprised you are standing so close."

He did not step away. Nichel sniffed lightly. There was no fear on him, nor could she detect treachery. Only determination, redolent of newly forged steel. "How could you have shown me?" she asked.

"With a spell. Well, I guess it's not really a spell." He shook his head. "It's complicated, but I can see the truth of things. Vagrants wear faces like masks, and the Sight—that's what it's called, this spell that is not a spell—removes the masks so I can see what lies underneath."

His eyes widened, and his scent changed. Hope, and optimism, like a spring breezes from the east. "You wouldn't need magic to see the truth!"

"What do you mean?"

"You stabbed him. He should have bled, but a vagrant's blood isn't red like ours. It's green, like ichor. Didn't you notice?"

Nichel remained silent. It would not do for her enemy or her lover-to-be to know of her fainting spell.

"Was there any trace of it?" he asked. "On the floor, maybe, or . . ."

Doubt, faint but unmistakable.

"The body," he said. "Have you already burned it?"

"Not yet."

"Then you believe me."

"I did not say that."

"You didn't have to."

Nichel fell silent. *Part of me does believe him.* Examining the assassin's corpse would answer her questions, if Jonathan had yet to dispose of it.

She turned on her heel. Aidan must have heard her feet rustle against the dirt.

"Nichel?"

She stalked away without another word.

AIDAN LOWERED HIS head against the bars and closed his eyes, listening to Nichel's retreating footsteps.

Coercion.

Gabriel's presence grew stronger. — *What of it?*

Aidan's hands choked the bars. He detected a teasing note in Gabriel's voice. If the portly little Cinder had been within reach, Aidan would have punched him.

Tell me what I need to do.

Chapter 33:
Investigations

ULESTREN FELL INTO step beside Nichel as she emerged from the Crevasse. The flame of her candle sent pale light shivering along the painted walls.

"Well, Clan Sister? Was I the Sand to your Silk, as you asked?"

Nichel's lips quirked in a bitter smile. "You were hard, Clan Sister." *Maybe not hard enough.*

"What is your next step?"

"The corpse."

Ulestren said nothing, only waited.

"What became of the assassin's body?" Nichel asked.

"I do not know," Ulestren admitted. "Jonathan said he would see to it. Half of your pack saw you safely to your chambers. The rest dealt with Aidan, and not gently."

"And Jonathan? Did he dispose of the body, do you think?"

"It would make sense. The Mother cannot pass sentence on the dead, and there would certainly be no place for a hired blade in *Daram Ogahra*."

Nichel's ears perked up. Her footsteps slowed, and her attention strayed to a wide corridor to her left. Ulestren paused at her side. "What are you thinking?" her clan sister asked. "That Aidan Gairden spoke the truth?"

"A walking corpse, sent to kill me and paint him the color of guilt." Nichel shook her head slowly. It was not color she had tried and failed to detect. It was scent, and Aidan had carried not even the faintest trace of guilt. Fear, frustration, determination, and compassion for her. That last heated her blood. She pushed it aside. *Only she who reigns within herself is queen.* "What do you think?" she asked.

"Our legends tell stranger tales," Ulestren said, shrugging.

"They do." Nichel squared her shoulders. "I am thinking, Clan Sister, that I should follow this trail, if only to discover where it leads." She caught Ulestren's gaze. The other wolf stared evenly back at her. "You disapprove."

Ulestren gave a bitter laugh. It sounded like a wolf's whine. "Not at all. For as much a part of me wants to see Aidan Gairden burn under the Mother's gaze at first light, I would be as insincere as an adder if I did not commend you for thinking as Romen of the Wolf had." She grinned. "Wise advice. I wonder who gave it to you."

Nichel's heart swelled with pride and love and loss. "Thank you, Clan Sister."

Ulestren nodded once. "What can I do?"

"Find Jonathan. Ask him what became of the corpse. If he has not destroyed it yet, tell him he is forbidden from doing so, and that I gave you the authority to make that command."

Another nod from Ulestren. Without a word she turned and loped away. Nichel felt another surge of pride. She had encountered no resistance from the speakers or other clansfolk since the *Nuulass* had possessed her that first, awful night, yet none obeyed her with as much alacrity as Ulestren. A sister in every way that counted, blood or no blood.

She winced. The language with which she had phrased her command for Ulestren to carry was unnecessarily severe. Jonathan did not deserve to be spoken to that way, not after all he had done for her since her parents had passed. At that, her eyes narrowed. Her parents had not died of old age in their sleep. They had been murdered. If not by Aidan, then by someone even more vindictive.

Nichel spared another glance at the passage to *Daram Ogahra* then resumed her quick gait toward the council chamber, hoping she would encounter no one there. She had another path to follow. Her hand strayed to where Silk should have hung at her waist. *You stabbed him,* Aidan had said. *He should have bled, but a vagrant's blood isn't red like ours. It's green, like ichor. Didn't you notice?*

As a matter of fact, she had not noticed. The *Nuulass* had sensed her weakness and pounced, determined to crush what remained of her self-control. Fighting it back had taken every scrap of spirit and willpower she possessed. Even so, she thought she remembered catching a trace of wrongness just before the assassin had emerged and Aidan had lunged at her. Or lunged past her. Nichel had thought, in that moment, that the odor emanated from Aidan. That he had gone from trying to convince her of his tale to trying to kill her. That pervasive smell, that wrongness had been brief, but it had been there. And it had smelled like something old and fusty. Something hidden. Then the wrongness had vanished and Nichel had acted on instinct, driving Silk into the assassin's belly before it could drive steel into hers.

Had it raised steel? Or had it only tried to grab her? After feeling the soft flesh of its middle give way, she remembered nothing. Not if the smell had lingered, and not what Aidan had done next. If her hunch was right, she would not need to remember.

Silk, lying discarded in the council room with blood caked on its blade, would tell her everything she needed to know.

— *CLOSE YOUR EYES.*

Aidan needed no further encouragement. His eyelids fell like curtains made from stone. Weariness crashed over him. The hard, uneven floor suddenly felt more comfortable. *I could fall asleep right now.* All he needed was to wrap a skein over his mind to shut out the voices, and to concentrate on his breathing—

— *I advise against that,* Gabriel said.

Aidan jumped as if poked.

— *We feel your fatigue,* Ambrose said with a note of worry. *You need rest.*

I'll see if I can fit a nap into my schedule, Aidan snapped.

— *We are only worried about you,* Anastasia said lightly.

All the fight drained out of Aidan, leaving only tiredness. *I know. I'm sorry.*

— *Pull yourself together,* Gabriel said, sounding not at all concerned. *The magic I will impart will not tax you at first, but will take its toll over time, like all shadecraft. Do what you must to stay alert.*

Aidan fidgeted until his right buttocks sat on a damp spot and his left buttocks jabbed into a pointed stone. He opened his eyes briefly, then closed them. The Crevasse was pitch black. There was no discernible difference between staring into its dark expanse and the backs of his eyelids.

— *Inhale,* Gabriel said. *Long and deep. Darken as you draw in breath. Just a sip, mind. Think of the Lord of Midnight's shade as fine wine: You savor it, you do not gulp it down like tavern swill.*

Aidan obeyed. His chest rose, and gooseflesh broke out across his skin.

— *Very good. Again.*

Flecks of ice swam through Aidan's bloodstream.

— *Once more.* Gabriel's voice sounded further away, as if it came from across the room instead of in his ear. Aidan let out a small shiver.

— *Now, exhale. Long and deep. As you do, push the shade back out of you. Let it ooze out rather than rush. Yes, just like that. Slowly, slowly. Excellent. Now inhale again and take another sip. Replace what you expel by pulling in just a fraction more.*

— *Dawn burn me,* Anastasia said from far away.

Aidan ignored her. He lost himself in his rhythmic breathing. Within moments he no longer felt a chill seeping through his flesh and hardening over his bones like ice. Gabriel continued to speak, but his voice grew muffled. As if he spoke above the surface while Aidan submerged himself in water. His ancestor's next words were as clear as crystal.

— *Open your eyes and tell me what you see.*

Aidan complied. He did not remember standing, but somehow he did, and not in darkness. The walls of the Crevasse, the air itself, shimmered a plum-colored purple. Outlines of objects and surfaces, such as the craggy walls, floors, and ceilings, were a slightly darker shade. The bars of his cage were gone.

— *Turn around.*

Dazed, Aidan did so. Too quickly. The world blurred, although not sharply, the way hills and ground sped by as one raced on horseback. Objects grew hazy, like a handful of sand flung beneath water. When the world grew still, he realized he had been facing the wall. Now he saw his cell bars. Aidan floated toward them. The bars blurred, growing closer, and then he was stepping through them. Not between them, but through them. He looked down and saw that his boots did not touch the ground. His legs, torso, and hands appeared misty and transparent. *A product of the spell*, he thought.

— *Not quite. Look back at the wall.*

Aidan directed his attention back the way he had come. A man in dirty trousers and a torn shirt slumped against the wall, chin tucked against his chest, eyes open but glazed as if in death. *It's a body*. His thoughts were sluggish and dreamy.

— *Not a body. Your body.*

Aidan drifted forward. Yes, it was his body, all right. Clothes filthy, hair disheveled, palms of his limp hands orange from gripping the corroded bars. Pouches sagged beneath his eyes. He straightened. *Am I dead?* The thought was dispassionate.

— *Look closer.*

Aidan did. His chest rose and fell, lightly and infrequently. *Fascinating*. He did not feel fascinated, though. He did not feel anything. *Am I a soul, then?*

Gabriel laughed, a crude and grating sound, the way one laughed at a dimwitted child. Aidan felt no anger or annoyance. He simply waited. — *Not a soul. A specter. You are detached from your body and can wander free, unchained from the limitations of flesh. Go ahead. Try it.*

Aidan intuited what "it" must be. He looked up at the low ceiling and floated upward. He did not have to push up off the floor. He had imagined himself floating and had done so. In midair he twisted, hovering parallel to the ceiling and floor. He glided along the ceiling and sailed back down.

It's like swimming, he thought. He pressed his legs together and wriggled them like fins. His shadow shot forward through the cell bars.

— *You are, after a fashion. Man must move with his feet on the ground. Shades operate under no such restriction. In this form, you can move through shadows as if they were water.*

The Crevasse consisted of blackness bordered by stone. Its expanse was like a basin filled with tenebrous water. Aidan swam in loops, testing this new method of movement. Ahead, he saw the outlines of the door through which Nichel and her wolf had exited. He stopped short in front of it. Locked. No matter: The shadows between stone door and stone wall beckoned. He shimmied through, his body flattening as thin as a sheet of parchment. Pouring through the keyhole on the other side, his shadow inflated back to his normal build and height. *What should I do now?*

— *Now,* Gabriel replied, *you convince your betrothed to stop acting the fool.*

"ULESTREN? JONATHAN?"

The council room threw her voice back at Nichel. Squinting, she listened. Her ears were as fine an instrument as her nose and eyes, able to pick up footfalls far down corridors. No sound reached her. Ulestren must have found Jonathan elsewhere. Wrinkling her nose, she entered through one of the passages ringing the hall. Stone and earth tickled her nose. No other scent mingled with them.

The seal trembled.

— *You search for hope where none exists,* the *Nuulass* said in a rumbling growl.

Nichel tensed. She realized she had not so much as thought of the Wild's Doom since leaving the Crevasse. Squeezing her eyes shut, she pictured the lake and took calming breaths.

Laughter, like sand sliding over stone. — *The boy-king lies. A broad pair of shoulders, a dashing smile, and you are as malleable as wet sand.*

Her confidence shook. The image of the lake wavered. Glowing red eyes formed in her mind. Its growl sweetened to a purr. — *Submit to me. Embrace me, and we will avenge the dead.*

The cave sharpened in her mind. Then Ulestren's words came back to her. Nichel breathed in and out, in and out. Gradually the *Nuulass* faded. The seal quivered once more and went still.

Nichel's eyes shot open. Anxiety crawled through her stomach, eating away at excitement. There was little time to waste. Just because she could not smell the wrongness here did not mean it was not present. *I did not smell it until . . .*

Eyes widening, Nichel hurried over to the effigy where she had stood the night before. Marlik the Widowmaker, chieftain of his clan centuries ago, towered over her. He was tall and spindly, like all of the Widowmaker clan, yet power radiated from his stone visage, as it radiated from all clan chiefs in life and after death. Nichel had stood with her back to Marlik's monument last night. And the assassin . . .

She stepped around the monument. The odor of rancid meat brought her up short, stinging her nose like a slap. There were layers to the room's scents. Dust. Dirt. Mold. And underneath, death.

Excitement fluttered in her belly. She had seen the Eternal Flame. Tyrnen Symorne had paid visits to Janleah Keep to meet with her father. Though she had never met him, Romen of the Wolf had respected the man, naming him wise and capable. *Surely such a man would not allow his dead soldiers to roam free without disguising their scents and rotten flesh. The right clothing to blend in among the living, a layer of flesh over rotten meat.*

A thrill rose in her. She had smelled many odors from Aidan in the time since he had been brought before her, and not one matched that which still lingered here.

Here. The assassin had emerged here, but where had he come from?

She took one step further, sniffing. The aroma dimmed. A second step, and it diminished further. *He came in from there,* she thought, eyeing an opening across from her. A third step, and the odor vanished.

Nichel froze. She sniffed, detected stone and dirt. *It's as if he vanished into thin air.* That was impossible. Perhaps the assassin had entered from another ingress. Turning, she retraced her steps to the rear of Marlik's monument, picked up the smell, and moved toward a different entryway. Three steps and the scent vanished.

She walked slowly back to the monument and leaned a hand against it. That his scent diminished did not surprise her. Smells diminished with time, like sound. A smell was freshest where it was most recent, weakest where it was oldest. That the assassin seemed to have materialized here no longer concerned her. He had fallen in the same spot. Which meant . . .

Her gaze dropped to the floor. It was spotless, as clean as it had been on the day the builders of legend had raised Janleah Keep. Nichel sniffed again and perceived a soapy scent she had missed before. Crouching, she saw that a large patch of stone had been scrubbed almost white, in stark contrast to the earthy colors of the rest of the stone. Someone had scoured the blood away.

Rising, Nichel rubbed at her nose with the back of her hand. The soapy smell loitered. She wanted it gone. Its cleanliness was unclean to her. Turning back around, she took a slow step near to where Aidan had stood. Death clawed at her nostrils again, and just as quickly a new scent replaced it. It reeked of flowers. *Perfume*, she realized. Suddenly, she sneezed. Nichel had just enough time to turn and sneeze into the crook of her elbow.

Nichel raised her head and just barely swallowed a scream.

Chapter 34:
Discord

AIDAN DRIFTED THROUGH the halls of Janleah Keep, studying his surroundings. Darinia's ancient builders had carved every hallway from a different material. Floors sloped and rose, curled around bends or jutted out at sudden angles. Walls of brick, then marble, then granite, then sandstone, then icestone, even myriad types of wood stretched up at variable heights, some lost in shadows above, others so low he would have had to crouch or crawl to progress. *If I were flesh*, he thought.

Every wall served as a canvas, displaying illustrations in paint or carved into stone. Each illustration was a tableau of people, places, and events from throughout Darinia's history. Aidan vaguely recalled some of them from sprinting through the Keep during his visits as a boy. Colors and images had passed in a blur as he ran ahead of Nichel, laughing, his longer legs keeping him just out of reach. Nichel had explained the pictures once. Had given them a name, said they proceeded in chronological order beginning at the Crevasse and culminating in a place called *Daram Ogahra* that outsiders were forbidden from seeing, let alone entering.

No colors whisked by him as he drifted along. All was black or purple, night or Dusk. Once, at twelve winters old, he had begged and pleaded with Nichel to show him *Daram Ogahra*. He had gone so far as to offer the kiss she had pursued relentlessly his past two visits. Her refusal had served to impress upon Aidan the significance of the hallowed place, and stoked the fires of his curiosity that much hotter.

Aidan thought of *Daram Ogahra* now and realized he no longer cared to see it. He was indifferent toward the sacred place, toward his predicament, toward Tyrnen. Toward everything.

— *You are devoid of emotions,* Gabriel said in his whispery voice. *Bodies are much more complicated than specters. As a specter, you are connected to your body, but only loosely.*

What happens if Nichel returns to the Crevasse and thinks I'm dead?

— *One assumes she would attempt to awaken you.*

Would she be able to?

— *Yes. Your specter would snap back into your body. The sensation is unpleasant.*

You have experienced it?

— *I make it a point to experience all things,* the scholar replied. *I considered it my duty as the greatest shade who ever lived.*

Greater than Aaren Bridgegil?

— *Focus on finding the wolf.* Gabriel went silent.

Aidan felt no pleasure at taking the scholar down a peg, nor did he feel shame for the childish rejoinder. He was nothing, floating through darkness.

Speeding forward, he rounded a bend in a corridor with marble flooring and tall wooden walls and arrived in a hall with two archways on either side. A drawing had been engraved into the stone above each: a wolf to his right, and an adder, a poisonous snake indigenous to Darinia, to his left. *Nichel is a wolf,* he reasoned. He glided through the opening and stopped short on the other side. Sconces lined a corridor fashioned from brick that glowed purple to his specter eyes. Their flames danced and popped, painting the walls with soft white luminescence.

He shied away from the light, aware of a lurch in his stomach, or where his stomach would be if he had one. *There are torches lining the passageway ahead. They make me feel queasy.*

— *Stay out of the light,* Gabriel said. *And try not to be seen. Light not only weakens you, it reveals you. You are a shadow without a body.*

Squinting, Aidan faced the sconces. Brightness overwhelmed him. The room swayed. He raised his eyes above the fire, the brightest points of light. Luminescence receded, fading to the purplish color that defined walls. Looking back the way he had come, he observed purple dimming to blackness. *Light magic, dark magic. Light. Dark. Each is the absence of the other.*

Above him, the ceiling glowed a plum color. Aidan swam upward until he felt his wispy form spread flush against it. In the same instant his perspective twisted. The ceiling became the floor, and the floor flipped over top him. Now the sconces hung like stalactites.

Tentatively, he oozed forward. His progress was smooth and steady. He wondered idly if this was what it was like to slither through grass as an adder. Ahead, his path grew paler. Light pooled at the base of sconces from where they hung from the ceiling, previously the ground. Between them were threads of purple as thin as veins. Their edges flickered as the flames danced. Aidan slid along, gravitating toward veins of shadow. He passed through one no wider than his small finger and felt himself compress, like wine flowing from the neck of a bottle. His perspective tapered to a fine point. Emerging, his vision widened. He spotted another tendril of pale darkness and wormed into it.

Spilling from yet another tapered path, Aidan spread into a puddle again. He was on the other side. The floor—the ceiling— was darker here. No torches stood ahead. He poured downward, willing his specter form to take the shape of his body. A moment later he drifted an inch from a floor made from an ebony-colored stone. He felt stronger now, further from the light. He righted himself until he drifted over the floor again.

Aidan proceeded, following the trail to another junction, this one with five openings. He found another wolf carving and followed it. When he came to braziers on the floor or torches hanging from walls, he puddled onto the ceiling and threaded his way through the darkest spots he could find. Once he came to a junction so brightly lit he cried out silently and fled back the way he had come. He regained his composure as he moved away from brightness. He followed corridors that took him around the impasse until he got back on track.

He arrived at a hallway that unfolded in a jagged line. Up ahead, a single torch painted brick walls white. Aidan ghosted forward, ready to swim along the walls or ceiling, then stopped. Footsteps behind him. Remembering Gabriel's warning about being seen, he dove headfirst into a patch of darkness along the floor. It swallowed him. Adjusting himself, he gazed up from his hiding spot and resisted a sudden instinct to flee.

Ulestren of the Wolf strode through the entryway he had used moments before, towering over him. Her face held as much emotion as he felt: her eyes were flat, her mouth set. Her skin glowed with a thin sheen of perspiration. She moved forward, her strides shorter than her long legs allowed.

Aidan rose, unfolding from the floor. Anastasia's words from earlier, aimed at Nichel, came to him. *Something is not right with that girl.*

He followed Ulestren, weaving in and out of shadowy tendrils and patches, until she entered the council chamber. She stopped in a doorway. Nichel was halfway across the room, sniffing the floor. Ulestren only stood, waiting. Aidan waited with her.

NICHEL SWALLOWED, THEN scowled. "You startled me, Clan Sister."

"My apologies, war chief," Ulestren said impassively from the entryway.

"Forgiven," Nichel snapped, then took a breath. Her tone did not match her words. "You startled me, that's all. It's been some time since I failed to hear even the quietest approach." She smiled.

Ulestren stared back. Discomfort crawled through Nichel's belly like worms. "Did you find Jonathan?" she asked.

Ulestren nodded slowly.

"Good," Nichel said after a moment. Ulestren's eyes never left hers. Nichel found herself temporarily at a loss for words. "Are you well?"

"I am," Ulestren said.

Nichel cleared her throat. Her eyes flitted around the council chamber and landed on the spot where the assassin had died. "Clan Sister, I searched for Silk but could not find it."

"Your knife." Ulestren nodded. "It was removed."

Excitement welled up. "It was? I thought you said . . . It does not matter." She crossed the distance to the doorway where Ulestren stood. "Where to? I—"

Perfume radiated from Ulestren in waves. Nichel's eyes watered. Through a haze of tears, she placed it as Heart of Lilacs. It had been her mother's favorite fragrance. Cynthia had carried it back from Leaston during a trip she and Romen of the Wolf had taken to negotiate more safe trade routes into the west and had given it to Nichel as a gift. Nichel enjoyed some of her mother's perfumes, but not Heart of Lilacs. Not wanting to hurt her mother's feelings, she had discretely given it to Ulestren. Her clan sister had accepted the gift with the proper respect and gratitude, then set it aside. Nichel had been neither surprised nor hurt. Ulestren was not of mixed heritage. She was Darinian, and wore the fragrances of her people: dust, dirt, sweat, and blood.

Why would she wear the fragrance now?

Nichel tried to smile. "Did you bathe in lilacs, Clan Sister?" The words came out thickly.

Ulestren did not answer right away. With great effort, one corner of her mouth rose in a smile that Nichel suspected was meant to appear friendly, but instead looked pained. "I like the way it makes me smell."

Nichel coughed. "You wear too much. You are supposed to apply it sparingly, in the crook of your arms and along your neck, for instance." She reached out to touch one side of Ulestren's neck and jerked her hand away.

"Is something the matter," Ulestren said. Her inflection did not rise as if asking a question.

"Your skin," Nichel said, resisting the urge to wipe her hand on her leg. "It is as cold as the Father's gaze."

Just then, Nichel's ears perked up. Shuffling footsteps from behind Ulestren. Her pack emerged from the gloomy corridor, filing through archways and lining up along the walls. Nichel took several steps back, cupping both hands over her nose. All the women reeked of flowers, sweets, and other perfumes. Grivah of the Eagle came last, and Jonathan followed a respectful distance behind her, hands folded in front of him. She caught a trace of his clean, soapy scent, but barely, buried beneath mounds and mounds of fruit and flowers.

Jonathan caught Nichel's eye and hurried over. "My apologies, war chief. I should have told you," he said quietly. "The perfume. You see, your pack, they . . ." He hesitated. "They're all wearing it. I don't know where they found it. Your mother's wardrobes, perhaps, but surely they would not enter her chambers without your permission."

Hesitantly, Nichel lowered her hands and took a small sniff. Countless fragrances burned her nostrils. Fresh tears welled up.

Jonathan rested a hand on the small of her back and leaned in close. "May I have a quick word, Nichel?" he asked.

"Of course," she said tightly. He typically used her name when they were in private. She felt a twang of guilt. She did care for Jonathan. He was a wise advisor and had been a friend. That was all he was. Friend and advisor, though she knew he wanted more.

"I'd been looking for you," Jonathan said. "I had hoped to warn you before . . ." He cast a fleeting glance at the women lined up around the hall. They watched, silent and unblinking.

"Warn me about what?"

Jonathan licked his lips. "The pack, Nichel. They—"

"It is time for you to decide, war chief," Grivah of the Eagle said.

Anger burned away her growing unease. Good. She liked the anger. Anger fused to her spine like steel. "I was not aware you were the one in charge of deciding when the time had come for your war chief to make a decision," Nichel said, fixing Grivah with a withering scowl.

Grivah of the Eagle only stared. They all did, even Ulestren, their expressions blank. A new fear struck her. *They know I can detect their emotions. Does my pack not trust me? Does Ulestren not trust me?*

"What is it you think I must decide?" she said, doing her best to sound annoyed.

"Aidan Gairden's fate," Ulestren said.

"He should have been kissed by the Mother the moment he showed his face in your realm," said Karta of the Spirits, her bald head painted in colors that shimmered when they caught light.

"Yet he continues to breathe our air and drink our water," said Xanada of the Tiger.

"We do not understand why," Grivah said.

"You must decide his fate. Now," Ulestren finished.

Nichel's throat had dried up. She shot a helpless look at Jonathan. He nodded and stepped forward. Relief swept through her. When he spoke, his voice was as stern as she had ever heard it. "Your war chief is not a woman to be pressured or goaded. I will point out to you that she is following in her father's footsteps, pursuing justice rather than—"

"Be silent, advisor," Ulestren said.

Jonathan's mouth hung open. Nichel's heart beat faster.

Ulestren stepped forward. "War chief. You are my sister and my friend." Ulestren stumbled over the words, no doubt embarrassed to express emotion before her peers. "But you have shamed your station in this matter, and your father's memory. The clans march to war. Many will not return. Yet you remain behind, hiding."

Nichel reeled as if her sister had slapped her. "How dare you? I am not hiding. You know that."

Ulestren did not back down. "We do not know what Aidan Gairden said to you when we left you alone last night, nor earlier when you visited him in the Crevasse."

Jonathan spun, shock and hurt twisting his face. "You saw him alone?"

Nichel went on the defensive. "I do not owe you an explanation."

"You are wrong," Ulestren said. "You have suffered great losses. And none of us understands entirely the matter of the creature inside you."

The seal trembled. Nichel's cheeks grew hot.

"So much has happened to you in such a short span of time," Ulestren went on. "But you are still the war chief. You challenged Guyde of the Bear, and you were victorious. However, we"—she gestured at the women fanned out around the room—"wonder if the speakers made a mistake. Your judgment is clouded. Aidan Gairden breached our borders. The assassin was his subject. Through him, Aidan made an attempt on your life. Yet he still lives." Ulestren's gaze settled on Jonathan. "Even you must believe this, Advisor."

Nichel glanced at Jonathan. His expression was pained. "Not you, too," she said softly.

"I gave you the benefit of the doubt," he said, voice tight. "You asked to speak with him alone after he arrived. I admit, the idea made me nervous. Yet he made no attempts to hide his approach, even though he could have kindled the Mother's light to attack directly or penetrate our walls unnoticed. He allowed me to Tie him. So, we adhered to your wishes. You may be the war chief,

Nichel, but if Aidan had showed even the smallest sign of hostility, I . . ." He stood straighter. "I would have opposed you. I won't apologize for that."

Jonathan spread his hands. "But the assassin. The assassin, Nichel! You are an intelligent woman. I have always believed it so, and yet you refuse to see the evidence of—"

Nichel looked at him sharply. "The assassin's body!"

Jonathan blinked. "What of it?"

"It's a vagrant. Or it might be. We're not sure."

"We, war chief? A vagrant? I'm afraid I don't follow."

Nichel spoke slowly and calmly. "Aidan told me that the Eternal Flame has the power to raise the dead and let them walk among us wearing the faces of friends and kin. He said that the assassin was one such abomination. Vagrants bleed the color of moss. I stabbed the assassin with Silk, but it's lost, and . . ." She shook her head. A dull, throbbing pain had settled in her skull. *Those dust-blasted fragrances.* It was difficult to concentrate. "The body, Jonathan. Has it been destroyed? If not, we must examine it. It could prove Aidan's innocence."

For a long time, no one spoke.

"The body has been disposed of, war chief," he said quietly.

"Disposed of?" she repeated. The hope that had bloomed in her chest wilted to nothing.

He nodded. "We would not dishonor you or your ancestors by allowing such filth to stain the halls of Janleah Keep."

"Stain," she mumbled through numb lips. She looked toward where the body had fallen after the man—*Was it a man?*—had attacked her.

"I cleaned up the blood myself," he said. He paused. "It was red."

Embarrassment colored Nichel's cheeks. She fought the impulse to look down at the floor. Her pack stared back, showing no reaction to her emotion.

Jonathan stepped forward and took her hands. "You inherited your father's gifts of reason and mercy. I commend that. But what you are saying would exceed even the limits of Romen of the Wolf's reputation for caution and compassion. Bodies risen from the grave . . ." He shook his head. "Please, Nichel. You must realize how this must sound."

Nichel teared up yet again, and not from the cloying odors this time.

"Please," Jonathan began. "We only—"

"You must do what needs to be done, war chief," Ulestren broke in. "If you do not, we will act on your behalf. Decide now."

AIDAN PLASTERED HIMSELF against a rough stone wall as Nichel's pack filed into the council room and spread out along the walls. Jonathan, the advisor, trailed a few steps behind them, wearing a troubled expression. Seeping to the floor, Aidan flowed forward.

Lamps ringed the monuments of the twelve war chiefs, each effigy at least twice as tall as Romen of the Wolf had been in life, and painted in shades of purple. Their white flames flashed and flickered. Aidan averted his gaze and took in the scene. Nichel stood at the center of the room, in the epicenter of the monuments. Jonathan and Ulestren extracted themselves from the others and went to her. The advisor gestured as he spoke. Ulestren stood stiffly. Their mouths moved, but their words came out garbled. As if they spoke in an unfamiliar tongue.

— *Have you found her?* Gabriel asked.

Yes.

— *Step into her shadow.*

Aidan studied the floor. Shadows extended from Nichel, her pack, Jonathan. Hers crisscrossed with Jonathan's. Aidan bled across the floor and flowed into Nichel's shadow. At the first touch, his specter snapped forward, stretching to her contours. When she moved, he moved with her, like clothing fitted to her body. Her shadow flared again, brightening, and now Aidan did feel something. It was an emotion, singular and strong. Hope.

— *She feels—* Aidan began.

— *We know,* Gabriel said. *We can sense how she feels through you. Now, breathe in. Long and deep, just like before. Do not exhale until I give the word.*

Aidan obeyed. He was deliriously happy, and he wanted that feeling to last forever. Breathing would help, so he did. Optimism swelled as his lungs filled, the way his heart swelled when he thought about Christine. He grinned, still holding the breath that was not a breath.

— *Exhale,* Gabriel said.

The breath that was not a breath drained out of him. A nimbus spread through shadow he shared with Nichel. It glowed a faint gold, like rays of Dawnrise through a leafy canopy.

— *Extraordinary,* Anastasia said.

Gabriel paid her no heed. — *Again. Send her joyful thoughts.*

He filled his mind with memories of simpler times. Before he could breathe in, Nichel's shadow darkened. Aidan's mood plummeted. Snarling, he looked up. Nichel faced Jonathan and her pack and was gesturing wildly. An image of him slumped against the wall down in the Crevasse entered her thoughts. *She's trying to confirm my claims,* he realized. He seized on that insight and inhaled, thinking thoughts of gratitude and trust, then expelled his breath in a whoosh. The nimbus rematerialized. It flared brightly, almost blindingly.

— *Caution,* Gabriel advised. *Coercion calls for a delicate touch.*

Aidan thought of the occasions he and Nichel had chased one another through Janleah Keep, riding horses through Calewind's streets and the snowy countryside beyond. He breathed in deeply and exhaled slowly. Patiently. Her shadow softened, as faint as pre-Dawn sky. A weak color, but preferable to a shade of black darker than a starless sky at midnight. Nichel did not feel happy and trusting, but neither was she angry and guarded.

— *You are a natural,* Gabriel said. His tone was even, almost respectful. *The Lord heeds your call effortlessly. You should be proud.*

At that, Aidan sensed uneasiness from Anastasia and Charles.

— *Ignore them,* Gabriel said, his voice low and cold. *Continue with your work. The frequency of Nichel's vacillations indicate you still have much convincing to do.*

Aidan obeyed. Each exhalation lightened Nichel's aura.

— *There it is again,* Gabriel said under his breath.

What? Aidan asked.

— *The darkness within her. Even as you sway her in one way, the darkness grows. Hurry, Aidan. A deeper conflict than your innocence or guilt wars within her, and you do not want to be close should she come out on the losing side.*

Abruptly Nichel turned from Jonathan and her pack. Something deep inside her trembled. Conflicting emotions rose up like a sudden blizzard.

Hope and despair.

Love and hatred.

Tranquility and anger.

The strongest of them—faith and love one moment, rage and fear the next—buffeted him from either side. It was chaos, a typhoon of raw passion that threatened to crush him. He gripped hands he could not feel together, as if holding on to a tree limb while a river rushed over him, desperately trying to tear him free and sweep him away.

A voice cut through the maelstrom. — *Concentrate,* Gabriel said.

It took Aidan what felt like hours to gather the strength to speak. *How?* The thought came at the height of another blast of rage and fear, turning his single word into a cross between a shriek and a bellow.

— *Watch her aura. Wait for an opportunity.*

— *No!* Anastasia's voice cut through him. *Look at what is happening to her, Aidan. This is not right. This is not your choice.*

— *Do not interfere, Mother*, Gabriel said.

— *Aidan, please,* the matriarch pleaded. *You are going to break the girl's mind. If she falls to madness, you will fall with her.*

Gabriel laughed. — *Typical of the Lady's disciples. You care nothing for outsiders, only your own.*

Aidan tightened his hold on Nichel's shadow. Her essence brightened and faded, brightened and faded. His emotions rose and fell with hers. He could feel his ethereal grip slipping. They teetered on a precipice.

— *Strike, boy,* Gabriel said.

— *Flee,* Charles said. *While there is still time!*

He rode the swell of her emotions for a moment longer. Then he acted. There was a flash, and then something shoved him. He was expelled from Nichel's shadow. The council room tumbled and twisted. When it stopped, Aidan was staring up at the ceiling. He lay on the floor, spread out like a rug. He looked down and saw that his ethereal form was translucent. He felt vague and indistinct.

I don't feel well, he said to no Gairden in particular, and was surprised at the steadiness of his voice. Mercifully devoid of feeling once again.

— Your body weakens, Gabriel said. He sounded exhausted. *Return to it at once.*

Aidan slipped in and out of dark patches until he poured out of the council chamber into a darkened corridor. For once, the voices in his head were silent.

NICHEL STIFFENED. BLINKING, she turned around. All save Jonathan watched her blankly. Her advisor's face was pale.

"Nichel?" Jonathan took a step toward her, extending a hand.

She waved him away, took two more breaths. "I know what needs to be done."

Chapter 35:
Inspection

FETER PLANTED HIS hands on his hips. "Each and every snake here would kill—really, truly kill—to slither out of this place forever. But you? You can't stay away."

Christine stood in the doorway of his domicile. His stormrobe hung from his thin frame like a curtain draped over a stick. "Where are you assigned?" she asked.

"Street sweeper and lighter in the north quarter." He snorted. "Honestly, university students are better suited to that work. They could light all of Sharem with a snap of their fingers. So could you. You should go in my stead."

"No, thank you," she said, stepping inside and closing the door behind her. "Very tempting, though."

Feter rolled his eyes then patted his robe. A few more pats and his face grew panicked. He got down on all fours and pushed aside his thin blankets and ration containers until he breathed a sigh of relief and stood up holding a folded sheet of parchment. Christine knew what it was and what was written on it without having to look. A day pass listed a Sallnerian's name, domicile, and assignment for the week. After the start of the next week, the thrall would be issued a new pass with new assignment details. The old pass would be burned.

"What's wrong?" Feter asked.

"Nothing's wrong."

He gave her a level stare. "I can tell. Always could. Let me guess. The audience with your father."

Christine shrugged. Feter made a sound of sympathy. "Listen, I can't let you stay here. You know that. But you should go find Lam. He's not working today."

"Why not? Did he get in trouble again?"

"No, nothing like that. Last I saw, he was sleeping in his domicile."

"Sleeping? At this hour?"

"The snowmen realize even snakes need to rest sometime." He threw an arm around her shoulder and steered her toward the door and outside.

"What's your hurry?" she asked.

"Running behind," he said.

Before he closed the door, Christine looked back and noticed an uneven plank in the center of his floor. It was slight, and she wouldn't have noticed except for an empty ration container that sat atop it, perched above the rest of the detritus littering his blankets. Then the door closed.

"Walk with me to the checkpoint?" he asked.

She shook her head, the odd protuberance already forgotten. "I'm going to wake up Lam."

"Good idea. You two should talk. He loves you, Chris. He's just feeling . . ." He shrugged one shoulder.

"Trapped? Caged?"

"The very words he used last night," Feter mumbled. "Not that I blame him. Not that any stormrobe blames him." He gave her a lopsided smile. "Must be nice to come and go as you please."

Christine swallowed a retort. Feter meant well, but he and Lam had always teased her about her mixed bloodline in a joking way that bordered on hostile. Christine and Garrett had been born on the Bridge, but they were not dependent on it. Not like the stormrobes, who worked for meagre earnings until the temple decided they had paid off their ancestors' debt and were free to look for gainful employment out in realms that despised them on principle, or until they dropped dead of old age, or exhaustion, or starvation, or some combination of the three.

Feter gave her an apologetic look. "Sorry, Chris. Didn't mean anything by it."

"It's fine. You'd better get going."

"Sure you're all right?"

Christine smiled. "Just restless." Eyeing her for a long moment, Feter nodded and set off down the lane. She watched him pick his way down the muddy street, his feet caked with muck. When he disappeared around a corner, she walked in the opposite direction. A few stormrobes huddled around a wet, unlit fire pit in the center of the lane. Others shied away from her as she passed, eyes fixed on the ground and arms at their sides, their empty hands in plain view. Christine tightened her mouth. It was her clothes, she knew. *They see my boots and think I'm some noble come to tour the Bridge.*

Rounding a corner, she swept by the pair of Wardsmen assigned to guard the mouth of the road. She could feel their eyes on her as she moved. *I have more right to be here than they do.*

Christine passed four more lanes of domiciles guarded by pairs of Wardsmen, then turned down another muddy road and walked until she faced Domicile 137. Her breathing quickened. She looked around. Sallnerians walked slowly, heads down and shying away from Wardsmen as they moved about. She took a deep breath and lifted numb fingers to the door. They tightened around the handle. She counted to three, then wrenched it open.

A man sat cross-legged on the floor. His head shot up. He yelped and scrambled to his feet. The heavy book he'd been holding thumped to the floor. Christine jumped and clutched a hand to her chest. Before her fingers came into contact with skin, she had kindled a sliver of the Lady's light, the words to set him ablaze perched on the tip of her tongue.

"Chris?" the man said.

She expelled the light and sagged against the doorframe. "Lam." She made no effort to disguise her irritation. "What in the name of Dawn are you doing in my home?"

Lam stooped over and plucked his book from the floor. Brushing dirt from the cover, he tucked it under an arm. "I come here to read sometimes, and to . . ."

"To what?"

Lam flushed. "To watch over your domicile."

Christine felt tears well. She brushed them away. When her vision cleared, Lam looked flustered. "Are you crying? Was it something I said? I didn't mean—"

"You did nothing wrong." *Damn you, Aidan Gairden.* "You're sweet, that's all."

Lam scratched his head. "It's nothing, really. Your father doesn't come by much, and you and Garrett are . . . gone. So, I thought, you know, I'd just dust every now and then, keep the place presentable."

"That's very kind of you. Thank you, Lam. Truly."

He cleared his throat. "I'm sorry for how I've treated you since you came back, Chris. Feter pointed out last night that, well, it makes sense, you being here."

Christine's face crinkled in confusion. Lam must have mistaken it for an indication of another teary outburst. "We don't have to talk about it," he said quickly.

"What are you reading?" she asked.

A clang of bells sounded from the front of the Territory Bridge. Christine glanced at Lam, who wore a deep frown. "Dinner already?" he mumbled. "It can't be." He shook himself roughly. "Go on ahead. I'll be right behind you."

Without thinking, she spun and hurried out of the domicile. She'd fallen into step with a tide of stormrobes before remembering that she was no longer obligated to obey calls for rations or head counts. A chill wind from behind sent shivers crawling up her spin. She glanced around and noticed a number of other heads swiveling. *A last gasp from winter?* she wondered.

The crowd pushed her forward. She slowed, looking for Lam. Suddenly, he jogged up beside her and took her arm. "Come on," he said, urging her forward.

Christine thought about reminding him that she could come and go as she pleased, then decided against it. The peace between them was weak, a bridge made of sticks instead of marble. She needed a friend. Aidan had grown up surrounded by family, attendants, and friends. Christine had had Garrett, Feter, and Lam. Garrett was lost to her. Lam and Feter were here. She could talk to them, and they would listen, and care.

Her eyes burned again. *Damn you, Aidan Gairden.*

Men, women, and children flowed out of domiciles and down lanes, the hems of their grey robes wet with mud. They spilled into a confluence in the wide, open area between the last checkpoint of the Bridge and the rows of domiciles. A line of Wardsmen—Christine did a quick count and arrived at twenty—

formed a wall along the path leading to the checkpoint. The wall parted to admit four dozen stormrobes. Feter walked among them, looking puzzled. Lam waved, and Feter nodded recognition.

"What are you doing here?" Christine asked as Feter hurried over.

Feter and Lam shared a hug and then pulled apart quickly, hands at their sides. "We were working, and the masters told us we were to report to the Bridge for some announcement," Feter said.

Lam glanced at Christine. "Do you know anything about this?"

She shook her head. The wall of Wardsmen parted again, and Christine ground her teeth. Terrence stepped through, flanked by two men wearing the emerald-colored robes of Torel's Dawn and a dozen disciples in red robes. Terrence raised his hands, letting his voluminous gold sleeves fall and bunch up around his elbows. The stormrobes were already quiet, but Terrence grinned as if they had only fallen silent at his gesture.

"You are here," he said, "to be notified of changes being made to your daily routines. Due to recent events, the Ward's presence on the Bridge has been increased. Six Wardsmen will patrol each lane at all hours of the day."

Christine and Lam shared a look. "You don't think," he began. "Last night . . . ?"

"Possibly. My father told me Terrence has been pushing to tighten patrols on the Bridge."

"Why?" Feter whispered.

"Because we're snakes and they're better than us," Lam said darkly.

"By that rule, everyone is better than us," Feter said.

"I'll talk to my father," Christine said. "He can overturn . . ." A thought occurred to her, and her blood ran cold.

"I'm sure your father had a hand in it," Lam muttered.

Feter shot him a disapproving look. "That's not fair, Lam."

Lam scrubbed a hand over his face. "I'm sorry, Chris. Your father does right by us as best he can. Christine?"

A chill swept through her. "He's powerless."

"Your father?" Feter said. "Of course, he isn't. He's the Second."

"Tyrnen is back."

Lam and Feter exchanged blank stares. Christine returned her attention to Terrence, who was still droning on.

". . . subject to spontaneous inspections." Angry mutters rose up from the stormrobes. Terrence made soothing motions. "This is not my doing," he said brightly. "Your behavior brought about these circumstances. Now, then. Materials found in your domicile that were not assigned to you will be confiscated, and the punishment for theft will be based on the value of the items found in your possession, with a minimum one month's penitence enforced in all cases." His smile widened. "These guidelines will be made effective immediately. The first inspection will be held today. Right now."

Nervous mutters rippled through the stormrobes. "Right now?" Feter whispered. "Can he do that?"

"Just watch him," Christine said darkly.

Terrence's arms dropped, and six snowmen broke away. Six disciples followed, one to a Wardsman. The group moved around the assembled stormrobes and made their way down the lanes, throwing open domiciles and stepping inside. Cries of anger and shock rang out from the assemblage. A few stormrobes made movements toward their domiciles.

"Remain where you are," Terrence said, sounding bored, "or you will be arrested and held for obstruction. This is your only warning."

Stormrobes froze in place, eyes flitting between Terrence and the sounds of Wardsmen tossing domiciles. A sheet was expelled from one doorway like a wad of phlegm. It settled in the churned mud. Sniffles and low sobs rose up.

"The Lady bestows her warmth upon those who have nothing to hide," Terrence said, hands clasped behind his back as he gazed over the assemblage like a stern father.

Feter growled. "Unconscionable. They have no right to . . . What is it, Lam? You look as if you're going to be sick."

Lam's face was bloodless. "The hatch, Fet. It's exposed."

Feter's jaw went rigid. "How? Why?"

"I, I left in a hurry," Lam said haltingly. "I was behind schedule, as usual, and I went to return one of the books and I just . . . I got careless."

Feter swore. Christine glanced from one to the other. "What are you two talking about?" She spoke in a low voice even though the muttering from the stormrobes was loud enough to mask conversation.

Feter ran a hand over his head. "Terrence said those with nothing to hide have nothing to fear. We have much to fear, Christine."

Lam swallowed. "There are . . . certain texts, and we have them, and we shouldn't. They're—"

Christine shushed him, thinking hard. "This hatch is in your domicile, Feter?"

He nodded.

"An unevenness in the center of the floor?" she said.

Feter hesitated, then nodded again.

Christine glanced toward the back of the assemblage, closest to the rows of domiciles. Her green cloak stood out amid the mass of stormrobes like a patch of earth between mounds of dirty snow. Although she could excuse herself anytime she wanted, disrupting an official temple action would draw unwanted attention to her friends, and would doubtlessly reflect on her trial. She stood on tiptoes, scanning the lines of domiciles. Wardsmen and disciples marched from hut to hut. They moved rapidly, ducking into one, throwing around blankets and spare robes and odds and ends, then hurrying out. *A benefit of stormrobes not owning much to search,* she thought.

Her stomach clenched. Feter's domicile was in the center of the sixth row and would be reached soon unless she acted. Christine let out a breath. She grabbed Lam and Feter by a shoulder. "I'm going to distract Terrence. Feter, how quickly can you reach your domicile without being seen?"

"A minute, maybe less," he replied.

She was grateful for his quick obeisance, but not surprised. Growing up, she had been the one responsible for concocting schemes. Feter had gone along with any suggestion she proposed, knowing they ended in harmless fun that cut through the tedium and despair of life on the Territory Bridge. Lam, meanwhile, had a tendency to nag her with questions. True to form, Lam opened his mouth.

"I'll explain later, Lam," she said. "Fet, get ready. Lam, stay here and do your best to look innocent. Yes, that's close enough. I'll explain the concept to you later."

Without another word, Christine strode to the front of the

pack. Heads turned to follow her as she moved. Terrence's brows lifted when she stepped out to face him. "Christine," he said.

"You don't seem surprised to find me here."

"Every nesting creature returns to its nest eventually."

"Snakes do not build nests, Terrence," she said calmly. "If you took as much time to open books as you take to open needless inquiries, you would know that."

"You will address me respectfully," he snapped. Behind him, the remaining disciples shifted from foot to foot. The snowmen stared straight ahead without blinking.

"Respect must be earned," she replied.

He narrowed his eyes. "You are disrupting Temple business, and you are not a Cinder, so you have no authority here. Stand aside, or—"

"I'm not disrupting anything. We're talking. But while we're on the subject, I do have a question about today's procedure."

"You have no right to question me."

"I'll ponder aloud, then. I cannot help but wonder—to no one in particular—if Disciple Terrence was granted permission by my father, the Second Disciple, to perform this inspection, given that the Eternal Flame is a participant in a trial and thus has no authority to execute decisions or arbitrate other matters."

While she spoke, the Sallnerians glanced nervously between Christine and Terrence. Then, one by one, heads shook. Murmurs of refusal grew more audible. Wardsmen and disciples had paused their searching to face the crowd, clearly wondering what was going on. As she watched, Feter slipped out from a narrow alleyway and crept across the sixth and final lane of mud and grime.

Terrence stood frozen. "Inspections are routine."

"This one isn't," Christine said. "You said so yourself: spontaneous inspections. You are an erudite man, Terrence. I'm sure I don't have to tell you what spontaneous means."

Terrence quivered with rage. "I am—"

"Perhaps I should go and ask my father. Just to be sure."

Terrence snarled. "I have the authority to . . . oh, what is it?" he roared at a disciple who had approached from behind and tapped him on the shoulder. The younger man flinched and leaned forward to whisper in his ear. Terrence's complexion darkened by the word.

Christine glanced in the direction of Feter's domicile. The door opened a hair before closing again. Nearby, a Wardsman turned toward it. Panic flared.

Terrence spun on her. "Very well," he thundered. Christine's skin grew warm as he kindled. She was a split second away from kindling to countermand an attack when he spoke. "Fall back into line. We're leaving," he bellowed in an amplified voice. With that he strode away, back down the path to the checkpoint. Pairs of white- and red-clad figures hurried forward from the lanes of domiciles. The Wardsman near Feter's hut glared at it for a moment longer, then huffed away. Packs of Sallnerians broke apart to let them through, their faces alight with victory.

When the last Wardsman and disciple had disappeared, cheers rose up from the Sallnerians. They surrounded Christine, shaking hands and patting her shoulders. She beamed stupidly, swelling with pride and humility. Over the commotion, three of the Wardsmen assigned to guard lanes of domiciles hurried over and gesticulated wildly.

Suddenly, Lam was beside her, pulling on her arm. "Let her through, let her through," he shouted. The crowd split, and Christine let Lam guide her to Feter's domicile. For a time, the sounds of their feet—his bare, hers sheltered in knee-high boots—squelching through mud filled the silence. Then he took her hand and squeezed it.

"Thank you."

Christine gaped at him. "What? No questions? No demands for an explanation?"

Lam shrugged. "You came through. You always do."

Christine clung to Lam's arm and hugged her to him. He kissed her hair. Idly, she wondered if they might have become more than friends, in another life. In this life, his heart belonged to another, and so did hers, but they shared a friendship unbroken by time and circumstance, and that was enough.

Lam glanced around and knocked gently on Feter's door. Inside, something heavy clattered to the floor. Looking concerned, Lam flung open the door. Feter wore a sheepish expression, clutching his left hand. Blood dribbled between his fingers, dripping onto stained, uneven floorboards. A short sword lay at his feet.

Christine pulled the door closed behind Lam as he rushed to

take Feter's hands. "You're hurt," he said.

"It's nothing," Feter said, giving Lam a tight smile.

"What in Kahltan's name did you do?" Lam asked.

Feter sighed. "The Wardsman in our lane turned his back. I thought I'd lift his sword. Just in case, you know, I got caught."

Lam made a sound of disbelief. "So, you thought stealing from a snowman would be better than only sneaking around?"

"I wasn't about to let any snowman or bloodrobe catch me," Feter said, mouth tight. "Not without a fight."

"Instead, you ended up losing a fight to an inanimate object," Lam snapped.

"I cut myself running. It's sharper than it looks."

Sighing, Lam smoothed back his hair. "Let's get you fixed up."

Christine stepped closer and got a look at Feter's hand. "That looks bad. Come outside and I'll heal you."

Feter shook his head. "No. None of *Her* light. Not ever again."

She recoiled at the scorn in her friend's voice. "But it could get infected."

"We don't need magic for this," Lam said. "I'll show you." He pulled Feter gently down to the floor. He reached for the end of the board jutting up from the floor.

"That's where I tripped," Christine said.

Lam hesitated. Feter gripped his collar. "We can trust her."

Lam gave Christine an appraising stare. Time seemed to stand still. "All right," he said at last. He pointed to the door. "Stand there. Don't let anyone in. Not anyone, Chris. Not even the Lady herself."

Feter snorted. "Not much chance of that."

Heart beating wildly, Christine moved in front of the door. With his free hand, Lam pulled on the long, rectangular floorboard. It swung back like the entrance to a bulkhead, revealing a long opening. Tight-lipped, Lam picked up the sword and tucked it out of sight. Then he rummaged around. Christine fought the urge to peer into the opening.

Lam straightened and withdrew two dusty bottles filled with a clear liquid. *Water?* Christine wondered. He reached in again and produced a cloth. It was a pristine shade of white. That piqued her curiosity more than the elixirs. A clean cloth on the Territory Bridge was as miraculous a discovery as . . . *Well, as a Sallnerian wedding the Crown of the North.*

Lam unscrewed the top of one bottle, pressed the cloth against its mouth, and upturned it. Turning it right-side up, Lam screwed the bottle's top back on and replaced it in the opening. He turned to face Feter, looking solemn. "It will sting," he said. "Be prepared. This would not be a good time to draw attention to ourselves."

Feter's hands shook. "Lam's tried it," he said to Christine, smiling shakily. "You should have heard him howl. Shriller than a Torelian grandmother who missed morning canticles." He gave a nervous laugh.

Christine swallowed, or tried to. Her throat was drier than the Plains of Dust. Lam pressed the cloth to Feter's bloody hand. Feter clamped his mouth shut. Breath hissed between clenched teeth. His eyes bulged.

"You're hurting him!" she said.

"No," Lam said calmly. "I'm healing him."

As she watched, Feter's breathing slowed, evening out. Easing Feter to the floor and tucking one of his thin pillows beneath his head, Lam reached into the hidden compartment again. This time he withdrew a tome bursting with yellowed pages.

"Sit down, Christine," Lam continued. "It's time we had a talk."

Chapter 36:
Agreements

AIDAN RACED THROUGH passageways. Archways and sconces passed in a blur of torchlight, and walls glowed shades of purple as he delved into lower levels of Janleah's Keep. Nearing the Crevasse, his thinking grew as dim and scattered as sources of light in the halls. He felt stretched in a way he had not when slipping through cracks in doorways and stretching along tendrils of shadow.

The entrance to the Crevasse resembled a toothless maw. Aidan flew down its throat and past rows of cages. His body came into view, slumped in the corner of the cage farthest from the entrance. His eyes were glassy, jaw slack, chest rising and falling intermittently. Aidan slowed and crawled back into his flesh. The world went from purple and white to utterly dark. A thousand icy needles pierced him from head to toe. Convulsing, he broke into a fit of shivering. His teeth chattered like dice in a cup. His boots drummed against the pockmarked stone floor. Reflexively he hugged himself, tucking cold fingers into his armpits. *What's happening to me?*

— *Like kindling, darkening saps a Touched's strength,* Gabriel said. *The difference is that darkening weakens at a trickle. When we kindle, we pull in the light we need and then release it all at once. To hold light for too long is to hold fire.*

Conversely, shadecraft unfolds over a period of time, bleeding you of the shade you imbibed.

— *Lovely,* Charles snapped. *What is my grandson supposed to do now?*

— *The same thing any Touched must do when our bodies and minds grow weary. Rest,* Gabriel said. *Kindle too much light, and a Touched comes down with the fever. Darken for too long, and sickness sets in. Chills, coughs, sniffles, a scratchy throat. What ancient Sallnerian scholars referred to as a cold.* He paused, then spoke in a softer tone. *Though you probably don't want to hear any more about that.* In a normal tone, he said, *Close your eyes and rest while you can, Aidan.*

— *He cannot rest, Gabriel,* Anastasia broke in. *We all felt Nichel's sentiment. She's coming for him.*

Memory of his time as a specter, of what he had done, cut through his chills. Aidan hugged his knees to his chest. He shook with disgust as much as cold.

— *What you did was wrong,* Anastasia said tightly.

Aidan turned and emptied his stomach. Mouth agape, he closed his eyes and let his head rest against the stone. It felt cool against his feverish skin. Almost comforting. He deserved no comfort. Memories of Nichel's clashing emotions battered at him. Tears ran down his cheeks.

— *We agreed that our sword-bearer had little other choice, my wife,* Ambrose rumbled. *We concurred. We must help him carry the burden of his decision.*

— *That is as may be,* she said. *But he deserves to sick up.* Her presence vanished.

No one spoke for a time. Eyes squeezed shut, Aidan concentrated on his breathing. It was the only sound in the Crevasse.

— *It is not easy to transition back to the flesh,* Gabriel said. *The detachment inherent in assuming spectral form was meticulously calculated. A careful equation of darkness taken in through inhalation balanced by the part of the brain responsible for . . . Well, never mind. You would not comprehend the calculations involved. Suffice it to say that detachment was made inseparable from spectral form in order to protect the shade from ethical quandaries that tend to arise when difficult decisions must be carried out.*

Anastasia came roaring back. — *You speak so calmly of violating minds and hearts. Of usurping wills . . . of violating . . . Did you shadewalk through life, Gabriel, to so blatantly lack compassion and decency for the struggles of your fellow humans?*

— *I learned from the best*, Gabriel said.

Gasps echoed throughout Aidan's mind. — *How dare you speak to your mother that way?* Ambrose thundered.

— *So sorry, Father. I forgot that you and Mother grow squeamish when those around you speak hard truths. A pity I am no longer flesh and blood, or you could exile me to a rotting jungle for eight hundred years as punishment for my impudence.*

When Anastasia spoke again, her voice was thick with tears. — *Where did we fail you, Gabriel? You were such a bright, precocious boy. We did not raise you this way. Dark magic is used to—*

— *To what?* the scholar said. His voice shook with emotion. *To raise the dead? To mold flesh and bone like dough? Yes, and so much more. Suncraft can be just as reprehensible. Aidan pointed this out, but still you refuse to see. To think. You did not raise me to think at all. You were content to banish your people—yes, Mother, they are your people—rather than attempt to understand what had made them turn away from your Lady. I never set out to violate or manipulate anyone, only to learn. To understand. No understanding was forthcoming from Torelian scholars. Even as Crown I was expected to drape myself in decorum and religion and laws that encouraged ignorance. So, I found my own way. I studied math and science. Who do you think taught the Ward how to calculate trajectories when the time came to hurl stones from trebuchets? Not your Lady of Dawn. And when difficult decisions arose, I saw to it that I had the means to make them without allowing myself to stumble over stones like ethics. And despite what you seem to want to believe, Mother and Father, I did stumble. At first. Then I did what needed to be done. As Aidan did. As you did. We are no different, save that I had the courage to look myself in the mirror every night before I laid that Dawn-cursed crown aside and tried to sleep.*

Dead silence, broken only by Aidan's shivering. His ears rang with Gabriel's words, but his eyes were so heavy. Raising his head felt like lifting a mountain.

Abruptly part of what Gabriel had said took on new meaning. He gave the revelation only a moment's thought, then smothered it with others: of Christine, of boyhood antics with Daniel, of his mother and father and simpler times gone forever.

— *So,* the scholar said in a voice not quite a whisper. *You figured it out.*

Aidan darkened and wrapped a skein over his mind. His shivering worsened slightly, but he no longer cared. All conversation ceased. He let his head fall back against the stone wall. His eyes slid closed. Nichel's face swam into view. With it came memory of the malice and hurt that had radiated from her in waves. He forced his eyes open. Nichel would come for him. Best to stay alert.

Numbness spread through his limbs. He no longer shivered. Without his ragged breaths, the silence of the Crevasse was deafening. Blackness closed in. His chest grew tight, as if the air squeezed like a vice. He considered burning away the skein, then remembered doing so required kindling. Kindling called for light. He was in the dark belly of the west, and he was alone. Aidan tried to sleep, but doubted if he could. Over time, his breathing evened out.

A loud click from down the corridor and his eyes flew open like uncoiled springs. A door creaked, and a faint ball of wavering light floated into sight. Footsteps, and Cinder Jonathan Hillstreem appeared holding a lantern aloft.

Without thinking, Aidan raised a hand toward the lambent flame. He craved its heat. Jonathan frowned and held the lantern away. "You could not even if you tried."

Aidan blinked, confused. Then he remembered. *I'm supposed to be Tied.* His arm shook from the effort of holding it aloft. He gritted his teeth. This was foolishness. He was not Tied, and Jonathan's flame gave off more than enough for him to work with. He could overpower the Cinder, bend and break the bars of his cage as easily as dry wood, and run. Away from Nichel, away from what he had done to her. Back to Christine.

Another surge of disgust rippled through his stomach. *What will she think of me now?*

Softer footsteps stopped behind Jonathan. Squinting, Aidan

could just make out glittering eyes at Jonathan's shoulder. Nichel.

He let his hand sink to his lap.

Nichel took a single step forward. Jonathan's lanternlight illuminated the left half of her body in pale light. The other remained lost in shadow. Her face was inscrutable. "I have made my decision," she said. "Will you submit to the Mother's judgment?"

"Yes," Aidan croaked, his throat as dry as the Plains.

Nichel sniffed once, as if testing the air. Then she gave Aidan a long, hard look. "He speaks the truth."

The handsome young Cinder came forward, jangling keys with his free hand. There was a click, and the door to Aidan's cell whined as it opened.

Gripping two bars, Aidan hauled himself upright. "Thank you," he said to Nichel.

Her brow rose. Jonathan grunted. "Compliance will gain you some measure of honor when you stand in the Mother's gaze, Aidan Gairden," he said.

The meaning of his words turned Aidan's tongue to dust. "You're going to kill me, aren't you?" he asked Nichel.

She cocked her head. "I am not going to execute you, Aidan Gairden."

Jonathan spun on her. "War Chief, you were quite clear. You said—"

"I said I understood what must be done. I did not say that meant bringing him before the Mother's Eye." She regarded Aidan. "My father would give him a chance to prove his innocence. Romen of the Wolf was a wise leader. You said so yourself, Jonathan. I will follow in his footsteps, though I fear my feet are too small to fill them."

Aidan's knees went weak. Coercion had worked. A bitter mixture of disgust at what he had done to her, and relief at being allowed to continue drawing breath rushed through him. "Thank you."

She continued. "You claim that the Torelian assassin is a walking corpse."

"I do."

"Cinder Hillstreem, you said you disposed of the body," she said.

"That is correct."

Nichel sniffed. "I smell half-truths, Jonathan."

Jonathan shifted his weight. "Dispose . . . a very strong word . . . a lapse on my part."

"Explain."

Jonathan licked his lips. "I intended to have your pack burn the assassin's body this morning, but we were concerned about you. I told them it would keep until tomorrow, and had it placed in *Daram Ogahra*."

Nichel went rigid. "You would defile that sacred place with an assassin's corpse?"

"It was only temporary, Nichel. I—"

"You will address me as war chief."

Jonathan stiffened. "I apologize. War chief."

"Accepted." Nichel turned to Aidan. "We will put your claim to the test. You will accompany me into *Daram Ogahra*."

"As will I," Jonathan interrupted. Nichel growled low in her throat. Jonathan's next words came out in a rush. "I insist on accompanying you, war chief. It is my duty. I am your advisor and a Cinder. More than a match for a Gairden while he is Tied."

Nichel considered him. "Very well. You will take us to the body, and Aidan will prove that it is one of these . . . vagrants."

Aidan straightened. "Lead the way." When she did not move, he gave her an inquisitive look. His blood froze as she spoke.

"If I find that you have lied to me, I will not wait until the Mother rises to pass judgment. I will kill you myself down in the dark. No more dithering, as my mother used to say." Her lips curled into a smile that vanished as quickly as it appeared. "Do we understand each other?"

Aidan bent over, massaging his calf. He needed to think. It was difficult. Exhaustion hung over his mind like a fog. The room swayed and he caught himself before he fell over. *What should I do?*

No answer. The skein held.

"Aidan Gairden?"

He looked up. Nichel and Jonathan were studying him. Jonathan gripped his lantern as if ready to swing it. Nichel stood with one hand on her hip, seemingly aloof, though her eyes were still sharp.

"What if I'm telling the truth?" Aidan said.

Jonathan snorted. Nichel ignored him. "Then I will return your sword, and you will leave unfettered."

"And the alliance between our realms?"

There was a long pause. "Restored," Nichel answered, "for as long as it takes to defeat our common foe. After that, I cannot say. The ground drinks the blood of the fallen, Aidan Gairden, but Darinians never forget that blood was spilled."

Aidan swallowed. He knew she spoke as much of the battle at Sharem as of her parents. "Agreed."

Nichel opened her mouth to say something more. She shook her head. "Cinder Hillstreem will lead. If you betray us—"

Jonathan placed a hand on her arm. She spun on him, features twisted in outrage. Then she noticed his expression, and her features softened. "Is this really what you want, Nichel?" Jonathan asked. He was smiling sadly. "Are you choosing him?" he asked.

"This is not a matter of choice."

"It is." His voice grew insistent, and his grip seemed to tighten, because Nichel winced. "You are choosing to believe him over me. The assassin's presence—"

"The assassin lies at the root of this problem," Nichel said, gently removing his hand. "Do you not see?"

"I do see," he said, sounding sadder than before. He turned and started down the passage.

Chapter 37:
Sunlight

CHRISTINE STUMBLED OUT of Lam's domicile with his book tucked under her arm. She craned her head and stared upward. Shadows cast from her figure and the huts along the lanes stretched out like black cloth. The Lady of Dawn simmered just above the western horizon. Her light would begin to fade soon.

No, she corrected herself. *Not the Lady of Dawn.*

Licking her lips and glancing up and down the lane, Christine formed one of the many new words she had learned this afternoon in her mind's eye. Then she spoke it.

"Sun. It's called the sun."

Blinking, she raised a hand as heavy as stone to shield her eyes. Staring directly into the sun could permanently damage one's eyes. Feter had told her that before she had left his domicile with Lam's book. For millennia, the Temple of Dawn's disciples had taught that staring directly into the Lady burned one's eyes because Her glory and radiance were too awesome for mortals to behold for long. According to Lam, and according to the Sallnerian scholars who had penned the book she clasped tightly to one thigh, that was wrong. It hurt because the sun is too powerful for human eyes to take in all at once. *Something like that,* she thought.

Two stormrobes drew nearer, gaping before hurrying by.

Sallnerians were not allowed to congregate in groups larger than two. Christine ignored them. A shiver ran through her. Of excitement or fear, she could not say. Whatever it was, it went on long and hard enough to rattle her teeth. Perhaps excitement and fear. A cocktail of discovery.

One of the Wardsmen at the far end of the lane turned and glared at her. Christine fixed him in her most imperious gaze. He dropped his eyes first. Turning, she took her time walking to the opposite end of the lane and turning past the Wardsmen stationed there, heading toward Domicile 137. Toward home. As she walked, she reviewed some of the other knowledge gleaned from her reading, and from Lam and Feter. Lam had treated Feter's wound with a jar of . . . What had he called it. *Some sort of healing agent. A . . . disinfectant?* Another strange word, followed by still another. *Medicine.*

Christine clutched the book tighter. Her mind went back to what Lam had said after he had introduced her to the concept of sun and sunlight.

"I know it's a lot to take in. I don't expect you to process it all at once, but I thought—Feter, too—that you deserved to know."

Christine took her time responding. "You would receive the Lady's kiss for this, Lam. Light, even my father could. If even one of these books were found in your possession . . ."

"It's worth the risk," Feter said. "The sum total of these manuscripts, of even one of them, is worth more than our lives." They stared anxiously at her.

"I won't say anything."

Both men sat back, looking relieved. "That doesn't mean I believe . . ." She waved a hand at the cavity, stuffed with jars of medicines, old scrolls, and thick books. "Any of this."

"Understandable," Lam said. He leaned forward, shuffling through his books until he found one with a golden orb emblazoned on a blood-red cover. "Here. Take this with you. Spend the afternoon reading from it. Go to my domicile. It's cleaner than yours." He sniffed. "And if you believe, if you don't think I'm stuffing your head full of lies and nonsense—"

"Like the disciples have done for time immemorial," Feter muttered.

"—then we'll tell you more."

"There's more?" she said.

Lam beamed at her. "There's always more, Chris. That's how learning works. If you knew the things our ancestors had seen and done, the discoveries they made . . ." He shook his head and held the book out to her. "Take this. Please."

Christine studied the book. She had never thought of herself as even remotely pious, but even holding the text, just looking at it, felt blasphemous. "Where did you get—"

Lam was ready for the question. "I'll tell you everything later. But first, just read that. As much as you can. If you still want to know more, meet me at your domicile around sundown."

"My domicile?" She had squeaked the words. To be caught on the Bridge holding this book could have dire implications on her trial. Being found with it in her domicile could have dire ramifications not just for her, but for her father.

Lam's expression was knowing. "Every day is a risk for Sallnerians, Chris. All I can tell you is that this one is worth it. We're trusting you. If, after reading, you don't believe, just return the book and we'll never speak of it again."

Silence fell. Slowly, Christine stood. "I'll read it."

Nodding, Feter and Lam watched her go.

Christine strode up to Domicile 137 and opened the door. She took a breath and stepped inside for the first time in seven years.

Domicile 137 looked much the same as when she had left it. Four thin blankets curled into rolls, four thin pillows propped behind the rolls, all stashed in a corner. The floor and walls were caked with dust. "Lam?" she said softly. No answer. *Am I early? Am I too late?*

Turning to go, her attention fell on a sheet of parchment sticking out from between the leftmost blanket roll and pillow, bedding that had belonged to her growing up. Kneeling, Christine pulled the parchment free and recognized Lam's flowing handwriting.

Can you believe what happened today? Some might not. We would forgive them that. From west to east, her teachings are set in stone, as are the beliefs she instills. Anyone would find them difficult to abandon.

Christine read the note again, then a third time. She slipped it between pages of her book and swept out of the domicile and down the lane, heading for the Bridge checkpoint. The Wardsmen stationed there were the same pair from her first night back on the Bridge. *Just last night*, she thought, amazed. She felt as if she had been home for weeks. The younger man stared sullenly but did not attempt to stop her.

Sharem's southern district was sparsely populated. Curfew fast approached. Stormrobes hurried along toward the Territory Bridge, most holding day passes in plain view. Christine scanned their faces as they passed. No sign of Lam or Feter. That was good. Assuming she had deciphered Lam's missive correctly, she did not expect to see either of them here.

She came to the long, tall iron fence that barred access to the Darinian district. On the other side, extravagant stone buildings sat abandoned. She glanced up. The Lady of Dawn—*the sun*—was a hazy golden ball. Christine estimated that two hours of daylight remained, perhaps three. Kindling, she focused on a space far across the other side of the bars and shifted. She appeared in the middle of a square, standing near a wide, marble fountain. In the center of the fountain, carved stone depicted half a dozen animals: bear, falcon, tiger, adder, meshia, and wolf. The basin was dry and covered in a light coating of dust.

Christine looked around. Although she knew the western district sat abandoned, she could feel eyes on her, staring through the empty windows. "Lam?" she whispered. Silence answered. Her boots scuffed against stone as she made her way deeper into the district. The sensation of being watched bored between her shoulder blades like a dagger point, then vanished abruptly, only to return again. Each time a low murmuring accompanied it, like a low breeze, except there was no breeze. Gooseflesh broke out on her arms, faded, then prickled again.

Christine froze. The prickling sensation was familiar. It reminded her of the drafts that slipped through the many cracks in Domicile 137's rickety door. She had last felt it when Aidan had . . . how had he phrased it? *Riding the shadows.*

Except that was not true. She had felt it last night on the Territory Bridge, a breeze without wind. *That's not quite right,* she amended. *It's as if I caught some sort of chill.* Christine resumed walking. Long seconds passed. Another itch between her shoulders. Tight-lipped, she strained her ears. Murmurs coalesced into words.

Christine's head whipped around and she kindled from the shadows stretching out from buildings. Only it was not kindling. It was the opposite of kindling, cold and darkness substituted for heat and light. Looking up, she concentrated on an open window and, repeating the murmured words, melded into its darkness. One moment she was down in the street. The next, she stood in front of Lam, Feter, and a dozen other stormrobes in a dusty, shadowy room, all watching her with neutral, unsurprised expressions.

"You figured it out," Lam said. Beside him, one corner of Feter's mouth rose in a half smile. He wore a bandage wrapped around his left hand.

Christine held up his missive. "It took me a moment or three. Are you sure this place is safe?"

"Security has been minimal," Feter said. "We come here when we need to talk."

"We?" she repeated.

"The resistance." Lam stood straight. "Meet . . ." He paused dramatically. "The Storm Guard," he finished, sweeping his arm in a grand gesture that took in the stormrobes huddled behind him. He listed off names, pointing them out as he went. "Undine, his brother Joske, Symon and his friend Berolt, and Thomassette and Tifaine you know. Their knowledge of herbs and medical treatments surpasses even my own, and my ancestors were at the forefront of those discoveries."

They waved at her. Christine waved back, uncomfortable. Christine had kept to herself growing up on the Bridge, confiding only in Garrett, Feter, Lam, and her mother. Lam rattled off six other names. Some, a middle-aged man named Tebald, looked vaguely familiar. Others, such as nine-winters-old Emy and her mother Jehanne, were complete strangers.

"It's a pleasure to meet all of you," she said. They murmured in reply. "Lam, would you please tell me what's going on?"

"First, do you believe me?" he asked. His expression was blank.

"It's not that simple."

"I think it is."

"That's why you don't do the thinking in this relationship," Christine said sweetly.

Lam scowled, but his face softened when Feter took his hand.

"Sorry," Lam said. "It's been a stressful few months."

"Because you've been forming a resistance," Christine said.

"Among other things," Lam replied vaguely.

"What is it you want to resist?" she asked, though the answer was obvious.

"The Temple of Dawn, its disciples, and the oppression of our people."

"And why am I here?"

"Because we want you to teach us."

Christine leaned back against a wall, careful to stay out of sight from the window. "Not dark magic." It was not a question.

Lam shook his head.

"I presume dark magic is among the forbidden secrets buried in your scrolls and books," Christine said.

"You presume correctly."

"And you were using dark magic last night on the Bridge, weren't you? That's what I felt, before you almost got both of us arrested."

"Yes."

"What were you doing with it?"

"It's the easiest way to sneak off the Bridge," Lam said. "When we need food, or extra clothing, or . . . other things."

"For the resistance," she said.

"We're dying out, Christine. Last winter was bad. Illnesses broke out and spread like the plague. A few others tried to escape. A few do every year. You know that. One was caught and executed. Two others died from infections from scalethorn. The disciples didn't lift a finger to help them. 'They shouldn't have tried to escape,' Terrence said. We've been thralls for too long. We're tired of paying for sins committed by people eight hundred years in the grave."

"Our ancestors were not buried in graves," Emy spoke up, clenching tiny fists.

"She's right," Lam said. "We and our loved ones have spent most of our lives on the Bridge, without adequate food, without clean water, without proper bedding or clothes. Those of us who earn our way off are subjected to the prejudice of realms who have been taught to despise us because of events that transpired so long ago only the Gairdens remember them."

"And who can trust them to tell us the truth about our

heritage?" asked Berolt.

"That's right," said Tebald. "We have only their word that things transpired the way the histories claim."

Anger stirred in Christine's belly, a desire to rush to Aidan's defense. "You question events chronicled in books," she said. "Yet you expect me to believe other books. Why?"

"Because we can prove every word in every passage in every book in our possession," Feter said. "It took a lot of reading. We read, and referenced, and cross-referenced. We conducted experiments of our own." His eyes shone with excitement and wonder. "You can track the sun's arc through the sky, Chris! The moon's, too. And the stars! The constellations. You saw the charts. Look for them tonight. They always appear in the same places, though some are brighter than others, but that's because—"

Lam placed a hand on his arm. Feter blushed. "I get carried away," he said.

"Where did you find these books?" Christine asked, hefting the tome Lam had loaned her.

"They belonged to our ancestors," Lam said. "Everyone you see here has traced their lineage back to the Serpent's War and beyond. Some of us are Touched, Christine."

"I'm not," Feter put in. "Not everyone on the Bridge can Touch, but most people here can do it. Dark magic isn't what the temple claims. It's just magic, just like light magic."

Christine bit her lower lip. Aidan believed much the same.

"Academia carries a repugnant reputation among the disciples," Lam said, "so my ancestors passed books to friends before they were killed or sentenced to the Bridge. Some of what we have are original copies. The others are duplicates, copied word for word and stashed away in new hiding spots. The ones in Feter's domicile are just some of the copies that exist. His family has less of a reputation than others, so no one thinks to search his quarters."

"Where are the rest?" Christine asked.

Feter and Lam shared a look. "We can't tell you, Chris," Feter said. "Not because we don't trust you. Obviously, we do. Every person in this room only knows of one or two private stashes. That's by design. Stormrobes who know nothing, or at least very little, can't succumb to torture and make confessions that would damn the rest of us."

Christine cast a critical eye on the gathering. Their faces were gaunt, and their bodies swam in grey robes. "Why do you need me?"

Lam's face colored. "Yes. Well. We get away with using dark magic only when there are no disciples around, and because most of them haven't been trained to recognize it. But the truth is, none of us are that good. We come here every now and then to practice, but we have no writings on suncraft. What you call light magic," he explained at her confused expression. "The disciples believe they weeded out Touched from our hereditary lines, but they make sure we're never in a position to learn anything about suncraft as a precaution."

"Did you know that the disciples used to test Sallnerian babes?" Feter asked. "And if they found it, the babes were thrown into the Great Sea, their heads dashed upon the rocks that serve as the walls to our prison." His face twisted. "Our ancestors grew adept at masking the gift in their progeny. One child per coupling, just like the Gairdens. By lowering a babe's temperature to near death, until the rise and fall of their little chests is barely perceptible, they are tepid to the touch, and the disciples sense no ability within them. It was difficult, at first. We lowered body temperatures too quickly. Not that the disciples cared if a newborn babe died in their mother's arms. One less snake to slither out into the realms. That's how they see it."

Everyone stared at the floor. Tears stained the cheeks of some older women. Christine's heart wrenched.

"There's still so much we don't know about shadecraft," Lam said, "and we know nothing about suncraft. Some of us have kindled. It's almost the opposite of shadecraft—"

"It is exactly opposite," Christine muttered, thinking.

Lam's face brightened. "See? If we had a teacher . . ."

At that, fourteen faces fixed her with hopeful looks. "Me?" she squeaked.

"Why not you?" Feter asked. "You're smart, Chris. Always have been. And you're powerful, too. People talk. Professors and disciples say your father brags about you any chance he gets."

"He does?" she said, as surprised by that as by anything else she had learned in the past half a day.

"He does," Lam said. "We don't need to go through years of

higher education. Just the basics. How to create light, how to throw fireballs . . ." He grinned. "You know. The fun stuff."

"We need to defend ourselves," Feter said, his tone serious. "The disciples aren't going to let us just walk off the Territory Bridge."

Christine held up her hands. "You're talking about my father. You're asking me to teach you ways to hurt my father."

"No, Chris," Feter said softly. "We're asking you to teach us how to defend ourselves. The last thing we want to do is hurt anyone. We only want to be free. The same as anyone else in the realms."

"That's another point," Lam said, talking faster with every word. "War is coming. You know the Gairdens. We could help them!"

"I just told her we didn't want to hurt anyone," Feter said.

"And you're right," Lam said. "But either Torel and Darinia will go to war, or based on what Chris told us, they'll ally to fight a common enemy. Either way, what do you think will happen to us stormrobes?"

"You'll get caught in the middle," Christine said quietly. Nobody said anything for a long time. "I don't know," she said at last.

Lam scratched at his nose. "I told you before that other Sallnerians can Touch. The truth is, Chris, I'm the strongest of us, but strength is relative. We need a leader, and none of us here is capable of that. You know what it's like to grow up on the Bridge. They starve, beat, and bully courage out of you. Maybe we'll never have to fight. I honestly hope it doesn't come to that. You could talk to your father on our behalf, if you like. I don't welcome violence. But make no mistake: We're going to do this with or without you, and we're going to do it soon. All of us would feel more comfortable with you leading the charge."

He licked his lips. "We know the Ward is camped outside the city. We can leave the Bridge during the confusion. We have to act soon, Chris."

"You saw how Terrence left," Feter added. "He'll be back, and it's only a matter of time until one or all of us are found out."

"What's stopped him from finding your secrets before now?" she asked.

"Your father," Lam said simply.

"My father hates Sallnerians as much as Terrence," Christine said. Even as she said it she knew it wasn't true. Couldn't be true.

Feter reached out to cup her cheek. "Your father could never hate you, Chris."

"Besides," Lam said, "not even the Gairdens hate Sallnerians as much as Terrence."

Christine pulled away from Feter and turned so they could not see her tears. Part of her wanted to say yes. To shout yes. To trample over the temple and its disciples and the centuries of oppression that had reduced her people to chattel.

Through a prism of tears, she glanced down at her belly. She scrubbed a hand over her face. "I can't lead your movement, Lam. I'm sorry."

His features darkened. "I can't believe this. You're siding with the Gairdens over your own people?"

"I'm choosing both," Christine said, her tone even.

"You can't do that," Lam said.

"I can, and I am. I said I can't lead your movement, and I meant it. I won't put myself in a position to betray Aidan again." Her jaw snapped shut before she could reveal her other, equally personal reasons to avoid conflict. Besides, what she said was true. Attacking a disciple was as good as attacking the entire Temple of Dawn, which could spark war. The last thing Aidan needed was to fight a war on two fronts. "I won't lead you," Christine said again, "but I can teach you enough to survive."

Lam narrowed his eyes. "You're trying to avoid getting your hands dirty. Teaching us makes you culpable, Christine Lorden, and you know it."

His use of her full name shook her, but Christine did not flinch. "You said it yourself, Lam. You'll do this with or without me. Crotaria does not need more bloodshed, but I don't want to see my people get butchered, and that's exactly what will happen if you stand against the temple as you are now. Just because I won't stand at the head of your . . . your Storm Guard doesn't mean I'll sit back and watch you die."

Lam and Feter looked over their shoulders at the rest of the group. "Fine," Lam snapped.

Christine raised a finger. "On one condition. Before anything happens, you'll give me a chance to talk to my father, and to Aidan."

Someone in the back snorted. "Gairdens are the true snakes. You can't trust them."

"Aidan is different," Christine said.

Shouts broke out, then Feter raised his hands. "I'll never trust a Gairden, but I do trust Chris. She's one of us." Many of the Sallnerians still looked angry, but a few nodded assent.

"When do we get started?" Lam asked.

Christine looked out the window at the street below. "Tonight. But do exactly as I say. We don't want to draw unwanted attention."

"To Sallnerians, all attention is unwanted," Emy said wisely. Nervous laughter greeted her words.

One by one they slipped into the shadows and congregated in a square deeper inside the district. Christine was the last to arrive. The others had arranged themselves in a semi-circle and appeared anxious.

"We don't have long," Christine said, glancing up at the sun. Another tremor ran through her. This time it was all excitement. Her mind positively hummed. There was so much to learn. Then she realized that for the first time since leaving him, she had barely thought about how much she missed Aidan. She could feel him somewhere in the west. She swallowed and took a deep breath. "Kindling is similar to . . . to darkening. Open your body and mind to the . . . to the sun, speak the prayer—the invocation you desire—and then release light and warmth."

She told them the word to create a small flame. "You may have to repeat it several times, depending on your level of strength. Let's spread out in a line. Stand a shoulder's width apart. We don't want to set anyone on fire."

Another round of nervous laughter.

"Raise a palm facing outward," she said.

There was a rustling like wind through leaves as fourteen hands raised to chest level.

"Now, on the count of three, kindle, and speak the word I taught you. One. Two. Three."

A flicker of light danced across Emy's hand. She gasped, then her face split in a grin. "I felt something! I felt it, Chris!"

Christine smiled. "Very good. Don't worry if it doesn't work the first time. Experience darkening may not count for as much as I thought." She did not believe this. It had only taken her a brief moment of concentration to jump between shadows. Still, she was more powerful than most, and had been Touching for years. It would not be fair to expect instant competence from everyone.

"Let's try again. One. Two. Thr—"

Four balls of fire shot across the square, tongues of flame trailing behind them. All four boulder-sized blasts exploded against a marble wall in the same instant. Debris flew everywhere. Christine stumbled back, blinded, a high-pitched ringing in her ears. When she opened her eyes, smoke rose in tendrils from the wall, reduced to slag. Blinking, she saw Emy, her mother Jehanne, Lam, and Berolt gaping at her, eyes wide in astonishment.

"I think you're catching on," Christine said weakly.

Chapter 38:
Conspirators

EDMUND'S EYES SHOT open. He lay still. Pitch blackness enveloped him. The room swayed and creaked. A chill ran up his spine. *What awakened me?*

Heavy footsteps, faint and growing louder. A door crashed against the wall. Edmund registered a short, stocky shape framed in the doorway against a night sky speckled with stars. The sight of it drove away all thought. Instinct took over. Swinging his feet to the floor he fumbled at his waist for Valor, realized it was not there. Silvery light reflected against something long and shiny poking out from beneath his pillow. He pulled the knife free and stood, legs braced to charge.

The shape raised a hand and spoke. Edmund could not make out its words and did not want to. He ran forward. Fire raced up his bad leg. He ignored it and bore in. The man in the doorway was too short to be a human. *A reaver?* Events from the previous day—was it a new day? It was too dark and he was too discombobulated to tell—returned in a rush of images. The Prefecture, the Anna-harbinger, Valor's broken blade, Jamian's ship. Undead Azure Blades and guildmasters.

Another flash as the Lord of Midnight's light glinted off steel. A sharp clang rang out as Edmund's knife bit into a *Sard'tara's* curved head. Edmund grunted. His arms shook. His opponent's face was taut with exertion, and in the faint light of the night sky Edmund recognized him. Hahrzen the reaver. Another soul lost to Tyrnen.

Edmund had a single breath to register a taller, lither shape in the doorway. The form brushed by him and hooked slender arms through his, wrenched them back and high over his head. Edmund struggled. It was no use. Hahrzen plucked the knife from his grip and tossed it aside. It clattered against wood beams. The second assailant kicked the back of Edmund's left knee. It buckled instantly. He sagged and was dragged backward.

"Damn you, General Calderon," the Hahrzen-thing rasped. "Hold still or—"

A third figure stepped into the doorway, holding a lantern. Fire flashed and the hands holding Edmund fell away. There was a grunt from behind him followed by a crash. His moment of distraction cost him. The Hahrzen-vagrant launched himself at Edmund and drove him back to the floor. Edmund kicked and flailed. A curved *Sard'tara* head against his throat stilled him.

"Will you stop and listen?" it roared in Hahrzen's voice.

Edmund thrashed harder than ever. "I'll be damned if I let you—"

"Edmund." Cyrolin, her tone controlled. She stepped forward to peer down at him. Another woman dressed in sea-green leather armor stood beside her, wariness etched on her face. It took Edmund a moment to place her. Nita, one of the Azure Blades from the Prefecture.

"They are alive," Cyrolin said.

Edmund stared up at Hahrzen. The reaver pushed himself to his feet and took a few steps back, levelling his *Sard'tara* at Edmund. "You're sure?" Edmund asked.

"Show him your hands," Cyrolin said to Hahrzen and Nita.

Warily, the Blades extended their right hands palms out. Edmund squinted and beheld thin cuts oozing red blood. "Ask me anything," Nita said.

Edmund pushed himself upright. "If Tyrnen or his creatures stole your souls, you'd have your memories. You'd know this place."

Hahrzen snorted. "I could have killed you a dozen times while you lay on your back like an upset turtle."

"Vagrants are snakes in the grass," Edmund said. "You won't

know one is nearby until it decides to bite you."

"The wounds are fresh," Cyrolin put in. "I cut them myself."

Edmund studied the new arrivals. Finally, he tossed his knife on his bed.

Hahrzen exhaled and lowered his *Sard'tara*. "I owe you an apology, Edmund. But you have to see things from my perspective. Your story didn't line up with that . . . with Anna's, and when you appeared ready to attack her . . ." He ran stumpy fingers through his wild hair. "You would have done the same."

Edmund steeled himself against grief that shot through him. "How did you escape?" Behind him, Cyrolin bent to right the chairs before Jamian's desk that had been knocked over in the commotion.

"Sit," the galerunner said to Nita. Tight-lipped, the Azure Blade limped over and dropped into Jamian's high-backed seat. For the first time, Edmund noticed a long gash running down her left arm. Cyrolin laid a hand on the wound and whispered. The lantern at her feet shivered and diminished.

Hahrzen sank into another chair, propping his *Sard'tara* in the crook of one arm. "There was pandemonium after you left. The Crown . . . whatever that creature who appeared as Annalyn Gairden was, she and some of the guildmasters started killing Azure Blades." His face darkened. "Some of the Blades joined in. Those who fell got right back up and attacked their fellows. The bloodshed was . . ."

He swallowed. "I had gore all over me, so I fell to the ground and played dead. I guess it worked, or I wouldn't be playing right now. The Crown said my name, so I stood. I was covered head to toe in the blood of my friends. I guess I blended in. The guildmasters told us to search the streets for you and Cyr—"

Cyrolin flinched at the moniker.

"—and when we did, I slipped away," Hahrzen said.

The reaver lifted his eyes to Edmund's. "That's when I found the body. Annalyn's, I mean. Except it was rotten and her blood and guts were the color of seaweed."

Edmund said nothing. His head felt tight, stretched near to tearing.

"I thought about going to Jamian's, but there were Blades everywhere," Hahrzen continued. "I didn't know who to trust, so I made my way here. That's when I found Nita."

Every head turned to behold the other Blade. Nita sat straighter in Jamian's chair. Color had returned to her face. "My journey was not so easy at Hahrzen's." She stared into her lap. "I killed Osphera."

Silence fell over the group.

"Dawn and Dusk," Hahrzen muttered. "I didn't realize. I'm sorry, Nita. It wasn't her. You must know that."

"I thought it was. It had Osphera's face. It was like Hahrzy said: The guildmasters attacked us. Osphera, she came at me. I defended myself." Nita sniffled and wiped at her cheeks. "I ran. I heard some coming after me, but I'm fast. I grew up on a farm and I'll be damned to shade if I'm not the fastest Blade you'll meet."

"We heard a summoning," Cyrolin said.

"Yes," Nita said, nodding. "That was me. I found my way to the bunker. It was deserted. I uncovered the horn where we hid it and I sounded it. I left the mark on the door and then left, and I heard another blast. Obviously, other cells heard the call or saw the mark, or maybe both, because when I got to the hideaway, a few of us were there." Her mouth tightened. "Too few."

"I sounded one myself," Hahrzen put in. Catching Edmund's confused look, he scratched at his beard. "Suppose you wouldn't know how a summoning works. Cyr, neither. Each cell's horn has a distinctive sound. Horns are only sounded in emergencies. A single blast from one cell indicates an emergency within that cell, and that all available Blades should report to their bunker. If another cell issues a summoning, that means what threatens one cell threatens all. All Blades are expected to make haste to the center and wait there."

"The center?" Edmund said.

"A central bunker," Nita said.

Edmund saw where their tale was going. "And when you got there, the vagrants—the undead—were waiting."

Hahrzen growled. "Not all the Blades at the center were these vagrants, but many were, and they claimed many more. We moved a second time, to another center. They were waiting there, too."

"Tyrnen has their souls," Edmund said quietly. The color drained from Nita's face. "I don't quite understand how it works," Edmund continued. "What I do know is Tyrnen can infuse corpses with souls and transpose the body into any shape, with any face. Souls possess the memories of the deceased."

"And any Azure Blade would be able to interpret the horn calls," Nita finished.

Edmund nodded.

"Shade and sand," Nita muttered.

"There have been no new arrivals," Hahrzen put in. "Not since we left, anyway."

"Left where?" Cyrolin asked.

"A third center, known only by each Blade who escaped the second. By that time most of us had some idea of what was happening. Upon arriving, we cut ourselves to show proof we were living."

"What brought you here?" Cyrolin asked.

Nita shrugged. "Dumb luck. You fled together, and you couldn't go to Jamian's." Her face grew tight. "Jamian is dead, too."

"Yes," Cyrolin said dispassionately.

Hahrzen raised his brow. "I suppose you would be the first to know."

"I wasn't, actually," Cyrolin replied, glancing at Edmund.

Hahrzen and Nita shared a look. "Everything you said back in the Prefecture," Nita said. "It was all true."

It was not a question, but Edmund treated it like one. "Yes. That's why Aidan needs the Azure Blades." Briefly, he explained again the situation in Torel and Darinia.

"We can't leave," Hahrzen said when he finished.

Edmund held his temper by the tail. "Why not?"

"Ironsail is our city," Nita said.

"With all due respect, you are mercenaries. Coin is your master, not the guild."

"And Ironsail is the only home we know," Hahrzen said. "Would you have us leave it to rot? We can still kill the dead and save the city."

"Killing vagrants does no good," Edmund said. "All Tyrnen has to do is transfer their soul to another body." He stared hard at Nita. "Are you prepared to kill Osphera again? And again? That is the fate that awaits you unless the Blades ally themselves with Torel's Ward."

Nita's eyes glittered with anger, and with tears.

"How do we stop them?" Hahrzen asked.

Edmund told them about Tyrnen's spirit stone. "As Aidan explained it, shattering the stone frees the souls trapped within it."

"Including your wife's," Nita said.

Edmund did not trust himself to reply. Greed shot through him, quickening his pulse. The feeling was welcome, even soothing. He knew not what fate awaited souls of the deceased. No one did, not really. Some believed they would find solace in the warm embrace of the Lady. Edmund had never been so certain. He did not need to be. Gairdens went to their bloodline's eternal resting place when their bodies expired. Anna would go there, too, and their marital bond guaranteed Edmund a place at her side. All he had to do was free her.

"Are you all right?" Hahrzen asked.

"Weary, that's all."

"You need more rest," Cyrolin said, suddenly by his side.

"You said the Eternal Flame has this stone," Hahrzen said. "I do not doubt you, but how could he control his minions from afar?"

Edmund considered. "The particulars are not known to me. I am not a Touched. Truth be told, I left such matters to Anna and her father."

"There have been no reports of Tyrnen Symorne in Ironsail," Nita said, frowning.

"It seems unwise," Hahrzen went on, "to rely on a single magical instrument for a task as important as subjugating souls."

"I've been thinking," Cyrolin said. She took a seat beside Edmund. "This object, the spirit stone, it sounds similar to the bond between captain and galerunner. Through the bond, captains are aware of their galerunner's location, emotions, and physical sensations." Her lips tightened into a thin line. "Jamian took advantage of this fact every time we . . . when we would . . ."

From across the room, Nita muttered something. Edmund thought he heard "men" more than once. Cyrolin shook her head. "Once, Jamian bonded a second galerunner, and dismissed her almost immediately. He likened the flow of both our emotions and locations to a storm." Shrugging, she went on, "I don't presume to know how this stone works. I would guess, however, that even a Touched as gifted as the Eternal Flame would be unable to command a great number of souls at once."

Edmund sat back, considering. Multiple spirit stones made sense. Tyrnen could not be everywhere at once. To conquer Crotaria's three realms, he would almost certainly appoint lieutenants, spies able to infiltrate stations of power and wrest them away so he could manipulate them. He had already done so, and successfully: The state of chaos in which he had found Calewind upon returning from Lake Carrean testified to that.

"We must consider the possibility that more than one spirit stone exists," Edmund said. The fist gripping his chest tightened. Two spirit stones, three, a thousand. It did not matter. To free Anna, he would scour Crotaria and shatter them one by one.

"Very well," Nita said. "Assuming the Eternal Flame is in the east—"

"We don't know that he's in Leaston, much less Ironsail," Edmund said. "It's possible he delegated, giving a stone to one of his servants."

"He does not seem like the sort of man to trust his underlings, judging by what you have said," Hahrzen said.

"Unless Tyrnen was assured that these servants would obey him implicitly," Edmund said.

"You know such a person?" Nita said.

"I do. My wife."

Chapter 39:
Compromised

THE SHOP HAHRZEN told them about was nestled in a far corner of South Haven. Like the buildings bunched up against either side, it was squat, dirty, nondescript. Stepping up to the back door, Edmund saw two slits. The first was level with his eyes. The second lined up with his waist. The lower slot slid open with a snap, revealing a pair of green eyes that glared at Edmund.

Hahrzen shuffled forward. "Tad sarar," he growled.

The slit snapped closed. There was a click and the door opened. Hahrzen strode through. Edmund followed and found another reaver standing behind the door, peering out into the night as they entered single file. "Sorry, Hahrzy. Protocol," the reaver said. Two other Azure Blades—one male human, the other a female reaver—seated at a long bench stood up, gripping *Sard'tara*.

"Protocol!" Hahrzen snorted. "Only the living were present when we relocated, Lanoden."

"Give it a rest," Lanoden grumbled, closing the door and sliding half a dozen bolts into place. "You're the one who made me swear to ask anyone and everyone."

"I know what I said. I was there. Where's Gewnan?"

"Resting upstairs."

"Rouse him. The general here needs to speak with him. It's urgent."

One of the Azure Blades at the table, an ebony-skinned man

whose hair hung in braids, took Lanoden's post by the door while the other man bounded down a hall and took the stairs two at a time. "This way," Hahrzen said, waving.

Edmund caught his arm while Cyrolin and Nita passed by them down a long hallway. "Gewnan's here?" he asked in a low voice.

"He's alive," Hahrzen said. "Just barely. Come on."

They entered the front of the shop. It was a large, square room. Furniture and tools—workbenches and tables, hammers and canisters of nails, saws of all shapes and sizes—had been shoved up against the walls. Sleeping rolls and three-legged stools had been spread out on a floor covered in sawdust. None were occupied. Azure Blades paced, clutching *Sard'tara* close. Edmund scanned their faces: harried, grimy, tired. In one corner, a woman and two dark-skinned men huddled together. They were middle-aged and dressed in expensive robes and glittering jewelry. Guildmasters.

Everyone looked up at their entrance. The guildmasters became aware of Edmund and stood. "You were right," the woman said shakily. "We should have listened."

"Tyrnen's deception fooled us all," Edmund said. "It cost my wife her soul, and my son nearly lost his head."

"We would like to keep ours," one of the robed men said.

Edmund began to speak. Cyrolin appeared at his side. He scanned her face, and what he saw there stole his breath. Confidence. Faith. Trust. Until tonight, he had been convinced her glower had been permanently fixed in place. "So do I," he said. "I might have a plan to do just that."

Every face grew grim and resolved. Footsteps bounding down the stairs in the adjoining hall announced the return of Lanoden. He waddled into the workroom and paused. Another pair of footsteps shuffled their way to him. Gewnan appeared, mouth puckered. The guildmaster's lips were as pale as his hairless cheeks. His eyes shone like blue diamonds.

"General," he said.

Edmund inclined his head. Four of the Azure Blades went to Gewnan. "I can manage," the old man said, waving them away. He shuffled over to a chair and eased into it with a sigh. Without prompting, the other three guildmasters dragged stools over and formed a circle. Edmund joined them. Cyrolin took a seat by his right side.

Gewnan lifted one knobby finger. Lanoden came over and leaned in. "Tighten security on the door," Gewnan said in a tremulous voice. "Front and back. We're all in one place."

"At once, Guildmaster," Lanoden said. He barked a few orders and disappeared down the hallway. All around, Azure Blades moved with purpose. Nita and Hahrzen flanked the front door. Several others stood to either side of boarded windows. A few dashed upstairs. At least four dozen fanned out around the group.

"I owe you an apology, General," Gewnan began.

Edmund shook his head. "Not necessary. Let's use our time to formulate a plan of attack."

"Attack?" Gewnan echoed, spreading his hands. "What is there to attack? I have seen men die and take to their feet as if disembowelment were no more mortal an injury than a grain of birdseed to the head. I have seen men bleed emerald blood instead of ruby. Dying is an inconvenience to the enemy we face." He paused. He'd been drawing deep, ragged breaths every few words. Edmund waited patiently.

"And that harbinger that wears your wife's face, also wields her magic. Annalyn Gairden is a powerful Touched. There are others like her, vagrants and harbingers, I believe you called them. Ironsail's Azure Blades have been decimated."

"How many still live?" Edmund asked.

"All you see here, and others hidden outside. No more than one hundred. There are tens of thousands more elsewhere in the east, but as for this city . . . I ask you again: what is there to attack, General Calderon? How can we kill that which cannot die?"

Edmund waited until the old guildmaster sat back. Sweat had beaded on Gewnan's forehead. To either side of Edmund, the remaining guildmasters had grown more crestfallen with every word. The survivor in him flared up. He could not let them surrender. He would not.

"The situation seems hopeless, but there may be a way to strike down Tyrnen's creatures in one fell swoop." He told them of spirit stones, and of his theory that there must be more than one. Gewnan and the other three guildmasters listened intently.

When Edmund finished, Gewnan sat forward. "What do these stones look like?"

"The one I have seen resembles a perfectly round, perfectly

smooth stone."

Gewnan puckered his lips. Color had returned to his face. "The harbinger, your wife, she cornered me at the Vault. If not for Lanoden, I would not be sitting here now." Coughs shook his thin frame. Nita took a step toward him, but the old man shooed her back. His face had turned beet red. "To think these Blades put their bodies, their very souls at risk to save an old man who has maybe one more summer in him, if he's lucky." His expression sobered. "Before Lanoden drove her off, I saw an object in her hand. I wasn't in the right mind to examine it closely, but I can tell you it was neither small nor round."

Edmund fought to swallow his disappointment. He must have done a poor job, because Gewnan held up a spotted hand. "Despite that, I have no doubt of the object's importance. It was thin and pointed at one end. Like a nail. And it glowed, white as the snow you Wardsmen wear. Lanoden was not the only Blade from my cell who came to my aid. There was another, a young woman by the name of Jess. She . . . got there first, and your wife . . ."

Gewnan's eyes were haunted. "Then the creature whispered something, and the spike glowed, and Jess rose again." He nodded. "Yes. I think that is the object we seek. If destroying it will destroy that creature and its followers, then destroy it we must."

The other three guildmasters murmured assent. So did Cyrolin. Edmund said nothing. He had no breath with which to speak. Until now, he had never considered that destroying any spirit stone other than Tyrnen's might set Anna free. Would the old man really trust Anna's soul with Anna herself? *Why not?* It all made sense: Tyrnen had commanded Anna to infiltrate the east and destroy the merchant's guild from within, stealing their souls and turning them into Tyrnen's subjects, all using the vessel that held her very essence in check.

A frisson of doubt nagged at him. Tyrnen had held the spherical stone at Lake Carrean. He had not seen the old man harvest her soul, but who was to say Tyrnen could not transfer souls between stones? What better way to protect his most prized possession: A Gairden?

Fury overwhelmed him, drowning skepticism. *Anna. A possession.*

Cyrolin touched his arm. "Are you all right?" she whispered.

Edmund looked up to find the circle staring at him. "I am well," he said, gently removing Cyrolin's hand. Her face colored. She stared at the floor. "I believe you're right," Edmund said to Gewnan.

"And destroying it will release the souls the creature has subjugated," Gewnan said.

"Yes."

"How do we do that?" asked the woman guildmaster, tall and lithe with skin as brown as the Plains of Dust.

"Are you four all that remains of the merchant's guild?" Edmund asked.

She nodded. "I am Cidra Galvi. This is Ande Kithmis"—she pointed at a short man, tan and bald save for a fringe of brown hair—"and this is Usmer Nyso, Osphera's sister." The other woman's brown eyes were red and puffy. She sat near Nita, who rested a hand on the guildmaster's shoulder. "Our numbers shrank from eight to three in the span of a night," Cidra continued.

"It's the attacks," Gewnan said. "The undead knew where to find us."

"We should be safe here," Cidra said.

"It's strange," Usmer said, dabbing at her nose with a handkerchief. "That they found our first center, I understand. If the corpses possess their souls, then they possess the knowledge of their lives. But how did they find the second? That one was unknown beforehand, decided on by summonings."

"Perhaps some of the dead followed us when we fled?" Gewnan suggested. He gave a faint smile. "Some of us do not move as quickly as we used to."

Cidra shook her head. "We did not flee until our Blades drove them away."

"Was Anna . . . was the harbinger with them?" Edmund asked.

Cidra shook her head. "If she was, we saw no sign of her." She tapped a lacquered nail against her lips. "Tyrnen seeks to usurp power from the merchant's guild by controlling our souls like puppets."

"It sounds as if that tactic worked all too well in Torel," Ande said.

Usmer sniffed, her expression thoughtful. "The vagrants that attacked our first two centers did not kill arbitrarily. Every soul and body they claim grows their ranks. One would think they would kill anyone in their path. But they did not."

Cidra frowned. She turned to Gewnan. "What do you think it means?"

Gewnan puckered his lips. One hand scratched at a bony knee. The other was thrust into a pocket of his robes. His eyelids drooped. He appeared to be dozing. Ande spoke instead. "Vagrants follow orders. They are puppets, as we now know. Whoever holds their strings has a target in mind." His gaze fell on Edmund. His was not the only pair of eyes that sought the general.

Gewnan abruptly came to life, waving a gnarled hand as if dispelling smoke. "Conjecture is useless. We're here and must make the most of our time." Removing his hands from his pockets, he clasped them before him and held Edmund's gaze. "Tyrnen and his creature won't see us coming, now that we've weeded out the dead from our ranks. Help us get close to the creature, and our Azure Blades can do the rest."

"No," Edmund said. "I will deal with the harbinger myself. I will break the stone."

Gewnan studied him. "Very well. Such an object is no doubt under the protection of the creature that holds it. You knew Annalyn Gairden best. How do you suggest we lure her out?"

"I don't think she'll be hard to find."

A thin eyebrow rose. "You have a plan," Gewnan said.

Edmund did. As he spoke, Azure Blades and guildmasters listened intently. Of the bunch, Gewnan seemed the most alert. As the night wore on, the shriveled little guildmaster began to shiver. He stuffed his hands into the pockets of his robe and focused on Edmund. When the general finished explaining, the first traces of grey light seeped through the boards covering the windows.

"It sounds simple enough," said Usmer. She stifled a yawn with a fist.

Cidra nodded. Her eyes were bleary, and her face was drawn.

Edmund rubbed his left leg. It had fallen asleep. Pins and needles peppered him. He gritted his teeth. "Old one," he said to Gewnan. "Do you feel comfortable with your task?"

"Don't you worry about me," Gewnan said in a voice that quavered only slightly. "I may be an old man, but I will do my part to make Leaston the way it should be." He betrayed his passion by giving a long, jaw-cracking yawn.

Edmund tried to fight back a yawn and failed. "We should get some sleep," he said. "An hour. Maybe two or three. Then we'll disperse, and . . . What in Dawn's name is that?"

At first the others looked confused. Then they heard it: A whistling noise, faint at first but growing louder. Cyrolin gasped and looked at her arm. Her hand snaked out and grabbed Edmund's wrist. "Get down!" she screamed.

The rooftop exploded. Dust, wood, and flaming debris rained into the shop. Flames bloomed in the grey sky, engulfing all they touched. Without stopping to think, Edmund grabbed Cyrolin and pulled her to the floor. She was shouting something, but her words were drowned by the roar of fire. Edmund fell over her, shielding her body with his own. Debris pounded and stabbed at his exposed back. He winced and gasped, more out of shock than pain.

As suddenly as it had begun, the bombardment stopped. He rolled off of Cyrolin and stared up at where the roof had been. The opening was uneven and ugly. Charred beams of wood and melted stone poked out like broken, rotten teeth. Screams sounded from nearby. Over them, Edmund heard a faint rumbling. Footsteps. Lots of them.

Edmund climbed to his feet and hauled Cyrolin up beside him.

"Are you all right?" she asked, searching his face.

"Not if we don't move."

Around him, Azure Blades and guildmasters stirred on the floor or swayed on their feet. All were covered in soot and grime. Many were bleeding.

Hahrzen carefully extricated Gewnan from rubble. "Alive," the reaver told Edmund tightly.

"Thanks to you," Gewnan said, coughing and sputtering.

Lanoden and two other Blades charged in from the back room. They were covered in filth. "What in stars' light—"

"Vagrants," Edmund snapped. "We've got to go. Now."

"The plan," Gewnan said between coughs.

"Is still in effect," Edmund said. "For now, we need to move."

He had to shout to be heard over rising screams and stampeding footsteps. Skull faces, decrepit and laced with mold and gore, sprouted around the edges of the gaping hole above.

They threw themselves through the opening and crashed to the floor with heavy thuds.

"Scatter!" Edmund shouted. He ripped his dagger free and hacked at the neck of the closest vagrant. After four swings the body crumpled. Undead surged in, rushing him from all sides. Wind buffeted him. He turned in time to see a cluster of vagrants lift off the ground and fly through the air, crashing into the far wall and dropping in a heap.

Cyrolin stepped in front of him, throwing her arms wide. "Go."

"Not without you." He grabbed at her arm, pulling. Cyrolin let him. They raced for the front door and Edmund threw his shoulder against it. It opened with a crash. Edmund maintained an all-out sprint for three heartbeats before his bad leg screamed. He sucked in breaths and fell into a limping gait. Something soft settled against his back, like a hand as light as a feather. It propelled him forward. With Cyrolin's cloud behind him, each step he took equaled ten.

Buildings blurred. Few faces occupied the streets at such an early hour. Those he did see registered surprise and then fell away as quickly as they had appeared. The road curved ahead. Edmund followed it. He could sense Cyrolin behind him, guiding them along alleyways and behind shops and residences and taverns and inns. The acrid scent of smoke and the sounds of screams faded, replaced by the Great Sea's tide.

Minutes later they slowed, stopped in front of a tavern. Edmund read the sign above the door. Reaver's Rest. Cyrolin threw an arm around his waist and walked casually through the swinging doors.

"How?" Edmund said. "The center was safe until we arrived."

"There was a traitor," Cyrolin said simply, pulling him along. Edmund bristled. He itched to move faster. "Be calm," she murmured, smiling and barely moving her lips.

He understood at once. They looked like any two people out for an early stroll. A middle-aged man with a bald pate and a spotless white towel hanging from his waist looked up from where he was taking chairs down from tables. "You folks thirsty this early?"

Cyrolin turned her most dazzling smile on him. "Is it early? We've been out all night."

The man chuckled. "Caught up in each other's eyes, are you?

Must be, else you'd notice you both look dirtier than the ground you walked in on. No offense."

Her smile grew more radiant. "We'll take a table in the back."

The man nodded and went about his work. In the furthest, darkest corner from the door, Edmund slipped free of Cyrolin and dropped onto a bench. "Was that necessary?" he said as the galerunner took the seat opposite.

"We don't want to attract attention," she said in a low voice. "People will be talking about what happened soon enough. Anyone who hears we were there . . . Word could get back—"

At that moment, a shrill blast from a horn pierced the early morning. The innkeeper jerked his head up from where he had been polishing a round table, features tight. He must have felt their stares because he pasted on a false smile. "Nothing to worry about." He returned to polishing. At another summoning, the innkeeper tensed. He tossed his rag onto the table and came to stand beside them.

"There's trouble a few blocks over," he began, hands on his hips. Another blast, deeper, followed by two more. The innkeeper frowned. "That's strange. They're supposed to regroup in the event of . . ." He cocked his head, nodded at two additional, higher notes.

"They're scattering," Edmund interrupted. Cyrolin glanced at him sharply.

"Yes, I . . ." The man blinked. "How do you know how to interpret a summoning?"

"The distance and pitch of the calls. You seem to know a great deal about the Azure Blades," Edmund observed. "How do you know them?"

"I retired five summers ago. Served guildmaster Gewnan for thirty-five summers, saved up, bought this place."

Edmund studied the man with renewed interest. His arms were tan and corded with muscles. Not so unusual for a Leastonian. What gave away the man's training were his eyes. Although lined with crow's feet, they were bright and vigilant. His hair was grey, but his rigid posture also spoke of intense training.

Three more notes sounded, two short and one long, low call. This time, the trio ignored them. Outside, two pairs of footsteps shuffled up to the swinging doors. "We're closed," the innkeeper called. The footsteps paused. Edmund could see two masked heads above the door, and below it, legs in dark pants and boots. Grumbling, they turned away. "You two don't seem surprised to hear summonings at this hour. Care to enlighten me?" the innkeeper asked.

Cyrolin's gaze flicked to Edmund. "Are you sure about this?" Edmund, staring right back at the innkeeper, nodded. Cyrolin shrugged. "I am a galerunner. I once belonged to Guildmaster and Captain Jamian Rolf."

"Once belonged?"

Her mouth became a thin line. "It is a long story. It will be longer still if you insist on interrupting."

The man narrowed his eyes. "Darvin Eppsom, galerunner."

"Well met, Darvin," Edmund said. "Care to sit? The lady is right. This will take some telling."

"I prefer to stand."

"Suit yourself," Cyrolin said. She withdrew a dagger from her belt. One of Darvin's eyebrows climbed.

"What does a galerunner need with a such a tool?"

"This galerunner needs you to prick the tip of your finger." She smiled broadly. "We need to know if you bleed like the rest of us."

Without hesitation, Edmund placed the tip of his right forefinger on the knife's head and pressed down. A dewdrop of blood welled up. Cyrolin followed his example, then wiped the blade clean on her shirt.

Darvin's eyes nearly popped out of his head. "You're both mad."

"No," Cyrolin said. "We're both alive. Can the same be said for you?"

"Best to do as she says, Master Eppsom," Edmund said quietly. Silence stretched between them.

Moving cautiously at first, Darvin backed to the swinging doors and reached out with either hand to brace himself in the doorway, like a drunk having trouble standing upright. He turned his back to them. Edmund and Cyrolin watched as he reached into either wall and pulled out two slabs of wood. They slid together smoothly.

Darvin calmly walked back to the table and touched a forefinger to the knifepoint. He held it up. Edmund saw a dewdrop of red blood.

"Satisfied?"

Cyrolin nodded and put the knife away. Darvin faced them. "I'll listen to your story only because I've observed more than my fair share of strangeness over the last few days."

"What sort of strangeness?" Edmund asked.

"Men with blank eyes where there should be life. The guildmasters holed up in the Prefecture since Festival began, an event they never miss a chance to attend so they can show off their status." He gestured to the closed door. "And the horns. Those most of all. Haven't heard summonings that urgent since pirates followed Guildmaster Gewnan back from the Storm Isles. Tried to follow, I should say. To their folly."

"What happened?" Edmund asked.

Darvin smirked. "I've talked enough. I believe you have information for me. If you don't, I'll kindly ask you to get out of my establishment and never come back."

Cyrolin watched Edmund, waiting. He nodded. She launched into the story, everything Edmund had told her and everything that had happened to them over the past two days and nights, culminating in their meeting the previous night and the attack that had scattered the last surviving guildmasters and their Blades to the winds.

"I knew you weren't one of them," Cyrolin finished.

"How's that?"

"Your eyes. And the fact that you knew Azure Blades and guildmasters were scattering and didn't attack."

Darvin chewed his lip. "Gewnan was alive, last you saw him?"

"He was," Edmund said. "Though moving slow."

Now Darvin's face did register surprise. "Slow? Really?"

"He is old," Cyrolin said.

"I suppose." Darvin scratched his head. "Old age can sneak up on you."

"This attack from some summers back," Edmund said. "How did Gewnan fare?"

Darvin laughed. "Better than me and any of my boys. I was cell leader, but old Gewnan? He put me to shame. We were on our way back from the Storm Isles, like I said. A ship appeared out of thin air and followed us. Gewnan got within a day's sight of North Haven and ordered his galerunner to turn around. Attacked the pirates head-on, and was the first man across the bridge after he gave the order."

"When was this?" Edmund asked.

"Six summers ago."

"And Gewnan led the charge?" Edmund said, incredulous.

"He's got the body of a man who's lived ninety summers but the spirit of a boy of fifteen." Darvin paused. "It might have been the sickness," he continued. "Four summers ago, a captain brought back goods from some far-off land, and sickness was among them. Gewnan caught it. Barely survived, or so I heard from the cells."

"Why are you telling us this?" Cyrolin said.

"Guildmaster Gewnan was good to me. Oh, he treated his Azure Blades roughly enough. Never a kind word for any of us, but never a mean one either. He was a man obsessed, you might say. Always looking for ways to extend the guild's power and influence. Anyone who slowed him down caught the rough side of his tongue."

Darvin laughed. "He only had rough sides. But not a one of us minded. He paid well, better than any other guildmaster. Kindness inspires loyalty in a man. But good pay? That inspires loyalty in a Blade. The kind that makes you die for a man. I'd have died before that, I think. I was a sneak before Gewnan brought me on, and not a particularly adept one. Still, I know things, and I've forgotten more than the younger sneaks I've seen bumbling around the city will ever know. If you need help, you've got it, no payment required." He gave them a cocky, half smile. "Must be a first for an Azure Blade, or for any Leastonian in any occupation, ever."

Edmund had gone silent again, staring hard at the floor. At last he looked up. "I'll take you up on that."

"Right," Darvin said, rubbing his hands briskly. "What can I do?"

Chapter 40:
Truce

GENERAL BRENDON GREAGOR leaned forward in his saddle. Beside him, his four lieutenants let out soft sounds of surprise. A heartbeat earlier the western horizon had been clear. In the next, clansmen crested a hilltop two leagues away as if out of thin air.

Their bodies were clad in armor or painted in markings. Their helmets were shaped like animal heads. Wolves with long, steel teeth. Falcons with beaks tapered to sharp points that glittered in the bright pink light of Dawnrise. Bears with maws frozen in a silent roar. The poisonous adder's triangular head, made up of dozens of tiny plates that resembled the serpent's scales, a forked tongue protruding from a closed mouth and drooping down the wearer's chin. Some hands clutched banners depicting animals or arcane symbols. Most clutched swords, halberds, axes, and clubs.

On and on they came, their numbers countless, oozing rather than boiling over the hilltop. Brendon let out a breath. They moved at a walk instead of a gallop, a good omen from the Lady of Dawn.

Through the lens, the clansfolk trembled. Brendon lowered his spyglass and stilled his trembling left hand. He turned to Lieutenant Moser on his left, Lieutenant Marrick on his right. "You remember the plan?"

Marrick nodded. Tight-lipped, Moser said nothing. From

behind, Lieutenants Christopher and Elliott each gave a muffled "Yes, sir."

"Talk like you've got steel in your spine and snow in your veins," Brendon snapped.

The lieutenants stiffened. "Yes, sir!" they shouted, voices ringing.

Acker snorted. The plates covering his cheeks, neck, flanks, chest, and back jangled. All mounts in the Ward had been fitted for full barding, but Acker could still sense Brendon's nervousness through all those layers of steel. Brendon scratched his ears. Acker grew still. Brendon closed his eyes, breathing in morning air that carried more than a trace of the decay from what Aidan had done weeks before.

Brendon flicked his reins and Acker started forward. Marrick's and Moser's horses clattered along to either side. Christopher and Elliott, and fifty thousand Wardsmen at their backs, stayed behind, watching them go. *All part of the plan,* Brendon reminded himself.

The hill descended smoothly. Brendon let Acker take his time navigating the terrain, still slippery from mud and loose grass. Clansfolk continued to spill over the distant summit. Squinting, Brendon saw eight hunched forms wearing dirty frocks at their head. Old crones, he realized. Their speakers. Gray hair the color and consistency of steel wool hung down their backs. Their arms were folded at their waists. The moment Acker set foot on even ground, Brendon halted and raised his banner. Marrick and Moser drew in to either side. The clans rolled forward, a league and a half away. One league. Half a league.

"Sir," Marrick said tightly.

"Hold." Brendon watched them draw nearer. The banner remained raised over his head, his arms as still as a mountain in a storm.

At last the clans slowed. The eight crones continued forward. One by one, twelve enormous men—some wearing armor, others bare-chested so that their sweaty chests covered in tattoos seemed to glow—broke away like sparks from a bonfire. They closed in around the women. The crones glided. Their escort moved in long, heavy strides.

Brendon's eyes narrowed. The dozen clansmen surrounding the crones appeared . . . different. Human, but less, somehow.

The tallest wore bearskin and a helm fashioned after a bear's head, but his exposed arms and legs were so hairy, his fingernails so long, that Brendon had trouble finding where the bearskin ended and the man began. Another, a tall and lean warrior whose face was hidden within a helm resembling an adder's head, exhibited pale skin that looked slimy in the Lady's growing light, pink fading to blue and gold.

A shiver threatened to disturb Brendon's calm. He suppressed it. The general sensed that these Darinians were harder and colder than any he had ever met, and that any weakness on his part would be tantamount to a wolf smelling blood on the deer that so boldly returned its gaze.

Fifty paces. Forty. Thirty.

At thirty paces away, the crones stopped. Their entourage stopped with them. As if one shared mind controlled all twenty clansfolk. One, the oldest of the bunch judging by a face covered in hundreds of seams and creases, lifted her eyes to the banner waving over Brendon's head. An "H" with a sword sheathed through its center bar.

"The time for talk has passed, Wardsman," one of the men said in halting common. It was difficult to tell who had spoken. Their helmets amplified their voices, giving them a resonate quality without revealing their mouths.

Slowly, arms burning from exertion, Brendon lowered the banner and placed it carefully across Acker's back. "I bring word of a truce," he called.

A breeze teased the long grass. The clansman who resembled an adder in both helm and body laughed softly, a low susurration. *Like a hiss,* Brendon thought.

"It is too late for that," the adder-man said.

"You insult us," said another deep voice. All the clansfolk stood frozen. "Where is your Crown? Where is your general?"

"I am General Brendon Greagor of Torel's Ward," Brendon answered.

Another low hiss. "What is this deception?" said the adder-man.

"Torel is not the deceiver, but the deceived," Brendon said. "Like our allies in the west, the north has been manipulated. We propose a truce. A renewal of bonds eight hundred years strong."

"Your Crown killed our war chief and his woman," a baritone

voice replied. "He slaughtered one thousand of our number not half a mile from where we stand."

"There will be no truce," another deep voice said. "We have come for blood."

Brendon kept his face smooth. "Where is your war chief?"

At that, some of the crones exchanged glances. One, short and bent-backed, grinned a toothless smile. "The *Nuulass* comes."

"The *Nuulass* comes," the other nineteen echoed.

Nuulass? The term—some sort of entity, he guessed—was unfamiliar. He ignored it. "I bring word from Edmund Calderon, retired general of Torel's Ward, and his son, Aidan Gairden, Guardian Light, King of Torel, Crown of the—"

A low rumbling filled the air. Brendon swallowed. They were growling. He ran his eyes over the assemblage. *The one in the wolf helm*, he decided. Eyes as red as hot coals stared back unblinkingly. Those eyes narrowed, and Brendon looked away. Not at the ground, but at the first crone who had eyed his banner speculatively, and who had remained silent ever since.

"The blood of Romen of the Wolf and Cynthia Alston is not on Torel's hands," he said.

"But the blood of those who returned to the ground here stains Aidan Gairden's hands," the eldest speaker said in a firm voice.

"Yes," Brendon said simply.

Beside him, Marrick and Moser stirred. The crones narrowed their eyes. The clansmen said nothing, did not so much as move. The crones gathered around the first, putting their heads together. When they parted, the first stepped forward. "I am Margia of the Falcon," she said. "I will hear you, Brendon Greagor."

Sensing there was more, Brendon waited.

"But know this," Margia of the Falcon went on. "The *Nuulass* has awakened. Its blood courses through our veins. It speaks to us through our war chief. Should she—should it—judge you guilty of treachery, you will die. Your Wardsmen will die. When next winter snows cover your land, they will freeze the blood that will run through your paved streets."

Another breeze caressed the grass.

"I understand," Brendon said, voice hollow but strong. He dismounted. Marrick and Moser followed suit. They led their mounts forward, and the clansmen broke ranks as they approached, forming a circular wall of flesh and armor that parted to admit Brendon and his lieutenants. Raspy breaths coming from deep within helms pimpled his arms with gooseflesh.

Margia of the Falcon stood at the fore of the cluster of Darinians. "Speak," she said.

"I do not know all the details," Brendon said. He raised gauntleted hands to show they were empty. "May I retrieve a message sent to me by Edmund Calderon?"

Margia nodded. Brendon peeled off his gauntlets and reached into a pocket, eyes steady on the speaker's face. He brought out the missive, unfolded it, and opened his mouth to read. Margia held out a wrinkled hand. Brendon handed it over.

The other crones crowded around Margia. Their eyes scanned the paper as one, moving from left to right, then back again. When she finished, she held it out to him. "The Eternal Flame. This is true? You swear to it?"

"The north swears," Brendon said.

Margia studied him. Behind her, the other speakers murmured. He thought he caught a name: Jonathan Hillstreem. It struck him as familiar, in a vague sort of way.

"Where is Aidan Gairden?" Margia of the Falcon said suddenly. "Why does he insult me by sending a newborn general to do his talking for him?"

Brendon gathered his courage. "He is in the west, with Nichel of the Wolf."

All at once the murmurs ceased. The clansman in the wolf helm growled. The adder-man hissed. As one, the clansmen closed in, trapping the three Wardsmen in a tight circle. Marrick and Moser reached for their swords, but Brendon raised a hand.

"The Crown of the North went to throw himself at Nichel of the Wolf's mercy." He did not know if this was strictly true. Christine had told him only that Aidan was in the west. Yet the words rang true to him. Of the royal family he loved as if they were his blood, only Aidan had been himself these past few months, except for the attack at Sharem, but even then, Aidan had only carried out orders. Brendon also disagreed with the war on Darinia, but it had not been his place to question, just as it had not been Aidan's place to defy his mother's ruling, misguided though it had seemed at the time.

"You disgrace the *Nuulass* by letting her earthly name pass through your lips," Margia said. Her words trembled with anger.

Brendon allowed himself a moment of absolute confusion—*Hadn't Margia referred to this* Nuulass *as an it?*—then banished it. He could not afford time to think, or to hesitate. Marrick and Moser clutched sword hilts but did not draw steel.

"My apologies," Brendon said. "I am not familiar with this custom. I only pass on news passed to me."

"Who said this?"

"One of the Touched."

"One under the Eternal Flame's control?" Margia said. Her lips peeled back. Then, with a great effort, she smoothed her expression. "Heel," she barked.

The clansmen went still. Growls and hisses died away. Once again Brendon was struck by the sense that these men were less than human. *Or more than.*

Margia and the crones closed their eyes. Their eyelids fluttered, as if some small insect scurried beneath.

"General?" Marrick whispered.

Brendon gave a slight shake of his head.

Minutes passed. Overhead, the Lady of Dawn grew brighter. Her glory melted away mist to reveal blue sky. It would be a glorious day.

The crones' eyes shot open. Brendon's throat moved. Marrick and Moser jumped. "Dawn and Dusk," Moser cursed hoarsely.

"The *Nuulass* remains in the west," Margia said. Her voice was dry, as if she had not wet her throat for days. Swallowing, she spoke again. Her words were stronger. "Our war chief lives. Yet danger lurks."

Brendon opened his mouth, snapped it shut. *Is Aidan the danger?* he had nearly asked. A question that would have doomed him and the north for certain.

"The *Nuulass* thirsts for blood. Your blood. Our blood. All blood," the old woman continued. Her face was expressionless, but the clansmen hunched further, shivering as with cold. Their weapons thudded to the grass. Hands hooked into claws.

"You have until the Father and his Vanguard reach their apex," Margia said. She fixed Brendon with eyes colder than any northern winter. "If our war chief does not stand beside us then, or harm befalls her in the interim, the North will die."

Chapter 41:
Ransacked

DANIEL DUCKED INTO an alleyway and sagged against a pile of scrap wood. He was filthy, exhausted, and covered in sweat. From behind him came a chorus of shouts and the steady pounding of hammers. Orange rays of morning light winked at him from between rooftops. He cursed and pulled his helmet over his eyes. If he could just sleep for five minutes . . . maybe five hours . . .

"Sergeant!"

Daniel ignored the voice. He was no sergeant. A hand shook him roughly on the shoulder. His eyes snapped open. Scrambling upright, a small golden pin fell from his collar and clinked against the stone. "What?"

Karter Rosen glared through bleary eyes. He pointed to the pin on the ground. "You'd better get used to that. People need to see order and rank."

Daniel stooped over and retrieved the pin, a single golden bar, and fastened it to his collar. "Dawn-burned thing won't stay fastened."

"You have to wear it."

"Fine. Was there something you wanted?"

"They're back."

"Who?" Then he gave a start.

Karter's face sobered. "Come on." He dashed out of the alley and into the crowded street. Daniel followed. His heart pounded in time with his footsteps. A steady stream of civilians and merchants flowed toward them. Daniel and Karter threaded their way through, barking for dawdlers to move faster. The sergeants had ordered all vendors to close up shop and evacuate into the east, west, and northern districts so the Ward could build fortifications without anyone underfoot. Storefronts sat dark and vacant, like harbinger eye sockets.

They raced through the center of Calewind, cutting a straight line into the western district. At Old Beld's smithy, they weaved behind his forge to an old hut. Cinder Toban Kirkus sat hunched on a bench, hands folded and head bowed. Scorch marks decorated his red robe like black ribbons. Refugees milled around him. They were farmers and peasants wearing cloth shirts and breeches, and boots stippled with holes. Bags drooped under their eyes. Their faces were tight and drawn. Three larger men wearing white shirts and pants covered in grime and blood huddled together and stared with dull eyes and open mouths. *Traumatized*, Daniel decided.

Hearing their approach, Cinder Toban Kirkus raised his head. Daniel ignored him. Alix stood with an older man and woman. She had one arm looped around the woman's neck, and her head buried against the man's chest. The woman's shoulders shook as she clung to Alix. *Her mother*, Daniel thought. *Must be.* The man had one hand placed absently on her shoulders, staring vacantly through red-rimmed eyes.

Daniel started to turn away. Then Alix raised her head, and he got a clear look at her as she wiped away tears. He took a step toward her.

Karter caught his arm. "Not now." He turned to Toban. "What happened, Hand?"

Toban Kirkus heaved a sigh. "Gotik's gone. Burned and pillaged," he said hoarsely.

"Vagrants?" Daniel asked.

"A whole pack of them. Twenty, maybe thirty. I took the tunnels, just like you said. Came out through a trapdoor that opened in the back of a barn. I heard screams and smelled smoke right away. The dead walked the streets, and they . . . they cut people down right where they stood."

The Cinder scrubbed a hand over his face. "I directed the

townsfolk down into the tunnel. Most of them made it. And now here we are. If I had . . ." His voice, raw and dry, trailed off. A Wardsman ran up and handed him a glass of water. Toban downed it in a single gulp. "If I had gotten there sooner, I might have been able to save more of them." His attention was fixed on a point in the distance.

"You can't think like that, Hand," Karter said. "Your efforts saved lives. I appreciate your courage. I know the Crown does, too."

Toban inhaled deeply. "Has anyone else made it back?"

Karter swallowed. "No." He stole a glance at Daniel, who could guess what he—and likely Toban—were thinking. Two scholars from the east, south, and west districts had been sent into the tunnels, but from what Aidan and Toban had told him, their ability as Touched was more suited to book learning than fighting and underground rescue missions.

"Well." Toban hauled himself to his feet. "I'm spent, but I dare not sleep. If I find a bed, I'm apt to never stand again." He regarded Daniel. "I believe you have something for me." Without another word, he set off toward Sunfall.

Daniel fell into step beside him. "I'm sure you did your best." He winced. The words sounded hollow.

Toban laughed. "The trouble with doing our best, Wardsman Shirey, is that sometimes our best is not good enough. Those people blame me for the deaths of loved ones. They might not say it, or even be conscious of it, but blame is there, and I feel it."

"That's grief talking," Daniel said. "They're glad to be alive. They're just in shock."

Toban said nothing. They ascended the mountain path and entered Sunfall in silence. The southern vestibule was empty. The doors to the throne room were closed. Toban slowed, letting Daniel take the lead. He guided the Cinder down corridors and out the side entrance leading into the eastern courtyard and climbed the stairs of the tower.

They found Tyrnen's quarters as they had left them: cluttered with books and scrolls and trinkets, air redolent with the scent of old wood, lantern oil, and parchment. Daniel loosed a breath he hadn't realized he'd been holding. Aidan had told him once that he found the tower room's smells comforting. He wondered how his friend felt about them now.

"What's the matter?" Toban asked.

Daniel jumped. "Nothing. It's just . . ." He shrugged, embarrassed. To his surprise, Toban did not laugh.

"I don't like it here, either. Yesterday, the Eternal Flame's tower seemed like the most wondrous place on Crotaria. I suppose that's still true. There may be more knowledge in this room than in the grand library of the Temple of Dawn. That moon book alone is worth one hundred times its weight in Leastonian marks." The light in his eyes faded. "Now I wish I'd never seen it. I wish I'd never seen most of what I've seen since our fates became intertwined."

Leaning his *Sard'tara* on Tyrnen's desk, Daniel rapped his knuckles against its surface twice, then dipped his hand into the secret compartment. He withdrew the moon book and held it out to Toban. The Cinder took it without comment, opening it to leaf through its pages. Daniel shivered and glanced at the window. grey clouds were rolling in. *Just the weather. Not the damn book.*

Behind them, the door creaked, and Alix stepped through. Daniel's heart lifted, and then dropped into his stomach. Her eyes were red and wet. *At least she knows her parents are alive.* A ray of the Lady's light broke through the cloud cover, filtered through Tyrnen's window, and glinted against the necklace around Alix's neck.

"What would you have me do?" Toban asked, looking up from the moon book. Distracted, Daniel turned back to him. His gaze fell on open pages. Words written in a flowing script mingled with elaborate diagrams, ingredient lists, and equations.

"You're asking me?" Daniel said.

"You are aware of the capital's defenses and which areas need fortifying, yes?"

Daniel chewed his lower lip, avoiding Alix's gaze. She folded her arms and leaned against the doorframe, watching him. Her face was stony. "I don't know," he mumbled. "Just use those spells, and the ones you already know, and go around and . . ." He waggled his fingers. "Magic things."

Toban's brow soared. "*Magic* things?"

Daniel removed his helmet and ran a hand through his hair. He could feel Alix's eyes on him. What she had said the previous day, the last time they were in the tower, came back. *You have a way with words.* He squared his shoulders. "They're going to hit hard. Hordes of them. Possibly—no, likely—at every gate." He studied the floor, thinking. "We need to do more than hold them back. They have overwhelming numbers."

"Yes, yes," Toban said impatiently. "But how?"

Daniel looked up. "Let them get in, and then break them apart."

Toban expelled breath slowly. "Risky."

"Calculated," Daniel replied. "I'm not saying to just open the gates and invite them in. We need to hit them hard outside. My point, they're going to break through. The Ward is preparing for that. It's why we're evacuating everyone into the northern half of the city. Once they're in, we need to do more than throw rocks and pour boiling pitch. Search through that book and find magic that causes as much devastation as possible."

Toban shook his head. "You don't seem to understand. Judging from what I've managed to glean from this book, and from my brief excursion through the tunnels, dark magic is not predicated on wanton destruction. Light magic is considerably more effective in that regard. It comes from fire. Fire destroys, yet it also heals. Dark magic favors deception and trickery."

Daniel's lips rose in a bleak smile. "Precisely. The southern district will be empty. Hit them hard outside to draw them inside, then, once they're in, they'll be like fish in a net. Light magic, dark magic. Use whatever you've got to skin them once we have them."

Toban's fleshy face split in a smile. "Magic things, in other words?"

"That's right."

Toban looked down at the book. "I'm alone, aren't I?"

"No," Daniel said. "There are still the inventors."

"They had a breakthrough," Alix cut in, stepping up beside Daniel.

"They've invented a lantern," Daniel said excitedly.

Toban gave him a flat stare. "Lanterns have been around for quite a while."

"It's no ordinary lantern," Daniel said, growing more animated. Knowing more about a subject than Toban delighted him. "They call it a lamp, but this type of lamp holds light the same way a jug holds water."

"You expose it to light during the day," Alix added, "and at night—"

"You kindle from it," Toban breathed. Daniel and Alix shared a smile. A moment later, her grin faltered and she turned away. Daniel's excitement faded. Right then, getting back in Alix's good graces meant more to him than fortifying Aidan's city.

"Dawn and Dusk, those useless intellectuals actually made something worthwhile," Toban said. "How many do they have?"

Daniel raised his eyebrows at Alix. He remembered, but he wanted to keep her engaged.

"I saw five, maybe six," she said.

The Cinder snapped his book closed and tucked it into the folds of his robes. "We will speak to the inventors immediately."

"We?" Daniel repeated. "Why do you want me to go?"

"Certainly not for your company. You will be my pack mule."

"I'm flattered."

"Best to be prepared," Toban said, as if he had not heard. "Would a man journeying through the Plains of Dust bring one water skin, or several?"

"All right," Daniel said. "As long as Alix comes, too."

Alix narrowed her eyes. "Why?"

"Because Emerus took a liking to you, and so did his friend."

"That old hag?" Alix snorted. "She's horrible. I'll bet she's never taken a liking to anyone in her life. I've seen more personality from dead trees. I'm only going because I care about the defense of this city."

"And because you have something that belongs to Emerus," Daniel said.

Alix's face colored. One hand went to the necklace at her throat. Turning away from him, she stalked over to Toban's right side and grabbed his fleshy hand. The Cinder extended his left hand, and Daniel took it, gripping his *Sard'tara* hard in his right. "Close your eyes," Toban told them. "Shifting is less jarring that way."

Daniel did as he was told just in time. The floor was ripped out from under them. Alix let out a gasp, and then a gust of wind scattered loose papers and toppled the stack of open books on one corner of Tyrnen's desk.

In a fraction of a second they jumped from Tyrnen's musty, book-logged tower to the clean, carpeted interior of the Spire. Daniel opened his eyes was immediately uneasy. Chairs, tables, and bookcases sat deserted. No buzz of conversation or rifling of pages came from the mezzanines above.

Toban brushed absently at his arms. "Someone just kindled."

"How close by?" Daniel asked.

"Two levels, at least," Toban sat, craning his neck to stare up.

Alix's hand went to the pommel of Jak's sword. "You don't think . . ." she began.

"I do," Daniel said.

"The lab," Toban said. His words were like a whip crack in the large, empty space. They charged across the floor. Toban reached the lift first. Daniel and Alix crowded on behind him. "Level three," the Cinder snapped.

A blue nimbus surrounded the platform, and it rose with a low *hum-m-m.* Sofas, chairs, bookcases, and rugs grew smaller beneath them. Level two appeared, identical except for green rugs instead of orange. The steady droning of the magical lift was deafening in the heavy silence.

Alix gripped his arm, her nails digging into his sleeve. "Look."

Daniel tried to swallow around the lump in his throat. As they flew above level two, bloodstains spoiled the blue carpeting. Bookcases had been overturned. Sofas and chairs had been gutted; feathers lay strewn like entrails.

"Where are the bodies?" Alix wondered aloud. But she knew. They all did.

The lift slowed at the third mezzanine, stopped flush with the railing. More bloodstains, no bodies. Toban slapped at the gate and rushed forward. Alix turned to Daniel. Her face was drained of color, lips pale as snow. *I'll die before I let anything happen to you,* he thought. What he said out loud was, "Stay behind me."

He raised his *Sard'tara* diagonally across his chest. He stepped off the lift, heard Alix fall in behind him. Another low *hum-m-m* signaled the disappearance of the lift. Alix gasped and went for her sword. Daniel looked up in time to see a large form hunched over the tables where Emerus had proudly displayed his creations. The figure straightened. Emerus. His face was waxen, his eyes blank. He raised his hand.

"Down!" Daniel shouted, and tackled Alix to the floor as a gout of fire rushed over them. Tongues of flame collided against the wall behind them and flew apart in sparks. The room grew brighter. Alix screamed, but the roar of the fire swallowed it.

Daniel opened his eyes. Alix trembled beneath him. Her head

was cradled against his heart, which was beating fast and hard enough to make him dizzy. "Are you all right?" he said, louder than he intended. He could still hear fire roaring in his ears. She nodded against him.

There were muffled shouts followed by a crash. Daniel stood quickly, extending a hand. She took it and he hauled her upright. All around them, fire devoured furniture and books. Smoke filled the space, stinging their eyes. Without another word they charged across the level, free hands clapped over their mouths and noses. Tendrils of smoke rose from the shattered table. Two of the four lamps, the rodules, had been smashed into pieces. Fragments lay spilled in the Lady's light streaming through the window. They did not glow golden. He had a sudden vision of punctured water skins, unable to hold liquid.

Toban was locked in a struggle against Emerus and the severe-looking woman. Their feet crunched against wood and broken glass. Toban had his hands wrapped around Emerus's throat. Emerus's face was blank. His right hand grasped a knife bent like a crooked finger. Its glassy blade grew brighter, flaring like the Lady on a summer day. *The Nail of Dawn*. It quivered in Emerus's grasp. Toban, purple-faced, strained to reach it, but Emerus was lankier and able to hold the weapon out of reach.

The old woman noticed Daniel and Alix. Her palms began to glow. Fire formed in her hands, swelling like a bubble. Heat filled the room. Daniel baked, roasting alive inside his steel and snow. Quickly, he measured the distance between him and the woman. It was too great. They were going to die here.

I'm sorry, Aidan. I couldn't protect you this time.

As suddenly as the heat had begun, it was gone, as if a bonfire had been doused. When Daniel's vision cleared, he saw the old woman on her knees. Jak's sword stuck out of her head. Her face had gone slack. Alix smiled shakily, then directed her gaze to Toban. The Cinder had one meaty paw wrapped around Emerus's robes. The other gripped the wrist of the hand holding the Nail. It shook, and Toban's face was purple with strain.

Toban's eyes found his. Panic clouded them. Daniel rushed forward, shouting, "Set fire to his robes!"

The Cinder's wide, terrified eyes narrowed. A moment later, fire forked up and spread over the inventor's white robe. Emerus pushed Toban away with astonishing strength and looked down at the fire racing over his chest, appearing more curious than alarmed. That moment of distraction was all Daniel needed. He swung his *Sard'tara* up in an arc, severing the inventor's bony hand at the wrist. Hand and Nail of Dawn clattered to the ground. Emerus stooped, intent on recovering the lamp. Daniel lashed out again. The harbinger saw the blow coming and jerked to the side. Its movement threw off Daniel's aim enough for Daniel's *Sard'tara* to pierce the undead inventor's breast. Emerus thrashed, trying to pull free. Panting, Toban dove for the Nail and, in one smooth motion, brought it up and drove it through Emerus's belly.

"Aim for the head," Daniel gasped. "Aim for the—"

Emerus jerked one last time, then fell still. "What in Kahltan's name," Alix muttered.

Toban pointed. "The knife! Something's wrong with the knife!"

Golden light drained out of the Nail of Dawn, emptying from pommel to the tip of its crooked blade. Emerus shook harder. His face turned pink, purple, red. He burst into flame. Daniel shouted and stumbled back. There was a blinding flash. When Daniel's vision cleared, a charred pile of melted bones sat at the base of the far wall. Red and green blood painted the walls and floor.

Daniel's stomach turned. He looked away, searching for Alix. She sat behind him, palms and booted feet flat against the floor, like a crab, gaping at the harbinger's remains. Her complexion was a pale shade of green.

"Look at me," Daniel said softly. She blinked and found him. "Are you all right?"

She nodded. "You?"

"Yes." Daniel rose shakily to his feet. Miraculously, his *Sard'tara* was still in one piece, though the shaft was scorched. Alix stood slowly, brushing her trousers.

Toban scrambled forward on hands and knees to inspect Emerus's body. "Dawn and Dusk," he cursed.

Breathing through his mouth, Daniel moved beside the Cinder. The Nail of Dawn was plastered to Emerus's chest like a melted badge. Toban reached for the remains, jerked his hand away with a hiss. Breathing hard, his robes and face damp with sweat, he heaved himself to his feet. They looked around silently, taking in the blood, the fire crackling contentedly along the carpeting, the pall of smoke.

Toban raised his arms, let them fall. "What now?"

Alix swallowed, coughed, and reached behind her neck. She held her lamp out to him. "I think you're going to need this," she croaked.

Chapter 42:
Right and Wrong Words

KARTER WRINKLED HIS nose. "You smell awful."

"And you're ugly," Daniel said. "At least I'll smell like a rose garden after a bath."

Karter's lips twitched. He sat at the head of a long table with slumped shoulders and half-lidded eyes. The other sergeants sat around them. To a man, they were covered in grime. The long table had been carried out of the throne room and placed in the center of the garrison training room, a vast hall lined with racks bearing swords, axes, spears, polearms, and other implements. Large rugs stained with oil, sweat, and blood lay at the base of each rack. Torches flickered on stone walls. There were no windows. The Touched felt soothed by windows, comforted by the Lady's light, but too many points of ingress made Wardsmen uneasy.

Daniel trudged over to the only empty chair at the table. Alix walked behind him, vacant-eyed and dirty. He pulled the chair out. "You should sit," he said to Alix.

"I'm only an honorary Wardsman. I'll stand."

"I insist."

Alix crossed her arms. "I'll stand."

Karter stood up and snapped his fingers at a Wardsman standing guard at the entrance. "Bring the lady a chair. She's earned a seat." The Wardsman hurried off, steel and snow jangling. The runner returned, set a chair, saluted, and hurried back to his post at the door. "Make room," Karter barked. Chair legs scraped against stone as the sergeants to either side of Daniel scooted down. Muttering, Alix dropped into her chair. Daniel sank down next to her.

Karter removed his gloves. "Report?"

"The Spire is lost," Daniel said.

"The inventors?" Karter asked.

"Dead, or . . ."

His words hung in the air. "We still have Cinder Kirkus," Alix said.

"How is the Hand?" Karter asked.

"As well as can be expected," Daniel said. "The inventors were working on artefacts called lamps that let Touched store light for later use. We think the lab was attacked so that the harbingers could get their hands on the lamps."

"Did they?" said another sergeant.

"Toban has the only remaining artefact that we know of," said Alix.

"How could the enemy have known about these lamps?" asked Raymond Porter.

Daniel sat back. "I think I know who's leading them." Briefly he filled them in on his past with Garrett Lorden. "Now he's one of Tyrnen's coconspirators." He snorted. "Sycophant, more like." Deriding Garrett bolstered his courage. "If I know about the tunnels, it stands to reason that Tyrnen and Garrett do, as well."

Karter chewed the inside of one cheek. "That would explain the attack in Sunfall."

"And the Spire," Alix said.

"I sealed the tunnel in the eastern courtyard," Daniel said. "The only one open is the one near Old Beld's smithy, the old hut next to it."

"It's such an eyesore," John Steele said.

"That's the point," Daniel said. "No one would think to look there. The Crowns of the North have known about the tunnels for centuries, I'd guess. There's an understanding between the Crown and the merchant's guild: As long as the sneaks don't steal any secrets or goods the north doesn't want them to have, they can come and go as they please."

Karter sat back, looking pensive. "We could assign men to guard the hut."

Daniel shook his head. "The tunnels are massive. Think of them like underground roadways. Five Wardsmen couldn't stop a large force if Garrett decided to enter the city that way."

"So we assign more than five."

"We're already undermanned at the gates."

"We could block it off," Kieran Wood suggested. "Pile a bunch of rocks in front of the entrance, or get Cinder Toban to, I don't know . . ."

"Good idea, but not good enough," Daniel said. A block of ice was forming in his belly. "Garrett has harbingers. A harbinger could blast through a mound of rocks or undo any magic of Toban's in a blink."

"Plus, we've got refugees to think about," Karter added. "None of the scholars have returned as yet, but Toban's appearance is a good sign."

Daniel stared at the tabletop. "I think we should close it."

Karter leaned forward. "It's only been a day. We have to give the others more time to deliver their messages. For Dawn's sake, Cinder Toban went to Gotik. That's the closest village to Calewind, and it took him hours to make his way home."

"Because Gotik was under attack," Daniel said. "And because he was too tired to harness the magic of the tunnels, so he had to walk."

A heavy silence fell. "What are you suggesting?" Karter said.

Daniel glanced at Alix. She nodded. Taking a deep breath, he shared his plan. An uproar broke out at the table.

"You can't be serious!"

"My family's coming from Tarion! It's a big city, they just need more time—"

"We're condemning those people to death."

"No, Shirey is condemning those people to death."

Daniel flinched. That last had come from Raymond. He did not defend himself. How could he? Raymond was right. They all were. Daniel and Alix sat mutely. At last, Karter lifted a hand. "Your brothers are not wrong, Sergeant," he said, holding Daniel's gaze. "You could be sentencing Torelians to death."

Daniel let out a long, heavy sigh. "Calewind's population is greater than every other city and village in the north combined.

If we don't act, tens of thousands will die. Every corpse grows Tyrnen's army."

Karter chewed his lip. "And the Crown? What of him?"

Daniel's head was pounding. "Aidan will be fine. He's a Touched, maybe the most powerful who ever lived. That's what Tyrnen used to say. We've got to think of Calewind. The plan to evacuate towns and cities in the undead's path was sound when we thought we had more than one Hand of Torel still in the city. But Toban is it. He's our only magical defense against what's coming. Against what's already outside our gates."

He looked around the table. "Tell me I'm wrong," Daniel said, almost pleading. "Tell me there's another way." They lowered their eyes. He turned to Alix, sick with desperation. She looked away from him, staring at her hands.

Karter straightened. "Best to do it now, then."

Daniel's limbs turned to stone. "Right now?"

"You're the one who said putting it off could mean—"

"No, you're right," Daniel said weakly.

Karter's expression held sympathy. "Should I call for Cinder Toban? Dawn knows where he is, with a whole city to magically fortify."

"I can do it. I'm a sneak, or at least, I was. All the sneaks know how to close a tunnel."

"Right, then," Karter said. "We're off to Old Beld's smithy."

"All of us?" Kieran asked. "We have our own positions to hold."

"They can wait," Karter said. "Last I saw, the crowd near the smithy had grown considerably. They're not going to be pleased."

"I don't blame them," Raymond said tightly. Daniel regarded him. The other man's eyes brimmed with tears.

Karter stepped in front of Raymond. "Blame him or don't. But you will do your duty as a Wardsman to the Crown."

They glared at one another, breathing hard through their nostrils. Raymond dropped his eyes. "My family," he whispered to the floor.

Karter clapped a hand to his shoulder. "I know. Mine, too." He looked away, blinking and swallowing. When he turned back, he had brought his emotions under control. "We swore an oath."

Daniel's respect for Karter swelled. "I'm still open to other ideas." No one spoke. No one met his eyes, not even Alix.

DANIEL HEARD THE crowd before he saw them. People from all districts stood crammed elbow to elbow or perched on the rooftops of surrounding buildings, talking animatedly as their legs dangled over the ground. Old Beld seemed oblivious to their presence. He brought his hammer crashing down again and again, pounding blade after blade after blade.

The ground in front of the crumbling old hut was clear. Daniel froze in front of it. He knew what to do, and how to do it. Once he did, there was no turning back.

The crowd grew quiet. He turned to see his brothers, sergeants all, fanned out around the hut. "What's going on?" called a man from above.

"Ward business," Karter barked. He turned to Daniel. "Get going."

Alix slipped through the line. "You heard the sergeant. Let's go."

"You're going with me?" Daniel said.

"Moral support."

"I'll take it." He opened the door to the hut and stepped inside. Alix squeezed in after him and closed the door. Daniel walked forward in three careful, measured steps. On the fourth, his boot met air. He turned, lowered himself to his knees, and groped around again until his foot met a rung on a ladder leading down.

"Careful," he said, descending. He could hear her shuffling around, and then the steady *clomp, clomp* of boots on steel rungs. Daniel's elbows brushed against the sides of the hole. It was narrow, and smelled of old, packed earth. Minutes later, his boots touched ground. He stepped off and back, giving Alix room to find her footing. Daniel groped at the rung, wrapped his fingers around a brass handle, and took out a flint pack. There was a flash, and he held up a lantern. Dim light filled the cramped, circular space. Behind him a tunnel led into darkness.

They set off down the narrow, twisty path. Inky veins ran along either wall, like an unravelling thread. The smell of old earth and stone grew stronger. Alix stepped closer to him. Their arms brushed together. He glanced at her. "I'm cold, and you've got the light," she said.

They walked on for a time. "Am I wrong?" he asked. "There's still time to think of something else."

"No, there isn't."

Their footsteps crunched against dirt and stones. "What will you do next?" he asked.

"Next?"

"After the war. After Aidan defeats Tyrnen."

"If that happens—"

"It will."

She glanced at him. "I've dreamed of seeing the other realms. Visiting Ironsail, working on a ship, saving up for my own and setting sail. Now that I know about these tunnels, there's nothing stopping me, I guess."

"Except not knowing where any of them lead."

Daniel caught her smile in the dark. "Except that."

"Where will you sail?"

"Anywhere."

"Crotaria's not so bad."

"You've seen more of it than I have."

"Not much excitement in Gotik, I gather?"

"Only if you don't count the arrival of peddlers from the east every spring. My mother positively quivered at the notion of buying new pots and pans this year." She reached out and touched a vein, then shivered and wiped her hand on her trousers. "Yuck. It feels like . . ."

"Like mud flecked with ice?"

She nodded, still scrubbing her hand on her leg. "What is it?"

"No one knows, exactly. There are theories."

"Such as?"

"Such as the blood of Touched who gave their lives to build the network of tunnels."

"Really?"

"That's one theory. Like I said, no one knows for certain."

"Wouldn't it be fun to find out?"

Glancing at her, he saw a familiar glint in her eyes. "I guess."

"You guess? You don't want to know?"

"No one can know everything, can they? What makes you want to see the world?"

"To see what's around the next corner," she said. The path sloped downward.

"Suppose you go everywhere, see everything. What then?"

"Well, I guess I'd . . ."

"You'd get bored again."

Alix did not reply right away. "It's different for you. Look at all you've done. You lived in Ironsail. You ran with a thieves' guild—"

"*The* thieves' guild," he said pompously.

"Your best friend is the most powerful man on Crotaria, maybe the world—"

"Don't tell him that. His head is already too big."

"And now you live in Calewind, the most fabulous city on Crotaria."

"You're forgetting the part where I almost died—more than once—fleeing from horrors straight out of a nightmare." He paused. "They really do come from nightmares."

"I see your point," Alix said. "But I still want to see it all."

"I'm surprised you hadn't left home sooner."

"Jak left first. Someone had to help my folks, farm boy. My father opened a lumber business. He taught me carpentry. Together, we—"

The slope ended. As they stepped onto flat ground, Alix stumbled. Without thinking, Daniel grabbed her around the waist. They stood for a moment, listening to each other draw breath. Then Alix wriggled free. "You wanted to talk. You've spent lots of words, but none were the ones I hoped to hear."

"I don't understand," he said.

She continued walking. The trail became sinuous. Up ahead, Daniel saw flickers of purple light. "You'll be able to see it," he said.

"See what?"

"I could take you to Ironsail, when all this is over. I have friends there."

"Sneaks?"

"Of course. And they have ships."

"Of their own?"

"Borrowed," he said solemnly.

Alix smiled. Before he could press his luck, they emerged in a waypoint. Arched tunnels ran along the walls from the ground all the way up to the shadowy ceiling. Glowing purple threads ran into the dark mouth of each tunnel. Netting clung to the walls like cobweb. Stone columns lined the cave. Ornate symbols had been hand-carved into each one.

Alix moved to the column nearest their tunnel and ran her

hand along it. "I wondered about these my first time through. Do they mean anything?"

"Most of them don't. But look along the bottom, on the other side."

Alix rounded the column and knelt. "The Gairden crest?"

"It indicates—"

"That the tunnel we used leads to Calewind," she guessed, rising.

"Right," Daniel said. "Most tunnels that open up on some major landmark exhibit some special marker in nearby waypoints. That way those who have to walk the tunnels—us ungifted—can be certain we're going the right way."

"Kind of like a second key? That seems dangerous. Anyone who meant the Crown harm could just follow this marker straight into the capital."

"Naturally. That's why whoever built this place planned ahead. Most waypoints don't have columns. Either you know the key to the tunnel you want, and you follow it from waypoint to waypoint, or you know where to look for special markers like this one."

Overhead, bats fluttered and keened. Alix hugged her arms, rubbing them briskly. "How do you do this?"

The reality of what he was about to do crashed into him. Cramps knotted his belly. Afraid to speak for fear of retching, he crossed to a small table covered in maps, writing utensils, rations. Crouching, he felt along the ground under the table until his nails dug into neat edges, like gaps between floorboards. He lifted a stone cover. Beneath it, in a shallow compartment, was a stick of what appeared to be chalk as long and thick as a forefinger. A towel lay beside it, neatly folded. Daniel removed the stick and went over to the tunnel where they had emerged. Alix followed, curious.

Daniel stopped in front of the mouth of the tunnel. The key, an "H" lying on its side, was carved into the stone. Beside it was a single vertical bar. Daniel raised the stick, and Alix gasped. It was stone slathered with the same viscous substance threaded along the walls of the tunnels. Tightening his grip, he pressed it to one side of the vertical bar and drew a line through its middle. When he finished, it resembled a cross. He stepped back. The threads running along the walls back the way they'd come faded, like the last of Dawnfall draining from the sky, giving way to darkness.

"Is that it?" Alix asked. "Is it done?"

Daniel tossed the stick into its secret compartment and replaced the stone cover. "Almost. Come on." He grabbed her hand and ran back into the tunnel.

"Why the hurry? What—"

Behind Alix, stone ground on stone. She yelped and ran ahead until she was the one pulling him onward. They turned and watched a stone barrier slide up from the ground to cover the egress into the waypoint, like a lower jaw closing. Without the soft glow of the veins, their lantern was the only source of light in the passage. Alix crossed to the barrier. "How did you do it?" she asked, running her hands over its surface. Daniel knew from experience that it was cool and perfectly smooth.

"The same way I sealed the one you entered the city by, and through which Aidan departed," he said. "Used a key. Now no one can come in or leave this way."

Hugging herself, Alix shivered. "Unless they have that . . . that key you replaced."

Daniel shook his head. "That's not how it works. Trust me." He gave her a tight smile. "Now we go tell the people of Calewind."

Alix stepped forward, resolved. "Come on. We'll tell them together."

ANGRY SHOUTS DRIFTED down the tunnel as Daniel and Alix climbed. He trembled like a man with fever. His hands were cold. One foot up the next rung, one after the other. If he stopped now, he would never be able to get started again. The cries grew louder with each rung he climbed. When his head brushed the trapdoor, he reached up and shoved it aside. He clambered up and out, reached down to help Alix.

"Ready?" she asked as they faced the door. Daniel couldn't answer. The tumult outside was deafening through the hut's thin walls.

"I suppose I have to be." He pushed open the door.

People crowded in, standing a dozen, two dozen deep. His brothers formed a tight ring, spears across their chests, straining to hold back the mob. Eyes fell on him, and shouts rose. Fingers jabbed at him. Daniel looked up and was relieved to see that the rooftops had been cleared. Then he paled. A single Wardsman stood on each of the three rooftops near the hut, bows or crossbows trained on the mob.

Someone brushed up against him. Daniel jumped and spun, saw that it was Toban. The Cinder stared at him gravely. "I will make sure you are heard." Toban raised his arms. Without stopping to think, Daniel began to speak.

"The tunnels," he said, and stopped. His voice boomed out over rooftops, sonorous as thunder. Its power startled him. Gradually, the people quieted, though they still glared. Tears leaked from eyes red with anger and grief. A hand squeezed his. Alix stood beside him, and nodded slightly. At her touch, his fear and guilt ebbed. He cleared his throat, and that did sound like a grumble of thunder. Voices rose from the crowd, but he spoke over them, smoothly and steadily.

"Last night, we sent our only remaining Hand of the Crown, along with half a dozen scholars, to nearby outposts in an attempt to evacuate our people and bring them into our walls. Only one, Cinder Toban Kirkus, returned. He and his charges, the people of Gotik, barely escaped with their lives. They were harassed by the Eternal Flame's undead. In the time since, Calewind has come under attack. People have died. The Spire has been lost. Our lieutenant, Anders Magath, a man who served the Crown proudly for more than forty winters, fell in the act of holding back abominations so that they would not reach you and your families.

"Due to those events, the Ward has sealed underground passageways for Calewind's protection. If you need someone to blame, please blame me. Sealing them was my idea. It was not my first, and I wish it had not been my last. I know you fear for your loved ones still outside these walls. They are my responsibility. I hope and pray that they still live, and you have my word as a sergeant of the Ward that my first act after the threat has passed will be to see to their wellbeing.

"But you are my responsibility, too. Mine, and the rest of the Ward's. Please, let us do our duty. The Ward are your servants. Cinder Toban Kirkus is your servant. Some might say the capital needs no fortification. There's a saying across all of Torel. I'm sure many of you know it. 'The Gairdens have ruled for more than eight hundred years, and after they've gone, Calewind will stand for eight hundred more.' I believe that saying will hold true, but not because the city's walls and roads are strong. Because Calewind's people are stronger. We are unbreakable. The enemy outside our gates is a threat greater than the army that followed at the heels of the Serpent King eight hundred years past. That makes it a threat greater than the Touched, or the Ward, or any Crown of the North has ever known. To survive, we must make hard decisions. I pray to the Lady this will be the last, but I will not make a promise I cannot keep."

Daniel's amplified words faded away. Children whined and fidgeted. Sniffs and low cries cut the air, faded away. Karter Rosen gaped at Daniel as if he had never seen him before. Cinder Toban Kirkus's face held an expression close to awe. He became aware of Alix's fingers still laced through his and stole a look at her. Her eyes shone and sparkled with the light of a thousand stars.

Heavy footsteps broke the spell. Slowly, painfully, Daniel wrenched his eyes from Alix's and turned back to the crowd. A man in the shirt, trousers, and boots of Calewind's working class had stepped up, halting at the chain of Wardsmen who barred the way forward. "I stand with the Ward," he said, gaze fixed on Daniel.

Dozens of voices echoed his words. Karter broke rank, stepping back to whisper in Daniel's ear. Daniel listened, nodded, and waited to speak until Karter returned to his place in the line. "The Ward gratefully accepts your support," Daniel boomed. He faltered as he felt Alix's fingers untwine from his. She remained by his side, hands folded behind her back, eyes fixed straight ahead. Feeling some of his newfound confidence slip, Daniel resumed speaking. "We have much to do to prepare for the threat we face. Please approach a member of the Ward in orderly fashion, and we will assign you a post."

He paused, and looked straight at Alix when he said, "All men and women are welcome and encouraged to help."

She beamed, though she did not turn to face him.

DANIEL AND THE Wardsmen worked for hours, sending men and women off to duties in one district or another. As they left, their backs were straight and firm. More lined up in front of Daniel than any other Wardsman. He found their attention flattering at first, then embarrassing, and then annoying. He was physically and mentally spent, and wanted nothing more than to—

Another woman stepped forward. Daniel's heart gave a nasty jolt. Mara waited with hands clasped at her waist. "Hello, Daniel."

"Mara," he replied. Frost dripped from his words.

Her smile slipped. "Word got back to the tavern about what you said, and how you said it. I always knew you would amount to something."

"You're here for assignment?"

Her mouth, still hanging from her last word, snapped shut. "Well, I . . . I was hoping you might need help with something."

"If you're not here to work, please go. I'm very busy."

She hurried from the hut. Daniel watched her go and caught sight of Alix talking with two men—one a Wardsman, the other in plain garb—to the left of the hut. "Excuse me," he muttered to no one in particular.

Hearing him approach, Alix turned. "There he is, now," she said. "Daniel, these two gentlemen and I were just talking about work to be done in the eastern district. Ryckert here just had a brilliant idea. He thinks that if we—"

"May I speak with you for a moment? Privately?" Without waiting for an answer, he pulled her down the closest alleyway.

"What is it?" she said, gently removing her arm from his grasp.

"Sorry. I just . . . I realized something while I was up there, you know, sermonizing to the whole city—"

"You should be proud. I am."

"That means a lot."

Her eyes searched his. "You said you'd realized something. What was it?"

Daniel took a breath. "Yes. I did. It was about you, and about us."

At the final word, her face closed up. "There is no us, Daniel."

"Alix, please, just listen."

Her gaze flicked back toward the congregation, settled on him. "Fine."

He took a deep breath. "We've been through so much together, and in such a short time. I care about you." He trailed off. For a fleeting moment, he thought he saw something in her eyes. It was bright, powerful, and warm, the same expression she had worn when he'd caught her staring at him during his speech.

"And?" she said.

"And . . . and that's it. I care for you."

The warmth in her eyes faded. "You paint with words the way Leastonian artisans paint with colors. But your words are also a knife, or perhaps one of your *Sard'tara*. They cut deep."

"I don't understand," he said hollowly.

Alix took a breath. "I'm not a child. Maybe I was, before I came up through the tunnel into Calewind. Before"—she swallowed—"before Jak. Not now." Her tone softened. "Inviting women to work and fight alongside men was a start. But for all your words, you didn't treat me like an equal before, when I told you—when I showed you—what I wanted."

"I'm sorry about that. I didn't mean . . . I didn't want you to—"

She raised a finger. "That's just it. You don't get to decide what I want, or what I should do, or what I need. I made my feelings known to you, and you threw them back in my face. That's not the way one equal treats another. That hurt. Just being near you hurts."

Before he could say anything, do anything, Alix walked away, swallowed up by the crowds in the streets.

Chapter 43:
The Man of a Thousand Spears

"SET IT WHERE?" Daniel asked, panting.

"Um-m-m," Toban said, not looking up from his book.

"Cinder," Karter gasped.

Toban lifted his head. His eyes took a moment to focus. "Yes? What is it?" Then he glanced down, noticing their burden. "Oh. The board. I need that."

Daniel gritted his teeth. A board he could have managed. What he and Karter carried, each lugging an end halfway across the city, was a beam twice as large around as Toban, perfectly smooth and squared at both ends. "Where do you want it?"

"The southern square."

"We are in the southern square, Cinder," Karter said, cheeks puffing.

"Oh. Yes. Um. Right here will be fine."

Daniel and Karter bent at the knees and set the *board* on the ground, letting out huge sighs as they straightened. "Careful," Toban said idly.

"Will there be anything else, Cinder?" Karter asked. Toban did not respond. His attention had already returned to *Approbation of the Moon*. Karter stalked off.

Daniel knuckled his back. Over the last six hours, the capital had become a flurry of activity. Men and women shouted and hustled. Wardsmen clutched armfuls of swords, shields, and axes to their chests; three women followed in their wake, carrying daggers and slim shafts of fletched wood. They distributed arms to groups of citizens—some dressed in fine robes, others in shirts and trousers—who turned to face sergeants pacing in front of them and shouting instructions on how to hold a sword, swing a club, chop with an axe. Two Wardsmen flanked the sergeant, overseeing practice.

Daniel caught sight of a small Torelian boy wearing dirty rags. He walked up and down the street leading into the southern square, carrying a metal pole the size of a shepherd's crook. The metal tip glowed red. The boy, no more than ten winters, strained on his toes to touch his pole to the top of each lamp. Upon contact a lamp flared into brilliance. Their effulgence did little to push away shadows. Half the lanterns on each street had been removed on Toban's orders. He had some trick up his sleeve, but could not be bothered to explain.

"Where would you like this one, Sergeant Shirey?" someone gasped from behind him.

Daniel leaped to one side as two men in plain clothes stumbled to a halt. They held a beam twice as long and thick as the one Daniel and Karter had carried. "Oh, er." He pointed vaguely. "Right there is fine. I guess. Thanks."

The men dropped the beam clumsily onto the ground near Daniel's foot. "Sorry, sir," one said. Embarrassed, they snapped sloppy salutes.

Fire heated his cheeks. "There's no need for that."

"Of course not, sir. Sorry, sir," the second man said.

"What would you have us do now, Sergeant?" the first asked.

"Are there more beams?"

"Yes, sir. Lots, sir."

"Um. Go grab another. I guess."

They saluted smartly. "Yes, sir!"

A breeze swept through the square. Like an ethereal messenger, it carried low moans from over the southern wall. Daniel shivered. *They're closer, or their numbers have grown. Or both.*

The men had gone pale. "We haven't been able to hear them before," one said.

Daniel's jaw clenched. Vagrants didn't need to breathe, to

speak, to make a sound. This, he guessed, was pure intimidation carried out on orders. He didn't have to guess whose.

"Just ignore them. They're outside, we're in here." When the men stared doubtfully, Daniel straightened. "You have orders. Carry them out."

The men jumped as if pinched. "Yes, sir," they said in unison, and ran off.

Daniel rubbed his temples. The sound of wood scraping against stone startled him. A Wardsman and a woman dressed in brown trousers and a dirty white shirt waddled forward carrying another beam. "Where would you like it, sir?" the woman asked.

Daniel pointed a couple of feet to his left. "There's fine."

Hissing breath through their teeth, they placed the beam so it came end to end with two others in a square. They formed the foundation of a trebuchet, or what would be a trebuchet. Wardsmen, women, and laborers swarmed in, fitting metal bracings where beams met. Toban marched over to stand beside him, tucking his book into his robes. "A bit of space, if you please," the Cinder said.

Toban glowered at the necklace around his throat. The glassy cylinder was half full. He rolled back his sleeves with a flourish and mumbled a few words. Tendrils of smoke curled up around the braces. They glowed white hot. Toban lowered his arms. "Very good. Prepare the sling and summon me when it's ready. I have other preparations to see to."

No sooner had he spoken than a voice called his name from high atop the southern wall. Daniel and Toban craned their necks, squinting. Wardsmen and volunteers patrolled the ramparts, tiny as ants from where they stood on the street. Each held a bow with an arrow notched. Wardsmen stood beside them, instructing others on how to notch an arrow, draw it back, and aim.

One of the Wardsmen noticed them staring, waved, called for the Cinder again. Toban waved back. "Those haven't been tipped yet," he muttered.

"Tipped?" Daniel asked.

"The arrows. I tipped them with dark magic. When they collide with a target, they'll . . ." He snapped his mouth shut. Suspicion clouded his features. "I shouldn't say much more."

"To me?"

"If you really are you, then I suppose it would be fine."

"I'm not sure what that means."

Toban's eyes narrowed. Abruptly he sighed, and his ponderous bulk deflated. "Forgive me, Sergeant. I'm exhausted."

"You should sit down," Daniel said.

"I'd never be able to stand back up."

"Does that help?" Daniel asked, nodding toward the lamp. The light it held had dropped to approximately one-quarter full. It glowed feebly, closer to the color of Dawnfall than midday.

Toban shrugged wearily. "This is the third cylinder I've consumed since earlier this afternoon. I drain the shade-cursed thing faster than our Lady can refill it. I shouldn't have drawn from it to fuse that trebuchet. Won't be able to kindle before long. Dawn and Dusk."

He started toward one of the two lifts that hauled people and cargo up to and down from the ramparts. Normally Cinders shifted Wardsmen up to the wall and back down to ground level. Toban had decided that his energy was better used elsewhere and had helped the Wardsman fashion a system of manually operated pulleys that ran up the side of the guard tower at each gate.

"Maybe you should rest," Daniel said, falling into step beside him.

Toban barked a laugh. "The south wall is but one wall. Three others need my attention."

Daniel nodded. "What did you mean by if I'm really you . . . I mean, me?"

"Well, we don't know if more vagrants came up from the tunnels, do we?"

"I sealed them," Daniel said defensively.

"I know," Toban said. "But who's to say we killed everything that crawled out of them before you did? Carrying out attacks on Sunfall by assuming the guise of people we know and trust would make for the perfect distraction to infiltrate other areas of the city."

Daniel swallowed. Toban had a point.

"They could be biding their time, waiting to strike, posing as any one of us," the Cinder continued.

"Even you."

Toban's eyes widened, then he harrumphed. "Nonsense. They could never duplicate my sunny disposition." He threw his head back and let out a booming laugh. Several nearby women—and more than a few men—jumped and shot him dirty looks. "Sorry, sorry," he said. Lowering his tone, he went on. "It does a man good to laugh, especially if he is to spend his final hours staring death in the face."

"Don't talk like that."

They had arrived at the lifts, square wrought from oak and large enough for four normal-sized men to stand shoulder to shoulder. Magically reinforced ropes ran through the roof and floor of a cabin with one sliding door. The cabin was connected to a steel loop bolted to the ground. The five Wardsmen assigned to the post took one look at the Cinder. Their faces fell in unison.

Toban opened the sliding door and stepped into the cabin. "Coming?"

"I've got plenty to do down here on the ground."

"This wouldn't have anything to do with your young lady, would it?"

The thought of Alix triggered a sharp pain in Daniel's chest. "I haven't seen her."

"Lovers' quarrel?"

He shrugged.

One of the Wardsmen moved to close the door. Toban raised a hand to forestall him. "Go find her, Daniel." The graveness of the Cinder's tone snared his attention. "These are uncertain times. Neither of us knows whether or not he'll see another Dawnrise. Your young lady is one of a kind. Have you slighted her in some way?"

"Why do you assume I did something wrong?" he snapped.

"You didn't?"

Daniel scratched the scruff of his neck. "I made comments in the heat of the moment. My meaning . . . I was trying to express that . . ." He let his hand fall to his side. "I don't deserve her."

"I have lived alone all my life," Toban said quietly. "It has been a good life, rich with knowledge and fine things and finer food. Knowledge was my mistress, and I pursued her to the ends of Crotaria and across the Great Sea to hold her in my arms."

Daniel said nothing.

"Granted, I have little experience with women," the Cinder went on. "My knowledge of them is purely academic. Theoretical. Men find them capricious and quarrelsome. To men, women take offense where none was intended." He raised a finger, smiling slightly, aware that Daniel and the Wardsmen assigned to lift his cabin were listening raptly. "Ah, but their offense is not imagined. It exists. It is simply too fine for men to see, like a cut one does not notice until it festers. Only when a man loses an arm does he realize he is bleeding, and it may be too late to stem the flow."

Toban levelled his stare at Daniel. "Do you want her back?"

"More than anything."

Toban nodded, pushed himself upright. "Don't go to your grave with regrets."

Daniel swallowed. His heart was racing faster than a Darinian stallion. "I will. I mean, I won't. Go to my grave with regrets. I'll find her right now. I'll—"

Toban's face grew distant. His eyes sharpened. "The tunnels have been breached."

Daniel blinked, nonplussed. "The tunnels? But I—"

"I set up a word using a spell from the book." Toban shrugged out of the cabin and extended a hand. Daniel took it. The world spun, and a gale of wind roared in his ears. In the next instant they stood in Sunfall's eastern courtyard, all well-manicured lawns and flowers. One bench sat askew, revealing an aperture leading underground. Familiar faces clustered around it. Alix's was the first he recognized. She held Jak's sword, frowning uncertainly at a pack of dirty people wearing simple clothing. Many had bare feet.

Half a dozen diminutive forms emerged from among the refugees. They were short and stocky, with long hair and beards pulled back in braided locks. Emerald-colored chest pieces mottled with splashes of blue rattled as they moved. Long earrings and gold chains jingled like loose coins.

Whispers swept through the onlookers. "Reavers! Here!"

Then another, rising up in excited tones: "The Man of a Thousand Spears."

Daniel's breath rushed out of him. The Man of a Thousand Spears, as he was known from shore to shore, was not a man but a reaver. He was short—last Daniel had measured, the reaver's head came up to his belly—but powerfully built. His skin was leathery, brown hair and beard well-groomed in a series of braided locks held in place by jewels that sparkled in the Lady's fading light. He wore an Azure Blade's sea-green uniform. He stood erect, one end of a *Sard'tara* resting against the ground. Situated next to him, the weapon stood twice his height.

Blue eyes colder than ice swept the courtyard. His gaze landed on Alix and her sword, then moved on, dismissing her. Daniel was not surprised. In Leaston, a woman wearing men's clothing and carrying a sword was as common a sight as mountains in the west.

The icy gaze found Daniel, bored into him, through him. Continued on. Daniel's temper simmered. *Dismissed again.*

Alix made her way to Daniel. "Do you know him?" she asked.

He nodded, unconsciously correcting his posture. "Rakian Shirey. He's my father."

Her eyes bulged. "Your father? But he's a . . ." She lowered her voice. "A reaver."

Rakian completed his survey of the courtyard. His eyes snapped back to his son. Daniel stood unable to move, barely able to breathe. Rakian opened his mouth, probably to bark some command. His eyebrows climbed up his forehead as six Wardsmen, twice as many men, and a handful of women spilled out of Sunfall and into the courtyard. They spread out, raising clubs and short swords and levelling spears.

"What's the meaning of this?" Toban said, striding forward. A flurry of activity answered him. One of the reavers shouted in a foreign tongue. The pack began to sway back and forth, like snakes in the throes of a charmer's flute. A low chant broke out, muttering stifled by layers of facial hair.

"There's no need for this," Daniel called.

Rakian stared at him. The chanting grew louder, the swaying more pronounced. Daniel was reminded of the way some of his brothers—namely Karter and his friends—acted after a night of imbibing. The Wardsmen and civilians positioned near the entrance to the courtyard had grown tense. His brothers, trained for combat at a moment's notice, raised shields and steel. The civilians looked ready to throw down their implements and run.

Daniel strode between the groups and glared at his father. Rakian raised a gauntleted hand and spoke a single word: "Elhe."

The chanting ceased. The reavers straightened and lowered their *Sard'tara*. Rakian strode forward, and they parted for him. Their heads swiveled to track him, helm tucked under one arm, scraping one blade of his double-headed weapon against the paving stones with every other brisk step. Unlike most reavers, he did not waddle. His stride was steady and measured. Some watched him fearfully. Most stares held reverence.

Rakian stopped in front of Daniel. Although he stood two heads taller, Daniel felt small. Rakian's eyes fell on the single gold stripe pinned to his son's steel and snow. "Who promoted you to sergeant?"

"Is it so hard to believe?" Daniel replied. Rakian held his gaze. "Where is General Calderon? I will speak with him." His perfectly enunciated speech cracked like a whip.

"He's not here, sir," Daniel said.

"Your highest-ranking officer, then."

Daniel did a quick scan of the brothers in attendance. Karter and the other sergeants were elsewhere. His stomach sank into his boots. "That would be me."

"You," Rakian said flatly.

"Yes."

"Where is General Calderon?"

"Leaston, at least I hope so."

"Your colonel, then."

"Colonel Greagor is gone, too."

"Where?"

"Toward Sharem, unless Aidan has—"

"Aidan? Aidan leads the Ward? Are there no lieutenants in Calewind?"

"There was one, but—"

"Are you the highest-ranking officer in the entire city?"

"I—"

"Last your mother and I heard, you were a doorkeeper. It is not the Ward's usual practice to promote a doorkeeper to sergeant without adhering to protocols for training and advancement."

"Last you heard? Who told you? Not me. I haven't heard from you since—"

"Mind your tone, Sergeant. You are addressing your superior."

A hand touched his arm. "Rakian Shirey," Alix began, "it's an honor to finally meet you. I've heard so much about—"

"Your name?" Rakian barked.

Alix jumped. "Alixandra Merrifalls, sir. Honorary Wardsman."

"Wardsman?" Rakian looked her up and down. Daniel saw Alix steel herself and couldn't stop a grin slithering over his face. *You questioned the wrong woman, Father.*

To his astonishment, Rakian nodded. "You seem fit, Alixandra Merrifalls. Though I cannot attest to your skill, it's past time the Ward allowed women to join its ranks."

"You . . . you think so, sir?" she said, sounding both stunned and pleased.

"I have for years. I made such a motion to Charles Gairden when he sat on the Crown of the North, but he wouldn't hear of it."

"You served in the Ward, sir?" she asked.

Rakian flicked his gaze to Daniel. "It seems you haven't heard much about me after all."

Alix blushed, and Daniel warred between embarrassment and anger. His father had forbade him from talking about his past. As far as Daniel was concerned, that included Rakian.

"Where is the Crown of the North?" Rakian asked, addressing Alix.

"Aidan is—"

"Not Aidan. Annalyn."

"Dead," Daniel said.

Rakian's expression did not change. "It's that bad, then."

"You know what's happening?" Daniel asked.

"I know only what I have seen. Palit was attacked by walking corpses late yesterday. I gathered my reavers. We fought the beasts off, but the village could not be saved. We led the survivors here." Rakian spoke each sentence in a clipped voice, the way any other man might describe the weather.

"Through the tunnels?" Daniel asked dumbly.

"Naturally," Rakian said. "Courtesy of one of your . . . old acquaintances."

"But I sealed them."

"Imperfectly," Rakian said.

Before Daniel could retort or demand an explanation—he was still deciding on which tone his response should take—footsteps pounded up behind him. A moment later, Karter burst into the courtyard. "I was on the eastern wall and received reports of a disturbance," Karter said. His eyes fell on Rakian, trailed over to the reavers. "Leastonian militia?"

473

"Azure Blades," one of the reavers muttered. The words were hard to make out, muffled by facial hair so they came out as if spoken through a mouthful of food.

"You've been quite loquacious today, Furus," Rakian said.

The reaver, Furus, shrugged.

"More refugees?" Karter asked Daniel.

"From Palit," Rakian answered, ignoring Daniel's glare.

"That far southeast?" Karter said. He scrubbed a hand over his face. "Dawn and Dusk, Daniel, you closed the tunnels."

Every head in the courtyard swiveled to fix him in a glare. He stared back defiantly at Karter. "I carried out the decision that we agreed was the best course of action."

"This tunnel was not sealed," Rakian said, flicking a hand at the bench. "Not fully. We just came through it."

Daniel could not decide whether he was more relieved that his friends and family from Palit had survived, or angry at his father for accusing him of not being able to seal a tunnel, or sick by the notion that, had he properly sealed the tunnel, he might have sentenced them to death.

"Where is my mother?" he asked.

His father stared at him, features stony. "Our house was the first to be attacked."

Alix gasped. To Daniel, she sounded far away. "Where is my mother?" he asked again. His lips felt numb.

"Take us inside," Rakian ordered Karter. "We have much to discuss."

Sergeants and reavers spoke, but Daniel only half listened. He sat slumped at the long table in the garrison. Karter sat across from him. Toban and Alix stood behind Daniel. He was aware of them and glad in a vague sort of way that they were nearby.

Rakian stood on an overturned crate at the head of the table. His helm rested on the surface before him. The reavers fanned out around him, the tops of their chests just visible over the tabletop. Furus stood at Rakian's right.

"The tunnels are still functional, then?" Karter asked.

"Calewind's, aye," Rakian said.

"Your son was a sneak," Karter explained to Rakian. "We thought he knew . . . that is, he told us he could—"

"He can, and he did," Rakian interrupted. "In a manner of

speaking."

Daniel did not bother to look up.

"There are two ways to seal a tunnel: magically, and manually," Rakian went on. "The steps Daniel took to sever Calewind's tunnels from the network were successful. So, too, was the process of removing it from manual usage."

"Manual?" Alix interrupted. "You mean by walking?"

Rakian nodded. "Correct. Daniel raised a barrier, preventing anyone from entering the passageway leading up to Sunfall's grounds." He raised a finger. "Except one who knows how to unlock it. The tunnels were formed by dark magic, and—"

Nervous murmurs rose up from around the table. Only Daniel, Alix, and Toban remained still. Rakian flapped a hand at them. "Torelians," he snapped. "As I was saying. The tunnels were formed by dark magic, and so too were the barriers that rise up to block a tunnel from use. The barriers rise in response to a key wrought from dark magic, the same key my son used to close the passageways into Calewind. Only, near the top of each barrier there is a small indentation, much like a keyhole. The keyhole is meant to receive a second key. When the proper key is inserted, the barrier can be lowered."

He directed a stern look at his son. "Had you wished to seal the tunnel more efficiently, you would have pocketed the key."

"I hid it," Daniel muttered.

"Not the stub. Every member of the merchant's guild knows about the second key," Rakian said, "and only guildmasters possess those keys."

"I never knew," Daniel said. "Why don't the sneaks have them?"

"A security measure. Sneaks smuggle goods and information to all corners of the realms. The guildmasters prefer not to give them more power than that. Should a sneak abuse a tunnel, or be captured and succumb to torture, a guildmaster may close it until such time as it is deemed safe to reopen."

"You're a member of the merchant's guild?" Raymond asked.

"I was."

"And you served in the Ward?" Karter said.

"I did," Rakian replied, sounding impatient. "Now that I have explained our sudden appearance, you will explain the creatures that attacked us."

All eyes fell on Daniel. He ignored them. Alix said, "They're called vagrants." She launched into a concise description of events that had transpired over the past month, many relayed to her by Daniel. Rakian listened, his mouth a thin line, his eyes bright and cold.

Daniel gave voice to what he suspected his father was thinking. "If only the keys a guildmaster possesses can open a sealed tunnel . . ."

"Then Tyrnen has most likely compromised the guild," Rakian finished. "General Calderon is in danger. Or already dead. These vagrants," Rakian continued. "They can wear the faces of the living."

"That's right," Karter said.

Rakian studied them. "Which means there could be spies among us."

Karter stole a look at Daniel, then cleared his throat. "I can vouch for every man who wears the steel and snow . . . ah . . ."

"Lieutenant," Rakian answered. "That was my rank in the Ward, and I never vacated it."

"I can vouch for my brothers, Lieutenant Shirey," Karter said. Another glance at Daniel. "But I'll be the first to admit I don't know every face in Calewind. If there was an ingress into the city that we thought had been . . . That is, if, during previous attacks, the enemy had infiltrated . . ."

Daniel closed his eyes. He knew what Karter was trying to say and appreciated that his old rival was attempting to say it so delicately. But there was no dancing around the truth. The fact that the tunnels were still open lent credence to the possibility that Garrett or Tyrnen could have slipped undead spies into Calewind during the commotion of previous attacks. That was his fault.

"How intelligent are these undead?" Rakian asked.

"They're controlled using a magical artefact called a spirit stone," Daniel said, not looking up. "The stone holds their souls, and whoever holds the stone—"

"So, we need to destroy this stone," Rakian said.

Daniel ground his teeth. His father detested interruptions, yet never hesitated to trample over others. Determined to have his say, he spoke in a rush. "Aidan's going to destroy it."

"Is there more than one?" Rakian asked.

The thought had never occurred to Daniel. He hoped it had occurred to Aidan. "I . . . I don't know. No one does," he said quickly as Rakian lowered his head to stare at the chipped and dirty tabletop.

"That would explain a great deal," said Rakian.

Daniel hesitated. "About what?"

Rakian raised his head. "A man led the attack on our village. A man in possession of his own soul, though his actions lead me to question that assumption. He butchered people indiscriminately, smiling all the while. Grinning. Perhaps he was mad. He seemed to enjoy killing, yet as I think back now, he did not partake in much of it. He hid behind his ranks, and his numbers grew with every . . ." Rakian caught his son's eye, and closed his mouth.

"What did this man look like?" Daniel asked. He thought he already knew.

"Tall," Rakian said. "He wore his golden hair in a braid."

Daniel was aware of Alix's hand settling on his shoulder, and that he was trembling.

"You know this man?" Rakian asked, leaning forward with stubby fists planted on the table.

Daniel nodded.

"Who is he? What does he want?"

"Me."

"You do have a flair for the dramatic," his father said.

Alix spoke up. "He's right, Lieutenant. Garrett Lorden has made his intentions toward your son known."

Rakian's visage was darker and more ominous than a thunderhead. During his youth, Daniel would have run as far as possible from such an expression, and had many times. Now, it brought a strange sort of comfort. Rakian was here, and in charge.

"What would you have us do?" Toban asked. He was looking at Rakian. So were the sergeants and reavers.

Rakian considered. "If I knew how to open the tunnel barriers, then so will the man who razed my village. We must take that into account. Set up guards around each tunnel and fill each shaft with rocks. As many as you can find. Rocks will not stop these . . . these harbingers from surfacing, but the guards will hear the disturbance, and we can be ready for them."

"We can't fight harbingers head on," Karter said.

"Of course not," Rakian barked. "Don't be foolish. I would not squander the lives of our brothers."

Daniel's eyebrows rose. *Our brothers?* But his father's words had had the desired effect. He watched as the faces of the sergeants underwent a dramatic change from exhausted to confident and resolved.

"By announcing their arrival in such a manner, they will aid us in springing a trap," Rakian finished. He directed his attention to Toban. "You're a Cinder."

"I am."

"You can orchestrate some sort of mechanism to deal with intruders who attempt to breach Calewind from below."

Frown lines creased Toban's face. "Not with light magic," he murmured.

"Am I to understand that you walk in the shade?" Rakian said quietly.

Realizing what he had said, Toban looked up. "No, Lieutenant. That is to say, not in ordinary circumstances. Your son, he—"

"My son?" Rakian's eyes pinned Daniel to his chair. "You're caught up in this?" And before Daniel could answer: "I should have known."

Blood rushed in Daniel's ears. "Actually, I'm carrying out the Crown's instructions."

Rakian's jaw worked. "Aidan's doing." He nodded to himself. "Dark times call for dark measures. I am not so squeamish as a Torelian. Very well, Cinder. Do what you must to protect the Crown and his people."

"As I have been doing," Toban murmured.

"Your men, Lieutenant. Are they willing to join our ranks?" Karter asked.

Daniel fought to keep a grin from splitting his face. "Have you ever heard of the Frenzy?" Karter shook his head. Daniel chuckled. "A reaver in the Frenzy is worth his weight in Leastonian coin. They—"

"The question was addressed to me, Sergeant Shirey."

Daniel trailed off. "I was only trying to—"

"May we speak privately?" Rakian said.

"Yes, sir," Daniel said stiffly. As if on cue, chairs scraped back and sergeants hastened from the room. Alix hesitated.

"You may go, Merrifalls," Rakian said without looking at her.

Alix began to turn as if compelled. Catching herself, she shot Daniel a supportive look and hurried from the room. The heavy door, carved from ebonywood, closed heavily behind her.

Daniel folded his hands on the tabletop. "Well?"

"I am sorry about your mother. I tried to save her." Rakian's voice grew strained. "There was nothing I could do."

Daniel stared at his hands. His eyes stung. "I'm going to kill Garrett Lorden."

"Only if I fail to reach him first."

Daniel's heart soared. He raised his head, believing Rakian Shirey would be wearing a grim smile. Instead, he was greeted by the stony expression his father always wore.

"You've made a mess of things. Again. I do not know who promoted you to sergeant, but I will acknowledge the rank only to show honor and respect toward the brothers of the Ward. You are not to make any decision without receiving authorization from me first. Do we understand each other?"

Torches chattered, murmured. Laughed. Daniel rose and pushed back his chair. "I'm going to leave now. Do I need your permission for that?"

"You have it."

Daniel turned on his heel and crossed to the door.

Chapter 44:
The Reaver's Son

DANIEL THOUGHT ABOUT walking Calewind's streets. He was too upset to sleep. Too upset, and too confused. Anger, grief, pride, and affection pulled him in different directions, four armies fighting for control and tearing their prize asunder in the process.

Stepping out of the garrison, he breathed in crisp evening air. Sunfall's western courtyard was in stark contrast to the eastern yard's manicured paths. Flagged stones, horses whinnying and snorting from stables, straw dummies rigged to wooden posts, and the garrison, a broad but plain stone building set flush against the palace's western wall. Daniel entered the stables and wandered up and down aisles of stalls. The sour scent of manure permeated the air. That didn't bother him. He had spent most of his boyhood on a farm. Such smells were familiar and more comforting than any perfume hawked by Leastonian peddlers.

Calmer, he exited the stables and entered Sunfall by a wide set of doors. Unmanned, of course. Braziers and chandeliers supporting hundreds of candles lit the western vestibule like midday. Daniel wondered idly who still bothered lighting every wick and torch in Sunfall. As if the thought had summoned him, a small boy appeared around a corner, holding a curved steel rod topped with a flame.

"I've seen you before," Daniel said. "You lit lanterns in the

481

streets."

The boy nodded. "I thought someone should do it, to keep Kahltan away." The boy grinned, and a chill crawled up Daniel's spine. The smile stopped short of the boy's eyes. Before he could dwell on it, Alix appeared and draped an arm around the boy's shoulder.

"I see you've met Zakary."

"How do you know him?" Daniel asked.

"Zakary lives in the house next to mine. Lived, I should say." She ruffled his hair. "He's always the first to lend a hand when chores need doing. Aren't you, Zakary?"

"I just like to help," the boy said. Daniel was impressed. At the boy's age, he'd spent every waking moment being conscripted into chores or scheming ways to get out of them.

"Where are Timothy and Eldera?" Alix asked Zakary. When the boy gaped at her, she laughed and said, "Sorry. You probably don't refer to your mother and father by their names."

Zakary smiled his weird smile. "They've bedded down at one of the inns in the north district."

"And do they know you're here?" Alix asked, hands on her hips.

When Zakary did not respond, Daniel stepped in. "He can stay. Someone needs to keep the shade at bay until Dawn."

"Is it safe?" Alix said.

Daniel nodded toward the two Wardsman standing against either wall far down the corridor. "Safer than it has been." Daniel knelt so he was eye level with Zakary. "Just stay in the main corridors so they can see you. Fair enough?"

"Fair enough," Zakary agreed. The boy strode away, pole held high.

"I thought you might need to talk," Alix said.

"You thought wrong."

"I'm a woman. I'm incapable of thinking wrong."

Daniel laughed. "You would have liked my mother." The words, and the reality they conveyed, tightened his throat.

"I'm sure I would have," Alix said softly.

"I would like to talk, I guess. But I thought you . . . I thought being around me was painful."

"It was. It is. But I decided to put those feelings aside for the moment."

"Good," he said. "I could use the company."

They walked stiffly, hands at their sides, heading the way Zakary had come, through galleries and halls until they rounded the turn leading to Aidan's quarters. The boy was thorough. Rows of bracketed torches bathed the corridor in warm, golden light. Daniel opened the door—brand new—stuck his head in, stepped aside, and held the door for her to enter.

"Such a gentleman," she said, passing him.

"It's how she raised me," he said, closing the door behind him.

"She did a good job." Alix pulled her legs up and tucked them beneath her, sitting cross-legged.

Daniel sat beside her, chest constricted. "Pieces of her upbringing stuck to me like burrs."

"What did she think of your involvement with the sneaks?"

"Wasn't too happy about it. But she was Leastonian. She knew about them. Everyone back east knows about them. People just look the other way, unless . . ."

Alix raised her eyebrows. "Unless you steal from the wrong people."

"Yes. Especially from the merchant's guild." Alix whistled, and Daniel put on an airy expression. "What can I say? I aim for the highest heights and climb higher still."

"Your father was on the guild, too. Couldn't he . . . ?"

Daniel laughed softly. "No. He tried, but not very hard. I don't think he wanted to."

"He didn't want to help his son?" She looked incredulous.

"Rakian is . . . Well, you've met him."

Alix traced her finger over the bedspread. "Your father is not what I expected."

"You could say I get my height from my mother's side. Rakian raised me, fed me, clothed me. My real father died when I was a babe."

"I'm sorry."

"Thanks, but I don't remember him. Rakian and my mother told me he was a seafarer, and a pirate. He died out on the Great Sea. My mother moved north with me. She had family in Calewind, and that's where she met Rakian. He was a sergeant. They became smitten. Rakian gave me his surname. He was promoted to lieutenant, and then one of his rivals got the better of him."

"Why?" Alix said.

"Because he's a reaver," Daniel said, leaning back against the wall and crossing one boot over the other. "Because he looks different than Torelians."

"He can't lose his rank for that."

"Not explicitly, no. This superior says he found Rakian bedding a woman of fair skin. This man, also a lieutenant, forged evidence of some wrongdoing and threatened to ruin Rakian's reputation unless he left the Ward."

"What did he do?"

"He left. Edmund was general by then, and would have stood by Rakian, but I think Rakian knew his reputation would be ruined no matter what his general believed. Torelians aren't exactly the most tolerant people. Rakian was different, and better than half the men on the Ward despite his stature, or from what I've heard. I was just learning how to walk when all this happened, so I heard everything from my mother. He took us back east, joined the Blades, and did quite well. He's a frugal man and saved enough coin to buy a tract of land. That tract grew into a field, which became a plantation. You can harvest damn near anything in Leaston's climate, and he did: fruits, vegetables, tobacco. Every harvest, he'd bring in goods by the wagonload. A dozen a week, if not more. Within a few years, he'd established himself as one of the most prosperous merchants in the east and bought himself a seat on the guild."

Alix shook her head. "I can't believe Torelians would do that to him."

"Rakian Shirey is incapable of doing anything wrong. Good people know that. So do the men he's brought to justice. He just had the poor fortune to be born a reaver who had the audacity to try and better himself in Torel."

Alix looked mildly offended. "We're not all so narrow-minded."

"No," Daniel agreed. "But tell me: How many dusky-skinned men and women live in Gotik? How many reavers? How many have you seen in Calewind, for that matter?"

She paused. "Very few."

"And would they be welcomed with open arms, the way they would in even the smallest, most remote village in Leaston?"

"Surely the Gairdens . . ."

"Aidan and his family are good people, and they rule the north, but they can't look after every single one of their subjects."

When she didn't answer, he closed his eyes.

"He's something of a stern man," Alix said after several moments.

"To put it lightly. Some men worship the Lady. Some men worship the Lord of Midnight. My father kneels at the altar of discipline. 'A man in control of his mind is in control of himself,' he likes to say."

"Sage advice."

"Oh, yes. He's a sage man, my father. The trouble is, my ten fingers have minds of their own. They like to touch things, and they're quite sticky. Some of the sneaks took notice and recruited me. I was six."

"That young?"

"Just young enough. Children are perfect, you see. They're small, nimble, and no one pays attention to them. They blend in. The merchant's guild doesn't mind sticky fingers unless those fingers happen to stick to their possessions. Or their secrets."

"That's what you stole? A secret?"

"A big one."

"Oh-h-h-h," she breathed. She propped her elbows on her knees and cupped her chin in her hands. "Tell me."

Daniel shrugged. "Oh, nothing much. Just proof of an affair between a guildmaster and the wife of one of his peers."

Alix gasped. "Who was it?"

"I swore never to reveal his name, and I try to keep my word. He was old, though. As old as the Lady Herself with a heart as black as midnight. All the sneaks despised him. His Azure Blades liked him only because his gold was good. Anyway, he knew that I knew, and my father knew that word of the affair would throw the guild into complete disarray. This guildmaster insisted that I be punished, as in my head removed from my shoulders. Rakian negotiated an alternative punishment."

"Which was?"

"Exile for life. We packed our belongings and moved to Palit, a quiet northern village that hugs the border separating Torel and Leaston. Palit makes Gotik seem as boisterous as the capital. My father settled back into farm life. My mother kept the house, and they both conspired to keep me out of trouble."

"Poor Daniel," she teased. "Your parents plotted and schemed to prevent you from returning to a life of crime. Life must have been so hard."

"It was hard!" His smile faded. He picked at the blankets. "They couldn't have stopped me had I wanted to leave. There's a tunnel in Palit. There are tunnels everywhere. I could have left and disappeared forever. Become a seafarer, like my father. But Rakian, it's like he could read my mind. He kept me busy, and never let me out from under his sight." His voice dropped. "Rakian hates me, I think. My sneaking cost him his place in the militia and the merchant's guild."

"I'm sure he doesn't hate you."

"You don't know my father. Militarism was his life. It was all he knew. Besides farming, I mean, but working a field no longer satisfied him."

"Sounds to me like money was his life."

"He still had plenty of coin and his plantation back east. He made a big show of selling it—part of his exile—but the new overseer was in his pocket. The overseer would report to him and run shipments of goods all over the realms. Rakian got the bulk of his profits and paid the overseer handsomely. In the meantime, he kept his farm in Palit nice and small. I think he liked the slower change of pace. He and my mother tried to live peacefully. I didn't. Eventually, Rakian got tired of me. He enlisted me in the Ward. I didn't argue. I wanted to get away. A man who earns the title 'Man of a Thousand Spears' is rather difficult to impress, much less please."

"I've been wondering about that. He's, er, well, not a man."

"Ask anyone he met in combat about that," Daniel replied. "You could, if they were still breathing. If you were to see him fight . . ." He inhaled and let out an explosive breath. "He's incredible. His *Sard'tara* seems to come at you from everywhere, and all at once, like he's got an army fighting alongside him. Doesn't matter how tall you are. Rakian Shirey will break through. He taught me everything I know, but Rakian's forgotten more in his lifetime than I'll ever be able to learn in mine." His visage darkened. "He's always willing to remind me of that. Going to the capital and enlisting seemed an escape, so I took it."

His throat tightened, and his eyes stung. "My mother always said she wanted a quiet life. I never managed to give her one."

Alix leaned close and rested a hand on his knee. "I am sorry about your mother."

Daniel did not respond. He was staring at her hand. Alix pulled it away as if burned. She stood hastily. "I should go. I doubt your father will afford anyone much time to rest."

He reached out and took her hand. She started to pull away, then went still, watching him. "I'm sorry for what I said to you the last time we were here together. It had nothing to do with you being a woman, or me viewing you as a lesser. It was me. I felt I didn't deserve you. Someone like you, with a doorkeeper?"

She stared at him for a long time. Slowly, she sat down next to him. "You need to understand something. I realize I am more forward than most Torelian women, but that is because I refuse to allow propriety or custom to stand between me and what I want, or whom I want. I do not give myself to a man lightly. The last time we were in this room together, we were lucky to be alive. We survived something terrible together. I knew what I wanted. Right then, in that moment, I wanted you. You do not choose what I want or deserve. I liked you when you were a doorkeeper, and I'd like you if you were still guarding doors, because I like you. I also know that if you want to explore what I think you feel as well, we will do so as equals. I will not be made to feel wrong or inferior just because I was born a woman in the north. If that bothers you, I will leave now and never speak to you again unless duty requires it."

It took him several moments to find his breath. "How could I be bothered? What you just said amazed me. You amaze me. Dawn, I missed you," he blurted.

At his words, all the tension drained from her. "I missed you, too. When I'm with you, I think about you. About how you know just when and how to make me laugh, and about how you make men and women follow you and believe in you."

Daniel's chest was tight. "And when you're away from me?"

"I still think of all those things. I also think about how damn angry you make me for thinking about you."

"I think about you, too," he admitted. "About your smile, about the way you chase what you want and sink your teeth into it when you finally get it."

"You're much the same. Perhaps that's why we work so well together."

He shrugged. "No one respects me now. Not with my father here."

"Does that bother you?"

"No," he said quickly. Too quickly. She glared at him. "A little," he admitted.

"You liked the respect," Alix observed.

"Yes. But not because I got to tell people what to do."

"People like Toban and Karter?"

"Especially Toban and Karter."

She giggled. "Why, then?"

"Because I've never been respected before. Sneaks aren't respected. They're tolerated by some, unknown by most. And a doorman in the Ward? Better to be unknown and unseen than a doorman. You heard how Karter talked to me before."

"I believe that was before you knocked him on his backside in front of your brothers."

"True. It's strange, though. I was happy as a doorman, or at least I thought I was. I was away from Rakian, the heir to the Crown of the North was my closest friend, and I had very little responsibility. Then I ran off with Aidan to protect his backside from all manner of horrors, and I felt . . . not important, but wanted. Needed."

Her brow furrowed. She tucked one leg under the other. "Time is a force, don't you think? It pulls us in its current the way a river can uproot the strongest, tallest, oldest tree. People must change, or time will tear them from the ground and wash them away. You have changed. You cannot go back to those throne room doors, no more than you could rejoin the sneaks."

"I know. I don't want to."

"Good. Because people still need you. I need you." She took his hand. "What do you want?" she asked softly.

He leaned in by way of answering, and their lips met. Their kiss was gentle, exploratory. He closed his eyes and felt her hands run up and down his arms. Where her nails grazed, pleasant shivers ran across his flesh. He reached behind her, cupping the back of her head and running his fingers through her short, chopped hair.

A knock sounded at the door.

He leaned his forehead against hers and was glad when she leaned back. "Why does this keep happening?"

Another knock. Muttering, he scooted out of bed and strode across Aidan's room while Alix sat up, fussing at her hair and clothes. Daniel opened the door to find Zakary standing in the hall.

"Your father summoned you," the boy said. His eyes sidled around Daniel to settle on Alix. "You and her."

"Of course, he did," Daniel said, staring at the ceiling. "Dawn burn the man."

Alix came beside him and took his hand. "Come on. We'll go together."

Chapter 45:
Furus the Furious

ZAKARY LED DANIEL and Alix into the garrison's main hall, where the rest of Calewind's command waited. Rakian stood at the head of the table. Daniel wondered if he had bothered leaving, or even sitting down. Toban stood beside Rakian, hands clasped behind his back. The Cinder's complexion was the color of cheese. He rocked gently on his feet. *The man needs sleep,* Daniel thought. *Dawn, but we all do.*

Zakary shifted his pole to his left hand so he could clap his right to his chest. Rakian returned the salute, then watched the boy go. The door closed behind him. Daniel slipped into his seat between Alix and Karter, and noticed his brothers staring askance at the reavers. Their expressions showed curiosity and unease. The Blades seemed unperturbed. They stood implacable, tiny mountains unruffled by wind or rain. Their eyes were vigilant, wide and bright.

Of the Azure Blades, only Furus seemed anxious. He shifted from foot to foot, his mouth puckered like the scar adorning his left cheek. His jewels clattered softly, mingling with the low chatter from the torches. Furus had always been impatient. His fellows had named him Furus the Furious because of the reaver's love of bruises, blood, and booze, and his willingness to incite activities that would lead to one or more of his three favorite things.

"I trust you had time to rest," Rakian said. He swept his gaze over those seated, and it lingered on Daniel. Color creeped into Daniel's cheeks, but he schooled his features. Nothing, not even his father, could ruin his good mood. His thoughts turned to the army of undead camped outside Calewind's walls. *Almost nothing,* he amended.

"Sergeants, you did a fine job rousing the people of Calewind to work," Rakian said. "That could not have been easy. They are not used to wartime conditions. I commend your efforts."

"It was your son's doing, Lieutenant," Karter said. The other sergeants murmured agreement. Alix gave Daniel's hand a squeeze under the table, and he squeezed back.

Rakian's bushy eyebrows rose. "Well done. You make your brothers proud."

"It was nothing," Daniel responded, flushing.

"To other concerns," Rakian said. "Cinder Toban tells me that he has fortifications to finish. However, I felt it prudent to give him time to rest. He has explained his lamp to me, but in his present state he lacks the constitution to kindle so much as a spark."

"I am willing to press on, Lieutenant Shirey," Toban said, straightening.

"I meant no insult. I understand little of how the Touched expend and regain their strength, but I recognize fatigue. You're of no use to me in your state."

Toban fumed. The Cinder's eyes found his. Daniel frowned, confused, until he realized that Toban was looking to him for assent. *No,* he thought. *For permission. Dawn and Dusk!*

Slowly, every head in the room swiveled to face him. Rakian's bushy eyebrows climbed higher. Daniel cleared his throat. "Um. Maybe you should rest, Toban. Cinder Toban," he amended. "None of us question your resolve. A lot sits on your shoulders. We need you, and you're at your best when you're alert."

All the fight drained from Toban's posture. "I am weary," he admitted. "I will rest for a short time."

"A wise course of action," Rakian said, watching his son.

Toban caught Daniel's attention and bowed. It was the deepest bow Daniel had ever seen a Touched grant anyone other than their Eternal Flame. Without another word, he exited the garrison. Daniel noticed that everyone was watching him. He cleared his throat again. "As you were saying, Lieutenant?"

Rakian pursed his lips. He jabbed a finger against a sheet of parchment on the table. "I have taken the liberty of dividing you into companies, and assigned you stations around the city. The city's populace and your brothers are working hard, but they require leadership. Spreading officers around the city ensures that fortifications continue apace, and that experienced Wardsmen will be close at hand should an attack come."

"I serve with you, Man of a Thousand Spears," Furus the Furious grumbled.

"You do," Rakian agreed. "I have assigned you to my company, as you requested."

Requested? Daniel thought. Furus usually preferred to work alone. On top of that, Daniel could not remember the Blade revealing any particular affinity for his father. He respected Rakian Shirey, but most men did. Beyond that, Rakian's and Furus' relationship was simple: Employer and mercenary.

"Who else serves in our company?" Furus asked.

Daniel knew what his father was going to say before he made a show of reading his parchment. "Alix Merrifalls, Karter Rosen, and Daniel Shirey. The rest of you, find your groups and depart to your assigned stations."

As one, Wardsman and Blades moved toward the head of the table. The two groups kept their distance at first. Then a reaver Daniel didn't recognize clasped Raymond's hand and shook it vigorously. Raymond smiled hesitantly. The two began talking. Other Wardsman and reavers read the parchment, found their contingents, and moved toward the door, Wardsman making small talk and reavers replying gruffly.

"What is it?" Alix asked.

Wordlessly, Daniel strode up to Rakian. Karter and Furus waited to either side of him. Rakian hefted his *Sard'tara* and watched his son. "Why does our unit need a fifth member?" Daniel asked through gritted teeth.

"Because we're going to be working around the two tunnels leading in and out of the city. You will direct our efforts, explaining the nuances of how the tunnels work in order to set up an advance warning system."

"Toban already did that."

"*Cinder* Toban's system warned him of intruders who still managed to breach Calewind's surface. Mine will be more effective."

"I could work alone."

"The last time you worked a tunnel alone, you bungled the job."

Daniel opened his mouth to retort. Alix's hand rested on his shoulder. He took a deep breath. "Fine. Shall we go?" He turned on his heel, and Alix fell into step beside him.

THEY PASSED THROUGH Sunfall's halls and debouched into the eastern courtyard. Alix shivered. The Lady of Dawn perched on the western horizon, and the evening breeze was cool. Daniel pulled Alix close. She let him, and they cut across the walkways to stand before the bench that led down to the tunnel. Rakian, Karter, and Furus joined them. Following Rakian's lead, they placed their weapons on the ground. Daniel noticed five pickaxes arrayed on the grass, damp and shiny with dew. Rakian hoisted one as easily as if it were a blade of grass.

"Take one and follow me," Rakian said. He pushed the bench aside, removed the covering, and descended into the dark. Karter and Furus grabbed two of the tools and followed. Daniel stooped and retrieved one, handed it to Alix, then picked up the last tool.

"There's probably something else you can do to help if—"

She raised a hand. "Listen?"

"What?"

"You don't hear that?"

"Hear what?"

"Listen," she hissed.

Daniel did, and he heard. Faintly, rising above the sounds of hammers and saws and feet and shouts, he perceived a steady droning noise. Like a child caught in a night terror and whimpering. Only the droning sound was not high, as a child's voice would be. It was low. A moan. More than one. Thousands, voices pitched in an endless lamentation of pain and un-death.

"They're still gathering," he said quietly.

Alix said nothing, her face pale.

Daniel took her hand. "You should go back to Sunfall. I'm sure there's something you can do—"

Alix put a finger on his lips. "Don't you dare," she said, voice steady and even a little sweet. She marched past him and climbed down the hole. Trying to pretend the vagrants' ceaseless wails did not exist, he picked his way down after her.

He expected the descent into the hole to leave them in pitch blackness. But, of course, his father was prepared. Lanterns lined the meandering path, casting a soft glow. Daniel studied the veins running along either wall. They were dark, empty, and cold. Up ahead, he could see the faint outline of the barrier that manually sealed the tunnel. Incompletely, as it happened.

They huddled in a tight bunch for several moments, a touch winded from the long trek down the ladder. Only Furus seemed unaffected. Lantern light reflected off faces shiny with perspiration, but Furus's skin was clear and dry. His puckered scar stood out prominently, and Daniel's eyes settled on it. The sight of it captivated him for some reason. It was as if he were seeing it for the first time, which was absurd, because he had known Furus his whole life, and the Blade had had the scar since he could remember.

Perhaps feeling his eyes, Furus regarded him. Daniel gave him a small smile. The Blade turned away, and Daniel's smile faltered.

Karter caught his breath first. "What's our assignment, Lieutenant?"

Rakian lifted his pickaxe and pointed down the path. "The Cinder laced these paths with some sort of magic to give those of us on the surface advance warning of trespass. However, it would be beneficial to waylay intruders down here for as long as possible. We will chip away at these walls, collect the stone pieces, and arrange them in rows up and down the path, like ribs. I will ask Toban to lace each line of stones with his spell, and they will detonate when crossed, bringing down the tunnel and rendering it impassable."

"What about more refugees?" Daniel asked.

"If they haven't arrived yet, they're not coming," Rakian replied. He buried his pickaxe in the nearest wall. Stone and bits of dirt scattered onto the floor. "No," Rakian said, waving Daniel and Alix away when they took up positions next to him. "Go further down the tunnel, toward the barrier. It's the only way to be sure we cover all our ground. Not you, Merrifalls. You stay with me." Daniel began to protest, but Rakian spoke over him. "Be romantic on your own time. Now is the time for work."

"This is ridiculous," Daniel said. "We're not children."

"I am your superior, Sergeant," his father said.

"It's fine," Alix said soothingly. "Splitting up makes more sense. We can complete the job and get over to the next tunnel sooner."

Rakian gave Alix an appraising look. Hiding a smile, Daniel went down to the far end of the path. Alix had played his father expertly. To Rakian Shirey, logic was like chocolate to a sneak. He felt a pang of hunger and glared accusingly at the barrier in front of him. There was plenty of chocolate just beyond it, in the waypoint on the other side.

Heavy footsteps came up behind him. Furus and Karter joined him, their pickaxes resting on their shoulders. Back up the way they had come, pickaxes rang against, and stones clicked over the hard earth. "Ready to begin?" Karter asked.

"Thrilled," Daniel said. Spreading his feet and bracing his legs, he gripped the shaft of his pickaxe in both hands and swung. Bits of earth and rock sprayed over his pants and boots. Pulling in a breath, he cocked the tool back and, exhaling, swung again. *I think I'd rather guard a door.*

Karter took up a position further down the same wall. He swung once, wrenched the tool out, and swung again. The wall behind them exploded. Daniel and Karter spun around. In Furus's huge grip, the pickaxe looked like oversized cutlery. In front of him, a huge chunk had been torn from the wall. "Dawn, you're strong," Karter exclaimed.

Furus made no reply. He heaved the pickaxe back and smashed the wall again. The hole widened into a crater.

"Why are we here?" Karter muttered to Daniel. "He could tear down both walls before the Lady sets."

Chuckling, Daniel returned to his work. The three men fell into a rhythm. Their pickaxes made a staccato pounding that mingled with their breathing. Before long, sweat plastered his underclothes to his steel and snow. Daniel let his pickaxe slip from slick fingers, undid his armor, and resumed working. Beside him, he heard the clatter of Karter's armor joining his on the ground. Both Wardsmen stripped to the waist and resumed working.

Across from them, Furus never ceased pounding. Daniel lost himself in the task. Idly, he realized he enjoyed it. The surface seemed far away, and so did the problems associated with it. His *Sard'tara* was above him, and at first, he felt a longing for it. Before long, he forgot all about it. Why did he need it? Down here, in this passageway, there were no vagrants, no harbingers, no Tyrnen, no Garrett Lorden. There was only the wall, and his pickaxe, and his body, and the release he felt in throwing himself at a problem he was capable of solving.

Sometime later, he lowered his pickaxe, breathing deeply, and looked around. Karter slumped against their wall further down. On the other side of the aisle, Furus had paused. He was staring up at the ceiling, as if listening to some sound on the surface.

"You two know each other?" Karter raised a dirty hand to indicate Furus.

Daniel nodded. "From when I lived in Ironsail, and then in Palit later."

"What was it like in Ironsail?"

Daniel propped his axe against the wall. "Hot," he answered. "Busy. Crowded. A lot like Calewind, really, but warmer, and with the smell of the sea hanging in the air, and the cries of gulls instead of ringing bells, and sand in the streets instead of snow."

"And the people. Do they all dress like the peddlers and vendors we have here?"

"More extravagantly. Any fabric you can imagine in any color you can imagine."

Karter rubbed one shoulder. "And the Azure Blades are like the Ward, but a militia?"

"Right. Anyone can join, provided they can undergo the training."

"Difficult?"

"Very."

"You never did it?"

"Never wanted to. I was perfectly content thieving and eating sweets."

Karter laughed. "That doesn't sound like a bad life."

"It wasn't."

Karter stretched his legs. "They say you came here because you were caught stealing."

"That's accurate enough." Daniel steeled himself, prepared to gently but firmly rebuke any questions about his past. Opening up to Alix had been difficult enough, not because of her persistence—he suspected he would have to get used to that—but because of the embarrassment and shame he harbored over getting his father exiled from the realm where he had worked so hard to build a life.

"I'm sorry I tormented you."

Daniel blinked. "What?"

"It was wrong," Karter continued, looking Daniel in the eyes. "I was jealous of you because you were Aidan's friend, and because you had such an easy job. I never gave much thought to the life you lived before we became brothers." He pushed himself up, walked over, and extended a hand. Daniel clasped it.

Karter flashed a grin. "I could use sweets right about now."

"There are plenty on the other side of that wall," Daniel said, jerking his thumb toward the barrier.

Karter groaned. "Don't tell me that." He hefted his pickaxe. "We'd better get back to it. Your father doesn't seem a man to look kindly on idleness."

"He's been known to accuse the Lady of not rising early enough."

As if he had been waiting for them, Furus lifted his and resumed pounding at his wall. He was halfway down, just ahead of their position. Karter swung once, twice, three times, and wiped a line of sweat from his brow. Turning to Furus, he said, "Could you tell me more about the Azure Blades? I've heard that no man can withstand the Frenzy, but I don't know what that means, exactly."

Furus did not answer, only continued to swing. Karter glanced at Daniel, frowning.

Daniel shrugged. "He's not talkative."

"Are they all like him? Reavers, I mean." Karter looked abashed. "I've never met one."

"Furus lets his actions speak for him."

Karter swung, his axe head biting into stone. "What was that they were doing in the courtyard? They looked like they were under some sort of trance."

"That was the Frenzy. I'm not sure how it works, exactly. Reavers aren't from the east. They're from someplace else. They go into a kind of . . . well, a frenzy, I guess, throwing themselves at enemies with abandon."

"Have you ever seen it?"

"Heard about it, from my father. It's not very pretty."

"But they're wearing leather. Steel and snow would stop them cold."

"*Sard'tara* are poisoned," Daniel said. "All they need to do is find one unprotected bit of flesh, and the fight's over. That's if you're facing a reaver in the Blades. If you're not, they pick up a kitchen knife and near cut you in half if they're in the frenzy."

Karter swung. "You grew up with Furus?"

Daniel chipped away at the wall. "He's been my father's friend since I can remember. When my family left Ironsail, he left his post and followed Rakian. He saved Nichel of the Wolf once. Furus, I mean."

Karter tried to halt the downward momentum of his pickaxe and lurched, off-balance. "The wolf daughter? The Crown's *betrothed*?"

Daniel winced. He'd hardly had a spare moment to wonder how, exactly, Aidan planned to handle that situation.

"When? How?" Karter asked, shaking Daniel from his thoughts.

Lowering his pickaxe, Daniel leaned against it like a cane. "My father told me of it. This was years ago, back in Ironsail. Nichel and her mother were visiting, and the merchant's guild made a spectacle of their arrival. Her grandfather sat on the guild. In any case, they were walking through the city—Nichel and Cynthia—and they were attacked by Darinians. Members of some rogue clan. The adder, I think. Nichel's grandfather had appointed a squad of Blades to watch over them. Furus reached them first and killed their attackers with his bare hands."

Karter's mouth fell open. "His hands?"

Raising his axe, Daniel turned back to the wall. "He paid the price for it. Isn't that right, Furus?" The reaver offered no response. "Those of the adder carry these special knives. If they cut you with them, you're marked. They can find you anywhere, like a hound given a scent."

"Dawn and Dusk," Karter breathed. "Is that how . . . ?" Glancing at Furus, he stepped closer to Daniel and whispered, "Is that how he got the scar?"

"Indeed. Shaped like a claw, just like the knife itself. But Furus doesn't care. He wears it like a badge of honor. He used to joke about it. What was it he said?" He furrowed his brow. "Something about his right cheek being payment for doing the right thing. Is that it, Furus?"

Furus swung and swung. Stone, dust, and dirt flew out of the wall. Shrugging, Daniel hacked at the wall again.

"Did you say his right cheek?" Karter asked.

"Right. I mean, yes. Correct."

"I see a claw-shaped scar on his left cheek," Karter said.

Furus went still, pickaxe raised for another strike.

"How did you come across that one, Furus?" Karter asked.

Daniel stared blankly at the wall. A chill swept through him, turning his blood to ice. In the next instant, the world exploded.

In one smooth motion Furus pivoted and slashed his pickaxe through the air. It whistled as it fell. Karter's face contorted from curiosity to horror. He pushed himself off the wall, one hand going for his pick while the other rose to shield his face. But Karter was slow, and Furus too strong. The metal spike shattered Karter's face, piercing bone and brain. Wet fragments sprayed like chips of stone. Daniel jerked as hot blood splashed his face. Karter's body sagged, but did not sink to the ground. Could not. The tip of the metal spike had burst through the back of his head. The sergeant dangled from it like a fish on a hook. Furus's head swiveled. His gaze settled on Daniel. That moment lasted an eternity. In it, the truth sank in. A vagrant. Daniel could see that, now. The vacant stare. The emotionless face.

Shouts from the far end of the tunnel. One deep and masculine. The other high and surprised. Two pairs of footsteps pounding toward them.

Alix's voice shook Daniel back to himself. Furus kicked Karter's body free and swung his pickaxe in a wide arc. Daniel ducked and launched himself forward, bringing his pickaxe up and around. Too slowly. He hated weapons like these: Axes and picks and heavy things. Spears were lighter and *Sard'tara* reached further. The dead reaver did not share his compunctions. He readjusted his swing effortlessly, bringing it up and around and then crashing down on the head of Daniel's axe.

Lightning raced up Daniel's arms. His pick dropped from nerveless fingers. Furus raised his weapon again.

Rakian barreled into him. They fell in a tangled mass of stumpy legs and arms and two picks, one red and shiny. When they stopped, Rakian sat atop Furus, pick raised. Furus's hand shot out quick as the adder he had killed and seized Rakian by the wrist. With his other hand Rakian bent the other reaver's arm back. There was a crack, and Furus's arm fell limply, his pick clattering to the floor. The vagrant's expression never changed. He thrashed soundlessly Rakian rolled backward in a tumble and came up to his feet. The vagrant skittered backward like a crab and then bounded upright, expressionless, dead eyes flittering between his prey.

Daniel became aware of movement to his right. "Alix!" Her eyes were wide and bright. Anger danced there. So did fear. "Go get help," he said.

She looked from him to Furus and back again. "Go!" Daniel shouted.

Alix turned and ran. Daniel and his father shared a look. Wordlessly, they began to circle, each moving in a different direction around Furus. The vagrant's broken arm hung useless. Daniel, still regaining feeling in his, sprang and aimed a kick at his old friend's chin. Furus's head snapped back. Green blood flecked, staining his teeth as if he'd eaten grass. Daniel waded in, jumping atop the vagrant and wrestling it to the ground. Rakian fell to his knees and wrapped the creature's legs in arms as thick as posts.

For the first time in his life, Daniel watched all color drain from his father's face. "Furus," Rakian said weakly. "How?"

The vagrant leered. "An imperfect copy," it grated in a voice choked with dirt, as if it floated up from a grave. "There was not enough left of the reaver's body to study such trifling details. I had to make do with this one." It paused, appearing to think. "Perhaps my master will paint me with your skin next, stout one." Then, in the span of a breath, it whipped away from Rakian and lunged at Daniel with its teeth. Daniel closed his eyes and tightened his hold on the vagrant's arms. There was a high whistle and a crunch. He opened his eyes. Furus's skull was a ruin of bone and green gore.

Daniel climbed unsteadily to his feet and slumped against the wall. Rakian sucked in breath. "There could be others," Daniel said.

Rakian nodded.

"Alix," Daniel said. They ran to the ladder. Daniel reached it first, bounding up, taking the rungs two at a time. His legs began to burn halfway up, and he was forced to slow, one foot for one rung. At the top, he crawled out of the opening flopped onto his back. He was covered in sweat and breathing raggedly. Shadows lengthened across the courtyard. Out of habit, Daniel inched away from any near him. Rakian pulled himself up and out, saw his son, and offered a calloused hand. Daniel took it and was jerked to his feet.

"Thanks," he mumbled. Wiping a damp curtain of hair from his eyes, Daniel scanned the courtyard. It was empty. The sounds of talking and hammering drifted up from the city. Their *Sard'tara* lay discarded near the bench. Daniel retrieved them. Handing Rakian's over, he saw his father's expression relax the moment the weapon touched his skin. They shared a look. *The Man of a Thousand Spears*, Daniel thought. *Plus one.*

"Merrifalls would not have gone far," Rakian said.

Daniel nodded and started toward Sunfall. As they reached the door, it opened, and Zakary came running out. "Sergeant! Sergeant!" he cried, coming up to Daniel.

"Who is this boy?" Rakian asked.

"A lighter," he replied. "What's wrong?"

"I have a message from the lady."

"You mean Alix?" Daniel said. "What does it say?"

"I can't read." Zakary handed him a folded parchment. Daniel opened it.

Southern gate. Attack.

"Dawn and Dusk," he cursed.

"What?" asked Rakian. Daniel handed him the note. Rakian read it and repeated the curse. Daniel was already moving. Zakary ran in front of him, just out of reach. They took the shortest route through Sunfall and hooked around to the southern courtyard. The entrance to the gate leading down to mountain path was unguarded.

"Where is Brinhem?" Rakian asked. "This gate should always be guarded."

Daniel offered no reply. Alix dominated his thoughts: her smile, the way she brushed her too-short hair away from her ears, the feeling of her breath against his lips.

Daniel, Rakian, and Zakary came storming out of the gate to

find Wardsmen and volunteers at their stations, building fortifications, moving supplies, running drills with weapons. Their brothers looked up as they passed. "Stay," Rakian barked. They stayed.

They raced through the streets, taking side roads and shortcuts instead of sticking to the main thoroughfare, which was clogged with wagons and men and women and supplies and makeshift camps. Wending their way around a cluster of homes, they emerged in the southern square. Alix stood in a ring of Wardsmen and civilians, worried and confused and then delighted. She ran and threw her arms around Daniel.

"I'm so glad you're safe," she whispered into his ear.

"You, too," he said, closing his eyes and holding her.

She pulled away first. "How did you know to come here?"

"I got your note," he said, holding up the parchment.

Frowning, she took it. "I didn't write this."

Daniel's gaze flicked around the square. "Zakary came for us. He said . . ."

The boy was gone.

Shaking her head, Alix tucked the note into a pocket and took his hand. "Come," she said, pulling him into the circle. Rakian stood across from him, between a sergeant, Kieran Wood, and a civilian, a woman Daniel didn't recognize. All the Wardsmen in the circle were sergeants, he realized: Gavin Kaurr was there, and beside him stood Jareth Byrn, shoulder to shoulder beside another civilian, a man . . . And then Daniel remembered the last time he'd seen him: Standing with a group of other beleaguered men, women, and children. One of the Gotik refugees.

"Who is that?" Daniel whispered to Alix, nodding discretely in the man's direction.

Alix shrugged. "No idea."

"But he was with your parents and the others from Gotik."

"Was he?" she asked.

At that moment, Zakary reappeared, squeezing in to stand on Alix's opposite side. "What's this about, Lieutenant?" Sergeant Raymond Porter asked. "We received the missive and came as soon as we could."

Rakian blinked. "I sent no missive. My son was attacked down in the tunnels. He received a note from Alix Merrifalls concerning an attack, here."

"I didn't write it," Alix said. "Zakary met me outside the gate in the north district. He said there was trouble here." She squeezed Daniel's hand. "I didn't want to leave you, but you were with your father, and I thought . . . " She trailed off, but Daniel paid her no mind. He was watching the others, listening.

"You summoned me," Kieran Wood said to John Steele, also holding up a parchment.

"No," Sergeant Steele said, "I . . ." The group dissolved into confused conversation. Rakian remained silent. A dark cloud passed over his face.

"Something's wrong," Daniel said, turning to Alix. "Let's—"

Alix was as pale as the snowy tabard he wore over his chainmail, her lips a thin, bloodless line. Zakary stood beside her, holding a knife to her throat. He had to stand on his tiptoes, but he showed no signs of strain. His other arm was wrapped around her middle, pressing her to him. A ray of the Lady's light glinted against the knife edge. Her body was as rigid as the boy's.

"What in Dawn's name do you think you're doing?" Daniel said hoarsely. The terror in his voice brought all conversation to a halt. Raymond shouted. Sharp hisses rang out as six swords were ripped from their scabbards.

Zakary pulled Alix closer. His lips peeled back in a rictus. "Tell them not to move, Daniel."

Thought and reason fled. Zakary's countenance was still that of a boy of ten winters, but his voice belonged to a slightly older man, its inflection of glee derived from inflicting suffering. Daniel's grip on his *Sard'tara* slackened. His fingers tightened before it could fall. Rakian recognized the voice, too. He crossed the distance in two long strides. Zakary saw him coming. His expression never changed as the hand clutching the knife to Alix's throat clenched. She spasmed, and a droplet of blood ran down her throat in a thin line.

"Stop!" Daniel shouted, panic cracking his voice. Rakian froze in mid-step. The other five sergeants held their swords in front of them, eyes flitting between Daniel and the boy.

"Tell them to throw down their blades," Zakary said.

"Do it," Daniel snapped. The clatter of steel against stone was loud in the stillness.

"Very good," Zakary said, sounding much like an adult praising a dog who has performed a trick.

"What do you want, Garrett?" Daniel asked.

Zakary's smile widened. "You know."

"Just tell me what you want and let her go. No Wardsman will try to stop you."

The boy's tongue poked out and ran across his lips, slowly, as if savoring a new taste. "I don't believe you." Turning to one of the civilians standing amid the sergeants, he nodded. The sergeants, absorbed as they were on the boy and his captive, failed to notice the way the expressions of the civilians went blank one by one.

Daniel did notice. "Look out!"

Too late. Another chorus of hisses rang out as knives were pulled from sheaths and buried in throats. Kieran Wood and Raymond Porter collapsed face down and thrashed, blood pooling beneath them. John Steele and Gavin Kaurr sank to their knees, gasping and choking, blood spurting through pawing hands. Jareth Byrn's eyes bulged as he cursed and wrestled with a vagrant that had grabbed him from behind. Expressionless, the vagrant adjusted its hold on its knife and sawed at Jareth's throat. Blood ran down Jareth in a freshet as his grip slackened. His hands dropped and hung limply. The vagrant released the body and Jareth fell in a heap.

Almost casually, Rakian batted away the knife of a raven-haired woman with one end of his *Sard'tara* and brought the other blade spinning up to cleave through her skull. Green, moldering flesh mottled the ground. The other vagrants turned, noticing this dissenter, and threw themselves at him. Rakian swung his *Sard'tara* from side to side, slicing at air and fleshy masks. One fell, then two, a third. The spear seemed to thrust and slice in every direction at once. Garrett had taken the Man of a Thousand Spears too lightly.

Two vagrants remained. They circled Rakian, faces blank. In front of Daniel, Zakary raised the hand that had been curled around Alix's middle, and his mouth formed two arcane words. Flame in a nearby lamp drained away, and Rakian's *Sard'tara* glowed white hot. The reaver cursed and threw it aside. His hands dipped to his waist, where Daniel knew he stored daggers. The vagrants leaped atop him and threw him to the ground. One pinned his arms while the other squatted beside him and held a dagger to his throat.

"You'd better soothe your father, Daniel," Zakary said.

"Lieutenant," Daniel barked. "Cease struggling and lie still. That's an order." Rakian calmed instantly. His expression was unreadable; Daniel had never seen its like on his father.

Screams rose up from the square. A stampede of footsteps from the west district signaled the approach of more Wardsmen.

"I want you to come with me," Zakary said. "There's something I wish to show you."

"No," Alix said, cutting off with a choked cry when Zakary pressed his blade against her skin.

"I'll go," Daniel said quickly.

"Ah, good," Zakary said. And with more strength than a boy of his stature should possess, he lowered the knife from Alix's throat and shoved her to one side, hard enough that her boots left the ground and she collapsed several feet away.

Zakary extended his free hand. "Shall we?"

Chapter 46:
Reunion

DANIEL'S WORLD DISSOLVED in a blur of senses: Alix's scream, Wardsmen and reavers storming the square, the coppery scent of blood pooling beneath the murdered sergeants. Then the world stopped spinning, and new sights and sounds and smells assaulted him.

They stood at the apex of a hill. Below, spread out across plains and hills and the charred remains of Gotik, stood vagrants. Tens of thousands. They faced him, bodies draped in steel and snow, or plainclothes, or single-colored robes, or covered head to toe in tattoos of animals and shapes and symbols, or lavish silks and jewelry, or flamboyant clothes. Torelians and Leastonians and Darinians and Sallnerians, all in varying states of decay. They stood as still as stone, holding swords and axes and crossbows and clubs at their sides.

"My army," said Garrett Lorden. Christine's twin brother came up on Daniel's other side, fingering a knife curved like a hook. The blade was frosty, like glass fogged over. Daniel spared it only a glance. Horror and shock rooted him to the spot.

"I taught them something," Garrett continued. "Watch." Tucking his knife away, he snapped his fingers.

Zakary raised the hand not clasped on Daniel's shoulder. A deafening roar poured forth from tens of thousands of throats. A wave of fetid breath snapped Daniel out of his stupor. He turned and retched. Bent at the waist, he wiped his mouth and stared. Four leagues north, tall white walls bordered Calewind. Sunfall sat perched above the capital, all gleaming spires and bridges and turrets.

"The Crown of the North," Garrett said. He gazed out at Sunfall. "It's to be mine, you know. He promised it to me."

Garrett turned back to his army. He crooked a finger and Daniel followed as if in a trance. They walked, vagrants parting before them like a ship cutting through waves. As they passed, the dead closed back in. They did not draw breath. They stood and watched, their heads rotating to follow him, moldering flesh or dry bone rasping over cloth or skin or bone.

Daniel was numb. He couldn't even feel fear. *I'm going to die*, he thought calmly.

At last they came to a rickety, high-backed chair. Garrett flopped onto it, draping one leg over an armrest and propping his chin on one hand. Three Darinian vagrants flanked the makeshift throne, hands folded beside their backs. Daniel flashed back to the tavern in Tarion—*the Fisherman's Pond*, he remembered— and thought, though he could not be certain, that these were the same undead who had barged into Aidan's empty room and . . .

He shuddered and looked away.

"It's hopeless," Garrett said, sounding bored. "Do you see that?" On his lap he held two sacks. Their tops were open. Daniel caught a glint of gold in the Lady's dying light.

Daniel did not respond.

"This is all for you, you know."

Daniel raised his eyes. "For me?"

Garrett nodded, smiling. "To introduce you to your extended family. Every ruler needs a pet. A dog to keep at heel. When Tyrnen gives Sunfall to me, you will be my—"

"I thought you were our friend," Daniel blurted.

Garrett threw his head back and laughed. "Aidan was a bounty. A job. Our orders were to befriend and waylay him until Tyrnen could collect him. Christine forgot that. She lost sight of the goal. Stupid girl. It's her Sallnerian blood. Traitorous and rebellious to the core. Like rotten fruit. Oh, sure, the apple may appear ripe on the outside, but inside lies a worm. I'm different. I know my priorities." His hands went to one of the sacks in his lap. He pulled out a fistful of Leastonian coins, let them drip between his fingers, smiling as they jingled and clattered back into the bag.

The clatter of coins in the absolute stillness unnerved Daniel. He thought about pointing out that Garrett was half-Sallnerian, too, then thought better of it. "You could have helped Aidan. He would have rewarded you," he said instead.

Incredulity spread over Garrett's features. "I see the judgment in your eyes. You! Judging me!" He gave a raspy laugh. "I know all about you, Daniel Shirey. A sneak. Just another word for thief. I came into my fortune honestly. I accepted a job, and I completed it." He flinched. "Nearly. But I won't fall short again. He wouldn't like that. Besides, I want that crown. And I want. My. Sword." His right hand opened and closed as if around a hilt.

Daniel laughed. He certainly did not mean to. He did not want to. Only, what Garrett had said was absurd. More than that, he was resigned. There was no hope of escape. Not from the center of Tyrnen's army. *If these are my final breaths, I'll spend them laughing at this madman.* He thought back to antagonizing the street tough in the Hornet's Nest, and provoking Karter just a few days ago. Outnumbered and outmuscled both times, but that had only made him laugh harder. As he did now, laughing until tears ran down his cheeks.

Garrett's hands went still, open in mid-clench. "Are you laughing at me?"

"Who else?" Daniel wheezed. "Your sword? Do you mean Heritage?"

"Tyrnen promised it to me," Garrett said. He sat perfectly still.

Daniel's mirth tapered off, chuckles and giggles fading to nothing. "Well," he said, wiping his eyes, "I'm sorry to inform you it isn't his to give. You have numbers on your side, Garrett, but no sense. You chose the wrong side. Aidan forgave your sister for her betrayal. He would have forgiven you, too. But it's too late for that."

"I don't fear Aidan Gairden. He is not as powerful as Tyrnen."

"No," Daniel agreed. "He's more powerful. Or has Tyrnen not shared with you the account of what transpired the last time he and Aidan crossed paths?"

Garrett brought both fists crashing down on the armrests of his throne. "This is what got you into trouble before. Or don't you remember? You interfered. You spoke out of turn. I was just trying to confer with my sister, and you got in my way." He took a deep breath, exhaled long and deliberately. "If you had known your place, I wouldn't have had to punish you."

The memory of cuts and bruises returned in a flash, then fizzled, replaced by comprehension that hit him like ice water. "Is that why you killed my mother?"

Garrett grinned. "I punished her in your place. I had hoped to kill your father as well. Tyrnen told me all about him. He seems like a dangerous man." He turned to Zakary, and a note of respect crept into his voice. "You should have killed Rakian Shirey."

Daniel followed his gaze and shuddered. Zakary's boyish face was gone, replaced by the tight flesh, empty sockets, and silent scream of a harbinger. "Rakian Shirey and the girl were left alive to force compliance," he said in a toneless voice.

Garrett brightened. "The girl? A blossoming romance? Do tell, Daniel."

"A refugee from Gotik," Daniel said evenly, "and an honorary Wardsman placed under my charge." Blood pounded in his ears.

Garrett snorted. "A woman in the Ward? Unheard of. How do you tolerate her? I certainly won't allow such flagrant disregard for tradition under my regime." Disdain was replaced by a sly grin. "I suppose there's room for advancement now that every lieutenant and sergeant who crossed your path is dead. If I didn't know better, I'd think you carried a plague."

Daniel's fists clenched. "You targeted them."

"Not at first. Truth be told, I had no idea you were in Calewind. I followed the sword my master planted, thinking to eliminate Aidan. Then I saw you, and you saw me. What a beautiful reunion we shared. I decided then and there that I wasn't finished with you." Garrett smirked. "I ordered my minions to infiltrate Calewind and follow its scent."

Daniel's mind raced. *How much does he know?* "To Aidan," he said.

Garrett waved a hand. "Aidan's in the west. I know that now." His grin showed teeth. "So does Tyrnen. But don't worry about that. You've got bigger problems. Thousands and thousands of bigger problems." He leaned forward, squinting at Daniel as if he were a particularly revolting bug. "You really are a fool. How many times will Aidan run away and leave you behind to incur

Tyrnen's wrath on his behalf?" He tsked. "I suppose every prince needs a whipping boy."

It took all of Daniel's willpower to remain standing. "Why don't you just kill me?" He realized he was resigned and was suddenly angry at his own resignation. Despite his best efforts, he would do the very thing Toban had warned him against doing. He would go to his grave—perhaps a hole in the ground, or the belly of some vagrant—with regrets. Alix, tall and headstrong and beautiful, swam in front of his vision. He hoped Garrett killed him now so she could be the last thing he saw.

"Obviously I'm going to kill you," Garrett said, rolling his eyes. "Not now, though."

"Why?"

"Because it's out of my hands," Garrett snapped. "I follow orders, and my orders are to give you a warning." He took a deep breath, looked skyward, and then spoke as if repeating someone else's words. "When next the Lord of Midnight takes his throne, my forces will storm Calewind's walls."

Daniel gaped. "Why would you tell me that?"

"Because your punishment is nearing its end. The first stage of the punishment I have planned for you, anyway. Your mother, your snow brothers. I had them killed to soften you up. To crush you beneath the weight of the responsibility you now carry across your gangly shoulders: Calewind's survival. Rakian will die, and your lady friend will die, and that will be your fault, too. They'll all be dead, and the blame for every broken body, every lost soul, will be laid at your feet."

Daniel's shoulder blades pinched together. His eyes flitted every which way, looking for something, anything he could use to . . . there. A discarded sword, old blood the color of dried mud staining its blade. Garrett followed his gaze. "That won't work," he said, the corners of his mouth lifting. "Zakary and his friends will protect me. Won't you, Zakary?"

Daniel scraped the last of his courage from the bottom of his stomach. "You won't kill me. You can't."

Zakary cocked his head. "We come and go from Calewind as we please. We must wait to tear down your walls, but we needn't wait to continue thinning your ranks."

Daniel's chest tightened. "We can still win."

Garrett smiled patiently. "No. You really can't. But do try. I'd hate for you to bore me."

"I'm going to kill you," Daniel whispered.

Garrett's smile melted away. "I've changed my mind. I'm going to keep you as a pet. A short time remains before the attack. Plenty of time for Zakary to break your mind and force you to—"

There was a gust of wind and suddenly Toban stood in front of him, eyes red and bleary. He blinked, saw Daniel. One meaty paw darted out and grabbed his wrist.

Garrett shot to his feet. "Stop them!"

Toban barked a clipped phrase and the world dissolved in streaks of color. Abruptly Daniel found himself facing Calewind's southern gate. Walls, huge and sturdy and safe, soared above him. They were still outside. From the other side of the gate, Daniel heard a din of shouts and stampeding feet. "Dawn and Dusk," he croaked.

"What is the title of the book you gave me?" Toban asked.

"What?" Daniel asked. A tidal wave of bestial screams pierced the air.

Toban's grip on his wrist tightened. "The title of the book. Quickly."

"It was something about the moon. *Appetite for the Moon?* No. *Aggravation of—*"

"Close enough. And its contents?"

Daniel caught on. "Dark magic. I'm me, Toban. Can we get inside, please?"

"Close your eyes," Toban said.

Daniel did. Another blast of wind kicked up, and the clamor from within Calewind rose to a cacophony. He smelled sawdust, sweat, horse manure, and blood, and knew without opening his eyes that they were back inside the walls.

"We're safe," Toban said.

Daniel almost laughed. They weren't safe anywhere. Didn't Toban know that? He'd seen Garrett's army. Daniel opened his eyes, and what he saw drove breath from his lungs.

The scraps of the Ward filled Calewind's main thoroughfare: fifteen hundred of his brothers, give or take several dozen who had been picked off over the last few days, held blades and shields that gleamed, but their steel and snow was scuffed and dirty. Days-old stubble covered haggard faces. Their eyes shone with fear. The Ward was, to Daniel's thinking, the most elite fighting force on Crotaria. They were also men. Flesh and blood. Anyone who believed Wardsmen ran toward battle were as mad as Garrett Lorden.

Civilians swarmed the southern square. Most wore tunics or frocks. Their faces were taut with panic. They held swords, axes, clubs, shields, and bows. Others clutched pitchforks in trembling hands. Women stood shoulder to shoulder with men. Six reavers stomped among them, bellowing orders. Old Beld and Helda, each as large as a bear and twice as ferocious, stood at the head of the army. Old Beld choked his smithy hammer below the base. Helda waved a rolling pin as if it were a baton, bellowing orders right back at reavers. Daniel thought briefly of relieving his brothers of their duties. Surely Old Beld and Helda alone could carve a path through Garrett Lorden's vagrants.

And then Alix appeared, shouldering her way to the front of the crowd and stealing his breath. She looked radiant in steel and snow that fit her perfectly. It was clearly an old uniform. Her tabard had not been pressed, her steel was dingy and dull. Yet she was beautiful. Seeing her in the steel and snow looked right.

She caught his gaze and broke for him. He met her half way. Alix threw her arms around his neck and buried her face in his shoulder. "I was going to come for you. We all were."

He breathed her in. *This might be it. This might be all we'll ever have.*

"As you were," a familiar voice shouted. "You have stations to man and tasks to complete."

The mob dispersed, many of the Wardsmen saluting in Daniel's direction. Rakian strode through them, face carved from stone. Daniel knew his father's body language—it was practically the only way he communicated—and saw deep frown lines etched in his face. Those lines signified a level of anxiety that, on any other man, would have manifested as complete hysteria. Daniel felt a pang of love and gratitude in his chest.

Rakian stopped in front of Daniel. "You shouldn't have gone along with that boy," he rumbled. Familial love became a flash of annoyance.

"Oh, enough from you," Alix snapped, stepping back and wiping her eyes. "He was beside himself with worry, Daniel. You should have seen him."

"You didn't let me finish, Wardsman Merrifalls."

"Sorry, Lieutenant," Alix mumbled. She grasped for Daniel's hand. He squeezed it.

Rakian's face softened. "I'm glad you're all right, son."

"Thank you," Daniel said awkwardly. They stood facing each other, both clearing their throats and shifting their feet. Alix rolled her eyes.

Rakian gathered his composure. "Make your report, Sergeant."

Daniel told them. About the size of Garrett's army, and Garrett's warning that they would attack at midnight.

Rakian listened, hands clasped, fingernails white. "Midnight. So little time."

"We're nearly ready," Alix argued.

Rakian scoffed. "This Lorden boy could give us until next winter and we still wouldn't be ready. Not without the full might of the Ward. Not without . . ." His gaze flicked to Daniel, and Daniel knew what he'd been about to say. *Not without a Gairden. Not without Heritage.*

Alix removed her helm and brushed a strand of too-short hair from her forehead. "Toban says the north and west defenses are prepared." She hesitated. "Just about prepared." She touched Daniel's arm. "You should have seen him when he heard what had happened. He was ready to battle Garrett's entire force on his own."

"How many would you estimate?" Rakian asked.

"More than we've got," Daniel said.

"An estimate, Sergeant."

"Ten thousand. Probably more."

Rakian's leathery face twitched. That was all, but Daniel could read him. *We're doomed.*

"He knows we've been preparing, Lieutenant. He's had spies in the city since the beginning. His army is camped outside the southern gate, but I don't think he'll concentrate attacks there. It makes sense for him to hit all at once."

"You would have us divide and conquer," Rakian said.

"We don't have much to divide, unless . . . unless we give Toban command of our numbers. He knows his defenses. There might be areas that would be better served with fewer or greater numbers."

"The bulk, yes. Not all."

"Half the Ward, plus the Azure Blades," said Alix.

"What about the north district?"

"I don't think it needs to be as heavily fortified as the other three," Daniel said, "unless Garrett means to make his men scale the Ihlkin Mountains and rappel into the streets. Unless—"

"They shift inside," Rakian cut in. He shook his head. "Cinder Kirkus has set a number of magical traps in the north. I'll have him add more." He waited.

"Sure," Daniel said, unsure what his father expected him to say.

Satisfied, Rakian nodded. "Take a moment to gather yourself, Sergeant, then you and Merrifalls get to the Cinder's side and stay there. He's our most valuable asset." Snapping a crisp salute, he turned on his heel and strode across the square, gesturing and barking commands.

"Dawn," Alix muttered, pulling on Daniel's arm until he fell into step beside her.

"Dawn, indeed. He must be exhausted."

"Why do you say that?"

"He seemed so . . . unsure of himself. Didn't you hear him?"

One corner of Alix's mouth tugged upward. "Oh, I heard him."

"I'm missing something."

"He was asking for your opinion, Daniel."

"He was?"

They rounded another corner and came to the Crown's Promise. It was crowded, but quiet. Conversation flowed in murmurs and whispers. Alix guided him to the table in back where they had met days—*Could it really only be days?*—earlier. A few Wardsmen sat there. They looked up, recognized Daniel and Alix, and saluted as they scooted off benches and pressed through the crowd.

Daniel's face grew warm. "That was odd."

"You're important to this city," Alix said. She nudged him onto a bench. Instead of sitting across from him, she piled in beside him. "Your brothers were the first to insist on mounting a rescue. That large, scary-looking woman—"

"Helda," he said absently.

"You must have been terrified," Alix said in a softer tone, rubbing his back.

"More for you than for me." He thought suddenly of Karter.

Only a few days ago, Daniel had despised him. Now he was dead. He was mourning Karter Rosen. "The world can be a funny place," he said, pressing his palms against his eyes, watching as stars bloomed over his vision.

"Tell me about it. Of all the people I'd expect to mount a rescue for you, the last would have been Toban Kirkus. Cinder Toban Kirkus."

Daniel laughed. Alix's smile faded. She stared at the tabletop. "This might be our last day together. This might be our last day ever."

"Don't talk like that," Daniel said.

Alix traced carvings and rings with a finger. "All my life, I've wanted more. When I was little, my mother kept me underfoot. I didn't want to be underfoot. I wanted to go outside with my brother. When I finally got outside, I wanted to leave. Jak went first, to Calewind. I vowed to follow. Then I came here, and I held Jak as he died. I thought I could avenge him. I thought I could be a part of something big."

She pinched the snowy cloth at her shoulders, let it fall. "I'm a Wardsman. Your father made it so. I was so excited, and proud. And then you disappeared. When I saw that you were safe, that was all I cared about."

"You were all I could think of, too," he said.

"Then we agree."

"On what?"

Alix looked at him steadily. "We don't have to stay."

Chapter 47:
Bridge Edict 794

FETER AND LAM faced one another, expressions pinched in concentration. Their faces were blotchy. Their stormrobes were spotted with perspiration.

"Can you still Touch?" Lam said tightly.

"As if I danced with the Lady among the clouds," Feter replied.

Lam snorted. "Absurd. You know for a fact that the sun is a star that burns with the ferocity of tens of thousands of—"

"Concentrate," Christine said gently.

Lam shot her an annoyed look, then took a breath and pressed his lips so tightly together they became a thin white scar. The other twelve members of the Storm Guard huddled around them, glancing from Lam and Feter to their forearms. Christine turned her arms this way and that to examine both sides. They were pale as ever. That surprised her. Constant waves of heat from the group's kindling warmed her skin as if she stood in front of the Eastern Pearl's hearth. So warm, she expected her skin to have turned bright red.

Lam and Feter quivered with exertion. Blinking heavy-lidded eyes, Christine stepped between them. "That's enough for now," she said. Her arms grew cool, signaling that no one within the immediate vicinity was Touching. "This is our third practice of the day. I've told you about the fever. The body not only craves rest between periods of strenuous kindling and darkening, it demands it. Let's get some dinner and get back to the Bridge before we're missed."

Feter raised an eyebrow. Tired as she was, Christine needed a moment to realize her slip. *Before we're missed.* She had lived among the Sallnerians on the Bridge for over two days and had even slept in Domicile 137 last night, finding that she preferred her childhood home's thin blanket and splintery wooden floor to the Eastern Pearl's decadence. Even a private bathtub paled in comparison to feeling welcome.

"All the others know how to Tie," Lam said, running a shaking hand through damp hair. "Emy can Tie me with her eyes closed."

"You can?" Christine asked the girl, impressed.

Emy, who sat on her mother's lap while Jehanne read from a book titled *Foundations of Kindling: Necessary Prayers to the Lady* that Christine had borrowed from the temple library, shrugged one tiny shoulder. "I had to look at him first, but once I could see his face when I closed my eyes, I could . . . feel him, I guess." She giggled. "I even did it with my eyes closed and my back to him."

"Nobody likes a braggart," Lam said, though he was smiling.

"That's remarkable," Christine said. "I'd like for you to teach me how to do that."

Emy gave a shy smile. "Sure. I mean, I'll try." Her face grew serious. "It's pretty hard to do."

"I want to try Tying one more time," Lam said.

"Lam," Christine began.

He pouted. "This is important, Chris. Sunset is drawing near. I won't get another chance until tomorrow evening at least."

"Running out of forged day passes?" Christine asked. Somehow her thieving friend had produced spurious passes for every member of the Storm Guard, each bearing a signature from a disciple claiming the stormrobe would be working in one area when in fact they were meeting in Sharem's abandoned western district. Every member of the group came and went from the Bridge individually or in groups of two, never the same two Touched in a group so as to avoid arousing suspicion. Once Christine decided they had made significant progress or needed a break, they filtered back to the Bridge one or two at a time.

Lam adopted an innocent expression. "One more time, Chris.

Please? Walk me through it again. If I don't get it on my first—no, my second try—we'll turn in. I promise."

Christine rolled her eyes. "Fine. One more try, and then we're done for the day. Don't look at me like that, Lam. A second try in your condition could burn you out. You do remember my lectures about burnout?"

Lam grumbled.

"Good," Christine said. "Would you like to help, Emy?"

The little girl opened her mouth to answer and yawned, long and deep. Christine laughed. "Feter, you try." Her friend faced Lam. "Now, Feter, kindle some of the Lady's . . . some of the sunlight. Just a small amount. You don't want to burn yourself." Slowly, her right arm grew warm, like clouds sliding away to reveal the sun. "Perfect. Now, a Touched does not need to kindle or darken for you to Tie them, but it makes them easier to detect, which suits our purposes. Now, Lam, concentrate on the warmth you feel emanating from Feter. In a combat situation there would be several sources of warmth or cold. We'll work on distinguishing one from another later. It's not so different from untangling string. Focus on Feter. Now kindle light yourself. Just a bit. There. Imagine your light fashioned as a needle, and thread it through the essence of kindling you feel coming from Feter and—"

From somewhere far behind Christine came a faint scuffling, like boot against stone. Emy pointed to the sky. Christine's arms grew doubly warm an instant before a ray of fire no thicker than her little finger shot into the air from Emy's hand. Shouts rose up from above the Darinians' steeples and elaborate domes.

Christine snapped her fingers twice. Heat and swirls of wind came from every direction as the Storm Guards kindled and shifted away, leaving her alone in the street. Alone except for Lam. "What are you doing?" she hissed.

Pale-faced, he tottered on his feet. "I can't Touch again. It hurts."

Christine cursed. "I told you about the fever. Don't you ever listen?"

"What?" he said feebly, and grinned at her. Christine draped one of Lam's arms over her shoulder and shifted. They materialized in a narrow alleyway that reeked of sweat, old clothes, and spoiled food.

"Can you walk?" Christine whispered. Lam took one tottering step and shook his head. "Fine. Come up with a story." She guided him out of the alleyway and into the dilapidated square that led to the Territory Bridge checkpoint. The two Wardsmen who had accosted Lam the night Christine had arrived were on duty.

"What have we here?" the younger one asked, striding out from his station with his chest puffed out. Christine glanced at Lam. Sweat ran down his face in rivulets. Her heart sped up, and she opened her mouth to weave a lie.

"I'm ill," Lam said weakly.

"Speak up," the Wardsman snapped.

Lam raised his head and glared. "I. Fell. Ill," he said, enunciating each word. The Wardsman's face colored, but the older man came forward.

"Where were you stationed?" he asked.

Lam wet his lips. "Temple courtyards. Pruning the vines growing over the lattices. Guess the heat just got to me."

"It's not so warm today," the younger man said.

The older Wardsman pressed one palm to Lam's forehead. "You're burning up. I suggest bedrest."

Christine nodded and dragged Lam through the checkpoint.

"Odd, that you two always come slithering back when trouble brews," the younger Wardsman called from behind them. Lam stiffened, but Christine ignored the taunt.

"Keep walking," she said.

The Territory Bridge was quiet. Wardsmen guarded mostly empty lanes. Behind her, Christine heard Emy and Jehanne catching up to them. "Don't say anything," Christine muttered under her breath when they drew near. "Go back to your domiciles. We'll meet for dinner."

Jehanne nodded tightly and pulled on Emy's hand. The girl gave Christine a petrified look. Christine smiled. "You did well," she mouthed. Emy beamed and, yawning deeply, let her mother drag her away.

Feter was already inside his domicile when Christine opened the door and staggered inside with Lam. The two dropped to the floor, panting. "How'd you get back so quickly?" Christine asked.

"Shifted right here," Feter said. He pointed at the ceiling. "Those cracks let in light. I knew I could shift anywhere *the*

Lady's light touches, so . . ."

Christine shook her head. "You've got to be more careful. For all we knew the Bridge could have been crawling with disciples and one of them would have felt kindling coming from inside a domicile."

"I panicked," Feter admitted. "I'm sorry, Chris. I'm not thinking clearly. I'm hot, exhausted, and not feeling so well." He went to Lam and cupped his cheek. "You look awful," he said with affection.

Lam sat slumped against the wall to one side of the door. His eyes were closed. "We kindled too much. Chris was right."

"She's always right," Feter observed.

Christine pushed herself to her feet. "I should go. It's almost curfew. We've done enough for one day. I mean it, Lam. No more kindling or darkening until after breakfast at least. We all need a good night's sleep."

"You won't get any argument from me," Lam said wearily.

"I'm going to pay a visit to the others," she said. "Discreetly, of course. I want to make sure they're doing all right. Lam, when you feel up to it, think of a time to meet tomorrow and spread word. Both of you, actually. Lam's the last person who should be seen sneaking around."

"You know," Lam said, his eyes still closed, "for someone who passed on the opportunity to lead our little movement, you're awfully dictatorial."

"I said I'd help. I'm helping."

"You are," Feter said, smiling faintly. He extended a hand and squeezed Christine's when she took it. "We couldn't have done any of this without you. Thank you, Chris."

Christine's chest swelled. It was so wonderful to be needed. Her eyes suddenly stung with tears. She scrubbed at them. *Damn you, Aidan Gairden,* she thought, but the words were lathered in fondness. She cleared her throat. "I'll check on you before I go to bed. Rest up a bit, Lam, then leave before—"

The door flew open, smacking against Lam's forehead. He grimaced and stumbled to the center of the domicile. Christine and Feter fell into line beside him. The older Wardsman from the checkpoint stood in the doorway.

"It's almost curfew," he said in his deep voice. "Each of you will need to retire to his or her domicile."

"Are you going to arrest us, then?" Lam said, eyes squeezed shut.

"It's just a warning," the Wardsman said. He cleared his throat. "I'm sorry about the door. I should have knocked."

Christine and Feter shared a look. A Wardsman? Offering an apology? Before they could comment, the man reached into his belt and withdrew a small, square-shaped parchment. "I've got a summons for Christine Lorden. You're wanted in the temple immediately."

Her breath caught. *The conclave has reconvened. That must be it.* She stepped out into fading daylight with the Wardsman. Her attention was so fractured that she did not even think to look back to wave goodbye to her friends.

FETER WAITED UNTIL Christine's and the Wardsman's footsteps had faded, then turned to Lam. "Are you all right?" he asked, gently prying Lam's hand from his forehead. He winced. A bruise was already beginning to form.

"Stupid snowman," Lam said. "I've got a headache starting."

"Do you want pills for it? I've got plenty."

"No. It'll be all right. I just need to sleep." He took Feter's hands. "I did not realize how late it was. I hoped to get back long before curfew so we could spend some time curled up with our books before dinner."

Feter's smile vanished. "Books," he said in a hoarse whisper. "I left one of our books in the western district!"

Lam frowned. "Leave it until the morning. I'll let Christine know and she can—"

"It's sitting in the middle of the street. No one's supposed to be in the west district." He smacked a fist against an open palm. "How could I be so careless?"

"A quick shift, perhaps," Lam said, though he sounded doubtful.

"We can't risk it." Feter smacked his palm again.

"What are you going to do?" Lam asked.

Feter chewed his lower lip. "Let them see me turn in for the night." He shooed Lam toward the door.

"What about my pills?" Lam asked quietly.

Feter peeled away his blanket and opened the secret compartment. He unscrewed a lid from a glass bottle and gave

Lam two white capsules. "They'll make you drowsy."

"I don't need any help with that. Feter?"

"What?" Feter said as he shut the trapdoor and threw his blanket overtop it.

"Be careful."

"Always." Feter gave Lam a peck on the lips and then, gathering himself, opened the door and loudly wished Lam a pleasant night. He stood in the doorway long enough for the Wardsmen standing at either end of the lane to see him, then closed the door. A moment later, he shifted.

CHRISTINE DID HER best to walk quietly. It was no good. No matter how softly she stepped, her bootsteps echoed through the Temple of Dawn's vaulted corridors. Most of them were abandoned. *Odd, for this time of day.*

Bells clanged overhead. Christine jumped. The silence had been so absolute that the bells had shattered it like a brick through glass. She quickened her pace, rounding a corner and hurrying down the long narrow hall toward the closed doors of the Hall of Morning. They were closed. Raising a hand to admit herself—she was in no mood to knock, and she had been summoned, after all—Christine paused. Were the Hall of Morning any other room within the temple, closed doors would have meant nothing. In this case, their closure was significant. The conclave met only at Dawn, convening to begin, continue, and end trials.

At that moment, the bells ceased ringing. Their echoes died away. Suddenly the Temple of Dawn seemed too quiet. Her belly tightened. She clasped her hands over it. The instinct to leave the temple and Sharem and Crotaria grew until her legs trembled with the urge to run.

The doors opened. Christine stepped forward briskly as if her legs could not abide stillness a moment longer. Seven of the eight gilded chairs were unoccupied. Tyrnen sat in the eighth, fingers steepled and propped under his chin. His cane sat propped against the chair. "You are early," he said in his strong, steady voice.

Christine turned to leave.

"A moment of your time," Tyrnen said.

"We have nothing to say to one another."

"I bring news of your betrothed."

Christine froze. She concentrated. *Still in the west.* Jealousy bubbled up. She suppressed it. "Is that why you summoned me here. To tell me what I already know?"

"I thought you might be interested to know that Aidan has won Nichel over to his side."

She fought to keep from panicking. *How can he know that? Perhaps he doesn't. This is Tyrnen. He lies like men breathe.* "That is why he went to the west, you old fool," Christine said.

Tyrnen's beard bristled, his lips quirking in a small smile. "He can be quite charming."

Christine's nails dug into her arms. "I'm leaving."

"Don't go far," Tyrnen said. "I have it on good authority that the conclave will resume soon and deliver a verdict." He tapped a gnarled finger against his chin. "Then again, perhaps you should go far. I doubt your peers will rule in your favor."

Christine had to force her hands to unclench. Her nails would draw blood if they bit any deeper. "You manipulated them. I should have known."

"I simply answered their questions. They know all about your collusions with Aidan, and how the two of you practiced dark magic to spirit across Crotaria."

"That's it? That's all you told them?"

"I also mentioned," he continued blithely, "how young Aidan has been a bad influence on you. Or perhaps it was the other way around. Did he teach you how to darken, or did you teach him? Either way, he is likely passing on his knowledge to Nichel. The Darinians do not know about their history. Their talent lies dormant. I am sure Aidan's hands will do a fine job coaxing it from Nichel's body, don't you think?"

Christine's temper surged. "I could kill you right now. I can hold more sunlight in my little finger than you could hold in your entire—"

"What a strange word," Tyrnen said. "Wherever did you hear it?"

Christine took a breath. "You speak in lies, old man. When the verdict comes in, tell my father to deliver a message to me himself. I will not appear before the conclave otherwise."

"Tell him yourself. He was in his study, last I saw him."

Her mouth went dry. "If you have harmed him, I'll kill you."

Sitting back, Tyrnen raised his hands. "You do not want to kill me. Believe it or not, I am the only one who has been telling you the truth."

Christine stormed from the Hall of Dawn.

TYRNEN WATCHED CHRISTINE go, not daring to move a muscle. "I believe you have heard everything you needed to hear."

From behind his chair came a stirring of fabric and popping of joints. Terrence came around to stand beside him. His pouty face was blotchy with anger. "The girl has used dark magic?" the Cinder said hoarsely. "You are certain? And . . . and a Gairden as well?"

Terrence's disbelief could not have been more undiluted if the Lady of Dawn had offered herself to Kahltan. Still. He had to be cautious. Calculating. "She did not deny it," Tyrnen said.

"No, but . . ."

"She asked if 'that was all' I told the conclave. As if that is not enough. And she reminded me I have no proof, words designed to reassure oneself that a criminal act will go undiscovered. Do you not agree?"

"Do you have proof, Eternal Flame?" Terrence sounded desperate.

"I do not, disciple. I know only what my eyes see and my ears hear. My eyes saw the Sallnerian stand right over there"—he indicated the empty portal—"while my ears heard her threaten my life and use a pagan word."

Terrence shuddered. "Where did she even learn such blasphemy?" His eyes widened. "The Gairden boy."

"Doubtless," Tyrnen said. "But my ears have heard even more. Certain members of Torel's Dawn have brought word of troubling rumors."

"What rumors, Eternal Flame?"

"Pagan rituals being performed right here in Sharem."

Terrence's voice went flat. "The snakes."

"I implore you not to let epithets slide from your tongue, disciple," Tyrnen said, his tone grave and disapproving. Despite his urgency to move plans along, he grew curious. "Why do you hate Sallnerians so much, Disciple Terrence?"

Terrence's upper lip curled. "One of the . . . a Sallnerian killed my father. He was a Wardsman and worked hard to provide for his family and make the . . . the Sallnerians as comfortable on the Bridge as he could. In return, the Lady welcomed him into Her embrace before his time."

Tyrnen fought a grin. He remembered Terrence's background, now. His father had been a bully and a petty thief, beating his Sallnerian charges for the smallest of infractions. His bullying extended further toward Sallnerian women. Sallnerian girls, to be precise, and one in particular. Eleven winters, Lessa had been when Wardsman Gaul Saowin had waited until she had reached the checkpoint to show her day pass and then dragged her deep into the scalethorn, forcing her to swear that she would never utter a word of what transpired there. She had, to her father, and that had been the end of Wardsman Gaul Saowin and Lessa and her father: Her father for murdering a Wardsman, and Lessa for speaking untruths toward a man who wore the steel and snow. Terrence's father had got what was coming to him, although Tyrnen doubted Terrence saw the matter the same way. *Perfect.*

"Ah," Tyrnen said, raising a finger. "But it was his time, Disciple Terrence. The Lady does not illumine the path along which Her plan unfolds."

Terrence bowed his head. "You are correct, of course, Eternal Flame. Thank you for imparting your wisdom."

"Nevertheless," Tyrnen continued. Terrence looked up sharply, confusion and hope warring on his face. "You are correct after a fashion. History shows that Sallnerians are as snakes in tall grass. They cannot help it. It is in their blood."

Terrence nodded, expression solemn, eyes aflame.

"These rumors were brought to my attention early this morning," Tyrnen said. "I would investigate them myself, but I thought you might want to handle the matter, now that your jurisdiction as Bridge custodian has been made official."

Terrence nodded. "I will gather a contingent and leave immediately."

"A word of advice, disciple."

Terrence, already halfway to the open doors, turned. "Yes, Eternal Flame?" He actually sounded impatient.

"Christine Lorden remains close friends with Lam of Domicile Four and Feter of Domicile Twenty. Were either domiciles searched during your first inspection? The one that ended prematurely?"

Terrence scrunched his face, thinking hard. "I . . . I do not know, Eternal Flame. I did not think to ask the Wardsmen or my peers for an account of which structures had been inspected."

"You must be more diligent in the future, Disciple Terrence. The night is long, but the Lady always rises, spreading her light to illuminate all corners. Remember that."

"I will, Eternal Flame."

Tyrnen flicked a hand. "Do your duty."

Terrence went. At last, Tyrnen permitted himself a smile. The flesh and mind were always so much more willing when the soul remained intact. Terrence would prove an able servant. Not as capable as the other in the west, but devoted.

Tyrnen pushed himself to his feet. Not all souls were as willing as Terrence's, and there was still so much work to be done.

NOT FOR THE first time, Christine cursed the temple's ward against shifting. She flew up the stairs two and three at a time, sprinting past disciples and pontiffs who eyed her with open contempt. Word of her trial had undoubtedly spread, probably directly from Tyrnen's tongue. *Or Terrence's*, she thought. *As if there's a difference.*

It occurred to her that she was pleased by the disciples' attitude. Before, they had looked upon Ernest Lorden's Touched daughter with suspicion or unease. Being unabashed in their raw dislike of her was more honest. She tried to convince herself that their prejudice meant nothing to her. Never had. Never would.

The door to her father's office was closed. Christine grasped the handle and hesitated. She had never entered this room without knocking. Muffled sounds came from within. She pressed her ear to the door. *Low talking? No.* Her chest went cold. Ernest Lorden was crying. She threw the door open. The Second of the Lady's disciples sat at his desk holding his head in his hands. His golden robe was creased and dull, bereft of its sunny glow. His hair was disheveled. He looked up sharply and stared at her with bloodshot eyes.

"Father?" she said softly.

"Chris," he said thickly, scrubbing his hands over his face. "Come in. Close the door."

She obeyed without thinking and came to stand beside her father. Hesitantly, she reached for him, then let her arms drop.

She began to ask if he was all right, but stopped short. *Of course, he is not all right. Dawn and Dusk!* Then she noticed the orange flowers sitting atop one of Ernest's mounds of parchments and books.

Her breath caught. *Begonias.*

Ernest slowly sat back in his chair. He looked older than Christine had ever seen him. "I miss her," he said simply.

"So do I. Every day." Her chest seized with guilt. *When was the last time I thought of my mother?* The answer came swiftly: When she had last set foot in Sallner. Not on the Territory Bridge that led into the realm proper. When she, Aidan, and Daniel had escaped some weeks ago.

Ernest drew a deep breath and stood. "You shouldn't see me like this."

"Don't be absurd," she said. "You are human, just like the rest of us."

His eyes drank in the room, coming to rest on the flowers. "Begonias were her favorite. She used to keep a garden of them out back."

Curiosity overcame her. "Here?"

"No. Behind her home. This was before you and your brother came along. She grew up in Domicile one thirty-seven, you know. After her parents passed away, it became hers. It was drab." He chuckled. "Hard to imagine, I'm sure. Your mother took it upon herself to plant flowers to liven up her square of yard. That was how I noticed her. I was still a disciple, then, though I had my eye on the station of Eternal Flame. I came to the Bridge as part of a routine patrol, as I had countless other times. But late one spring, I saw this bright, beautiful patch of color. It stood out, and the splash of color did the Bridge good."

He smiled. "And then I saw your mother. I'd seen her before, of course, but that time was different. Standing beside her flowers, she was even more beautiful. More colorful. More vibrant. I had to talk to her. I gathered my courage. My mind was blank, so I stated the obvious: 'Your flowers are beautiful.' The compliment startled her. Startled her into smiling this awkward, uncertain smile. Guarded. But I saw her in it. I looked past the old, torn clothes, and the dirt on her face, and I saw her. Like the Lady peeking out from behind clouds. I fell in love with her. It wasn't the easiest choice, but then, it wasn't a choice at all."

The light in his eyes faded. "She was sick before we married. I didn't notice. I should have fought harder to take her away from that place. I didn't pay enough attention."

"You were too busy." Christine's words were stone encased in ice.

Ernest simply nodded. "I made poor choices. I chose the Temple of Dawn when I could have taken my family elsewhere. I wanted both. I wanted it all."

Christine's expression grew wintery. This was no time for her father to regret losing a family he had neglected. Then she chided herself. "I wasn't here for her, either," she said softly.

Ernest frowned. "What happened was not your fault. You were a child, Chris. There was nothing you could have done for her. She wanted me to help you and your brother."

Christine tried to suppress years of anger and resentment, but pettiness got the better of her. "We hardly saw you. I didn't even realize you were my father until Lam told me during one of your visits. Your official Bridge tours. Garrett and I flourished in spite of you, not because of you. I love you, Father. Some days I'm not sure how, exactly, but I do. But for you to imply you helped either of us, any of us, is an outright lie."

She forced herself to stop, surprised to find she was breathing heavily. Her face glowed with heat. Her hands shook at her sides. "I'm sorry," she said. "Not for how I feel, but because this was not the time or place to express it."

Ernest had stared at his desk during her tirade. "I cannot deny I've been less a father and more an authority figure to you and your brother. I did not know how to nurture, and even if I had, there were complications in my spending too much time on the Bridge."

"You could have taken us away! You said so yourself!"

"I helped you and Garrett to leave."

Christine shook her head. "Bridge Edict Seven hundred and ninety-four states that we could not be bound to the Bridge because of our mixed blood."

Now he did look up, giving her a half smile. "And who do you think wrote that law?"

Christine blinked. "When did that happen?" she asked, even though she thought she already knew.

"Shortly before you and your brother turned ten winters old.

It was my first official act as Second Disciple. You were a gifted child, Touched by the Lady. I knew you would not and should not be confined to the Territory Bridge. You were so intelligent, Christine. I did not want you to be a bird trapped in a cage."

Christine sank into a chair across from Ernest. "Mother. Did she know, too?"

Ernest folded his hands atop his desk. "She did. She was so proud when you were born. I saw to it that you were born away from the Bridge and performed your testing myself. Had she been any stronger, she would have done something desperate to get you away from the Bridge. She was bold, your mother. So, I confided in Tyrnen. He had long been a friend. It was his deciding vote that elevated me to Second, and there I stood, not even one full day as Second Disciple behind me, asking him to amend the law so that any Sallnerians also of Torelian or Leastonian descent be free to go. I did not specify an age. A wise decision, I think."

"Why would Tyrnen agree to that?"

Ernest gave a slow shrug. "He recognized your talent, and expressed interest in your education. And I assumed at the time he was being fair and just."

Christine knew her father meant no harm, but his words stung. *Fair and just to anyone with a drop of northern or eastern blood.* She shook her head. "We just walked away. Garrett and I left Sharem. No one tried to stop us."

"That is not technically true. Unbeknownst to me, you and your brother schemed to leave. You were scheduled to attend an examination related to your schooling. When you did not arrive, and when Garrett could not be found, what had happened became clear. Your premature departure caused quite a commotion within the temple. A number of disciples pointed to your actions as proof that Sallnerians could not be trusted and argued that your debt still stood."

"Terrence?" Christine asked sourly.

Ernest nodded. "Fortunately, I had Tyrnen's backing. He could not countenance holding any of mixed blood against their will. So, you see, he is not all bad."

No. He only values one realm's blood less than another's. "Why didn't you try to help Mother?" Christine asked.

"Her debt was insurmountable. She had inherited her mother's and father's when they entered the Lady's embrace.

Those, added to her own, made it impossible." Ernest's throat moved. "I wish I could have done more for her, Chris. I'm sorry. I live with that regret, that and so many others, every day."

Christine pounded her fist against the chair's armrest. "Sometimes the law is foolish." It was a childish thing to say. She did not care.

"Most of the time," her father replied bitterly.

Christine's mouth fell open. "I don't think I've ever heard you speak ill of temple edicts."

"And you will not. Certainly not in a place where I could be overheard." He licked his lips. "I could have left the temple, but I did not. After you left, and your mother's passing before then, I thought I could do more good within the temple." He shrugged, looking embarrassed. "I was still ambitious, Chris. Just for different reasons. Nobler reasons."

"You were always so strict with me. That's why I left."

"I never worried about Garrett. His appearance favored his Torelian blood. You were not so lucky. Your mother and I worried over you constantly. After she died, I never wanted to let you out of my sight. But that would not have been fair, either. So, I let you go. It was better to lose you than to see you subjected to the sort of treatment your mother endured." He made a sound of disgust. "That I stood by and allowed her to endure."

"You never mention how she died. I know she was sick, but that's all."

"Chris, please."

"No, Father. I need to know."

Ernest said nothing for a time. "It was her lungs, we think. Her breathing grew increasingly labored. The healers came to see her and said there was nothing they could do."

"Did they do their best, Father?" she asked, voice hard. "Or was she just another snake?"

"I believe they did their best, yes. I studied healing as well. I understood their diagnosis. There was nothing the Lady's light could have done for her."

Her hands began to shake. "Did you ever wonder if she might have lived if there were other remedies? Other forms of treatment?"

Ernest went still. "Ah," he said softly. "How long have you known?"

The room swayed like a ship in a storm. "You know?"

"All pontiffs elevated to disciple know. Before this conversation proceeds any further, you should know that science and medicine could not have saved your mother. And even if they had, they would have condemned her in the same stroke. Do you think the temple would have stood idly by if it came to light that there existed a power outside their control? Those who administered such treatments would be branded heretics and burned, and your mother and I right alongside them."

Christine swallowed. "When I was little, I believed the temple existed to help people. Then I grew up. I saw the way everyone looked at me, and I realized it was full of liars and hypocrites."

"That is unfair," her father said softly, "and untrue. People are people, Christine. Never mind the color of their robes or whether they wear a crown or a helm or a fusty old cap. There are some in the temple who care only for wealth, and power, and control. But there are others who gain satisfaction from helping their fellow man by performing acts of mercy and charity. I believe that is what the Lady wants, but scripture and motive can be twisted to serve other ends. Deeds, not race or robe or even thoughts, speak volumes."

Christine considered that.

"I presume Feter and Lam have shown you their private stores," Ernest said.

She shot forward in her chair. "How do you—? Father, you can't—he didn't—please, he—"

He raised a hand. "I won't say anything. I have no proof, only knowledge of his ancestry and their possessions. Documentation that is, coincidentally, stored in my office, in a secret vault that only I can open."

"Do they know that you know?"

"They do not, and I would prefer it stay that way. Were Lam or Feter to become aware, they might assume that the Second could shield them from penalty. I could not. There is only so much I can do in my position. The station of Second is not what it once was, especially with Tyrnen back at the Temple of Dawn."

Christine let the meaning of his words sink in. "You believe me?"

There was a long silence. "I believe in you," he said at last.

Christine turned away.

"Chris, please understand my position. I know what dark magic is capable of, which allows me to conceive of the sort of profane arts of which you have accused Tyrnen. Could the dead be called from the graves? That, I believe. Is Tyrnen capable of such action? Yes. All men are capable of any action that will gain them power. That, and the fact that you are my daughter, lead me to believe in you."

"And the rest of the conclave?" she said stiffly.

"They are proving more difficult to convince. Few here could believe the Eternal Flame would commit such blasphemy. You know something of my history with Tyrnen. I have trouble reconciling the fact that a man I admired, who backed my ascension through the temple ranks and who helped my children make a bid for freedom, could commit such deeds. However, I am more pragmatic. Terrence is a zealot. He views the Eternal Flame as the earthly manifestation of the Lady Herself, and thus incapable of doing wrong. If the scriptures tell him to believe something, to do something, he will. It is that simple for him and men like him."

"But you're the Second! Surely that must count for something."

"Not if I stand alone. The Second is only a man. Tyrnen is the Eternal Flame, and is, thus far, beyond reproach. Consider his accomplishments: Elected unanimously by his peers to ascend to Eternal Flame, and hand-selected by Annalyn Gairden to educate the one and only heir she could produce."

Christine's brow furrowed. "I didn't know he'd been unanimously raised to Eternal Flame."

"The only Flame in our history to hold the honor."

Something nagged at Christine. "Who chose him?"

"For as bright as you are, you did have a habit of daydreaming during lessons. If you recall from your lectures, a committee of eight disciples are nominated from within the Temple of Dawn to—"

She waved away his explanation. "I know that. I asked who chose him. The eight."

"Well, let me think. That was many years ago." He pursed his lips. "Now I think about it, at least half of them were members of his Torel's Dawn."

The world seemed to tilt. "Kahltan help me," she breathed.

"Watch your language."

"They're harbingers," she continued breathlessly. "They've got to be."

"Who?"

"Torel's Dawn. They were there, Father. They assured Aidan and me that they had seen Tyrnen's duplicity. Reporting it to you was the reason they agreed to accompany me here!"

Ernest scratched absently at his beard. "Can you give me proof?"

She threw her hands up. "I told you, I—"

"And I told you that without proof, I am powerless. What would you have me do, ask Cinders hand-chosen by the Eternal Flame himself to let me cut into their skin to see the color of their blood?"

Christine stared helplessly. "What else can I do?"

"Tyrnen has flatly denied your accusations. With some sort of proof, I could form a committee to challenge him. Absent that, there is only one other person on Crotaria whose word is equal to that of the Eternal Flame's."

Her stomach sank. "Aidan is still in the west."

"When will he return?"

"I don't know." It took all her willpower to stop herself from tearing her hair out in frustration. *Damn you, Aidan Gairden.* "Tell me what to do," she said.

He drew a breath. "Wait. I will talk to the conclave. At the very least, I can delay a verdict. Gather proof if you can, but avoid arousing suspicion. There is little I can do to protect you."

"I don't need protection from Tyrnen. I can handle him, and Aidan would chase him to the far end of Sallner if any harm came to me."

His eyebrows rose. "Now, why would the Crown of the North take such a personal interest in you?"

"Why is that so surprising? Because I'm Sallnerian?"

"Do not try to change the subject. What is your relationship with Aidan Gairden?"

Christine thought of telling him everything, then decided against it. "We are friends."

"Friends?"

"I can't have this discussion with you right now, Father. I'm exhausted."

"Very well. Where will you stay?"

"On the Bridge," she said, and raised a hand to forestall him. "Whatever the other disciples think of me—and if they have taken Tyrnen's side, I doubt it is kind—I am still a Cinder. I am, Father." Her gaze flickered to the flowers. "Besides, I need to feel close to my mother tonight."

A lump formed in Ernest's throat. "She would like that."

THE NIGHT AIR was cool, but Christine wanted to walk. She roamed Sharem's eastern district. Fewer people wore costumes than yesterday or the day before. The Festival of Blossoms neared its end. Streets were less crowded, and vendors shouted tiredly about their wares. She barely heard them. Three of her father's words from earlier replayed in her mind, like an echo that never faded. *People are people*, he had said.

She followed the street's curvature to Torel's quarter. Streets were straight and orthogonal; homes and shops were tidy and white. Wardsmen patrolled. Some gave her a passing glance. Others ignored her. Still others stopped and watched suspiciously as she breezed on by them. *Never mind the color of their robes or whether they wear a crown or a helm or a fusty old cap,* Ernest had said.

Christine turned south, cutting through the temple's sweeping lawns and manicured paths toward the gate that barred entrance to the Sallner quarter. It was closed. More to keep snakes inside their pens, she knew, than to keep anyone out. A torch flickered nearby. She kindled and materialized on the other side. Of stormrobes, there was no sign. That was not surprising. Curfew had long since passed. Her lips thinned. The district was quiet, as it should be. Yet something felt wrong.

Her two least-favorite Wardsmen stood at their post near the checkpoint leading onto the Bridge. Both spotted her at the same time, and then Christine was surprised. Each man wore conflicting expressions. The younger Wardsman smirked, his eyes shining with arrogance. The older snowman with flecks of snow in his beard gave her a solemn look. His eyes shone, too, but with . . . Christine could not say. Not arrogance. Not pride. Not derision for her.

The older Wardsman stood. "Good evening, Mistress Lorden. May I recommend staying elsewhere tonight? A chill wind came down from the north, and a lady like yourself can afford better bedding than what the domiciles offer on nights like these."

A knot formed in Christine's stomach. His words and tone were cordial, but his eyes were like a cipher. Bright and intense. He was giving her a warning. *But of what?*

Christine kept her voice even. "Thank you, Wardsman, but I will stay with my people tonight." Pride ebbed at her nervousness. The Sallnerians were her people. She had people.

He dipped his head. "Wardsman Jony, my lady. If there's anything I can do, you need only ask."

Dimly, Christine felt a flash of guilt. She thought back to her encounters with Wardsman Jony and realized he had never been anything but . . . well, not polite, but not rude or contemptuous, either. He did his duty. Unlike his younger companion, he never threw his weight around. Wardsmen were prone to that behavior. Sallnerians were like toothless dogs or clawless cats, easy targets for men looking to lash out at targets unable to fight back.

Deeds, not race or robe or even thoughts, speak volumes, her father had said.

The younger Wardsman looked back and forth between them, their exchange twisting his smirk into one of befuddlement. Christine hurried by. *A chill wind from the north.* What could that mean? Fronds wove a tight canopy above. Soon, trees and leaves and scalethorn gave way to rock walls. The Great Sea battered them. The scent of burning meat permeated the night air.

Breath died in her throat. Up ahead, campfires in the center of each lane winked like stars. Stormrobes milled around a larger fire in the dirt square ahead of the domiciles. Red-robed disciples and snowy Wardsmen encircled them like white trimming on the edge of ashy fabric. Firelight glinted off drawn steel. Shouts punctuated the smell of meat, strengthening in pungency with every step she took. The Wardsmen formed a solid line that held back tides of Sallnerians. Disciples stood just behind them. Some rubbed their hands together frantically, their faces pale and haunted. Others appeared calm. Still others wore smug smiles.

Christine broke into a run. Features crystallized as she drew nearer. The faces of stormrobes were taut with fear. Shouts became moans of horror. Tears stained cheeks, glittering like diamonds in the firelight. The bonfire was not a bonfire. It was a stake, piles of kindling littered around its base. Flames roared, giving off waves of heat strong enough to make Christine squint.

A small, blackened body hung suspended, held in place by a cord wrapped tightly around its neck. Fire licked its feet, belly, chest, crawled up its arms. Its face was purple and bloated, eyes and mouth open wide in a silent scream.

Emy.

Chapter 48:
Storm on the Bridge

CHRISTINE STUMBLED TO her knees and retched. A curtain of silky black hair fell over her eyes. She brushed it away and pushed herself upright. Through a screen of tears her gaze landed on Jehanne. She stood in the front line of the assemblage of stormrobes. Two Wardsmen strained against her, red-faced, but she did not push against them. She sagged in their arms, her body wracked by sobs.

A hand touched her shoulder. Christine threw it off and raised her palms. "Chris, don't!" Feter. Tears streamed down his cheeks.

Her hands went limp. "What happened? What in Kahltan's name happened?" She was screaming. She didn't care.

Feter could not speak at first. He swallowed a sob and took her hand. "I was on my way back with the book, but there wasn't enough light left to shift. One of the snowmen stopped me. Emy was near the bonfire. Some of the Wardsmen were on their way to douse it, but Emy saw what I held and she, she kindled and she . . ."

"The fire," Christine whispered. She was staring dumbly at the mob of stormrobes, snowmen, and disciples gathered around the fire. People were screaming, crying. Wardsmen jostled stormrobes, trying to keep order. Most of the disciples wore expressions of horror or revulsion.

"They took her, Chris," Feter said. "None of us knew what to do. We were afraid, and they took her and, and now she's—"

One of the disciples took a step back and raised his hands. His mouth moved. Although Christine could not make out his words over the tumult, his gestures implied he was calling for order. Terrence. He never called for order. He demanded it. The sight of him burned away sadness and horror. Christine stormed up to him, grabbed him by a shoulder, and spun him around to face her.

"What have you done?" she screamed. "She was a child! A child, you—"

Terrence slapped her hand away. "The snake was caught with printed material considered blasphemy. When I ordered her to turn it over, she refused. I ordered her arrested. When she resisted, she was given the Lady's kiss immediately. Justice has been served, Christine Lorden."

"You have no authority," Christine grated. Smoke crawled down her throat like razor blades, sapping her voice. Her eyes stung with unshed tears.

"On the contrary," Terrence said. "The Eternal Flame has granted me full authority on the Bridge. In fact, he indicated that certain thralls were hoarding contraband having to do with pagan rituals. My Wardsmen are searching domiciles now. Should evidence be found, the guilty parties will join the child."

Christine realized the Bridge had gone quiet. "I will not allow you to get away with this," she said. She began to kindle from the fire that gnawed at her friend.

"Ah, ah," Terrence said, holding up a hand. "You are under investigation, Christine Lorden. You do not have my permission to flee. To do so would be tantamount to admitting guilt." When she said nothing, did nothing, his face split in a triumphant grin.

Terrence's words had not stilled Christine. Behind him, familiar faces inched their way to the front of the line of stormrobes. There, to her right, stood Thomassette and Joske. Beside him she saw Joske's brother Undine, hands clenched. To her left, Lam held Feter's hand so hard his knuckles were white. Feter's cheeks were tear-stained, but his lips were stitched in a thin line. Tebald, Berolt, and Symone eased up beside them. Their faces held fear, shock, indecision. Christine willed herself to appear calm. She caught each gaze one by one. One by one, their faces grew resolved.

Triumphant cries came from the lanes of domiciles. Four Wardsmen emerged, their steel and snow clattering as they jogged forward. Jehanne chose that moment to look up. Slowly, almost imperceptibly, she straightened. The Wardsmen holding her appeared not to notice. Their eyes followed the steady approach of their brothers, who clutched armloads of books and bottles and scrolls.

A cramp squeezed Christine's stomach. One hand clutched her belly. She kindled ever so slightly and probed her body. No damage. Everything was normal. She breathed a sigh of relief.

The Wardsmen dropped their discoveries at Terrence's feet. The disciple bent down, retrieved a book, thumbed through it, nodded, and tossed it into the flames. Gasps rang out from the crowd. Terrence eyed them with renewed interest. "These items are blasphemous. They contradict our Lady of Dawn's scriptures. Lies. Filthy, sacrilegious lies. I expect nothing less from snakes. Are these items known to many of you?"

Silence but for the crackle of flames. Stooping, Terrence picked up a bottle and pulled the cork. He sniffed its neck, made a face, and hurled it into the fire. More cries.

Terrence thrust a finger at the group. "As I thought. There is a conspiracy on the Territory Bridge. One steeped in heresy. You defy the Temple of Dawn and the Lady's servants who work tirelessly to see to your wellbeing. No longer. No one leaves this Bridge, no one so much as moves until Wardsmen and disciples have interrogated you. Should you be found guilty of complicity in . . ."

One moment Christine was staring at Jehanne. In the next Jehanne stood in front of her, putting Terrence between them. The Storm Guard surrounded them, a tighter circle within the larger ring of stormrobes and Wardsmen and disciples.

Trailing off, Terrence lowered his arms. His eyes flitted from Jehanne, to Lam and Feter, to Tebald. They landed on Christine and narrowed. The Wardsmen drew swords and levelled spears and advanced. Terrence lifted a hand and they stopped, watching him. The disciple let his hand fall.

"You taught them this," he said to Christine. It was not a question or a supposition. Terrence did not bother to ask how over a dozen Sallnerians had come to learn how to kindle and shift. He simply knew. She stood frozen, unsure what to do, hands clutching her belly. "Such teachings are forbidden. The Eternal Flame told me of the paganism you practice with the Gairden. He has no proof, as of yet. But this? It was you. It must have been."

The members of the Storm Guard watched her. Christine wet her lips. "I did."

Terrence's eyes bulged. "You confess your crime? Vile serpent! You will burn for this! You will—"

Jehanne strode forward and slapped him. Terrence staggered back, one hand clapped to his cheek. He gaped at the woman, then lowered his hand and studied it as if it were something new and foreign. "How dare you?" the disciple whispered. His eyes quivered with rage and flitted from one stormrobe to the next. They landed on Lam and Feter, who stood with hands clasped. The disciple thrust out a palm but Lam knocked it away.

"You will not harm him," Lam said. Feter stepped forward and encircled an arm around Lam's waist.

Without sparing another thought for Terrence, Jehanne went to the stake. Mumbling, she swept one hand out before her. The flames sputtered and dwindled. The rope strangling Emy's neck snapped. Her body tumbled forward. Before it could hit the ground, Jehanne caught it and let her daughter's dead weight carry her to her knees. She buried her head in Emy's singed hair and began to sob, rocking the body in her arms.

Terrence paid her no mind. He was gaping at Lam and Feter. "You . . . you're both . . . That is forbidden!"

"We're in love, bloodrobe," Feter said, raising his chin. "Is love a crime in the eyes of your god?"

Terrence turned purple. "Wardsmen! Arrest them all!"

Chapter 49:
Blossoms

EDMUND DECIDED HE hated boars. Not that he had ever been fond of them.

Beneath the Dawn-cursed mask, his hair was damp and curly, and his breathing echoed and rasped. Sweat soaked his clothing, a thick brown shirt with long sleeves, trousers, boots. It was his true disguise: a reveler more interested in food and drink than in an elaborate costume.

Men, women, and children packed the Pincer's Heart, pressing their way forward through tides of colored robes, costumes, painted faces, masks. One flaxen-haired woman adorned in shimmering robes wore a golden orb atop her head. Fiery tendrils sprouted every which way. *The Lady of Dawn walks among us*, Edmund thought. *If only.* Men were half-clothed. So were women. Tan chests and backs glistened with sweat. The night sky was speckled with stars, and the din was incredible: shouts and yells and laughs and a deafening drone of conversation.

A hand gripped his arm. He slid his eyes to his right, saw only plaster around the narrow slits of the mask's eyes, and cursed. He swiveled his head. Through the eye slits he saw a short, slender figure draped in simple attire—loose shirt and pants, boots—wearing a horse head. Cyrolin. Rotating his head and squinting through the slits, he scouted for ordinary field beasts. That was the agreement: heads of beasts, plain clothes for bodies. He could not find . . . There. Two other boars, masks identical to his, and one boar half the height of the other. Nita and Hahrzen. On either side of the boars walked Gewnan, Cidra, and Usmer. They wore no costumes. They wanted to be noticed, and would be: Their guildmaster's jewelry flashed in the light of torches, stars, and Kahltan.

Edmund inched along, mentally seeking calm. This was his ritual. Before battle, he closed out the world until he was able to focus on his breathing. His Wardsmen believed him unafraid. Edmund the Valorous, they called him. He knew their names, their backgrounds, their habits, strengths, weaknesses, the names of their wives and children. But they did not truly know him. All men who marched toward battle felt fear. Even Edmund the Valorous.

This time was different. He was surprised to find that serenity draped over him quickly, a solid wall without cracks through which terror might worm its way into his heart. It was not that he was unafraid. He was just . . .

Cyrolin squeezed his arm, pointing. Lanoden loitered near the stall where Edmund had bought his chest, feigning an interest in the merchant's wares. Darvin stood opposite him across the square, hefting melons and cantaloupe. Edmund ran his dry tongue over dry lips. Other Azure Blades had entered Pincer's Heart. All carried *Sard'tara* and wore their sea-green leather armor. All walked, milling through the crowd. Everywhere he looked, he found oddities. Azure Blades who wore similar armor, shouldered a similar weapon, but stared straight ahead with flat, impassive gazes.

A large contingent of Azure Blades strode several paces ahead of him, bunched together in a cluster. They shouldered aside anyone in their path, and no one dared challenge them. Their faces were as hard and emotionless as stone. Edmund touched Cyrolin's arm. The horse head gave a slight nod. They followed the group, moving deeper into the marketplace. Edmund's chest constricted. Not with fear. Excitement. Digging into his right pantleg, he withdrew a plain short sword and raised it high into the air.

Azure Blades with red blood coursing through their veins

sprang into action, converging from all sides toward the cluster of undead in front of Edmund. Lanoden replaced a jewelry box and began shouting and waving his hands. Opposite him, Darvin tossed a melon back onto a cart and pressed his way toward them. Gewnan, Usmer, and Cidra pushed and shoved their way toward Edmund.

Cyrolin gripped his forearm so hard her nails dug through fabric and bit into skin. He hardly felt them. The crowd parted before him, and there she stood at their center. Anna, resplendent in a blue gown with lace trimming, jewels set in her Dawn-kissed hair and—

". . . looking so beautiful as you do today," he breathed.

One corner of her mouth rose in a tremulous smile. "You probably say that to all the Crowns."

"I never said it to your father."

She threw back her head and laughed. The sound, high and surprised and genuine, carried through Sunfall's throne room. That space would soon fill up with laborers, visitors from afar, and revelers. Up above, nobles and Hands of the Crown would fill the balconies. None of the Wardsmen—two at the doors, a dozen lining either wall—paid them mind. Almost none. Daniel Shirey gawked openly. Edmund grimaced. That one will never grow up, he thought.

Edmund took Anna's hands in his. They were cold and clammy. "Why are you nervous?" he asked softly. "You'll do fine."

As if in answer, a swell of cheers rose up from Sunfall's southern courtyard, loud enough to permeate Sunfall's walls.

"I'm not nervous for me," she whispered. "I'm nervous for our son."

"He'll be fine. He's got me to guide him. Better yet, he's got you."

She squeezed his hands. "He's got us." She glanced at Heritage, sheathed at her side. Hilt, curved guard, and ruby Eye poked out above the scabbard. "And more, besides. Isn't that so, Father?" Tears welled.

Heritage was still. The Eye, normally flashing and flickering like lightning behind storm clouds, was dark. Anna frowned. "Peculiar," she murmured.

Another roar from beyond the palace walls. Edmund wiped

*away her tears with a thumb. "It's almost time. He'll be here
soon."*

*Still distracted by the sword, Anna was slow to look up.
"You'll be here to meet him?"*

"That is the plan."

*Anna beamed. Edmund basked in her radiance the way
northern men basked in the first day of spring. In her radiance,
and her confidence in him. To take care of her, of their boy, of
their family.*

He had failed them. He had failed her. He had—

Light flashed. Squinting, Edmund came back to himself.
Pincer's Heart. The crowd, pressing in and undulating like the
Great Sea. Vagrants. And in front of him: Anna, clutching a
splinter of what appeared to be frosted glass. What little spit he
could muster dried in his mouth.

A hand smaller and frailer than Cyrolin's gripped his left arm.
His sword arm. Gewnan frowned, studying him. Edmund
nodded. The old guildmaster pivoted, heading for Anna. Usmer
and Cidra followed in his wake.

The harbinger spotted the trio. A wicked grin twisted her
features. Edmund started after them, tightening his grip on the
short sword. He wanted Valor, missed its feel in his hands, but
any steel would do. Absently, he registered surprise at Gewnan's
pace. Even hampered by the crowd, the old guildmaster seemed
revitalized. He took strides that seemed more appropriate for a
man thirty winters younger.

He began to follow in Gewnan's wake, pulling Cyrolin with
him. A bolt of pain shot up his left leg. He gritted his teeth and
pushed forward. Gewnan and the women slipped through the
undead Blades, who clashed with their living brethren closing in
from all sides. A few screams rose above the commotion. Azure
Blades living or dead had no room to swing *Sard'tara*, so they
stabbed and pushed.

Edmund held his sword flat against his right leg. All he had to
do was get close and, while Anna was distracted by Gewnan and
the other two—

Osphera and Jamian drifted in from one side, walking
alongside three other guildmasters Edmund did not recognize,
though their robes gave them away. They took Edmund in at a
glance and then dismissed him. He was just a man in a costume.

Edmund moved on. His eyes were on Anna. She held the spirit stone as he did his sword, firmly in hand and pressed between her palm and leg. Hidden to everyone except those who knew to look for concealed weapons.

Anna looked up and spotted him. Her eyes, very much alive, seemed to see straight through the mask. Her wicked grin broadened.

"Cyrolin," he started.

Something hard as steel yet at once soft and fluffy slammed into his back. Cyrolin took off and Edmund walked after her. Each step carried him as far as a leap. Vagrants carrying *Sard'tara* lunged and cut at him, but he was a feather on a breeze. No, he was a breeze, fast and there and then gone, sweeping past and leaving them in his wake. The harbinger drew closer. The shard in her hand was like fogged glass. She saw them coming and stabbed, but Edmund and Cyrolin were faster. He closed the gap in one final step. In the same motion he brought his sword arcing up.

There was a crack like glass shattering against stone. Anna stumbled back into vagrants that collapsed like tall grass in a wind. Gewnan stared down at them grimly. Cidra and Usmer came to either side of him, pale and wide-eyed.

Edmund ripped off the boar's mask and stared down at the harbinger. Cyrolin, standing beside him, removed her horsehead. She was saying something, but Edmund failed to hear her. He heard nothing, saw nothing except Anna. Her jaw was slack, and so was his. *I've done it, son. You've got your mother back. She's free. Thanks be to the Lady, she's free!*

Anna's mouth snapped shut. She sat up. Behind her, vagrants rose and leered. Edmund gaped. What was happening? He had shattered the stone. He looked for it and saw two broken pieces of glass at Anna's feet.

Glass. It made no sense to him. Then Cidra screamed. He watched Gewnan pull a shard of fogged glass from his robe, long and curved, and slash it first across Usmer's forearm then Cidra's, like a serpent striking twice in one blink of an eye. The guildmasters stared uncomprehendingly. Then their faces contorted, and the shard in Gewnan's age-spotted hand flashed twice. Life leeched from Usmer's eyes like water through a sieve. Cidra's gaze became expressionless.

As one they lunged at Cyrolin. Edmund started for her. Anna took one step forward and her hand snaked out, wrapping around his throat. Her skin was cold as ice. It froze him in place. "Chasing another woman?" the harbinger purred. "I'll remember that, husband."

Edmund allowed confusion and panic one last moment to breathe, then dismissed them. They had no place on a battlefield, and the Pincer's Heart had become one. Screams rang out as vagrants tore away fleshy masks. Azure Blades who still drew breath attacked, stabbing armor and putrefied flesh. Guttural roars filled the air as vagrants pressed forward despite hilts jutting from chests and bellies.

Nearby, Hahrzen fell to his knees, hands pressed to his belly. Blood pooled around him. The spirit shard in Gewnan's hand flashed, and the reaver jerked upright and threw himself at his former allies. Cidra walked smoothly to stand beside Jamian and join him in a two-on-one assault against an Azure Blade holding two pieces of a broken *Sard'tara* in either hand.

"The heads, you fools!" Darvin's voice. The retired Blade was holding back three vagrants, his *Sard'tara* spinning and flashing. "Sever their heads!"

Anna's hand tightened. Stars bloomed in Edmund's vision. He struggled. It was no use. She held him like a vise. The sword! He still held it. He flicked his wrist so that he gripped it like a dagger.

Anna's eyes never left his. "Go ahead. Kill me again."

The sword trembled.

"Sever their heads!" Nita shouted, taking up Darvin's cry. Skulls caved in or rolled from shoulders and toppled to the ground where they shattered like clay vases. Anna shot a furious look at Gewnan. Edmund knew that expression well. His wife was impatient, anxious, ready to move on to the next item on her agenda.

Now. He needed to strike now, while she was distracted. It would be so easy. But she would know. She would feel. She would remember. He thought of Aidan, hopefully marching beside Nichel at the head of the clans, on their way to join the Ward and stand shoulder to shoulder against Tyrnen. His boy needed him. Anna needed him.

Anna was right in front of him, and he could not kill her again. He could, however, kill Gewnan. Edmund's attention slid to the guildmaster. To wrinkly, mottled skin, and cold eyes. "What did he promise you?" he gasped out.

Gewnan lifted his eyebrows and leaned in. Edmund was dimly aware of the old guildmaster replying when a ringing filled his ears. Spots bloomed across his vision. Blackness crept in. He wished it would take him and be done with it.

Anna's hold loosened. She was scowling again. "This is not wise. He should die, here and now."

"Patience, creature," Gewnan said. "Our orders still stand."

Her gaze burned with hatred. Edmund's anger flared. *Creature.* She was his Anna, inside if not out. An idea took shape. He let his arms dangle at his sides. "What did he promise you?" Edmund asked again.

The old guildmaster grinned broadly, revealing pitted gums. What few teeth remained were yellow with age. "Immortality and a crown."

"The east is not a monarchy."

"Things change. Realms grow and adapt. The merchant's guild has governed Leaston by committee for centuries, and to what end? So that fools like Usmer Munerel and Rakian Shirey can pretend they deserve an equal say in the direction of our trade and commerce? So that bastard children from faraway lands can walk among our people as equals?"

"They are hardly equals," Edmund rasped. "Galerunners are slaves."

The old man's eyes widened. "Precisely right! And I will free them by sending them back to their islands and jungles. No longer will our realm be ruled by committee. I will be the committee. The Eternal Flame promised me life unending, and autonomy to rule the east in his name. One ruler, one law. An isle of life in a sea of the dead. Oh, yes, I know what the Eternal Flame has in store for Torel and Darinia. Useless realms. Nothing but ice and snow in one, sand and mountains in the other. Inhospitable. Leaston will be a paradise: lush jungles, verdant fields, cities spread out before the Great Sea."

"And you at its head," Edmund said.

Gewnan stared at him as if he were a slow child. "The Eternal Flame is the head. I am the hand destined to guide Leaston forevermore. That is why Jamian and the other guildmasters had to die. They wanted to bring in more outsiders. More bastards.

More dilution."

"The people you propose to rule will never allow it."

"On the contrary, they will welcome it. I will represent stability in a world overrun by death." He swept his gangly arm out, taking in the battle. "They will see me as the one who rallied the Azure Blades and saved the east from destruction. From you. Word of our council meeting has spread. How you attempted to kill your wife in cold blood, and how you attempted to manipulate the merchant's guild, distracting us until your Ward could flood across our borders and subjugate our people. Fortunately, Annalyn and I were there to stop you. Leastonians will rally behind me. What's more, they will worship me." His eyes glittered.

Edmund's fingers, slick with sweat, choked the sword's hilt. "You're mad."

Gewnan laughed, an ugly rasping sound like parchment against stone. "And you are defiant to your last. The Flame has use for you, General. I think you'll find—"

Anna's eyes widened. That was all the warning Edmund needed. A blast of air slammed into his back and hurled him forward. Anna, caught up in the current, flew with him. Her grip slackened. Before he could think, before he could hesitate, Edmund slashed. They crashed to the ground and Edmund scrambled upright, sword raised in a defensive stance. The wind current had thrown off his aim. Anna lay on her back, green blood spurting from a ragged slash across her throat. She did not move. Choking back tears, Edmund buried his sword in her skull.

Soon, my love. Soon.

But not yet. He spun. Vagrants swarmed around Cyrolin. *Sard'tara* jabbed and cut. Every time one drew near, Cyrolin flicked a hand at it and the blade jerked back as if yanked from behind. Air currents ruffled clothing. Cyrolin's hair flew wildly, curtaining her face one moment and streaming behind her the next. A swarm of green-and-blue-clad forms flooded into the Pincer's Heart from every entrance. *Sard'tara*, hundreds if not thousands, flashed and swung and cleaved. Edmund saw Darvin climb atop an abandoned fruit stand and heft his weapon high, pointing and shouting.

Edmund clenched his jaw. Cyrolin could hold her own. The Azure Blades would sweep away the dead. That left Gewnan.

He looked back to see the old man charging at him, swinging the shard wildly. Edmund raised his sword. Closing the distance would favor Gewnan's shorter weapon. He stepped back, and his left leg buckled. He dropped to one knee and had just enough time to raise his sword over his head. Sparks flew as cursed stone collided against steel. Gewnan pulled back and swung again. Again. Again. The power behind his attacks sent tremors up Edmund's arms. *He's as strong as a man half his age!* Instinct corrected him. Gewnan only appeared as frail and thin as old paper. He was a harbinger. Infirmity made perfect camouflage.

Gewnan clutched the shard like a dagger. Edmund tried to rise, but pain lanced his leg. He thinned his lips and fended off thrusts. Sweat broke out on his forehead and stung his eyes. He dared not blink. All the shard had to do was break skin. Anna had been dead a month, and that was painful enough. An eternity without her defied comprehension.

There was a pause in Gewnan's onslaught. Fatigue registered on the old man's face. Gripping the shard in both hands, he roared and brought it crashing against Edmund's sword. The steel snapped in half, and Edmund's fingers went numb. Gewnan gave a triumphant howl and kicked out with one of his bony legs. His foot caught Edmund square in the chest. He toppled onto his back. Breath left his lungs in a whoosh. Dimly, he heard the sword's broken blade skitter along the street.

Gewnan stood over him, blotting out the Lady's light. "You are beaten," the old man whispered. His attention went to the spirit shard clutched in one fist as if drawn to it. His shriveled tongue ran over dry, chapped lips. "You have proven uncooperative, General," he began, halting at first, then growing excited. "You are a liability to the Eternal Flame. He wants you by his side, but in this case, circumstances . . . I'm sure he would understand if . . . Yes. This is best. I had no choice. He'll understand, will probably thank me, reward me with . . ."

The old man's gibbering faded. Relief swept through Edmund, warm and comforting, like lying beneath layers of blankets with Anna as they dozed before the hearth in their bed chambers. Aidan's face swam into focus. He had his mother's sharp mind. He would have convinced Nichel by now. They would stand together at the head of the Ward and the clans, more than enough to throw back Tyrnen's undead. And Anna . . .

Edmund turned his head. Anna had risen to her feet. Her head dangled from her neck by a strand of flesh. Blood the color of human waste drooled from her torn throat, staining her robes. She staggered toward Cyrolin. The galerunner seemed unaware of the harbinger's approach from behind her. Cyrolin swung her arm wide in a backhand. Four vagrants flew away and landed in a heap.

Anna raised a hand. The air rippled around it. Cyrolin sensed her kindling and spun. Too late. There was an ear-rending eruption and a blinding light. Cyrolin fell back, and—

A streak of lightning smashed into Annalyn's legs, sending chunks of flesh and bone scattering in all directions. Anna fell to the ground with a wordless scream as crimson mist from twitching stumps sprayed over the white blanket of snow. She stared up, mouth agape, eyes opened wide, her scream trailing off in a hoarse whisper. She flopped around on her back and began to inch backwards, gibbering in fright.

"NO!" he screamed.

Edmund struggled to reach his ruined, twitching wife. He raised his bloody hand and reached toward her. Tears spilled down his cheeks, cutting a path through the drying blood on his face. Then he shuddered, gasped, and went still.

Fresh tears bloomed. Edmund had lost consciousness. That was what he had told Aidan, later. That the wounds incurred at the hands of the vagrants and the harbinger wearing his face had overwhelmed his senses and sapped his remaining strength.

It had been a lie. Seized by creatures he could not accept were real, face-to-face with his own face, betrayed by a man he had respected, if not trusted, forced to watch his wife die. It had been too much. In the final moments of Anna's life, when she had needed him most, he had become a boy again. Small and scared, quivering beneath a thin blanket. All those nights at home, listening to his mother and father scream at each other, flinching at the sound of glass bottles shattering against walls. Hiding had been easy. Beneath his blanket, he could pretend to shut out the angry voices, the screams of pain, the slow, heavy tread of his father's footsteps drawing closer.

At Lake Carrean, Edmund had been injured and utterly stunned by what had unfolded. He had also been afraid. That was why he needed to save her. Not only because he loved her.

Because he needed to see her again and hear her repeat the lie he had told himself over and over since he had returned to Lake Carrean to find her body lying in the snow. *"I know you did your best."*

And to believe it. Because he had to. Because it was all he had left.

There was a flash of light and a wave of heat. Cyrolin screamed. Edmund's eyes shot open. Anna advanced, swaying on her feet, lolling head bobbing. Cyrolin scrabbled back on her hands and knees. Her front was singed. Burned, but alive.

Chapter 50:
The Vale of Spirits

AIDAN'S JAW DROPPED as the embossed, marble doors swung inward, admitting them onto the first level of *Daram Ogahra*. Torelian scholars translated the Darinian words to Vale of Spirits. It was melodious, and evoked tranquility, especially for the generations of clansfolk who rested here.

Daram Ogahra was circular, like a bowl. Five tiered levels wrapped around a cavernous chamber as wide as Calewind and twice as deep. Light from the Father and his Vanguard poured in from the mountain's open peak high above. Each tier consisted of a broad road paved in pale marble that glittered in the soft, night light. Ornate lamps bordered each curved street, spreading pools of golden light. Between them, mausoleums towered over wide courtyards. At the center of each courtyard stood a monument, an effigy of the dead buried within. A thin layer of dust carpeted the lanterns and monuments, but the marble, gold, and silver bore no signs of wear. *Few things are as eternal as Darinian craftsmanship*, went a saying in the north.

Aidan became aware of a muted rushing sound. *The Mother's Bosom,* he recalled from his studies. *Janleah Keep is the source of all water in the west*. His throat constricted with thirst. At the same instant, a medley of scents caressed his nostrils. Flowers and perfumes, no doubt to mask the smell of old bones and decay.

Given the Vale's expansiveness, Aidan suspected there must be tens of thousands of clansfolk entombed within. Every clansman, woman, and child who had died in the centuries since builders had transformed the largest mountain in the west into Janleah Keep, and the second-largest just beside it into the Vale.

Aidan glanced at Nichel. Her face was a pale shade of green, and she sucked in air through her mouth instead of her nose. Thunder rumbled overhead. He squinted upward, as astonished by the sound as by setting foot in *Daram Ogahra*. Rain in Darinia was as rare a phenomenon as snow over Leaston's beaches.

Nichel glared up at the sky. "An omen," she muttered.

"Indeed," Jonathan said from behind her.

Nichel cleared her throat. "Aidan. Do you remember when you tried to—"

He gave her a small smile. "Of course. You wouldn't let me."

Nichel's lips curved. Just a little. Jonathan glanced between them. "Would you care to invite me into your joke?"

Nichel's hint of a smile fell away. "Aidan asked to see *Daram Ogahra* relentlessly when he was a cub. A boy," she corrected. "I would not allow it."

"Certainly not," Jonathan said. "It is a sacred place, not to be defiled." His unspoken words hung between them. *Not by the likes of you.*

"Shall we proceed?" Aidan said.

Nodding, Nichel gestured for Jonathan to guide them. The Cinder gathered his blue robe around him, as if chilled, and turned right down the vast street of the first tier. Aidan's head twisted this way and that, soaking in every courtyard, every monument, every mausoleum, sights few not born of Darinian blood had ever seen. He wished he held Heritage so his Grandfather Charles could see. He had loved history and spent hours each night poring over historical texts and reciting names, dates, places, figures, and facts.

I wish you could see this place, Grandfather. It—

Abruptly, he remembered the skein. A pang of loneliness struck him.

Jonathan walked in front of him, turning with the curvature of the road. Nichel brought up the rear, several paces behind Aidan. *In case she decides I can't be trusted and needs room to pounce.* His loneliness deepened. For the first time since becoming sword-bearer, Aidan missed his family. "Who lights the lamps?" he asked, more out of a desire for communication than interest.

"The sentinels," Nichel said. Aidan was unfamiliar with the term. His lips formed the beginning of a question when he detected a strange note in Nichel's voice. Her face was scrunched, as if trying not to vomit. She caught him looking and smoothed her features.

They walked on. Aidan sifted through memories of lessons about Darinian custom and culture, but his mind was cloudy. His feet began to drag. Fatigue, held at bay by curiosity, threatened to drag him to the ground. Another rumble of thunder, and raindrops sprinkled down. Aidan winced as drops cold as ice touched his skin. His chills returned.

A sizzle to his right caught his attention. Raindrops peppered the lamps, sending flames into spasms. More hisses broke out all around *Daram Ogahra* as raindrops collided with fire. Aidan licked his lips. A plan took shape. One step further and he let himself stumble. He pitched to his right, spilling into the street beside the lamp.

Nichel started to rush over then caught herself, face torn between concern and indifference.

"Sorry," Aidan mumbled. "I'm exhausted, and thirsty."

"We can drink below," Nichel said, tucking a strand of damp, curly hair behind one ear. "The Mother's Milk is cold and refreshing."

"Stand up," Jonathan said gruffly.

Aidan made a show of trying, rising to one knee. "I can't," he admitted, breathing heavily and infusing his voice with shame. *Gabriel would be proud.*

"Help him up," Nichel said.

Jonathan made a sound of disbelief. Then he extended a hand. Aidan took it, grunting. He let his body go slack so the Cinder had to do most of the work. Jonathan pressed his lips together, bracing his legs to maintain balance. Which meant he was too distracted to see the flames shrink ever so slightly as Aidan kindled from the lamp, sipping rather than guzzling. The effect was instantaneous. He gasped as heat spread through him, melting the chill.

Standing upright, Aidan had stopped shaking. Traces of his

chill still lingered, but muted, like pre-Dawn frost melting on a spring morning. When he tried to step back away from Jonathan, he tottered. He threw a hand out and caught the lamp to steady himself. This was no ruse. Although kindling had thawed some of the chill caused by assuming spectral form, exhaustion still clawed at him. For a Touched near breaking, there was no substitute for rest.

He murmured a prayer. Conversation rushed in.

— *he back?* Anastasia was saying. *Aidan! Thank the Dawn!*

— *Please do not do that again,* Grandfather Charles said tightly.

I'm sorry, Aidan said, and he meant it. His heart swelled at the sound of his grandfather's voice. He wished the old man was here.

— *From now on, if you want privacy, just ask,* Charles went on, sounding relieved.

I will, Aidan said. *I . . . Hold on.*

Nichel was frowning. "Lead on, Jonathan."

Jonathan scowled at Aidan before turning and continuing down the road.

— *What is happening?* Ambrose asked.

Aidan filled them in as they walked along. They passed four more mausoleums before a wall rose up on their left. It was tall, at least four heads higher than Aidan, and its surface was rough and spiky, like stucco. Paintings and illustrations covered its surface. The stories of the chieftains and their kin buried on this tier, Aidan guessed. There was an arched opening in the center of the wall. A stairwell descended to the second tier. Wall sconces, one on either side, cast orange light against the walls. Jonathan entered the stairwell. Their footsteps and Nichel's breathing were loud in the enclosed space.

At the bottom they stepped onto another broad street, this one painted blue. Mausoleums even more lavish and colossal than those on the first tier marched along either side of the road. Jonathan paused, looking this way and that. Aidan scrubbed the back of one arm over his nose. The heady aroma of perfume and flowers was heavier than it had been on the tier above.

— *More prestigious chieftains and their families are laid to rest on lower levels,* Charles said. Aidan fought not to smile. His grandfather's voice shook with excitement. *Their descendants visit their tombs and decorate them with exotic fragrances that can only be made with flora indigenous to the west. Oh, I wish I were there with you, Aidan. What a privilege you're experiencing.* Some of his sprightliness faded. *If only the circumstances were less dire.*

Aidan's gaze flitted nervously. Shadows clung to alleyways between buildings. He strained his ears, but heard nothing except for the hiss of raindrops tasting flame. *It's so quiet down here. And still.*

— *Naturally,* Gabriel said. *Nothing in* Daram Ogahra *has moved for years.*

Nichel marched up to Jonathan. One hand was clasped over her mouth and nose. "The assassin. Where is he?" Her words came out muffled.

Frowning, Jonathan tapped a finger to his lips. "I don't know, precisely," he said, peering around. "I asked the pack to bring it here, but I did not specify a tier."

Her eyes narrowed. "You walked as if you knew where you were going."

"I assumed it would be on the first or second tier. I did not specify—"

"Enough." Nichel's body went rigid. Taking a deep breath, she removed her hand and sniffed lightly. Tears welled in her eyes. Aidan and Jonathan stepped toward her. She waved them back, sniffed again, then set off to the right. Aidan started to follow. Jonathan threw a hand across his chest.

"Walk behind me," the Cinder said.

"I thought I was supposed to stay between you two," Aidan said evenly.

Jonathan's face went red. "If any harm befalls her, I will kill you myself." Without another word, Aidan set off after Nichel. He had to jog to catch up. She covered ground in large strides, almost seeming to lope.

Another covered stairwell rose on their left, bordered by mausoleums. Nichel bounded down, pausing at the bottom to wait for Aidan and Jonathan. Here the street was painted red. Overhead, thunder cracked and lightning flashed. The rainfall picked up. Fat drops plastered Aidan's dirty clothes to his skin. His hair stuck to his forehead. He swept it away. Water ran along red paving stones. *Like blood.* Visions of Sharem flashed through his mind. He forced them down.

Nichel's nostrils flared again. She turned right. They followed the road in its wide loop until a third wall appeared, leading to a third set of stairs. Aidan labored for breath as they descended. "Why are the stairs so far apart?"

"A defensive measure," Nichel called over her shoulder. "Centuries ago invaders breached Janleah Keep and attempted to loot *Daram Ogahra*. Our builders did not make it easy. There was a battle on the fourth level. The invaders died there. Blood flowed down the streets. It took the sentinels weeks to scrub it all away."

Aidan shivered as he hurried along. Her tone had been clipped until mention of the battle. Then it had grown thick, as if with desire. *For what? Blood?*

Nichel did not slow when she reached the fourth tier. She pivoted and marched left. Aidan barely registered vaults as sweeping and luxurious as Torel's grandest temples as he followed. His legs throbbed. If any of these tombs held a bed, he would gladly curl up next to old bones and sleep. A wall rose up on their right and they hustled down the stairwell. Aidan described their placement to his family.

— *It's a brilliant architectural move*, Charles said. *The Vale could have been built so that stairwells led straight down to the lowest level. Erecting them in a different location on each tier would confuse and waylay enemies.*

There was no street on the fifth and lowest level, only perfectly smooth flooring paved from a multitude of stone from all around Crotaria: icestone, marble, polished granite. Fluted columns stretched into the air, straining to touch the stormy sky. In the center was a mausoleum as majestic as Sunfall. Rain cascaded down walls of gold and white marble. Behind it, water from the fall crashed into a stream half as wide as the streets above. Frothy waves rushed along the wall and disappeared into Janleah Keep. *The water must circulate through the mountain*, he thought.

Dozens of lamps surrounded the tomb, unlit by rain. Only the silvery light from Kahltan and the stars lit the monument. He noticed vaguely that the light filtering through the rain seemed . . . blurry, as if swimming with dust motes. Then he fixed his attention on Nichel, who seemed oblivious to the downpour. She rotated slowly, sniffing. Aidan caught himself admiring her wet, brown skin. Christine's smile flared in his mind and he looked away.

Nichel pointed. "There." She strode ahead. Squinting, Aidan saw a stone slab in the courtyard before the entrance to the palatial burial chamber. It rested beneath a stone awning. A single body wearing plate mail beneath a snowy tabard lay face-up on its surface. *The assassin.*

Aidan and Jonathan hurried under the awning, glad to be out of the rain. Two lamps, the only manmade sources of light not extinguished by the storm, bordered the slab. Rain fell in curtains over the awning. Nichel moved up to the slab. It came up to her chest. Hieroglyphics adorned the sides: a babe painted all in black and cradling a small hatchet; beside it, a man-sized figure hefted a spear high over his head; and, finally, the ghostly form of some wild beast rising up from a black body that lay supine. A layer of light brown paint covered the side of the slab and served as a backdrop. The Plains of Dust, Aidan guessed, where all clansfolk began and concluded their cycle of life.

— *This must be where they prepare bodies for internment*, Charles said after Aidan had relayed what he was seeing.

The Torelian assassin lay face up on the slab. Its visage was pale, eyes closed, arms folded across its chest. It still wore the snowy mail and cloth of a Wardsman. Aidan leaned closer. Two holes punctured the mail. Holes punched by Nichel's knives: one ragged around the edges, the other smooth, a clean entry and exit. Nichel had noticed them, too. She probed a finger into the smooth, then brought it close to her face for inspection, rubbing thumb and forefinger. Aidan's heart leapt into his throat. Her features were blank, neutral. Her hand went still. She held it out to him.

They were bare. His heart plummeted into his stomach.

Jonathan came around the other side of the slab. "I believe you told the war chief the blood would be green," he said.

"I don't understand," Aidan muttered.

"I think I do," the Cinder said. "It's quite simple, really. You lied." His eyes caught Nichel's and held them. "About everything."

Aidan wasn't aware he had clenched his fists until his nails bit into his palms. He wished Heritage was at his side. He looked over at Nichel, who was watching him carefully. *She's waiting for me to explain.* "Cut it open," he said.

Nichel's brow furrowed. Then she looked to the body, and back to him.

Jonathan snorted. "What good would that do?"

"The body is rotten, it's probably been in the ground for centuries, you'll see," he said, speaking faster.

"Ridiculous," Jonathan said. "Nichel—war chief—this foolishness must end. Aidan Gairden told a lie, and you did him the courtesy of testing it. Your father would be proud of the wisdom and compassion you have shown an enemy, but—"

"I am not your enemy," Aidan shouted.

Jonathan's features tightened. His hands shrugged free of voluminous sleeves. Aidan's skin grew warm. He sent a desperate plea to his family. *Tell me what to do!*

— You must focus on Nichel, Anastasia said. *Without Heritage, there is no way to help her see past the lies Tyrnen has constructed.*

Aidan's eyes widened. *That's it!* "It's a mask," he blurted out.

Nichel did not raise her head. Her eyes held him in place.

"The vagrant," he continued, pointing at the assassin's face. "They wear masks of flesh to hide their skulls."

Neither of his companions spoke for a long moment. "We all do that, Aidan," the Cinder said.

"Just . . ." Aidan began. Grunting with impatience, he lunged for the assassin's face. Jonathan, perhaps believing that Aidan was going for Nichel, raised a palm. Aidan's skin warmed and the firelight nearest the Cinder trembled again. Nichel reached forward, grabbed a fistful of the assassin's face, and pulled.

There was a wet snapping sound as flesh tore free. Nichel stumbled back, caught her balance, and gaped at the mask in her hands. Its features were slack and stretched. One half of the mouth drooped toward the floor.

Color drained from Jonathan's face. Aidan barely noticed. His attention was on the exposed skull of the vagrant. Specks of green mottled it. Moss sprouted from its yellowed, gnarled teeth. *Tyrnen didn't put much effort into this one.* All the vagrants he had encountered since that horrific night two of the creatures had cornered him in Sunfall's sword chamber had been indistinguishable from the living. This one looked shoddy, disposable. A tool fashioned for a task, to be disposed of once the work was finished. *No,* he amended. *Two tasks. To implicate me, and, if that failed, to see Nichel dead.*

Swallowing, Nichel let the mask fall from limp hands. When she looked up, tears swam in her eyes. From the moment Aidan had been dragged into the Keep's council chamber, her features had been carved from stone. A war chief hardened by battle and loss. Now she looked like what she was: A girl of fifteen winters who had seen too much and lost even more. His heart went to her. Part of him, a part deep inside, wanted nothing more than to go to sleep and never wake, lost in memories of the good days before his sixteenth birthday.

Nichel crossed to him and rested one of her calloused hands atop his. "I believe you."

Her words were like a sieve. Anxiety drained from him. He squeezed her hand. Nichel took his touch as an invitation to come closer and pressed against him. Awkwardly, he hugged her, patting her shoulders.

There was a strangled cry from behind them. They turned to see Jonathan staring at them, face twisted in horror. Nichel's expression became sympathetic. "Jonathan," she said softly. "Aidan did not lie. Please understand what this means."

Raising one quivering hand to his mouth, Jonathan pointed at them. Aidan tensed, preparing to kindle. But no heat flushed his skin. Gooseflesh broke out over his arms as he realized Jonathan was pointing behind him. Aidan whirled, right hand going for Heritage but grasping air. His eyes fell on the spot where Jonathan was pointing, and his throat seized up.

The vagrant stood awkwardly atop the slab, its legs bowed as if rising from a crouch, its skull tilted. White mail rattled as it straightened, then fell away, clasps and plate crashing to the stone slab and sliding off to clatter onto the floor. Its body was a ruined husk: shriveled and desiccated, spotted with dabs of mossy flesh.

Nichel's hands flew to her belt. One fist closed around the hilt of a knife with a broad, serrated blade. The other closed on air. She brought her empty hand up and glared at it as if returning empty-handed was its fault. A low growl rose in her throat. At the sound, the vagrant straightened. It screamed, high and shrill, and leaped at Nichel.

Aidan never stopped to think. He kindled. The flame topping the lamp behind him shrank. Aidan bit off an incantation and slashed one hand out in front of him in a wide arc. Fire roared out of his open palm in the trail his hand followed, whipping through the vagrant's putrefied neck at the same time Nichel drove her knife into its chest with both hands. Its head dropped to the floor and rolled, bumping up against the base of the slab. The force of Nichel's two-handed thrust sent its skeletal body flying out over the stream, where it landed with a splash.

Nichel gasped and darted to the edge. She fell to her knees and plunged her hands into the frothing water. "We have to find it! We have to get it out!"

Aidan started toward her. A firm hand on his shoulder pulled him back. He whirled to face Jonathan. The Cinder was red-faced and spluttering. "I Tied you. Deception!"

Aidan flung his hand away. "Not now, Cinder Hillstreem. Your war chief needs us."

Looking over Aidan's shoulder, Jonathan saw Nichel kneeling over the water. He shouldered past Aidan, who followed. Nichel rose at their approach. "I couldn't find him," she said softly. The roar of the falls nearly drowned out her words. "He was washed away."

Aidan stared into the current. "Where does this lead? Maybe we can . . ."

Nichel shook her head. "No. It runs through Janleah Keep, and to certain mountains out on the Plains." Her complexion was pale. "This is the Mother's Bosom. Our largest source of water. And I've corrupted it. Death taints life. My people are doomed."

She convulsed. Her mouth moved. Aidan leaned in and caught the words *Wild's doom* but did not understand what they meant.

Jonathan spun on Aidan. "This is your fault. Your duplicity led directly to—"

"Enough," Nichel snapped.

"War Chief, he deceived us. He can Touch! He has somehow unTied himself from . . ."

"I know," she said.

Jonathan's mouth hung open. "You . . . you know?"

"Yes. I smelled warmth on his skin when he pretended to stumble up above."

Jonathan's chest heaved. "How can you condone—"

Nichel shivered again. When she went still, she appeared focused. Resolved. "Because he saved my life." She faced Aidan.

"Thank you, sword-bearer. I hope you can forgive how I treated you. I was . . ."

"You were heartbroken and lost," Aidan finished. He gave her a sad smile. "I understand. I lost my mother, too."

Her mouth tightened. "The assassin. He . . . it played dead. It was waiting for something. What?"

Aidan did not know, and at that moment, he did not care.

— *What happened?* Charles asked.

The vagrant assassin attacked us.

Aidan realized Nichel was looking at him strangely. "You talk to them?" she asked.

"Yes."

"How?"

"Through my connection with Heritage. I hear them, up here." He tapped his forehead.

Nichel's eyes widened. "In your mind? You hear their voices?"

"Constantly."

Her forehead creased. Aidan braced for her inevitable observation: *Yes, it's wonderful sharing my head with eight centuries of Gairdens who come and go as they please, picking through my thoughts like Leastonian sailors pick over driftwood—*

"Does it pain you?" Nichel asked. "Their thoughts, crashing through your mind like a stampede of meshia when all you want is peace?"

Aidan detected a pleading note in her voice, as if his answer were critical. He opened his mouth to answer in the affirmative, then paused. "Yes. But it's also . . . It's wonderful. We do not always get along, my family and I. But they support me no matter what. That's how families work. If given a choice between inner quiet and perpetual chatter, I would choose the talk."

Relief painted her features. "I would like to talk to you about that, and other subjects, once we leave this place."

Aidan's cracked lips split in a grin. "We're friends. We have lots of catching up to do."

"Yes. Friends," Nichel said, blushing. "Jonathan," she said, turning to the Cinder. "Aidan needs his sword. Where did you—"

She went still. Her nostrils flared. "We must leave. Now."

"What is it?" Aidan said. Then he heard something. At first, he thought the rushing in his ears was the water; they still stood near the falls. Then it grew louder and more solid, like bundles of sticks rustling in a heavy wind.

Movement in his periphery. He looked up in time to see a torrent of vagrants pouring down from the tombs above them.

Chapter 51:
Rabid

DEATH REIGNED IN *Daram Ogahra*.

On the four levels above Nichel, the dead rushed from shadows and scrambled atop burial chambers. They held rusted swords, axes, daggers, polearms. Tattered clothes caked with mold hung from bones like loose skin. Patches of putrescent flesh stippled faces, ribs, and limbs, peeking out from old cloth and rusted armor. Many of the undead hoisted bones like clubs. They wore helms in the shape of animal heads: lions, bears, adders with fangs tapered to points, falcons with hooked beaks, wolves with rows of pointed teeth. All perched on the shoulders of moldering bodies that staggered and lurched. The air rang with howls, screeches, roars.

The seal trembled.

Nichel shoved the *Nuulass* down deep. "Run!"

She sprinted forward. She knew Aidan and Jonathan followed. Their scents—freshly fallen snow and soapy freshness—stayed close. She vaulted over the slab where the vagrant had lain and raced toward the stairwell up to the fourth level. Entering the shaft dampened the cries, but only slightly. Within the cramped passage, three throats drew ragged breaths.

Two skeletal shapes rushed down the stairwell toward them. Nichel leaped at them, shoving them back and hacking and slashing and stabbing with Sand. Arms tore free from bodies with wet or dry snaps and fell to the ground. Fleshy lumps flew from chests and bellies. Emerald blood splashed the paved road, walls of tombs, columns and effigies. Vagrants fell, but did not stay down. Those missing arms and legs got back up or dragged themselves toward her, snapping and hissing. Dry, bony fingers grabbed at her ankles. More vagrants along the winding road from both directions.

"Get down!" Aidan called from behind her.

Nichel threw herself to the ground. A wave of heat rushed over her back. Streaks of fire cut through the mob like blades, severing skulls from necks melting bodies that spread over the road like mud. "Their heads!" Aidan shouted above the clamor of bones and screams. Not screams of pain. Vagrants, Nichel had come to realize, did not feel pain. They lived un-life. She started to rise when a warm hand gently pressed into the small of her back, pushing her back down to the road. Jonathan's sudsy odor grew stronger. He spoke a long string of strange words. Undead stampeded closer. She struggled against Jonathan's hand. She wanted to leap up and be with Aidan. To die in his arms when the end came.

Jonathan stopped speaking. Heat crept up her arm. The ground trembled. Nichel's eyes popped open just as columns of fire burst from the road and engulfed vagrants like dry kindling. She wrapped her arms over her head to shield her face from the heat. When the columns dissipated, piles of ash and steel melted down to slag covered the street.

More cries sounded from above. Nichel raised her head. Vagrants still perched atop mausoleums and monuments on the first, second, and third tiers of *Daram Ogahra*. More climbed behind them, jostling the ones up front. She gasped as bodies fell, raining down to lower levels. Others did not wait to be pushed. They threw themselves off, limbs twisting and flailing in the air. Heavy crunches and wet smacks resounded over the steady churn of the Mother's Bosom below and behind them. Bodies shattered against streets and tombs.

For a moment, all was still. Nichel watched, horrified, as a pile of bones flew together, knitting a body. Another pile rose. Another. Still others began to claw at the ground, pulling themselves forward and down to lower tiers. Jaws worked, opened wide in screams. They charged. Above them, more vagrants fell and jumped.

Two pairs of hands hauled her to her feet. Nichel took Aidan's face in her hands without thinking. He was covered in sweat. His dirty shirt and trousers clung to his skin. Deep bags had settled under his eyes. "*Conah*," she whispered for the first time in his hearing.

"I'm all right," he said. His words slurred. He stooped down to pick up a desiccated leg. Green blood seeped from it, running down the bone. Aidan hefted it. He looked awkward, like a Darinian too young for a hunt but determined to mimic the adults of his clan. All around them, the crunch of bodies crashing against stone and wild, piercing cries grew louder.

Aidan shoved her forward. "Go!"

Nichel stumbled, but moved no further. If Aidan died, she would die. He was all she had left. She had to save him.

The seal trembled.

— *I can save him. Free me.*

She hesitated. The *Nuulass* sensed her indecision and pounced. A surge of rage and hate coursed through her like fire. Weariness drained away, and bloodlust washed in. Nichel shoved the Wild's Doom back down into its prison but held on to the wild anger it had brought with it.

— *You used me!* it roared, sounding far away. Not far enough. *You are my weapon.*

Nichel growled and raced down the street, leaping over mounds of ashes and liquefied flesh. The road looped around in a wide arc. She followed it, staying near the center. Vagrants spilled from above. Ornate doors sealed for centuries flew from their hinges and skidded across the road in front of her, sending up sparks. Nichel leaped a door made from marble and ran onward. Jonathan and Aidan followed. Another wave of heat baked her skin. Every hair on her body stood erect as lightning lanced down from the sky. The road exploded, throwing up chunks of stone as small as pebbles and as large as a man's head. Vagrants flew apart, spraying skulls and limbs. Green gore slapped her face, arms, chest. It was cold, and as thick as paste. Viscous blood painted everything.

So much death. So much violence.

The seal trembled.

Nichel ran on. The covered stairwell leading up to the third tier appeared. She sniffed. Freshly fallen snow behind her. Close, but not close enough. Jonathan's soapy scent clogged her nostrils.

"Help Aidan!" she called over her shoulder, and plunged up the stairwell. She collided with a line of vagrants. The touch of their cold, slimy flesh repulsed her. Vomit crawled up her throat. Nichel swallowed it. She had no time for weakness. None of the torches were lit, and Aidan and Jonathan could not safely use magic in tight quarters. Fortunately, the vagrants were at a disadvantage, too. The stairwells had been built for solemn processions of clansfolk descending one after the other. Nichel spun Sand in her hand and punched a hole through the skull of the vagrant in front of her. It dropped. She caught it before it hit the ground and shoved it against the rest of the undead crowding in. They stumbled back, giving her room to breathe and stab. Again and again Sand thrust out. Again and again its coarse steel punched through frail bone and rotten flesh.

The stairwell was black as pitch without torchlight. Squinting, she made out sharp outlines of forms jostling and crowding the entrance above. Another growl rose deep in her throat. Nichel bent at her knees and surged forward. Vagrants fell back, one after another in a long line. Silvery light filtered in through the entrance. Sand thrust and cut and carved. All too quickly the stairs were carpeted in bodies and skulls. Nichel leaped over them and out onto the third tier. Vagrants streamed toward her from both sides, a flood of bodies and corroded steel.

"Down!" Jonathan yelled.

Nichel threw herself to one side. Torches up and down the road winked out and three columns of flame grew from the ground. Bodies disintegrated and flew apart. Olive-colored blood ran over stone. Nichel never lost momentum. She rolled to her left and sprinted up the street. A stitch in her side flared with every breath.

Another wall up ahead. "Stairs!" she called just as vagrants spewed out of the opening. Nichel stopped dead. They were trapped.

Aidan stumbled up beside her, throwing an arm over her shoulders to catch himself. She supported him without thinking, holding him close. His eyes no longer looked tired. They were bright, and took in the stairwell ahead. All the torches had been extinguished, depleted for Jonathan's spell.

He removed his arm and took her hand. "Hold on to me," he rasped. She squeezed harder. Aidan extended his other hand to Jonathan. The Cinder paused.

"What is the meaning of—"

"Do as he says, Jonathan!"

Jonathan took the Crown's offered hand. She gasped as cold deeper than the one Torelian winter she had experienced gushed into her, through her. Ice ran through her veins, freezing her blood. On Aidan's opposite side, Jonathan had risen to his tiptoes. Shock painted his face. "Step with me," Aidan said. They walked into a pack of shadows as words Nichel had never heard but were somehow familiar passed through his lips and—

Darkness, and the sense of impossible speed. So fast the air threatened strip flesh from bones—

—and they emerged in *Daram Ogahra*. Below her feet the road was painted blue, and the tombs bordering the lane appeared smaller than when she had last looked. Nichel gasped again. "We're on the second tier."

Jonathan jerked his hand away and clutched it to his chest. "Dark magic," he said slowly. His look weighed Aidan on new scales.

Nichel peered over her shoulder. Behind them, vagrants clogged the staircase down to the third level. "How—" she began.

"Keep going," he said. His voice quavered.

Nichel nodded and hurtled down the street. Sweat dripped from her. She glanced up. *One more. One more. Hold on,* conah. *Hold on.* She passed a mausoleum on her right.

In the next instant her ears rang and the world spun. Tombs, street, and night sky twisted and tumbled in her vision. A sudden jolt followed by agony in her left side and the world went still and blue. *The sky?* She blinked, and realized she was staring down at the painted road. Nichel winced. Her left side throbbed, one giant bruise.

Slowly, painfully, she pushed herself to her hands and knees, climbed to her feet. *Aidan and Jonathan.*

What she saw froze breath in her throat. One of the mausoleums had exploded in an eruption of marble, gold, and paving stones. Two shadowy forms stepped out, bowing their as they ducked through the doorway. They unfolded to heights three times greater than Romen of the Wolf. Their shoulders were broad, their bodies draped in leather armor. *Sentinels*, she thought vaguely. Guardians of *Daram Ogahra*. Reanimated in living death, but in subtler ways than the moldy bodies that had dogged her steps.

Their skin was sallow, but did not hang from their bones in bloody tatters. They might have died an hour ago, a day at most, except for their faces. All trace of expression and personality was gone. Their skin stretched tightly over their skulls. Empty sockets stared at Nichel. Their mouths hung open. Strips of flesh ran between lips.

Nichel spared them a cursory look. Jonathan lay in a heap beside Aidan, who was sprawled against the foot of a sarcophagus. Blood oozed down his head. She limped over to him and fell to her knees. "*Conah. Conah.*" She held a palm to Aidan's mouth.

Nothing. No breath. None of the teases or jests that had driven her mad as a little girl yet somehow made her love him more. No life. Aidan was dead.

The sentinels spoke guttural words. The fleshy bars that covered their lips like the bars of cells in the Crevasse shuddered and trembled. Beside them, two torches snuffed out. The sentinels raised glowing palms. Her vision swam, covered behind a blur of tears. She looked up, and rage burned the tears away.

The seal trembled.

JONATHAN'S EYES FLUTTERED open. Agony struck everywhere at once. His head pounded. He stared up at the Father's Vanguard, breath hissing through his teeth, back arched so he lay propped up on elbows, fists opening and closing. Rain fell in a torrent. With a gasp he fell onto his back. He squinted and covered his mouth and nose, breathing from behind his cupped fingers. Distant shouts reached his ears. Were they what had awakened him?

No. A chill ran through him. It had been a particular battle cry he had heard only once before. A dawning of the Mother's Light he would never forget. Memory cut through pain. *Daram Ogahra*. Aidan Gairden's innocence. Undead, spilling over the tiers of the Vale like the Mother's Milk. And that cry. *Nichel. The*

Nuulass!

Jonathan turned and saw her. The woman he loved sat on her haunches across the road, in the mouth of an alleyway between two tombs. Aidan lay at her feet. His eyes were open, staring at nothing. *He's dead. The Gairden line is dead.* The realization brought no joy or sorrow. He was numb.

Nichel's curly hair draped her face like a curtain. Her fists pressed against the sides of her head as if trying to hold it together. Three pairs of legs half as big around as stone columns walked past him, a veritable forest of legs. He looked up and saw sentinels. They were crossing the street and headed directly for Nichel, who had not looked up from Aidan's body. Each carried a knotted staff topped with a yellow jewel.

I have to reach her. Jonathan sat bolt upright. His stomach heaved from the sudden movement. He gritted his teeth and pushed himself to his feet. "Nichel!"

The sentinels paused in the middle of the road. Three heads turned slowly to consider him. Jonathan gasped. Each face was a taut mask of death. They turned and strode toward Nichel. "War chief! We've got to run. We—"

Nichel threw her head back and let out an ear-splitting howl. She spasmed and was jerked deeper into the darkness, as if an unseen hand had grabbed her by the hair. The sentinels lumbered closer, nearing the mouth of the alleyway. Sounds emanated from the shadows: gasps, screams cut short, scraping and kicking. Grunts. Growls. Thunder boomed overhead, and the downpour intensified. Breathing hard, robes soaked with sweat and gore and rainwater, Jonathan half-ran, half-limped over to the sentinels and grabbed the one closest to him by an arm. It paused again, staring down at him. Jonathan threw his weight against it. He might as well have tried to shove Janleah Keep.

Its companions stood in the mouth of the alleyway. The one in front raised its staff. The yellow jewel flared, burning away shadows. Jonathan beheld what they had hidden and screamed.

A hulking form strode out of the alleyway on all fours. The woman he loved was no longer a woman. The *Nuulass* resembled a wolf, but larger and hairier than the biggest of the beasts that ran with the clan. Its hair was black. Red eyes burned like coals. Yellowed claws as long as Jonathan's hand extended from all four paws. Even on all fours, it stood eye level with the sentinels' chests.

"Nichel?" Jonathan whispered.

The beast swung its head toward him. Red eyes simmered. Jonathan's bladder let go. The beast's nose twitched. It took another step forward at the same instant one of the sentinels swung its staff. Claws flashed in the light of the Father and Vanguard above and the dead sentinel flew apart. Jonathan, who was still gripping a sentinel by the arm, jerked as the undead shrugged free. The remaining two raised their staffs and made guttural noises. The *Nuulass* bounded into the lane and snapped its jaws once. The sentinel Jonathan had tried to impede was bitten in half. Its legs crumpled in a heap while its upper torso dropped to the street and began to drag itself toward the *Nuulass*. A clawed hand lashed out and smashed the skull to bits. The body fell still.

In the same breath the *Nuulass* spun and pounced on the last sentinel. Her weight drove it to the ground. Its staff flew from its hands and clattered against an obelisk to one side. Claws and jaws flashed. The sentinel went limp, its head a pile of bony shards.

"Nichel?" Jonathan said hoarsely.

The *Nuulass* froze. Still on all fours, it stood on hind legs and loomed over him. Its lips had peeled back to reveal rows of long, curved teeth fixed in a vulpine grin. Ropes of saliva hung from its jaws. Its eyes swam with blood.

Jonathan's throat seized. His mind screamed at him to run but his legs refused to obey. Another sentinel lumbered down the curved road, eyes fixed on the beast. Jonathan glanced around for a brazier, for any source of warmth and light, but found none. The lone sentinel took another step. One more and it would be on her. On it. The undead raised its foot and Nichel barreled into it. The sentinel flew apart. As Nichel moved, Jonathan saw what lay behind her: A still form in the alleyway, covered in red and green blood. Aidan Gairden.

Jonathan took a step toward him at the same moment Nichel whirled. Her—its—angry red glare froze him to the spot. Movement to one side distracted Nichel. Jonathan stole one last glance down at Aidan Gairden, whispered a quick prayer to the Mother and Father above, then ducked his head and charged past Nichel, who had once again become a whirlwind of flashing claws and snapping teeth. A howl rang out from behind him. His stomach shriveled. He looked straight ahead, tearing off down the thoroughfare in the direction of the stairs leading upward to the first level. The *Nuulass*'s cry went from mournful to furious. Four pairs of heavy paws crashed along behind him, gaining ground. The road trembled, shaking dust from crypts and effigies.

Jonathan clenched his teeth and ran faster. Eyes flitting from side to side, he cursed. Every brazier he passed had been upended, coals and ashes scattered along the paths, or snuffed by rainfall. Light filtering down from the opening in the mountain cast a cold, pallid glow. The Father had already passed, sailing toward the eastern horizon. Not that he could have used it. He had no proficiency in dark magic.

Hot breath caressed his neck. Jonathan moaned and ran faster. A desperate plan flew together in his mind. It was foolish, lunacy. It was also his only chance of surviving to reason with—

Nichel's heavy tread stopped. Jonathan became aware of a shadow pooling over the ground in front of him an instant before a great weight struck him square in the back. The ground rushed up and he slammed into it. Breath left his body in a whoosh. A soundless cry passed through his lips. He tried to rise, to crawl forward, but a great weight pinned him to the stone. He could feel hot breath that reeked of the grave against the back of his head. Something warm and wet dripped onto his neck. He closed his eyes, praying that there was enough of Nichel left inside the demon to grant him a quick death.

Shrill calls pierced the air. Unable to move his head, Jonathan rolled his eyes upward. Vagrants boiled over the monuments ringing the first level above, spilling onto rooftops and clattering to the street. Bones knitted together as they picked themselves up, their cries growing louder. From where he lay, Jonathan saw a forest of decaying legs and bony stalks stamping toward them. He squeezed his eyes shut and then cried out as Nichel launched herself off him and leaped into the swarm with a bellow that shook the world. Skulls, limbs, torsos, and weapons spun through the air and clattered against tombs and the distant mountain walls. Four sentinels trudged past him and waded into the fray. Nichel swatted at them, cleaving through torsos with great sweeps of her arm. Their bodies broke with a series of crunches and wet snaps. More vagrants charged up the stairs from the lower levels, the stairway retching them out into the street.

Groaning, Jonathan pulled himself upright. He cupped his hands over his mouth. "Nichel! War chief! Wolf daughter!"

Jonathan crouched behind a nearby sarcophagus as bones and rotten limbs flew past him. When he looked up and over, she was standing over him, red eyes burning. Vagrants rushed up behind her, cutting and biting. Roaring, Nichel spun away, sweeping vagrants from her path. Jonathan sucked in a breath and ran, shouldering past vagrants who bellowed and screeched but did not give chase. Nichel plunged after him. Vagrants threw themselves at her, keening as they swung their weapons or grabbed hold of limbs and ears and neck. Their cries cut off with sickening crunches as Nichel ripped through them. Jonathan flinched as a rusted blade twirled through the air near him and grazed his cheek. An ear-splitting roar shook the ground, and the booming gait of her footsteps quickened.

Jonathan let out a gleeful cry. The staircase, wide and smooth and flanked by two lit torches, was just up ahead. There was a crash behind him. He chanced another look back and saw that Nichel had barreled through a monument to one side. Her impact had reduced the monument to rubble. With dawning horror, he realized she was trying to flank him. Nichel bounded out of the wreckage and batted at smaller monuments and stones. They flew from her like sheets of parchment buffeted by wind.

Terror lit a fire under his feet. There were no vagrants to slow her. Without something to kill, she was like a boulder careening down a hillside with no obstacles in its path. Desperately he kindled from the torches up ahead, fixed the vicinity at the top of the staircase in his mind, and gibbered out a prayer. Wind kicked up around him just as Nichel leaped, claws outstretched and jaws parted wide—

—and bit through empty air. Dust and dirt flew in a torrent as Jonathan materialized on the first level. Without pause, he threw himself inside the open doorway of the nearest tomb and hunkered down in the dark, breathing raggedly. His body shook and burned. He rolled his eyes to look around. It was not a tomb, but a simple home, one of many where a sentinel had lived. Spacious yet sparsely furnished, the stone structure had a square window on each wall, blanket rolls on the floor, discarded armor and staves within reach.

A low growl echoed up from the stairwell. Jonathan crawled on hands and knees to the nearest window and raised his head to look out. Nichel burst from the stairwell, howling and swinging her head from side to side. Ducking beneath the window, he clapped a hand over his mouth to stifle the sound of his breathing. Outside, Nichel growled and spit. Then she fell silent. Heavy footsteps padded closer. A sniffing sound came from above. Jonathan swallowed and held his breath. He looked up. A nose, black and shiny at the end of a long snout, twitched in the aperture.

Slowly, silently, Jonathan eased himself to the floor and pressed himself flat. This was not how he had imagined his end. He had thought he might earn a peaceful death after many years spent advising Romen of the Wolf, and the wolf daughter after him, and perhaps her children after that. Their children. He had loved her. He still loved her. Nothing would change that. Her betrothal before birth had not. The reemergence of her feelings for Aidan had not. Her transformation into a bloodthirsty demon out of Darinian legend could not.

He listened to the far-off roar of the Mother's Milk pouring into the stream, her Bosom. He glanced up. Nichel's snout had disappeared. From far below he heard wild cries and a rush of footsteps. More vagrants. This was his chance, probably his last. He would wait until the undead showed themselves. Then, while Nichel was busy tearing them apart, he would flee. The doors into Janleah Keep were close. They would be closed, but no matter. He could kindle to open them. Assuming the torches near the entrance remained lit.

The yells and rattle of the vagrants rose to a crescendo as they dashed up the stairs and raced out onto the streets. *Have to risk it.* His heart hammered so fast and hard his body vibrated. Gathering the tattered remains of his courage, he pushed himself to his knees and peered out the window.

Two blood-red eyes stared back at him.

NICHEL DID NOT see Jonathan Hillstreem's ghostly white face gaping back at her. She saw man meat. Meat that could flee and hide and think and stalk.

— *Kill*, the *Nuulass* thundered. *Kill. Kill. Kill.*

Deep within herself, in the cave, Nichel tried to speak up. To order the *Nuulass* back into its prison. It ignored her . . . and after a last feeble attempt, she stopped fighting. She wanted vengeance. The *Nuulass* knew that. The red eyes were massive. They filled the cave, casting a blinding red glow over the walls, the floor, existence. In its thundering voice it ordered her into the pit to be sealed away forevermore. The *Nuulass* was in control now.

With a roar of triumph, she swung one great arm and brought down the wall behind which the man hid. He screamed and fell back. It stalked through dust and debris, its perfect sight lighting up the darkened interior space. The man was gone. It heard him, moaning and panting as he shoved his slender frame through the window on the far side of the room. The *Nuulass* bounded forward and snapped at his legs before they tumbled through the aperture and out of sight.

Anger and anticipation pulsed through its veins. The kill was everything. It lived for killing, but the hunt was nearly as gratifying. *Run, man meat. Run.* Its voice reverberated through every core of the woman. It charged through the opening it had made. A band of the not-men stood in its path. It made short work of them, hammering and slashing until bones and flesh littered the ground. A horde of the giant not-men lumbered up the stairs. It ignored them, sniffing, and then bolted down the street. There he was. Just ahead. Arms flailing, legs faltering. She could smell his weakness, his fear. He pitched forward, almost falling before he righted himself and plunged on.

Saliva flooded its mouth and ran down its jaws. It bounded forward. Not-men rushed at it from side passageways, but they were fewer in number now, but they were of no consequence. Their meat was rotten to the core, but it enjoyed the crunch of their bones against its limbs and between its jaws. The *Nuulass* pounded forward, its form perfect. Its prey grew closer, closer still. It opened its jaws, already tasting ripe flesh and hot blood flooding down its throat.

A sound from behind. A man's voice.

Deep inside, Nichel froze. *Aidan.*

The *Nuulass* struggled to exert dominance. — *Impossible. Impossible!*

Up ahead the great stone doors loomed. They were close and flanked by man-fire. The man-fire vanished in a hiss, mourned by the tendrils of smoke that rose in their wake, and the man-meat's form glowed. The *Nuulass* growled. Man-fire seared. It gathered all its strength and lunged. Ornate stonework, mountain walls, and road blurred as its body took flight. It stretched out its claws, straining. It believed that if the woman could but taste living flesh, the battle would be won. She would no longer fight. The man turned, his mouth opening in surprise, and the *Nuulass* drove him to the ground again.

The voice called. Faintly, still far behind. Nichel of the Wolf took to her feet and sprinted away from the pit, from the seal. The *Nuulass* reared its head back, snarling and snapping at the night sky. Suddenly the man's arm shot out and threw fire, not at its face, but near it. The heat and brightness made the *Nuulass* cringe. Anger surged. It jammed its prey's arms to the ground and then reared, jaws opening wide.

"Nichel!"

Nichel of the Wolf's presence strengthened, like orange and purple bleeding into dark sky as the Mother assumed her throne.

"Nichel! Nichel!"

She wrested control from the *Nuulass* and turned to look. Aidan collapsed at the top of the stairs.

He lives!

Nichel's voice penetrated the vile thoughts of the Wild's Doom, a storm of ghastly images of blood and tearing meat and sharp teeth and death. It shrank from her will, and she capitalized, banishing it down, down into its prison. Nichel screamed as her bones and flesh shrank and twisted, folding in on themselves. When she opened her eyes, she found herself lying on the ground near the doors. She sat up, dimly noticing that her clothes hung in tatters. Cuts and bruises mottled her dark skin.

Arms enfolded her. "We're almost free, Nichel."

Jonathan? He pulled her to her feet. Nichel threw him off. Aidan was upright and moving, running at a limp on the first level, halfway between the stairs and where they stood. Vagrants rushed him from both sides, threatening to engulf him. Nichel did not think. She ran for him. Her knives were gone, but she did not need them. Rage pumped through her, suffocating the sharp, throbbing pain from what felt like a thousand cuts and bruises.

One of the vagrants turned as she drew near. She pounced on it, kicking and punching and scratching. It crumpled beneath the fury and chaos of her attack. The others raised weapons. Nichel paid them no mind. Fury washed over her, so hot and acidic it made her stomach churn.

— *Free me,* the *Nuulass* purred. Its red eyes glared from the depths of its cave. *I can save him. We can save him!*

Nichel lifted its seal slightly, like raising one side of a rock to see what hid beneath that edge. Madness coursed through her. She slammed the seal back in place, but strength gleaned from the demon remained. Nichel flung vagrants aside and called his name. Aidan reached for her, and she seized him and pulled him free.

Tombs and monuments blurred as she ran, her fingers intertwined through Aidan. She nearly dragged him behind her. Wind rushing through her ears drowned the sound of pursuits.

There was a loud, reverberating *creak*. She narrowed her eyes and saw Jonathan, his small form growing larger as she closed the gap between them. He was leaning into one of the doors and grunting with exertion. The door was opening, but not quickly enough. A crack of darkness stood between the doors, widening slightly as Jonathan strained against it.

Nichel could not stop now. Her momentum was too great. She lowered her head and careened into both doors. They flew and the three of them tumbled into the darkened hallway. A moment later, there was a *boom* as the stone slammed closed.

Chapter 52:
Embrace

AIDAN FELL AGAINST the embossed doors and slid to the ground. His chest heaved. Blood ran down the gash on his forehead, stinging his eyes. He closed them and all at once his body grew heavier. *I could sleep right here*, he thought. Warmth suffused him like a blanket. His eyelids weighed as much as anvils.

The door shuddered. Aidan jerked and scuttled back on all fours. The doors gave another jolt. Muffled wails, mournful and bloodthirsty, seeped through the stone.

"They'll hold," a weary voice said. Jonathan Hillstreem stood across the corridor between two braziers. He was doubled over, hands braced on his knees. Green gore stained the front of his robes. Aidan's skin warmed as the flame to his left diminished. "Are you all right, Nichel?" Jonathan asked, straightening.

Nichel stood by Aidan. She looked as haggard as he felt. Splotches of vagrant blood matted her curly hair. Her body was covered in cuts and bruises already starting to ripen. What remained of her clothing hung from her glistening body in bloody strips of leather, exposing more skin than it concealed. Wordlessly, she offered him her hands. Aidan went cold. *What are you?*

Shame heated his face. *You're my friend. You've always been that.* He reached for her. Her hands, small and delicate yet rough, took his and pulled him upright as easily as if she were lifting a book. The corridor spun. He placed a hand against the wall to steady himself, and suddenly pressed against him. Her lips found his. He began to pull away, but her arms held him like steel cords.

Aidan stopped fighting. Her body was so warm. So alive. He closed his eyes and kissed her back. Her breathing quickened.

A moment. That was all he gave himself to celebrate surviving. He pulled away and gently pried Nichel's hands from the back of his neck. Hurt and surprise painted her face. "You're wounded," he said.

"You're alive." Nichel wrapped her arms around him and rested her head against his chest.

Aidan stared past her. He was, but it had been close. He had tried to kindle and felt a cold shock, like breaking through the surface of a frozen pond, followed by a burning sensation. The pain had lasted no longer than an instant, but it had been agony. Like fire racing through him.

— *You nearly burned out,* Anastasia said.

Aidan's vision landed on one of the braziers near Jonathan. He extended a hand toward it and kindled. Flame shrank obediently as warmth coursed through him. He let out a shuddering breath. He could Touch, but it hurt.

— *You need rest,* Anastasia urged. *I know this is not the most convenient time or place, but you must listen to your body.*

Nichel shook in his arms. He heard her sniffle. Unsure what to do, he patted her hair. She pulled away abruptly, wiping her eyes. Aidan's eyes lingered on her exposed curves, ran over her bronzed legs, rose to her full breasts. He cleared his throat and turned away, making a study of the corridor. His cheeks grew hot, and he could feel Nichel's eyes on him.

Jonathan crossed to them. "You're bleeding!" he said, cupping her face in his hands. "Let me heal you." Aidan watched Jonathan run his hands over Nichel's bruises and gashes. She squirmed, frowning at him. Her eyes found Aidan and she gave him a small smile. One by one, her wounds closed. Only blood remained as proof of what she had endured in the Vale.

"That is the best I can do for now," Jonathan said. He turned to Aidan and his mouth worked silently, as if groping for words. "I need to heal the Crown of the North."

"I'll be all right," Aidan said. He took a step toward them, and the world teetered.

"Nonsense," Jonathan said. He crossed to Aidan, rolling up his sleeves. "This will take but a moment." He brushed Aidan's hair back and hissed in a breath. As bad as the cut must look, it felt even worse. Every beat of Aidan's heart sent a spike of pain through his head. Jonathan cupped Aidan's head in smooth hands. A brazier flickered, and Aidan let warmth suffuse him. Spikes faded to jabs, faded to nothing. The memory of aches and pains remained, but his exhaustion seemed even greater.

"There," Jonathan said. His frown did not match his satisfied tone. "You are diminished, Crown. You need rest."

Nichel came to his side. "I will take you to a bed."

"I'll be fine. I'm already getting a second wind."

Nichel gave him a dubious look, then bit her lip. "*Conah*," she said. Her voice quivered. "I could have . . . You might have died because of me. Because of my misguided anger. I beg your forgiveness." Tears cut through blood drying on her cheeks.

Aidan shook her head. "Nichel, I won't hear any more of this. We had not seen each other in years. Your parents journeyed to Torel and never returned home. You had every reason to doubt me. I would have doubted you had our situations been reversed."

"I still ask your forgiveness."

"Then you have it, on one condition."

Nichel steeled herself. "Name it."

"We have a saying in the north. 'Winter buries our past, and spring brings new life.' Let the past stay in the past. Agreed?"

She gave him a tremulous smile. "You are a wise man, Aidan Gairden. I knew you would be."

"It took hard lessons to acquire that wisdom."

She put a hand on his arm. "Your mother."

"Yes."

"You will avenge her."

"And you will avenge your parents."

Nichel's expression hardened. "From this moment forward, the alliance between Darinia and Torel is repaired."

"Thank you. Now our people must know."

"You will take us when the Mother sits her throne." She raised her eyebrows questioningly. Nichel knew about shifting and understood Aidan could only perform the spell during daylight hours.

Jonathan stepped up beside the war chief. "The underground passages would be quicker." He considered Nichel. "Perhaps you should both rest, whatever path we choose. You need your strength."

"If there is a way to leave immediately, we must take it," Nichel said. She gave Aidan a level stare. "There is other news our peoples must hear."

Aidan frowned, confused.

— *Your betrothal,* Grandfather Charles said.

Nichel seemed to take his shocked expression for delight. She reached for his hand. He stepped away, and her smile slipped. The knot in his stomach tightened, but he steeled his resolve. *Better to do this now.*

"Cinder Hillstreem," Aidan began.

Jonathan waved as if dispelling an odor. "Few men have survived what we endured together. I, too, owe you an apology. Please, Crown, call me Jonathan."

Aidan smiled weakly. "Accepted with friendship." The two men clasped hands. "Jonathan. May I have a moment alone with Nichel?"

"Of course," the Cinder said, too jovially. "As adviser to the war chief, I do insist on staying close, especially given what we just endured. I suppose down the hall is close enough." Without another word, he walked quickly down the corridor and paused just around the bend. He did not turn back to face them.

Nichel stood close to Aidan, smiling the way she had when they were children. As if she was privy to some secret that he was too thickheaded to figure out. "We should not have this conversation here," she said.

"Then where?"

"My bed."

Aidan opened his mouth to protest. Before words could escape, Nichel eased herself up on her toes and kissed him. He pushed her gently away. "Nichel. Please." He scrubbed his hands over cheeks bare of stubble. "So much has happened. We haven't seen each other in so long, and now we have a war to fight. Side by side, as it should be."

"As it was promised long ago."

"There is so much I have to tell you," Aidan said.

At that, Nichel hugged her chest. "I have secrets to share as well."

"You go first," he said quickly.

She was silent for several moments. "Aidan, what did you see in *Daram Ogahra*? Just before we escaped."

Images flashed through his mind: A beast, huge and monstrous, larger even than the wolves that roamed untamed forests in the north. It had turned and fixed him in its gaze, red eyes blazing like pits of fire. The beast had convulsed, shrank, taken on human features. That was when the vagrants had overtaken him, and then Nichel was there, pulling him to safety.

Gasps resounded through his mind.

— *The* Nuulass, Gabriel said in a low tone.

Aidan had questions, but now was not the time. He kept his face neutral. "I saw a lot of dead bodies trying to kill me."

Nichel swallowed. "What else?"

"I saw . . . I don't know what it was. It looked like an enormous wolf."

"And then?"

He considered. "The vagrants piled onto me. I couldn't see much of anything. I thought I was going to die. Then I saw you, and you saved me. Thank you, Nichel. I owe you my life."

Nichel studied him for a long time. "You are my life, *conah*. You are all I have left. I will never let harm come to you again. This I swear."

I'm not familiar with that word, Aidan thought.

— *Darinian for "beloved,"* Anastasia said quietly.

Aidan was speechless. The knot in his stomach tightened. *I'm going to break your heart.*

Nichel blushed. "I'm sorry. It's just that I've lost everyone. I will not lose you. Not now that I have you back."

He took her hands. "Thank you. I care for you, too."

At that, Nichel averted her eyes.

"What's wrong?" he asked.

She stepped back. "You are exhausted," she said, staring at the floor. "Jonathan was right. The Mother will rise soon. You should rest. My chamber is nearby. Walk until you see the wolf over the doorway on the left. Follow that hall to its terminus."

"Nichel, I—"

Without another word she turned on her heel and ran down

the hallway where Jonathan had gone. The Cinder turned as Nichel brushed past him. Jonathan glared at Aidan before hurrying after her. Aidan lingered, listening to the crackle of torches. He contemplated going after her, but thought better of it. Nichel had suffered so much confusion and loss since losing her parents. Not only that, what they had experienced in *Daram Ogahra* had to have been traumatic for her.

Once again, his mind recalled the wolf with its burning eyes, hair as dark as night, long teeth and fangs.

— *If she left,* Ambrose said, *you should follow. You cannot afford for your alliance to break down again.*

It won't. She needs time alone. So do I.

Aidan touched his lips. He could still taste Nichel, her urgency and the life pulsing through her veins. It all felt familiar. He and Christine had survived unthinkable crucibles, only to end up lying together. *No,* he thought. *That was different.* It was. He had been attracted to her from the start, and she to him. Only her involvement in Tyrnen's schemes had tempered his lust. When she proved her trust to him, they consummated feelings that had been building for days.

No, Aidan realized. That was false. More than false, it did Christine an injustice. Bedding her had signified lust budding into deeper feeling. His thoughts turned to Christine. Not just her body, but her smile, her laugh, the way her eyes lit up when he said her name. The thought of her made his heart swell and ache.

I love her.

The words rang true. Tears welled, and he did not raise a hand to brush them away. He was suddenly desperately lonely, and only she could make it better. *I want to tell her. I want her to hear those words.*

His grin dissipated. *Nichel needs to know.* Aidan looked back the way he'd come. *Not now. After.*

He set off in the direction Nichel had indicated, glancing up occasionally to note the symbols engraved above entryways and passing through portals marked with a wolf. The halls were murky, each path lit only by a few torches. His footsteps echoed along winding corridors. He quickened his pace, only to drag his feet and stumble. Aidan planted an open hand against the nearest wall, steadying himself.

— *You need sleep,* Grandfather Charles said. *I have heard the*

Darinians stuff their mattresses with goose feathers.

— *Where will Nichel sleep?* Gabriel asked, sounding overly casual.

— *You need to tell her about Christine,* Ambrose said.

— *Yes,* Charles agreed. *The sooner the better.*

Aidan considered throwing another skein over his mind.

— *I understand your reticence, grandson,* Charles said. *But your alliance is still tenuous.*

— *The longer you wait to tell her of your feelings for the Sallnerian girl,* Gabriel began.

She has a name.

— *Gabriel meant no disrespect,* Charles interjected. *More to the point, he is correct. Given the darkness inside of her—*

— *Nothing a wedding cannot fix,* Gabriel said.

Aidan decided to change the subject. *You referred to her by a specific term, Gabriel. A . . . lass of some kind.*

— *The* Nuulass, Gabriel said. *Darinian for "the Wild's Doom."*

What does that mean?

Gabriel scoffed. — *Does it sound pleasant?* He went silent for a moment. *The Darinians are an ancient people. Older by far than Torelians, Leastonians, or Sallnerians. The history of all three peoples combined amounts to but an instant compared to that of the wildlanders.*

I wish you wouldn't call them that.

— *It is not an insult, Aidan. They are the wild the doom refers to. The* Nuulass *represents their doom.*

How?

— *I do not know, exactly.* Gabriel sounded troubled. *What you saw down in the Vale seems relevant somehow. Nichel took the form of a wolf. I do not know what triggered it, but I sensed an ancient ferocity within her. It was of nature. Of Crotaria itself.*

— *And of Kahltan?* Anastasia asked.

— *Of shadecraft, yes,* Gabriel admitted. *Though it is a magic with which even I am unfamiliar.*

If it originated in Sallner, Aidan thought, *perhaps Christine will have heard of it.*

— *The Sallnerian girl?* Gabriel said. *She knows nothing of her past.*

Aidan stopped. *I told you to call her by her name. If you insult her again, I'll—*

— *You will what? Bash yourself in the head?*

I love her, Gabriel. You will respect her.

— *You are too young to recognize love.*

I wager I understand more about love than you.

— *You think so, do you?* Gabriel's voice was low and dangerous.

I know so, Aaren Bridgegil.

Shock rang through Aidan's mind.

— *Yes,* Gabriel said, unperturbed. *I did wonder how you figured that out.*

The rhythmic *clomp, clomp, clomp* of his boots against the stone sounded like drumbeats. Aidan came to another juncture with four doorways, two on either side. He inspected them, found a wolf head etched over the second portal on his right, and took it. *You dropped enough hints. You're the only Touched I know who speaks of the relationship between magic and the sciences. You talked to me of calculations and trajectories, and I saw your notes in the margins of* Approbations of the Moon, *a book you wrote, of course.*

— *What makes you so sure?* Gabriel sounded both curious and pleased.

You attributed spectral form to Aaren Bridgegil, and then later you spoke as if you had invented the spell. You are prideful, Gabriel. Every time I paid compliments to the shade, you grew testy. You couldn't stand for someone else to receive credit for your genius.

— *Do you deny his charge, son?* Ambrose asked coldly.

— *I do not.*

— *The most notorious, reviled shade of our age,* Anastasia said in a low voice. *How could you, Gabriel? How dare you?*

— *I dared only to learn. To taste forbidden fruit. I did nothing unlawful.*

— *Practicing dark magic is unlawful,* Ambrose said.

— *Dark magic has saved Aidan's neck countless times within the past week alone, Father. Ignorance should be made unlawful, not the pursuit of knowledge.*

Was there ever an Aaren Bridgegil? Aidan asked.

— *A sobriquet,* Gabriel replied, *designed for my protection. It was a simple disguise, merely an anagram of my name. I will* confess that not every spell in my book came from me. Some came from my grandparents, the Thalamahns. Perhaps you've heard of them? Dark magic is in our blood, Mother. It exists within every Touched. To deny it is to deny ourselves.

— *We hunted for you for decades,* Anastasia continued. *Even after your father turned Heritage over to you. To think that we brought you into this world. To think that a shade held Heritage and wore our crown.*

— *Aidan is my successor, then. Whatever you feel toward me, you must feel toward him.*

— *Aidan was right,* Anastasia said after a moment. *You do not know what love is. How could you? You maneuvered us like stones on a board. You mocked us behind our backs.*

— *We all have reasons for what we do, Mother.*

Aidan could stay quiet no longer. *You treated people like disposable baubles in your pursuit of power.*

— *Do you imply that you are any less depraved?* Gabriel shot back. *What you did at Sharem was no better. Invading Nichel's mind to coerce her into sparing your life was no better.*

Aidan shook with rage. *I will make amends for that.*

— *You will never make amends for that. You are no better or worse than I am. You are just as big a fool and hypocrite as my mother and father and every single Gairden who has drawn breath for the last eight hundred years. You know what it takes to wear our crown, yet you have not made even a fraction of the difficult decisions I was entrusted with during my reign.*

What do you mean?

— *Do you think your mentor stumbled on my words by accident? He was my pupil, boy, just as you were his.*

Aidan's shock froze him in mid-stride. Gabriel had taught Tyrnen? When? The histories said nothing of—

There was a slight, barely audible creak.

NICHEL RAN THROUGH Janleah Keep's twisty corridors. When she realized Jonathan would not give up pursuit, she slowed, taking up the graceful and deadly stride of a wolf.

"Nichel? Why did you run?" he said, coming up beside her. "What is it? What did he say?"

She kept walking, facing forward. "Nothing."

"If he offended you, or hurt you in some way—"

"It was not what he said, Jonathan. It was . . ." Nichel wiped away tears. "I made a mistake."

He brightened. "Oh?"

She felt a twang of guilt. *It is time to settle this.* Nichel took his hands. "Cinder Hillstreem. What happened tonight has changed everything. I love Aidan. I have loved him all my life. You know this."

He nodded, mouth tight.

"Even if I would have found him guilty before the Mother's Eye . . ." she began.

"I know," he said. "An advisor and a war chief's daughter—"

"A war chief," she corrected.

"Of course. But, war chief—"

She shook her head. "I was too formal before. You may call me Nichel. We are friends, Jonathan. Good friends."

He flinched as if slapped. "Nichel," he said awkwardly, as if pronouncing her name for the first time. "I will not apologize for how I feel. I hold strong feelings for you, whatever our stations. We have grown close since your parents . . . I thought . . ." He searched her eyes for some sign he might have missed. She watched hope drain from his face.

"You were my pillar, Jonathan. I thought I had lost everything. I had lost everything. Now I know the truth. Now I have my vengeance and know where to direct it."

The seal trembled. She ignored it.

"Your father had a saying," Jonathan said. "The wolf sees clearest in the dark."

Nichel squeezed her eyes shut. She remembered Romen of the Wolf quipping those words at her, over and over. Only now did she understand them.

Jonathan let his hands fall away. "You choose him, then?"

Nichel considered. "My father made that choice for me, before I was whelped. Now, I make it voluntarily. I choose Aidan."

"Very well." His voice was soft, a sad caress. "I will remain by your side, war chief. If you will still have me."

"Of course. I value your counsel, as my father did."

"That makes me glad." His face became serious. "Then as your advisor, you must listen to me. Yes?"

Her lips quirked. "If your words are wise."

"I only speak wise words, war chief. And my words are for you to sleep. You and the Crown of the North have a difficult fight ahead."

"Of course. I will bed in my parents' chambers."

"A move you should have made long ago," he said gently.

Nichel nodded.

"I will send your pack to stand guard outside your door. They will bring dinner along as well. Or perhaps breakfast, given the hour."

"I'm not hungry." Her stomach let out a plaintive growl, like a *Nuulass* cub. Jonathan's eyebrows rose. "Send Aidan food, however. I did not feed him properly."

"It will be as you say, war chief."

Nichel frowned. "Now that I think of it, where are they? Ulestren and the others."

"You used misdirection to prevent them from following you into the Crevasse and freeing Aidan."

She blushed. "Even so, they should not have stayed away so long."

"That is true. Perhaps they still wait in the council chamber. I will disperse them between the two of you."

"With food for me as well. Meat, if there is any," she said in a rush.

He smiled. "I thought you weren't hungry."

"Do not make jokes when your war chief is hungry."

"Cooked?" he asked, though he knew the answer.

Nichel hesitated a moment before giving a quick shake of her head. He nodded and turned to go. "Jonathan." He paused in an entryway. Above it was an engraving of an adder, coiled, bearing its fangs to strike. "Did I . . . The *Nuulass*. I don't remember what—"

"You cleared our path," he said, giving her a small smile. "You controlled it, just as we trained for."

"Thank you." She held his gaze a moment longer. "I am sorry things cannot be different."

Jonathan inclined his head and disappeared through the archway. Beside it stood an effigy of her father. The builders had constructed it after he was named clan chief. His lips were parted just slightly, as if privy to some joke. The builder had caught Romen of the Wolf in good humor, a state in which his wife and daughter had known him best, though only in private. *The wolf sees clearest in the dark.*

Touching her father's folded arms for support, Nichel closed her eyes and visualized the cave. Darkness engulfed her, and the image became real. Jagged, uneven stone poked and cut at her bare feet. Green and blue light reflected off wet walls. Before her was the seal. It took the form of her mother's sapphire ring, a wedding gift from Romen of the Wolf.

I want to talk. Will you behave?

The seal trembled.

I need your word. I am your master and war chief, and will no longer tolerate your subversion.

A warm wind gusted the darkness, teasing her hair. At the back of the cave, red eyes appeared. Flames rose from them like eyelashes, licking and spitting. They floated closer. The wind grew warmer until Nichel felt as if she stood before a bonfire. "That is close enough."

Nichel spoke aloud, standing in the corridor of Janleah's Keep, but the *Nuulass* obeyed. It growled. The sound reverberated through her mind. *You came to my aid in* Daram Ogahra.

— *You deceived me.*

Did I have to?

The *Nuulass* did not answer.

You are a part of me, she thought. *That is why I was able to usurp control.*

— *No, wolf-woman. I am not part of you. I am you. I am the Wild.*

You are the Wild's Doom.

— *One is the same as the other.*

Then why do I have to fight you?

— *You do not fight me. You fight yourself. You fight your instincts, your craving for blood. Your teeth broke flesh and you wanted more, to feast, to drink—*

The *Nuulass* lunged and the seal trembled. It clawed its way up her throat. Nichel pictured the lake. Her enemy laughed and redoubled its efforts. She fell to her knees and gagged, clawing at her mouth. Rage coursed through her, setting her blood to boiling. Suddenly she thought of Aidan, remembering the feel of his lips against hers.

The cave returned but the *Nuulass* recoiled as if flung away. It snarled and snapped and spit. She could just make it out, a vague outline punctuated by fiery eyes, fangs, claws. It was massive. Nichel held firm to the memory of her moment with Aidan.

Stop.

The *Nuulass* froze. It let out a roar that shook Nichel to her core. She did not look away, did not so much as breathe.

— *You want this,* it growled.

I do not, she thought back. *I want you to tell me what you are.*

— *I am the Wild's—*

No! No more riddles! What is my doom? How will my people die?

— *What has lived forever cannot die.*

You will answer me directly.

— *You have the answer you seek.*

Nichel bared her teeth. It was right, she knew. If it was her, and she was it, she knew what it knew. *How? How do I find the answer?*

— *You know, but have forgotten. The Wild's Doom is a memory long buried.*

Nichel picked up her mother's ring and held it above her. She opened her fingers and the ring stayed. It began to spin. The *Nuulass* howled and was gone. Scowling, Nichel opened her eyes and stalked away from her father's statue. The wolf may see clearest in the dark, but she was still blind.

She walked, not noticing where she was going and not needing to. There was no artery of Janleah's Keep she could not follow to get anywhere she wanted to go. Unburdened by navigation, her concentration turned inward. The *Nuulass* called itself the Wild's Doom. Foreigners who did not understand Darinians referred to the clansfolk as wildlanders. To her people, that was the gravest insult imaginable. But where had the term originated? The Plains, her home since her birth, were wild. Untamed. Her father had been the first clan chief and war chief in generations to attempt gentrification. All the chiefs welcomed caravans from the north and east, provided traders stuck to assigned paths. To wander from those paths was to invite death from the elements, or clan chiefs who viewed them as lawbreakers.

If the Plains are the wildlands, then we are wildlanders.

She stopped, chewing her lip. The *Nuulass* had said that it was her. That it was the Wild. The Darinians were wildlanders. Could the *Nuulass* exist within all her people? It must. But why had it only manifested in her? And what had aroused it? She thought back to the night it had emerged, and she knew.

My anger. My rage and my grief.

On the night she had challenged Guyde of the Bear, she had lost everything. Romen of the Wolf, her mother, her *conah*, and at Guyde's killing blow, her life. Looking up at him standing over her, she had thought her anguish and ire would consume her. And it had.

We are the Wild. We are our doom.

The *Nuulass* said nothing. The seal held steady. Feeling petulant, she stamped her foot. Why did it go silent now? *If I am the* Nuulass, *if all Darinians are it and it is us, then I should be able to answer that question.*

At that, the answer materialized, as if simply waiting to be summoned. Because she was calm. Rational. In control.

Nichel walked, concentrating on breathing and counting her footsteps. Anything to maintain control. The corridors were quiet and empty. It was dark, but her sharp eyes pushed back the darkness. When next she minded her surroundings, she found that her feet had carried her outside her chambers. Nichel thought again of Aidan and how he had tasted. Her body tingled with excitement. Nichel approached the door, hand raised to knock. She let it drop. *I'll see him in the morning. Not long from now. The Mother will rise soon, and we will begin our journey.*

A muffled thump from behind the door. Nichel paused, sniffing. Freshly fallen snow and crisp morning air, and perfume. Wrinkling her nose, she stepped away. Some of her pack was with him. *Inside?* Jealousy flared up, then reason prevailed. *Jonathan sent them, and Aidan is wounded. Better to watch over him from inside the room than from without.*

Her parents' chambers were not far from her own. She glanced idly at one of the braziers that lined the winding corridor, then stopped and examined it. The flames had died. Embers smoldered. Anxious, Nichel scanned up and down the hall. Each and every brazier had grown faint, huddled against the shadows reclaiming Janleah's Keep. When they had passed through, the braziers and torches bracketed to the walls had bathed their path in light.

How long were we in Daram Ogahra? *Hours?* No. That did

not ring true. She broke into a run. By the time she saw soft light pooling out from beneath large stone doors, all thoughts of the *Nuulass* and Aidan and lapsed time were forgotten. A soft, blue glow emanated from the right-hand door. Three red spots pulsed from the left door. Her hackles rose.

Outfitting doors on their bedroom had been her mother's idea. Cynthia once told her daughter that she had broached the subject to Romen of the Wolf on the morning of her first day as the war chief's wife. She respectfully pointed out to him that she would not feel comfortable sharing a bed with her husband in a room into which anyone could look at any moment. Romen of the Wolf needed no further convincing. He had been fixated on Torelian and Leastonian society. Naturally, the speakers had been appalled by the idea. Darinian builders crafted doors for the other realms who commissioned their talents, but they had no place in western culture. Doors encouraged secrets. Romen had listened patiently. When they grew quiet, he had observed that stone doors would enhance the security of Janleah Keep. By the time they had retired to their bed that first evening, stone had been cut, smoothed, fitted, and mounted.

Cynthia had broken into a fit of laughter at the memory. Nichel had giggled, too. She had marveled at her father's cleverness and found her mother's laughter infectious. Romen had ordered the builders to imbue their doors with protective magic. The red stones glowed to signify the number of inhabitants in the room, and only those who knew how to touch them would be able to gain entry. There were three individuals inside the room, and the blue stone's glow communicated that at least one person within knew how to open Romen's doors.

Nichel clenched her fists, wishing that Sand and Silk were at hand.

The seal trembled.

— *Embrace me,* it whispered now. *Use me.*

She steeled herself.

— *I will obey. Only first, embrace me.*

Nichel opened the seal. Just a sliver. Wrath filled her. The doors flew open like two sheets of wood hanging by threads. Nichel rode her fury like a wave, bounding over the threshold and landing in the center of the chamber. The scent of perfume crashed into her. It was strong and pungent, as if she had stormed into a garden overgrown with fruits and flowers. Nichel clapped her hands to her face and stumbled back. She began to cough. The *Nuulass* shook free and fled back to its prison.

Everything in her parents' chambers was as it had been before Romen of the Wolf and Cynthia had departed for Torel. Their bed was made, another of her mother's habits. The stone floor was unadorned and dusty. Her mother's wardrobe stood closed against one wall. Beside it sat a small, round table surrounded by three stone chairs, one three times the size of the others. Two of her pack—Lynntak of the Temporal and Ipadia of the Adder — stood by it, setting out a platter of meat, dining utensils, and a stone flagon. Her pack mates stared at her with flat, unsurprised expressions.

Nichel was nonplussed. "How did you—?" she began. Then: *There were three spots on the door.*

"You taught me once," a voice said from behind her.

Nichel whirled. Ulestren of the Wolf leaned against the wall near the doors. Her clan sister appeared unruffled, every bit the wolf at ease. Her arms were folded across her chest, the heel of one foot propped against the wall. Her expression was flat. Tall and lithe, Ulestren pushed off the wall and strode forward. "The doors," she said by way of explanation when Nichel did not answer. "You taught me how to open them. When we were cubs."

The blend of perfumes was cloying. Nichel's head began to pound. She closed her eyes and massaged her head between the thumb and forefinger of her right hand.

Ulestren gestured toward the platter. A hunk of raw meshia filled its center. Blood pooled around it. "Eat."

Her nose caught the meat's scent, which mercifully cut through the perfumes. Another growl escaped her. "I'm famished. Thank you." She sat at the table. Nichel resisted the urge to tear the meat with her bare hands. She insisted on the implements. It was her way of fighting back against the *Nuulass's* savagery. She picked up knife and fork, holding them the way her mother had taught her.

"Thank you," she said again. "I'd like to eat alone."

Her pack mates did not move. They stood watching her. Irritation rippled through Nichel. Sometimes even her clan sister crossed boundaries. "Jonathan told you to bring this to me, yes?"

Lynntak of the Temporal nodded.

"Then he probably also told you what happened in *Daram Ogahra*."

"He did," said Ipadia of the Adder. "We are glad you are well."

"Then you can understand why I would like to be alone."

"The Cinder told us to watch over you," Ulestren said.

She rolled her eyes. "His caution is . . ." She couldn't describe it as unwarranted. It wasn't every day an army of the dead rose up and tried to kill her. She sighed. "Outside, then. To be blunt, your perfumes make my head ache." A thought occurred to her. "Did you go through my mother's things?"

Ulestren waved to the other two. They fell into a line and strode out of the room, taking up positions around the doors. "We will be out in the corridor if you need us, war chief," her clan sister said.

"I'm so grateful," Nichel muttered.

"Eat."

"I will!"

Ulestren's hands raced across the stone as she stepped backwards out of the room, and the doors swung closed. Nichel ran a hand through her hair. *I do not remember teaching her, but . . .*

But they had been fixated on Cynthia Alston's collection of clothing and sparkly baubles when Ulestren's mother and father had given her permission to stay with Nichel inside Janleah Keep, where only the war chief and his clan resided. Other clansfolk entered only for gatherings, or on business with the war chief, or to drink from the Mother's Bosom.

The cloud of perfume seemed to have followed her pack out of the room. Her head was beginning to clear, and the smell of the meat grew stronger. The *Nuulass* growled. Ignoring it, she leaned forward and inhaled, long and deep.

Nichel slammed back in her chair, gagging and clawing at her nose. Her stomach roiled and bile climbed her throat. She turned and retched. Her eyes popped open, but did not see. Memory gripped her. She was back in her bedroom, naked and swimming in sheets soaked with sweat, sitting up only to empty her stomach into the stone basin Jonathan had held for her, stroking her hair and making soothing sounds. She had been grateful to him for that, but had wanted her mother. Those two weeks were lost to her, swallowed in a haze of delirium. Jonathan had told her about them in the dark days that followed.

That smell.

She straightened, pushing herself up to a sitting position with shaky arms. The meshia sat on her plate. Hesitantly, she sniffed and immediately pinched her nose shut. It was there. Faint, but there. A trace of putrescence. Like the vagrants in *Daram Ogahra*.

Nichel shot to her feet. Her chair scraped against stone and fell back with a clatter. *Poison. Ipadia of the Adder.* She grabbed the platter and hurled it across the room. It shattered spectacularly. Stone fragments rained to the floor. Her meshia hit the wall and fell with a splat.

The door opened. A cloud of perfume wafted in, making her eyes water. Nichel cupped a hand over her mouth. "Ipadia has poisoned—"

Ipadia's foot drove Nichel's breath from her lungs and sent her tumbling backward. The room spun in a blur of colors. Instinct took hold and she rolled through the blow and came up in a crouch, fingers and feet gripping the stone. Ipadia of the Adder charged forward, Lynntak of the Temporal at her side. They were unarmed. Nichel rolled and swept one leg out as she shot up. Lynntak had closed the distance and got tangled in the war chief's kick. She went down hard, sprawling face-first against the floor. There was a sharp crack. She lay limply for a moment, then pulled herself back up. She turned, and Nichel gasped.

Green blood painted her face.

Ipadia and Lynntak closed in, punching and kicking. Nichel circled them, deflecting and dodging as best she could. There was a flash of light against steel and a sharp stinging sensation that ran up her right arm. She hissed a breath as pain lanced through her. Nichel lashed out with two backhand slaps.

The seal trembled.

— Embrace me.

Emotions broke in her mind like a storm. Love and hate, fury and tranquility, sadness and bliss. They pulled in opposite directions, greedy hands threatening to tear her apart. The *Nuulass* hammered at her will with every beat of her heart.

— Embrace me.

No! She would not lose control again.

Her struggle with the *Nuulass* had lasted only moments.

Nichel sprang at them and then feinted, rolling around Lynntak and bolting for the corridor. Out in the hall she whirled and ran her hands over the doors. They flew forward. Before they slammed shut, she caught a glimpse of Lynntak and Ipadia standing still, watching her.

Nichel staggered, clutching her right arm. A thin red line ran from the back of her wrist halfway to her elbow. *Ipadia's dagger.* She lurched away from her parents' chambers and toward her own. *Aidan. Get to Aidan. Make sure he's—*

She smelled Jonathan's soapy aroma before she saw him. She tensed, expecting attack. Her advisor shuffled into view, blue robes swirling. His arms were spread, palms out and fingers splayed. Then his eyes glazed over and he crumpled to the floor. Blood bloomed from the dagger sticking from his back. She stared at it, bewildered.

Ulestren stepped out of the shadow behind him. Her clan sister bent, withdrew the knife from his back, and wiped it on Jonathan's robes. *Silk.*

Straightening, Ulestren's face split in a smile that did not touch her eyes.

Nichel's reality shook. She threw out a hand to steady herself. That was when Ulestren raised her other hand, the one not holding Silk, from behind her back. Her clan sister extended a closed fist, unclenched her fingers. A gold ring with an amethyst sat on her palm.

With a flick of her wrist, Ulestren threw the ring. It clinked against the floor and then rolled, wobbling to a stop against one wall. Nichel gaped at it. *Aidan's ring.* Numbly, she bent to pick it up. Fear gripped her. Rage blossomed, and the seal trembled. She slipped the ring onto a finger. The cool band felt good against her skin, which had gone feverish.

Nichel looked up in time to see Ulestren grip Silk and launch herself at the war chief. *Ulestren is dead*, Nichel thought numbly. *Aidan is dead, too.*

The *Nuulass* charged, roaring and clawing for control. Nichel held it by a thread. Silk flashed. Its hilt clipped her forehead and emotions and thoughts finally stopped tumbling.

Chapter 53:
Point of Fate

CYROLIN STAGGERED TO her feet, but Edmund did not see the galerunner. In his mind's eye her red hair was brown, her stature short, her eyes vivacious and filled with love for their son and their life together. In his mind's eye, Anna was alive, and this was his chance to keep her that way.

Strength and purpose filled him in the breath it took for Gewnan to plunge the spirit shard toward his chest. Edmund's hand locked around the old man's wrist. He squeezed his fingers tight and wrenched. There was a loud crack. The sound was satisfying and life-affirming, as was the guildmaster's thin cry. Edmund felt no pity. He no longer saw a terrified, old guildmaster. He saw Tyrnen.

Gewnan's hand went limp. The spirit shard slipped from his grasp and clattered to the ground. In a blur Edmund scooped it up and jabbed it into the old man's throat. The shard winked, faded. Red blood sprayed and bubbled, splashing Edmund's shirt and pants. Gewnan clawed at his torn flesh with yellowed fingernails. He took one last, labored breath, and his eyes faded. Suddenly, his mouth closed. He rose to his feet and stared blankly at Edmund.

Edmund scrambled to his feet, mentally shouting down the spike of pain shooting through his left leg. Red blood. Gewnan had been human. Only now did he serve in death. Edmund's visage went stony. He pitied harbingers and vagrants. They were puppets that danced on strings. He had no pity for Gewnan. The guildmaster had fallen in with Tyrnen of his own free will. His soul deserved eternal torment.

A scream caught his attention. The harbinger shambled toward Anna, his Anna, who dragged herself backward. The spirit stone quivered. It warmed in his hand, glowing with a soft, pale light.

Footsteps pounded from his right. He spun and saw two vagrants rushing in. Cursing his leg, he raised the shard like a dagger, wishing futilely that he had Valor. He could have stopped them already, could have—

The shard flared. The vagrants froze. Their arms clapped to their sides. Weapons dangled from still hands. They stared at him without expression. For a moment, Edmund gaped at the shard. Then he turned back to his Anna. She had stopped moving. The harbinger who dared to wear her face and smile and life like a costume was weaving back and forth, almost falling, head lolling from her neck to down around her shoulders. Slowly, she extended her arms and opened her palms over Anna. No. Over Cyrolin.

Edmund raised the shard high. "Stop!"

Every undead stopped. Nita, facing down three vagrants, her clothes tattered and face bloody, drove her *Sard'tara* through exposed skulls. One by one, the vagrants crumpled. Shouts erupted as awareness swept through the other Azure Blades. Vagrants fell, a few at first, then dozens.

An idea came to Edmund. "Leave them! Leave them!"

Uncertainly, the Azure Blades lowered their weapons. Nita was saying something, but Edmund didn't hear. The harbinger stood still. Suddenly, Cyrolin kicked out with both legs. The creature collapsed, sprawling face first. Remarkably, gruesomely, her head did not tear free.

A lump rose in Edmund's throat. His leg finally gave out and he dropped to his knees. Tears blinded him. He brought the shard in close. He knew, down in the part of his heart that had blackened and died with Anna, that she was imprisoned in the glassy fragment he clutched in his fist. She was under his control, an instrument to be shaped to his will.

Cradling the shard like the first flower of spring, he whispered to it. The shard flickered. Anna fell and did not rise again.

His hands went limp. Dimly he heard the shard rattle against the street. He did not care. Edmund's chin tucked against his chest. He realized his was crying and could not bring himself to stop.

"It's all right." Cyrolin was by his side. Hands, smooth and soft, cradled him. "I'm here, Edmund. I'm here."

DANIEL'S FEATURES TIGHTENED. "What are you saying?"

Alix wet her lips. "I'm saying we could leave. Not just us. We could evacuate the whole city. Think about it. We didn't finish sealing the tunnel near the palace."

Daniel said nothing, only studied her. Alix folded her hands over his. "Look, I'm going to tell you something, and you'd better listen carefully because I don't expect to say it again for a long time, if ever." She took a breath. "You were right. I've already lost my brother. I've got my parents here with me, now, and you. I can't lose you."

Swallowing, he searched for words. "Suppose we can go down into the tunnels. What then?"

"Anything. You could take us anywhere. Ironsail! We could go to the east, all the way to the coast!"

"And everyone else?"

She shrugged. "Ironsail is a huge city. There'd be plenty of room for everyone."

"Calewind is bigger than Ironsail."

"Well, yes, but, look, any part of Leaston that isn't a bustling trade city is farmland or jungle, right? We could build houses. New cities! People could start over, make new lives for themselves." One corner of her mouth tugged upward. "And us, Daniel. There could be an us past tomorrow."

"I could get us a ship," he said slowly. "We could sail around Crotaria, see the realms where the galerunners come from."

"Galerunners?"

He grinned. "They ride the winds. You should see them. They're Touched who control the Lady's breath to direct ships wherever they want to go. We need only point in a direction, and they could take us there." At her expression of wonder and delight, his heart soared. He entertained a fantasy, then. The two of them on their ship, cutting across the Great Sea. His arm around her as they stood at the prow, watching the horizon draw steadily nearer, yet never quite within reach. An endless chase, an endless adventure with Alix by his side.

"That sounds beautiful," she said. "Let's go talk to your father. Preparations will need to be made. We—"

"It's a beautiful dream, Alix. I hope it can come true someday."

"It can come true today. All we have to do is leave."

He cupped her face. "Suppose we did as you say. Suppose we fled to Ironsail. Or Tarion. Or, shade and shadow, into Sallner. We could never get away, Alix. Not for long. Garrett Lorden would pillage, plunder, and kill everything and everyone until he found us. His army would grow, and they would pursue us to the farthest edge of Crotaria and back."

Smiling sadly, he brushed a too-short strand of hair from her eyes. "We can't run. There's nowhere else to go."

Blinking hard, she let her hands slip free. "I'm sorry. I don't know what came over me."

"You're afraid. I am, too."

"You don't look it." He took her right hand and placed it to his chest. Her eyes widened. "We could use your heart as a battering ram to break down the walls belowground," she said.

He gave a strained smile. "I'm not scared. I'm terrified. Being out there, surrounded by more vagrants that I could count, drove home the hopelessness of our situation. Truth be told, I thought about doing exactly as you suggested. I wanted to get back to you and run, as far away as our legs could take us. Just us. Forget about my father and everyone else."

"What stopped you?"

"You. Your courage. Your belief in me to do what was right."

At that, she winced. "Do you think me a coward?"

"No. Never. We're all allowed a moment of panic. Dawn, I've had more than one."

"I was ready to act on mine. I still am."

"So am I. But we won't."

"Why?"

"Because I'm not a doorman anymore. Even though, just between us . . ."

"Even though you want to be," she guessed.

He shook his head. "That's just it. That is what I was going to say, only it would have been a lie. I don't want to be the person I was a few days ago. I want to be the person you believe in, the person who all those people out there were willing to risk their lives to save." Sighing, he slumped back and stared at the ceiling. "Damn that Aidan Gairden. He's worn off on me."

"He was afraid, too?"

"Oh, yes." He laced his hands behind his head. "If you want the truth, I'm the only reason he made it back alive."

"I believe it."

"You do?"

"I do. After all, you're the reason I'm here."

"Dawn," he mumbled. "If I'm understanding you correctly, what you're saying is that I'm right . . . again?"

She elbowed him. "I'm saying you might have a point. Might."

They were sitting close, now, noses only a hair's width apart. Unable to wait another second, Daniel leaned in and kissed her. After a long time, though not long enough, Daniel glanced darkness through the windows. The sound of moaning, like a keening wind, could be heard through the sturdy walls.

His chest tightened. "It's almost time," he said.

Alix's mouth tightened, but she nodded and scooted from the bench. Waiting until she was upright, he extended a hand. She took it. They walked out together into the empty streets. The moans grew louder.

To Christine, everything seemed to happen at once. Wardsmen rushed in with weapons raised. At the same time the assemblage of stormrobes broke apart. Screams filled the night. The grim resolve that had painted the faces of the Storm Guard melted into confusion and sudden fear. Feter pulled Lam close, shielding him from two Wardsmen who grabbed at them. Tebald and Joske cowered before a Wardsman who prodded at them with his spear. Blood bloomed on Joske's grey robe. He stumbled back and fell, clutching one arm.

Christine was only vaguely aware of the chaos. Terrence had turned away and set eyes on Jehanne, who still clutched Emy's ruined body. Terrence lifted a hand. The flames shrank. Terrence's palm glowed as Jehanne looked up.

Damn you, Aidan Gairden.

Christine kindled and pointed at Terrence. The disciple burst into flame with an ear-splitting shriek. Lam and Feter flinched and fell back, scrambling to get away. Terrence slapped at the conflagration as it chewed through robes and flesh and hair. Abruptly, he jerked. His scream cut off, and he toppled to one side. His body spasmed and went still.

No one moved. Lam and Feter looked from Terrence to Christine. Haltingly, they climbed to their feet and went to her. Their mouths moved, but she could not make out words. She stared at her hands. *I killed a man. A living, flesh-and-blood man.* It didn't seem true. Couldn't be. Someone else had committed murder, and she, Christine Lorden, had only witnessed it. Then her skin grew chill. Shadows sprang up around Lam, Feter, Jehanne, and the others. Their lips worked. Christine studied them, fascinated, until their words became clear.

"Storm Guard! Storm Guard!"

Her eyes fell on Emy's body. Small, full of potential. Ruined.

Christine raised a fist. Her ears rang. Her thoughts were scrambled. Fireballs shot out of outstretched hands to collide with Wardsmen and disciples. Screams cut through the night again. Lam and Feter ran to Christine's sides, flanking her. They pressed forward, the other members of the Storm Guard falling in behind them as they left the Territory Bridge and marched on Sharem.

GENERAL BRENDON GREAGOR'S left hand shook. He swallowed and faced fear itself.

One league away, on the hilltop where the Shared Wood had once harbored trees that had grown for centuries only to be reduced to ashes and blackened stumps, tens of thousands of clansfolk cavorted and pounced, stumbled and fell writhing on their backs. Overhead, Kahltan sat his throne, round and full and bright as a silver coin. Clansfolk threw back their heads and brayed at the night sky.

Acker snorted. Brendon scratched between his ears, but the soothing gesture did no good. The horse sensed his anxiety. Oddly, Lieutenants Moser and Marrick sat in silence. They flanked him, Moser on his left and Marrick on his right, gazing across the expanse of charred plains and rolling hills that separated them from the Darinians. Their mounts, too, held steady. Barely seemed to breathe. Over the tumult from the Darinian camp, Brendon heard the restless creaks and jangles of Wardsmen. Torel's Ward, the northern army, his army, stood arrayed behind him, fifty thousand men in full steel and snow, fifty thousand hands clutching sheathed swords or spears held parallel to rigid bodies, or bows nocked with arrows cut, sharpened, and fixed with steel and stone points that very morning thanks to the aid of one hundred disciples who had lent their magic to the proceedings.

Those fifty thousand men and one hundred disciples fidgeted, waiting. Ellis stepped up beside him, hands folded within the sleeves of his crimson robe. "Midnight approaches," the disciple said. Like Brendon's lieutenants, his face held no expression, his eyes absent of emotion. He had been that way since escorting Cinder Keelian out of Brendon's tent to the shifting ground where the woman had shifted back to the Eternal Flame's side. No further word had come from Tyrnen, or Edmund, or Christine Lorden, or Margia of the Falcon.

Brendon clutched his left wrist and squeezed until he lost feeling in his fingers. He let his hands fall to his sides and slowly drew his sword, raised it high in his right hand. Thousands of swords hissed from scabbards, cutting through the night air and drowning out the wild cries from the Darinians. There was a rustling noise, like leaves being swept along a wide street as ten thousand longbows were pointed upward. Other lieutenants galloped up and down the lines of archers, shouting trajectories. Marrick and Moser stayed close to their general.

Ellis glided forward to stand beside Brendon. He was smiling. Brendon looked away, disgusted. His gaze landed on the Darinians. Their revelry seemed to have reached its climax. Whether naked or armored, every clansman had fallen to his knees, holding heads in hands and wracked by spasms, looking for all the world as if something inside of them was desperate to break free.

Brendon's lips moved in a silent prayer to the Lady of Dawn, hoping with all his might that She might hear him from where She walked on the far side of Crotaria. His right arm dropped. Before it fell, the Darinians' fitful seizures slowed until their bodies became still. He watched tight-lipped and pale-faced as the mass of bodies rippled and parted. Fumbling at his waist, Brendon raised his looking glass. An old woman, shriveled and hunched and wrapped in white cloth, shuffled forward. She looked up and caught his eye, never slowing in her steady, shambling gait. Her wrinkled face appeared calm, giving no sign that she had been overcome by some pagan ritual only moments earlier.

"What is this madness?" Ellis snarled. "Do your duty, General. Attack."

Brendon glanced at him. The disciple's face was twisted in a snarl as animalistic as any Darinian's, yet no emotion reached his lifeless eyes.

"You do not give orders, Cinder Ellis," Brendon said, surprised at the evenness of his voice. Brendon heeled Acker's flanks and raced forward. Breath misted out in front of him. Two other pairs of hoofbeats closed in. He did not look around as Moser and Marrick rode up to either side. They met Margia near the spot where they had convened before. She raised an eyebrow, her frock whipping in the cool night breeze.

"I came alone, General," she said.

Brendon pulled his helm free. "I did not ask my lieutenants to accompany me. I meant no disrespect."

"We do our duty," Moser and Marrick said together. Brendon turned to each. They wore no expression, only stared down at Margia of the Falcon from their mounts.

Margia remained silent. Time stretched interminably. "You do us no disrespect. Far from it. You are both steward and adjudicator. Were it not for your level head, our realms might have spilled yet more blood, good for nothing more than wetting the earth."

She waited. Brendon stayed silent, unsure of what to say. He had only carried out Edmund's orders.

"Aidan Gairden does not threaten Nichel of the Wolf," Margia said at last. "They are allies. Our war is at an end. Our armies will unite."

Brendon could have kissed her. "I am glad, Margia of the Falcon. Thank you."

"Do not thank me," the old crone said. "The war chief speaks through the *Nuulass*, and the *Nuulass* speaks for Darinia."

Brendon blinked, unsure of exactly what she meant. He sorted through her words and grasped the salient information: The north and west were allies. "Do you know where Aidan and Nichel of the Wolf are now?" he asked.

Margia did not answer. Not with words. A low cry rumbled

deep in her throat. Gooseflesh peppered Brendon's arms and legs. One hand went to his sword. Just as his gauntleted hand closed around its hilt, Margia of the Falcon sprang at Moser. Her teeth sank into his throat. The lieutenant slid from his saddle noiselessly. Before his body hit the tall grass Margia bounded over to Marrick and tackled him from his horse. The lieutenant struggled, his steel and snow rattling. Like Moser, he did not cry out, or grunt, or shout, or call for help. There came a wet tearing sound. Marrick's legs jerked once, twice, and went still.

Brendon pulled his sword free and braced himself as Margia of the Falcon climbed unsteadily to her feet. When he saw her, he choked down a scream. Blood the color of grass stained her mouth and chin, dribbling down the front of her dress.

"The dead walk, and Nichel of the Wolf and Aidan Gairden are in danger. We must go to Darinia. We must—"

The ground shook beneath their feet. Stones, ash, and bits of dirt bounced and danced. Margia's head whipped to the west, where a tide of men wearing moldy clothes and steel and snow and Darinian armor and the emerald leather of Azure Blades boiled over a hilltop. Their heads shone as white as Kahltan, skulls and empty sockets where flesh and eyes should have been. With a thunderous roar that turned Brendon's spine to ice, the undead charged down the hillside, fanning out in a stampede set to collide with the clans and Torel's Ward.

Margia stood calmly. "The war has begun."

AIDAN GAZED AROUND. Like Nichel, her quarters exhibited an incongruent medley of color and sparsity, a reflection of her mixed bloodline. Her walls and floor were bare, but a fine wardrobe stood against the far wall. Within, shelves held Leastonian garments sewn by her mother and Darinian jewelry forged by the most renowned silversmiths in the west. Her four-poster bed, draped with blue silk sheets, sat in a far corner. Nichel had told him once that her mattress was unyielding, like the ground on which her nomadic clansfolk slept. A brazier, small and close to the floor, stood in the corner opposite the bed. The sight of it reassured him, though only slightly.

What was that noise?

— *What noise?* Grandfather Charles asked.

Aidan trained his ears, but heard only the occasional pop of the fire in the corner. He wrinkled his nose as the scent of berries assaulted it. A flicker of movement from behind the sheets draped over Nichel's bed caught his eye. It was a silhouette, small and slender, as if glimpsed through mist. "Nichel?" he rasped. His throat had gone dry.

A soft, humorless laugh ghosted out from behind the sheet. Before he could move, the silhouette stirred. Long, tanned legs swung over the side bed. A hand gripped the edge of the curtain and threw it back. It was one of Nichel's pack, the one with fiery hair and freckles. She was dead. Her eyes were glassy. Blue lips peeled back to reveal teeth spotted with blood. Her clothes were blackened, and burns marred her flesh.

Aidan kindled from the brazier on instinct. Scalding heat rushed through him. Hastily he released the light back into the fire. Gasping, he fell to his knees, beating his hands over his chest, his legs, his arms, his face. The pain was gone, but the memory of it was strong. He tried to stand but fell back. The vagrant charged at him. He raised his hands to shield his face. Without Heritage, without the ability to Touch, he felt like a babe exposed to the elements. Fists and feet rained down on him, hammering his limbs, chest, his neck. Voices careened through his head. Ambrose and Anastasia and Gabriel and his grandfather and dozens more.

The vagrant's leg took him full in the face. Stars exploded across his vision. A sharp ringing in his ears drowned out his family. All but one.

— *Aidan?*

That voice, her voice, was precious to him. He slid down the wall, just clinging to consciousness.

Mother?

Another kick took him on his temple. Pain and blackness rushed in, swallowing Annalyn's presence from his mind.

Continued in

The Twin Crowns: Book Three of the Gairden Chronicles

Acknowledgments

NO BOOK COMES together without a lot of help, which means a lot of thank-yous are due.

Heritage was my first novel, and for years, a solo venture. I keep a journal for every project, no matter how big or small, and spent nearly eighteen months feverishly writing and then discarding ideas until I wrote the first draft in late 2005. The book grew from there, benefitting from the experience I gleaned as a working writer, but most of all from Margaret Curelas, who gave Aidan and his pals a home at Tyche Books in 2013. From that moment on, the Gairden Chronicles became a team effort, even during the eighteen months—my magic number, apparently—rewriting *Point of Fate* from 2015 through 2017. Margaret has been a steadfast editor, sounding board, and confidant ever since. Without her, neither *Heritage* nor *Point of Fate* would have been half as good.

I don't have one biggest cheerleader. I have two. The first is my mom, whose greatest gift to me is a willingness to talk when I'm in the mood to listen, and to listen when I'm in the mood to talk. She reads, she critiques, she encourages, she supports.

My wife, Amie, has been through ordeal after ordeal between the publication of *Heritage* and the arrival of *Point of Fate*. She says she's not strong or brave. I say she's spectacular at humility. She's even better at being supportive. She's the first to hear my story ideas, the first to weigh in on them, the first to interrupt me while I'm trying to chill with video games and ask, "Have you written <Book X> yet? I want to read it!" We've walked a long, winding, rocky road, Amie Christine, but we're still here, and you're still strong and brave whether you can admit it or not.

Last but never least, thank you, Reader, for buying this book— the best type of encouragement you can show an author. And if you read *Heritage* and have been waiting four years to find out what happened, thank you for hanging in with me.

Glossary

A

Alston, Cynthia:. Wife of Romen of the Wolf and mother to Nichel of the Wolf.

Alston, Nichel: Daughter of Romen of the Wolf and Cynthia Alston. Before birth, she was promised to Aidan Gairden, next in line to become Crown of the North.

Apprentice: Third rank of a trained and educated Touched. Apprentices wear an orange band.

Architect: A Touched who applies his or her magical abilities to architecture.

Avivian River: River that runs north to east through Crotaria.

Azure Blade: A mercenary under the employ of a guildmaster of Leaston, or the entire guild. Azure Blades are trained as competently as any Wardsman, though their allegiance is to coin, not crown.

B

Band: See "Cinder band."

Bridgegil, Aaren: One of the most notorious shades to ever walk Torel, third in infamy only to Dimitri and Luria Thalamahn.

C

Calderon, Edmund: General of Torel. Father of Aidan Gairden and wife of Annalyn Gairden.

Calewind: Capital city of Torel and the site of Sunfall, home to the Gairden family.

'cin: See *"Ordine'cin."*

Clan Chief: The leader of a Darinian clan.

Cinder: Fifth and final rank attained by a Touched over the course of their formal education.

Cinder Band: Golden band with an embedded amethyst signifying the rank of Cinder. Worn on right forefinger.

Clan: A tribe of Darinians united under the leadership of a clan chief.

Creed: A professional pursuit or occupation selected by a Touched following his or her graduation.

Crotaria: Main continent divided into four realms: Torel in the north, Darinia in the west, Sallner in the south, and Leaston in the east.

Cyrolin of the Winds: A galerunner bonded to Captain Jamian Rolf.

D

Daram Ogahra: A subterranean city deep in Janleah Keep where the Darinians entomb their dead. *Daram Ogahra* consists of several layers, and each layer boasts more ornate tombs, roadways, and treasures than the ones above it. At the bottom, in the very center, rest the remains of Janleah of the Wolf, the first war chief in the west.

Darinia: Western realm of Crotaria made up of hot, dusty deserts. Home to the clans of Darinia.

Darinia's Fist: The combined warriors of all Darinian clans, united under the leadership of the war chief.

Dark Magic: The inverse of light magic, also known as shadecraft. Northern scholars believe shadecraft to be rooted in death and only practiced by those who worship Kahltan, the Lord of Midnight. In Torel, shadecraft is forbidden and punishable by death.

Darken: Drawing on cold and shadow for the purpose of casting a spell born of shadecraft. Any who can kindle can also darken. Thus, all Touched are able to practice suncraft and shadecraft, though the Temple of Dawn has worked for centuries to suppress that knowledge.

Disciple of Dawn: A Touched devoted to serving the Lady and spreading her word.

Domicile: A one-room dwelling on the Territory Bridge where a Sallnerian family lives. Sallnerian thralls are to report to their domiciles at or before curfew, and can only depart their domiciles if they carry a day pass issued by a Disciple of Dawn or other authority figure.

Duskwood: A nondescript cottage of magical dimensions where prophets of the Lady of Dawn guarded the Serpent's Fang for eight hundred years. The Duskwood could be entered only by invitation. However, once an invite had been extended, any Touched could follow the trail to the cottage and the location of the Serpent's Fang.

E

East Road: The main road between Ironsail, Leaston's capital city, and Sharem.

Emerson, Matias: A revered Disciple of Dawn charged with guarding Terror's Hand, the cursed weapon infused with Luria Thalamahn's soul.

Eternal Flame: Leader of all Touched on Crotaria. The Eternal Flame swears no fealty to any ruler or realm, but is expected to act according to the laws of the realms.

Eye (of Heritage): A magical ruby embedded within the hilt of Heritage. Through the Eye, Gairden ancestors can guide their descendants and pass along knowledge.

F

Father, The: Known as Kahltan by Torelians, Sallnerians, and Leastonians, the Father is a luminescent orb that rules from the night sky. His Vanguard, the glittering pinpricks that surround him, are the spirits of fallen Darinians who left the mortal realm to join the Father in his wild ride across the sky.

Feter of Domicile Twenty: A Sallnerian thrall on the Territory Bridge, and a childhood friend of Christine Lorden.

Fever, the: Kindling saps the strength of the Touched as they cast spells. As they grow weaker, tiredness sets in, recognizable by the onset of a fever that worsens until they rest.

G

Gairden, Aidan: Son of Annalyn Gairden and Edmund Calderon. Prince of Torel and next in line to become Crown of the North.

Gairden, Ambrose: Patriarch of the Gairden line. Husband of Anastasia Thalamahn Gairden. *Ordine'kel* comes from Ambrose's exemplary skill in combat.

Gairden, Anastasia Thalamahn: Matriarch of the Gairden family and daughter of Dimitri Thalamahn and Luria Thalamahn. *Ordine'cin* comes from Anastasia's potent magical abilities.

Gairden, Annalyn: Crown of the North, wife to Edmund Calderon, and mother to Aidan Gairden.

Gairden, Charles: Father of Annalyn Gairden and grandfather of Aidan Gairden.

Gairden, Gabriel: Son of Anastasia and Ambrose Gairden, and the first offspring of the Gairden bloodline following the Lady of Dawn's blessing. Gabriel was a famous scholar, though his research was conducted behind closed doors, away from the prying eyes of his family.

Galerunner: A Touched, usually a woman, raised on a faraway island across the Great Sea and trained to manipulate the wind in order to greatly increase the speed of ships. Leastonian sailors—many pirates, though the merchant's guild would deny it—seek out the youngest of these Touched, transport them back to Leaston, and sell them to captains, who bond them and enlist them in training by other bonded galerunners. A galerunner's bond to her captain is magical in nature, and exists for as long as the captain lives, or until he disbands the bond. The bond forces galerunners to comply with any order issued by their captains. Noncompliance results in the appearance of the verrucae, a rash that spreads across the galerunner's body and increases in severity, ending in death. Obeisance is the only cure for verrucae.

Goddess of Light: See "Lady of Dawn."

Gotik: A small village in Torel, a few miles south of Calewind.

Greagor, Brendon: Colonel of Torel's Ward.

Guildmaster: A member of the merchant's guild in Leaston.

H

Hands of the Crown: Touched hand-picked by the Gairdens to govern cities, towns, and villages in the name of the Crown of the North, though their allegiance ultimately lies with the Eternal Flame.

Harbinger: One of Tyrnen's vanguard of enslaved souls, harbingers are reanimated corpses infused with the soul of a Cinder, and thus able to Touch.

Healer: A Touched specializing in the art of healing.

Heritage: Magical sword passed down from generation to generation in the Gairden family.

Hillstreem, Jonathan: Advisor to Romen of the Wolf and a Touched.

I

Ihlkin Mountains: Mountain range that borders Crotaria.

Inventor: A Touched who specializes in researching and executing breakthroughs in magic.

Ironsail: The capital of Leaston and the largest port city in all of Crotaria.

J

Janleah: Janleah of the Wolf, clan chief of the wolf clan and the first war chief of Darinia.

Janleah Keep: The largest city in the west named in honor of Janleah of the Eagle, the first war chief of Darinia.

K

Kahltan: Known as the Lord of Midnight by Torelians and Leastonians.

'kel: See "*Ordine'kel.*"

Kietel, Lotren: General of Torel's Ward killed by invading barbarians.

Kindle/Kindling: The process by which a Touched casts magical spells granted to them by the will of the Lady of Light.

L

Lady of Dawn: Goddess of Light. Also referred to as the Lady. Individuals "Touched" by the Lady can wield magic by praying to her.

Lake Carrean: A lake nestled deep in the woods near the border between Torel and Leaston, and the site of Queen Annalyn Gairden's death at the hands of Tyrnen Symorne, Eternal Flame.

Lam of Domicile Four: A Sallnerian thrall on the Territory Bridge, and a childhood friend of Christine Lorden.

Lamp: An object capable of storing light that a Touched can use to kindle at any time, much like a water skin from which one can drink when one needs water.

Language (of Light), The: An ancient, universal language used in spell casting. The Touched draw in light and release it as a spell by praying in the Language of Light.

Learner: First rank of a trained and educated Touched. All learners wear a dark blue band.

Leaston: Eastern realm of Crotaria ruled by the merchant's guild.

Light Magic: Magic drawn from a source of natural or manmade light and heat.

Lion's Den, The: The most prestigious magical university in all Crotaria, located in Sharem.

Lord of Midnight: See "Kahltan."

Lorden, Christine: A powerful Touched at only seventeen years of age. Sibling of Garrett Lorden and daughter of Ernest Lorden. Half-Torelian, half-Sallnerian. Growing up, Christine lived in Domicile 137 with her brother until she left the Territory

Bridge.

Lorden, Garrett: Sibling of Christine Lorden and son of Ernest Lorden. Unlike his twin sister, Christine, Garrett exhibits Torelian features. Also unlike his fraternal twin sister, he is not a Touched.

Lorden, Ernest: Second of Crotaria. Father to Garrett and Christine Lorden, and a Torelian.

Lorden, Monumei: Mother of Garrett and Christine Lorden, and a Sallnerian. Formerly Monumei of Domicile 137 before marriage to Ernest Lorden. Monumei died of an illness when her twins were very young.

M

Magath, Anders: Lieutenant in Torel's Ward. Gruff but fair, Magath has earned the respect of all who serve under him.

Merchant's Guild: A council made up of the men and women who govern Leaston.

Merrifalls, Alix: A farm girl who grew up in the Torelian village of Gotik, dreaming of big cities and bigger adventures.

Merrifalls, Jak: A farm boy who left the tiny village of Gotik to join Torel's Ward. Jak is stationed in the Torelian capital of Calewind, a place under the weighty influence of the Gairdens and the Disciples of Dawn, but large enough that Jak can indulge in his lifestyle without scrutiny, provided he takes precautions.

Meshia: a large, horned creature that roams the deserts in the west. A favorite meal among Darinians, especially cooked over an open flame.

Mother, The: Known as the Lady of Dawn to inhabitants of Crotaria's other three realms, the Mother is praised by Darinians for the light and heat she provides.

N

North Road: A main road running up from Sharem into Calewind, the capital of Torel.

Nuulass: An ancient source of primal energy unique to Darinians. Those who know of the *Nuulass* both revere and fear it.

O

Ordine: "Guardian" in the language of the Darinians. A gift bestowed on the Gairden bloodline by the Lady of Dawn. *Ordine* manifests itself in every Gairden in one of two ways: *Ordine'kel,* or *Ordine'cin.*

Ordine'cin: "Guardian Light" in the language of the Darinians. Bestows a Gairden with the gift of magic. A Gairden gifted with *Ordine'cin* is stronger by far than the strongest Touched outside of the Gairden bloodline, though the talent must be nurtured by study and practice.

Ordine'kel: "Guardian Blade" in the language of the Darinians. Bestows a Gairden with Ambrose Gairden's skill in combat, though teaching and drills are necessary.

P

Philosopher: A Touched who spends his or her days studying and pondering magic, Crotaria, and the mysteries of the world beyond the home continent.

Plains of Dust: A desert in Darinia that stretches on for hundreds of miles.

Q

Queen of Terror: See "Thalamahn, Luria."

R

Reaver: A diminutive race that hails from far across the Great Sea. Short and stout, reavers have skin as brown and tough as leather, and tend to let their beards grow long. They serve as militia in Leaston, no different than the Azure Blades that protect eastern cities and the guildmasters who pay them.

Rite of Heritage: Ceremony that culminates in the official anointment of a Gairden king or queen.

Rite of Provenance: A rite by which the blood kin of a fallen clan chief or war chief can challenge a newly appointed chief in a battle to the death. If successful, any who invoke the Rite of Provenance assumes a position of leadership. If unsuccessful, they are quickly forgotten.

Rolf, Jamian: A captain and guildmaster on Leaston's merchant's council.

Romen of the Wolf: War Chief of Darinia. Husband of Cynthia Alston and father to Nichel of the Wolf.

Rosen, Karter: A sergeant of the Ward stationed in Calewind.

S

Sallner: Southern kingdom of Crotaria.

Sanctuary: A resting place for Gairden souls located within the Eye of Heritage.

Saowin, Terrence: A priest of high rank within the Temple of Dawn, and close confidant of Ernest Lorden, Second of the Touched.

Sard'tara: A halberd with a curved blade at either end. Used exclusively by Azure Blades in Leaston, each *Sard'tara* blade is coated in one of many types of poison—some designed to stop the heart instantly, others intended to draw out death, making it as agonizing as possible.

Second, the: Second in command of the Touched after the Eternal Flame of Crotaria.

Serpent's Fang: A cursed sword forged and wielded by Dimitri Thalamahn, Serpent King. It resembles the Gairden's ancestral blade Heritage in form, though its steel is black and a sapphire rests in the center of its pommel rather than a ruby. Like the Gairden's ruby, the Fang's sapphire is able to contain souls.

Serpent King, The: See "Thalamahn, Dimitri."

Serpent's War, The: A devastating war waged by King Dimitri Thalamahn and Queen Luria Thalamahn of Sallner.

Sharem: A trade city located at the heart of Crotaria where all four realms meet.

Shift: Magical method of transportation dependent on the Lady's light.

Shirey, Daniel: Wardsman. Best friend of Aidan Gairden and a Leastonian.

Shirey, Rakian: Father of Daniel Shirey. Known as the "Man of a Thousand Spears" for his proficiency with *Sard'tara*.

Snake: A racial slur that refers to Sallnerians. They have slanted eyes, but the slur also references their corruption under the reign of Dimitri Thalamahn, the Serpent King.

Sneak: A band of thieves in Leaston, or so rumors suggest. The existence of the sneaks is widely contested. The merchant's guild of Leaston does not condone their actions, but the sneaks bring in goods and coin, so the guild would not proscribe the sneaks' actions, either—if they existed.

Soldier: A Touched devoted to defending Crotaria in times of war.

South Road: A main road running down from Sharem to the Territory Bridge, which leads into Sallner.

Speaker: A Darinian elder who interprets the will of the Mother and Father.

Spirit Stone: An orb of a glass-like material able to entrap souls. Whoever holds a Spirit Stone commands the souls within it.

Steel and snow: The armor and clothing worn by Wardsmen.

Sunfall: The ancestral home of the Gairdens, rulers of Crotaria's eastern kingdom of Torel.

Sword Chamber: A magical chamber where Heritage rests when not in use. Only Gairdens may access the chamber.

Symorne, Tyrnen: Eternal Flame of Crotaria. Mentor to Aidan Gairden. Travelled to Torel shortly after Aidan Gairden's birth in order to petition Queen Annalyn Gairden for permission to assist in the mentorship of her magically gifted son.

T

Tarion: The second largest city in Torel.

Temperdine: Leastonian city renowned for art and clothing.

Territory Bridge: A strip of land leading into the main body of Sallner, the dead realm of Crotaria. What remains of Sallner's population lives on the bridge in communities closely guarded by Wardsmen from Torel's Ward.

Thalamahn, Luria: Queen of Terror. Co-ruler of Sallner before she was executed at the end of the Serpent's War and a confessed Disciple of Kahltan.

Thalamahn, Dimitri: The Serpent King. Co-ruler of southern kingdom of Sallner and a confessed Disciple of Kahltan.

Tied: The process of severing a Touched's connection to their magic. A Tie can only be performed and removed by a Touched.

Torel: Northern kingdom of Crotaria ruled by the Gairden bloodline.

Torel's Dawn: Elite group of Cinders under the direct command of the Eternal Flame. Torel's Dawn serves and protects Torel and the Gairden family, though they still answer to the Eternal Flame, like all Touched.

Torel's Ward: Army of the kingdom of Torel.

Touched: One blessed with the gift of magic.

Tunnels: A network of subterranean passageways that extends through Crotaria's four realms. Virtually all cities and towns, even the smallest villages, have at least one ingress and egress into and out of the tunnels. The sneaks utilize tunnels to move goods and information.

V

Vagrant: A reanimated corpse under the command of a shade and often in the guise of the living so they can move undetected. Unlike harbingers, a corpse need not be infused with souls to be reanimated as a vagrant, though any who lack a soul will also lack memories, thoughts, emotions, and autonomy.

Vale of Spirits: See "Daram Ogahra."

Valor: Sword wielded by Edmund Calderon.

W

War Chief: A Darinian clan chief who holds the power to lead all Darinian clans during times of war.

Ward, The: See "Torel's Ward."

Wardsman / Wardsmen: A fighting man in Torel's Ward.

West Road: A main road running across Darinia and into Sharem.

Wielder: Second rank of a trained and educated Touched. All Wielders wear a purple band.

Wildlander: A pejorative term for Darinian.

Z

Zellibar: Darinian city renowned for the work of its metal smiths.

About the Author

David L. Craddock lives in northeast Ohio with his wife and business partner, Amie Kline. He writes fiction, nonfiction, and author bios, usually his own. He is the author of the Gairden Chronicles series of epic fantasy novels for young adults, and the bestselling Stay Awhile and Listen trilogy that recounts the history of World of WarCraft developer Blizzard Entertainment and Diablo developer Blizzard North. Tag along with his writing adventures online @davidlcraddock on Twitter, and at www.davidlcraddock.com.

CPSIA information can be obtained
at www.ICGtesting.com
Printed in the USA
FFHW02n0748091018

9 781928 025931